Dirty Wars

Nicolas Brentano

ISBN: 978-0-9572640-6-9

SIFIPUBLISHING
WWW.SIFIPUBLISHING.CO.UK

info@sifipublishing.co.uk

DIRTY WARS is available in all Ebook formats from Amazon, Smashwords, Ibooks and most other retailers

The author wishes to thank Simon Fraser for having had the courage to accept to publish this book and - the decision once taken - to provide invaluable guidance and support to a novice in the arts of fiction-writing, publishing, and especially in the uncharted domain of epublishing.

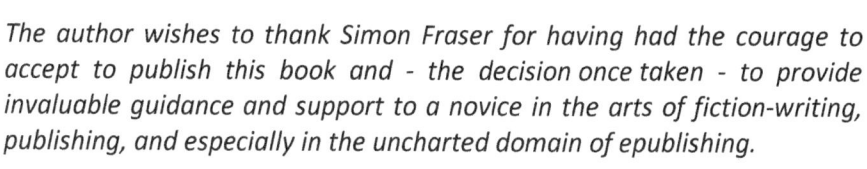

Cover photo by kind permission of Patrick Andraste

www.andraste.com

The Dirty War (Spanish: Guerra Sucia) was a period of state terrorism in Argentina during the 1970s. Victims of the violence included several thousand left-wing activists and militants, including trade unionists, students, journalists, Marxists, Peronist guerrillas and alleged sympathizers. Some 10,000 of the disappeared were guerrillas of the Montoneros (MPM), and the People's Revolutionary Army (ERP).

Montoneros (Spanish: Movimiento Peronista Montonero-MPM) was an Argentine leftist urban guerrilla group, active during the 1960s and 1970s. The name is an allusion to 19th century Argentinian history. After Juan Perón's return from 18 years of exile and the 1973 Ezeiza massacre, which marked the definitive split between left and right-wing Peronism, the Montoneros were expelled from the Justicialist party in May 1974 by Perón. The group was almost completely destroyed by 1977, during the Dirty War..........although their "Special Forces" did fight on until 1981. In late 1979, the Montoneros launched a "strategic counteroffensive" in Argentina, and the security forces killed more than one hundred of the exiled Montoneros, who had been sent back to Argentina after receiving special forces training in camps in the Middle East.

Autoerotic asphyxiation has at times been incorrectly diagnosed as murder and especially so when a partner is present.

(All above: Wikipedia)

See also Glossary at rear of book.

The social, political and economic events which form the backdrop to this account are based on reality. The opinions expressed about these events are however those of the protagonists and any similarity with real events or persons living or dead is purely coincidental.

Dirty Wars

May 2007

The rain dripped off the brim of his beret onto the telescopic sights of the Heckler & Koch rifle. It was the MSG 90, a 7.62mm high precision version, fruit of a little deal with some drug runners in Paraguay. A sniper's dream, overkill for this job. The humidity was fogging up the lens. He wiped it with the cuff of his shirt and took another look down the scope. From where he was lying in the oleander shrubbery on the edge of the well-kept lawn, he had a clear but oblique view of the bedroom door, which opened out onto the covered *galeria* of the simple colonial house standing a hundred metres away. It had been raining heavily since about three thirty in the morning and he was beginning to regret not having brought some form of ground sheet. His waterproof poncho was trapping the rain as much as it was protecting him from the ground. It was now six thirty and he had been lying there since before daybreak. The beast must surely be let out soon . . .

Over to his right, smoke had started to curl up from the metal chimney on the roof of the manager's small bungalow. Probably brewing their first *mate* of the day. With this downpour, they would certainly not move until the rain had stopped. It was their day off and the manager and his plump little wife had no call to get out of bed, plans to go into the nearby town almost certainly shelved on account of the rain. Even their mongrel watchdogs would be curled up in their wooden kennel under the veranda.

Over the last week, he had been building up a picture of the habits of both the owner of the house and his manager, supplemented by the occasional gossip in the *pueblo's* café. An ugly church with a crumbling facade, the unprepossessing municipal offices, general store and a couple of bars surrounded the main square with its concrete park benches, wilting oleanders and a decaying bust of Peron. Only the road around the square and the main road running north and south out of town were paved. The other streets running off into the one-storey residential parts of town were muddy and would, when the winter rains came, become impassable except for horses or the odd four-wheel-drive. A typical small town in a remote part of the Province of La Pampa where strangers were not so common. He had picked out the

3

more ill lit of the two bars on the square. To get the locals to drop their guard and give him a few tips about possible local employers, it had taken only a few drinks and a credible story of having been fired by a vindictive farm manager for having bedded his mistress in the neighbouring province of Cordoba.

A week ago, he had watched the manager and his little wife ride into town on their ageing 125 Yamaha, their three-year old daughter squeezed between them. They whiled away their day off watching the TV in the café and visiting the Chinese-run supermarket, stocking up on basic groceries. He had sought their advice on possible work, but had been given little reason for hope as regards their employer.

"He runs a very tight little farm, works us all far too hard – there are two of us permanent, and occasionally a couple of others come to give us a hand with the castration and branding the cattle. Frankly, I can't see him hiring anyone else – not with beef prices where they are. Anyway, he's an *hijo de puta* – we've thought of leaving a couple of times, but it's not as if there are many jobs on offer around here... and going back to Santiago del Estero isn't really much of an option. No work up there. Sorry, *che*, not to be more helpful."

He had paid for their Cokes, overruling their protests, and watched them load up on the Yamaha.

She would be quite sexy under the warm blankets drawn over their little wooden bed. His thoughts began to drift....

The sudden opening of the veranda bedroom door snapped him back to the job at hand. The large Argentine *dogo* waddled out. It was getting on in age, like its master, probably the same level of arthritis, although it remained a very powerful example of its breed. A hand pulled the door shut, leaving the hound to do its first patrol of the day. Lying in the bushes, he was downwind from the house and the rain would dampen any sound, so there was little cause to be concerned that the beast would spot him at this range. He fixed the crosshairs of the scope on the dog's head, as it looked up at the heavy clouds and laboriously shook off the drops of rain. It was coming down a lot harder now and the occasional roll of thunder suggested it would go on for some time more. A quick glance towards the manager's house. No sign of any movement from there. The dog was moving along the side of the house, out of sight of the bedroom. He let it go another few metres and then squeezed the trigger. With a faint 'plop' from the silencer, the dog crumpled into a heap under a eucalyptus tree on the edge of the lawn. It was now only a matter of waiting, the rifle firmly sighted at head level on the veranda door. The rain increased and another roll of thunder crashed after a particularly brilliant flash of lightning. The thunder had even drowned the faint sound of the shot. With his right hand, he quickly swept up the ejected shell case, curled his finger round the trigger once more and waited. With the smaller 5-round magazine, he still had four shots, more than enough.

Another glance at the manager's house. All quiet, no sign of their dogs, with the wind in the right direction, even the scent of the *dogo* would not have reached them. Ten minutes passed before he caught the sound of a bedroom window sliding open. It was on the side of the house away from the manager's house, so that he could only get a profile of the head, which briefly looked out and whistled once, before ducking back in again. He waited. Another short whistle, but in vain. The owner would not be very keen on a waterlogged dog coming back to his bedroom.

This time the veranda door slid fully open and an elderly man, wrapped in an ageing blue dressing gown, without slippers, shuffled out to the edge of the lawn keeping just under the veranda roof. The cross-hairs were fixed on the centre of his forehead. The old man moved slowly towards the corner of the house, keeping under the veranda. The cross hairs followed steadily. The veranda stretched down the side of the house, away from the manager's house. The old man rounded the corner, the cross hairs shifting to the left temple. The target stopped and gave another whistle, just as another burst of lightening lit up the scene. A couple of seconds, the thunder began to roll on the horizon, a steady squeeze of the trigger and the old man crashed forward on his knees, coming to rest with his forehead on the edge of lawn. He could have been struck by lightning, so neatly had the shot dovetailed with nature's tensions. Blood began to spread in the wet grass from the huge gash on the other side of his skull, caused by the round spinning inside the softness of the brain before exiting.

"Time to be getting out of here," he muttered to himself, pocketing the second shell case. He checked the manager's house. Nothing had changed.

He crawled backwards through the bushes to the gap in the cattle wire through which he had come. Then, moving along the narrow, water-logged ditch which ran between the muddy driveway and the line of eucalyptus trees stretching as far as the entry gate, he made his way back to the earth track which linked up with the main road a couple of kilometres east. The trace of his boots would very soon be washed away by the water running down the ditch. He followed the track up to the point where, tucked into some thick shrubbery, he had left his battered 4L Renault. Wrapping the H&K in an old oily horse blanket after carefully drying it off, he stowed it with his riding tackle in the back. He gave it a light pat of appreciation. It had been a good day when the Paraguayan intermediary had delivered the smuggled weapon to his door in exchange for a large wad of dollars. That wad had been replaced a number of times over by the contracts which the H&K had enable him to execute on behalf of this anonymous client. At times he wondered as to the client's identity, but quickly realised that the less he knew, the better. He climbed into the driver's seat. With the heavy rain, he had seen nobody. Carefully, he edged the car onto the dirt track, which was rapidly becoming as slippery as soap and headed slowly away from the house. The bald tyres and the continuing rain would leave very little evidence of his presence. The first truck to come through would inevitably plough up the waterlogged surface, wiping away any final trace.

August 2007

As he pushed open the front door of his flat and reached for the hallway light switch, Eduardo was grabbed by the front of his jacket and dragged inside. Losing his balance, a sweeping blow to the side of his head sent him tumbling across the small hall and through the opposite door into the sitting room. Before he could begin to get to his feet, he was pinned to the ground, a knee thrust brutally into the small of his back. The force seemed enough to crack his spine. A second assailant followed up with a kick to his right hand, followed by a couple more vicious kicks in the region of his kidneys, which left him retching with pain, fighting to get his breath. Expert hands frisked him and relieved him of his small Bersa 9mm service automatic. A click as the magazine was released and thrown away into a corner of the room under one of the cupboards. He felt himself being picked up by the shoulders, spun around to face his attacker, and then propelled with a head-butt into one of the armchairs. The room was in darkness, but through the tears which the blow had released, he could make out the silhouette of two large men facing him. He curled up in the chair as a way of protecting his body, trying desperately to clear his thoughts.

One of his attackers switched on a table light behind them, so that they remained in silhouette. The two men were of medium height, around one metre seventy, jeans, leather jackets, well-worn trainers, a simple balaclava concealing only the top of their faces. A Browning 9mm Hi Power automatic, pointing steadily at his head. He could just make out that one had a moustache, the other clean-shaven. From their overall build, they must be in their early forties.

"Put your hands where we can see them," the instruction came in a low voice. Eduardo complied, resting his left hand on the arm of the chair, whilst his bleeding right hand hung limply towards the floor. From the lilt of the sentence, he could just detect the accent of someone from the province of Cordoba.

"Where's your laptop?"

Eduardo pointed in the direction of a sliding ledge under his worktable. The second man stepped over towards it and, having pulled out the power plugs and the mouse, scooped the laptop into a briefcase lying on the table. They must have brought this case with them, he didn't own anything like it.

"Keep any work files here?"

He shook his head, immediately regretting it as the pain, which was now throbbing from his neck upwards, instantly shot through his skull. It felt as though it was beginning to burn into the back of his eyeballs.

"Sure about that?"

Again Eduardo shook his head, slowly this time.

"Certain!"

Stealing a surreptitious look around the room, Eduardo noted that everything seemed to be pretty much in its place. They had either only arrived a few minutes before him and had not had time to turn the place upside down, or they were relying on him to hand over whatever they were looking for.

The man holding the Browning spun one of the wooden dining chairs round so that he could sit on it facing backwards towards Eduardo, resting the automatic on the armrest, unwavering.

"Take this by way of a courtesy call, Subinspector Eduardo Falcioni!"

Emphasis placed on the "subinspector."

So they knew who he was, which suggested far more than a simple break-in. As it was, everything about the attack indicated that these men had come with some purpose which had little to do with trying to steal his hi-fi or TV set.

"It's a courtesy call, Subinspector, but it comes with a message. I'll make it very short. The case of the Englishwoman. Make sure it gets nowhere. Forget about it, *che,* bury it. And don't get any bright ideas. Whoever sent us here tonight can track your every move. At the slightest hint that you're being overzealous to solve the case, it won't be just a little visit like this. Which would be a shame for Florencia. Or maybe, we'll drop in on Florencia as a starter and then visit you afterwards."

So they also knew the name of his girlfriend. He made as if to ask a question, but before he had even got out the first word, he was cut short.

"Shut up, you've got the message, that's all that matters."

"Yes, but..."

He got no farther, as the other man stepped up beside him and delivered a crashing sideswipe to his face, which lifted him out of his armchair.

As he lay crumpled on the ground, the two men turned on their heels.

"No room for being *vivo*, nothing smart. We're off now, but remember, we can come back any time. This was just a small taste of what will happen next time. Ciao, Subinspector. Let's hope we don't have to meet again."

As he began to pick himself up, he saw the two men quietly leave through the front door, pulling it closed behind them. Following them was clearly going to be a bad idea. All he could think of doing was to step into his unlit bedroom to try and catch a glimpse of them as they left the building. It was dark outside, the street lamps weak in this part of town. As he watched through the edge of the net curtain, two figures emerged from the direction of the front door of his apartment block and stepped between the parked cars along the pavement to wait. Within less than half a minute, a dark Renault van appeared, stopped and they climbed in through the back doors. Part of a team, apparently with some form of radio or cell phone communications.

His head was splitting, his spine and kidneys slowly serving up a duller pain. Switching on the light in his bathroom, he looked at himself in the mirror. The last blow had opened up a superficial cut with what was rapidly becoming a dark bruise spreading over the left-hand side of his face. A right-handed blow. After plunging his face into the cold water of the basin, he gingerly dabbed at it with a soft towel, before returning to the sitting room and pouring himself a large brandy. Not always recommended if there was any risk of concussion, but what the hell.

As he sat in the armchair, trying not to put too much weight on his back and side, he went over what he had been able to retain about his two visitors. The message could not have been clearer. They were obviously only concerned with the investigation into the Englishwoman. If the only item they had taken was his laptop, they were presumably hoping to see whether it would throw any light on how far his investigation had gone to date. Surprising that they had not attempted to interrogate him any further about how far he had got in his enquiries. Only explicable on the basis that they were either not really interested, which suggested that they might have some other way of tracking his progress, or that spinning out their time together could have compromised their identity. The links between the police and criminal world were incestuous and well documented. Eduardo had instinctively been on the lookout for anything which might suggest that his visitors actually came from the same stable as his own. Two or three things pointed in that direction. Firstly, the 9mm Browning they carried, standard Policía Federal issue, although also readily available in criminal circles, given the frequency of handgun theft from police *Comisarías* round the country. A gun whose design was getting on for a hundred years old. A version had been manufactured for many years by Fabricaciones Militares, the Argentine government armaments group, making it one of the commonest sidearms in the business. Secondly, the professional and efficient way in which he had been frisked, which suggested practice, not something that the common criminal usually indulged in. Finally, most blatant of all, the reference to the fact that whoever had sent them also had ready access to what he was doing in the investigation. Even if his two attackers were not moonlighting policemen, it sounded as though their boss might sit somewhere centrally in the system. Not a comfortable thought.

How much would they be able to extract from his laptop? Probably little, as he tended to shift any work he might be doing backwards and forwards between his office and his flat on a memory stick. He checked his pockets. It was still safely tucked away in his trouser pocket, having escaped their rapid search. Fortunately, the laptop was also fairly new, he had not yet transferred much of his personal stuff onto it. They would no doubt discover his address book and personal e-mails, or at least some of them, since he preferred to use hotmail rather than Outlook. Most of his mails would be sitting on the hotmail server. Much would depend upon the sophistication of the analytical capacity thrown at his computer. But for now, with the way he was feeling, he needed support of a more personal kind.

11

CENTRO

INVESTIGACIÓN

ECONÓMICA

July 2007 : POLITICAL COMMENTARY

That president Kirchner should have finally decided that his wife would be the official candidate at next October's presidential elections probably comes as less of a surprise than might be expected, even though ruling candidates are not often inclined to give up power. However, this is a transfer between husband and wife and one must assume that he feels totally confident, particularly when confronted with so unimpressive an opposition, that she will win with ease. Given the line-up, with everyone still scrambling to find a decent team, the president's wife can probably sleep quietly in her bed. The only shadow revolves around concerns about his health, which may or may not have been a factor in his calculation, but are unlikely to have been the prime rationale behind his decision. Economic problems firmly on the horizon include both the rate of inflation and the potential energy crisis. But government resources, particularly with the price of soya in the US $ 330 – 350 range on the Chicago markets, are sound, particularly with the record harvest of this year in Argentina.

Turning to the recent scandal surrounding the Minister of Economy, Felisa Miceli, aside from the actual facts of the case, which may not come as much of a surprise to those accustomed to the way in which power is conducted in Argentina, more interesting is the time taken by the President to resolve the issue.

Finding an envelope in a ministerial private bathroom containing about US$50,000, in cash may be regarded as commonplace, not only in Argentina, but possibly elsewhere. As our readers will recall, the discovery was made by security guards in the early hours before the arrival of the Minister, carrying out instructions ironically established at the time of the much hated military junta in the 1970s, probably following the terrorist attack on the family home belonging to the Vice Minister, Walter Klein. In the interval, the President has shown unwavering support for his errant minister - until yesterday! Closing ranks around her was the order of the day, typical of a government which has not yet learned that to admit a mistake may be a way of resolving it. Perhaps the President hoped that some obsequious judge would back off pressing charges. If so, he was wrong. Is this a sign of vulnerability at last, or the recognition that society cannot be frightened off as easily as in the past? As each new explanation for the origin of the funds was trotted out by the Minister, the situation only became more unmanageable and more ridiculous. Even the opposition, usually hard pressed to find a united front with which to attack the government, has found a way to seize this opportunity. The resignation of a Minister of Finance in such turbulent circumstances would normally send ripples through the markets. Is it a sign of market sentiment that, under this government, when a Minister of Finance is little more than a figurehead, these sordid events have not even appeared as a blip on the radar?

A bit of scandal like this enlivened the monthly economic bulletin. Pressing 'save', Leandro Flemming turned to the latest Central Bank figures for money in circulation.

A crashing sound from his front door interrupted the analysis.

None of his friends announced themselves quite so violently. A little care being in order in these times of growing insecurity, he ducked into the small hall and stood to the side of the entrance doorframe.

13

"Who's that?"

"Eduardo, open!"

"You on your own?"

"Yes, don't worry, just open!"

He slid the chain off the door and opened it. His godson, Eduardo, stumbled in, clutching his rib cage. Catching sight of his swollen, bruised face, Leandro took a quick look onto the landing and up and down the stairs as far as he could see without going through the doorway, then pulled the young man inside, closing the door and repositioning all the bolts.

"Next time, pick a fight with somebody your own size or preferably smaller!"

Not for the first time, he thanked the day that, on buying the flat, he had installed a reinforced door with an armour plated lining and heavy, multiple bolts.

Propping up Eduardo with his arm across his back, he walked him unsteadily towards the couch, onto which the young man collapsed, groaning softly.

"What the hell happened? Car hit you or something? You look terrible!"

Eduardo shook his head gently to avoid setting off the pain again.

"Some brandy, if you have any."

"Are you sure? Any chance of concussion or worse?"

"Probably not, so let's have some! Anyway, I've already had some earlier!"

"What've you been up to now? Nasty profession you've chosen, I always said so. Hold this against your eye, while I get something. You're sure nothing's broken?"

"Perhaps a rib or two, they kicked pretty hard!"

"You should be in hospital, not here. Come on. Let me take a quick look. I'm no doctor but I've had the odd cracked rib or broken collarbone from rugby."

Eduardo gingerly slid out of his coat and jacket, and lifting his shirt, let his godfather examine his rib cage.

"Does this hurt?" Leandro asked, pressing the lower side of Eduardo's chest.

"A bit."

"And when you take a deep breath?"

"A bit, but nothing too terrible."

"You may have been lucky."

Eduardo was soon awkwardly propped up in an armchair in a position to keep the pressure off his ribs, sipping brandy and holding a wad of Kleenex to his face to staunch the bleeding, which had started again above his eye.

"Okay, if you're feeling up to it, start at the beginning."

"They must have followed me when I left the *Comisaría*. Had a faint feeling that a car moved out when I drove out of the courtyard of the station. Traffic was heavy on Las Heras, five o'clock, everyone on their way home, I couldn't be sure. And frankly, I wasn't really looking for anything."

"They? Who's 'they'? How many were there? What the fuck is this all about?"

"Two guys attacked me in my flat, less than an hour ago. Could have been *canas* in plain clothes. What with the car possibly following me home, and the van in which they left, there might have been up to five or six involved. Certainly there was a van, a Renault I think, with a driver, waiting for them, because they pulled away fast once they left the flat."

"*Por Dios!* Why should anybody be attacking you like this? Couldn't it have been just a simple robbery?"

15

"Slow down, uncle. At this stage, I'm not sure what it's all about, but I've an idea. Two men attacked me as soon as I opened the front door of my flat. They must have been waiting for me. They got me on the ground very fast. Frisked and disarmed me, then kicked me to bits. Finally, after warning me off, they left with my laptop. I don't keep any valuables in the flat – even if I had any anyway - and things usually get rougher when you can't give these people what they want. It might have been a lot worse, but it clearly wasn't money they were after."

"Warning? What kind of a warning? People don't just break into a flat and beat you up to give a warning, do they? Linked to any particular case you're on?" Leandro asked.

"I don't know whether I mentioned... it was actually in the papers, with my name in there... I'm involved in that case a couple of weeks ago where an Englishwoman was murdered at that boutique hotel, L'Hotel."

Leandro shook his head.

"Don't think you said anything. What makes you think there's a connection?"

"One of them made it very plain that I should forget about *la inglesa*. He knew my name, also knew about Florencia. That's much more worrying."

"So you think he was referring to the hotel case?"

"Can't think that he meant anything else."

"Seems strange. Why should anyone want to attack you over that? Was there a drugs angle to it?"

"Nothing more than a bit of personal consumption. At this moment, I can't think. But clearly there must be more to this than I thought to begin with."

"Relax. Take your time."

Eduardo sat silent, clearly trying to order his thoughts. Then he shrugged his shoulders. A grimace of pain flitted across his face.

"Puta madre, my head hurts. Not to mention my ribs. I'm sorry, uncle, but I think I'd better get to bed after all. Let's continue this when I'm feeling up to it. I'm a bit confused at the moment."

Eduardo got up unsteadily, finished the last drops of the brandy and made his way to the door. Leandro moved forward to help him, but was gently waved aside.

"Sure you'll be all right? You don't look great. And presumably, somebody's going to ask questions tomorrow when they see you looking like that."

"I'll think of something."

"You're coming with me. I'm not letting you go like that. With concussion, you never know."

"No, don't worry, please, uncle."

"Shut up!"

Slipping into his coat, Leandro put his arm around his godson and led him carefully down the stairs. On Bartolome Mitre, he stopped a passing taxi.

"The nearest *policlinica,* please."

An hour later, the tests having shown little more than some severe bruising, he dropped Eduardo back at his flat.

"Don't worry, I can make it upstairs by myself. Thank you."

With Leandro's help, Eduardo slipped out of the car carefully. In the doorway, he turned

"I'd like to tell you a bit more about that case. For a variety of reasons – which often happens - it's not going anywhere, but I've a feeling the reasons are a bit more unusual this time. Would you be prepared to listen? I do need some fresh thoughts on all this. Could we meet some morning over a coffee?"

"Sure. Give me a call tomorrow, I'll be back home as of five. If you feel worse, give me a ring at once."

He gave his godson a careful hug to avoid the bruises.

Back at his flat, Leandro sat thinking in the unlit drawing room about his relationship with his godson. Godson? As only Leandro and his wife Elena knew, the circumstances of Eduardo's birth were nothing if not unusual.

Francisco Falcioni and Leandro had been pilot and co-pilot - navigator of a two-seater FMA IA 58 Pucará attached to the Argentine Air Force's Grupo 3 de Ataque, flown to the Malvinas in mid-May as replacement for aircraft losses inflicted by an SAS raid. Returning from a ground-attack mission in the wake of the British landings at San Carlos on 21 May, the twin turbo-prop ground-attack aircraft had run into heavy ground fire. Penetrating the armoured fuselage, a round had instantly killed Francisco, blowing off the back of his head. A further glancing explosion from a Stinger missile had nearly destroyed them in the air. The dual controls getting no response, Leandro had just managed to activate his Martin Baker ejector seat at very low altitude, coming down behind Argentine lines. Quickly recovered by his own forces and brought back to Puerto Argentino, he had been repatriated to Comodoro Rivadavia on the mainland on one of the last transport flights out the next day.

After a physical check-up, which had confirmed that no serious damage had been done, Leandro had been granted five days leave to rest before resuming duties. For reasons which he could now only dimly remember, he had decided there and then to seek out his partner's widow. He had been a witness at their marriage a couple of days before their departure for the islands, and the thought of what she must be going through had pushed him to take the long-distance bus back to Buenos Aires. On arrival, Leandro had gone straight to the small flat into which the newly-weds had moved on the eve of Francisco's return to the air force battalion.

Leandro had knocked on the door of the second-floor flat, which, after he had answered Leonor's tearful query as to who was outside, she had opened to let him in. As he walked through the door, Leonor turned away, to look through the rain-spotted window onto the darkening street below, her shoulders shaking with her sobbing. He stepped up close and put his arms around Leonor's shoulders, the only way he felt he could convey his compassion to her. She turned and pulled him towards her. Awkwardly, he had taken out his handkerchief and given it to her. She stepped away from him and mopped her eyes, before collapsing onto the small sofa in the barely furnished little sitting room. A few removals boxes still stood around in corners, most unopened. A bare bulb hanging from a wire in the ceiling shed a dismal gloom, which could have done little to improve her emotional state of mind.

Leandro couldn't think of anything remotely appropriate to say. They sat in silence, staring into the semi-distance, her sobbing the only sound above the traffic from the street below. After a while, he got up and went into the kitchen to look for something to drink. A half-empty bottle of whiskey stood in a corner by the sink. He poured a couple of fingers into a tumbler for her, as well as one for himself, and came back into the drawing room. At first, she shook her head, but as he continued to hold it outstretched towards her, she finally took the glass, although it was some time before she actually sipped any. He downed his glass almost straight away and then sat there, again in silence, waiting.

"It's so unfair," she had finally murmured, shaking her head. "Of course, unfair is meaningless – especially after the Belgrano sinking…. And I really don't want to know how it happened or what happened to Francisco, please understand…." her voice trailed off.

Silence had seemed to be the only option and they continued to sit there, motionless. He watched the evening sun go down through the scudding rainclouds on the windows of the buildings opposite and the room had grown darker.

"Have you eaten anything?" he finally asked.

She shook her head.

After some persuasion, Leonor agreed to his offer to take her to the bar below the flat. Their plates virtually untouched, only a bottle of poor red wine passed between them. After paying the bill, he had taken her hand as they stepped out onto the pavement. He explained that he would have to be re-joining his base the next day, trying to find a way to say goodbye in the most painless manner possible. He sensed that he had completely failed to bring her any consolation, to offer her a way to diminish the pain. As she stood turning the key to the ground floor door, he had felt her hand tighten around his and, after a momentary hesitation, pull him into the entrance passage.

Dawn next morning had found them side-by-side in the small bedroom. On waking, he found it almost impossible to understand quite what had happened. On getting back into the flat, she had pulled him close, as if she recognised that his embrace was the only way that he might silently convey his sorrow and sympathy. They had stood for some time in the unlit drawing room, saying not a word and then, to his astonishment, she had led him to the bedroom. Their lovemaking had been short but soft, Leonor taking the initiative, as if she had found this way to throw off some of her pain. At first, he resisted gently, unable to understand why she might be doing this so soon after the death of Francisco. Finally, he had realised that this was probably the only way that he could help her. So they had made love, with him putting more tenderness into the act than he could ever remember having done in the past.

Convinced that, once they were both awake, the strangeness of what they had done would shatter any benefits that it might have brought, he had slipped away while she lay asleep, leaving the telephone number of the staging airbase on the little side table in the drawing-room. He caught the next bus back south, much of the trip taken up trying to unravel the meaning of this extraordinary episode. At first, he had tried, guiltily, to analyse whether he was in any way responsible for what had happened. But by the end of the trip he was sure that it was she who had led the process, that it was she who had needed it and that he had had little choice but to play his part. What to do next? He could find no answer, and by the time he was back in the islands, he gratefully escaped into the tensions of fighting the war.

No phone call had ever come while the war lasted into mid-June. The final terrible moments of the Argentine defeat had left them all exhausted and shamed. His only consolation had been to have seen action in one of the military arms which had at least demonstrated its full capacities, by the boldness of its actions, doing something to preserve the honour of the country alongside the success of the Exocet attacks on the Task Force. As one of the pilots who had been shot down, clearly demonstrating courage in the face of the enemy, Leandro had been spared the ambivalence and neglect, even recrimination, which had shamefully been reserved for the army's returning soldiers and officers. Although this had made it psychologically a little easier to bear, it had left him with little desire to remain in the Air Force. He had presented his resignation within a few months.

His commanding officer had expressed genuine regret at losing a battle-hardened pilot, but since nobody at the time had any idea where the armed forces, let alone Argentina, was going, he had given Leandro little cause to withdraw his resignation. By mid-September, Leandro was back in Buenos Aires, looking for something to do. As a pilot who had seen action, he was well received by future employers, who seemed anxious to put the experience of the war behind them as fast as possible, and could see a variety of reasons to employ someone who clearly fitted the mould of a 'war hero'. By October, Leandro was sitting behind a desk and earning a salary.

Then one day, in early November, when spring had brought warmth and the first feeling of hope back to the city, his mother had called to say that a letter had arrived for him from Salta. At first, he couldn't think of anyone he knew in Salta, not even amongst those with whom he had fought. So it had been a few days before he had dropped in on his mother to pick up the letter. Sitting in a nearby cafe, he sliced open the envelope with the stem of his teaspoon. It was from Leonor.

She had left Buenos Aires within days of their night together to return to La Caldera, a small village just north of the city of Salta, where her parents ran a guesthouse. The first part of the letter thanked him for his friendship with her dead husband and reminisced about their courtship, the wedding at which he had been the witness, and how little time they had been able to spend together before Francisco had set off on his last flight. No reference was made to their night together, but the next paragraph brought him the news that she was expecting a child the following month. She said no more, but left him a telephone number. That evening, after a long fight with the decrepit telephone system, he had finally had a short conversation with her, in which she had made it plain that they must meet as soon as possible. The connection had collapsed before they had been able to take it any farther, and by the time he got through again, they found it difficult to make sensible headway. Coming together was all she asked for and he had promised to try and get up to the north-western province as soon as he could arrange it.

A week later, she had met him at the Salta central bus station and they had driven in her father's broken-down Renault to a cafe on the central square. As they sat there under the arcades, with the evening sun going down between the fronds of the large palm trees framing the cupolas of the cathedral church, the early evening bustle of *salteños* stopping off for a drink or a chat at the cafe tables surrounding the square, she slowly recounted what had happened and why. Francisco had failed properly to make love to her on the night of their wedding, but both of them had been content to put this down to the tensions of war and the knowledge that on the next day he would be going back to his squadron. The disappointment of that night had made their parting even more painful, but failure to return to base would have been even worse. So, embracing each other by the folding doors of the long-range bus, they had prayed that fate would be kind and that, as soon as the war was over and he could return to Buenos Aires, all would be made good.

Francisco's death in the downing of his aircraft had put paid to that illusion, but the sudden appearance of Leandro within days of the crash had triggered something inside her which even today she could not explain. She had wanted a child by Francisco more than anything, but if that was not to be, then perhaps a child by his best friend might somehow provide a replacement for the son or daughter that she would never have by Francisco. Their night together had been totally uncalculated, but coming so soon after their wedding night, she had felt that nobody would be in any doubt that her child was Francisco's.

Leandro had been unable to find any convincing reason - or indeed any desire - to argue against this state of affairs. To propose marriage was clearly not what she wanted, nor had she even hinted at such an idea. From the café, they had moved to a nearby restaurant, where she had done everything to de-dramatize the situation. She had confirmed to him that her parents and all her friends were convinced that this was the child conceived with Francisco and she could see no reason to dispel the illusion. Leandro's offer to provide financial support, or even to be present around the time of the birth, were brushed aside. She was asking nothing of him except his silence, which he was only too happy to give. Fatherhood had never loomed large in his thinking, and somehow this version did not seem to match its criteria anyway. After the dinner, she had driven away to her parent's house, leaving him a phone number. He had spent the rest of the night on a bench in the bus station, waiting to travel back to Buenos Aires.

In late February 1983, a short letter had arrived announcing the birth of a boy, in good health and christened Francisco Eduardo after her late husband. She seemed to refer to him more often in the letter as Eduardo and he guessed that this was a way of minimizing the pain. He had replied with a letter of congratulations, which could have been picked up by anyone, promising to keep in touch and accepting her offer that he be Eduardo's godfather.

Over the intervening twenty-four years, Leandro had seen Eduardo pass through a normal childhood - at least as normal as any single parent arrangement might be - into his teens, largely spent as a boarder at a school near Hurlingham in the western suburbs of Buenos Aires. Far from his home, Eduardo had often had little choice but to fend for himself, breeding a dynamic single-mindedness, which had fed through into his chosen career with the Policia Federal, where he had rapidly pushed ahead of his age group. In the harsh environment of police work in a city such as Buenos Aires, Leandro had watched Eduardo mature far faster than his peers. Looking back, Leandro could feel only a good measure of satisfaction that his 'son' had turned into the energetic young man he had just driven home. A young man Leandro loved as a father, a love which his official 'guardian' role had allowed him to show with little fear of the truth being uncovered. But the evening's events filled him with a feeling of deep anxiety, which he must allay by finding some way to help.

Two days later, Eduardo came through the swing doors and looked around the large café, shaking the drops off his raincoat. The late-morning regulars in the London City bar, on the corner of Avenida de Mayo and Calle Perú, were buried in their newspapers, small cups of coffee and the remains of savoury *medialunas de grasa* on side plates, cigarette stubs slowly accumulating in ashtrays. The café's proprietor being untroubled by any non-smoking ordinances of the Government of the Ciudad Autonoma de Buenos Aires, over the decades its pale ceiling had acquired a yellowish patina from the thousands of regular smokers who made up his clientele. Although not nearly as beautiful as some of the other cafes of its period, with its black and white floor and wood panelling it still figured in the tourist guidebooks as one of the better preserved old-style cafes, of which Buenos Aires had retained more than most other cities round the world, along with Paris, Madrid and Milan or Rome.

It being mid-winter and a rather cold winter at that, there were fewer tourists, usually distinguishable by their cameras and open guidebooks, soaking in the *vieux monde* atmosphere in which the city specialized. This was a cafe for middle-aged regulars, men and women not too fashionably dressed, in the daily habit of spending the morning at one of the small square wood or marble-topped tables for an hour or two, stretching out a couple of coffees. The low hum of conversation was broken only by the rustling of newspapers being turned or refolded and, in the background, the waiters reeling off the orders. Bringing a touch of colour, a sprinkling of secretaries from the nearby offices. The passing shower had brought more in off the pavement than usual.

Eduardo quickly spotted his godfather seated in his favourite corner near the last window looking out onto the street. His overcoat and long-suffering beret lay perched on the top of the chair on the other side of the table. In Argentina, the Basque beret was usually associated with farmers in the *campo*, so for a town dweller like Leandro, it was something of an affectation, although in truth he only wore it on cold winter days. Eduardo could see that he was shaking his head over

25

some article he was reading in La Nación, intermittently tapping an unlit cigarette on the tabletop. He walked over and stood silently beside the table.

Leandro looked up.

"*Hola*, Eduardo, you look a lot better. Rather less as if you had walked into a number 11 *colectivo*! Sit down!"

He stretched out a hand for a firm handshake and gestured to the seat opposite. After bending to give his godfather a kiss on the cheek, Eduardo, slewing off his raincoat so as to put minimum strain on his sore ribs, sat down, rubbing his hands to get them warm.

"First of all, I need a strong coffee."

"Fine."

Leandro gestured to the waiter, who had watched Eduardo's arrival from the bar. Weaving his way between the tables, impeccable in his dark shirt, long black and white striped apron, his hair slicked back like some 1920s gigolo, he belonged to the older school of cafe waiters, stuck in a time warp of the 1920s and 30s. Which in no way altered the fact that they were some of the most efficient waiters on the planet, able, without taking a single note, to retain multiple orders from tables of ten people or more.

"What will it be, Señor?"

"A *cortado*, that'll be fine."

"Anything else, Señor?"

"Oh, okay, and a couple of *medialunas de grasa*. They are so good in this place."

Eduardo was hesitant about plunging straight away into the events of the previous evening and deliberately sidestepped Leandro's look of obvious curiosity.

"So what are you shaking your head over, uncle Leandro? Another bit of governmental scandal, I'll bet."

"You're right, these people haven't a clue what they're doing. They think we're all fools, that they can spin us any old rubbish, and that we'll swallow it. And you know what the trouble is? They're probably right, our capacity for self-delusion is unlimited. How did we elect people like this in the first place? I don't know, I even voted for them back in 2003. I must have been crazy. But I don't suppose you want to hear me on that subject again. You had your fill at the *asado* last Sunday, I don't doubt. Meat was good though, wasn't it? The *chinchulines* were spectacular, and Elena's puré of pumpkin was out of this world. I had a great snooze after that by the fire. Must be showing my age! Anyway, tell me a bit more about all this. What the hell have you been up to for this to happen?"

Eduardo still hesitated, waiting for his coffee.

The waiter came over balancing a small round tray on one hand, the *cortado*, a glass of cold sparkling mineral water and the croissants on a separate plate, neatly laid out. With a flourish, he laid them out in front of Eduardo as if he were dealing a hand of cards and tucked the ticket under the aluminium napkin holder.

"Another coffee, Don Leandro? "

"No thanks, I've already had more than I should this morning."

As Eduardo sipped his *cortado,* Leandro watched his son over the top of his half-rimmed reading glasses, relieved to see that the boy appeared to be on the mend. Eduardo was obviously trying to make up his mind about something, but Leandro knew from experience that it was best to let him take his time.

"How's Florencia? She was looking very pretty on Sunday, I thought."

"She's working too hard, I would have liked to get her away for a week or so, not too late for the snow as it's good this year. It's been a long time since we had a break. But now with this, I don't see myself on skis just yet. Trouble is, the prices down south have rocketed, set for foreigners with dollars, not us underpaid policemen with pesos."

He smiled wryly at his godfather and pulling it across the table towards him, picked up the newspaper, skimming through to the domestic news pages, clearly looking for something.

27

"Did you see this?" he said, pointing at an article halfway down page sixteen, speculating on the murder of an English polo fan in Recoleta a couple of weeks earlier. The story had been out of the news for some days, but now the paper had returned to the case. The gist of the article was that the police were making little progress in any direction.

"Yes, I was reading that, since you mentioned it as being the possible cause of the attack. On the face of it, as far as I recall, it looked like a rather outlandish bit of sexual sophistication, something about being chained and asphyxiated, wasn't it?"

Eduardo did not immediately answer the question.

"It's all a bit strange," Eduardo began. "Had a meeting with Fonseca yesterday morning. You know, he's my immediate boss. Left word that he wanted to ask me a few questions. Tricky fellow, so I went prepared. Can't remember whether I mentioned it the other night, but at the time, I had a strong feeling the guys who beat me up may actually have been in the police. So had to make up my mind whether to tell Fonseca the truth about someone warning me off, or some other story. Depended upon whether or not Fonseca might know why I had been attacked. Was even wondering whether he could be behind it in some way. However, thinking it over, I came to the conclusion that he probably didn't know anything about it. Mainly because, being my superior, he could so easily just tell me to pack it in, without going to the lengths of beating me up. And it's not as if I had been constantly chasing him to push the investigation forward."

Eduardo took a mouthful of the coffee before continuing.

"So the more I thought about it, the more I came to the conclusion that, whoever wanted me to freeze the investigation had to be someone outside our team. Possibly someone even unknown or unsuspected by Fonseca. I went prepared to tell him some story about having got too close to a couple of small-time drug runners, they'd beaten me up in the street, no point in mentioning the loss of my laptop. So when he asked me why was looking such a mess, that's what I told him. Watching him closely, I think he bought it. In fact, from the discussion after that, I was left with the impression that he was relaxed about my continuing a routine investigation on the Englishwoman. He did however make it clear that I wasn't getting any free travel to England or anything like that."

"From what you've told me in the past, Fonseca's a complicated bastard at the best of times. Fingers in lots of pies and that will certainly include the drug scene. Presumably he could try and check out your drug story."

"That's what I was thinking. On the other hand, there is little that he can formally do about it. In case I've misread him, I must just assume that he'll be watching me more closely. As to the case, it's moving very slowly. To be more precise, it's almost at a standstill."

"But you think that your present appearance is connected to it?"

Eduardo continued to avoid answering his direct questions.

"Fonseca asked me to join the team right from the start because of my knowledge of English, thought we would need to speak to the police in London, and their Embassy was involved also. She was quite a well-known lady in certain polo circles. That's close to the British royal family, as you know. Apparently she was around when one of the Princes came over a few years ago, down at Lobos or some place in the Province of Buenos Aires."

"Yes, I remember, there was a bit of a scandal. He had to go home early, something about not being able to guarantee his security, wasn't it?"

"Yes, something like that, though they say he was living it up a bit more than he should."

"I'm sure he was, if he's anything like his grandfather. When the Duke of Edinburgh came to Argentina in the mid-1960s, I'm told he had a very good time. While *la reina Isabel* stayed behind in London."

Leandro watched Eduardo taking another bite from the croissant. He wiped his mouth on a paper napkin and looked over at his godfather.

"I know you want to hear why I look as if I've done a couple of rounds with Monzon, but let me come to that in a minute. Let me tell you a little about the case first."

He waved to the waiter for another coffee before continuing.

"In spite of all our efforts, the case doesn't seem to make a lot of sense. We believe that the killer was a woman, or at least, the English girl came back to the hotel with another woman. You don't have to be strong to asphyxiate someone that way. To date, we haven't been able even to determine whether it was murder, or just a bondage session gone wrong. These Europeans have very complicated tastes in sex." He paused. "Still, I don't know why I say that, we've had a few cases like that in Argentina in the past. Anyway, the other woman just walked away from it, we've got the CC video of her leaving ... since when, no trace. She appears very calm from the back and even waves over her shoulder to the night porter."

"What have you been able to put together so far as to what happened earlier in the evening? Do you know where they met?"

"It coincided with the annual agricultural show at the Rural, so we spent time tracking through the horse-breeding and polo crowd, but as you know, they are not crazy about the police crawling over their life-style. The English woman seems to have known a lot of people on the circuit, both here and in England. We're only just beginning to get a picture of her. Nobody seems to know anything about the other woman, no recollection of their meeting that night. Or at least, if they do – which is possible – they aren't telling. There were a lot of parties on the fringe of the Rural, in town, in Pilar and Hurlingham and out in the suburbs – Martinez and San Isidro."

"If you're here and telling me all this, I presume that you think there is something I can add. Although sex and drugs are not really my speciality. I'm better at interest rates and economic development. On top of that, is there any kind of professional confidentiality that you're ignoring? That boss of yours, Fonseca, would your talking to me be okay with him?"

"He doesn't know I'm seeing you and nor should he, he'd be really pissed off. But I would doubt that he has any cause to make a link between us, being your godson, so I've no reason to think that our relationship is actually a problem. However, it could be a real problem if he suspected that I was discussing the case outside police circles. But for reasons I'll explain in a minute, the shape of my face now seems actually to be part of a way of trying to prevent just that. Give me a minute. I'm getting there."

Leandro knew what his godson meant. From what he heard from Eduardo and on the basis of a single encounter a few years earlier, he knew that Fonseca was nothing if not complex. Only interested in his own career, which meant that he had cultivated key friends in high places whatever the government of the day.

"Okay. Take your time."

Eduardo searched the bottom of the coffee cup in vain for another mouthful, before looking out of the window at the crowded pavement on Avenida de Mayo. The shower had passed over and the late morning office crowd was hurrying past, turning the collars of their overcoats up against the cold. A pretty brunette on the other side of the plate glass had stopped by the entrance to the metro to answer her cell phone, the wind picking up her coat to reveal an elegant leg. Catching a glimpse of Eduardo's undisguised admiring gaze, she flashed a rapid smile and turned towards the street to continue her conversation. Eduardo grinned.

Leandro caught the look on his godson's face. Pretty girls never failed to get his attention, however much he might have been going out with Florencia for more than five years now. Still, given his own relationship with Sam, Leandro was in no position to pass judgment on anyone. Anyway, Eduardo was a handsome fellow, like his father had been at his age, having inherited the very dark eyes of both his parents. Leandro's pale blue might have been a give-away!

"It's hard to tell what to think. An Englishwoman arrives late at night at her hotel, accompanied by another woman, apparently of similar age. The Englishwoman was forty-three, but the other woman could be younger, though we are not sure of that. They go up to her hotel bedroom, no room service, a couple of hours later the other woman leaves, apparently calm and relaxed, and about nine hours later the hotel management finally open up, to find her asphyxiated on her bed."

Eduardo looked over at his godfather.

"The next bit gets more rough. Is that okay with you?"

Leandro gestured to him to go ahead.

"Very well. Her head was encased in some kind of hood to restrain her breathing, her wrists and ankles tied to the ends of the bed with chains, clearly having had some kind of extreme sexual activity. Her cunt was

31

lubricated and there was a large dildo under the bed. Time of death established as approximately coinciding with the other woman being there. Where did they first meet? We still don't know. The other woman? Disappeared into thin air. We showed a short extract from the CC tapes to a number of professional hookers and high class escort agencies, the kind that usually see extra business round about the time of the Rural Show. No-one recognized the other woman. Not that there is a lot to see, but girls usually recognize a fur coat or a hairstyle belonging to the competition. Nor did any of them have any contact with the Englishwoman. We also asked around the transvestite and small transsexual community, which also tends to get busier at show time, but again no connection. So it looks like someone who is not on the circuit, a gifted amateur if you like. Except that it all went wrong."

Eduardo paused to drink some of the fresh coffee the waiter had put beside him, before continuing.

"But the question is, did it really go wrong? Because if it did, the other woman appears to have been pretty unconcerned about it, from the little that we can tell about the way she left the hotel. She gives a wave to the night porter as she goes out the door, and is then seen strolling down the street until she gets out of range of the hotel camera. Nothing more after that. We weren't able to trace any taxi, which might have picked her up round the corner. We checked the airports and even the bus terminals – though she doesn't look like the type to take a bus. Nothing. The CC tapes at Aeroparque and Ezeiza show nothing like the profile – or at least anything that does, we've followed up with the airline check-in counter to get a fix on who it might have been. Tall thin blondes in expensive clothes turned out to be just that, wives of rich businessmen, off to Europe or Punta del Este for a long winter weekend. We ended up with about ten names of women who just about fit the profile, height, long silvery blonde hair, expensive clothes, slightly Asiatic features - though we don't place too much importance on that aspect - but their records were clean and certainly not enough to warrant a trip to Europe to track them down. In the case of two of them, we even went so far as to talk to them on the phone or to their husbands. They were tucked up in bed at the time and we would make too many waves if we started to try and undo their stories. But now Fonseca is putting on an act of getting bored with the story and attempting to shut the files unless something new comes in. In some ways, I'm not sure I don't agree."

Eduardo paused briefly, but since Leandro showed no sign of asking a question, continued.

"Even before my attack, there was something niggling away at the back of my mind. That we were looking at something a bit different. Not to mention that we hardly want to relax if there's a sadomasochist female killer on the loose in Buenos Aires, capable of seeing off rich tourists. Not much to go on, I know. Part of me says I should not waste any more of my time – and perhaps not yours either. But with this attack, it's a different matter. My hunch may be right, though I don't know what the reason is."

"Could we get back to the attack? It's all very well hearing about what the jet set gets up to on a quiet night in Buenos Aires, but it's actually you, Eduardo, my godson, that interests me."

Eduardo grinned.

"Okay, you're probably right."

For the next five minutes, he rehearsed what had happened in his flat two nights before. Leandro looked more and more worried as the story progressed.

"Don't worry, uncle. Thanks to you, apart from some heavy bruising, we know that there's nothing serious. Time and swabbing my face and chest with arnica will probably reduce the swellings pretty fast."

"Have you said anything to Florencia about it yet?"

"Not in so many words, though she was clearly shocked to see me when we met last night. I stuck to the same story with her as well, not to get her worried. She'll probably put it down to my drinking habits!"

Eduardo grinned again.

Leandro thought for a minute.

"So what are you actually going to do? The message passed by your friends the other night seems to have been pretty clear. If you think Fonseca wants the story to die, it looks as if you should play along with that, not only to keep on his good side, but just to keep alive."

Eduardo paused before replying.

"As you can imagine, I've spent quite a bit of time thinking about that in the last forty-eight hours. The easy course would certainly be to forget about it and move on. But, you know me, I'm pig-headed by nature, always more inclined to do the opposite of what other people expect of me."

"As some of your schoolteachers would be the first to confirm."

Eduardo, although usually getting good results at school and then at university, had often shown a tendency to push the boundaries, particularly in areas in which he saw the hand of petty school discipline. As his guardian, Leandro had on numerous occasions been asked to call in to the school to hear about another one of Eduardo's escapades.

"I don't think that you can just ignore what happened the other night. Of course you won't. But this kind of direct action, which I suspect rarely makes it into the newspapers, hasn't died out in Argentina. There is sadly an endless supply of people specializing in this kind of intimidation and, as you know better than I do, some of the cases don't just end up with bruised ribs."

"I know. I see some of them pretty regularly."

Leandro weighed up what he had heard so far. First of all, there was his concern for the safety of his son. But there appeared to be something more to it than that. He sensed somewhere that it could make a change from reading Ambito Financiero and the Economist. There was exoticism in the story, a rich European victim, some kind of *crime passionnel* on the fringes of Buenos Aires's upper class, a hotel situated in the most fashionable *barrio* of the city, home to its rich and powerful. A part of town in which the social group could be expected to close ranks and bury their scandal as fast as possible, and for which a compliant conservative press would be rapidly persuaded to give up the story. He had seen it a number of times before. The subeditor of one of the leading dailies killed by his boyfriend in his elegant flat in Recoleta, the story had lasted at most a week and then silence. Or a jealous husband killing his errant wife in their gated community home in the northern suburbs, paying off doctors, maids, ambulance men and a few more to make it look like an accident – even though she had three bullet holes in the back of her skull! Leandro's curiosity was aroused.

"On the face of it, all quite exciting, definitely a change from my usual reading, but... Can I really be of any use to you? Without a bit more in the way of hard facts, it's hard for me to tell whether I can do anything except listen. Would it be possible to see some papers? Want another coffee?"

"I would have to be careful of course. I could try to bring some papers round to your flat later this week. It's okay, thanks."

"I think I need one. *Mozo*?" he called to the waiter, who was passing between nearby tables. With thumb and forefinger, he indicated a small espresso, lifting his index to show only one. The waiter nodded and placed the order at the bar.

"You said 'asiatic' features – so you did get a shot of the other woman's face."

"Well, that's stretching it a little. We were able to get a half-second glimpse of her reflection in the lift mirror when she gets in on the way up to the room and a brief view when she steps out again on her way down. We blew it up as far as possible. We get a rather flat face, with large almond eyes heavily made up and a very full mouth, impossible to fix the age. Not much to go on, but it looks Chinese or Japanese – not that that really fits with being blonde and with her height, she's taller than the average Asiatic. Although that doesn't mean that there aren't tall Chinese. But silvery blonde? In all the other images, her hair is in the way or it's just the back of her head. We even showed it to a number of hairdressers in the Palermo and Recoleta area of town, since she had a small red bow in the back of her loose hairstyle, like one of those ornate French combs, just to see whether any of them recognized the hairstyle. Nothing either."

"Sounds as though you've been trying quite hard in the space of a couple of weeks, all the same?"

"Yes, Fonseca was very keen at the beginning of the investigation, sent us scurrying in all directions, following every possible lead. I met a lot of polo players and their girlfriends, mistresses, wives, ponies, dogs. Also the escort agencies – the job has to have some compensations..."

"I wouldn't say too much to Florencia about that, if I were you," Leandro interjected, laughing.

"I know, but it makes up for the lousy salary! Even the transvestites were something. But compared to that television crossdresser – what's his or her name? - something 'de la V' – they looked very tame and ugly. She's actually quite handsome, if you like your women strong. Anyway, no leads there."

"Even dear old Argentina seems to be moving into uncharted sexual territory. Never thought I'd hear you admiring a transsexual! "

Eduardo blushed slightly.

"But you said that Fonseca is now putting on an act of getting bored? Perhaps he can't see a quick kill to enhance his reputation."

"I say 'act', because since a week he's started systematically closing down some – but not all - the avenues of the investigation, telling us to drop it, but not giving any real reason. I suggested that we should do something about the English angle, try and find out more about the victim's contacts in the polo crowd there. I had a brief chat with a man in Special Branch in London and he seemed to be saying that a bit more digging in the county polo milieu might help. But Fonseca killed that one very smartly, admittedly on the grounds that we didn't have money to send youngsters like me off to Europe to have a good time. But there was something about the way he said it that made me wonder."

"It being England, it's got delicate political overtones, what with the islands and all that. Something smelling of cooperation with the English wouldn't go down too well, either with the diplomats in Palacio San Martin, or with the President in the Casa Rosada. Britain's pretty much off the radar as far as this government's concerned.

"Or more precisely, on it, just as long as they can send an Exocet into some British position at the UN."

Leandro looked up at Eduardo, noting the sudden edge of bitterness which had crept into his voice at the mention of the Malvinas. Not surprising, with his father buried on the islands.

He stretched out a hand to touch Eduardo's sleeve and felt him stiffen.

"I don't know, what do you want to do with all this? Do you have any idea about how I could help?" Leandro repeated his earlier question.

Eduardo sat silent for a minute. Then, leaning across the table, he continued.

"My analysis is the following. Tell me what you think, though obviously I need to show you more of the files. To begin with, it's not a routine murder case. It's got overtones that we don't have much experience in dealing with in Argentina. This is a country in which jealous husbands shoot their wives' lovers, or drug runners settle scores. Or else the odd purely political killing, perhaps a journalist who writes one story too many about someone close to government, like the case of that journalist murdered in Pinamar in the 1990s. Many of these cases never get to court, a judge is instructed to sit on it until it's forgotten, usually in the political cases. Secondly, it's got a clear international dimension, it being an Englishwoman as victim. That's also a bit different, we tend to kill among Argentines, foreigners don't usually play a part, or if they do, its drug runners from somewhere else in South America, Peru or Colombia or Mexico. We know how to deal with them, we speak the same language and we can liaise with their police forces without much trouble. Here, we need to be able to communicate with Europeans, and – to make it more complicated – with Brits. At least, that looks like being a possibility. So that's an angle where your experience and language skills could be very useful, given your origins and connections. You've mentioned that you've worked with people in London on financial investigations in the past. And as I recall, you lived there for a couple of years. Thirdly, we're not moving in the usual lower middle class strata of the population, we're touching on a social group in which the police rarely gets through the door. Where a few well-planted phone calls in the right places can shut all of them up very smartly, and in which even the press often drops the story in case they harm a major shareholder or relative of the founder."

Eduardo pointed at the newspaper.

"That's why I was a little surprised to see this story resurfacing today. By rights, La Nación should have lost interest by now. It's not as if there has been any development in the last few days to bring the story back to the surface. Maybe the journalist has had a tip off of some kind. If so, it's unlikely to be coming from us. Maybe someone else is taking an interest. Who? I don't have a clue at this stage, but it's intriguing nevertheless. Those are just a few of the reasons why I think it merits a serious look, something which Fonseca is showing every sign of wanting to avoid. What do you think?"

Leandro had been nodding his head slowly as Eduardo listed his ideas. He stuck a deformed but unlit cigarette between his lips, and played with it with his tongue.

"Yes," he said slowly. "Yes – all of that and perhaps some more."

He hunched his shoulders a bit and stood staring down at his newspaper. The waiter set his cup of coffee down beside it, and took away Eduardo's used cup and plate, sliding another ticket under the napkin rack. Leandro picked up his biro and began to jot a few words in the margin of the paper.

"There are certainly some interesting and intriguing angles to the story. The British connection may be something I can help on. And it's nothing if not a bit exotic, definitely a change from economic statistics. Something inside me is twitching to find out more."

Leandro went on.

"So I am definitely interested, above all if it can help you to get out of any further trouble. As my godson, that's my number one motive. But, frankly, without a look at the papers, I probably can't add much more at this stage. I'm sure your summary is pretty complete, but you know what I mean."

"Thanks, uncle, that's helpful. Obviously, you would need more information to work with. It won't be easy, I'll see what I can do. Give me a few days and I'll come back to you."

Rising from his chair, and after exchanging a kiss, he picked up his coat and made his way out onto the street through the swing doors. The rain seemed to have stopped. Leandro watched him leave, then turned back to the newspaper. La Nación finished, he picked up his cell phone and made a call to his ex-wife Elena. She was good when it came to Eduardo, having acted as a surrogate mother to the boy during term-time for many years. She might have some ideas about whether he should get involved on this case. He also was curious to know whether she had detected anything about Sam.

Elena had found a profitable little niche doing research for one of the foreign banks in the City, which she was able to do pretty much when she liked, mainly working from home. So he was confident he would find her in. However, an ex-husband should never arrive unannounced.

He stayed sitting at his table, looking out at the windswept street. He might even stay a bit longer and have one of their delicious toasted ham and cheese sandwiches. He began to jot a few ideas down on the side of the newspaper. The more he thought about what Eduardo had told him, the more it intrigued him. If somehow he could help Eduardo to escape from any further direct action by parties unknown, that was the most important.

Maybe Sam might have a few ideas too. Letting her in on the plot should certainly provide material to satisfy her insatiable curiosity as regards his work.

May 2007

Looking back on it, Leandro was sometimes surprised by the speed with which his relationship with Samira had evolved in the three months since their first meeting.

On a warm autumnal Sunday in late May, he had strolled along Avenida de Mayo, the elegant avenue which stretches west from Plaza de Mayo in front of the Casa Rosada, the presidential palace, towards the imposing edifice of Congress, built at a time when the nation clearly still believed in strong democratic institutions. In the last decades of the nineteenth century, the planners of Buenos Aires had looked to Europe and Washington for inspiration. It was probably no coincidence that Avenida de Mayo boasted the same width of road and pavement as the Avenue de l'Opéra in Paris. Attempts by the municipality to regulate the height and style of the buildings had gone the same way as most attempts at administrative control in Argentina, so that a disparate proliferation of more and more imposing buildings had imparted to the Avenue a personality and beauty all its own. From the east end in Plaza de Mayo, one could look all the way west to the imposing dome of the building of Congress. The Avenida, whose resilient plane trees somehow survived the onslaught of an interminable stream of deafening, exhaust-belching buses and taxis, was crowded. The sun was shining and some of the girls, perhaps sensing that winter was only just around the corner, were still bravely flaunting the ubiquitous tight jeans and T-shirts, which, as they all knew, never failed to capture the attention of the opposite sex. Leandro had to recognise that he was probably no exception.

Buenos Aires was the city of Leandro's birth. He had grown up here, watching it change slowly over the years. Life in Buenos Aires shaped his view of how life should be lived, a certain pace, a certain feel. Only when travelling to Europe had he appreciated the extent to which his birthplace somehow perpetuated a style of life which had all but vanished in so many other large cities in Europe. He loved it even more for that reason. In any listing of the globe's top ten real cities, as opposed to urban sprawls of more than five million inhabitants, Buenos Aires would certainly find its place. To him, a city meant vibrancy, perpetual movement, scents and sounds, not necessarily all pleasant. The roar of a passing *colectivo*, spewing noxious exhaust fumes onto passers-by, mingled with the scent of a grilling *asado* in the nearest restaurant, or the trail of perfume left by a pretty girl passing him on the pavement. Above all, a powerful if indefinable personality distilled from the warm intercourse of the *porteños*, as residents of the Argentina's capital were known, harking back to the days when everything entered and left the country through its docks. This intercourse was shaped by the physical dimensions of the metropolis, sprawling over two hundred square kilometres along the southern bank of the Rio de la Plata, by its history and indefinably by the way that people moved through its spaces. For many of the wrong reasons perhaps, including inefficient governments, political turbulence and economic disasters, Buenos Aires showed fewer signs of the indiscriminate forces of modernisation and commercial real estate development than so many other great metropolis. Ever since Buenos Aires' architectural heyday in the early decades of the previous century, intermittent phases of economic boom interspersed with wrenching economic chaos had ensured that few developers had built with the long term in mind, preferring architectural solutions ensuring a quick profit.

In spite of the worst that poor planning and undying municipal corruption could inflict, shabby multi-storey apartment blocks could not totally conceal the beauty and charm of elegant one- or two-storey townhouses in the city's distinctive late colonial and turn of the century style. Buenos Aires in the 1920s must have been one of the most beautiful cities on earth. This was the Buenos Aires which he knew, which he could not imagine ever abandoning.

This feeling for the lifeblood of the city explained his love of the tango, a unique music which had emerged from the docks of the city, a music of older men, men who had loved, been cheated, betrayed. In this respect, he was not typical of the average Anglo-Argentine, few of whom felt any particular empathy with the tango. Probably too *latino*. The lyrics nostalgically scrolling visions of rejected passions, of jealous lovers, of violence, of frustration, deeply distilled from the depth of the Argentine psyche, were almost unique in the world of music for often being geographically identified with real streets and *barrios* of the city. San Juan y Boedo, Pampa, Sur – the names of these streets also the names of the most famous tangos. As the lament of the *bandoneón* struck up, the nicotine-stained voice of an Edmundo Rivero or Julio

Sosa would seamlessly transport dancers to a street corner, a café, a suburb, which true *porteños* could visualize, where many had grown up, which they could almost smell.

Leandro had settled into a table at Café Iberia. His copy of La Nación unread on the wicker chair next to him, he was enjoying the salty taste of the *medialuna de grasa*, and sipping a bitter, unsweetened espresso, observing the passing crowd over the top of his half-moon reading glasses. The last days of May were special. And this year even more so. Twenty five years ago, almost to the day, he had been given a second chance in life, surviving the crash of the Pucará. It was a time to be thankful.

It was on that Sunday morning that he had first met Samira, a student at the Universidad de Buenos Aires, who had sat down at the table beside his on the pavement, their backs to the bay windows of the bar.

His eye was immediately drawn to the girl. Certainly good-looking and very sexy. At first glance, he wondered whether she was Argentine. Unlike most examples of her sex and age group, for whom straight long hair, most often blonde, falling to the small of the back, was the norm, her hairstyle was short and carefully sculptured to frame a striking profile. Argentine girls tended to adopt a natural look. This girl's make-up was stylised, verging on the artificial, with perfectly tapered, arched eyebrows over large, surprisingly pale green eyes, elaborately made up. Below the straight nose, a full, brightly rouged mouth, above a firm, slightly pointed jaw. Her face was broad, the forehead high. There was something faintly familiar about the face. A film perhaps? The rest of her appearance betrayed an impeccable, clearly personalised, sense of style. In tapered black jeans descending from a narrow waist, through the unbuttoned opening of a short, well-cut dark grey woollen jacket, he could make out strong breasts under an off-white silk blouse with open Chinese collar. Her shoes also looked expensive. He wondered who was paying for all this. She would have been more at home in Paris or Rome than on the pavements of Buenos Aires. Although he guessed that she must be in her late twenties, maybe early thirties, she exuded an air of unusual maturity.

A well-thumbed edition of Oscar Wilde lay flattened on the table beside her cup of coffee. He had caught a glimpse of the cover page as she set it aside to take a look at the menu.

"Oscar Wilde? What brings you to read that?" he had shot at her. It must be the first time anyone has used a nineteenth century *maricón* to pick up a twenty-first century girl!

Quite unfazed by the direct approach, she had paused a couple of seconds before turning in his direction.

She noted the pale blue eyes in a slightly broad face, a hint of Paul Newman, though the rest was definitely *latino*. Black hair slightly dishevelled, but – thank God – not that scruffy length so beloved of Argentine males. Strong, apparently in good physical shape. A certain elegance about the way he dressed, even if the slight wear of the cuffs suggested that this was an old, if favourite, jacket. Mid forties? Unusual.

"Sorry?"

He could see that she had rapidly scanned him from top to toe. The small smile at the corner of her mouth suggested that she was not wholly disappointed by what she saw.

He repeated the question, with a broader grin, now that she was looking at him.

"Oh, he's my favourite author. Have you read anything by him? He's fascinating. I love him. But perhaps not for everyone."

She wondered whether he would have even heard of Wilde. He didn't look the literary type, although you never could tell these days.

Ignoring the veiled, if possibly justified, challenge to his intellect, Leandro had to confess that he had never read any Wilde.

"Oh, but you should. You do speak English, don't you?"

"Certainly, my great-great-grandparents stepped off the boat from Glasgow with some of the first Aberdeen Angus. Between us we made the country."

She laughed, easily, relaxed, leaning back in her chair.

"Tell me more about Wilde," Leandro suggested slyly, inwardly a bit ashamed to have to betray such ignorance.

Quite unselfconsciously, she had launched into a surprisingly erudite explanation of her interest in late Victorian England. A world in which elegance, wit and sexual nonconformity had been so humorously distilled in the mind of a single man, whose intelligence and creativity had not been sufficient to protect him from bigotry and jealousy.

"Though it's arguable he couldn't – wouldn't – save himself."

Her reading list proved impressively wide. Proust, Gide, Zola, Baudelaire, names not unfamiliar to him, but never read. Others – like Huysmans – of whom he had never even heard. Her fascination with the *fin d'epoque* aesthetic, culture and lifestyle was manifest. She spoke of Wilde almost as if she had known him personally.

"Wilde was very interested in fashion. He even designed dresses for his poor wife, Constance. Of course, he also dressed outrageously. I love that about him. Although Oscar Wilde might not have agreed with me, I think the fashion of the day was so beautiful. All those elegant women in their long bustle skirts, tight corsets, the inevitable parasol. Beautiful! So blatantly sexy, that hourglass silhouette! Did you ever see Nicole Kidman in Portrait of a Lady? With Malkovich? Fantastic film. The cameraman constantly focusing on the back view of Kidman, her train sweeping from side to side."

"No, can't say I've even heard of the film. Sounds as though you recommend it. Though all those skirts and stays might make things a little complicated, if you see what I mean?"

"You should also read the book. By Henry James. An American. Another great writer. Not that Wilde admired him."

He began to wonder whether this conversation had not got out of his depth. The intellectual type. But then again, with those looks?

"Do you always start intense conversations like this with men you don't know?"

"No, not usually. But then you started it, not me," she fired back

The lecture on Oscar Wilde seemingly at an end, she moved over to his table.

With no trace of embarrassment, she switched to a blatant investigation of Leandro, his work, his private life.

This was something rather different from the average pickup. Leandro even wondered who had picked up who.

From the way she looked at him, which she did with little attempt at concealment, he guessed that his overall looks and physique were not entirely wasted on her. Women were generally attracted to his regular features, the combination of his Nordic blue eyes with a more aquiline Mediterranean profile inherited from his mother. Frequent visits to the gym, the combination of broad shoulders and a narrow waist, coupled with the fact that he was about ten centimetres taller than the average Argentine, ensured as much success with women as he felt manageable.

Nearly an hour later, she stood up to leave. Leandro had to move fast.

"It's a lovely day, have you any other plans? I'm not going to let you escape that easily." He looked up at her. Her momentary hesitation rendered the answer superfluous. "How about some lunch?"

"Why not, what's on the menu? Apart from you? You're one of the better things in town today."

Leandro ignored the blatant approach, inwardly delighted.

A taxi ride took them to one of the riverside restaurants specialising in barbecues near the Jorge Newbery downtown airport.

"When I was a small kid, there weren't any of these smart restaurants down here," Leandro commented as they stepped out of the taxi. "There used to be a line of ramshackle little sheds with makeshift barbecues, each one a bigger health hazard than its neighbour. Somehow, I bet it was more fun. Then they closed them all down and these dull restaurants took their place."

Having ordered two large *bifes de chorizo* with *papas paille* and a good bottle of merlot, the mutual probing continued. She had travelled extensively in Europe and the Middle East, from where her family stemmed, and showed herself untypically interested in politics and economics, revealing a rare knowledge of international affairs compared with Argentine women of her age. Her English, from the few

46

phrases she dropped, was flawless, and like many Argentines of a certain social class, she sprinkled her conversation with English and French phrases. Although he usually found this irritating, in Samira it somehow felt natural and unpretentious.

The demolition of more than one bottle of merlot seemed to render her more perceptive and bold in her questioning, with every glass he poured.

How old was he? Was he married? What was his job? Who were his favourite writers? Film directors? Foods? He saw no reason to be anything other than honest on all these subjects.

By the end of lunch they had established a common love of James Bond movies - she had even read Ian Fleming in the original - Woody Allen, Sting, Handel, Italian cars and – in his case – Italian women, in hers, Italian men. The only serious point of difference seemed to be whether Daniel Craig – her view – was a better Bond than Sean Connery, although they could easily agree on the worst, Roger Moore. She was clearly passionate about the cinema. Running through it all, a shared love of Argentina, that throwback to the best and worst of times gone by. As the world seemed to be accelerating fast towards extremes of cheap hedonism, this rich, vast land preserved values – as well as vices - which they agreed were fast going out of fashion everywhere else. Politeness, compassion, time for others, well-polished shoes, empty spaces, alongside massive corruption at the highest levels of power, economic mismanagement, violence. A powerful cocktail! As he looked back on it later that evening, Leandro could not remember any first encounter, which even remotely resembled the five or six hours he had spent that day.

In the late afternoon, as the sun was beginning to go down, they walked back towards the centre of town through the parks of Palermo. The leaves had begun to fall, the grass still yellow after a long summer. Just as he was about to suggest prolonging the encounter over dinner or maybe a movie, she turned to him, as if suspecting what was coming, and silently handed him a slip of paper with her cell phone number. Then, dropping a soft kiss on his cheek, she waved down a cruising taxi. Sliding the large sunglasses, which she wore like a braid on her dark hair, onto the bridge of her nose to prevent any further eye contact, she lithely slipped into the back seat. All he could do was gallantly close the taxi door and, somewhat bemused, follow the back of her head as the cab re-entered the stream of traffic.

Outmanoeuvred, he would have to be quicker next time. She might be some fifteen years younger, but she had little to learn when it came to tactics.

A movie. She reminded him of some movie actress. Not one of the stars. It would probably come to him when he least expected it.

He had allowed a week to go by, resisting the temptation to pull the slip of paper out of the pocket of the jacket he had worn that day. Finally his curiosity, given the impression she had made, got the better of him. The first couple of calls went unanswered. It was only a few days later that his cell phone finally rang on his bedside table around eleven thirty in the evening.

"Hi, it's Sam, sorry not to have got back to you sooner. Sure you'll understand. Been very busy," she said, with no trace of remorse in her voice.

"Don't worry, quite understandable."

She had given him the diminutive of her name, but had seen no reason to explain why such a silence might be understandable and she certainly made no attempt to explain it.

"We're having a public play reading of Oscar Wilde's 'The Ideal Husband', which I thought, given your track record, might have been of interest... You might pick up a tip or two," she had chuckled.

He remembered that, somewhere near the end of the first bottle of merlot, he had told her something of his current ex-matrimonial status. At the time, he had wondered whether it might appear a bit too obvious, yet here she was playing it back to him in a more subtle manner.

"It's next Thursday evening in the UBA auditorium, starting at six thirty. If you're interested, I'll leave the ticket in your name. Not that it costs anything anyway, so don't get too excited."

"I should be able to manage that. If something gets in the way, I'll give you a call," he responded, perhaps a little too cautiously.

48

"That's okay, hope you can make it."

She promptly rang off.

On reflection, he suspected that his hesitation wasn't going to make her lose any sleep.

Over the next few days, he caught himself frequently thinking about his meeting with her. That she was very sexy and good-looking, he had not the slightest doubt, but then, so were a number of his short-lived affairs since leaving Elena. That her worldly intelligence and self-assurance set her aside from the rest, however, was much clearer, as evidenced by her intellectual bandwidth and the way she dressed. In spite of the abrupt separation after their lunch and the week's delay in ringing him, he consoled himself with the thought that she might be genuinely interested in seeing him again.

At ten minutes past six on the following Thursday, he showed up at the entrance to the auditorium. Asking around, he found an assistant holding a number of envelopes with courtesy invitations, including one in his name.

With the usual minor delay and confusion of such events, the play reading finally began around six forty-five. The auditorium seemed to contain more adults than young students, perhaps symptomatic of the new reality that Argentina's younger intellectual class was fast shrinking under the onslaught of the Internet and pop culture. Some ten chairs had been aligned on the stage. The actor-students filed in, a copy of the play in their hands, Sam the last to emerge. Before the reading began, one of the young men provided a brief introduction to Oscar Wilde and to the play, and then identified those who would be reading the main parts. Sam had been given the role of Lady Chiltern.

Leandro's command of English, totally fluent given his Anglo-Saxon origins and education at the bilingual school St. Andrew's, allowed him to enjoy every twist and turn of Wilde's humorous and devastating commentary on late Victorian marital infidelity. Although it was only a reading, each of the young actors clearly enjoyed putting as much of their own personality as possible into their parts and Sam revealed a certain acting talent, reinforced by her impeccable English. Leandro regretted that he had not followed up on a fleeting idea of picking up a copy of the play before the reading.

At the point in the play in which Mrs Cheveley attempts to blackmail Lady Chiltern's husband into financing a canal project in Argentina, which he condemns as 'a commonplace Stock Exchange swindle', an ironic ripple of laughter went through the audience and someone called out "As always! *Nada nuevo!*"

He found himself following the play closely. Whilst it was obvious that the presence of Sam was largely the reason, he was also intrigued by Wilde's portrayal of a world in which politics, fidelity and honour could be presented with such a light touch, the latter ultimately conditioning the other two. In the real world which he knew, the concept of honour had long ago disappeared from both politics and even from marriage. Somehow, he now understood better some of the things that Sam had been saying over their lunch together.

Although there had been a couple of defections during the reading, most of the audience stayed to the end and rewarded the actors with a few minutes of appreciative applause. As the audience filed out, Leandro remained standing in his row. The cast stayed and were now chattering gaily among themselves on stage. He saw Sam step to the side of the group and signal to him to wait in the entrance hall.

"I told them that my uncle had come to see me in the play," she explained with a grin as she joined him about ten minutes later.

"Uncle? Indeed. Ah well, I suppose that that's what people of my age get reduced to!"

But the squeeze she gave his arm was consolation enough.

"Come along, uncle Leandro, I'm hungry– and thirsty, very thirsty!"

"I like it when you get an uncontrollable urge."

"Yeah, I know, it's my best feature."

He stopped and grabbed her by the shoulders.

"I love it. Woody Allen! That was so quick."

"I know."

"Except that that was supposed to be my line, not yours."

"I'm glad to say you don't look like Woody Allen."

"No, I'm also glad about that."

In the weeks following the play reading, Leandro and Sam saw each other on a regular basis. He would come back from his offices in San Isidro or business in town to find her curled up on his couch, often with a book taken off his shelves in her lap. He was gratified that she loved his apartment on the top floor of the central block in Pasaje La Piedad. Off Calle Bartolome Mitre near the corner of Parana, a couple of blocks from the Argentine Congress building, it was one of the city's rare '*pasajes*', these little gated streets, which in France would have been called 'cités', or in London perhaps a mews. Accessible through a locked wrought iron gate at both ends, with no traffic and no more than two hundred metres long, he had chosen it for its calm and privacy. His flat provided a view of the elegant mansion on the other side of the street, but also enjoyed maximum luminosity, since not all the opposite side was built up.

The little *pasaje* struck her as something out of time, taking her back to the *fin de siècle* atmosphere she so loved. Walking through the wrought iron grille into the little street, she claimed she could almost hear the sound of hooves and carriage wheels on the cobbles. A small sign still showed the way for access by horse drawn carriages!

On evenings such as these, it was with a sense of some consternation that he realised that the mere sight of her lying there reading produced an almost instantaneous sense of arousal. He couldn't remember any other girlfriend who had had quite this effect. With her full breasts, slim waist, perfectly proportioned thighs and long legs, their curves enhanced by the tight cashmere sweater and designer jeans she so often wore, she projected a strong, provocative female sexuality. Her predilection for tall thigh boots rising above the knee did little to detract from the effect! Her look, transmitted over the internet, or in fashion or society magazines such as ¡Hola!, meshed in with the relentless diffusion on his computer desktop of strong images of the new woman. Powerful, dominating, beautiful, apparently totally self-sufficient, men seemed to play only a minor, subservient role in their lives.

When his arousal became irresistible, she would respond unhesitatingly, her appetite for sex clearly on a par with his, her lovemaking leaving him in no doubt that he was what she wanted most at that moment. Though clearly not the first man in her life, he couldn't have cared less.

At other times, she would find ways to convey to him that she valued her independence, disappearing without trace for three or four days at a stretch. Just occasionally, she would even inflict this on him at the weekend, to make her absence doubly felt. He told himself that this was probably as much as he deserved, given their age difference. No doubt she had other friends. He was nevertheless surprised at the degree of restlessness, and even moodiness, which such acts of abandonment provoked in him.

"Were you always in the financial research business? All those boring statistics. I thought you had more in you," Sam had teased, on a cold drizzly evening in June.

They had abandoned the idea of going to the cinema. She was lying the length of the couch, the back of her head resting on his chest, twisting strands of her dark hair between her long fingers. Looking around the room, with its bookshelves and record and DVD collections, she could see the span of his interests. Although she knew that he was definitely interested in sex, she knew that there was more, probably a lot more, to this man Leandro. She needed to explore it.

The central heating had steamed up the windowpanes and it was a good evening to be indoors. Ben Webster was playing 'Stardust' in the background. Sam had appeared about an hour earlier, just as the rain was starting, a copy of La Nación open at the cinema page. Last year's Woody Allen, Scoop, was still playing in their barrio. But a look through the window at the wet cobbles outside had got the better of their energy. Anyway, neither was a fan of Johanssen.

"Inquisition beginning again, is it? Okay. Here we go. I think you may have heard some of it before, so tell me. Though it's going to be hard without a drink."

He hesitated, but then decided to get the drink later.

"When I came out of the Fuerza Aerea in 1982, I had to do something to prepare myself for life. So I went back part time to university and for three years I studied law and economics. I tried to keep up with a business course, but to be frank, few businesses were looking very promising in the days of Alfonsín. In 1986, I got married to Elena. The same year, I started to work in a small, privately-owned bank in the financial district, but two years later moved to Citibank, one of those big, impersonal institutions which provide good training, but which are not much fun. In 1990, by which time Alejandra was about two years old, Citibank sent me to their London office and, as a family, we spent a great couple of years there. London was cheaper in those days and we were able to find a little flat on the edge of Chelsea, with Alex going to the kindergarten round the corner. Those were great days in London, before all the money flooded in. One summer, we rented a small cottage out beyond Oxford. Although it was only ten years after Malvinas, it was as if nothing had happened. We even took a trip up to Scotland to find where my family had come from. That's probably when I acquired my taste for whiskey. Then things began to look up back here when Menem's Finance Minister, Cavallo, brought in the convertibility programme in 1992. So I came back.

Leandro paused.

"Jesus, you sure you want to listen to all this...? How about a drink? Not sure I can keep this up otherwise."

"Thought you'd never ask. Yes to the drink, and yes, I want you to go on. I only have a vague idea of what you get up to, when you're not thinking of sex. I've a funny feeling that you're a bit more than just a boring economic analyst."

Carefully setting her head on a large sofa cushion, he slid out from under her and got up to fetch a bottle of white wine with which he filled their glasses.

She sipped her wine.

"So what are you up to now?"

He returned to the couch and her head resumed its place, this time near the base of his stomach. Overcoming the temptation to move straight to the more physical part of the evening, Leandro accepted that he owed her more in the way of explanation.

"You could say that I fell into it by accident. An old friend of mine was working for Techint - you know, the large engineering firm - and he told me that they were looking at a very complicated deal, in Central Asia as I recall. They were trying to collect delicate information on one of their competitors. It was one of those conversations that was not supposed to go anywhere in particular, but, on thinking it over, it struck me that there must be organisations, which could provide what Techint was looking for. At that time, I was on the research side of Citibank back in Buenos Aires. The biggest name in the corporate intelligence business in those days, and maybe still today, was a large American firm called Kroll. Techint had already approached Kroll, but without much success. This was long before post-9/11 Afghanistan, although even then the Americans were quite involved in that area. I said I would do some research. It turned out that a number of obscure organisations had sprung up in places like London, Washington and Paris, selling political and security information to large corporations. Often staffed with ex-spies, one or two of them were already present in Argentina and other parts of Latin America as well, having found good business negotiating in kidnap cases. You probably saw the film with Russell Crowe and Meg Ryan, in Colombia as far as I can remember. What was it called? Something like 'Proof of Life', or whatever the phrase is when you need to show that the hostage is still alive in order to get paid. Anyway, this was before the days of Google, so finding them and making contact was not all that easy. Given my Scottish roots and my contacts from the time in London, I started off trying to find someone in England. To cut a long story short, I finally was able to get in touch with one of these firms. They're called Frobisher. After the Elizabethan navigator. Once we had got over any residual hesitation post-Malvinas, in their usual pragmatic fashion, the *ingleses* proved perfectly willing to help, for a price!"

"And did they produce what Techint wanted?"

"Apparently. In the end, the people in London hired me as a part time stringer, which struck me as a lot more interesting than studying boring balance sheets. That was also a time when British companies were trying to get involved in Menem's privatisations, so they occasionally came to me - on behalf of some client - to get my views on how the privatisation would be run, or who they needed to speak to to push a deal, that sort of thing. Obviously, these were small beginnings, but most of all it got me interested in this line of work. Like everything, it's a lot about who you know, just as much as what you know. Some of the deals were quite big and they paid well, with a large bonus in a couple of cases."

"But given what happened to you in Malvinas, didn't you feel uncomfortable about working with the English? After all, they had killed one of your best friends and no doubt many others."

Leandro paused before replying. He had told Sam about Francisco, though not about the fathering of Eduardo.

"You're right. I did give it a lot of thought at the beginning and it wasn't easy. But at the same time, I needed to put the war into perspective. Ten years had passed, Menem was rebuilding bridges with the UK. British companies were getting involved in the privatisations, Gas del Estado for instance. All the more, as you say, given my family roots. Argentina, apart from the Malvinas, goes a long way back with Britain. They invaded us twice at the beginning of the nineteenth century, and we kicked them out each time - which may have been a mistake, except that we might have ended up as boring as the Canadians - and it's after that that my ancestors came here from Scotland. They settled here and intermarried and became Argentines. But like many in the Anglo-Argentine community, they never completely lost touch with their native land."

"Yes, all that's true, but the war.... surely that was very different?"

"You have to remember that, at the time, in 1982, I was already serving in the Fuerza Aerea. They had trained me as a pilot and navigator, and when I joined up, there was no talk of war, except with Chile. We nearly went to war with them in late 1978. Luckily the Pope intervened. But with England? Good heavens, at that time - and I'm talking about 1981 when I joined - there were strong historical ties going way back, particularly in the Armada. Half its ships came from British shipyards. So it was more than ironic that the one who was really pushing for war was Anaya, the head of the Navy."

He paused again, looking out of the window at what had now become a downpour.

"And when the war came, to be frank, it was as much a surprise for us as it probably was for the British. For a hundred and fifty years, the British were Argentina's main commercial partner, since Canning was quick to recognize our independence. Trade and finance were the backbone of our relationship. Baring Brothers nearly went bankrupt lending money to this country. So many little details. How many of our restaurants or hotels have English names? London Grill? That one had to change its name at the time of the war. But Claridges, Clarkes, Brighton? Or look at a map of Argentina and count the English names of towns. Hurlingham, Open Door, Banfield... and many, many more. It's not just in *my* blood. It's part of the national bloodstream as well. You for one should know the influence of the English on our schools. Even in a simple village school, the kids are often dressed in a tartan skirt and blue sweater – as if they were at an English prep school! You must have seen that."

Sam nodded.

"Don't I know. Carry on, Leo, please. I want to understand. The war...."

"Obviously, I had to make a choice, it wasn't easy. I'm sufficiently Argentine deep down inside to have my own ideas about the merits of the Argentine or the British case over the islands. But it's far from clear cut. If I look back on it now, it's obvious that the war was madness and a terrible tragedy for the six hundred or so young Argentines who gave their lives. And for the two hundred or so who died on their side. It's hard for me to find any rationale for the sinking of the Belgrano. But remember, we had attacked them and, for a country that saw off Napoleon, the Kaiser, Hitler and - to some extent - even the Soviet Union, it was always unthinkable that they would just let us get away with it. For that, I blame our diplomats. Our Foreign Minister, Costa Mendez, ardent Anglophile until that moment, suddenly found himself kissing Fidel Castro in an effort to drum up Latin American support for the Argentine cause. I hope he found it uncomfortable. But his ambassadors should have warned him, always assuming that they even knew what was coming. All these thoughts came to me after the war. At the time, in the final analysis I hadn't many options. I had to console myself with the idea that we were professionals on both sides, doing our job, however unpleasant - and it's certain that there's nothing romantic or glorious about killing other people - and we simply had to get on with it. For someone like me, with something inside me splitting me down the middle, it was the only rationale that could work. I still lie awake at nights about it sometimes, it doesn't go away. Especially the friends who died. Like Eduardo's father, one of my best friends. Perhaps I would put it like this. I deeply regret what happened in the war, I regret every Argentine who died. But I can't find it in my heart just to blame it all on the Brits. We started it. That was our mistake and we paid for it. And now we seem to be heading back in the wrong direction again. But that's another story."

He took a long drink.

She noted that his voice had, at certain points, broken very slightly. Raising her head, she pulled his face down towards hers, kissing him softly. She could feel the tenseness flow out of him and, gratefully, he prolonged the kiss.

They were silent for a minute or two.

"But now, you're actually working with the British. Doesn't that mean you've begun to take sides in some way?"

As so often, the incisiveness of her questions sometimes took him unprepared. Again he thought before replying, disguising it by giving her another kiss.

"The trouble with you, Sam, is that you're just too fucking curious for your own good. As I said before, I regret, but I cannot blame. The world back in 1833 when they kicked us out of the islands was a very different place. I believe we have to find ways to adjust to the new reality that there are two thousand Brits living on the islands. Shouting and screaming about it won't move the needle on the dial. I supported the approach which Menem took, along with his Foreign Minister, Guido di Tella, trying to get closer to the islands. It was always going to be a long haul. But I believe in building bridges with the Brits. Kicking them in the teeth never got anyone anywhere. History has shown that. However, right from the start, I made it clear to the people in London that I would help them, but not get involved in anything which, in my sole judgement, would work against the true interests of Argentina. They were pragmatic, said it wasn't a problem. And on the whole, we've kept it that way. As I told you when we met, I now do economic research at a little 'think-tank' which I set up in San Isidro with a partner. We publish regular reports on the economy, on trade, and occasionally also go out on a limb on local politics. It pays the bills, we have a good client list and they value our inputs. At the same time, it allows me to keep my lines open with the people in London. Perhaps I shouldn't be telling you this, but the people here don't know much about my links with the people there. And to be frank, I prefer it that way. It avoids difficult questions. In the end, I remain the judge of what's a conflict of interest, and what's not. So much of the work I do with the Centro draws on purely public information, which is presumably available also to the people in London."

"So, let's have it, what are you working on now?" Sam asked, rolling over to rest her chin on his stomach. She began to nuzzle it towards his crotch.

"Ah, wouldn't you like to know?"

"Yes I fucking well would," she insisted, digging her slightly pointed chin deeper in the direction of his groin, slanting her eyes towards his.

He held her gaze, wondering how far he might go with her. She did have the loveliest eyes! But he remained cautious.

"Frankly, nothing very exciting. Nothing for London anyway."

"You're just trying to fob me off," she complained, with a look of petulant disappointment.

"At the moment, it happens to be the truth. Maybe if I get something more exciting, I'll let you know. It's actually quite hard to write anything interesting, given the futility of what this government dresses up as an economic policy."

After a pause, while she finished her glass, she returned to the charge.

"Oh well, give me another drink. But you haven't broken off with those people in London, have you?"

She seemed to want to confirm something in her mind.

"No, though as I just said, there's not much going on at the moment."

That seemed to put an end to the conversation, although Leandro was left with a strange feeling that some of this curiosity might be a little more than small talk. If their relationship was to be short-lived, probably the less said the better. But he did want to get her inside him more. And not just physically.

She changed the subject.

"I suppose with a surname like Flemming, the English must have felt more relaxed. But frankly, there's not much of the English left in you, either in your appearance or in the way you behave" and she thrust her hand swiftly into his crotch. "If you see what I mean...."

"Yes, I see what you mean!" he gasped. "Come here and stop being so curious. And by the way, I know the Argentines call everyone from Britain English, but Flemming is Scottish – a big difference! Now it's my turn to do a little investigation."

Pulling her towards him, his hands slipped under the pale silk blouse she was wearing. As usual, she was sexily and expensively dressed. He sometimes wondered what he was doing with a girl who daily wore a different set of clothes roughly equal in value to his monthly pay packet.

His hand softly began to caress her large, firm breasts and she curled voluptuously. Perhaps some sensual torture would be in order. Her turn to work for it!

"By the way," he said, "where does that name Samira come from? I bet your parents had trouble baptising you with a name like that, here in Argentina. Presumably it stems from your *turco* antecedents."

She laughed.

"Oh, I was baptised Maria Claudia Haidar. Ghastly! But as far back as I can remember, my father called me Samira, which I much prefer."

"So do I!" He buried his hand farther down her blouse. "Definitely! So tell me about your family."

"If you think I can concentrate like this...."

"Business first, pleasure afterwards."

But he didn't remove his hand and she made no attempt to escape it.

"So I must work for my reward. Ah well...here goes. My turn."

She rolled over again and leaned back in the couch. His hand followed. She tried to focus her thoughts.

"To start at the beginning, my great-grandfather, Abbas Haidar, came to Argentina in 1919 from Syria."

"When the Turkish Ottoman Empire collapsed. Which is why we call all you people *turcos*."

"Right. He brought money apparently and set up some kind of trading business in the province of Entre Rios, in Gualeguay, where my grandfather was born. His mother was also Syrian. They brought a large family and I have cousins all over the place. Not that I see much of them. Oh God, you're killing me! Stop a minute! If you want me to go on."

Leandro did not relent.

"Very well. Have it your way. As I was saying, my grandparents moved to Buenos Aires, where my father was born. He was the one to break the pattern by marrying my mother, who was a mixture of Italian and German. Technically that meant that he's no longer considered a proper Druze."

"That explains a lot. I wondered where your height and green eyes came from. Not to mention that brain of yours."

His fingers were circling her nipple.

"Jesus...! Probably. Maybe I also inherited the fact that I am a bit more methodical about life from that side. Oh, God, stop that! If you want me to go on...."

His fingers paused.

"Carry on."

She took a deep breath, before continuing.

"There's nothing the matter with the Arab brain. It's the religion which screws us up. Same with the Christians!"

"That's another subject."

"Luckily there's quite a lot of the Italian which, mixed with Semitic, produces a pretty explosive result."

Now it was the turn of her hand, which had found its place between his legs.

"Okay, okay. You haven't finished so no rewards yet. Are both your parents still alive?"

She paused and looked away, withdrawing her hand.

"No, my mother died about nineteen years ago... of cancer. I was twelve."

It was his turn to withdraw his hand.

"I'm sorry, Sam," he said.

They were silent for a moment.

"I'm very close to my father and he spoils me a lot."

"I had noticed. That's a lovely blouse. And those boots are from Perugia or some shop like that, I would guess. Must be worth a small fortune. I'm surprised you can allow yourself to be seen with a scruffy fellow like me."

"Don't worry, we'll soon have you sorted out. Anyway, you're really not that scruffy. Or if you are, it's sexy. Although I was just thinking that maybe a quick visit to Ralph Lauren on Alvear mightn't go amiss. It's pretty much your style. You know, upper class, Brit, yachting."

He snorted.

"Yachting! I hate ropes and sails. All that wet and cold! And who do you think is going to pay? Hardly the cheapest place in town and anyway, it might give my partner the wrong idea, that I was taking too much out of the business."

"As my friend Oscar once said 'anyone who lives within their means suffers from a lack of imagination'."

They both laughed. His hand had renewed its mission.

"Christ, don't stop! I love it. Yes, like that! And again!"

She was silent for a few moments, her eyes shut, enjoying, before continuing.

"This takes a superhuman effort, Leo, but... as I was saying before you so rudely distracted me, you'll see, when you're least expecting it, I'll get you through the doors of Ralph Lauren. I'll soon have you looking presentable, fit to be seen in public with a girl like me. Yes, my father likes to make sure that I've enough money. Having lost his wife, he probably likes to give me the things, which he would've given her. I can't complain and I don't want to disappoint him. That being said, I'm not sure that I am as conservative as he might like. Probably lucky that he doesn't know about my tattoo, the little one. It's very small and discreet anyway. It would probably give him a heart attack. Just to remind you...."

He'd seen it, kissed it often, but she still unbuttoned her blouse down to the waist, revealing the tiny, beautifully drawn star riding slightly off centre on the top of her left breast, like a small medal. He kissed it again.

"I had noticed it."

She pushed his face away and closed her blouse again, though leaving his hand inside. There were many more sides to her she wanted to show him. But it was not yet time.

Leandro's hand appeared temporarily to have lost interest.

"Hey, don't stop!"

"Don't stop what?"

"You some kind of Gerald Ford? Can't do two things at once? Concentrate on what I'm saying and caress me?"

"Oh, sorry."

The look on his face showed little contrition, but his fingers had resumed their focus on her nipple.

64

"That's more like it. I don't work for nothing, you know."

She arched her back, thrusting her breasts forward, her nipples straining against the soft blouse. She wanted only one thing. Leandro inside her, deep inside her. Yet first she must earn the full reward.

"You see, my family on my father's side has something of a tradition of wives or mothers being lost at an early age. Not only did my mother die prematurely, but my father's grandmother - that's to say, my great-grandmother - also died young, which seems to have left an emotional stain in the family. She was killed in Syria in the uprising of the Druze against the French in the mid-1920s. The French troops bombarded the town of Hama, which the Druze rebels controlled. She had gone back to visit relatives and was killed in the artillery fire. My great-grandfather never got over it. It seems to have left a mark down through the next generations. Maybe none of this means very much to you, but as I once told you, my family is Druze by origin. This little gold and enamel star I wear on a chain around my neck? Like the tattoo, it's the Druze star. Do you know anything about the Druze?"

Leandro thought for a minute. "Frankly, not much... virtually nothing. I have a faint recollection of a name beginning with J, Jum something or other during the Lebanese civil war, but apart from that... and of course I had noticed the star, but didn't really give it any special significance."

"You never even asked. But if I've anything to do with it, one day you will understand its significance," she responded rather mysteriously. "You're thinking of Walid Jumblatt, leader of the Druze in the Lebanese civil war. Anyway, I'll tell you a bit more about the Druze some other time, it will take far too long now. Now I'm in a hurry to be paid for my revelations! In my opinion I've more than earned my reward."

"I'm not at all sure that you have, there's a lot more I need to understand about you. But what the hell!"

She stripped down to her soft silk and lace lingerie. "Expensive, very expensive La Perla, bought in Rome", as she had informed him on a previous occasion. As usual, she kept on her thigh boots. The rest of her clothes were sprayed across the floor.

On that evening, as they made love, he was again captivated by her extreme sensuality, reinforced by her total lack of inhibition. So unlike most of his previous girlfriends, for whom sex sometimes seemed to be an unadventurous one-way street, in which the man was expected to choose the itinerary. Sam regularly made the running, setting the pace, frequently signalling to him to pause and wait. While, quite unselfconsciously, she masturbated, her fingers expertly thrusting, caressing, arousing, it was clear she also intended him, the observer, to share the pleasure she was experiencing, albeit in the mind.

"God, you're so beautiful when you do that. I could sit and look at you for hours, your body, your cunt, your fingers sliding in and out. Just watching you...."

She was unbelievably erotic. Having brought herself close to climax, she would invite him, more passionately, to bring her to final orgasm.

Sometimes, she complained that he came too fast. That was something nobody had accused him of in the past. Rather the contrary.

"One day I'll pay you a trip to Cairo to meet Abbas, he'll teach you the ways of *imsak*. Then there will be no limit to your ability to please me. What was good for Aly Khan should be fine for you! And he fucked Rita Hayworth, no less."

"Comparing yourself with Gilda, are you? Just a touch conceited? The hair colour – red, though you're much darker - might be right, and the city also, but the likeness certainly stops there," he added, with a touch of cruelty.

She had slapped his face, hard. Then covered it with kisses.

Imsak, she explained, was a technique developed in the Islamic world to allow a man to remain erect for many hours, a major challenge when faced with a harem! Though it might demonstrate that she had had a number of mature lovers, he had decided not to worry about it. On second thoughts, he had to admit that there might be areas in which he could improve his game.

Further details of her childhood emerged slowly in the course of these evenings together. Without brothers or sisters, and with a father who was often away in the provinces on business, she had often been left to her own devices as a child. As a result, she had matured more swiftly than other girls of her own age. Most of her girlfriends belonged to the traditionally large Argentine family, in which ceremonies such as birthdays, marriages and christenings seemed to monopolise the calendar, ensuring that the nucleus of the family, however large, remained solidly bound together. In contrast, Sam had been a loner, occasionally invited to someone else's birthday party, but rarely able to return the hospitality.

"In that respect, at least, we've something in common," he commented. "I was also an only child, something of a rarity in Argentina. I never really knew why my parents didn't have any more children. Not that I was unhappy, but like you, I could feel the difference when in the company of friends with lots of brothers and sisters. My parents weren't particularly strict. Probably my father's influence. Prepared to let me get on with my life. He died a few years ago, but my mother's still alive, though not in the best of health. One day I'd like you to meet her."

Sam's more solitary childhood had also fostered an unusual capacity for reading. Associated with what he rapidly discovered was an exceptional memory, particularly of the written word, this had fed a far-ranging appetite for information on a wide range of subjects. Her fascination with English and French literature of the late nineteenth century proved to be only one area of interest, albeit a crucial contributor to her thoughts.

A spell in a convent run by Cistercian nuns had left her with a view of the Catholic Church, which she described as 'claustrophobic'. A healthy scepticism for any form of dogma and general resistance to mind-numbing, repetitive book learning, as well as to the petty rules and conventions imposed by the nuns, had often brought her into confrontation with her spiritual guardians. The situation had finally led her father to the conclusion that some alternative educational system might suit her better. So, at around the age of sixteen, she had gone to an English-style college in the northern suburbs of Buenos Aires where, although she initially had no difficulty in scoring high marks in her academic subjects, her strong personality and sense of independence still led to bouts of friction with the school authorities. Sam's Semitic origins, whilst not necessarily provoking anything which might be regarded as clear racial discrimination, had nevertheless set her apart. Her powerful good looks and the fact that she was a few centimetres taller than the average, only reinforced her 'nonconformism'. When combined with the fact that she was maturing much faster than her classmates, she soon found herself hanging out with a group of young men easily five years her senior and already with their schooldays behind them.

His attempts to discover why, now aged thirty-one, she was back at university aged nearly ten years older than her fellow students initially ran into a series of uninformative, side stepping responses.

"Oh, you know, I wasn't in a hurry," or "Just a late starter!"

"But your English? It's exceptional. Where does that come from? St. Mathews can't get all the credit, surely?"

"No, that's thanks to my father. Somewhere, deep inside, he's an Anglophile. On the one hand, he's never really forgiven the French and the English for slicing up the Middle East to suit their ambitions. But between the two, he remembers that the British supported the Druze against the French in the 1920s. He's grateful to them for that. What's more, like so many Argentines, he respects what they've given to the world. Tolerance, democracy, things like golf. He's a fanatic."

"And rugby, never forget rugby!"

"Of course. How could I? That puny body of yours had to come from somewhere."

From their first day together, she had shown interest in his marriage and the fact that he had a daughter some ten years younger than herself. From the way he spoke of Elena and the circumstances of their decision to live apart, she detected that she must now form part of some triangular emotional relationship in the mind of Leandro. As far as he could tell, she appeared totally relaxed about this state of affairs. He made no effort to conceal from her the occasions on which he would drop by to see Elena or Alex, and she showed no sign that this in any way troubled her. The absence of any kind of formal divorce, the persistence of a solid dialogue between Leandro and Elena born of many years together, seemed to her both normal and evidently a contributor to his peace of mind.

A month or so after they had met, as they sat on a rainy June evening sharing a cheap bottle of cabernet sauvignon in a crowded pizzeria, she had begun to speak about her life after leaving St. Mathew's.

"Since I know that you are a voyeur at heart, I'll tell you a bit more about my wilder early days."

Leandro looked up from the menu.

"Good, now I can tell I've got your attention! My first real affair, even before I left school, was with the son of a well-to-do *estanciero*. His family owned a few thousand hectares in the region of Pergamino, as you know one of the richest agricultural areas of the province of Buenos Aires. Those were the good days of Menem, when a peso was worth a dollar and, given the profits being made by his dad at the time, he wasn't short of money. Instead of pouring over books, most of my evenings were spent in places like Embers or the other bars and nightclubs in San Isidro and Vicente Lopez. I enjoyed being driven home in his sports car in time to catch a shower and breakfast, before making a bleary-eyed entrance into class."

"And a few extras doses of marijuana or Chivas Regal no doubt sharpened your learning skills."

Sam merely smiled.

By the time she had scraped through the final classes at St. Mathews, she was neither prepared for, nor indeed interested in, going to university. So the good life continued and had seen one or two younger, and perhaps not so young, men following in the footsteps of the first good-looking polo playing *estanciero*. Then, when she was twenty, her father had stepped in and sent her to finishing school near Lausanne.

"I hated the idea, all those snobby upper-middle-class English girls mixed in with the daughters of Colombians and Venezuelans. And the odd Argentine. Luckily, my year was pretty wild. I had a great friend, a half-Chinese, half-English girl, Swallow - such a beautiful name - her mother was from Hong Kong. Lots of money. I'm not quite sure what my father thought was being 'finished', but it was mainly champagne or *glühwein* on the mountain slopes. But it did do a lot of good for my English."

Her gaze drifted.

"Anyway, enough of that."

Although she obviously belonged to a later generation than his own, Leandro was struck by the social non-conformity of her early sexual encounters. Not for Sam the old-fashioned, but still prevalent, talk of *novios* and *novias*. Argentine parents were quick to pin this label on boyfriends or girlfriends, as if it somehow made the relationship more respectable. Which did little to ward off youthful promiscuity, as he suspected, watching his own daughter.

Though the world had clearly become a more complex place in which to grow up, he envied the younger generation their greater freedom, even if Argentina might still not be the Sweden of South America. Listening to Sam inevitably reminded him of how much more difficult he had found it to get his first girlfriends between the sheets.

"As soon as I heard the word *novia*, I used to run a mile."

"So what are you doing now with a guy as old and decrepit as me?"

He pushed his chair back and lit up his one cigarette of the day.

"Always self-pitying! Wouldn't you like to know? It's probably all the expensive restaurants you take me to," she said, her arm gesturing towards the garishly illuminated pizzeria in which they were sitting.

"Obviously, I can imagine that's a major factor in your calculations."

They laughed.

"No doubt, when finally some big contract with your friends in London comes along, we'll be able to afford something a little better. In the meantime, though, a good restaurant would also be better for my figure. These pizzas make for a lot of extra work on the treadmill. But, don't worry, I'm not after your money."

"Luckily for you. I can't think why some women get the idea that I have a pile of dollars tucked away somewhere. After all, they only have to look at the state of my clothes or even the fact that on some days, I can't seem to afford even a razor blade."

She stretched out her hand and stroked his unshaven cheek.

"Luckily, I like it that way."

She leaned across the table to kiss him.

He turned and made a sign to the waiter to bring another bottle of the wine they were drinking.

"Who's driving this evening?"

"I guess we'll have to take a taxi. I can pick the car up from the parking lot tomorrow morning."

"That's okay then. But whilst were on the subject, what are you doing with a girl of my age? I would have thought that something in her late thirties, perhaps a divorcee, a walking advertisement for botox in all the right places, preferably without children, would have suited you better, a man of the world like you."

She teased him with her eyes.

"I thought that it was only around fifty that men started to look at girls half their age," she added.

"You're not half my age, at least two thirds, so don't age me prematurely. And frankly, with your record, you're almost a divorcee anyway."

"What do you mean? You don't know what you're talking about. It's me who has to be careful before hitching up with men who have spent the last ten years or so moving in and out of relationships."

"Speak for yourself. Anyway, it's not ten years, only a couple since I left Elena."

The waiter appeared with another bottle and Leandro filled their glasses.

"Are you implying that I've been anything other than stable in my relationships?" she asked.

"Well, there aren't all that many really good looking girls like you, at your age, who haven't already got hitched up. In Argentina, by the time girls are approaching thirty, people begin to wonder. In some ways, you're over the hill already. You've almost admitted as much. Not to mention the way you make love. That certainly wasn't taught you at that convent!"

"God, with a remark like that last one, you've got a fair bit of learning to do. You are out of touch! Nowadays, it's very common for girls to go into their thirties without having done the obligatory walk down the aisle. Not to mention the fact that marriage is going out of style anyway, although rather less so in Argentina perhaps than in places farther north, I'll grant you that. That's not to say that Argentine men don't get a little nervous when with a woman - as opposed to a girl - near their own age. As to where I may have been educated.... And by the way, what's the matter with the way I make love? Never had any complaints so far!"

She took a mouthful of the cabernet before continuing.

"To be frank, the marriage scene in Argentina is anything but idyllic. When I look around, all I see is loads of girls fussing over their babies, with nothing else to talk about, just waiting for the husband to fix the summer month on the beach in Punta del Este or the skiing holiday down south. Or worse, beginning to look for the signs of a man who is already moving on to his first extramarital affair."

"Yes, I can see that that's not really your style," and Leandro smiled, "not your style at all. And I bet that you don't have all that many friends among the fairer sex, or am I wrong?"

"No, not many. At least, not of that variety."

Samira's expression changed imperceptibly, but Leandro still caught it.

"We've still got to do some work on this bottle," he changed the subject.

That evening, looking across the table at Sam, he drank in what he saw. Her image was definitely Parisian, the stylized make-up serving to emphasise the darkness of her eyes, the elegant curve of her eyebrows plucked to produce a perfect, tapering arch. In the corner of each eye near the tear duct, a small black dot emphasized their almond shape. He wondered where that detail had come from. The full richness of her lips was lightly heightened by the hint of a transparent gloss.

Her very dark red hair, hennaed, encased her face like a helmet, reminding him of the 1920s, shorter at the back, carefully shaped points sweeping forward towards the corners of her mouth, a fringe cut just above the eyebrows. At times, her perfectly symmetrical features, the skin lightly bronzed, seemed to give her something of the appearance of a baroque mask. Add to this a physique moulded by assiduous spells at a neighbourhood gymnasium, and Leandro, to his own bemused surprise, realised, not for the first time, that she had, in the words of Cole Porter, completely got 'under his skin'.

He watched her long, strong fingers clasping either side of the wineglass, fingernails perfectly shaped. He raised his glass in a toast to nothing in particular. She raised hers, but this time she did not hold his gaze for more than a fraction of a second.

Their lovemaking that night seemed a little less passionate on her side, as if she were distracted by something. They had been together for over two months, but Leandro still felt that he was only slowly getting to understand his mysterious new companion. Large areas of her personality and life remained closed to him. Areas he would make it his business to penetrate.

August 2007

In the late afternoon following his breakfast meeting with Eduardo in London City, Leandro had made his way to his ex-wife's flat. Elena opened the door to let him in. Slapping his hands to get the blood flowing again, he slipped out of his damp coat and dropped into his old armchair. It felt good. Elena watched him. He could see that she was doing a quick inventory.

"Yes, I know I need a haircut and a shave."

"Yes, and your sports jacket and grey flannels need a session at the cleaners. Doesn't anyone look after you?"

The retriever came in from the kitchen and sprang up in delight at the sight of his old master. Leandro leaned forward and stroked him furiously.

"He really misses you," she said. "Maybe you miss the dog more than me ...."

"You're looking good."

He looked at her appreciatively, wondering whether there was not a man somewhere. A bit of sex did wonders for Elena. Yet what right did he have to feel jealous?

"Actually, in spite of your haircut and stubble, so do you for a change, Leo. Presume you've got someone looking after you. Want a drink? Or is it a bit early even for you?"

He ignored her initial remark.

"Half past six in the afternoon is no ways too early. What've you got?"

"There's a bit of the old malt left over at the back of the kitchen cupboard. You must have forgotten to take it with you last time. Bring back memories of London."

He nodded and she walked into the small kitchen, switching on the ceiling spots. From the back of one of the cupboards, she produced a dusty bottle of Glenmorangie and as she reached up to get a glass off another shelf, she felt him come close up behind her. His hands rested on her hips and began to slip down towards the hemline.

"Okay, Leandro, nice try, we've been there before, seen it, done it..." as she gently pushed his searching hands off her buttocks. "It's always like this, haven't seen me for a month, think it gives you rights."

Though she had to admit to herself that there were still occasions when she would have welcomed Leo in her bed.

He chuckled and turned back into the sitting room. She poured out a glass for him, "No ice", and a small red wine for herself, setting them down on the side table between the sofa and his armchair.

He watched her under half-closed eyes as she moved round the kitchen. She still showed substantial traces of the good figure, which she had when they first met in 1980, when he was taking his flying lessons in the Argentine Air Force and she was the Brigadier's secretary on the air base at Palomar. He had brought his personal file into the Brigadier's office for review and squatted on the side of her desk, as she clattered away on the old IBM ball typewriter, pretending not to take any notice of this good-looking young *porteño*, who was clearly making a quick pass at her. Her thick dark auburn hair suggested traces of Irish ancestry – she had a grandfather who had come out from County Cork to build the railroads at the end of the nineteenth century – and it married well with her pale skin, the gift from a Piedmontese mother.

He had been in luck. She had just dropped her last boyfriend and was not averse to going out with someone new that Saturday night. The smoke-filled evening in Don Torcuatos's only nightclub, Africa, had ended in the back of his jeep in San Fernando down by the river. He could still feel the smoothness of her skin as he watched her now, that tinge of sensuality in the way she moved, a sensuality which had caused him many a moment of jealousy as he watched the eyes of other men following her across the parade ground or between the tables in the canteen.

They had kept in touch when the war ended and after a couple of years together, not without the occasional interlude of other affairs, she had finally married him in 1986, with their daughter being born a couple of years later. They had enjoyed two years of freedom without children to worry about.

"How's Alex?"

"Fine, she was here an hour or so ago, bringing me the usual load of clothes to wash! All very well having one's children move out on a whim of independence, but it would be better if they could not only afford the freedom but also the washing machine."

Alejandra was their twenty-year-old daughter who, unlike most girls of her generation in Argentina used to staying at home until a husband finally took them away, had decided to move out to share a flat in the Barracas area of the city. A rough district, which nevertheless concealed some beautiful early twentieth century art deco town houses, turned into flats by enterprising young architects.

"The flat-sharing with Nouria seems to be working out."

Nouria was the flatmate, five years older, an extremely good-looking student of half-Lebanese extraction, studying psychology at Buenos Aires University, where Alejandra had now enrolled.

There was a brief silence, as both parents left their concerns about the two girls unspoken. It was early to jump to conclusions, but they both knew what the other was thinking.

"Alex says you have a new girlfriend."

"Does she, indeed? Where did she get that from?"

"Nouria apparently. She knows her."

"Ah, the *turco* gossip shop, I bet. Well, she may be right."

He got up and walked over to the window, looking out into the darkened street below. She detected he wasn't going to fall for the bait.

"Eduardo came to see me this morning," he said, without turning round.

"How is he? Still happy as a detective?"

"Looks like it. He's on an interesting case. You probably saw it in the papers, Englishwoman murdered in a hotel in Recoleta."

"Yes, a couple of weeks ago, wasn't it? Something about another woman being involved.... Why did he come to you?"

"He seems to think there is some way I can help him from the sidelines. Probably is. Even if it goes no farther than helping him to clear his thoughts. It's quite a strange case. Some aspects which suggest that it goes beyond a simple lesbian affair gone wrong."

"That's not your normal area of expertise. Needing a bit of extra titillation on the side? Sex, at least professionally, has not been an area of research for you, as far as I know. Mind you, now that you're a bachelor and what with so much porn on the Internet, perhaps he was right to come to you."

"Don't be so catty. It doesn't suit you."

He felt himself blush. She spotted it and laughed. She hoped the internet wasn't contaminating his sex life. Knowing him, not wholly unlikely.

"So what are you going to do? Do you think you can help him?"

"Some rather nasty angles to it, including the way in which the victim was killed. Even though it happened in a hotel, with closed circuit TV everywhere, they haven't been able to track down the woman who came in with her that night. Seems to have disappeared into thin air. On top of that, the victim was English, moving in fairly wild polo circles... and as you can guess, they don't like the police trampling over their lifestyle.

"Not really your scene either, you being more rugby than horses."

"Whatever happened to that whiskey?"

She poured him another glass. She had brought another glass of red wine for herself, which she began to sip, looking at him over the rim, trying to assess how he was surviving on his own.

"So you're looking after yourself? All your usual needs being adequately met?"

She narrowed her eyes in a wicked fashion which he knew only too well.

"Sure! As you can see, I'm surviving."

"A bit more than just surviving, I would say."

He smiled and delayed his reply with a sip of the whiskey.

"Okay. But nothing too serious, don't worry."

He caught himself lying, a new habit now that they were separated.

"Why should I worry? I'm sure this Arab lady takes good care of you. Anyway you're your own master now and I can hardly expect you to go into a monastery just because you and I decided that we would keep more of our relationship intact by spending less time together."

"What about you?"

She pretended to look coy and stretched out the pause to tease him.

"Ahhh! Wouldn't you like to know?" She smiled. "Perhaps you should dedicate some of your research to me."

"As I recall, one of the things we agreed on was that we were not going to get in the way of each other's lives, and if things changed for one of us, then the other would simply have to adapt. Most of all, I want to preserve the best of what we had – or should I say have - together... avoid the situation so many of our friends seem to have fallen into, breaking up in a destructive fashion, where the children end up being the principal victims."

She smiled again. That was part of the deal they had struck and, for now, she certainly did not intend to break faith with it. Although neither of them was as young as they might have been, both remained attractive and attracted to the opposite sex. In a country in which fidelity was hardly everybody's watchword, emotional or even purely physical attachments were a part of daily life.

Their decision to split had somehow evolved without any particular crisis. He couldn't even remember very clearly how it had come about. One evening, the conversation had imperceptibly slipped towards a measure of agreement that, given their age, each still entertained a view of life which somehow seemed at odds with being constantly together. A taste for change, sex with another person, had been part of it, coupled with a shared view that, if conducted in secret, behind the others back, the damage would be much greater.

"Perhaps we should just split up," Elena had suddenly thrown at him. "Not a divorce, maybe not even very formal, but a change nevertheless. Probably less destructive for Alexandra. What do you think? If we don't like it, we just come back together."

Leandro had initially been taken aback by the simplicity of the idea. Somehow, that wasn't the way things were done. You either stuck together, or you split up. But on thinking about it and talking it through with Elena that evening, they had finally decided to give it a try. Being less formal, less terminal somehow, had made it more bearable for Alejandra. Largely because she entertained the secret hope that they would always come together again. So, for some two years, they had run their lives that way and, on reflection, the damage seemed manageable. Sometimes they had discussed a current affair, often it had gone unspoken.

This evening, Leandro saw no harm in being a bit more transparent.

"I've been going out with a girl called Samira. Couple of months now. She's about ten years older than Alex, very intelligent... and experienced. Like so many of the younger generation, she doesn't seem to be at all concerned about the kind of fidelity which you and I would have thought natural at the same age. These young people seem to be very relaxed on that score. Not sure what that means for the future of marriage, but, for someone like me, it certainly makes things easier. So why shouldn't we old folks take advantage of the fringe benefits of the younger generation's moral revolution?"

"Cynical bastard!"

But she was laughing.

"Let's drink to that! "

He lent across and they clinked glasses with a look of mock seriousness.

As she got up to go back into the kitchen, he sensed – not for the first time - that he was not necessarily totally convinced that they should have split up. No time limit or preconditions had been set as to whether they might come together again someday. She was right, he was a bit of a cynical bastard - and for the time being, perhaps it was easier to leave it at that.

"Do you want to stay and have something to eat? Or we can have a delivery. I don't know, pizza or maybe even some sushi. Or we can go around the corner and have a steak, if you're feeling short of a bit of cholesterol."

"What have you got? I'm relaxed, a bit of home cooking would make a nice change."

"Frankly not much."

"Then let's go around to Rueda next door, you can pay for me!"

She laughed.

"That's the price you pay for going independent. No pay cheques guaranteed, so you have to fall back on your ex-wife. Pretty embarrassing, but I'll fund you this time."

Ten minutes later, they had found a corner table in the bar around the corner. Its walls were decorated with photographs of Juan Manuel Fangio, his Formula One Mercedes and Maseratis, and other racing memorabilia of the 1950s. So much more attractive than the later generation of national heroes like Maradona. In those days, you would have had trouble being a national hero and publicly high on drugs. Leandro's passion for cars came from an uncle's stories of Fangio's victories at Monza and Nurburgring, his epic battle against Mike Hawthorne at the German Grand Prix in 1957 and similar tales.

Elena smiled as she followed his gaze.

"How's the Alfa?" she asked.

Leandro's second - or perhaps third - secret love was his 1964 Giulia TI Super, with the 1600 twin cam engine, white, as driven by the Italian police in the early 1960s and occasionally visible in films of the period, their sirens howling through the narrow streets of Naples or Rome. Not a beautiful Alfa, muscular rather than feminine, with its squared off body and chopped tail. Having been imported for a motor show, but never nationalised or re-exported, it had taken quite a lot of bureaucratic manoeuvring to get the papers to release the car from customs, where it had been sitting abandoned for about twenty years when he had found it after the Malvinas. Too much of his early monthly salary had gone to pay for the work of an Italian mechanic in San Fernando, who, having been brought up in the 1940s and 50s in the Alfa factories in Milan, had leaped at the chance of completely stripping the car down to its bare bones and rebuilding it. It was probably the only example in Argentina and Leandro was careful not to make it too visible or tempting. As a result, he would only bring it out for the occasional rally, but to his taste, it spent too much time in the garage, never a good thing for a car.

"Oh, she's fine. About time I gave her a run."

Elena smiled at the feminization of the car.

"Are all your passions feminine? Even I occasionally miss the noise of that exhaust," she quipped, knowing that even something as banal as the growl of an Alfa engine was part of a man's internal addictions.

They smiled and raised their glasses to honour the rasp of a four-cylinder Alfa Romeo engine.

19 August 2007

Three days passed and Leandro was working that Sunday afternoon on the latest review of the Argentine economy for insertion in their weekly bulletin.

CENTRO

INVESTIGACIÓN

ECONÓMICA

August 2007 : POLITICAL COMMENTARY

Unlike many observers, it is our view that the Argentine economy, although to a certain extent insulated against the worst effects of the current financial crisis, nevertheless carries a number of significant weaknesses, which may well come home to roost in the medium term.

In spite of the fact that the government currently enjoys a fiscal surplus as well as a commercial one and can count on reasonably solid foreign currency reserves in the Central Bank, the fiscal position itself is to a large extent built on an asymmetric foundation. Creative accounting is concealing the fact that public sector expenditure is rising far faster than fiscal income. Subsidies and hand-outs, fostering non-productive activities or sustaining unprofitable ones, will ultimately erode the tax base. Populist policies such as facilitating early retirement will only accelerate the need for pension requirements. On the balance of trade front, the first six months of this year show that imports are growing nearly 5 times faster than exports. A strong currency, maintained to ensure commercial competitivity in foreign markets is hardly keeping track of inflation. Any sudden devaluation would feed through to costs and prices very fast.

> On the political front, President Kirchner's truce with parts of the Peronist movement may enable him to hold the ring into the foreseeable future. Nor is it likely to change in the run-up to the October elections. The balancing act between traditional Peronist strongholds such as the unions and an urban middle-class grateful to him for having steered them back from the crisis of 2001 is, to say the least, unusual, but he appears able to hold it together. Only a failure to confront inflation, preferring instead blatantly to manipulate the official statistics, is showing any sign of a potential crack in the edifice.

It was not a reassuring prospect for any investor, Leandro thought.

Eduardo arrived punctually at half past seven with a bulging leather satchel tucked under his arm.

Leandro waved his godson in the direction of the long worktable, which stood facing the windows of his living – dining room. The building dated back to the last decade of the nineteenth century, with high ceilings, wood panelling and – one of Leandro's more treasured possessions – an array of mahogany bookcases rising to the ceiling on the three walls away from the front window, which he had rescued from the demolition of an old lawyer's offices. The shelves were filled with books covering a wide range of interests - the history of Argentina, the Malvinas campaign, antiques, economics and music. Also his Ian Flemings and P.G. Wodehouse, alongside a large collection of jazz, tango and classical CDs and vinyl records, accumulated over the years.

A rarity in Buenos Aires, an open fireplace, logs smouldering in the grate, sending out a rich aroma of eucalyptus. Logs that Leandro would bring back on a Sunday evening from his place up in the river delta.

Eduardo glanced at the bursting shelves, catching a glimpse of himself aged fifteen climbing on a chair to pull down some volume that had attracted his eye. Bittersweet memories of rainy afternoons spent in his godfather's drawing room, back in the days when Leandro was still married to Elena, leafing through books about the war, which had taken his father months before his birth. Elena would sit next to him and talk quietly about his life at school or ask about his friends, standing in for his mother so far away in Salta. One of the shelves higher up contained a collection of photographs of the campaign, including one of a wrecked aircraft spread across an open hillside. To one side, a model of the Pucará in which his father had died – and Leandro had survived - alongside a photo of the two men standing below the cockpit.

He laid the satchel down on the large table, which Leandro had hastily cleared.

Leandro stepped into the small kitchen adjacent to the larger room and flicked on the ceiling lights to illuminate the work surface.

"What do you want to drink? A coffee, although it's perhaps a bit late? Or a glass of wine? I've a nice merlot from Neuquen, if you want to try it?"

Eduardo paused. It was probably going to be a long session.

"Better a coffee, on second thoughts."

"Coming up. Make yourself at home. I've cleared the table for your papers."

Eduardo began to unpack the files and folders. A couple of angle-poise lamps were clamped to each end of the worksurface to provide good light for reading. He made separate piles, the crime scene, the telephone and CC recordings, a couple of personal files, and a folder of emails and letters with other parts of the police force, as well as the results of Interpol traces. Leandro, leaving the Italian coffee machine to warm up, watched over his shoulder. Eduardo had always been methodical and tidy. Just like when he was at school, bringing in his homework. He was touched that his son was showing this level of confidence in him.

Leandro walked across the room and turned down the volume on the stereo, fading the Bach into the distant murmur of the traffic from the street at the far end of the *pasaje*. The fugues, played by Glen Gould, combined the tension and orderliness, which helped him reflect and concentrate when working.

"Where shall I start?" Eduardo asked after a moment, when he had checked that he knew where everything was.

"How about the beginning?" Leandro suggested, smiling.

Leandro pulled up a couple of deep leather armchairs, 1930s recoveries from the flea markets of San Telmo, and placed them facing each other along one side of the worktable. With notebook and biro, he settled himself in one and looked across expectantly at Eduardo. At that moment, the coffee machine began to splutter in the kitchen, and after a couple of minutes, he was back with a large French-style green coffee cup with a gold rim, stolen from a café off the Champs Elysées many years earlier, which he placed beside Eduardo on the table. He settled back into his chair again and watched his son pick up the first of the crime scene folders.

Eduardo began by passing over a set of photographs, which showed the English woman pinioned to the bed as she had been discovered by the hotel manager and maid when they finally opened up to see why she was not answering her wake-up calls. Leandro studied them carefully, noting the signs of seemingly consensual sadomasochistic sex. The woman's tight black leather breeches tucked into stiletto heeled boots of black patent, the crotch pulled wide open to reveal her genitals. Long black latex gloves reaching above her elbows. Silver chains and padlocks stretching from her wrists and ankles to the bedposts. Finally, the crucial twist of erotic stimulation, a black latex hood encasing her head, pulled down to form an airtight seal round her neck. The hood had only a single small hole over the mouth.

"A brain deprived of oxygen enters a semi-hallucinogenic state called hypoxia. Combined with orgasm, the rush is said to be like cocaine and highly addictive. Found that the other day," Leandro murmured.

Near asphyxiation was far from everyone's taste as a driver to orgasm, but it was a deviation which was shared by a surprisingly large number of men and women alike, who had discovered in the effect of being strangled or deprived of air an added stimulus to unleash the desired, explosive climax.

Each silver chain was padlocked to an elegant leather cuff buckled around the wrist and fastened to the bedposts at the head of the bed with another padlock. Similar cuffs and chains had been stretched from her ankles to each corner of the bed. At this end, in the absence of bedposts, the chain had been taken down to the feet of the bed on each side and then run along the floor before coming up at the other corner.

Another set of close-ups showed a large inflatable black rubber dildo, which had fallen under the edge of the bed. Photographs had been taken of her wardrobe, a white satin blouse draped over a chair, a woman's fur coat on the floor, the dressing table and the bathroom, as well as a number of general shots of the hotel suite. Scandinavian simplicity with a bit of zen thrown in for good measure. There appeared to be no signs of any form of struggle.

"Presumably this kind of scenario relies on things being done methodically and carefully. Needs a sense of absolute security for the person prepared to come close to death, or at the very least to a blackout, for sexual fulfilment?"

"That's right," Eduardo confirmed.

More photographs showed the mirrored wardrobe on the far side of the room. A detective was carefully taking out the woman's clothes and laying them on the damask-covered couch near the window, onto which the early afternoon sun was streaming through half-drawn curtains. The clothes looked expensive, a mink coat, a shot of a New York furrier's label, some silk dresses, a lot of sexy lingerie. A Louis Vuitton medium-sized suitcase was tucked behind the sofa and another LV carry-on stood next to it.

As Leandro studied them, Eduardo interjected the occasional comment by way of explanation.

"She had quite a wardrobe of expensive clothes, some sexy leather stuff, mainly from Germany and Italy, a few items of latex, more the kind of clothes in which she could have gone to a wild party – and no doubt she would have turned a few heads in the process. The rest of her clothes, also expensive, from Paris and New York and London. Plus a few weird bits and pieces – you know, straps, a small whip, chains, stuff like that. In all enough to make up her full airline allowance. We found two large suitcases. We know she came in ten days earlier on British Airways from London, First Class, and had a return booking for two days after we found her."

As Leandro turned over the photo of the dildo, Eduardo explained.

"She appears to have been suffocated with it, if that's how you describe it being stuffed into her mouth through the only breathing hole of the rubber hood as far as the back of her throat. With her hands shackled, she would not have been able to remove it and would have suffocated very quickly. Not nice! We're pretty sure this is what happened, although the dildo was under the bed when we arrived. The manager said they found her with it sticking up from her mouth, but immediately pulled it out in a last minute attempt to bring her round."

Leandro grimaced.

"She had asked for a wake-up call at twelve thirty, but the front desk, getting no reply, had finally decided to come in at quarter past one that afternoon. That's when they found her. By that time, she'd been dead about eight or nine hours."

A copy of the woman's British passport lay next to a small purse on the dressing table. The photo page gave her as Janet Mary Williams, born Norwich, June 28, 1965, which made her just forty-two.

Leandro stopped shuffling the photographs and looked at the list of belongings apart from her clothes and toiletries. "I see she had a laptop, but there doesn't seem to be any sign of a mobile phone. A bit strange for a foreigner, wouldn't you say ?"

Eduardo looked over at him from behind his empty coffee cup.

"I'll come to that, but, if you don't mind, can we follow the same sequence of analysis that we did? In other words, first impressions first? That way we can check our logical process." When Leandro nodded, he went on. "Just on the basis of the photos, how do you interpret the scene?"

After a minute's thought, Leandro began slowly.

"Strong stuff. Not a scene I know much about, though I've taken a quick look at some of it on the net since you told me about it. From the little I've gathered, this is not the kind of game you play with someone you don't know pretty well – and trust! Anyone who allows themselves to get into this position surely has to have total confidence in the partner. As far as I've heard, it's playing on the edge of suicide, or at the very least unconsciousness. When things go wrong, you have to be sure that the partner not only knows when things are starting to go wrong, but also how to pull you back from the abyss fast. You wouldn't go down this road with anyone you didn't know and even less someone who might be seen as an amateur. That at least suggests that they already knew each other, and possibly very well, but also that they might even have played this sort of game together before."

He paused a minute and shuffled through the photos once more.

"So far you're doing well, uncle. You should have been a detective," Eduardo said admiringly.

"Next, I would've thought that this is more often something you do in a safe place belonging to one of the partners, rather than in a hotel – just because if something does start to go wrong, you don't usually want the hotel management to be the first to know. So that's the first strange thing that comes to mind. However, taking a risk on the location might just be acceptable if you felt very safe with the person, although not really recommended. But doing it with a stranger? I would have thought very unlikely. Which confirms, to my mind, that they knew each other, and possibly pretty well. Why, given that, the other woman should have decided to play dirty and commit murder, that's another question altogether and at first glance, doing it in a public place makes it seem even more irrational. Did you find any trace of the other woman in the bedroom?"

"Not a thing, not a print, not a cigarette end, no lipstick on a glass, not even a bit of fair hair to match what she showed in the lift. There were plenty of stiletto heel marks in the carpet, but nothing to go on. I'll tell you more about that when we get onto the other woman."

"Okay carry on, take me through it whichever way you want."

"What you've just said is pretty much the way we saw it at the start as well. That being said, Fonseca seemed very reluctant to bring in the boys from the vice squad. Said we could handle it, didn't want to be seen to need help, the usual pride he shows. So we were fishing a bit to begin with. *Crime passionnel*, blasting your mistress with a .38, or staging a riding accident is about as exotic as it gets in this country. Maybe even getting someone to run over your wife's lover or your husband's mistress, but this stuff with chains and so on tends more to suit the gay or trans-sexual community. To be frank, we don't see a lot of this kind of thing. That's not to say that we didn't also take a look at the transsexuals and transvestites, there's still a lot of them around, though they've become more discreet now that they've been given territory of their own to strut their stuff. Not that the English woman was a TV or trans, she was all there from day one."

"But no-one had set eyes on her in the TV community," he continued, "and the description of her companion was either too imprecise or she does not seem to have been known in that neck of the woods. Anyway, the hard sex scene in Buenos Aires, SM, that kind of thing, is pretty small, and those that are involved all seem to know each other. It's also very hard to penetrate. The last thing they want is something to go wrong, so that we come snooping round their upper class clientele. We shook the tree pretty hard, but nothing dropped out. Let me play you the CC footage, just so that you know how little we have to go on as regards Lady X – by that I mean her killer."

Eduardo had been plugging in his laptop whilst speaking and he waited for it to fire up. He skipped through the desktop icons and finally turned the screen round to face Leandro so that they could watch a grainy copy of the hotel camera recordings. The first one showed the street outside and a cab pulling up at the front of the hotel. Eduardo commented quickly on the movement of the two women through the lobby into the lift. Then the sequence about an hour later, when the blonde woman emerged from the lift and, at a confident and unhurried pace, walked to the lobby, paused, looking away from the camera, to let the night porter open the front door and, with a friendly wave, exit onto the dark pavement outside. There she had set off to the left in the direction of the corner round which she disappeared. No taxi or car had appeared in the next five minutes and there were no more CC cameras on which to rely as to how she travelled after that.

"She appears to have phoned down about five minutes before leaving, apparently impersonating the victim. We presume it was she, as by this time the Englishwoman was no doubt dead. She told the porter something to the effect that her friend would be leaving in five minutes, so please to be ready to open the main door and also that she, the Englishwoman, was not to be disturbed until after midday. Pretty cool, assuming it's the killer. The porter said that the voice sounded a bit muffled, but the accent was definitely foreign. He couldn't be sure whether it was an English accent or perhaps French, but anyway he had no reason to doubt that it was the hotel guest. He had glimpsed her a few times on other late night arrivals, but had not really chatted with her."

"Did they have a recording of this call?"

"No."

"Go on."

"Well, we tried to put together as much as we could about Lady X, merely on the basis of the CC footage, which is all we have anyway. Silvery blonde hair, about one metre eighty, though we don't know what she was wearing in the way of heels, probably quite dramatic, given the whole scenario, which makes her pretty tall when dressed. Slim, judging by the cut of the fur coat and although we looked for them, we couldn't find any clear stiletto heel imprints in the bedroom carpet with which to work, so perhaps not very heavy either – that would confirm her being slim. Mind you, by the time everyone had crashed around the bedroom, you would have had trouble finding a print from an elephant! Not sure about the features, apparently Asiatic, judging by the glimpse we catch of her in the lift mirror and on her way back down. Here's a blow up of that shot."

He handed Leandro a heavily pixelated photograph of a woman's face, three-quarter view, the silvery blonde hair covering at least half her features. Leandro was able to pick up the outline of a small straight nose, most of a wide and apparently very full red mouth, and huge eyes, heavily outlined in what appeared to be dark mascara.

"You're right, there is a real almond shape to her eye, though she looks tall for an Asiatic. She would certainly be a very tall Thai or Japanese, I would think. Can't be many of them in BA, she would have been spotted by someone. Perhaps Chinese? Any photofit done? "

"We worked with the porter and he produced something, but it hasn't rung any bells with anyone."

Eduardo pulled out a mock-up, which showed a tall woman of indeterminate age in a long fur coat, slim build and pronounced Asiatic features under the long hair.

"He commented that it was very hard to determine how old she was, her features were very smooth and pale. In fact, he was more fixated on the large red lips and dark eyes than anything else. Said she was very striking."

"Asiatics are usually hard to put an age to anyway, so that figures," Leandro commented. "I once sat next to a Chinaman on a flight thinking he must be about mid-40s. Turned out he was nearly seventy!"

He stretched his legs towards the warmth of the hearth.

"Perhaps we're needing something a bit stronger?" he suggested, putting down the papers he was holding. He walked into the kitchen and opened the corner cupboard.

"Whiskey? Or wine? Not a great selection, I fear."

"Whiskey will do fine. No ice thanks," the younger man replied.

Whilst Leandro was in the kitchen, Eduardo pulled open one of the files on the table and began to lay out some more papers. With his glass beside him, Eduardo resumed the story.

"These are the bits of info we were able to pull together on the day of the murder. Nothing very useful, I fear, trying to piece together the night before and the next twenty-four hours. There's the results of our sending out a call to the airports and the ferries to Uruguay. Not much there, nobody fitting our description seems to have surfaced anywhere. Nice whiskey, by the way! We sent out a signal within an hour or so of discovering the body. Just in case Lady X might have skipped out earlier, we also looked at the CC TV in Aeroparque, Ezeiza and Buquebus from about six am onwards, but no tall Asiatic women anywhere and nobody with an Oriental name on any of the manifests."

"Then, of course, we looked at the hotel guest list, but nothing strange there. Only fifteen guests reserved in the hotel that night, twelve of them foreigners. The three locals we checked out, but frankly found nothing to connect them in any way. A businessman from Cordoba, a polo player from San Antonio de Areco and one reservation who never seems to have turned up. That one was perhaps a little strange, but the reservation had been made over the phone and we weren't able to take it very far."

He took a swig and savoured it. Leandro had introduced Eduardo to the pleasures of Scotch whiskey on a fishing trip when he had taken the fifteen-year old down south in the spring. He did not regret it.

"Then there's the results of the taxi trace. The cab that brought them picked them up outside a bar in Palermo Hollywood, around two thirty in the morning. They were alone, by that I mean no male seems to have said goodbye to them. The driver couldn't be sure which bar they came from, there are about three or four on that street, next to each other. They climbed into the back of his Renault. He thought it was the English woman who gave the hotel address, which makes sense since she was staying there. The other woman kept her face buried in the English woman's hair, so he hardly got a look at her, though he was able to confirm that she seemed tall. He can't remember them talking much and had the impression that they were quite busy with each other at the back. That much caught his attention, lesbians are usually more discreet in a taxi. The Englishwoman paid and left a largish tip. That's all we got from that source, nothing we couldn't have worked out pretty much for ourselves."

"And the bars?"

"We did those and were a bit luckier. A waitress at El Reposo served them. They came in around one thirty in the morning and ordered a couple of tequilas each. The waitress was struck by the blonde's fur coat and though neither of them removed their coats, she seems to remember the blonde wearing a kind of high-neck dress of some silvery, shiny material. She also remarked on her smooth skin and large mouth, but at this stage, she was wearing large dark glasses, so nothing on the eyes. She couldn't confirm the Oriental angle. She did notice that when they walked out, the blonde was a bit taller than the Englishwoman. She recognized Williams from the photo we put together after cleaning her up a bit. But again, nothing hard to go on at all."

"What do you know about the earlier part of the evening? They must have met somewhere."

"According to the hotel, the Englishwoman went out around eight thirty that evening. We see her on the CC TV, it's 20.33. She hadn't ordered a cab, and since we see her on the front door camera walking away down the street, we've no idea whether she picked one up or was met. About twenty minutes later, we catch her coming through the turnstiles at La Rural, apparently alone. There were a number of official parties on that evening. Although we glimpse her again a couple of times on other cameras, it's hard to pin down whether she is with anyone and certainly no sign of Lady X. She seems to be moving round the show with some of the polo crowd as far as we can tell. We know that she had friends there, so we started to see who knew her and what light they could throw on her friends and movements."

"That can't have been easy, many of them regard themselves as living on a different planet, as far as I've heard."

Eduardo nodded.

"Frankly, nothing, no-one even the slightest bit helpful, though some of them knew her or had seen her. But nothing about that evening."

"Can we go back to the hotel CC?"

"Three video screens stand on a shelf in front of the manager's desk, one covering the rear of the hotel, the other the pavement outside and the last the lobby and bar area. They don't have any on the floors or in the lift. The tapes we saw cover the period from nine o'clock in the evening until nine in the morning."

Eduardo fast-forwarded the tape to around 2.30 in the morning and then advanced it more slowly up until 2.52 am. The images were at least in colour, although dark out in the ill-lit street. A black and yellow Buenos Aires cab, a Peugeot, drew up at the door of the hotel and after the time taken to pay him off, two women in dark fur coats stepped out of its sliding door, the darker English girl emerging first, followed by a taller, slim woman with very luxuriant, long blonde hair falling over her face. They had both been only side-on to the camera and had waited less than a minute, backs to the camera, for the night porter to unlock the front glass doors.

"Did you get the taxi number?"

"Yes, AEB 239. As I said, we spoke to the driver."

The tape switched to the lobby images. The two women had rung the night bell of the hotel. The night porter had responded promptly and could be seen picking up the keys and then walking to the glass entrance. He unlocked it and the two women swept through the glass doors into the elegant modern lobby, the English woman pulling her room key out of her purse, slightly in front and partly hiding the blonde, whose hand she then held.

"Muchas gracias, good night, *buenas noches*," the English woman had thrown to the night porter as they moved to the lifts.

"She gives a friendly wave to the concierge, but as he told us, he only caught a glimpse of two good-looking women in long fur coats disappearing into the lift. It was just before three in the morning, and he noted their arrival in the book. During the Rural agricultural show in July, the hotels always see a stream of wealthy clients returning from late night parties, so there was nothing special about this."

The blonde could be seen in profile, but her hair fell forward covering much of her face and when they turned to the lifts, only her tall silhouette remained in the frame, standing to the right of the English woman. The dark fur coat was clearly expensive and fell to her ankles, her silvery hair covering slim shoulders. She did not turn round again to the porter and stood quietly beside her companion until both of them stepped into the lift. Although the English girl turned towards the camera to press the floor button, the other woman could just be seen looking straight ahead, as if examining herself in the rear mirror of the lift.

"But the fact that one of the women was not staying in the hotel? Would it be normal not to ask questions? "

"If it had been a man with a younger woman, they might have, but in this case... two women, you know, there don't seem to be any rules about that."

"Go back again, Eduardo, let's run it again, to get a better look at her."

Eduardo wound the tape back and then played it on slow. The frames jerked forward one by one, the figures on the screen stepping out of the taxi and across the pavement.

"There, stop it, let's have another look."

The blonde was facing to the right towards the hotel and they could just catch sight of a rather flat profile, heavily made up features, large dark eyes and a well-shaped mouth with heavy lips.

Eduardo took another sip of whiskey and paused as if to clear his thoughts. Leandro took advantage of the silence to begin to ask what had been at the back of his mind since Eduardo first came to see him in the café a few days before.

"Shouldn't we stop a minute and just ask ourselves where all this taking us? This is perhaps not the first case you've discussed with me since you decided to join the police, but it is certainly looking like one of the most complex. You and me need to be pretty clear about the whys and wherefores of our even talking about it. I don't need to tell you what Fonseca would say – let alone do – if he knew you were here, even without that pile of police documents, which should presumably never leave your office. Don't get me wrong, I am not saying I don't want to help – or even that I can't – but it would be smarter to try and at least clear our thinking a little before we both – and especially you - get in too deep. Maybe you disagree, but…"

"No, you're quite right. We need some ground rules."

A week had gone by since Eduardo's briefing of Leandro. There had been no new developments as far as he knew, and he had been taken up dealing with an enquiry from Frobisher in London. It had been an exceptional winter, with snow even falling in Buenos Aires in July for the first time in nearly a hundred years. In spite of the late-August cold, he had coaxed Sam into accompanying him out into the Delta for a weekend in his rustic shack on stilts up river.

The tumbled-down hut stood about a kilometre up a side stream off the River Urión, one of the main arteries in the Delta. He had found it one winter's day on a fishing trip with a friend in the late 1980s. Having failed to catch anything but a few skinny catfish, they had stopped for a barbecue on this stretch of the river. As they sat watching the steaks roast over the embers, one of the islanders had come rowing past in a battered dinghy, the water spilling in over the gunwales. He had waved to them in an untypically friendly fashion. Islanders were rarely forthcoming with strangers, inevitably regarding visitors from the capital with ill-disguised suspicion, almost denying their existence. They had offered him some of their *asado*, an invitation which he had readily accepted, particularly when they waved a bottle of red wine in his direction.

In spite of his dishevelled and frankly intimidating appearance – a long scar ran down his right cheek and a couple of fingers were missing on his left hand - he turned out to be friendly, appreciative of their gesture. He lived about half a kilometre farther along the stream, in a hut inherited from his parents, where he now lived with his common-law wife and five children. Leandro and his friend mentioned that they quite often came fishing in the Delta, which prompted Carlitos, as they discovered he was called, to ask whether they had any kind of base for their trips. The 1980s were a time when an increasing number of *porteños* were discovering the mysterious tranquillity and charm of the network of rivers on their doorstep, a process which the resident *isleños* watched with mixed feelings. To them it meant that officialdom and interference would begin to impinge upon their traditionally anarchic way of life. The Delta was in many ways a lawless area, controlled by anonymous island caudillos on virtually feudal terms. Here the rule of law rested on a knife in the back on a dark night or the mysterious explosion of fuel tanks on your neighbour's boat. But the islanders were not so reclusive as not to see that the *porteños* also brought cash and business from which they might profit.

"My aunt just died, no kids. She left a house and nobody is going to go and live there. It might suit you, so that you wouldn't have to come and go in the day."

Without fully knowing why, Leandro found himself at the end of the afternoon a few thousand pesos lighter, by way of down payment. Carlitos had led them upstream and shown them his aunt's house on stilts, sitting in a clearing some fifty metres back from the riverbank. Probably attributable to the bottles of red wine they had drunk with the barbecue, even the squalor and unkempt appearance of the house had not been enough to deter him. The garden - not exactly the word - had been a rubbish tip for decades, with empty oil drums sharing space with a rusty bicycle, a straggling pile of empty beer bottles and all manner of machinery and building materials. However, on closer inspection, the walls appeared solid, the bathroom facilities non-existent and the remaining furniture just about good for a bonfire. He had jumped up and down on the floor to test the boards, finding them generally solid, as also the wattle and adobe walls. The *quebracho* piles of the jetty sunk deep into the mud also appeared strong and likely to last a few more decades.

As they drove back along the Panamericana highway towards Buenos Aires that evening, Leandro could not help wondering what had got into him. Luis Miguel, his companion, had watched him in astonishment as the negotiation proceeded, but had not felt that it was any of his business to get in the way.

"You'll have some work to do on that place," he commented.

"Some? I haven't a clue how much, but at that price, it should be manageable. Anyway, you can never tell when a place like that won't come in handy. somewhere you can lose yourself completely."

In the ensuing months, in spite of Elena's barely concealed reticence, the deal had been done on a totally informal basis. A sum of money had changed hands, but there were no papers to back up his title, a problem he was content to push into the future. Come the spring, a team of Paraguayan builders and carpenters had installed themselves in the vicinity of his new house and, under his intermittent supervision, had put on a new roof, installed some basic sanitary facilities, re-floored the wooden terrace from which he could look out onto the river, and changed the planking on the jetty. A coat of pale ochre paint on the outside, dark green on the new zinc roof and whitewash inside had completed the transformation. A large and very alcoholic *asado*, with all the builders and painters, as well as Carlitos' family and relations, had celebrated the end of the restoration. Carlitos' wife, Juanita, had been recruited to come in once a week to clean up the place and, in exchange for a monthly contribution of half a dozen bottles of rough wine, Carlitos undertook to watch over the property. He had proudly shown off a dangerous looking shotgun to demonstrate his ability to deal with all-comers.

In the 1990s, Leandro and Elena spent frequent weekends up the river with Alejandra, joined on occasion by friends. To the child, this watery jungle in which she only had to bury a stick in the ground to find a sapling a week later, where coypus and otters dived into the water with a resounding 'plop', where fish could be had on a string with a piece of cheese, had provided a wonderland of animals, birds and insects in which she revelled every time they went there. Summers were spent plunging off the jetty into the slow-moving river of brown molasses, winters in front of the log fire. For a number of years they had survived on kerosene lamps or candles at night, until finally one day Leandro had shipped in a diesel generator to provide power and more comfort, albeit at the price of silence.

Among his wider circle of friends however, Leandro had deliberately spoken little of the house nor revealed its whereabouts. At the back of his mind, he had clung to the idea, expressed that first day when he had seen the house, that at some point in the future it might provide him with an escape hole. So the fewer knew where it was, the better.

Once Alejandra had grown into her teens, she no longer joined them upriver as often as before, preferring to stay behind for the parties organised by friends in the northern suburbs. As a result, Elena had also shown increasing reluctance to spend the weekends lost in the Delta, and Leandro's visits had become more intermittent. For a couple of years after the turn of the millennium, he had rented the house to a writer, who appreciated the peace and quiet of the weekends. But although this served to maintain the overall condition of the place, it was never an economic proposition. When he and Elena had separated, it was agreed that he would keep the house, in which Elena by this time was showing little interest. The expansion of wealth, which had accompanied the years of President Menem through the 1990s, had seen an exponential increase in the number and horsepower of the motor cruisers and launches which now swept up and down the Delta on Saturdays and Sundays. Fortunately, the narrowness of the side tributary ensured that hardly any of these intruders ever made their way to his hideout. By way of precaution, Leandro had never invested in anything flashy by way of launch, preferring an older and less eye-catching wooden hull of the 1980s, equipped with a V8 in-line Ford Falcon petrol engine. Although the risk of fire or explosion was technically greater, it was easier to look after and he never started the engine without taking the precaution of first lifting the hatch to release any fumes, which might have accumulated. A friend had been blown into the water on starting the engine without checking!

It was Saturday night. He and Sam had dined off some rather tough steak and potatoes in their skins, cooked over the embers of a fireplace well stocked with *quebracho* logs, a reddish ironwood from the northern provinces of Argentina, which burned slowly, throwing off an intense heat. A good bottle of red wine, a gift from Sam, had been followed by one from the small cellar he kept up river. A couple of brandies and some bitter Lindt chocolate serving as dessert, they chatted, the cut and thrust of these late night discussions a prelude to the vibrant sex which usually followed. He dozed off watching the *quebracho* glow in the fireplace.

The controls were useless, however hard he pulled on the joystick, the Pucará continued its sideways slide towards the rocky hilltop now a mere three hundred metres below. The smoke from the starboard engine enveloping the cockpit gave him nothing more than an intermittent view of the landscape rushing up towards him. He caught a glimpse of one or two figures staring up at him from their foxholes. In the seat in front, he could just make out the slumped shoulders of Francisco, the back of his head a red gash of bone and brains through what remained of his flying helmet. The roar of the wind and the other engine blotted out all thought, and the roll of the aircraft was causing him to lose consciousness.

"God, that fucking dream again! When will it ever go away?" he groaned.

Sweating profusely in spite of the cold, he sat bolt upright in the bed. The fire had gone out in the grate, leaving only a dull glow from the embers in the darkness. The sound of water lapping beneath the floorboards broke the silence.

Trying not to disturb Sam, he got out of bed and moved across to the window, pulling the curtains aside. The south-easterly wind combined with incoming tides at the mouth of the Rio de la Plata had raised the level of the river, so that it now flooded most of the islands in the Delta, a common phenomenon which never ceased to fascinate him. Over the ages, the Parana River had carried the silt and vegetation from the Pantanales of Brazil and Paraguay downstream to form this mosaic of islands. Looking out, he could see the dark silhouettes of his *casuarina* trees standing in the middle of what was now a shimmering lake stretching across to the opposite bank. It was a very cold winter's night, the cloudless sky and the brilliant half-moon bathing everything in tones of silver and black. He could see from the direction of the ripples as they came in from the river that it was still rising, but since the old fisherman's hut stood on stilts nearly two metres high, there was little risk of the water coming through the floorboards. He opened the window, listening to the soft wind playing in the branches of the trees by the edge of the river. The launch, still on its moorings, was now floating quietly halfway up the lower trunks, on a level with the top of the jetty's handrail.

Sam stirred in the bed behind him.

"Has the river come up? Oh, let me see, Leo, I love it."

Pulling the heavy blanket around her naked body, she joined him at the window.

"How beautiful it is," she whispered, pulling him in under the blanket with her.

For a flash, her gesture reminded him of similar moments when he and Alejandra as a child had stood looking out onto the rising waters. She had shared his fascination for the transformation in front of her eyes of land into liquid, and on summer nights, they had sat out on the balcony watching as the waters rose and fell.

"The fire's gone out."

Sam shivered.

Taking some pinecones from the basket, as well as a couple of solid pieces of *quebracho*, he bent over the grate, fanning the embers with a newspaper. The dancing shadows of the flare from the pinecones lit up the room. In a flash, Sam was back in the bed, pulling up all the blankets she could lay hands on. With the clear sky, the temperature had fallen to around five or six degrees.

"Get back in, you'll catch pneumonia!" she ordered.

He was hardly under the blanket before her hand had found him. Slowly, gently working him towards the erection which she finally took into her mouth, her tongue flicking, her lips pumping. Repeatedly drawing his penis deep into her throat, she made as if to swallow him entirely. Blowjobs were a Sam speciality.

As they finally lay entwined under the mound of blankets, he couldn't resist the line from 'Manhattan'.

"How many times a night...? How often can you make love in an evening?"

"Well, a lot."

Sex didn't seem to get in the way of her capacity for total recall.

"Yeah, I can tell. Well, a lot is my favourite number."

Giggling, she squeezed herself under his arm.

Sam was by no means the first of his girlfriends to share his retreat, but unlike most of the rest, who had only barely disguised their impatience with sacrificing the nightlife of the capital in favour of a cold and draughty riverbank, she had responded enthusiastically to every opportunity to escape. Not that she was particularly adept at tying knots or manoeuvring the large boat, usually preferring to stretch out on the couch at the rear end of the cockpit to take in the wintery sun.

But that didn't matter, since what she lacked in on-board skills, she more than made up with her evident enjoyment of their secret bolt-hole.

He got up once more just after sunrise to put more logs in the fireplace. As the sun pushed through the trees outside, he observed Sam sleeping, only the crown of her dark hair emerging from below the mountain of blankets. Like for almost everyone, the first moments of waking from the semi-somnolent state of early morning were a time when everything seemed more uncertain, problems loomed larger and life seemed to make less sense. As he watched her, he couldn't help wondering how long his relationship with Sam would last. Why a girl like Sam, who, he had not the slightest doubt, could take almost any man off the street, might want to prolong their affair. She had once made a remark to the effect that none of her previous men had come close, at least in Argentina, to providing her with the same combination of intellectual stimulus and skills as a lover. Clichés about girls seeking out father figures only left him wondering whether, given his age, that was good or bad. After more than three months together, he had to confess that there were still vast recesses of her life and of her psychology about which he knew too little. Her body, on the other hand, held fewer secrets.

He crept back beside her under the blankets. She stirred. His soft caressing initially provoked little response.

"Leave me alone! I need another hour's sleep at least. No, don't! You know I can't resist that! You're such an insatiable shit, Leo. Now I know what you mean by a lot. Stop it! Oh God... Alright, but more slowly. Yes. Yes. Again..."

They woke a couple of hours later to the noise of someone stepping onto the veranda at the front of the house.

"It must be Carlitos," he whispered.

"I'm just leaving you some eggs, Don Leandro."

Leandro pulled a blanket round his shoulders and opened the front door a crack.

"Many thanks, Carlitos. Everything all right?"

"Quiet at this time of the year. But very cold! Cover yourself properly when you take that kind of exercise."

Leandro could see a broad grin on the villainous face.

He laughed.

"And give my best wishes to the Señorita."

"I'll leave your box of wine in the kitchen, where Juanita can find it."

"*Muchas gracias*, Don Leandro. Take care."

"You too."

25 August 2007

On that same night, some five kilometres farther upriver, a different scene had been playing out. Built on stilts like everything in the Delta, this house was modern and extremely spacious. The central heating, fired by a large boiler in one of the outbuildings, was producing an ambient twenty-five degrees. The owner, small, wiry, in his early fifties, wearing only a pair of short black lederhosen, stood in the entrance to the bathroom, interrogating the two heavily-built men standing in front of him. He was sweating and physically excited. He tried not to show it.

He had been preparing himself for this moment for several weeks. The uncontrollable inner pulsations of desire to plunge, however momentarily, into that fusion of horror and ecstasy which the next few hours would bring, had taken his brain totally hostage. Able to concentrate on other matters during the hours in the office, no sooner had he returned to his apartment, than his evenings - and worst of all - his nights would become a sinister whirlpool of images and emotions, so strong that his body, his mind, no longer seemed his own.

The unquenchable desires filling such moments grew stronger day by day, week by week, until only the ritual on which he would now embark could bring release. It was sexual, but also so much more. Since those first, tentative initiations, the yearning had become uncontrollable. Questions of right and wrong no longer concerned him. At times he felt as though, like some kind of incubus, he would generate renewed life from the coming act. Yet once fulfilled, he also knew he would suffer, like a mediaeval martyr at the stake, until the desire grew again inside him, silently, steadily, to be quenched once more.

"Are Maria and Estela locked in their quarters?"

The older of the two men nodded, the cracking of his knuckles betraying his unease. There were some things he preferred not to have to do. But the boss was the boss.

"Is this one safe? Where was she picked up?"

"José picked her out of the line queuing for their papers at the immigration office on Jujuy. She struck him as by far the prettiest and she was happy to go along with his offer of a cushy job and a large salary as a maid. She's Bolivian."

"Yes, I took a look at her when she arrived. Are we sure she's no relatives here, no official trace of being in the country already?"

"José interrogated her quite closely and he thinks that it'll be very hard to identify her. She never got as far as filling out any papers."

"That's good! Bring her in, Mario, and get her fixed. And you, Cacho, you run the camera. There will be the usual large envelope for both of you at the end."

With that, the older man slid open the door of a large closet in the bathroom and stepped into the inner chamber which it concealed. At the centre of the house, its very existence disguised by the layout of the surrounding rooms, the walls were lined with a gleaming black soundproofing material. One wall was entirely covered by a mirror.

He sat down on a stool opposite a white aluminium medical examination chair, upholstered in black simulation leather, and waited.

A few minutes later, Mario and Cacho came through the entrance from the bathroom, dragging a young woman by the wrists. Naked from the neck down, screaming hysterically. Her head was encased in a tight black latex hood, leaving only her mouth visible. Struggling furiously, she was pushed down onto the chair and immobilised with straps at ankles, waist, wrists and neck and a ball-gag forced into her mouth, fastened behind her head. Unable to move, the only sound was now of her sobbing. Through the thin latex, it was just possible to detect her eyes darting from side to side in terror.

He studied her. She was lean, with proud young breasts and good legs. Pale brown skin. A tiny gold chain on one ankle, another round her neck. Somehow, her figure was too good for someone from the *altiplano*. A town girl more likely, perhaps even a prostitute, given the gold chain. Strangely, he felt relief that he preferred them pretty. It made it seem almost normal. He waited for her to calm down a little, then leaned forward and, spreading her thighs apart with one hand, inserted the fingers of the other between her labia. The girl screamed and reared up in the chair as far as the straps would allow, but no amount of jerking and contortion could escape the thrust of his fingers. Then, with his other hand, he began to masturbate.

Mario stood over her, hands on her shoulders. Cacho filmed, never allowing the camera to stray away from the girl's body and head, careful to avoid any frame of Mario or the *patron*. Only the latter's hand would be visible.

As the session proceeded, a long hard dildo replaced the probing fingers, which he thrust in and out like a piston. Her labia swelled out of all recognition, drops of blood began to appear on the floor between her legs. Briefly at times, the girl seemed to relax, as if accepting the horror of what was being done to her. Muffled screams gave way to whimpering, to his mind almost of pleasure. Then panic and pain would take over again as her gagged screaming filled the room. Keeping up the relentless penetration, he visibly became more aroused.

The end came suddenly when, after nearly half an hour and on a signal from the *patron*, Mario enveloped the girl's head in a thin sheet of plastic, closing off her only access to air. Her head crashed from side to side, her gagged mouth visibly sucking vainly for oxygen, the screams unbearable. Within less than two minutes, her body went limp. The older man rose, having attained a feeble orgasm, and, pulling up the zip on his pants, left the chamber.

"You know what to do now. Take it as far away as possible," he threw over his shoulder. "And, Cacho, leave the film on my desk."

He walked slowly to the veranda and poured himself a large vodka, before sitting down in a cane armchair. He watched the river glide past silently. Everything was peace, calm, most importantly inside him, as if an escape valve had been opened, the unbearable pressures of the previous weeks suddenly released. He felt physically lighter. He would sleep well tonight. It was always like that.

27 August 2007

The mongrel ran along the bank of Arroyo Sabalos, the little boy chasing along behind, dribbling an ageing football. His ragged blue and white striped number 10 football shirt showed where his loyalties lay. It was late afternoon and the sun was beginning to sink over the trees on the far riverbank. The dog stopped suddenly, barking furiously and making little dashes back and forth into the long grass tussocks by the edge of the jetty, where a small accumulation of floating bottles, plastic bags and broken branches had collected. At first, the boy paid no attention and went on kicking the ball along the path in the direction of his parent's shack, a hundred metres away. Only when the dog had not caught up but remained barking loudly behind him, did he stop.

"Come on, *perro*, let's go."

He put his fingers to his lips and uttered a shrill whistle. The dog still paid no attention, but continued to scrabble at the edge of the reeds.

"Come on," he called again. Seeing that nothing was going to bring the dog back, he retraced his steps along the bank, ball under one arm.

At first, he couldn't quite see what all the fuss was about, but as he bent down and parted the long reeds, he caught a glimpse of a pale hand breaking the surface of the water, the arm disappearing into the brown and turgid water at the edge of the stream.

"Shit! *Perro*, let's go, let's go - now!"

He dropped his ball and ran off in the direction of his house. The mongrel finally followed, still barking.

An hour later, an Alucat 850 patrol boat of the Prefectura, one of the shallow-draught waterjet models they had bought from the Damen shipyard in Holland, moored against the jetty. Two sailors climbed out wearily and signalled to the boy to follow them. A third stayed on board.

"Okay show us what you found, *chico*."

"It's over here, take a look," he called back to the two men, one of whom was lighting up, his back to the evening breeze. For a moment, they all stood there in silence, looking at the hand rising from the water. One of the sailors pulled out his cell phone and tried to get a photograph of the hand and the surrounding bank, but it was already too dark.

"Probably drowned somewhere and got carried here by the river. Though there's hardly any current to do that," he murmured.

His colleague called up the San Isidro base on his walkie talkie.

"They say pull the body out and bring it to the mortuary in San Fernando."

"Okay, let's get on with it, I'm getting late for my dinner."

The greasy and mud-stained, but visibly well-shaped body of a dark-skinned young woman lay in the rough grass in front of them, her long black hair plastered over her face and neck, a strangely bloated look on her face, her eyes wide open. She was naked, breasts standing up incongruously from her torso, her back arched, her legs half bent upwards. But it was the gash between her legs, which focused their attention.

"She can't have fallen in naked and drowned, girls don't do that. She looks as though she's from the north, what d'you say ? See those rather narrow eyes and high cheek bones. And she's pretty dark, too. It's almost as if she had seen something that scared the shit out of her, those eyes! And her cunt! *Madre de Dios!*"

The little boy stood beside them, fascinated by the sight of the woman. She faintly reminded him of a pin-up he had seen on the wall of his father's workshop, over the bench, next to the picture of the Virgin Mary. He tried not to look at her genitals. Finally, he picked up his ball and pretended to lose interest.

One of the sailors bent down and pulled her hair away from her face and neck.

"That's a nice gold chain she's wearing round her neck."

"Yes, and she's another one round her ankle. Maybe some kind of pro, they often wear that kind of thing."

"Where did you get that, Franco, what the fuck do you know about that kind of thing?"

"I saw it in a magazine we picked up on that cruiser we searched the other week."

"Tampering with the evidence again, were you?"

They laughed, nervously.

"Okay, let's get on with it. But it's clearly not a simple drowning. We'll have to have the forensics take a look at her, I suspect. Okay, give us a hand."

The other sailor dropped his cigarette and, between them, they carried the stiff body onto the back of the patrol boat, where they wrapped it in a tarpaulin.

"Come on, Felipe, we'll drop you off at your home, and then you can tell us how you found her."

They walked along the riverbank until they came to the ramshackle house on stilts where Felipe's father was waiting. He pulled the little boy to his side. He was shivering from the early evening air, the iconic number 10 still just visible in the fading light.

"We'll need him to make a statement. Be back tomorrow, as it's getting a bit late now and we have to get the body to the forensic team as soon as possible. You had better be present as well, as he's a minor."

The father, never keen to get too close to the forces of law, merely nodded.

He watched them unhitch the launch and reverse out into the river with their macabre baggage on the rear deck propped up against the large exhaust manifold. He turned back into the dimly lit shack, pushing Felipe in front of him. The dog followed, but a swift sidekick left him outside for the night.

"You have to admit, the girl had balls! After all, she must have known that the people on that plane were senior members of the government. For example, Espinoza, president of our great new energy company Enarsa, Claudio Uberti, a top official as well. No, she had to have guts to stand in the way of that lot. And on top of that, she's very good-looking!"

"Trust you, Miguel, to focus on the girl, rather than expressing concern about the obvious criminality of what was going on."

"Listen, Alberto, if in this life, and particularly in this country, we were to focus more on the corruption than on the girls, we would have committed suicide a long time ago."

Francisco, from the other side of the table, joined the argument.

"We have the best of both worlds, the corruption to get us out of trouble when things go wrong, and the pretty girls to console us if, even after we've handed over the bribe, we're still in trouble."

They all laughed.

Leandro watched them. These lunches, every Thursday at noon, of which he attended about one out of two, in the same restaurant near the corner of Montevideo and Sarmiento, inevitably raised his spirits. When all was said and done, with people like this, Argentina was virtually indestructible. Always taking the same table, a group of about ten or twelve good friends from university would come together to shoot the breeze and kill a few bottles of wine. The group varied from one week to another. A couple of engineers, one or two lawyers, an architect, an economist and a pair of doctors. They had hunted together when young. The chase continued, as much crap being talked now as when they were twenty-five years younger! Politics, football, rugby, religion, sex - lots of sex - were subjects on which everyone always had an opinion, inevitably varied. Whilst one half of the table was busy talking about the latest match between River and Boca - what else? - his side of the table was discussing the scandal of the Venezuelan businessman stopped a month ago at the downtown airport with a suitcase containing nearly a million dollars.

"No, as I said, you've got to admire her. Six in the morning, an official government plane coming in from Venezuela, going through the VIP section at Aeroparque. A couple of senior government officials on board, with this Venezuelan guy, Antonini Wilson. Where do they get names like that? Tells her his suitcase contains books, since it's showing up dense on her radar screen. The other officials with him must have been making it pretty clear that she shouldn't be too inquisitive. But she persists and gets him to open the suitcase. And what do they find? Nearly a million greenbacks! Which, furthermore, she confiscates. She gets my vote any day. They're even offering her a centrefold in one of the men's magazines."

"I wonder whether you'd be paying as much attention if she was ugly."

"Alberto, that's an unworthy remark!"

"With you, Miguel, it's entirely appropriate. By the way, who was that on your arm, the other night at the cinema, Patio Bullrich?"

Miguel looked slightly disconcerted.

"I don't know who you're talking about. Anyway, what night?"

Few secrets could be kept around this table, except from their wives or mistresses. Leandro smiled.

Just then, his cell phone began to vibrate in his jacket pocket.

"Hi there! What's up?"

Sam.

"I need to see you in a hurry. I know you're at one of your macho lunches, no doubt claiming to have been in bed with half the women on this planet. Can you make it?"

"Sure, I can skip the dessert. You'll just have to pay me a coffee somewhere else. Where do you want to meet?"

"In front of the Alvear Hotel. Shall we say in about half an hour?"

Leandro looked out of the huge plate glass window beside their table. It was a fine afternoon, the grey cold of the weekend in the Delta had given way to the blinding glare so characteristic of these late winter days in Buenos Aires. The late August sun, lower in the sky, seemed to bounce off the city's streets and pavements, blinding drivers and pedestrians alike.

"I can pick up a taxi. See you there in half an hour."

"Love you."

"Me too."

She hung up.

"Now who's that?" Alberto asked.

"None of your goddam business!"

"Ah, just as I suspected. You divorcees have all the fun," Alberto added with a tone of mock bitterness.

"And some married ones as well."

Leandro passed a one hundred peso bill across the table.

"Got to run. Here's my share. If there's any left over, you can give it back to me next week."

Respecting the formal ritual, he circled round the table, shaking hands with each of them in turn.

"He's got a pressing business engagement," Alberto announced to the group. "And when I say pressing...."

Leandro shook hands with the waiter, who always looked after them.

"See you next week, Negro. I've left the money with Alberto."

He had no difficulty in finding a taxi cruising slowly past the restaurant entrance.

Fifteen minutes later, he was standing in front of the large newspaper and magazine kiosk located at the main entrance of the Alvear Palace, considered the finest of Buenos Aires old generation of hotels. He picked up a copy of American Vogue magazine and idly began to turn the pages.

"Proper little voyeur, I see."

He turned. Sam was laughing at him. As always, immaculately turned out. A tobacco coloured suede coat, dark blue roll collar up to her chin to keep out the cold, a matching beret set at a perilous angle on top of her perfectly combed hair.

"I didn't know you were a fashion buff. Maybe you could become my fashion advisor."

She continued laughing.

"Actually, when I was much younger, reading Vogue or Elle was a pretty innocent way to find a lot of photographs of very good-looking girls," he confessed, slightly shamefacedly.

"I love it!"

"Twenty years ago or so, fashion was fashion. There were recognisable trends. But now... There isn't any more fashion. It's all shapeless, tasteless, all over the place. In those days, fashion designers still wanted women to look beautiful. Nowadays, I'm not so sure. Perhaps people like Lagerfeld. But the rest..."

"Lagerfeld indeed. Whatever next? I'm impressed. I'll have to take you along with me when I go shopping."

"You don't need an expert. You're spectacular as you are."

"Yes, but do you really think I'm sexy enough?" she coyly asked, opening the top half of her coat and turning slightly away from the less than disinterested gaze of the kiosk owner. The blue turtleneck sweater was clearly a couple of sizes too small for her. Leandro studied the proud spheres of her breasts, made more arrogant as Sam arched her back.

"Well, I'm not sure..."

114

Leandro adopted an expression of deep uncertainty.

"Really? Then we'll have to do something about that. Right away!"

Taking Leandro firmly by the arm, she strode under the arches of the hotel entrance into the main lobby, past the admiring doorman. Once inside, she indicated to Leandro to take a seat and marched up to the reception desk.

"Good afternoon, Señorita Haidar."

"Good afternoon, Leonel. I need a room for one night. Have you got anything? Non-smoking of course and preferably quiet."

Leonel consulted the computerised guest register.

"Well, Señorita Haidar, we have a couple of rooms. But one of them will only be ready in about an hour or two."

"Then I'll take the other one."

Sam placed her American Express Platinum card on the counter.

"We have your details, don't we, Señorita? And those of your father, of course."

"Of course."

Armed with the electronic key, she signalled to Leandro to join her by the lifts.

"I'm not sure what to make of all of that. They seem to know you very well. Not your first time, I would say," he commented, not without a tone of irony, as they stepped inside.

"I just knew you'd say that. No, I stayed here with my father for six months over the end of last year when we were having our flat redecorated. I'm just trading on that. Anyway, shut your mouth, I've got a better use for it."

Even when the lift doors opened on the third floor, Sam had not released Leandro from the kiss. To a bemused hotel guest waiting to take the lift down again, she flashed a broad smile.

"Terribly sorry to keep you waiting. Some last minute business to attend to."

Taking Leandro again by the hand, she marched off down the passage, reading out the numbers on the doors as she passed.

"Here we are."

They spent the best part of the afternoon making love, languidly, luxuriating in the crisp sheets of the king-sized bed, enjoying the change of surroundings. Not that there was any real risk of their relationship going stale, but Leandro had to admit that making love to Sam in the anonymous, five-star surroundings of the Alvear Palace was a stimulating change from 'your place or mine'.

They had ordered a bottle of Baron B Brut Rose, a favourite, and scrambled eggs with smoked salmon, the eggs not too firm. A charming waiter, almost certainly gay, had brought it to them on an elegant trolley, the tablecloth pristine, the silver stamped with the logo of the hotel, a solitary rose in a flute vase. Being early September, the sun was now going down, bringing the buildings on the other side of the Avenida Alvear into shade.

"This is the life," Sam sighed.

"You're lifestyle, I know," he teased.

"Yes," she stretched the word out. "We really should do this more often."

"Oh dear, is my flat beginning to pall?"

"Your flat, not really, you know I love it. And you? Definitely not!"

"At least that," Leandro muttered with undisguised relief.

"Stop playing the victim. It doesn't suit you."

After a pause, she continued.

"You see, that's Argentina for you. The government may be corrupt, inefficient, and generally shitty. Not that I want to get into that discussion. But in spite of it all, there's still a lifestyle here like no other.

And not just because Leonel downstairs treated me like some long lost relative. In reality, the people in this country, if you take away the politicians and a few of the rich businessmen - those who have always lived off the state, in other words off our taxes - if you take those away, what are you left with? Some of the nicest people on this planet. Perhaps made easier by the fact that the last decade of wealth seems to have brought out the worst in so many others. What do you think?"

Leandro was lying on his stomach on the far side of the bed, his chin cupped in both hands, studying the silhouette of this girl, who had so clearly begun to reshape his life. She really had spectacular tits! He rolled over onto one side.

"I think this is a pretty heavy conversation, when all I want to do is just go on looking at your breasts. It's not the first time, Sam, when other girls would be pulling out a cigarette, you pull out a topic for a profound philosophical discussion."

She kicked out at him across the bed.

"I'm being serious. Trying to ensure that your brain doesn't just become addled by sex."

"Could be worse things in life."

"Oh, shut up and be serious."

"But I don't want to be serious."

Seeing the look of frustration on her face, he relented.

"Oh well, no getting away from it. Was it to discuss this that you called me away from my lunch?"

"No, I wanted to fuck you. I've done that. Now I need something else."

At least the agenda was simple!

He pulled himself up the bed and, piling up the pillows next to her, lay down with an air of one resigned to his fate, his head nestling against her breast. None of his other girlfriends had ever seen fit to challenge him both physically and intellectually in the same bed. This girl was different in so many ways. He paused to collect his thoughts. Another glass of Baron B. Then he was ready to start his speech, after an artificially long sigh to drive home his reluctance.

"Okay! Argentina? Here comes a lecture on Argentina. You asked for it. You and me, we're both Argentines. Like all Argentines, our roots are very mixed. Unlike the Americans, this nation has generally failed to instil the sense of patriotism, which one finds amongst the Yanks. We think we have, but I don't believe it. Yes, we're all very patriotic when it comes to football, some of our literature, take Borges, or on topics like the Malvinas. Like everyone, we take offence easily if our nationhood is attacked. But only too often, it's just a defensive posture. Somewhere along the line, in the early decades of the last century, the values of what we call the generation of the 80s, people like Roca, Urriburu, Carlos Pellegrini and others, began to fade. Perhaps because we had it too easy. As we all know, at the end of the First World War, Argentina was the seventh richest country in the world. And where was that wealth spent? We allowed the foreigners, often the English, to make the investments, in the railroads, in the ports, in the meat packaging plants. Our upper classes, the *estancieros*, with nothing to do while the harvest ripened and the cows munched the grass, packed their large families off to places like Biarritz, or Paris, or London, where they spent it. Our fortunes were made by people who owned thousands of hectares. Not like the Americans, the Pierpoint Morgans or the Carnegie's, who ploughed their money into steel, infrastructure, railroads. And made America what it is today."

She stretched out a hand to cover his mouth. She was listening to him closely, almost as if they were sitting opposite each other across a café table, not lying naked in each other's arms.

"I know all that, Leo. That's the official version. Arguably, that's the negative side. The side immortalized in 'Cambalache', you know, the bit in that tango which says '*Hoy resulta que es lo mismo ser derecho que traidor*' – 'There's no difference between an honest man and a traitor', and finally that terrible phrase, '*El que no afana es un gil!*', 'If you don't steal, you're a fool!' It's one of the few tangos I know. I hate tangos. So depressing! But the words are even truer today than when they were written by Discépolo seventy years ago. But leaving all that aside, what I was talking about were the other, the positive values. Human values, not just balance sheets. I know our balance sheet has been disastrous. Six years ago, the world had written Argentina off. We had financial meltdown. Nobody thought we would recover in under ten years. Yet here we are, in 2007, and look at us. And whatever anybody may say, especially our dear President, who thinks he's the one who did it, all that's thanks to the little guys, to the *campo*, to half a million farmers spread across this land, who have turned this country round. From the abyss into which our politicians and civil servants had dragged us."

"This is getting really heavy. I need another glass of champagne."

Leandro slid off the bed, returning with the ice-cold bottle and filling their glasses.

"You've actually got a hell of a physique, Leo. Did anyone ever tell you?"

"I tell myself every time I look in the mirror. Do I detect you're changing the subject?"

"No, not at all. But I don't want to talk about politicians. I want to talk about ordinary Argentines. They're the ones I admire, the ones I love. From the taxi drivers, the waiters, through the people who put petrol in your tank, you name it, the people we deal with every day. I've lived in France, in England, the Middle East. We've got something special."

"I know what you mean. The English are very tolerant, well meaning, educated. I first discovered that the day we surrendered at Port Stanley – or Puerto Argentino, as we baptised it for those terrible seventy-four days. They had just defeated us, we all looked and felt fucking miserable, we hated them for everything they had done to us. And yet, they didn't seem to hate us. They treated us like human beings. I'll never forget that."

He paused. She stretched out a hand and took his, giving it a squeeze. She knew that those events still cut deep. He continued.

"One way and another, the English are some of the most civilised people on this planet. They love animals. And they invented rugby. But, as you were saying, even leaving aside the weather, I'm not sure I'd trade in my life in Argentina for a little house in the Cotswolds. Last time I was there, in England I mean, a couple of years ago, there was just too much money floating around. I'd known it in the early 1990s, when I was at Citibank. In those days, London felt like a series of villages, people knew each other, they had time for each other, it was all much more informal. Hard to pin it down, but somewhere they seem to have hardened. Now they seem to judge you by the horsepower of your engine. Perhaps it's the fact that we, the Argentines, have been so regularly abused by our leaders that has made us compassionate, helpful, loving. Those are qualities which you find still in places like Italy. It's no coincidence that we're the only Latin American country with such a high proportion of Italian blood. Whilst on the one hand it's probably the source of our chaos, it's also what saves us. Perhaps you don't agree."

Sam didn't reply at once, but got up to look out of the window. The sun had gone down completely and the streetlights of the Avenida were reflected off the windows on the upper floors of the building opposite. As so often, her response surprised him.

"I wonder what Wilde would have made of the London of today," she murmured, without turning round. "In his day, it was aestheticism, which slowly slipped towards hedonism. That's what fascinated him, drove him. Writers like Huysmans, Proust, Gide. Today, the hedonism has simply become materialism. I wonder what he would have made of the internet, of today's art, people like Damian Hirst?"

Surprised by her digression and aware of his own relative ignorance when it came to literature or art, Leandro waited until she looked at him again before continuing.

"I don't know. That's your area," he replied, lamely.

She smiled and came back to the bed.

"Sorry, I didn't mean to change the subject. Carry on with your psychoanalysis of us Argentines."

He relocated his head on the softness of her stomach, before continuing. He resisted the temptation to place his hand between her thighs. There would be time for that.

"As you know, large parts of the population actually believe that, somewhere, somehow, God's an Argentine. We believe in miracles. Just before we destroy ourselves at the bottom of whatever pit we've chosen to throw ourselves into - usually a choice made quite irrationally - we believe that the hand of God will stretch down and catch us. It's the only way that you could explain why an Argentine, behind the wheel of a powerful car, will pull out and overtake into the face of an oncoming car with all its lights flashing. How often do we sit by and watch that sort of suicidal behaviour? We even think it's normal! Somehow, we always believe that nobody is going to call 'Game over!' And then, when the miracle has happened, it becomes just another piece of our neurosis, fuelling yet another visit to the psychiatrist, as we try and analyse why God should have saved us. Part of it may come back to the fact that we Argentines really are good people, the kind of people that God would want to have on this planet. And I suppose you could argue that our never-ending crises are evidence of the existence of the Devil, trying to spoil God's game."

Sam was silent for a moment, thinking over what he had just said.

"I rather like that interpretation. All that Italian blood is certainly part of the answer. That's why I feel a strange mixture of passion and adrenaline in my veins whenever I go to Rome, but also when I come back here. In both places, family is so important. Perhaps it's something I missed out on. That may also be something that gives me more resilience, a stronger will to fight. Although you could argue that all that family warmth, the womb into which Argentines withdraw at the weekend, surrounded by grandparents and grandchildren.... it's arguably what makes them soft. Unwilling to take risks. And because of that, the politicians, and before them the military, have been allowed to get away with murder, often literally. The people who govern us seem to have a better understanding of our own psychology than we do. That gives them power. These people now, the Kirchners, I'm really afraid that they've worked it out. It's something I'd like to change. But I don't know how."

She looked down, sadness in her eyes. Now it was Leandro's turn to squeeze her hand.

"Let's not spoil this afternoon by worrying about the fate of Argentina. It'll survive. We'll survive. We'll find a way to do something about it. As you say, God will. He always does. Now I want to enjoy the sensation of being a kept man, taken to expensive hotels and fed smoked salmon and champagne. So, if you don't mind, I've lost interest in your brain. There's another part of your anatomy I'd like to reconnect with."

His fingers had found her clitoris.

"And I was just thinking that I ought to check out your horsepower...."

Astride his erection, she towered over him, her breasts caressing his tongue, his lips. Her hair falling forward, framed her large eyes in shadow. Suddenly it hit him.

"Rita!" he gasped.

"What?"

"Rita! Mulholland Drive!"

It had suddenly come to him. Rita – Camilla – the girl who had made steamy love to Naomi Watts. David Lynch's film. That was the face he had been searching for since their first meeting.

"I never understood that film!" was her only response.

September 2007

Leandro turned over the letter and held it up to the light to see if there were any obvious watermarks. The envelope wasn't any more informative.

He looked over at Eduardo.

"You say you found this under the door of your flat? Did no-one see who brought it? How about the *portero*?"

"He said that a young man had delivered it by hand, but left no name. The *portero* pushed it under my door."

It was the first week in September and Eduardo had suddenly rung Leandro asking for an urgent meeting.

"It's addressed to you, but what makes you think that it has a connection with the Englishwoman's case?"

"How else do you interpret the reference to polo?"

"Maybe, but that's hardly conclusive."

"Except for the fact that it's the only case I'm working on and for which my name has appeared in the papers."

"True. Let's go through it, line by line. No date, no address, nothing to indicate where it's come from. Have you had a graphologist look at it to see whether it's a man or a woman?"

"Not likely, if you read what he writes. Let's assume it's a man, shall we?"

Leandro started to read the letter.

Dear Inspector Falcioni. I believe that you are currently investigating a rather difficult case and that you may not be making a lot of progress.

"That could apply to a lot of your work," Leandro commented.

I believe that I may be able to add a few pieces to your investigation. However, if you in any way reveal the fact that you have received this letter, not only are you personally likely to be in grave danger, but my help will immediately come to an end. The polo circles in which you have been trying to make some progress, although not irrelevant, will prove a dead end, unless you know exactly where to start and who you are dealing with.

"Have you got any other cases in which polo players or that crowd are in any way involved?" Leandro asked.

"No, the Englishwoman's the only one at this time. We were taking a look at a possible prostitution ring last year, but the trail on that went dead. There's no doubt that a lot of that goes on. They bring in girls from Brazil and even from as far away as Paris or Moscow. Some of the Colombian polo players are almost certainly also a channel for drugs, which flows as freely as the Johnnie Walker. The trouble is that a lot of it takes place in the estancias out in the province, you know, Cañuelas or beyond Pilar. As a result, it's pretty difficult to get a look at what's going on."

Leandro went back to the letter.

You will find that certain trails lead to Europe, in ways which you will find hard to follow. Going through Interpol or more formal channels will almost certainly lead nowhere, and anyway, others will become aware of the fact that you have moved the enquiry in that direction. That is something which will almost certainly not only put an end to your investigation, but even possibly your life. You may believe that this is being melodramatic, but I can assure you that I have good reason to warn you. Until I have been able to learn from you how you might proceed, and indeed, whether you are even interested in doing so, I will not add anything further to this letter. Although you do not know it, the pool in which you are fishing contains some of the most dangerous individuals in the Argentina of today. Catching and destroying them will serve to remove one of the buttresses of the system which is currently strangling our country. But without my help, and without every precaution - which means evading the eyes of a system currently devoting enormous resources to protecting itself from just this kind of investigation - you will achieve nothing and indeed only make matters worse. If you are interested in pursuing this contact, place a copy of La Nación on the rear window-ledge of your car for two days starting the day after tomorrow, when it is parked in the side street behind your flat. Do not attempt to watch it. If you wish to continue and I see the newspaper, I will send you a second letter, which will provide a first piece of evidence that I know what I'm talking about.

The letter was unsigned.

Leandro put the letter down on the table.

"Very mysterious. Very. What are you going to do?"

"I already have. I placed La Nación in the back of my car this morning."

"What makes you so sure it's not some kind of trap?"

"Frankly, at this stage, I haven't the slightest idea, but equally, I don't see what the downside could be. The next letter should be more interesting. If it provides some clue to the identity of the writer, we're obviously going to be faced with the decision whether to maintain anonymity between us, or try and go after him, to speed up the whole process. On balance, I don't think the latter is actually an option, since by the sounds of it, the source will dry up without our finding out very much more. What's your view?"

Leandro thought for moment.

"I tend to agree. Obviously everything is going to depend on what kind of information this person will start passing you. He seems very convinced that the material, which he can provide is potentially highly explosive. It may be a sign of his self-importance, but on balance, unless he's some kind of sensation-seeker, it seems as dangerous for him as he suggests it may be for you. Any indication as to how soon a second letter might come after the business of the newspaper? We'll just have to wait."

Eduardo shrugged his shoulders. "I'll keep you posted. Sorry, but I've got to rush. If you've any further thoughts, I'll come round. My suspicion is that this isn't the kind of subject we should be discussing, even on our cell phones."

"I agree. Just give me a buzz and we can meet at the cafe as usual."

A week went by with no news from Eduardo. Then late one evening, Leandro's cell phone carried a text message suggesting that they meet in London City over breakfast next morning.

Eduardo was already there when he pushed through the doors.

"I found this when I got home last night."

Eduardo passed him an envelope identical to the one they had been examining a week earlier.

Having ordered a coffee and a *medialuna*, Leandro pulled the single sheet of paper out of the envelope. It only took a couple of minutes to read the brief typed script.

Dear Inspector.
From my last letter, you will have worked out that I know that you are working on the murder of the Englishwoman in the hotel back in July. This is no simple murder, but the first time that a certain group of people very close to the centre of power have committed a mistake and broken surface. For many reasons, you will be allowed to make no formal progress in the investigation and any visible attempt by you to push the case will certainly place you in real danger. Whether or not you have realised it, you have become a target yourself for a person who has almost unlimited power and certainly no scruples about doing anything to preserve that situation. I am in a position to pass you information which will lead you in the right direction, but I cannot tell how, given the fact that you are yourself under observation. Ultimately, only you will be able to make use of this information properly.
Therefore, before we go any farther, two questions need to be answered. The first is how we can more directly but safely exchange information. The second is how, once you have the

information, you propose to make use of it. A face-to-face meeting between us is not possible, so I am sending you an e-mail address, which you may use once only, presenting your ideas on how we can best communicate. Although electronic surveillance is now within the reach of many governments, few have the resources to conduct any systematic screening of e-mails or similar systems. Even so, we must find a way to run a sequence of digital communications, each one different from the last.

When you have found the solution to this, send it to me at the following mail. Once I have received your message, that mail will in turn be replaced by another. Do not contemplate Facebook or Twitter or similar media.

The letter ended on a Hotmail address.

"Cryptic, but not very informative!"

Eduardo nodded.

"It makes you wonder whether it isn't in fact a trap being set by this mysterious person he refers to. By sending a mail, it might actually provoke the consequences he is warning me against."

"It's obviously a possibility, but if such a person exists - or group of persons - there would be little to be gained by advertising themselves in this way, particularly if they are as discreet as the writer seems to imply. There are plenty of ways of stopping you on this case, but stimulating your curiosity would not, to my mind, be one of them."

Eduardo thought a minute.

"You're probably right. But all this business with different e-mails. I'm not very good at that kind of thing."

"I have a guy who probably knows how to do these things. I could have a word with him, better that I do it, so that there's no direct connection with you. Give me forty-eight hours and I'll see what I can do. All we can say is that this looks like being a slow and complicated process. On the other hand, if the original crime was a bit exotic, this seems to add some pretty interesting new dimensions. How do you feel about going on with it? After all, the risk seems to have increased tenfold."

He studied Eduardo's face, which had gone expressionless.

"Oh, I don't know, given the line of business I am in, this was never going to be just sitting behind a desk in some warm office. Let me turn the question round, uncle. Are you interested enough to help me, because, if we take what he says at face value, it rather sounds as though my ability to do certain things or to go to certain places – if that's what it's about – may be heavily circumscribed?"

"Yes, that had occurred to me. It's too early to say. But as you move forward and gain this person's confidence, one of the things which he appears to lay a lot of store by is how you're actually going to act on the information he provides. And for that, maybe someone like me could come in handy. At this stage, I don't think you should reveal the fact that you've discussed his letters with anyone. Until you've a clear idea of what it is that he is going to provide, there's little point in showing too much of your game. So I suggest we leave that question unanswered for the time being."

Leandro got up and waved to the waiter that he was leaving cash on the table for their coffees.

"I'll get back to you just as soon as I have any thoughts on this business of the e-mails and communications. Take care."

Eduardo buried himself in his newspaper.

Leandro again met Eduardo in the cafe.

Leandro had arrived ten minutes early and set himself down at a corner table near the back from where he could observe all comings and goings. If Eduardo's cell phone was being tapped, he might arrive accompanied. As he watched, the manner in which the waiter and the barman received all those who came through the door suggested that they were regulars, who often dropped in for a drink on their way home from the office, and therefore almost certainly of no interest. Eduardo arrived punctually.

"Followed?"

"Not that I could see. I slipped out of the office about forty-five minutes ago and have been trawling the bookshops and video stores, which provides an opportunity to check out faces. What news?"

"According to my friend Juan, who's good at this kind of thing, it should be quite easy to set up a system of revolving e-mails or even of Skype identities. Obviously, it remains to be seen whether your friend is prepared to go on Skype. It might be a little too close for comfort for him. Juan suggested that a way of adding an additional layer of protection would be to use Internet cafes to communicate. Obviously one can never rule out that a *locutorio* might be under police surveillance for drugs or something else, but probably only someone like the NSA in the States could run systematic coverage. And part of the process apparently revolves around your avoiding the kind of phrase which sets alarm bells ringing... anything remotely linked to drugs or the idea of shipments, for instance. One idea he put forward would be a series of Yahoo or Hotmail names, which might work in sequence, changing with the numbers or letters from mail to mail. Obviously, the first challenge is to get agreement from this person to what is involved. I presume you haven't used the e-mail he provided yet?"

"Not yet."

"Let's just think this through for a minute."

The attack on Eduardo in his flat on the one hand, and on the other the appearance of their informant – to whom they now, for no particularly logical reason, decided to give the codename of 'Sarmiento', one of Argentina's political founding fathers from the late 1880s - added up to a picture, which was not only confusing, but also potentially physically dangerous. On the negative side, a brutally clear warning to have nothing to do with the hotel murder, as demonstrated by the attack on Eduardo. On the positive side - if that was what it was - the fact that Eduardo had been associated with the investigation by someone who appeared willing to help. Leandro was not sure whether the sudden appearance of Sarmiento, seemingly opening the way to a series of new leads, adequately outweighed the risks which the violent attack had only too clearly presaged. Ideally, he would have preferred that his son find a way to abandon the case. But he knew that simply sitting still and doing nothing was not part of Eduardo's nature.

"With all that has happened in the last months, I'm not sure how much this is really my scene, but there we are. Makes a change from currency rates and inflation. Have you had the slightest hint that whoever may be behind the attack on you is still interested? That's what worries me most."

"Since we don't know who it is, it's pretty hard to tell. I've been watching the behaviour of people around me. Nothing suspicious there. However, the slightest mention of the case with Fonseca seems to produce an immediate instruction to get on with more important things. He claims that the judge has closed the case for the time being and that therefore I should forget about it."

"Remind me who the judge is."

"Etchenique. He keeps very much in the background, but has a reputation for pulling the chestnuts out of the fire for high-ups in the government. As you know, the present lot is a little rushed to line their pockets and hasn't got a lot of time for detail and tying up loose ends. Some of the cases have reached the papers, but a lot of them never get anywhere near. Some of that is reckoned to be thanks to Etchenique."

"Yes, the name rings a bell. Anyway, I think we need to weigh up just how much exposure you can take on this. If it were just a simple murder case, I'd be tempted to recommend strongly that you drop it. For health reasons. But the arrival on the scene of Sarmiento seems to suggest that the murder is part of a wider picture. Much more complicated. That might obviously be an even stronger argument to drop it. Yet somehow, I don't get the impression that that's what you want to do. If you're not going to drop it, then for my part, I'm actually more intrigued. As they say, two heads are often better than one in this kind of situation."

Eduardo was nodding in agreement.

"Before we go any farther, Eduardo, I think we should agree how we play it between us, in such a way as to make progress, but at the same time to minimize the risks for you. Obviously, we must avoid giving anyone the idea that you and I are working on this together, so I suggest that from now on we keep our meetings to the apparently social. As it is, we tend to get together at the weekend at someone's *asado* and the occasional drink is probably in order. Maybe we should also meet more often at Elena's. She won't mind, in fact she may be delighted."

"I suppose you're right. I haven't said anything to Florencia, but I do have a girlfriend to think of. Thanks by the way for the idea of the rotating mails. I'll take another look at it and then, if I think I can manage it, send it through to Sarmiento."

Eduardo rose from the table and they embraced.

"Keep me posted."

"I will, uncle."

Leandro sat down again and ordered another coffee. If his son could not be persuaded to abandon the case – after all, being a detective, why should he? – then his father must do everything in his power to help him.

On the following Monday, Eduardo found an e-mail on his computer. It came from the second in the series of agreed e-mail addresses. He was surprised by the speed with which Sarmiento had accepted his proposal on communications.

The contents were brief.

Connect:
The shooting of Juan Carlos Suarez
Sosa
Dead women in the Delta
Switzerland.

He went round to Leandro's and passed him the text.

"What's this?"

"A certain Juan Carlos Suarez was killed with a single bullet through the head about four months ago on his *campo* in the province of La Pampa. They also shot his dog. High velocity bullet, soft nosed, they never found the weapon. The local police found no trace of the killer, though there was some suspicion surrounding a guy who came into the local town around that time, but disappeared just after the murder. Apparently, it was raining heavily on the day of the killing, so no tyre marks were found on the dirt road leading to his place. His workmen also heard nothing. As to the Delta, there have been a couple in the last year. Seems to be a favourite place for dumping ex-girlfriends! In fact, there was one a fortnight or so ago, an unknown woman, possibly from the north or Bolivia, washed up on Arroyo Los Sabalos, some way towards Parana de las Palmas. Didn't drown, dead before she entered the water, asphyxiated according to forensics. No signs of physical violence, other than some very heavy sexual activity. No-one knows who she is. As to Switzerland, I don't understand."

"And this is somehow supposed to connect with the hotel killing? "

"Presumably."

"What do you know about Suarez?"

Eduardo looked at his notebook.

"Aged 55, born in Rio Tercero, in the navy, evacuated from Malvinas June 1982, went back to his base, reached the rank of *cabo primero*. Seems to have been associated with some of the excesses of the 'dirty war', but owing to his lower rank, was never brought to trial and would have been swept up in Menem's amnesties. Retired to his small farm in La Pampa and just about scraped a living. No wife, no known relatives. The shooting was not connected with any robbery, so it had all the appearance of a contract. At least, that's what the local police believe, but they were never able to produce any real evidence and the case was closed. I had a quick word with the local Comisario, who sounded pissed off that anyone was taking an interest. In fact, he strongly hinted that it was best left alone. That single fact is the only reason, at the moment, why there might be some connection."

"Did Suarez have any local enemies?"

"Seems to have kept very much to himself. A few years ago, apparently someone daubed some graffiti referring to ESMA on his car, so presumably there is something there. I guess we would have to get in touch with the Madres de la Plaza de Mayo, who no doubt have a file on people like Suarez."

"Yes, except for one thing. Sarmiento - whoever he is - has suggested that these stories are connected in some way with the current government, and, as you know, the Madres are close to the Kirchners. So chasing after information on Suarez with them might get back to the wrong people. We would have to be very careful. An alternative route might be to try and track down his commanding officers from the time of the 'dirty war'. Not that they will necessarily be keen to help either."

"I've asked a colleague in San Fernando, who covers events in the Delta, whether he can provide me with a bit more detail about any dead girls. I may have something next week."

"And Sosa?"

"Not a clue. There are about three hundred in the phone book alone."

"How are you going to respond to our friend?"

"In order to keep up the series, I have to acknowledge his mail to the next in the series. I guess I thank him and wait for the next instalment. Maybe I can ask him to be a bit more explicit about the Swiss connection."

Eduardo got up and left the café. Leandro stayed behind and settled down to the read the paper. All this was tantalizing, but certainly not getting any clearer.

Almost a week had passed when Eduardo again rang on the Saturday morning to suggest an urgent meeting two hours later at a bar on which they had previously agreed. Leandro again made a point of arriving first and placing himself at a table which would allow him to observe Eduardo's arrival. Eduardo appeared looking flushed.

"Bit hectic, all this avoiding being followed. Anyway, I'm pretty sure that nobody was behind me. Did you see anything as I arrived?"

"No, nothing special. So what's the news to warrant this urgent meeting?"

"I found another note from our friend, not an e-mail this time," and he pushed a single sheet of paper across the table to Leandro. As before, the message could not have been more cryptic.

Film record of torture. El Pozo June 1980.
Meet the librarian.
Perú 857, fourth floor B.
Password: Gualeguay.
You are expected.

"What do you make of that?" Eduardo asked.

"Hard to tell. The word 'librarian' suggests some kind of document collection, but what of, God only knows. Do you have anything on the address?"

"I looked it up. Home to Miguel Angel Sosa, age sixty-five, unmarried, no record. Was in the Navy in 1980, is on a list of lower ranks associated with the atrocities of the *dictadura*, but doesn't seem to have been prosecuted at any time. Sounds a bit like the other guy, Suarez. Presumably benefited from the various amnesties, which led to the trial of senior ranks only."

"So that explains the name Sosa in the previous message. The only way to make sense of this is presumably to see Sosa. Hard to tell how risky it would be to call on him. At this stage, we have to assume that whoever doesn't want this to go any farther knows of your involvement, but not necessarily mine. If that's the case, then it should certainly not be you, Eduardo, to take any followers to this address."

"'Fraid so," Eduardo replied slowly. "That's what I think too. But I'm really not keen to see you so close to something which has now clearly taken a new turn, taking us back to the events of the *dictadura*. I'm sure I don't need to tell you that things tend to get very messy when you come anywhere near all that."

"Yes, I know. Up to now, our friend was taking us in the direction of a killer of women. Add to that some kind of Swiss dimension. Now, he suddenly throws in more information, given what he told us about Suarez, which somehow reinforces his reference to El Pozo. Do we know anything about El Pozo? Sounds like some kind of interrogation centre at the time of the military. Although how all this is connected to the hotel killing, I can't see at the moment. But...."

He paused, before resuming.

"Unless we call on Señor Sosa, we're not going to find out, are we? We've got to decide who goes to see Sosa, but I've a nasty feeling it's going to be me."

Eduardo was silent for a minute.

"I'm sorry, uncle. I guess that is the only route. However, we can take certain precautions. There's a bar almost next door which has a reputation for distributing. I'll get a couple of my boys to pay them a call. I'll keep back in one of our cars, but in such a fashion that I can keep an eye on the street. We'll go in a police car with flashing lights, which should at the very least distract anyone interested in you, and possibly even keep them away. Then if for any reason somebody wants to know what I'm doing there, I'll claim that we had a tipoff. Let me set it up and I'll give you a ring in which I'll mention a time. Assume it's for the following day."

"Sounds good. I'll expect your call."

Eduardo got up and exited through the swing doors of the cafe. Watching through the large plate glass window, Leandro's attention was drawn to a thickset man in a leather jacket throwing away his half-consumed cigarette and ambling slowly after Eduardo. Leandro had a feeling that he had seen him leaning against the side of a closed newspaper kiosk on the edge of the pavement throughout their meeting. As if he had always been on the edge of the picture. Leandro hadn't seen him arrive, so could not be sure. Whatever the case, there was little point in turning this into a three-man convoy. He would alert Eduardo when they next met.

Eduardo's call came next morning, setting the time for three pm the day after. Leandro decided to take a look at the area on the afternoon of the call, dropping into the bar suggested by Eduardo for a toasted sandwich and Coke. Perú was a fairly busy street. Having paid, he strolled past the door of number 857. He could see that there were about twenty flats in the building. The name Sosa didn't appear anywhere, though there was certainly a flat on 4B and the system seemed to have an intercom.

The next day he was back in the bar, but was careful to leave as soon as he saw the reflection of the police car lights on one of the buildings opposite. As he walked away, he caught sight of two young men and a uniformed policeman go through the door of the bar. Some twenty metres farther up the street he could see the patrol car parked with someone in the backseat, presumably Eduardo.

He rang the bell of 4B. After a pause, a man's voice, sounding frail, asked who was there.

"I come on behalf of Gualeguay."

This time the delay was nearly a minute.

"Could you repeat that?"

"Gualeguay," he repeated.

"What's it about?"

The voice sounded more nervous.

After a moment's thought, Leandro replied.

"I need to see the librarian. It's about an old document."

This time the delay was even longer.

"I'll send someone down to open the door. Please wait."

He turned with his back to the door, watching the street. Apart from the police car still parked on the opposite pavement, and a bit more noise coming out of the bar, things appeared quiet. Hearing a key being inserted in the lock behind him, he turned again to face a middle-aged woman, her hair pulled back in a bun and an apron over a simple black dress. She invited him in.

"He told me to let you in and to go and pick up some groceries. Please, Señor, come in."

He found himself alone in a dark, dilapidated hall with a line of grey metal letterboxes for some twenty flats along one wall. There being no lift, he set off up the two flights of stairs. He met and heard no-one. Reaching the second floor, flat 4B was on the right, apparently on the inside of the building looking onto the inner courtyard, rather than onto the street. The door was off the latch. Hesitating slightly, he pushed it open slowly. The hinges were rusty, making a low creaking sound. Stepping into a very small hallway, he could see a door open in front of him.

"*Hola?*" he called.

There was no reply. He crossed the hall and walked cautiously into the room. Little light filtered through the half-open curtains, but as his eyes grew accustomed to the semidarkness, he could make out the shadow of someone sitting in the corner. Something metallic glinted on the armrest. The revolver motioned him to sit down on the hard-backed chair by the table. He sat down. For a minute or so, nothing happened and he was unsure how to start the conversation.

"Who are you? Who sent you?"

The voice may have been frail, but the barrel did not waver.

"That's a little difficult to answer."

Given that he had no way of identifying Sarmiento, it might be hard to persuade the old man of his credentials. However, there was a chance that this might play in his favour.

"You see, Señor Sosa, your address and the word 'Gualeguay' were given to me anonymously. I received a message which suggested that I should look to you for something that happened at an interrogation centre known as El Pozo in June 1980. I should ask for the 'librarian'. I presume that must be you."

"How do you know my name?"

He lied, since he was by no means sure that any reference to the police wouldn't produce quite the wrong result, even a bullet between the eyes. The barrel was now pointing higher, still as steady as before.

"I saw what might have been an electricity bill on the floor in the hall with your flat number."

The old man wasn't impressed.

"I paid my electricity bill last week," he responded curtly, with a trace of annoyance now creeping into his voice, making it stronger.

Things were getting more complicated. Having been given so little to go on from Sarmiento, Leandro had somehow assumed that he would be expected, not treated as a potential threat.

"As I said, I was just given this information. Of course, if you're not the librarian or this is the wrong address, I'll leave quietly."

There was a silence of about a minute, as the old man seemed to weigh things up. Although the revolver did not move away, Sosa finally seemed inclined to give him the benefit of the doubt.

"There are only two people who would link my name with 'Gualeguay'. Neither of them wish me any harm, as far as I know."

He paused. Steadying himself on the side of the table, but not changing the aim of the revolver, the old man got slowly to his feet.

Leandro sat deliberately still, both hands in full view on the table. The old man moved across the room and switched on the ceiling light, which threw a pale yellow glow around the room. A battered old TV stood in a corner. On the wall, a number of black and white photographs showing groups of sailors, some obviously taken during the Malvinas campaign on the islands.

"I see you were in Malvinas. So was I."

The old man did not reply. Pulling a set of keys from a cigar box on the mantelpiece, he opened a wall cabinet containing a number of glasses and some decorative plates. With his left hand, he removed the glasses, leaving one of the shelves bare. Changing keys, he unlatched what appeared to be a tiny wall safe, keeping an eye on Leandro all the while. From the back of the aperture, he took out a small box. He then shuffled over to the table and sat down opposite Leandro. Only then did he put down the revolver and look Leandro in the eye.

"As you see, I have decided to trust you. But you must understand that what I am doing now could cost me my life. And perhaps yours also."

Leandro nodded. Hardly reassuring!

Sosa opened the box to reveal a number of USB memory sticks, one of which he extracted.

"June 1980, you said. This should be the one. Be so kind as to get the computer which is on the desk over there," he said pointing towards a small oak writing table which stood in the opposite corner.

Leandro stepped across, pulled down the lid and lifted out a battered Acer laptop and its power cable, which he brought back to the table. The old man showed him where to plug it in. He powered it up and they waited a minute or so, without exchanging a word. When the screen had finally settled, the old man slipped the USB stick into one of the ports.

"You're younger, so can probably manage these things better than I can," he said, sliding the laptop across the table towards Leandro. "You'll see files with the years, open the one for 1980 and find June."

Leandro opened the folder for June. There were six small movie files.

"What am I looking for?"

"I don't know. You mentioned El Pozo." The old man pulled his chair slowly round to sit next to Leandro. "As you can see, three of them relate to El Pozo."

He paused and looked at Leandro hard and long, before adding.

"This is very bad stuff. Are you up to it?"

Leandro wasn't sure how to reply.

"I'll have to be."

"If it's any help, two of them relate to male terrorists, and one to a woman. That's number three."

Leandro thought for a moment. He hadn't come here to indulge in some kind of sadistic voyeurism and the whole affair seemed to him to be turning very nasty. At the same time, he had not only put himself in danger, but very probably the old man as well. To stop the process now would do nothing to solve the case or in any way reduce the heightened level of danger which he increasingly felt he was personally approaching.

"Okay," he said, swallowing hard. "Let's try number three. The trouble is, I don't really know what I'm looking for."

The old man stared at him in surprise.

"It's probably none of my business, but what are you looking for?"

Some explanation was in order. Leandro briefly said that he was involved in helping someone to solve a murder involving two women, which was why he had opted for the third film in the set. He imagined that Sosa knew the identity of the person who had given him the address and password but that he, Leandro, did not. From the look on Sosa's face, he could not tell whether he believed him. However, Sosa appeared prepared to leave it at that. Leandro double-clicked on the third film.

The quality of the black and white film was extremely grainy and at first, it was difficult to see what was going on. But Leandro soon made out the scene of a woman, partially undressed, tied to a chair illuminated by a single white-shaded bulb hanging from the ceiling. He could distinguish someone in uniform standing in the foreground just in front of the camera and apparently another figure, again in some sort of uniform, behind the woman's chair. Her body sagging on the hard wooden chair, the woman was screaming and sobbing by turns. Only her wrists tied behind the chair, and the hand of the person standing behind resting on her shoulder, kept her from slipping to the ground. Her eyes were wide with terror and pain, and between each scream, her breathing was rasping through the wet towel held over her nose and mouth. Standing outside the arc of light, Leandro suspected the presence of a fourth person, betrayed by a slight shadow falling into the pool of light. The man immediately facing the seated woman was talking, his soft lilting accent from north-western Argentina somehow incongruous, given the terrorizing effect of his quiet but relentless questioning. The sound was bad, but Leandro could just make out the questions.

"Come on, *chica*, we know you have names, we know that you've been a courier for the Montos. Why prolong this anymore? Try harder to remember that night in Tucuman in June last year. Who else was there?"

Only the sobbing continued.

"You're just not trying!" the interrogator spat out with disappointment, and poured another pitcher of water over the towel, whilst the person standing behind the woman's chair pulled her head back so that the water would soak deeper into the towel and block out the air over her nose and mouth.

Leandro now realized that the figure behind the chair was that of a woman wearing uniform. The victim's head twisted and jerked violently side to side in her attempts to find a small loophole somewhere in the towel, but the woman blocked it on both sides. She convulsed and the pool of fluids falling under her chair from between her widespread legs grew thicker and darker as she strained every muscle in her body to escape from the suffocation which was draining her. This time she fainted and, once the towel had been removed, it took some violent face slapping to bring her round again, her head sunken onto the heaving breasts bulging through her thin blouse, blood stained and grimy from residence - God only knew for how long - in the cells of the torture centre.

As he watched, she tried to raise her head again, weakly scanning the blackness outside the pool of light, where she seemed dimly to be searching for someone other than her torturers. From the shadow, Leandro again detected this presence. Now, suddenly, this fourth person leaned forward into the light and Leandro could see that he wore some kind of mask over his head, presumably to maintain his anonymity. In silence, this observer passed a slip of paper to the interrogator, as if to guide his questioning.

The first interrogator picked up the water bucket beside him and sluiced away the filth on the floor to drain down a pipe somewhere in the corner of the room. A second bucket of cold water, this time between the legs, caused the prisoner to tauten upright, her head steadied by the woman standing behind her. The towel was kept over her mouth as she retched and sucked in air through her nostrils, choking on the water at the back of her throat.

"It's okay, now let's try a different approach," Leandro heard the *cabo* say.

The woman pulled the towel up so that it now covered her victim's entire face, yet lifting a corner so that a little air could still get through to her mouth. Then she seemed to take the girl's pulse, and after a minute, nodded to the men standing opposite.

The angle of the filming changed as whoever was holding the camera moved to the side. The hooded observer, now more clearly visible, stepped into the pool of light, pulling up another chair on which he sat down to face the prisoner. He was dressed in a T-shirt, jeans and wore a black stocking over his head. He straddled the chair, facing the woman. The camera panned briefly to show him unzipping his trousers, whilst simultaneously stretching his other hand between her legs. She snapped her legs together, but it was too late. Slowly the observer began to caress her genitals. At first, she resisted. With his other hand, he appeared to caress his member in time to hers.

Her breathing had settled down and in what might have been a state of semi-consciousness, her body seemed to accept the movement of his fingers.

The lens shifted to a close-up of the victim's head. The sound just captured her beginning to moan in what appeared to be a grotesque mixture of pain and pleasure. The observer nodded to the woman behind the chair, who pulled the victim's head back, tightened the towel all over her face and began to pour water onto it. As the holes in the towel became waterlogged and air impossible to drag in, her body contracted violently in a combination of suffocation and sexual contortion, her head pulling from side to side. Leandro watched, appalled, as a sound of panting seemed to come from the observer's hood. The camera caught her as she finally passed out and slumped in the chair. With a few more strokes on his own member, he came onto the front of the wooden chair. He stood up stiffly to adjust his trousers.

The woman untied the prisoner's hands from the back of the chair and between them they dragged her inert body across the floor to a door at the back and out into a passageway.

Just as the film began to fade, Leandro caught the words of the observer.

"She knows what we want to hear, I'm certain of that."

The film died in a rough snowstorm. Sosa was silent. Leandro remained motionless, paralysed by what he had witnessed. Like everyone else in Argentina, he had endured accounts of the crimes committed during the military dictatorship, but this was never enough to prepare anyone for a glimpse of the real thing. He got up and walked to the window, which he opened and began to gulp in fresh air. Sosa remained in his chair. After a moment, Leandro turned and looked at him.

"What a nightmare! You can imagine so many things, but it never seems to come anywhere close to reality."

The old man nodded.

Leandro went back to his chair. The silence lasted a minute or two. Then Leandro began.

"Frankly, I haven't a clue whether all this in any way relates to the murder I'm looking at. For a start, it was more than twenty-five years ago, so any connection is hardly obvious. But tell me, why do you keep these films, what purpose do they serve?"

Sosa thought for a minute.

"They exist because some of the people who were committing these crimes at the time seem to want to preserve them for posterity. God only knows why. Didn't the Nazis also film the atrocities they committed, whether in the prison camps or in the mass slaughter of populations in Russia or Ukraine?"

Leandro was surprised by the analogy, not that it wasn't appropriate, but rather that Sosa, who had almost certainly never been anything more than a simple *cabo*, should have known about such things.

"You're surprised," Sosa interjected. "Over the years, after leaving the navy, I've had plenty of time to think about why men do such things. Argentina at that time was living a kind of madness which I was trying to understand when I emerged from the nightmare. I've read books about what the Nazis did and seen films on TV. You know, History Channel, things like that."

Leandro nodded.

"But that doesn't explain why they exist today. As I recall, General Bignone, the last President after Galtieri, seeing that elections were coming, ordered all the records destroyed. So how did this survive?"

"The answer is that one of the senior officers, perhaps now sitting somewhere under arrest, gave instructions in the late 1980s that all these films should be destroyed except one set. I was working for him at the time and, out of some form of loyalty – I must have been mad - I accepted his instruction to hide them. Very few people have known of their existence. Obviously, the person who sent you. I was instructed to show them to anyone who came using one of the passwords. You're one of these people," he added, his hand raised in a gesture of helplessness.

Leandro was silent, before asking.

"Do you think there is any purpose in looking at the other films for June 1980?"

"I really don't know," Sosa replied, shrugging his shoulders.

"And another thing," Leandro asked. "Is there any way of knowing who those people are? Without names, it's hard to tell what one can do with the film."

"In each folder, there is also a scrap of paper, which gives a little information on each film. See if you can find something."

Leandro opened the folder again and found a document divided into six short parts. One related to film number three. It gave the date as 20

June. Then three names. Juanita. Suarez. Burkart. At least one was missing. Which one was the victim? And the other two? Could this Suarez be the same as the one shot on his farm? Other than Juanita, was Burkart male or female? Sosa could not throw any light on this.

"I am sorry to say, the kind lady that looks after me and opened the door for you will be back any minute now, she's already been gone longer than I expected. Have you any way of taking a copy of this?"

Leandro dug into his jacket pocket and found one of the USB memory sticks, which he usually carried around between his home and office computers. He slotted it into another port on the Acer.

"I don't know how to do these things," Sosa responded. "I'm too old."

"Don't worry, our grandchildren do these things far better," said Leandro, with a wry smile.

To copy the films in the June 1980 folder took five minutes. When finished Leandro extracted the stick and stood up.

"Señor Sosa, I am most grateful to you, although, to be frank, I cannot at this moment tell where all this fits in. I will leave you now. Is there anything I can get for you? To thank you for your trust?"

The old man shook his head.

"Don't worry. It's time you left."

He remained seated and stretched his hand across the table to Leandro. Leandro took it in both of his and held it tightly for a moment. He could almost physically feel the pain which Sosa carried deep inside him.

"May God take care of you, Señor Sosa."

Then he turned and left the way he had come. On a sudden afterthought, he came back into the flat and, with his handkerchief, which he dipped in the washing-up liquid he found by the sink, carefully wiped the surfaces of the computer, the mouse, the USB and the power cable, as well as the chair and the door handle. The old man watched him, in some surprise.

"You can never be sure," Leandro explained, rather lamely.

Shaking Sosa's hand again, he left the flat.

He looked at his watch. He had been there for about forty-five minutes. He opened the front door cautiously and looked across the street to see if Eduardo's car was still there. It was, but it now contained the other policemen. He stepped out onto the pavement and made his way towards Estados Unidos. He'd only been walking for a minute, when the patrol car passed him, its lights flashing.

Later that evening, he had postponed Sam's visit to the following day and was waiting for Eduardo to make contact. He switched on the television and zapped through the news channels. On one of them, his eye was caught by a live transmission from an ill-lit street, which the streaming headline announced to be Calle Perú and 'breaking news'.

"Perú. That's where I was a couple of hours ago. What the fuck?" he muttered to himself.

The journalist was standing in front of a police line, with a number of patrol cars, lights flashing, farther down the street. With growing anxiety, Leandro listened to the journalist explaining that an old-age pensioner had been murdered in his apartment at around seven that evening. He was visibly revelling in the gory details of the assassination, which had apparently involved an automatic weapon. There was a momentary flashback to the scene of more police cars and an ambulance arriving, followed by a shot of the entrance to the building. Number 857.

"Jesus. That's my building!"

At that moment, the phone rang. It was Eduardo, from a public phone booth.

"Quickly, switch on Channel 24!"

"I'm on it. *Carajo*, what's happening? I can't believe it!"

"It looks like Sosa. Because I was doing a job in the same street earlier this afternoon, the officer in charge from the *Comisaría* 2da. rang me about fifteen minutes ago and asked me to get round there. Frankly, I don't know how he knew I was there, although with his *Comisaría* only two blocks farther down the street, someone may have spotted our patrol car. Anyway, it may give me a chance to take a look."

Leandro paused to think.

"For Christ's sake, be careful. I don't know how your systems work, but it's certainly strange that he should have got in touch with you so fast."

"Don't worry, I will. If I were to refuse to go, that would look worse. I'll be back in touch as soon as the picture is clearer."

Leandro sensed Eduardo was on the point of hanging up and he shouted down the line to hold on.

"What is it?" Eduardo snapped, clearly under stress.

"If you get a minute alone, there may be some keys in a cigar box on the side table or mantelpiece. One of these will open the wall cabinet. Behind the glasses on the second shelf, the other key will open a wall safe, very small. Inside, there should be a box about the size of a cigarette packet. Try and get it before they do."

"Do my best."

The line went dead.

Leandro poured himself a large whiskey and sat back to watch the rest of the news.

He flipped to another channel and then another, but none of them carried the story. Channel 24 seemed to be the only one and, by the looks of things, had got there early. Whilst it was always possible that the victim might not be Sosa - after all, the victim had not yet been identified in the news programme - he had a sinking feeling in his gut that it was.

He slept very badly that night.

Leandro had been in his early teens when the military had taken over on that fateful twenty-fourth of March of 1976.

For the previous couple of years, he could remember listening to his parents complaining of the chaos and violence into which Argentina was so rapidly sinking, following Peron's return in 1973 from his long exile in Madrid. Leandro had been dimly conscious of the fact that, even at that range, the old dictator had been able to manipulate the elections which the military had been prepared to call, even though they knew that the much-loathed Peronists would probably win. The same Peronists they had so violently ejected in 1956. Peron's stand-in, Hector Campora, had gone on to win and then invited the ageing dictator to return. Peron's arrival had been marked by violence and shootings at Ezeiza, where he was supposed to land, and his plane had been diverted to another airport. Some fifteen people had died that day alone, with right wing guerrillas taking on members of the Peronist Youth Movement. Peron had been pulling the strings of the various extremist groups for a number of years from exile in the Puerta de Hierro in Madrid, playing off the right-wing factions, whose origins lay in the trade union movement, against the left wing and Marxists, including the Montoneros, under the leadership of Mario Firmenich, and the People's Revolutionary Army, the ERP, led by Mario Roberto Santucho. The level of political violence was high, epitomized by the curtain-raising act of the Montoneros with their assassination of ex-president Aramburu in 1970, seen by them as the brain behind the overthrow of Peron in 1955 and the subsequent disappearance of Evita's corpse. The army, acting alongside paramilitary forces, had been slugging it out for a number of years already before they finally took matters into their own hands. Peron's death in 1974 saw the presidency pass to his widow, Isabelita, an ineffectual former nightclub hostess, now like the Czarina with Rasputin, totally under the spell of the evil Lopez Rega, commonly referred to as 'El Brujo', the sorcerer. Even before the military coup, it was estimated that, between the guerrilla movements, the Argentine Anti-Communist Alliance, the infamous 'Triple – A', inspired and coordinated by Lopez Rega, and the military themselves, the victims already ran into thousands. A pre-

Christmas ERP attack in 1975 on an armoury in the Province of Buenos Aires alone left more than ninety civilians dead, the army summarily executing their ERP captives and burying them anonymously in one of the city's main cemeteries. It was a time of systematic violence and bloody reprisals by all parties.

The military coup, when it finally came, was passively - and even in many circles, enthusiastically - received by large segments of the population, sick and tired of the corpses littering the streets, the bank robberies, the kidnappings. With the implicit blessing of the Argentine Roman Catholic Church and even to a certain extent of such people as Kissinger, then Secretary of State in the United States, the military easily shouldered what they saw as the crusaders' mantle, to rid the country through their programme of National Reorganisation of all trace, political, cultural, even sexual, of what they considered contrary to the true spirit of Argentina. Democracy, although facilitated by one of their own prior to the return of Peron, had failed. Only an implacable military dictatorship, executed in such a manner as to leave little trace of their actions, would eradicate the cancer they clearly detected at the heart of the nation. And, in the process, ensure several decades of their own rule.

In the first few days following the coup, the army moved in force into universities, against the unions and any institution they considered subversive. Arrests and disappearances spiralled, with a significant proportion among the youth of Argentina, as the military rounded up and dealt with the list of some seven to eight thousand susbversives whose removal they considered essential to the task, a process technically referred to as 'Final Disposal' - 'Disposición Final'. The methods used largely owed their inspiration to the worst practices honed by the French in Algiers in the late 1950s, subsequently peddled, like the product of some sinister Alliance française, by French military attaches to the armed forces of the developing world. In the Latin American military dictatorships, they had found a receptive audience for 'el metodo francés', the French method. Though he was a couple of years younger, Leandro could detect what was going on, hearing about it, often in terrifying detail, from the elder brothers of his school companions. However, the rule of fear bore ample fruit and for the next five years, the military literally got away with murder. Looking back, he was forced to admit that a certain middle-class, which included his parents, had sat tacitly by, asking few questions, afraid to confront.

Timidly at first, the Mothers of the Plaza de Mayo had begun their vigil and international sentiment had slowly turned. For a long time, however, large segments of Argentine society continued to shut their eyes. When somebody disappeared, the neighbours too often consoled themselves by assuming that there must have been 'good reason'. The pursuit of 'subversive elements' reached grotesque proportions, with one arm of the military, for example the Air Force, raiding the detention centres of their brothers in arms, maybe the Navy, to steal their detainees and whisk them away to their own underground torture chambers. It was a simple way to inflate the inter-services head count. In such a context, the potential for systematic theft of property was commonplace. Raids on the houses of suspects often ended with the sight of the captors piling TV sets, refrigerators, hifi, even whole libraries and other household goods into the back of their trucks.

Once in the detention centre, torture, rape, enslavement and, in innumerable cases death, were the norm. Being dropped alive, often, but not always, drugged, from helicopters or aircraft flying over the sea proved just one way of disposing of the evidence. Except that the tides weren't always so compliant and bodies washed ashore. The most notorious of the interrogation centres, which numbered more than three hundred up and down the country, had been the ESMA, the Navy's Mechanical School, an elegant building standing beside Avenida Libertador on the way to the northern suburbs. The Kirchners had, as part of their flagship human rights policies, turned it into a museum to the disappeared, *los desaparecidos*.

Their ignominious defeat in Malvinas had sealed the fate of the military. Not only could they not run the country, they couldn't even fight a war. Democracy returned with President Alfonsin and a process of uncovering the past and establishing the truth began. Although too young to have had any direct involvement, Leandro nevertheless followed with shame and anxiety the seemingly endless litany of revelations, of mass graves discovered, of identities revealed, of children painstakingly restored to their true parents.

With the events of the last hours, it was as if he had been hurled straight back to that time, much more directly, more violently, to a past he had hitherto only read about. However many articles and books might have been written on the subject of what had gone on in the cellars of places like the ESMA, visual images were virtually non-existent. He had seen interviews and discussions involving victims, but, through the lens of time and nature's instinctive ability to insulate itself against unbearable horror, the impact had inevitably been quite different. The scenes he had witnessed that afternoon had left him numb.

Had the end of the horror been an illusion? Why should those events be part of the murder of an Englishwoman in a Buenos Aires hotel? Was the 'dirty war' still being fought somewhere in the shadows?

The following afternoon, he received a call from Eduardo, again from an outside phone. He arrived at Leandro's flat forty-five minutes later. Eduardo took in his godfather's dishevelled appearance.

"You look pretty rough, uncle," he commented.

Leandro tried a grin.

"The fact is, I'm not used to all this. I slept very little last night and have only just caught up with a quick siesta this afternoon. Most of the people I meet as I go about my business survive a little beyond the three hours of Señor Sosa. What a mess! I need a coffee. What have you brought?"

Eduardo opened an envelope and displayed a series of crime scene stills.

"Were you able to get into the wall safe?"

"No, I wasn't alone for a minute."

"That's probably bad news. Presumably they'll find them, unless someone else – his killers – got to them first. Did you even see whether the safe was open?"

"Yes it was, but I couldn't tell whether it was the killers or the police who found it. A set of keys were still hanging in the little door."

Shrugging his shoulders, Leandro looked at the photographs carefully, one by one. They showed the small sitting room, in which he had spent part of yesterday afternoon with Sosa, in a state of shambles. The chair on which he'd been sitting lay flat on the floor, partially broken, the carpet pulled to one side, the standing lamp horizontal.

"That's the chair I used."

The next photos showed Sosa crumpled in a heap against his armchair, his head lolling on his chest, his right arm extended, the revolver still held tightly. A series of large dark patches which extended from his left thigh to his right shoulder traced the spray of bullets which had killed him. A line of small black holes could be seen in the wallpaper behind his chair.

"Poor bastard. He didn't deserve this. Got mixed up in something way beyond his control. Though to be frank, he knew he was in danger."

The next series picked out different angles of the room, the smashed doorjamb and Yale lock. There were shots of the kitchen, bathroom and his small bedroom, which seemed in good order. Finally, some photographs of the stairway and hallway.

"Poor old man, he certainly gave me the impression that speaking to me was a risk, but neither of us could ever imagine it would come to this - and so fast."

Looking up at Eduardo, he went on. "Any idea who could have done this? And how come so soon after my meeting? Any way you look at it, we have to assume that it might have been cause and effect. But how could they know so fast?"

"That's what worries me more than anything. The guy from *Comisaría 2da.*, although he hadn't got very far in his enquiries, hinted that he saw some connection between my being there and what happened. He doesn't know why and, as far as I can guess, neither thinks that I had been with Sosa nor - thank God - has any reason to put your name in play. It tells me however that my little distraction is going to be taken apart higher up. Luckily, I can just about justify it. He gave me this set of photographs to jog my memory, though how they might is far from clear."

Leandro was shaking his head in disbelief.

"By the way, the old man seems to have got off a couple of shots, two of the chambers on the revolver had been fired and it looks as if he may have hit one of the attackers. There are drops of blood leading out onto the landing. Good for him anyway! A revolver against an Uzi is hardly fair, but he must have sensed that something was coming through the door."

Leandro doubted how much of a consolation this might really be.

"Surely someone must have heard or seen something as it was going on? Sosa's gun didn't have a silencer. How could they get away so easily?"

"The automatic they used was certainly silenced, so the noise they must have made breaking down the door, some of the scuffling and Sosa's two shots inside the flat were probably the only noise. Most of the other people in the building, according to my contact in the other *Comisaría*, are elderly and retired - probably deaf - and certainly smart enough to keep their doors shut if they don't like the sound of something happening in their building. They probably still have the reflexes they acquired at the time of the *dictadura*, when they were younger. On top of that, it seems they got away through the inner courtyard and out through one of the buildings giving onto Chacabuco, the street behind. They certainly didn't reappear out of the front door."

Leandro sat in silence, before replying.

"Something, somewhere must have triggered this coincidence. The three events, beyond my actual visit, seem to be - correct me if I'm wrong - the original message from Sarmiento, you're putting a name to the address and our phone calls agreeing how we were going to play it."

"Exactly. I think we have to work on the basis that Sarmiento isn't playing a double game. If he were, I can't see what the purpose is. If they want to pin something on me, or simply kill Sosa, they wouldn't need to go through this elaborate ritual. So on balance, I don't think it's Sarmiento."

Leandro nodded in agreement.

"As to our phone calls," Eduardo continued, "I suppose it's always possible that they've got as far as tapping your phone, but at this stage, that strikes me as very unlikely. You haven't been what you might call 'visible' enough so far, I would've thought. We've only had a couple of meetings apart from those at Elena's. Not unless our normal meetings, mainly in family circumstances, are being tracked through me. I've been pretty careful, and haven't really detected anything of that kind so far. Finally, there's my looking up the Perú address. That strikes me as the most likely, since it could have been done by monitoring my computer use at the office. I have to admit that that's what I did when we got the message. Fucking stupid of me! Apart from that, for all we know, whoever killed Sosa knows of some connection between him and the hotel killing, a connection which neither you nor I have yet worked out. Or have you? I still don't know what you found at Sosa's."

Eduardo looked enquiringly at Leandro.

"I'll come to that. But the first conclusion that strikes me is that this whole affair has, since Sarmiento's message, moved into very different waters, clearly extremely violent for anyone remotely connected to it. That means we've got to be ten times more careful in everything we do. We'll have to set things up very differently from now on. And whilst on that subject, you really need to stay very alert to being followed. When you left the other day from the cafe, I had a nasty feeling there was somebody behind you. So from now on, we really have to cut back on meetings."

Eduardo looked shocked, but said nothing.

After a pause, Leandro went on.

"On this memory stick - and for the love of God don't take it anywhere near your office or mainframe - you'll find six short, horrifying, amateur takes of the torturing of what in those days presumably passed for 'suspects'. Filmed at an interrogation centre called El Pozo. Better to have a stiff whiskey in the other hand. Whilst at Sosa's, I watched one, number three in the June series, in which some poor woman is being - I think the phrase is - water-boarded, as well as being sexually abused. There's no limit to man's capacity for horror. Of the four people in the room, three are identified. The fourth, man or woman - one doesn't know which - is not given a name. What's the connection with the hotel murder or Sarmiento? Far from clear, but presumably he can help us on that one, otherwise why send us there?"

He slid the memory stick across the table. They both sat thinking in silence for a minute or so.

"I'll take a look at it. I guess I'm better prepared for this kind of thing than you are. I'll remember the whiskey. It's Thursday today, I think we need to let the dust settle a bit, avoid seeing each other, certainly at least until the *asado* on Sunday. In the meantime, a bit more may emerge on Sosa."

"We also need to think how we can get Sarmiento to throw more light on this. Have you got another internet rendezvous any time soon?"

"As you know, in principle, depending on which email address I use, I should be able to get to him any day of the week. So if you can think of something, let's go for it. Anyway, I'd better get back to my desk, who knows what hell may have broken loose following last night."

He got up, gave his godfather a hug and made his way towards the door.

At that moment, the doorbell rang downstairs and Leandro went to the kitchen to take the intercom.

"It's Sam," he said. "About time you met her. Suggest whatever happens, we say nothing about Sosa."

Eduardo nodded, though his expression betrayed that he was not particularly happy at the prospect of meeting Sam. When young, he had regarded Leandro and Elena as second parents and their breaking up had undoubtedly affected him, although obviously not as much as it had their daughter, Alejandra. Leandro had already detected that his godson viewed his post-marital relations with a certain degree of reserve.

In response to another brief ring on the front door, he let Sam in. She was in one of her more provocative moods, huge dark glasses hiding her eyes, her clothes a favourite combination of red and black. Under a long light raincoat, with a hood which framed her face, black jeans, which looked as if they'd been painted on, tucked into stiletto-heeled boots, under a loose red cashmere sweater with a high collar.

"I love the feeling of tight clothes on my body, the caress of soft wools and silks", she had once explained to Leandro. "Can't get enough of it. You might call me a sensualist."

From what she had told him about her icon, Oscar Wilde, Leandro suspected that she, like the nineteenth century aesthete, dressed in large part to create maximum impact on those around her. Watching Eduardo, Leandro could immediately see that she had done exactly that. He smiled quietly as Sam marched straight across the room, put her arm firmly around Eduardo's neck and kissed him. To his credit, he also responded without hesitation.

"From the photograph, you're Eduardo. Not that your photograph does you any justice!"

She looked back at Leandro with a big smile, challenging him to be jealous.

"Good looking fellow, though seems a bit worried. Hey Leo, jealous already? Don't worry, he may be young and virile, but...." She left the sentence unfinished.

"I told you he's a very handsome fellow, and Florencia – his *novia* - has no intention of giving him up!" Leandro responded emphatically.

Eduardo looked slightly embarrassed.

"Have I interrupted something? I hope so. Something you're going to tell me about?" Sam responded. "Something to do with Lady X? "

Eduardo shot Leandro an angry glance, clearly disapproving of the fact that Sam seemed to be in the know.

"If you must know, yes," and turning to Eduardo, he went on. "I probably should have warned you that I might mention the case to Sam. At a certain point, it occurred to me that a bit of female intuition might come in useful in trying to understand a case involving two women. I've explained to her that it's extremely delicate and told her about the attack on you. When you get to know her better, you'll realise that she is not the gossiping kind. What's more, she might actually be an asset, as she has easy access to the polo fraternity. I think we both agreed that that's a hard one to crack, since they run a mile when they see someone like you."

Eduardo looked back at him steadily, apparently unconvinced.

"You mean, I might be able to get involved?" Sam rapidly asked.

"It's something that's been going through my head, but to be honest, I haven't discussed it with Eduardo yet and obviously he would have the last word as it's his case."

Sam turned expectantly to Eduardo, but said nothing. Putting on a look intended to transmit maximum reliability, she sat down in one of the armchairs and crossed her legs.

Eduardo hesitated. Sam's confidence had thrown him off-balance. He was afraid that he might to some extent lose control of his case, but

Sam's ease of access to the polo community - though he had no way of judging - could open up a new avenue. He sat down at the table and poured himself some more whiskey.

"It's a possibility, uncle. Have you thought it through in practice?" he said, looking at Leandro.

"I don't think we have to make it very complicated. I've been pulling together some of the polo magazines and also the Sociedad Rural publication after last July's show, since they are usually full of photographs of all the socialites getting together. Sam has moved in that crowd in the past and might have some ideas about some of the people. What do you think, Sam?"

She uncrossed her legs, rose smoothly from her chair and moved over to the table. Her initial frivolity had given way to a look of focused concentration that Leandro had noted in the past, whenever she was reading or discussing more serious matters. A slight frown creased her high forehead, her eyes a little narrower.

"Certainly, I could have a look, though of course I haven't been in that crowd for a year or so. But they don't change that much, and from what you mentioned, both Lady X and her victim weren't either of them so young, so they may well have been moving in a crowd I've met before."

Leandro was struck by the speed of her response. He could also see that she'd got Eduardo's attention. He went over to the bookcase and pulled out a pile of magazines, which he placed in front of her.

"Suggest you flip through these. Eduardo, you should do the same, if you haven't already done so, to see whether the Englishwoman is in any of them."

Sam pushed half the pile across the table to Eduardo, without a smile.

"This may take a little time, if we have to study each photograph."

Turning to Leandro, "Suggest you ring up a takeaway and get some food in for us."

"Yes, ma'am," said Leandro, curtsying. "What's it to be? Sushi? Pizza? *Empanadas*?"

"Haven't had sushi for a little while. Healthier. As long as you have some good chilled white wine."

Looking across the table at Eduardo, she asked, "Or are you one of those Argentines who can only eat meat? "

Somewhat nervously, he grinned. Leandro suspected he was not used to girls quite as forthright as Sam.

"No, I'll eat sushi any day. Good idea."

After about twenty minutes, Sam set aside the magazines.

"There are a couple of photographs in each of these on which I may be able to help. This one, taken at the Rural, shows some of the polo players I know. This guy in the corner was a boyfriend of mine," she said, pointing at one of the social pages.

"Eduardo, what's the date of the murder?" Leandro asked.

"27 July, the day after the inauguration of the Rural."

"Same evening therefore."

Eduardo studied all the photographs of that evening on the page. One of them showed a more general view of the cocktail party. The captions listed most of the people in the photographs.

"Have you got a magnifying glass?"

He moved closer to the light, then suddenly looked up.

"I have a feeling that this lady over in the corner might be the Englishwoman," he said, pointing at the photo. "It's a side shot, but the hairstyle, and what looks like a fur coat, seem to match. Do you think your ex-boyfriend was at the same party?"

He seemed reconciled to the idea that Sam might be a new member of the team.

"Possibly. Of course, that doesn't mean that he necessarily knew her, but it would at least be a start."

Eduardo was beginning to betray some excitement at what, it seemed, could be a new lead.

"We have to think this through," Leandro mused. "This happened nearly two months ago. You can hardly walk in and start asking questions," he said, turning to Sam. "For all we know, given the fact that we've never been able to identify Lady X, she may still be around. However, the polo season will soon be getting into full swing, so all kinds of people will be coming and going as we run up to the Palermo finals at the beginning of December. That makes it as good a time as any to do a little snooping around the polo crowd. The trouble is, you, Eduardo, are likely to be shown the door very fast. I don't think I have the right credentials either, being more a rugby man. I've been looking at the names in the captions, and although many of them ring plenty of bells on the social front, I can't say that I move in that crowd. Add to that, if I do bump into anybody I know, they're likely to be intrigued to find me there."

Sam coughed.

"I don't know why you're taking so long to get to the point. It's not usually your style. It's obvious that in this case I can go where neither of you two can. And I'm dying to do it!"

Leandro and Eduardo looked at each other and then at her. She had caught them by surprise. She continued, visibly enjoying their embarrassment.

"On balance, I can't see that a little socialising could be all that dangerous."

"Unless of course your old boyfriend starts to take an interest again. With his bank balance, I don't feel that secure," Leandro replied, adopting a depressed look.

"Aaah," Sam replied. "I'm told he has a Porsche now."

"Shit!"

"That could be very tempting."

She grinned.

"Don't worry, I'm told that he's completely under the spell of a domineering Italian lady, who has even more money than he has. Mind you, a bit of competition is what I enjoy most."

Her eyes glazed over.

"What do you think, Eduardo?" Leandro asked.

Eduardo paused before replying.

"Well, on the one hand, given everything that has already happened, this case is clearly at a standstill. On the other, we need to be extremely careful with every move we make. But a little innocuous socialising doesn't - on the face of it - necessarily seem so dangerous."

Looking at Leandro, he continued. "But I'm certainly not going to take the responsibility for a final decision."

Leandro walked over to the window and looked out. After a moment's thought, he turned and looked at the two of them.

"It strikes me that we need to tell Sam a bit more about the case before either she or we take a final decision as to whether she gets involved."

"Yes, please do. It's what I've been waiting weeks to learn."

She sat down, crossing her legs again, looking from one to the other expectantly.

"If you insist on looking that seductive, your chances diminish by the second," Eduardo responded.

Leandro was struck by the speed with which Sam had turned Eduardo from caution and suspicion to the beginnings of a flirtation.

Almost mockingly, she sat up straight, placing her hands on her knees, as if waiting for instructions. Her eyes, however, were anything but serious.

"When you've heard some more, you may think twice."

They proceeded, between them, to take her through the history of the case, with a brief description of the murder itself, the little they knew about the two women, the attack on Eduardo, and their lack of real progress. Nothing was said about either Sarmiento or Sosa, though there was a suggestion that some of this might have roots in the time of the military dictatorship and the dirty war. This seemed to make Sam even more attentive, though Leandro was not sure why.

At one point, Leandro appeared to be about to reveal the existence of Sarmiento, but Eduardo interrupted him. This was an asset which needed total protection for as long as possible. Leandro caught the message in time and made vague reference to a police informer to the vice squad. Finally, Eduardo went back to the question of Lady X and explained that both the victim and her murderer appeared to have been connected to the polo crowd, as the victim at least had been at the Rural parties on the night of her death.

At one point, Sam interrupted them.

"You said the hotel was called L'Hôtel? There's a hotel in Paris by that name, in the Rue des Beaux Arts. I've stayed there. And do you know who else stayed there?" she added, looking at Leandro. "Oscar Wilde! In fact, he died there. Isn't that an amazing coincidence? Just a tiny detail that gets me more interested."

As she listened to their exposé of the crime, Leandro realised that the idea of Sam's involvement had probably been ticking away somewhere at the back of his mind for a week or so.

Sam was silent for a while, looking at the photographs in the magazine.

"Well, it's not a pretty story, and by the looks of it, the connection may be very tenuous. On the other hand, I can't see much downside - even a certain upside, like making Leo jealous," and she dismissed him with a wave of her hand, "in having a good time... again!" she added, looking at Leandro.

"Bitch!"

She laughed at the expression on his face.

"Oh dear! It's so terribly easy to make you jealous."

"I think it's too dangerous," Leandro said firmly.

"I knew you were going to say that," Sam immediately shot back at him. "Let me be the best judge of that. I'm not one to take unnecessary risks... only calculated ones."

"I can't help you," Eduardo commented.

"Frankly, I can't see what risk there can possibly be with my attending a few parties and watching a few matches... except to Leo's peace of mind. And I can deal with that! So it's settled. Do I get expenses?"

"Whatever happened to the gallantry of the Argentine male? With all the money swimming in that crowd, a girl like you shouldn't have to lift a finger."

"I was only joking."

The doorbell rang announcing the arrival of the sushi.

October 2007

Given recent events, it looked as though the relatively quiet life which Leandro had been leading in recent years might be a thing of the past. The attacks on Eduardo and the killing of Sosa bore all the hallmarks of a situation in which he might quite rapidly and unexpectedly find himself the target, at the very least of a break-in, but possibly of a mugging or even an attempt on his life. The most he had ever taken in the way of precautions was to leave a baseball bat in his umbrella stand in the hall. Perhaps erroneously, he preferred to rely on his overall strength and physical condition which, although his rugby playing days might be over, he still maintained with a few weekly sessions of Canadian air force fitness routines. But he had to admit that his good physical condition, moulded many years ago when he had been one of the fastest and strongest wing three quarters of CASI, the San Isidro Athletic Club, was unlikely to be sufficient to face up to any kind of concerted aggression. The attack on Eduardo had shown that they might come in strength, whoever they were.

The next morning found him opening the door of a gun shop incongruously called 'El Amigo' in a side street not far from the Colon opera house. Since his time in the military, he realised that he had lost touch with the masculine fascination with killing, whether human or animal. Large posters of triumphant huntsmen holding up the dangling head of a stag alternated with target cut-outs of sinister advancing soldiers. The display cases presented a range of rifles, revolvers and automatic pistols, hunting knives and even crossbows. He should have consulted Eduardo before coming here, but the grey-haired salesman, spotting what looked like a novice, was soon explaining to him the relative merits of a variety of revolvers and automatics, extolling their range, accuracy or stopping power. As to the administrative formalities, this was simple paperwork, which the salesman would be happy to handle on Leandro's behalf. Señor would only have to sign here and here and then find time to visit the firing range in the Circulo Militar, on Plaza San Martin, where the salesman's good friend Juan would take Señor through the paces required to satisfy the authorities that Señor was not a public menace with a gun in his hand. The fact that Señor had seen action in Malvinas and done basic weapons training was obviously a guarantee. After about half an hour of listening to the options and weighing some of the guns in his hand, Leandro selected a Bersa 9mm automatic. The salesman extolled its reliability and the fact that the magazine held thirteen rounds, an above-average number for a weapon of such small size. Leandro had to admit that just holding its compact body in his hand brought back powerful memories, even a slight quickening of the pulse.

"What is it about us males, that we always seem to react predictably, whenever we take a gun in our hand?"

The salesman smiled, understanding.

Having put down a deposit and provided all the basic information which the salesman required to fill out the form, which would be sent to the RENAR registration authority, he decided to get Juan's seal of approval straight away.

Catching a taxi the few blocks down Santa Fe, he stepped out in front of the elegant portico of the Circulo Militar, the Argentine military's social headquarters. Argentina had imported the British tradition of men's clubs in the early twentieth century. Political, financial and social elites thronged the Jockey Club's elegant Parisian-style townhouse, the Brazilian Embassy opposite, the French embassy with drooping tricolour to its left, in the upper-class quarter known as Barrio Norte. Leandro had also lunched occasionally in the Circulo de Armas on Avenida Corrientes, but it was a boring modern building compared to this Parisian style hotel, with its ornate portico, matching the Ministry of Foreign Affairs on the other side of Plaza San Martin.

Leandro had always felt an instinctive aversion to membership of any institution, which he suspected was good at manipulating the future of the country with impunity behind the scenes, yet singularly averse to taking risks when the chips were really down.

Stepping through swing doors into a side building of the Circulo, he was greeted with a powerful smell of chlorine, which he soon traced to the club's swimming pool in which a number of elderly gentlemen were laboriously completing their daily lengths. Farther down the corridor, an ageing sign indicated the *Administración*, in which a portly lady, with what appeared to be her grandson on her knee, was busy colouring the child's painting book. In response to his enquiry, she indicated that the firing range was a floor below in the basement. Continuing along the cream and brown coloured walls of the corridor, Leandro found a staircase leading down under the central courtyard of the building. Following the intermittent crack of gunfire, he pushed open the door.

"Are you Juan?" addressing a strongly built man in his fifties.

Juan pointed to the yellow, work-site style earmuffs he was wearing to indicate that he had not understood the question. Behind him, two men, wearing similar earmuffs, were firing handguns down the thirty-metre range. Once they had emptied their weapons and were winding their targets back to the firing point, Juan came over, removing his earmuffs. Leandro gave him the form supplied by the gun shop.

"What kind of gun do you want to use?"

"I'm buying a small automatic, a Bersa, so anything that you have like that will probably be adequate."

Juan opened a cabinet on the wall and produced a Browning 9 mm.

"It may be bigger than what you're buying, but it should do."

"Okay, I'm sure that's fine."

Juan took him through some basic safety steps and showed him how to hold the automatic, using his left hand to clasp under his right in order to steady his aim. Leandro had a brief flashback to his days of recruit training. Earmuffs on and feet apart, he took aim at the small target at the end of the shooting alley, with a faint sense of acting in one of the mind-numbing American police series which he occasionally zapped on TV. Unprepared for the buck of the first round, the bullet just clipped the edge of the cardboard. Juan, using a small pair of binoculars, told him where the shot had fallen.

"You need to hold the gun more firmly and squeeze, don't pull."

Leandro knew that he had usually achieved good scores on the firing range and was disappointed by his first shot. This time, whilst tightening his grip, he made the effort to relax his shoulders and breathe more slowly. The next five shots were grouped much more neatly in a radius of about ten centimetres, although down and left from the centre of the target.

Juan wound back the target.

"Very good, sir. Clearly not the first time you've held one of these things."

With that, he filled in, signed and dated the bottom of the form, adding the rubberstamp of the Circulo Militar.

With something of a feeling of childish *macho* self-satisfaction, Leandro returned to the gun shop, where the salesman expressed suitable admiration at the cardboard target Leandro showed him.

"The paperwork should be through in a couple weeks, so if you want to drop in then, I'm putting the Bersa aside for you."

Leandro had to hope that he would not need it before then. He also knew that whatever he might be able to do in the peace and calm of a firing range might not be achievable in a more confused situation.

8 October 2007

Eduardo and Sarmiento had now been in contact for more than four weeks. Given everything that had happened, especially the murder of Sosa, Eduardo had, as agreed with Leandro, suggested in one of his mails to Sarmiento in early October that more progress might be made if the exchanges could be less cryptic and ideally face-to-face. The reaction from Sarmiento had initially been completely negative. But, as Eduardo pointed out, Sarmiento had reason enough at least to contemplate some more direct form of communication, if only to give Eduardo the opportunity not only to pose questions, but also to get replies in real-time and thereby hopefully to make more rapid progress. By dint of further mail exchanges, they had been able to set up a Skype arrangement, in which Eduardo would make the connection from a public Internet cafe. Given the fact that a number of these *locutorios* might already be under surveillance from the Policía Federal, Eduardo first had to establish which cafe might not yet have attracted police attention and, on that basis, stake a claim to be interested in it, in the hope of keeping his colleagues away. He finally found one tucked away a few blocks behind the Congress building.

The first Skype connection served to break some of the ice, although Sarmiento limited himself mostly to monosyllabic responses. Eduardo deliberately showed no interest in the identity of Sarmiento, but concentrated instead on trying to fill in some of the gaps in the information he had provided. Sarmiento, for his part, was more interested in how the investigation was progressing. Eduardo saw little reason to tell him about the attack made on him, since this might scare Sarmiento off completely. At the back of his mind, Eduardo could still not completely rule out the possibility that Sarmiento might in some way be connected to those behind the attack. The less detail Eduardo provided, in particular about the involvement of Leandro and Sam, the better. He therefore confined himself to describing standard steps in the investigation, the profiling of the victim, review of the CC tapes and so on. To his surprise, Sarmiento, on the occasion of their second Skype conversation, forcefully accused Eduardo of not really trying. In response, Eduardo explained to Sarmiento that the scraps of information he had been serving up were sadly lacking in sufficient substance for Eduardo to pursue. The murder of the librarian, Sosa, was very concrete, but as Eduardo tried to explain, difficult to relate to the hotel murder. How did Suarez or Switzerland fit in? Confronted with this criticism, Sarmiento appeared to lose patience and cut off the call. Five minutes of patient texting finally got him to resume the conversation.

"Don't misunderstand me, Señor, but at this point it's not so obvious how they connect. The murder in a Buenos Aires hotel of an Englishwoman, keen on polo, in the year 2007, doesn't obviously tie in with the actions of the military dictatorship some thirty years before. I need some help here and I suspect only you can give it. The fact that Señor Sosa paid for it with his life shows that we're dealing with something very unpleasant, as you have tried to suggest, but I will need more to tie the two together."

There was a pause at the other end.

"I see what you mean. Apologies if I appeared impatient. The link is there, but it will take some explaining. Probably better that I do this in writing, to ensure clarity and save time. Leave your car in the usual place for the next few nights, with a gap in the rear passenger window sufficient for me to drop in a thin envelope."

Sarmiento hung up as soon as Eduardo had confirmed that he understood the instruction.

Eduardo wondered how long he would have to wait.

Only a few days later, an early Saturday morning, Eduardo found a dark grey envelope on the floor mat behind the driver's seat of his car. Inside were half a dozen closely typed sheets of paper.

Dear Inspector Falcioni,
To place the story in context, I must explain to you at the start that there are three strands running together in the events which you are investigating. So far, only one of these is clear to you, namely the murder of an Englishwoman in a Buenos Aires hotel in July of this year. From the events in Calle Perú, you are aware of some connection back to the events which took place under the military dictatorship of Videla and Galtieri between about 1976 and the fall of the military in 1983 after the disgrace of the Malvinas. The third strand, which is totally invisible to you at this stage, relates to a complex and vicious blackmail operation of which I am the victim. I suspect that I am not the only target of this operation, given the scale and professionalism of its design, but I can throw no light on who else might be a victim. I merely suspect this to be the case. I must also tell you that I cannot put any names to the perpetrators of the blackmail, since it has been handled in an exceedingly sophisticated fashion, precisely to ensure that the victim cannot trace where the blackmail is coming from. God knows, I have tried as discreetly as possible, given that the blackmail is now into its fifth year, but without success. Alongside the financial blackmail also hangs a clearly stated threat either to discredit me, or to kill me or members of my family, should I make any attempt to identify the blackmailer. It is

176

precisely because the murder of the Englishwoman was intended to send a clear message, in a manner which I will explain below, that on the one hand I am forced to take the precautions which I do and to which you have kindly consented, and on the other, that I have finally decided that I must act to put an end to the inferno of the last years.

What I'm about to tell you is an expression of my trust in you. At this stage, it is my view that my identity, were it to be known to you, would not significantly improve your chances of making progress in your investigation. I must therefore seek your promise that, whatever you do, you take no steps of any kind to identify me, since, were this to become known to the blackmailer, it would without the slightest doubt provoke my assassination or that of a member of my family. He has already killed once. He will again. With my disappearance, any chance you might have of eradicating a cancer which sits at the heart of our politics would almost certainly vanish. Perhaps a moment will come when we may meet face-to-face, but not yet.

The reason that Janet Williams was murdered is that she was very close to me. Some 10 years younger than me, she had been my mistress for more than 8 years, and I had been successfully able to conceal her existence from my wife and family, as well as from my entire circle of friends. I know that you have been trying to identify her friends and contacts, but you will find no trace of me. Tragically, I apparently failed to conceal her existence from my tormentor, for reasons which I believe I have now worked out. Within a day or two of her murder, the blackmailer, using the untraceable form of messages (of which more below) which are the hallmark of his style of operation, had sent me a clear message that her death should be taken as an indication of the lengths to which he could go. And if that was not sufficient, in the post I received her cell phone, which contained detailed photographs of her lying on her bed in the hotel, clearly already dead. Until that moment, I had no reason to believe that he, or indeed anyone else, was aware of her relationship with me. The fault - unforgivably - is mine, since about a month earlier I had delayed payment and failed to provide him - or her, as it is not totally apparent that I am dealing with either a man or a woman - with a plausible reason. I should say that I am 99% certain that it is a man.

The basis for the blackmail is twofold. On the one hand, my affair with Janet, which would not of itself justify the level and the duration of the payments being sought. As I said, I never suspected that the blackmailer was even aware of it. The second is financial. And once again, I must place my reputation and even my fate in your hands by revealing its nature.

It will come as no surprise to you that funds way in excess of the Central Bank's reserves sit in Argentine bank accounts offshore. It has variously been estimated that several hundred thousand, perhaps even a million or more, middle and upper class Argentines keep substantial assets behind the doors of banks in Panama, Virgin Islands, Austria and Switzerland, to name only some of the countries where banking secrecy prevails. Many more accounts sit relatively unprotected in jurisdictions such as the US or the European Union. I belong to the group which has chosen the land of the cuckoo clock to conceal part of my assets from the predatory hands of governments characterised by an infallible gift for corruption, but less by a gift for building Argentina up to become the country it so obviously deserves to become - and has been in the past.

By means which are not clear to me, my blackmailer obtained substantial evidence regarding my assets in Switzerland, including the identity of the bank and even details of the accounts under which the funds were held and by whom they were managed. By some means or other, this person was able to build up a picture not only of the scale of the funds which I had deposited, but also of the manner in which I was spending them. When the blackmail began, I was presented at one and the same time with evidence in the blackmailer's possession regarding my assets, and vivid testimony of the lengths to which he - or she - would be prepared to go should it occur to me to take any steps to avoid the blackmail. The evidence provided not only included a detailed picture of my family, my friends and our way of life in Argentina, with details of our cars, the schools attended by my children, the hours at which they left the house or returned, the way we spent our weekends. It also warned me to look out for an event which would serve as a warning of the consequences which might follow should I fail to cooperate, whilst at the same time being explicable in the more normal course of things - or at least what passes for almost normal in Argentina. A mere 10 days later, the family retriever disappeared from our quinta in the northern suburbs of Buenos Aires, only for its severed head, including the collar with address tag still attached, to be deposited at the main entrance of the gated community where we live. Whilst no one could determine the purpose of such brutality, the message was clear for me. Not content with extracting a very significant monthly payment from me, the blackmailer has added a particularly nasty additional twist. Once a month, I receive an e-mail with a link to a website, highly protected, for members only, it's URL constantly changing, specialising in paedophilia or some similar abominable sexual deviation. But occasionally also what I believe is called a "snuff movie", in which one is forced to watch the dying moments of some terrified victim, killed "on camera". From this, I am instructed to download one or other video or set of appalling photographs, thereby apparently turning me into the kind of pervert for whom no jail sentence is adequate punishment. I need hardly tell you the consequences of these enforced perversions becoming known to my family and social circle. Failure to make the download inevitably prompts a vicious reminder. The blackmailer has clearly put in place some digital method of checking that I have not only downloaded, but also that the material remains stored in my computer. Are these spies called something like "cookies"? I once attempted to delete a download and very rapidly received a message warning against any further attempt.

I need not elaborate on the details of the emotional, and to a lesser extent financial, nightmare which this situation has generated. But at last, the murder of Janet has finally produced a shift in the relationship, which I cannot fail to exploit if this torture is to be brought to an end. Firstly, because it is the first occasion, of which I am aware, on which the blackmailer has taken so highly public and visible a step. In the process, he may have focused too much on the message he was sending me and overlooked any collateral benefit which it might provide to me. By this, I mean that, in the process, it has brought me an ally in the person of yourself. Someone who, if armed with appropriate clues and information, may perhaps help me to unwind this drama, whilst simultaneously solving the crime. If I am writing you this letter, it is because you have provided me with sufficient proof that you are prepared to take the investigation farther. My one ambition is of course that in the process you should destroy the blackmailer.

So far, I have provided you with two of the components. The third is much more complicated. What is the link to the torture and horrors committed at the time of the military dictatorship? I do not believe that the connection is necessarily of a purely political nature. I personally can find no ideological or political link between the blackmail and anything that may have happened during those terrible years.

The only connection that I can see, for which I have as yet no rational explanation, is the fact that my father served in the Army and was, at that time, a high-ranking retired officer. He was not directly involved in the events of the "disappeared", though of course many of his friends and colleagues probably, or certainly, were. I came to my military service just after Malvinas, so was in no way a participant. The connection is more tenuous. Part of it can be found in phrases or expressions used by the blackmailer in his written communications. On occasions, an oblique reference has been made to the "dirty war", to the "disappeared", to the tortures. One thread running through the messages is the suggestion that somehow all this is justified by the iniquities perpetrated by "your fascist military bloodline" or by "your class which has always buried the poor in the ruins of your capitalist tyranny". On one occasion, the blackmail was described as a just revenge against those who had stripped Argentina bare, and the name of Martinez de Hoz, Videla's Minister of Finance, was given as an example. Argentina has had many unsuccessful Ministers of Economy, and Martinez de Hoz was not necessarily the worst. However, in the minds of parts of the general public and particularly of the left, his economic policies at times almost rival the criminal tortures committed in cellars around the country.

Much of this language resonates today in the passageways of the current government machine. That didn't however seem to provide a sufficiently solid base for making any connection with my situation, until one day, my father, who is now well over 90, passed me a letter he had received from one of his old army colleagues. We all know that Argentina is a profoundly divided society, never able to come to terms with its past and seemingly unable to see into the future with optimism and confidence. Not like our Brazilian or Chilean neighbours on whom we so easily look down - or at least have for most of the last century.

The letter reached my father from a retired Lieutenant General, now under arrest along with many of his fellows in the barracks at Campo de Mayo. As you know, the current government moved rapidly to bring forward trials and investigations which President Menem had seen fit, in the interests of national unity, to halt or even amnesty. Somehow, this letter had got to my father through the censorship. The author did not conceal the fact that he had participated in some of the terrible activities perpetrated at the Naval Mechanical School. In the letter, he expressed the firm belief that a group hidden inside the current government, not content with putting the Armed Forces back on trial, were actively taking direct steps to eliminate certain members of the Armed Forces who might, for different reasons, have escaped the investigations which took place during the 1980s or for whom insufficient evidence had been produced to lead to trial. In the letter, reference was made to the existence of additional evidence, which had so far escaped the attention of the judicial process. This included the films held by Sosa. We now know what happened to him. I do not know whether you were able to follow up information I provided to you before he was assassinated. But I have reason to believe that there is a connection between one of the films, of which I provided the date, and the blackmail. Somehow, my father's colleague had become aware not only of the fact that direct action might be being taken, but he also made reference to other forms of pressure being brought to bear, and blackmail was one of the ways mentioned. He implied that the funds being raised in this manner might be being used for secret activities, the purpose of which he could only suspect.

Not having seen the films, I obviously cannot comment on whether the connection is real. If in some way you were able to get hold of them in time, you may be able to make the link.

From the same source, my father received the identity of Sosa and the passwords which I provided to you. When I spoke to him, he implied that his contact had been very insistent that someone should learn of the existence of a particular film, the date of which I provided you. Somehow, something on that film would connect with the conspiracy of the secret funds. Obviously, I cannot tell whether you were able to make contact with Sosa before his death nor what you may have been able to find out. I can only hope that it may have been of some use. Whatever it was, the poor man gave his life for it!

I cannot emphasise enough the fact that the contents of this letter, were they to fall into the wrong hands, would almost certainly lead to my death or to that of members of my family. I have placed my fate and theirs in your hands. Yours.

Having read it through a couple of times, Eduardo brought the letter round to Leandro's flat the next day. He found him reclining with a couple of Quilmes six-packs in front of the television, totally absorbed in the World Cup rugby semi-finals, in which the Argentine Pumas faced an old rival, the Springboks, at the Stade de France in Paris. The Pumas' victories against Namibia and then Ireland, and only ten days earlier against Scotland, had brought parts of the country to fever pitch, with the names of Juan Martín Hernández, Felipe Contepomi, Agustín Pichot, and Patricio Albacete suddenly capturing the national imagination in a manner which almost rivalled Maradona. The voice of Miguel Simon, commentating, could be heard in every bar and café around the country. Eduardo had to control his impatience, not being a rugby fan, as he sat watching his godfather shout and jump in sympathy with each Argentine move and tackle.

"Shit! That's fucking disappointing!"

Leandro tossed the can across the room as the final whistle blew on the South African victory, 37 – 13.

"Contepomi the man of the match again. But I wouldn't mind laying my hands on that New Zealand ref, the bastard. Though to be frank, we did make rather too many mistakes. I guess we shouldn't complain, we had a fantastic run. We beat Ireland and took our revenge for what they did to us in 2003. And we were fourth overall. Who would have imagined that! It'll change rugby forever in this country. About bloody time too."

He stood up and looked out of the window for a minute or so, as if needing to find solace. The he turned to Eduardo.

"So, *chico*, what have you brought to cheer me up?"

Leandro read the letter carefully. At the end, he looked at Eduardo, a smile spreading over his face.

"Amazing! Congratulations on having brought Sarmiento to this level of confidence. It's a pretty terrifying story, but it's a real breakthrough. I know he specifically asks you not to, but have you been able to check anything, even discreetly?"

"A couple of things. I was able to find a list of the retired senior officers in the Army still alive in 1976 when Videla took over from Isabelita and the dirty war began, or at least moved inside the government. The list is quite long, nearly two dozen. At that time, the Armed Forces had a habit of promoting a lot of people, who then sat around until they could retire and begin to draw a pension, or even better in those days – not any more - pick up lucrative jobs in such places as Fabricaciones Militares. As you can imagine, it's not easy to find out what they were all doing at the time. The military were busy covering their tracks, not only as regards what they were doing in the war against the Montos and ERP, but also on the business side. All their Christian principles of defending the nation against the threat of Marxism and Fidel Castro lived conveniently alongside a system of massive corruption, which, I suppose, has never been very absent in so many of our countries in this part of the world."

"Some pretty heavy deals were cut during the time of the junta, not only in armaments purchases, but also in infrastructure, in energy, in transport," Leandro interjected. "It was under the military that we began to build our biggest dam with the Paraguayans at Yacyretá. A lot of people on both sides of the frontier got very rich on that one, long before the topsoil was ever moved."

Eduardo nodded.

"You're right. I had a word with one of my sources, ex-military himself. He tells me that a number of senior officers, some of them retired, acted as intermediaries or fixers in many of these deals. The commissions were enormous! I wouldn't be surprised if that weren't the origin, or part of it, of our friend Sarmiento's wealth, the money in Switzerland, thanks to his father. I'm bound to say that I find myself torn on the one hand between wanting to help Sarmiento in the interests of solving the murder, and on the other of trying to take the lid off the whole business of corruption in the state, and particularly at the time of the *dictadura*. I don't know what you think?"

Leandro pondered the question, not an easy one to answer.

"I know what you feel, but frankly, at our level, chasing corruption is a waste of time in this country. It's endemic. Not until we get a leadership which realises that corruption eats the heart out of our nation, and starts to do something about it concretely, at the highest level, is it worth the likes of you and me losing sleep over it. It can be done, and obviously public pressure can help, but it has to come from the top. It's been done in some countries - but with the present government, all you're doing is making yourself a target. Plenty of people think that this lot are far worse than Menem, and that's saying something! But given what has already happened, I'd say you shouldn't provoke them any more than you absolutely have to. My instinct would be to concentrate on the murder and, even more interesting, what he seems to tell us about where this blackmail is coming from. Who knows, that may even lead us to the question of corruption. In fact, I would be very surprised if it didn't."

"I suppose you're right," Eduardo replied, hunching his shoulders. But the look on his face indicated that he was finding the decision a hard one to swallow.

Leandro continued.

"When you started digging into what the Englishwoman had been up to, do you think you found any trace of Sarmiento? After all, he's telling us that they were having a long-standing affair. Was there any sign of someone like that in what you've been able to throw up?"

Eduardo shook his head.

"Another thing," Leandro continued. "If she and Sarmiento were having an affair, what's she doing with another woman? I know you haven't been able to track down who she was with, or rather, left the party with the night she died. That still surprises me. Yet Sarmiento doesn't seem to have picked up the fact that his mistress was killed by a woman, although some reference did appear in early press reports. He says nothing about that. Perhaps, like all good Argentine *machos*, he doesn't want to admit to himself that his mistress might also have girlfriends."

"You're right, I'd thought about that and was planning to find a diplomatic way to ask him if he could throw any light on who she was with that night. Though it sounds to me, from what he writes, that he and she were rarely if ever seen together in public. Which probably means that he wasn't with her at any time the night she died."

"Another intriguing bit of what he writes relates to how the blackmailer might have been able to find out so much about him, his bank accounts and so on. Unless he left his bank statements lying around somewhere here in Buenos Aires, I wonder how the blackmailer was able to find out about his Swiss bank, how much he had in his account, enough to make the blackmail worthwhile. Tracking his movements, his family and so on, would be easy, but bank accounts are something else. Unless of course Sarmiento was being indiscreet or inefficient. That being said, I'm still amazed how many Argentines continue to use credit cards here in Buenos Aires paid for out of a Swiss bank account. One of these days, someone is going to get a nasty surprise. People simply underestimate the level of information which electronic banking leaves by the wayside."

"Somewhere in what he writes there's also a suggestion that this blackmail operation is aimed not only against him, but against a number of other people. Pulling all that information together wouldn't be easy. It would be nice to have another Sarmiento, but that's too good to hope for. What Sarmiento makes clear is that, had it not been for the murder, he would still be terrified - and paying."

"I wonder whether the cell phone might tell us something."

"That's right. It makes the connection between the killing and everything else. As to the phone, just as there were no prints anywhere in the hotel, I bet there won't be any on the phone either. Though its log might tell us something about who she was calling – always assuming that Lady X was one of them."

Eduardo thought for a minute before continuing.

"When you put it all together, it's a nasty picture. Blackmail, murder, pornography extending to paedophilia, all thrown together in a cocktail on the margins of the darker side of our political system. With roots possibly going back to events which took place in the torture chambers at the time of the military. Faced with this, where do we stand? Practically our only asset is your girlfriend, chasing virtually the only lead we have."

"You don't need to tell me," Leandro responded gloomily. "It's about time to check out what she's been able to dig up. If our precautions so far have been reasonably successful, anyone watching to see whether the investigation into the hotel murder is making progress will, I presume, detect little movement. At least, that assumes that you haven't been active on the case since you're beating?"

He looked questioningly at Eduardo.

"That's right. Probably the only connection, and a very tenuous one at that, is my having been nearby when Sosa was killed, which might also look like a coincidence. Nobody has come back to me on that one since the day I spoke to the guy in the *Comisaría 2da*. And I certainly haven't done any more digging. As to my connection to you, that's probably explicable enough in innocent terms. From you to Samira, that's quite a jump. On balance, although we can see a link between all these pieces, including you and Sam, that's not to say that these people can see the connections."

Leandro pondered a moment.

"You're probably right. Frankly, I would doubt that they're going to make a habit of bumping off people in the same social milieu, and almost certainly not using the same method, namely Lady X. So, for the time being, Sam is probably fairly safe just going to parties and keeping her eyes open. I haven't heard from her for a day or two, so I'll get in touch."

Leandro suspected that her absence might be connected in some way to the fact that, on World Cup Rugby days, he tended to lock himself away with the TV or join a group of fellow rugby men for a tribal session of drinking, shouting and cheering. Sam had made it very clear to him that this was a setting in which she did not feel at all at home. By today, she had been out of touch for over a week and he was getting worried, not to mention physically and emotionally frustrated.

His attempts to call or leave messages on her cell phone had initially produced no result. He suspected that her absence might be a way of keeping the cutting edge of his affection well sharpened. When they finally did make contact, her behaviour betrayed nothing. As regards Lady X, Sam had nothing to report so far. The polo season was still in its early stages and the international crowd would not be arriving until early November. They would have to be patient.

"I think we'll have to leave it at that for today. By the way, any more signs of your being followed?" Leandro asked his godson.

"No, obviously I've kept my eyes open. Driving around usually provides a good opportunity for spotting a tail, but no sign. So perhaps the man you saw the other day outside London City was a coincidence."

"Let's hope so. Just take care."

28 October 2007

The proximity of the presidential elections in late October led to Leandro receiving a brief from Frobisher to make an assessment of likely future Argentine policies, in the event of the victory - largely discounted by everyone anyway – of Nestor Kirchner's wife, Cristina Fernandez. The signals coming from the Kirchner camp had been confusing, with some speculation directed at the personalities likely to survive into the next government. After some five years of the Kirchners in power, a large segment of middle class Argentine society was looking for a change of faces, particularly some of the more aggressive personalities, such as Gustavo Moreno, the Commerce Secretary, whose strong-arm tactics with business were beginning to grate.

Leandro, a recognised member of the clan of political and economic analysts, had little difficulty in arranging a series of meetings with the better-informed observers and politicians. Through good contacts, he was also able to have discreet discussions with a small number of people, whom he had known for a number of years and who he had reason to believe were close to the otherwise hermetic power structure which the Kirchners preferred. Decisions being usually taken behind closed doors, there never having been a single full Cabinet meeting since Nestor Kirchner had become President, there were even those who questioned the legitimacy and constitutionality of some of the major decisions taken under the current Presidency. Intolerant to criticism or opposition, the Kirchner duo preferred to bludgeon decisions out of their ministers on a one-to-one basis. As such, power was entirely concentrated in the hands of the family.

By the end of the week, he believed that he had been able to put together an analysis of where politics might go when the President's wife was elected. He sent off his report and received an appreciative response from London.

The Presidential election, when it finally came on 28 October, provided few surprises. With 45.3% of the vote and a sufficient lead over her nearest rival, there was no need for a runoff.

November 2007

Sam and Leandro had seen each other intermittently in October. Then at the beginning of November, she had flown off to Europe for ten days, giving him a vague explanation, something about having to do some business for her father. He had decided not to press her on this. By mid-November, having returned, she suddenly and without warning appeared to break off contact completely. What had happened in Europe?

After a few days silence, he finally decided to do something which he had never done before, namely go round to her flat unannounced. He took a taxi to fashionable Puerto Madero, the old port area of Buenos Aires, which had been completely redeveloped over the preceding decades. Armed with her address, he found himself looking up at a modern block of flats standing on Pierina Dealesi, overlooking the inner waterfront. Everything appeared to be glass and stainless steel in the lobby which he could see through the wide plate-glass door. Presumably her father was funding this as well.

Somewhat to his surprise, the main door was open and a usually vigilant *portero* nowhere to be seen. He hesitated, wondering whether he should first ring the bell of her flat on the cube-shaped chrome stand by the door. Then, seeing that the *portero* had not appeared, he went through, passing across the entrance hall and pressing the button to the fourth floor. Each floor had only two flats on either side of the small lobby onto which the lift opened. He stepped out and walked over to press the bell of 4B. There was no reply.

He rang again and waited. After a moment, he heard a door opening inside and the sound of steps approaching.

"Who's there?" The voice was Sam's.

"It's me. Leandro."

There was a silence on the other side.

"I heard nothing from you. You didn't answer my messages or calls. I was worried."

"Just a minute."

The sound of her walking away was followed by what he thought was the low murmur of voices, and then she was back.

The door opened.

"Come in," she said.

Although the embrace and kiss were warm, he sensed that she was tense. She was wearing a pale yellow silk dressing gown and a pair of Moroccan *babouche* slippers – and nothing much else as far as their embrace allowed him to detect. She led him towards a small glass table near the picture window looking out onto a balcony. The appearance of the place was contemporary, with a large dark grey leather sofa and two immense matching armchairs, surrounding a low black lacquer coffee table. A single abstract painting in the style of Rothko covered one wall, a huge black and white photograph – he suspected by Helmut Newton - on the other, a tall bookcase filled with hard covers, paperbacks and magazines taking up the entire opposite wall. The floor was glistening black laminated parquet.

She sat down and motioned him to the chair on the other side of the table.

"Some coffee?"

"Black, small, please, the usual," he replied.

She was not alone, that much was obvious. Almost immediately, the half-suspected source of his uneasiness materialised, with the silent appearance of an extremely beautiful Asian girl from what seemed to be the only bedroom. She wore a dark silk peignoir, over which her jet-black hair cascaded to her waist. She was bare foot. And beautiful.

If Sam was in any way embarrassed by this new insight into her private life, she showed no sign of it.

"This is Lamai," she said simply, introducing him as well. "Could you make the coffee, Lamai?" Turning to him again, she added, "Lamai means soft in Thai, I think it fits her so well."

"Very appropriate." His tone was slightly dry.

Lamai smiled.

"Of course, Samira, I'll make the coffee."

Leandro detected a rather charming accent. She made her way to the kitchen.

"I was worried," he began again.

Sam laid her hand over his.

"You shouldn't have been," she said firmly. "I was going to ring you today. I've got so much to tell, some of it really important. But I had to be careful, for reasons which I'll explain. Obviously, we can't discuss this in front of Lamai. Can we meet this evening?"

He was fascinated by the ease with which she could step out of one relationship into the other. It suddenly made him feel rather old and he said as much.

"Every time we meet, I find there's some new dimension to you. Really hard to keep up. I'm not as young as I was!"

She laughed and softly stroked the side of his face.

"Don't worry, you're really young for your age and all this will make you even younger."

She smiled again. He could just about manage a wry grin and shook his head.

"This is Argentina," he said, "and I suspect some of us still have some catching up to do with the rest of the world. Adapting to it."

"I hesitated before I let you in, but it only took me half a second to realise that if anyone could adapt to this little surprise, it would be you. And you certainly shouldn't think that this is embarrassing either for me or for Lamai. The trouble is, the Catholic Church has left so many of you men unprepared for what in other parts of the world is rapidly becoming the norm."

She looked at him compassionately.

Lamai brought three diminutive cups of coffee with a sugar bowl on a small Japanese lacquer tray and sat down with them at the table. Out of the corner of his eye, Leandro studied the porcelain beauty of her face and her diminutive proportions. He had never been particularly attracted to Asian female beauty, but trust Sam to find a pearl. He smiled at her and she smiled back, quite unselfconsciously.

It was obvious that the conversation could not turn to what really interested them both. Having finished his coffee, he got up to take a look at the books on the shelves. Apart from the English language classics which he expected to find, predictably Oscar Wilde and a number of other writers of that period, he noted books relating to the events of 9/11 and some, mostly in English, dealing with the Middle East, Islam and Judaism. Next to a framed photograph of a handsome woman wearing a chador, an open book face down on the table bore the title 'The Rage and the Pride'. Also a number of photographic coffee table books, not only Helmut Newton, but also Mapplethorpe, David Hamilton and others, strewn over the shelves.

"You're certainly interested in Islam and the Middle East," he remarked, turning to her. "I know you've mentioned it a few times, but I see that it's much more than just a passing interest. Who is this woman Fallaci?"

He wasn't going to say anything about her taste in photography – not yet at least.

"Certainly," she replied, "we've never had a proper discussion on the subject. But it's something that I am really interested in and feel strongly about. Oriana Fallaci? You've not heard of her? Shame on you. She's an inspiration. But let's have dinner tonight and we can discuss it farther."

This by way of confirming their meeting that evening, in a manner which should not attract Lamai's attention.

"Fine, let's meet at my place for a drink at about nine."

Turning to Lamai, Sam said. "Don't worry, you're not expected to attend this political discussion."

Lamai showed every sign of relief.

After going out onto the balcony to admire the view, Leandro left. She accompanied him through the front door into the small lobby by the elevator and, out of sight of Lamai, pulled him towards her, pressing a silent kiss on his mouth, while her hand found his crotch. He looked into her laughing eyes and pressed her against the wall, his thigh deep between her legs. She pushed him away gently and without a word, went back into the flat and closed the door, leaving him in darkness to wait for the lift. Since their first meeting, Leandro had more than once had the impression that Sam was only too often just one step ahead.

Sam arrived punctually at nine. She breezed through the door, clearly with no intention of referring to the events of the morning. As far as he could see, she had not given it a second thought and apparently did not expect him to either.

He had spent part of the day going over their meeting in his head. That a lover might two-time him with another man he considered par for the course – however undesirable - in a city where predatory males abounded. This was however the first time that one of his lovers - at least as far as he knew - was also having an affair with another woman. He had obviously read about it in magazines, the phenomenon of 'bi' was certainly not new to him conceptually speaking, but this was the first time that he had knowingly become part of such a triangle.

The more he thought about it, the more he was forced to recognize that this might be the way the world was going. Or, more accurately, had gone, perhaps whilst he had not been watching too closely. By the early evening, a couple of whiskeys behind him, he had come to the conclusion - at least it seemed persuasive, if perhaps out of character - that, if this was the way Sam wanted to deal the cards, it might be rash to play the part of the jealous lover. She would certainly find separation easier than he.

"What'll you have to drink?"

After putting on some of her favourite Al Green, a CD which she had given him, she dropped into the armchair.

"I think some champagne is called for."

"You seem very pleased with yourself."

From behind her chair, he took her breasts in both hands. A combination of the whiskey and his reflections during the afternoon had led him to the conclusion that, with Sam, a frontal attack was likely to be the more promising strategy. She tilted her head back and kissed him, a long, penetrating kiss.

"So how about that champagne? I think you'll find I've earned it."

"Coming up!"

An ice bucket, a bottle of Chandon Extra Brut and a couple of filled glasses on the table between them, he sat down opposite her.

"I haven't seen you for too long," he began, almost as if they hadn't met that morning.

She threw him a quick glance as if to check that he really had decided to take the situation in his stride. His steady gaze reassured her.

"As you will soon discover, for various reasons, I felt it better not to be chasing around in the polo crowd and at the same time making time to see you. They're a tough bunch and, if I was going to play my part to the full, I thought it best to be completely available."

"I'll skip what you might mean by completely available. But a little call to tell me might not have come amiss."

"You're right, Leo. Sorry."

Although he thought that he detected a look of genuine contrition, he wondered whether this was really the only reason Sam had been out of touch for so long. From the episode that morning, it was likely that her behaviour might be dictated by all manner of different priorities, which would vary from day to day.

She stretched out her glass and he refilled it. She leaned back in her chair.

"Here goes. It didn't take me long to get in touch again with Alvaro, my ex-boyfriend, when I got back from Europe. I got myself invited to a party by a mutual friend and from there, one party led to another. In November anyway, the polo scene is very active with all the preliminary games leading up to the Argentine final in the first week of December. I met his Italian girlfriend, and made a point of ensuring that she was on my side. Not so easy with such a jealous lady from Milan, but anyway, you know me, we became fast friends. Or at least, as much of a friend as that kind of lady will tolerate."

Sam made a grimace to convey what she really thought of the Italian.

"The main thing was that she should be relaxed about my moving in the same circles. Around about the tenth of November, word began to go around that a very large, wild party was being planned by one of the English players out in Pilar. A lot of them have bought houses out there, it's quite a Brit community, with a lot of money and a pretty crazy lifestyle. As you know, they seem to have an unlimited capacity for drink. Sadly, they sometimes get so drunk that they fail to perform - whether on the playing field or in bed! Luckily you don't seem to have inherited that particular Anglo-Saxon gene!"

She laughed, before continuing.

"Anyway, I got myself invited to this party three nights ago, last Saturday, that's the seventeenth. Everyone was there, obviously all the locals, but also people from Colombia, Yanks, Swiss, French and Italians. Even a sprinkling of Chinese and Arabs. The alcohol and everything else flowed. What was interesting was that there were also quite a lot of Argentines who had nothing to do with polo, even one or two politicians. And then there were the groupies - from all over, certainly some of them whores, paid for by the Colombians or possibly the Chinese. Pretty high-class most of them, flown in from Paris or London - even from Moscow, they're some of the prettiest of the lot these days. I was with a guy called Marcelo, who breeds polo ponies in the province of Buenos Aires. He's chased me in the past and clearly hadn't given up. Don't worry! For a start, he wouldn't begin to understand a situation such as Lamai."

She watched his reaction.

"Until this morning, I didn't think I would either. But as you predicted, I seem to - or have to - adapt fast."

"I didn't doubt it for a minute."

She smiled before continuing. "Anyway, the party started around one in the morning, everybody was already pretty gone by then. It's a big house, with lots of rooms, some bungalows outside, a vast pool. Everything you need to make people happy on a night like that. If I was going to be of any use, I had to drink less than the rest and find a way not to inhale!"

She suddenly stopped.

"What about Eduardo? Shouldn't he be here?"

"I thought we'd spend the evening just the two of us. I'll pass on anything of interest to him when we next meet. As you know, we're trying to avoid being seen together too often."

"Of course."

She sensed the unspoken reason for Eduardo not having been invited.

"Anyway, by around three, Marcelo had collapsed, so I wandered around a bit on my own. I found a quiet corner out on the veranda. After a few minutes, I felt that someone was standing watching me behind my settee. A tall blonde, round about forty-five I would guess, beautifully sculpted features and a hell of a body. Might have been a facelift, but if so, must have been a disciple of Pitanguy, the Brazilian wizard. Hard to tell whether she was one of the pros or with someone. I thought I'd seen her earlier in the evening with a small guy, bit older than her, but he seemed to have disappeared. She was also pretty extravagantly dressed, with shiny black jodhpurs, knee-high black boots with ten centimetre heels, a large *faja* studded with all kinds of silver coins, obviously an antique piece, expensive. Anyway, she stood there for a while, and seemed to be studying me. I ignored her and so after a while, she moved away. I saw her again a couple of times later in the party and every time, she was looking at me. To be frank, she scared me a little, sent me some pretty strong vibes. Round about five in the morning, a lot of people had disappeared, presumably round the house. At some point, I came across Alvaro with his Italian girl, trying to find some champagne. Marcelo having disappeared, he offered me a lift back into town. Somehow, in spite of the fact that he'd had far too much to drink, we made it back and decided to get an early breakfast at La Biela. Over coffee, I asked him about this lady. It turned out that he didn't know much about her, but his Italian cow, Antonella, did. According to Antonella - and she got it from some of the other girls, polo regulars - this woman doesn't live in Argentina. She thought someone had mentioned Switzerland. She regularly turns up on the polo circuit in Argentina, but also in such places as St. Moritz, for the winter matches on snow in February, and in France and England in the summer. She's some kind of hooker, allegedly very expensive and - so she'd heard - very 'complicated'. Specialises in very - but very - wealthy partners, company presidents, sheikhs, that kind of thing. Antonella was told that she may be Latin American, apparently speaks impeccable *porteño*."

"Eduardo only has a few seconds of closed-circuit TV of the woman who came into the hotel with the victim. My guess is, it may not be enough for you to match it, but let's see if we can get it over here. One piece which does fit with what we have is the possible Swiss connection. What happens now in terms of parties? Are you likely to disappear again? Though, if she is the killer, the last thing we would want is for you to get too close to her and end up like the Englishwoman." Seeing Sam's smile, he went on. "I mean that seriously, Sam, Lady X is not to be played with lightly."

"Well, there's another party with rather the same crowd at the end of the month, on the Saturday. We're in the middle of the play-offs between now and the end of the first week in December. It would be strange if I were suddenly to disappear. To be frank, unless she's also in the kidnapping business, I should be able to avoid her clutches."

"Let me think about it. We should also discuss it with Eduardo."

"And you haven't even congratulated me!" Sam said, putting on a petulant look.

"Shit! Sorry! Sam, you've done a great job so far and you more than deserve your champagne," he said, filling her glass again. As he bent across her, her right hand swiftly moved under his belt. He gasped.

"If you think you can get away with just a few glasses of champagne, that's frankly not good enough," she murmured, her tone almost threatening.

In the love-making that followed, as passionate and unconventional as any night they had spent together, Leandro found himself wondering momentarily whether the newfound knowledge of Sam's bisexuality wasn't driving him on to greater heights, as if in some way he was seeking to convince her... although of what, he was not very sure. As he lay in the darkness, Sam finally sleeping by his side, he wondered whether he was driven by jealousy of Lamai. Possibly. He sensed a certain stimulus at the thought of this exotic rival.

By the next evening, using the letterbox in Elena's block of flats, which they had set up as a way of innocently exchanging messages and objects in a manner which avoided meetings, Leandro had obtained an extract of the CCTV footage. Sam came round to have a look.

"To be frank, it's almost impossible to tell. The woman I saw at the party was a blonde, though the platinum sheen in your video actually looks more like a wig than anything natural. In terms of the figure, and the height, judging by the lift door and the exit door, they're about right. However...." She paused. "Can we freeze frames of her by the lift?"

She moved the frames forward one by one and amplified one or two on the screen.

"The profile doesn't seem to match. This woman in the lift has a very flat profile and, from what you can see, a very large mouth and slit eyes. That's what catches your attention most. That's not however the image I have of Lady X at the party."

"Well, it's probably as much as we can get out of it. Other than you're going to another party and meeting her again, I don't see how we can take this any farther," Leo said, his tone betraying a certain disappointment. "What do you think?"

"I gave it some thought today. I can't see any reason not to go to the next party, in about ten days' time. In fact, Marcelo already rang me, very apologetic for having crashed out at the last one. I suspect he'll be much more protective this time, which should be useful and ensure I don't get mixed up in anything too dangerous - other than his driving."

"Okay, she may not even be there anyway."

Although he had finally given in to Sam going to the party in the hope of meeting Lady X again, he was now in fact even more concerned for her safety. Was this in some way linked to his discovery that her sexual inclinations were more unconventional than he had expected? Her bisexuality meant that, given the fact that the murder at L'Hôtel was apparently the product of a lesbian relationship, Sam now appeared more vulnerable. However much more complicated and violent Lady X might be than the norm, he fervently hoped that the next step in the search for the murderess would not appear to Sam as yet another opportunity for adventure. There were times when he cursed that man Wilde!

December 2007

4 December 2007

Sam only reappeared two days after the party. As before, she had succeeded in staying out of contact and he did not this time feel like dropping in unannounced. A text message suggested that they meet for lunch at Sotto Voce, a fashionable Italian restaurant on Avenida Libertador. From the choice of venue, Leandro placed a bet with himself that she would be bringing some interesting news and wished to be rewarded with a good, expensive, meal. He was to win his bet.

She had exchanged her customary boots and trousers for a tightly fitting skirt and pale rose-coloured blouse. She looked like a top of the range business executive out to impress the chairman. Suspecting something of the sort, he had gone to the trouble of putting on one of his better blazers and even managing a tie. She acknowledged the effort with an appreciative smile and nod of the head, but could not resist adjusting the knot of his tie.

As she sat down next to Leandro, she turned to the *maitre d'*, who was clearly delighted to be given the opportunity to spread Sam's napkin across her lap, and promptly ordered a couple of glasses of champagne.

"Of course, Señora, right away!"

She did not bother to correct him as to her marital status.

"So what have you got to tell me? Fuck it, I'm more scared than curious."

She was looking far too pleased with herself, like a cat over the proverbial bowl of cream. He dreaded to think what she'd got herself into.

She was clearly determined to maximise the impact of her news and, ignoring his question, sought his advice as to which delicious pasta she should choose and, with a frontal assault on his macho territory, also made the choice of wine, an expensive merlot from the Catena vineyards. The champagne duly arrived, and, lifting her glass and looking him in the eye, she said. "Well now, I don't know whether to frighten you straightaway or just leave you suffering until the coffee."

"For Christ sake, Sam. All you're doing is scaring the shit out of me! And wrecking my appetite."

"Yes, I can see that and it's great. Maybe with the main course...."

Leandro sighed.

"Okay have it your way. Try putting some olive oil on this bread, it's delicious. But then, you would know that." He changed the subject.

During the *antipasti*, she asked him to tell her who he knew in the room and whether he had any scandal or other information about them. Looking around, he spotted a dapper, middle-aged banker, who to his certain knowledge had been involved in more than one major piece of fraudulent business during the Menem presidency, at the time of the later privatisation deals.

"It clearly hasn't done his reputation any harm, judging by the fact that he's lunching with one of the current directors of the Central Bank. Nasty piece of work he is, too. And over there, on that table, the little fair-haired guy, used to run a small finance company specialising in buying up profitable businesses, selling off the best parts at a profit and leaving the banks holding the baby. Not short of a buck or two, as a result."

He briefly explained how these things were done.

"Nice business, finance in Argentina," she commented. "One day, I'll introduce you to my father. Listening to him, you'll be able to add a few more stories of that kind to your treasury."

The *farfalle a l'arrabiata* finally arrived for her. He had ordered a *picata milanese*.

"That looks delicious," she commented, pushing her plate in his direction to beg a sample.

"Yes, it's very hard to get veal in Argentina, this is one of the few places. But you also made an excellent choice. Now for Christ's sake, stop stealing my food! Are you going to tell me what happened? The tension is beginning to get seriously in the way of my appetite."

She laughed.

"Well, if we're sitting here, it's obviously a sign that my party wasn't wasted. Just pour me some more wine, please."

Raising his eyes to heaven in exasperation, he filled her glass.

Finally, having demolished half her *farfalle*, she began to describe the evening two nights previously.

She had arrived with Marcelo in his new Audi, the fruit of a profitable summer polo season in Europe, when the party was already well underway.

"Very much the same crowd as on the previous occasion. For the first hour or so, I looked in vain for Lady X or for the small, slightly older man who appeared to be accompanying her at the previous party. However, around about three am, with the party now spread out across various drawing rooms, I saw her arrive, this time apparently alone."

Sam and Marcelo had continued dancing, but at some point, he had got caught up with a bunch of polo players in a long discussion about the upcoming finals. Sam, not being very interested in the subject, had drifted away, found herself some more champagne and settled on a small couch in one of the side rooms to which a few couples had retired, away from the deafening loudspeakers and flashing lights. She was talking to a girl in a group just behind her when she sensed someone joining her on the sofa.

"I turned and found myself looking directly into the eyes of Lady X. Her eyes are beautiful, very dark blue-grey, cold at times, but also capable of a lot of softness," she continued.

"That kind of remark is really scary coming from you."

"A really handsome woman, a broad face with high cheekbones and good bone structure - very athletic, expensively dressed. Exudes sex! Oh, and by the way - you'll love this – spectacular tits!"

The woman, who introduced herself as Carla, had made some comment about the noise and the heat of the dance floor. Concealing any initial surprise, Sam had responded by moving over on the sofa and giving her name. In the usual Argentine fashion, they had exchanged a kiss on the cheek.

"Again, she was pretty provocatively dressed. Presumably, at her age and - if what Antonella told me is correct - in her profession, she probably has to be. She was wearing a pair of beautifully cut soft black leather *bombachas*, tight at the ankle, inserted into low ankle boots with very high heels, and a plain Thai silk golden yellow blouse open to the waist, pinned over her breasts with a large golden brooch in the shape of a riding crop. More expensive gold jewellery as well. I guess the riding crop is some kind of marketing."

"Not a detail missed. Typical women!" Leandro interrupted her. "You don't usually dress like a maid, so what were you wearing? I'll bet you chose something to see if it would attract her."

Sam smiled. "You bet! In fact, I could have been part of Lady X's team - whatever the sport may be that she plays."

"Jesus, Sam, you really sail close to the wind."

"And don't tell me you don't like it that way."

Shortly after the introductions, a young man, black haired with a small goatee beard and sharp aquiline features, had joined Carla, bringing her a whiskey on the rocks. It turned out that he was from Jordan. Sam and he had briefly exchanged the traditional Arabic greeting. *"As-Salāmu 'Alaykum." "Wa alaikum salam."* This had naturally provoked the curiosity of Carla. Sam had continued the conversation in Arabic for a few minutes. Tawfiq, the young Arab, pulled up an armchair and joined them.

"The three of us talked about polo, about Argentina, the usual. Obviously, I was trying to see if anything that Carla said could in any way suggest or confirm that she really was Lady X. About the only thing that in any way fits is the fact that at some point she let drop, firstly, that she lives in Switzerland, and, secondly, that she had been here in Argentina in July. I can't say that sitting opposite her for half an hour in any way provided a match with the image of the woman in the lift.

From the way she treated Tawfiq and the way he responded, I would certainly think that she is in the line of work suggested by Antonella. And I suspect that Tawfiq has little hesitation in getting his money's worth. From something she said, it looks as though the expensive Breguet watch she was wearing was a recent courtesy of her Arab friend. No doubt peanuts for him. Anyway, by the end of our little chat, I had Tawfiq's phone number and e-mail, should I ever be at a loss in Jordan or the Gulf, and I had her e-mail and a Swiss cell phone in case I was passing through. And she now has my cell phone number."

Sam looked triumphantly at Leandro.

"So there, I think I earned this lunch. What do you think?"

Leandro shook his head, though finding it hard to conceal a grin. He thought for a moment before replying.

"No-one could say anything other than 'mission accomplished', as far as hooking up - if you'll excuse the expression - with Lady X is concerned ... if Carla is Lady X. As you say, a couple of things fit, but we're some way from what Eduardo might call a positive identification. Presumably, you also have a surname for Carla? That might allow Eduardo to do a little discreet research."

"Bodmer," Sam replied.

"Fine. I'll pass that on to him. So is this Madame Carla sticking around for the finals next weekend?"

"Tawfiq said that he would be staying and he looked across at her. She seemed to confirm it. She also mentioned something about Punta del Este, though it wasn't very clear to me when she was planning to be there. And it didn't sound as though Tawfiq was going with her."

Leandro toyed with his *tiramisu*, trying to think through more precisely what progress had been made.

Carla might be Lady X, but equally she might just be an expensive hooker, who happened to move in the same circles as the Englishwoman murdered in the hotel. He was worried by what, given the manner in which Sam had described their meeting, looked like Carla taking the initiative to get alongside Sam. A lot depended upon how much one believed that she was Lady X. Was she somehow connected with the people who had attacked Eduardo, was the Swiss connection the one suggested by Sarmiento, was there somewhere also a link to the murder of Sosa? Finally, was someone pulling the strings behind all this? If all this was the case, Sam might well have enabled them to get closer to Lady X. More worryingly, it seemed to have allowed Lady X, and anyone who was behind her, to get closer to them. So these people – whoever they were - could be pulling the strings, not Eduardo and Leandro. And if that was not enough, Sam was now also likely to be in far greater danger than he had imagined possible.

He kicked himself inwardly for having allowed this to happen. He was in two minds about presenting this analysis to Sam at this stage. But, to be fair to Sam, he felt that he had little choice. She heard him out in silence.

"So what's the next step?" she finally asked.

"Not sure..." He paused. "I'm not sure that we have anything firm to go on to link Carla with the hotel murder, however superficially she might fit the description. What's your impression? Was it pure coincidence that she sat down next to you?"

"Far from it, the way she looked at me didn't fit with someone who was just feeling a bit hot and sweaty on the dance floor. Anyway, my guess is she never sweats. For some reason, I seem to interest her. Her parting kiss was more than a mere formality."

"God help us! This is moving far too fast and potentially in a very dangerous direction."

"I don't agree. In practice, I can set the pace of this pretty much as I like. She may have my cell phone, but that's not quite the same as telling me what to do and when. If we want to slow it down, I can always be otherwise engaged."

She paused and stretched her hand towards him under the table to caress his crotch.

"In fact, I've every intention of being otherwise engaged. And the sooner the better. Let's get the bill."

Back at his flat, as he was putting some slow jazz on the CD player, she returned to their lunchtime conversation.

"The little guy you pointed out at the other table, the one who bought and sold companies. What was the technical term you used?"

"Asset stripping. Why?"

"Well, I've brought the assets. I've done my share. Now you do your bit."

She twirled in front of him.

He didn't need a second invitation.

To the lingering notes of Ben Webster and Coleman Hawkins in 'Prisoner of Love', she proceeded to give him a striptease act which - for a moment - had him wondering whether she might not have been able to fit in a semester at the Actors Studio before auditioning for something in Pigalle. Not that he had ever been there. Or was this some kind of dress rehearsal for Carla?

10 December 2007

A week later, the finals of the Argentine Polo Open on the previous Saturday had brought the predictable victory of Ellerstina, fielding the world number one Cambiaso, over La Dolfina, for the third time in a row. Sam said she would be attending with Marcelo. Leandro watched it on television in his flat. He paid close attention when the cameras panned across the elegantly populated stands, in the hope of spotting Lady X.... or more likely, Sam. By the end of the match, 16 – 15, he had worked his way through a reasonable amount of Scotch, but could not claim to have seen either of the women he was looking for. Given the post-final parties, Sam only made an appearance on his cell phone two days later.

"Tawfiq was there, but no sign of Carla," she opened, rather tersely. "He said something about her having left Buenos Aires a couple of days earlier. Didn't tell me where she went and, frankly, it didn't seem appropriate for me to press him too hard. Anyway, he'd found a replacement in the form of a voluptuous Russian, a good ten years younger than Carla, and even more dangerous looking.... if that's possible. Where do they find these girls?"

Skipping her last question, he replied, "Ah well, perhaps safer that way," not fully concealing a hint of disappointment.

She picked it up immediately.

"You see, you do want me to try and find her. I can tell from your tone of voice."

"The real problem is that, even if we were to be able to satisfy ourselves that Carla is Lady X, how much farther would that take us? As you know, my first priority is to protect Eduardo. Catching Lady X would no doubt solve that one. Carla only interests me in that context." He ignored her sarcastic laugh at this point. "It's what surrounds Carla - if indeed it does - and how this might help us to identify whoever attacked Eduardo. Somehow, it doesn't seem likely to be Lady X sending in the thugs to beat him up. It's got to be something - or someone - else."

"Well, I'm not sure that I can throw much light on that," she replied, her tone slightly impatient, as if to suggest that all this rationalisation was not her prime concern. She changed the subject. "By the way, my father is renting our place in Punta del Este sometime in January and he's asked me to go over next week and see about setting it up. We usually spend Christmas and New Year there as well. What are your plans? I'm not going to sit on a beach for six weeks by myself. So if you're not there...."

She allowed Leandro to draw his own conclusions.

Leandro wondered whether Lamai might not be part of the scene as well, but thought better of asking.

"To be frank, I'm not a great fan of Punta, myself. However, if you're there, that's different. I'll probably be working up until about the twentieth. Give me a few days, I'll organise something. What part of Punta is your house?"

"It's beyond La Barra on the way to Jose Ignacio. It's relatively secluded, up an unmade track into the pinewoods. Good view of the sea, though. My father, being the workaholic he is, tends to come and go only at the weekends, so I'll be in residence. Of course, it's by invitation only, no exceptions."

"Of course."

"Let's talk later in the week, I'll be getting over there in a couple of days. My cell phone obviously works over there as well. Ciao!"

The phone went dead. Leandro shook his head. This was getting serious, what with his holidays and his private life now being organised by someone just a little bit older than his daughter. On further reflection, however, he was forced to confess that he secretly quite enjoyed the feeling.

He turned back to the commentary he was writing. Although Cristina Fernandez de Kirchner was only formally taking over from her husband as Argentina's fifty-second President, at that very moment, it was not too early to put down some preliminary thoughts as to how she might perform.

CENTRO

INVESTIGACIÓN

ECONÓMICA

December 2007: POLITICAL COMMENTARY

The consecration in power this month of President Cristina Kirchner, the wife of outgoing president Nestor Kirchner, is likely to provide some indications of the continuity of what is being presented as a winning formula. Any concerns which independent observers may have about the probable level of inflation this year, which many see in the region of 25% at least - when the official, government figure is nearer half that - or about the almost total lack of productive investment, leading to potential bottlenecks in the production cycle - all these realities are unlikely to get a look in. Nor are more troubling signs of the way in which the Kirchners see the exercise of power, most recently exemplified by the unresolved scandal of the $800,000 in the Venezuelan suitcase, likely to keep anyone in the Government awake at night.

Picking a fight with the US, by trashing its President, may go down well with certain nationalists and xenophobes – of which Argentina has never had a shortage – but looks like a risky strategy in a world of economic and political interdependence. The Monroe Doctrine may no longer apply in the way it did 150 years ago, but that's not to say that the White House doesn't have the last word when it comes to the World Bank or similar institutions lending to Argentina.

Although rapid growth and a more satisfied consumer may lie at the heart of the government's current economic strategy, there are plenty of signs that things may be slowing. The increased cost

of borrowing and the ever-growing weight of taxes are bound soon to make an impact. The current government's appetite for export duties, alongside the tax levied on bank cheques and social security contributions, one of the principal sources of their funding, will ultimately rebound. The absence of capital investment, not only at the level of inward foreign investment, but even locally, will certainly lead to a worsening of the energy crisis and the saturation of what installed capacity already exists. An increase in inflation, the other side of the current model, although hotly denied and disguised by the government through various tricks, is nevertheless clearly visible at the level of the provincial statistics, as well as in figures produced by independent economic observers. The figures for this year 2007 range anywhere between 25% and 28%, in line with the target we originally announced over six months ago. At these levels, it becomes a vicious spiral. High consumer spending will also have an effect on the balance of trade, as local production bottlenecks are compensated by growing imports. As a result, next year's trade balance could be a mere 50% of the figure expected for this year.

Of all this, the present government appears blissfully unaware, expounding the virtues of "EL MODELO" to all those who care to listen, though the audience, at least outside Argentina, seems to be leaving the conference hall.

He paused and took another sip from the whiskey glass. This would have to keep the clients happy over Christmas.

Since they were splitting forces, with Eduardo remaining in Buenos Aires, the two men agreed to meet at Elena's flat for a final stocktaking before Leandro left for Uruguay.

Eduardo had taken virtually no formal steps in the murder case since September. The sighting of someone possibly following him, although not repeated as far as he could tell, suggested that his room for

215

manoeuvre remained limited. They must assume that any traceable attempt by Eduardo to follow up leads should be avoided at all costs. For his Skype communications with Sarmiento, Eduardo had now purchased a small laptop, which he kept carefully hidden outside his flat, contacting Sarmiento from different cafes or bars with Wi-Fi in which he could find a quiet corner. He not only kept communications to a minimum and as short as possible, but only made contact once he had taken precautions to ensure that he was not being followed. He had taken Florencia partly into his confidence on the assumption that any observer, seeing him using his laptop in the company of his girlfriend, would more likely ascribe innocent motives to what he was doing.

All in all, only Sam appeared to have the freedom of action necessary to make progress.

"Though I don't disagree with you, you've got to understand that she might pay a very high price for that. From now on, she has to know as much as we do, so that she can fully assess the risks she's taking. The only thing that we should, perhaps, hide from her is the nature of the dialogue with Sarmiento. Whereas she needs to know the facts, perhaps she doesn't need to know how we came by them."

Eduardo agreed.

"The most important items of information that we're still missing, and without which, to be frank, we're just wasting our time, strike me as the following. Is Carla Lady X, what is her connection to someone high up in government running a blackmail operation, and who is that person? If we don't think Sam can get the answers to these questions, I believe you, uncle, have to stop her going any farther."

"That may be easier said than done!" Leandro commented with a wry smile.

They agreed to keep in touch via Elena as often as either saw necessary. Leandro gave his godson a hug as they parted, catching Eduardo by surprise with its warmth. Might the woman Sam be having a good effect right across his godfather's emotional spectrum?

20 December 2007

Although Leandro and Sam had exchanged phone calls every two or three days, it wasn't until just before Christmas that Leandro was able to find a seat on the Buenos Aires - Punta del Este direct flight. The small plane taxied to the white terminal building. He waved to Sam waiting for him on the other side of the perimeter fence. Collecting his suitcase, he emerged onto the hot tarmac of the parking area. She was looking extremely bronzed and as usual, perfectly turned out, in a pair of dark coffee brown shorts, a white linen safari-style shirt and Roman gladiator sandals. More at home in St. Tropez perhaps than Uruguay. He dropped his computer and suitcase on the backseat of the little white Peugeot. Carving her way unhesitatingly round the outside of the queue at the exit to the parking area, she slid in under the nose of a large Mercedes with darkened windows and fed in her parking ticket. The irate blast of a German horn was greeted with a cheery wave out of the window.

"You really know how to make friends," Leandro commented dryly.

"He would do exactly the same to me, given half a chance."

Her attitude to driving was totally in character. Amply above the speed limit most of the time, although never suicidal, she twisted and turned along the back roads, expertly using the gearbox and – with the windows down and the slipstream playing in her hair - clearly enjoying the rasp of the exhaust. He loved her expression of concentration, the fluidity of her handling of the gearstick, the occasional smile she threw him to convey her enjoyment. He had missed her, badly.

Lined with majestic eucalyptus trees, the route she had taken provided a shortcut to avoid the centre of Punta del Este, leading northeast to the back of the low hills which ran parallel to the shore on the Atlantic coast, with its string of increasingly overbuilt villages stretching up towards the Brazilian border.

"There's still time for you to wash off the slime of Buenos Aires in the sea, if you like," she threw at him with a sideways glance.

"Thanks. I didn't think I smelled that bad. A good drink in a bar looking towards the sun setting behind Punta del Este will be ample remedy this evening, followed by a good meal at your expense, given the hard work I've been putting in."

From the back roads, she emerged onto the main coast road at the southern entrance to La Barra, fortunately going in the opposite direction to what was already an unbroken queue of cars leaving the beaches and heading back south towards Punta. Leandro tried to recapture his memories of La Barra some twenty years earlier, when its simple little houses only stood a couple of rows deep on either side of the main road. This evening, as far as the eye could see, serried ranks of little white Mediterranean-style houses stretched towards the tree-lined hills behind what had once upon a time been a fisherman's village. The number of houses had doubled in the last ten years.

For about two months of the year, this coastline was invaded by thousands of Argentines, now joined by Brazilians, for whom late December and January in Punta del Este constituted the only socially acceptable annual holiday. Argentines had been investing here for over half a century, so much so that it had often been said that if the Argentine economy caught a cold, Uruguay - and Punta del Este in particular - would catch pneumonia. Land prices had spiralled, bringing rapid and rich rewards to the local population, which now lived off the uncritical spending habits of the Buenos Aires upper and middle classes. With little planning control, the Argentines - and now the Brazilians - were throwing up lavish holiday homes, often characterised by massive picture windows providing a surprisingly intimate view of their owners as they sipped their *caipirinhas* in the evening. Beaches and roads had become increasingly congested and the sound of traffic hardly ever let up, as teenagers - as well as their parents - streamed back and forth from the nightclubs from two in the morning until breakfast.

Parking the car on the main street and hiding his suitcase under a towel, they made their way down a side road to one of the fashionable bars near the edge of the sea.

With a couple of strong but not too sweet *mojitos* on the low table in front of them, she settled herself close to him on the comfortable white canvas settee, as they watched the red ball of the sun dipping into the sea beyond the skyscrapers of Punta.

"So, is the house set up? When's your father arriving? You've clearly been taking advantage of the empty beaches before the hordes arrive. And by the feel of it, you may even have lost some weight," his hand feeling its way around her waist and up below her breasts.

Without replying, she produced a couple of photographs from her small bamboo and black canvas handbag, which she handed to Leandro with the kind of conspiratorial smile, which he had by now come to associate with yet another high risk initiative.

One of the photographs showed Sam in a dark pink bikini perched on a bar stool, apparently in some beachside restaurant or club. The stool behind her was occupied by another woman, somewhat older, her bronzed hourglass body also wedged in a diminutive bikini, her face in profile framed by a mass of ash-blonde hair. The second photograph showed the two of them again, reclining on beach lounge divans, a small table with drinks between them, this time with both of them looking into the camera, eyes hidden by massive dark glasses. The statuesque proportions of Sam's companion were not lost on Leandro.

Leandro felt a shiver in spite of the warmth of the evening. Sam grinned.

"Thought you'd like that!"

"If it's who I think it is, I don't like it at all."

"It's exactly who you think it is," she replied simply.

"Fuck it, Sam, what *are* you playing at? If this is the killer, you're mad. And if it's not, I'm really not sure how to read the photographs. Go ahead, give me the story. But first I need another *mojito*," and he signalled to the passing waiter to bring two more.

Sam had been in Punta del Este for little more than a week when Carla had rung her.

"She claims to have caught a glimpse of me on the beach the day before, but the company she was in didn't allow her to come across straightaway. She's staying in a house about halfway between Manantiales and Jose Ignacio, where she's apparently been since the beginning of the month. We agreed to meet for lunch the following day by the poolside at La Posta del Cangrejo, you know, up the road. It's very fashionable."

Carla had turned up in a silver Mercedes convertible, one of the latest small SLK models. She was by herself and allegedly lonely, given the fact that the main body of visitors would not arrive until just before Christmas. She let drop that she had, in the interval, made a very brief round-trip to Switzerland, but was now expecting to stay into the middle of January. Sam's idle conversation had not served to establish the ownership of the house, nor indeed what or who was keeping Carla in Uruguay.

"At the end of lunch, she took a phone call, some forgotten engagement. She suggested that if I had nothing better to do, I should come to her house when I felt like it. She sold me on its seawater horizon pool, concealed from any neighbours, with a beautiful view out towards the Atlantic. I didn't want to appear too eager, so I promised to try and get there a couple of days later. Actually, I was dying to get there."

Leandro shot her a glance.

A further phone call two days later had led to an invitation to a late lunch and, following Carla's germanically precise instructions, Sam had parked the Peugeot in among the pine trees in front of a house surrounded by a pale ochre painted wall topped with several strands of unattractive looking razor wire. Closed circuit cameras strategically placed at each corner and a couple of aggressive black Dobermans added to the impression that uninvited guests might not be so welcome. A ring on the doorbell brought Sam face to face with a maid dressed in a very short black skirt, white starched blouse and surprisingly high heels.

"From the way she spoke, I would guess that she was Bolivian or even possibly Peruvian. But she was tall, her crew-cut hair dyed blonde, slightly punk. Much more self-assured than what you usually find in the way of maids in this part of the world. Not to mention her figure! She led me through a hall, the walls covered with fearsome 1930s-style German expressionist painting, all tortured faces and bodies."

"Since when have you become an expert on German Expressionism, whatever that is?"

"You always underestimate me," she replied acidly. "And in so doing only reveal the extent of your ignorance, your total lack of culture!"

Leandro had no reply.

Crossing a wide sitting room with large sliding glass doors, she had found Carla virtually naked, face down on the edge of the pool, her powerful tanned physique gleaming with sun oil.

"She must do a lot of bodybuilding to get a shape like that. Sun oil and a little black leather Brazilian thong, all she was wearing! Pretty impressive!"

She watched his reaction.

"Listening now, are we? Men are so predictable. It gets better. By the end of it, you're going to be going to be pleading with me to introduce you."

Leandro made a gesture as if to indicate that nothing could be farther from his mind.

Carla had pointed Sam in the direction of a small blue and white striped tent off to the side of the pool, in which to change. On emerging in her diminutive Brazilian bikini, she had been greeted by the maid holding a perfumed bottle of sun oil, which she silently offered to apply. Having decided that her bikini top was distinctly overdressed, Sam had accepted, submitting her body to the not unintrusive hands of Carla's exotic assistant, after which she found herself lying next to Carla on the teak deck beside the pool.

"Just let your imagination wander, Señor Flemming."

After a light lunch served by the maid, Carla had taken her on a guided tour of the house.

"Very modern, two very large bedrooms on either side of the drawing - dining room on the upper ground floor, same level as the swimming pool. You go down some interior steps - everything in pale grey marble, cool like the mistress, always assuming it's actually her house. I'll get to that later. Downstairs, servants' quarters, very modern kitchen, then on the other side, a large gymnasium and sauna, filled with various machines – serious American equipment - and mirrors all round, even on the ceiling. Floor of glistening black marble this time, but covered with lots of black shiny padded vinyl mats. She apparently spends a lot of time in there. You can see the result. Given the slope, the house seems to be built into the side of the hill. There seem to be other rooms at the back."

"Do you think it's her place?"

"Hard to tell. She implied that it belonged to a close friend and that she had constant access to it, whenever she wanted. I don't think she rents it, no sign of any suitcases standing around, which might indicate that she has a wardrobe there as well. From her appearance and from the way they spoke to each other, the Bolivian is her personal maid, probably accompanies her everywhere. At one point, I even thought that she said something to the maid in what sounded like German to me. Oh, and by the way, there was a pretty tough looking – although handsome - guy wandering around outside the property when I left."

Late in the afternoon, Tawfiq had rung Carla's house and they had agreed to meet for dinner at one of the better fish restaurants in downtown Punta del Este overlooking the yacht basin. At dinner, Tawfiq had been accompanied by a handsome Saudi lawyer, apparently in Uruguay to prospect real estate opportunities on behalf of a minor member of the Saudi royal family. The evening had ended at around four in the morning at one of the nightclubs along the coast.

Leandro listened in silence, trying not to give any hint of his mild irritation that all this had been going on while he sat in Buenos Aires, bent over his computer. Sam was not the kind of girl who would easily tolerate any attempt to put down boundaries on her behaviour. To his surprise, as if reading his thoughts, she put her arm around his neck and planted a long kiss full on his mouth, as if sensing his momentary insecurity.

"So, that's the story so far. All this formal reporting to the boss gives me an appetite. Where are we going?"

After the drinks, they walked across the road to a small bistro which, since the crowds had still not arrived, was empty and quiet. Over a dinner of properly grilled fresh fish, Leandro attempted to map out some kind of strategy going forward.

"Let's try and see where all this is going. Assuming that Carla is Lady X, you've obviously done a fantastic job in getting alongside her, though frankly, it scares the shit out of me. I'm sure that in any normal situation you can look after yourself, you're a big girl now, but this is far from a normal situation. We have every reason to believe that Lady X - call her Carla – may have actually murdered someone. For all we know, the Englishwoman may not even have been the first. One thing that struck Eduardo was the confidence - even nonchalance - with which Lady X left the hotel, whilst her girlfriend lay upstairs, suffocating to death. So Carla isn't squeamish. That's one thing. The other, and that's much more difficult to assess, is how Carla might be connected with people in high places in the Argentine government."

Seeing Sam's raised eyebrow at this last remark, he went on. "Sorry. It's time I let you into a little bit more information."

Leandro told Sam about the existence of their informer, though in a manner to disguise as far as possible how the connection had been made. He summarised the exchange of messages with Eduardo, his own visit to Sosa and the latter's murder within hours of his visit. Without going into much detail, he explained the existence of the library of torture films and mentioned the case of the murder of Suarez, which Eduardo had still not been able to tie in completely with all the rest.

She listened closely, asking only a few questions about the film library. Although the events under the military dictatorship were virtually over when she was a small child, like for many Argentines, this was an episode in recent history which instilled a high level of anxiety, alongside a certain morbid curiosity. The sudden emptiness which she sensed in the pit of her stomach was brought on by the realization that seemingly ordinary Argentine men - and the occasional woman - the kind you might meet at a barbecue or on the beach, had at one moment in their lives, and on an unparalleled scale, indulged in torture, rape, murder, as well as the deliberate abduction of children. And all this ostensibly in the name of anti-subversion, the protection of the state, with the less than silent blessing of the Argentine Catholic Church. As she grew older, she had come to realize that, below all the charm of the Argentine character, there seemed to run a fault line which was hard to explain and which, given the right circumstances, could come to the surface.

"I'm not a fan of some of the people in the Madres de la Plaza de Mayo, but one can't help admiring what they've been able to do, to bring some of these people to justice," she said softly.

"If it's something that interests you, we can talk about it someday."

"It certainly is. It's one of the great contradictions of the Argentine personality, which never ceases to amaze and infuriate me."

She stopped for a minute and frowned. "Not sure whether it might not have been nice to know some of this before you set me off on the trail of Lady X."

Seeing the expression of embarrassment which her remark had provoked, she leaned across the table, took one of his hands in hers and tenderly kissed the inside of his palm.

"Make you feel bad, Leo, don't I? What a look of guilt! Don't worry, I won't let you forget this in a hurry! I'll find a way to send the bill."

Leandro remained silent.

"How do you think Carla connects with this business of torture and the military?" she went on.

"Frankly, at this stage we don't know. She might have been involved in some way and cleared out of Argentina when the military were thrown out in 1983. If she's Lady X, it might explain where she picked up some of her murderous habits. How old would you say she is?"

"Mid or late forties, though she has a very good skin, amazing figure and is extremely fit, so I suppose she could even be a little older."

"That would suggest that she would have been in her early twenties at the time of the military. Offhand, I can't remember how much women were actually involved in the tortures - at least, on the other side from the victims."

Leandro paused.

"But it's something to look into. No doubt, Eduardo can provide some information. Come to think of it, there does appear to be a woman somewhere in the background in the film I saw. I wonder... I suppose it's possible. That would be a pretty scary connection."

Leandro paused again to fill their glasses, watching the expression on Sam's face.

"Does all this change things for you, Sam? Nobody could blame you if it did."

She sat thinking, sipping her wine and looking out into the street, where the first young passers-by were studying the menu. When she finally replied, Leandro detected a look of unusual seriousness, but also total calm.

"Hard to tell," she began. "Obviously, Carla may be even nastier than we already suspect, involved in some terrible things nearly twenty-five years ago or more. She must have been very young at the time. Late teens or just twenty. But to be frank, if I'm going to be scared by anything, it's much more likely to be by something that Carla may have done in the last few months than anything she did so long ago. So in terms of the physical danger which she may represent, I'm not sure that things have changed all that much. What has changed - and at this stage, I can't work out what it may or may not mean - is the broader context, which you seem to be suggesting she may lie at the heart of."

She paused again before continuing.

"That might not be very relevant somewhere in Europe, but we're down here in Uruguay, with Argentina just across the water. These atrocities were being perpetrated on both sides of the River Plate. We may think that, after twenty-five odd years, most of this is history. But what you told me about Sosa and Suarez suggests the opposite. Add to that the threats to Eduardo, and there is obviously more going on than a simple sadomasochistic session which went wrong - if it went wrong."

As usual, Leandro could not fault her analytical faculties.

"You should certainly not take any rash decisions. Neither you nor I have any professional or moral responsibility for pursuing this. I only got involved through the attack on Eduardo, my godson, and somewhere along the way, you climbed on board. With hindsight, I was

225

crazy to let you get involved. But then again, somehow - perhaps stupidly - I imagined that you weren't going to do much more than a bit of reconnoitring in the polo world. With your customary flair for doing the unexpected, you seem to have drilled down into the heart of the crime. And now, we've got to get you out of it."

"Who said anything about getting out?" she replied sharply and finished her glass of white wine.

"*Puta madre*, what's the matter with you, Sam?"

"Nothing... nothing at all. I simply don't think that it's just an 'in' or 'out' decision. Leaving aside the matter of the murder - not all that simple, I'll grant you – you, or should I say *we*, are dealing with something much more worrying. Namely, that thirty years after the events, there are still people going around killing and possibly even torturing in the name of those events, no doubt as a way to avoid being brought to justice."

He detected, not for the first time, a look of contained fury in her eyes.

"As you know, I've seen injustice before, my months in the Middle East taught me all about that, and about the ability of men – why is it always men? - to inflict unlimited hardship and cruelty on others in the name of religion or politics. This isn't the moment to start a long discussion on all that. You know as well as I do what happened in Argentina in the 1970s. A clash between extremist left and right-wing politics expressed via ruthless terrorist groups, at times manipulated at the highest level of Government, pitted against an equally ruthless far-right nationalist military, inspired by the Catholic Church and its more sinister offshoots, such as Opus Dei. Not to mention a measure of tacit support from places like the US. And those involved were not above trying to do deals with the very people they were torturing, throwing alive out of aircraft into the River Plate, generally disappearing. Used as a transitive verb."

She paused, as if the forcefulness of her reply had made her slightly breathless, before going on.

"It really makes me sick! And now we see that, whatever Argentina may think it has been able to achieve since the return of democracy in 1983, it's still there, bubbling away under the surface with ambitious -

and vicious - men still fighting their nasty little battles. All this reminds me of what I saw on the West Bank. Except that we don't have anything like the same justification."

She glared out of the window and he saw her fists clench. The fierceness of her voice only partially caught him by surprise.

A few months earlier, having watched a news item on television about a violent demonstration in the Occupied Territories, she had begun to tell him about a time she had spent in the West Bank. It was connected with her Druze ancestry. Sam was in her mid-twenties and partly at the suggestion of her father, had decided to spend some months visiting the region from which her family had come, following on from a trip to Paris and London. After two weeks in Damascus, which - however beautiful parts of the old city might be - she had found totally oppressive under the Assad regime, she had made her way first to the Druze region, Jebel al-Druze, and then to Hama where her great grandmother had died. There she had found relatives and spent some weeks living with this minority in modern Syria. She had already done a lot of reading about the history of the Druze and their religion. Sitting around with some of the older men and women in the village, Sam had listened to stories about the courage and resistance of their religious minority going back over the centuries. She had come away with a feeling that this community, emasculated by a series of totalitarian governments of which the Assad family was only the latest manifestation, had lost its way and, in the process, lost a lot of its religious and moral courage and purity. She had left Syria profoundly discouraged.

From there, she had gone to Jordan and, after a spell helping out in a Palestinian refugee camp, to the West Bank. There she had rapidly made contacts among her generation of students, which had led her into the heart not only of the Arab-Israeli confrontation, but also into the violent rivalry between Hamas and Al Fatah. She had made friends with a couple of girls about her own age, Hamas activists, involved in supporting Palestinian villagers near the wall which Israel was building to quarantine the Arab sector. She had described to Leandro her involvement in a series of minor clashes between Arab farmers and the Israeli army, as the latter, escorting a team of bulldozers, sought to clear land for the wall. She had felt pride in the defiance shown by the women, standing in the front line opposite Israeli soldiers, who, to her surprise, also included girls of about her own age. The courage of the

Arab girls in the face of armed soldiers, as well as the sight of women shouldering the same risks and hardship alongside men in the Israeli armed forces, had made a deep impression. One morning, the Israelis had temporarily detained her, as well as some of the other Arab girls, and she had been subjected to lengthy questioning by an Israeli woman officer.

"She was young, handsome, extremely tough, but showed a lot of psychology in the way she handled me. In a strange way, in spite of all that separated us, I was left with a profound feeling of waste, of futility, that human beings - especially women - of such courage and quality could not find a way to make peace and work side-by-side. She very soon worked out, because of my accent in Arabic, that I wasn't a resident. My Arabic is fluent – I used to speak it as a child with my father, but even so. From there, she dug up my Druze lineage. I discovered that there was actually quite a large Druze community living in Israel, in the north of the country near the Syrian border. Next day, my Israeli interrogator told me that I also had relatives on the Israeli side, which left me pretty confused, I can tell you. At the end of the afternoon of the next day, I was released. I came very close to staying on in the West Bank, but my father, as soon as word got back to him about what had happened to me, piled on the pressure, and I finally came back. Somewhere, I feel that this was a cowardly decision. At the same time, I realised that I was pretty much all that my father still had left."

On another evening, as he and Sam sat eating some of Volta's delicious ice creams on Avenida Libertador, the conversation had turned to the question of relations between the sexes. Sam had again harked back to her West Bank experiences. She had contrasted the courage shown by women of her age, prepared to risk physical violence for a cause in which they believed, with the vast majority of Argentine women, lulled by the relative comfort and well-being of Argentina's male-dominated society. Nor, in her opinion, were Argentine men much better.

"I mentioned the Israeli intelligence officer who interrogated me."

Leandro nodded. "The day they picked you up?"

"Yes. She was very impressive. She told me a lot about her life, probably as a way to get me to talk about myself. In the space of that afternoon, I learned one important lesson. She had been brought up on

228

a kibbutz, you know, one of those farming communities which the Jews founded when they moved into Palestine. She said that the question of gender had simply not been an issue in that small community. Men and women were equal, shared the same burdens, prepared to take up arms alongside each other to defend themselves. No discrimination of any kind. When she left the kibbutz and started to work in Tel Aviv, she had suddenly been hit by an awareness of the discrimination which our societies practice between the sexes. All this business of woman's liberation, glass ceilings, all that stuff. It just didn't make any sense to her. And another thing she said. At the end of the day, the principal obstacle to having the courage of our convictions is fear. The fears that we carry around inside us. Ever since then, I've tried to make sure that this kind of fear doesn't end up preventing me from doing what I want, what I believe in. Fear, even in little things. You know, the way that men dominate a conversation. And we women sit there, listening politely, waiting for our turn to speak."

"I don't think I could accuse you of that," Leandro interrupted.

"You see, even that's a typical *macho* reaction. In that remark you just made, you're implying that somehow I'm overbearing. As if speaking one's mind first was somehow a male prerogative. But I'll give you that, Leo. You practically never transmit the message of having some kind of innate male superiority. Here in Argentina, it's called machismo. But there's nothing specially Argentine about it. It's the same everywhere. One of the things I love about you, is that you don't send that kind of message."

"Why should I? There are times when I think you're far more intelligent than I am. Certainly more courageous. Anyway, perhaps there are a few more things you love about me."

"Now you're fishing for compliments."

"No I'm not. I really believe that. And even if I didn't," and Leandro chuckled, "I get such a kick out of watching you expound on any subject that interests you passionately, that it all makes it worthwhile."

She kicked him hard under the table and snatched half his ice-cream by way of punishment, before going on.

"Mmm, I should have taken that bitter chocolate. It's much better than mine. But we're straying from the subject. How many men have you met in this country, who are really prepared to take a physical risk for some moral value? Far too many of them are either drawing-room radicals or, sadly - and that's by far the majority - can think of nothing more adventurous than the next visit to Punta del Este or the beaches of the Cote d'Azur. That's the way that Argentine men are and that's also the way they like their women. As decorative as possible and - above all - as unchallenging as possible. Argentine men don't like women to be too intelligent. Though there are exceptions... apparently. Luckily!"

She had shot him a glance, before coming out with a remark so typically Sam.

"By the way, have you noticed how many middle and upper class Argentine men over forty – don't worry, you're an exception, otherwise I wouldn't be with you – wear a really mean look on their faces in everyday life? It's almost as if they needed to assert their dominance over women by looking menacing. Argentine women on the other hand – when the botox and the facelifts allow – have a kindly, compassionate expression on their faces. We really are the better sex."

"God, you can be mean!"

Leandro revelled in Sam's moments of passion, when her eyes would fire up, her beautiful hands slicing the air to make a point. In a strange way, she even made him feel slightly afraid.

"Well, I certainly wouldn't describe you, Sam, as unchallenging. You're right, of course, and part of the problem lies in the fact that, as so often in our poor country, we come up with half-baked, spur of the moment solutions, then shift our ground when it suits us. How did we deal with the aftermath of the dirty war? First, we gave some of these people an amnesty, then the next government comes along and takes it away and starts locking them up again. If you look elsewhere in the world, you see examples such as South Africa with its truth commission, which found a way through the minefield. But for that, they needed a Mandela. We don't have any of those."

"Sadly. Part of the problem may be that power in Argentina is only about making money as fast as possible. Oh well ...."

Her tone was full of bitterness. For some reason, Leandro was left with the impression that something even more important to her had gone unsaid. This evening, as they now sat in the seaside restaurant, he saw the same look in her eye as she stared out of the window. She threw her napkin onto the floor beside her and stood up.

"Let's not prolong the usual discussion of Argentine politics. It only too often leads nowhere. I suggest that you get a good night's sleep, me too, and we get back to this tomorrow."

Noting a fleeting look of disappointment on his face, she went on, firmly. "For once, I feel that our spending the night together might not be so conducive to clear thinking. And although, after the weeks we've been apart, I want nothing more than to be fucked by you, please don't argue."

He sighed.

"You're probably right... just this once."

She dropped him off at the entrance to the building in which he had rented a flat. He stood beside her car door, holding his suitcase. Then he bent down and kissed her through the open window. She didn't linger.

"I'll come round and make you some coffee - say ten o'clock?" she said briskly.

"Fine with me."

He watched her drive off.

Next morning, he was roused by the incessant ringing of the intercom in the kitchen. A towel wrapped around his waist, he let her in.

"I bought some coffee, jam, milk, butter and croissants, as I guessed that this rental would come with an empty fridge. Sleep well?"

Until he had had his shower, he could rarely articulate sensibly, so he kissed her and disappeared into the bathroom, sidestepping her probing hand against his towel. By the time he emerged, she had set up a breakfast table for two on the small balcony and a strong smell of coffee was coming from the kitchen. By way of precaution, he leaned out over the rail to see whether the next-door apartments might be occupied. As far as he could tell, all were shuttered, presumably because their owners had not yet arrived or the rentals had not yet begun. Whatever they might be about to discuss, he wasn't keen that the neighbours should be part of the conversation.

Sam emerged with the coffee and the warm croissants.

"Fantastic day. So what's the plan?"

"I'll have to spend a little time renting a car, as I suppose we may need more than yours and we won't always want to be seen together. After that, you name it."

"Unless you've got some particular agency, I know there are a couple of rentals in town and we could go there first."

For a while, they sat in silence while he got through a couple of croissants and his first cup of coffee. She looked out towards the sea. Then, as she poured him a second cup, she began.

"Well, I did my thinking. And what do you suppose is my decision?"

From the half-malicious, half-serious look in her eyes, he was pretty sure he already knew the answer. He noted the word 'decision'. Her mind was made up. To play her along however, he pleaded ignorance.

"I trust you've taken the wisest course," he responded, adopting his most serious, paternal tone of voice. "Most of all, as I explained to you last night, neither Eduardo nor of course the lover who sits before you, want you to feel that you have to put your life at risk. If you don't think that, for whatever reason, you can get the three answers we need, namely, are Lady X and Carla one and the same, what is her connection with the blackmailer, and finally, who is the blackmailer - these are the answers we need - if you don't see your way to getting them, then we refuse to allow you to continue. So before you tell me your decision, that's the framework."

She dipped her croissant into the coffee, before continuing.

"By the way, did I ever tell you that you're so sexy when you're being serious. Never mind. Refuse? Who are you guys to refuse? Of course, I realise all that. Perhaps the word 'wisest' doesn't immediately apply to my decision, but, to my mind, it's the only option we have."

For a second, he even wondered whether she had decided to pull back, but the illusion was short-lived.

"I am convinced that we have to continue, and that I can get those answers. And, most critically, that I'm the only one who can. The more I thought about it during the night, the more it became clear to me that we've probably been playing this in too amateur a fashion. To assume that someone isn't tying up the loose ends - someone unknown to us, whose existence we only suspect but have not begun to identify - strikes me as a risk we can no longer take."

He interrupted her. "That's not entirely true. As you know, our weakest link on that front appears to be Eduardo, but he and I have put in place a number of ways of communicating, which should at least escape superficial observation. The only lead we have is someone who you may or may not have seen in the company of Carla at one of the parties. All the same, you're right, that's not enough to go on by any means and we must put in some serious effort to try and see who that might be. If only to give Eduardo a better chance."

"Which makes our ability to keep close to Carla all the more important!" She spoke almost triumphantly. "And to be frank, though you may be the sexiest man this side of the Equator, I'm not sure that you have what it takes to get close to that lady."

Seeing his machismo beginning to react, she rapidly added. "I mean financially, of course! God, you men are so predictable!"

She laughed, before continuing.

"Whatever the reason, and I've a number of ideas on that score, Carla seems keen to have me around. Reasons? Could be one of many. Obviously, the least favourable is that they've worked out what we are up to and are hoping either to mislead us, or – worse and perhaps more likely - get rid of us. Or more precisely... me." She paused. "The more I thought about it, however, the more I wondered whether they would in fact go to all the trouble. What happened to those poor men in Argentina suggests that, for these people, a bullet in the back of the head is the quickest and cheapest way of solving things. On that basis, I or you or both of us would probably already be dead."

Leandro nodded. "Unless of course there are actually interested in trying to find out how much we know and why we're interested."

"True."

She went on.

"The other interpretation, more reassuring obviously than the first, is that Carla has her own reasons which, perhaps, have nothing to do either with the murder or our interest."

She paused to look out towards the sea.

"Given what we know - or think we know - about Carla, you'll forgive me for not regarding that interpretation as particularly reassuring either," Leandro interjected.

"Perhaps not, but then, it seems unlikely that this lady can cruise her way through life leaving a trail of dead lovers. Not good marketing!"

Leandro looked up sharply at the word 'lover', but she avoided his gaze. He immediately sensed that to pursue her line of thought farther might lead them into destructive terrain. Sitting around a breakfast table was not going to be the right setting for this topic.

"You're probably right," he commented lamely.

She shifted in her chair and helped herself to some more coffee.

"So what you're saying, Sam, is that you're prepared to keep up the connection with Carla, but that we need to handle it - or rather our contacts - much more carefully. That obviously makes a lot of sense, however inconvenient."

"Carla is very, very smart and, I would suspect, also very jealous of certain kinds of relationship. She certainly draws a clear distinction between business and pleasure. Don't read too much into what I'm about to say, but my suspicion is that I currently fall into the latter category. But please understand, this isn't the moment nor the place to take that subject any farther."

She threw him a look, which seemed to signal the end of that discussion. But how did her decision to pursue Carla fit, if only emotionally, with his relationship with Sam? He was not sure that this was safe ground, but somehow any ambiguity seemed even less attractive.

"Are you trying to send me any messages about the relationship between us?" he asked, after a moment's silence.

She spun round and looked him straight in the eye.

"What the shit are you talking about?" she flashed back at him.

"You're a very clever man, Leo," she continued, "and I'd be surprised, if I had to spell everything out for you. As a man, you're close to the ideal combination, at least in my opinion. The brain of an Anglo-Saxon in the body of an over-sexed Argentine lover. British neurons and Latin libido. Just think how terrible it would be the other way round."

Leandro could not conceal a smile as Sam continued.

"One day, which is probably not now, when we've got a good bottle of French brandy between us, I'll be more than willing to fill in any small gaps in your knowledge. Though as I say, my guess is that they are very small. Perhaps I'm not entirely what you're used to in terms of Argentine girlfriends, but then again, if I were, I suspect you wouldn't be here at all. Somewhere inside you, there's something which I can recognise. And, although you may not perhaps have thought it through completely, you see something in me which resonates strongly with part of you."

She got up from the table and came round to stand behind him, placing a hand on each side of his neck. He tilted his head back. She did not lean down, but remained upright, looking out towards the sea, caressing his neck with her strong fingers all the while. He found it soothing, given the damage wrought by hours in front of his laptop.

"For the time being, you're just going to have to trust me. As you know, my affections can be compartmentalised. Then it's a matter of which compartment is in the top drawer and which in the bottom. If you see what I mean. I'm not going to flatter you by telling you where your compartment sits, it might make you conceited.... or depress you. Anyway, the levels sometimes change from week to week or even day-to-day. Let's just work on the basis that we trust each other, but that we are also transparent and - the kind of word you no doubt understand - accountable."

He closed his eyes, preferring not to respond visibly.

"Can we get back to business?" she asked.

He nodded. He would have to leave the subject there for now.

"Fine, then. What do you suggest as regards how we see each other and how we communicate?"

She seemed to be handing him back the initiative.

"Well," he answered, tentatively, "as a first step, we need to try and decide what we're dealing with. The options range, I would have thought, from no-one being interested in us or you, right through to a situation in which, for reasons which we cannot as yet determine, they are on to us. Though I tend to agree with you that, if that were the case, you and I might not be having this coffee and enjoying the view. So whilst that is a possibility, it's probably not the case, at least not yet. However, we do have to try and check whether, for any reason, Carla - or perhaps someone behind her - is trying to understand where you're coming from and why. In other words, we should probably assume that you're being checked out and that, in the process, this could lead them to me, and then, possibly from me to Eduardo. That would have the

236

effect of closing the circle and placing not only Eduardo, but also you directly in the firing line. And come to think of it, me too. This possibility means that we have to do a number of things in parallel. Firstly, obviously, any light you can throw on why Carla is taking an interest in you would be very useful. Secondly, we have to make sure that, if you're being followed, they don't just simply trip over me. Perhaps we haven't been very smart since I arrived yesterday, but we'd better be careful from now on, whilst we look at the third precaution, which is, to my mind, to try and find a way to determine whether anyone is following you or trying to track your movements or phone messages, all that kind of thing."

She was nodding in agreement, still standing behind him.

"Do you mind sitting down so that I can see your eyes?"

She gave him a final sharp jab between the shoulder blades and then moved round in front of him, still standing, this time with her arms folded across her breasts, her bronzed legs parted. He resisted an overwhelming urge to put his hand between them.

"As regards seeing each other, much though it pains me, since I was looking forward to appearing on the covers of Caras and ¡Hola!, with you on my arm, I fear that we will just have to make do with more discreet rendezvous away from the paparazzi. If we meet here, once most of the flats have filled up, which, given Christmas is only a couple of days away, should happen tomorrow or even from today onwards, I suggest that you vary the floors to which you take the lift. Either walk up or down to this one. Primitive, but it may work, if anyone actually follows you into the building. Also, drive into the underground car park, so that you make it harder for anyone to follow you. I fear that, until we're certain that nobody is following you, I just won't get to see your place."

He thought for a minute before going on.

"From the spy movies I've seen, one of the easiest ways to see if you're being followed is when you're driving. Think of all our favourite James Bonds. That means looking in the mirror and making a mental note of who is behind you every time you look. On top of that, as soon as I get a car, I can follow you to see what's happening behind you."

"This is getting better by the minute," she interrupted, now sitting down opposite him. She giggled. "When are you going to pass me my gun and a licence to kill? You'd make quite a good James Bond. And me... let me think. I've always kind of liked the name Pussy Galore."

"It's actually not such a laughing matter, but heck, one has to enjoy life while it lasts. Anyway, in the words of the immortal Q, shut up, double O seven, and listen, I haven't finished." He quoted Q in English.

"It's 'pipe down'. Not 'shut up'."

She corrected him, also in English.

What a memory! He paused, temporarily thrown off his train of thought, before continuing slowly.

"If we establish that they are really seriously following you, then I suppose we will have to assume that they will also be tracking your phone calls. Though how they might do that over here in Uruguay is not clear. However, as a first step, let's buy a couple of 'pay as you go' local cell phones, which it'll take them even more time to get on top of. We can do that this morning anyway. Then after that, let's see. Finally, it occurs to me that we should agree on some underground, public parking place, where we meet discreetly, so at least I can get my hands on you," he finished, smiling. "Clearly a lot will depend on whether we can find any trace of your being followed. If there isn't any, that may make things easier."

"Time is passing, why don't we get going? Learn by doing?"

"Fine. We'd probably better start applying the new rules of our relationship right away."

Turning his chair around, but remaining sitting, he put one arm round her waist to pull her down towards him, whilst slipping the fingers of the other hand between her thighs, seeking her vagina. Not for the first time, he discovered she was naked under the tight skirt she was wearing. His finger began to caress her clitoris. Her hips swayed softly in response.

"I can't remember any rules covering this," she muttered.

"Next time, as they say, read the fine print."

It was well past noon when he finally roused himself in the large bed. Resting his chin in one hand, he studied Sam's uniformly bronzed body sleeping by his side, facing him. The sheets had fallen away revealing a tiny triangle of paler skin in the area of her vagina. She must have been putting in a lot of hours in the raw by her father's pool – or maybe Carla's. Their ferocious lovemaking had borne all the hallmarks of their separation since before the Argentine polo finals. The softness and warmth of her proximity aroused him again, and his fingers slipped between her legs. Although still asleep, she was moist. Softly, he stroked her. Her body responded languidly. He would let her sleep.

Naked, he walked across to the open balcony door and sipped some of the cold coffee which had remained on the table. Soundlessly, she crept up behind him and now kneeling with lowered head in front of him, took his half-aroused penis deep into her mouth and began a blowjob as sensual and subtle as any she had ever performed. The dark red of her hair, like a helmet, contrasted with the faint sheen thrown by the sun on the smooth, taught skin of her back, as her face moved in and out, her eyes looking up at his. No woman he had ever known had shown the skill which her lips and tongue deployed every time. In response to a comment he had once made, she had merely said that she had a good Palestinian teacher to thank for this. He remembered thinking that she seemed to have picked up more than just a political commitment to the cause of nationhood during the six months she had spent in Jordan. His final explosion came propped against the inner corner of the balcony, Sam's face upturned, eyes half closed, lips parted.

Given that they had now agreed that they should avoid being seen together, Leandro left the building first, with Sam following about twenty minutes later. Since shops and offices remained closed until well after four pm, he stopped off at a pavement bar before finally making his way to the office of a small car rental company, owned by a friend in Buenos Aires. Remembering Sam's parting words of advice, he rented the most common form of small four-seater hatchback he could get. He wasn't quite sure why she had been so insistent that it not be a saloon. The girl behind the counter gave him an address where he could pick up some 'pay as you go' cell phones. Finally, he spent an hour checking out a series of Internet cafes, noting their addresses and opening times. From one of these, he made a phone call to Sam to confirm that he had 'done the shopping'.

"See you in thirty minutes outside the southern exit of the Disco supermarket on Pedragosa. I'll park there a few minutes beforehand. From there, I'll drive home which, being some ten kilometres, after passing the stretch known as Balneario Buenos Aires, beyond La Barra, should give you an opportunity to check things out. When I pass Calle 30, I turn off left into the pine woods on one of the next roads. That way you'll also get an idea where the house is."

"Yes, but I won't follow you off the main road. There'll probably be very little traffic and I would stand out."

"Okay, good luck. We'll fix up how we meet later after that."

Some twenty-five minutes later, Leandro drove slowly towards the southern exit of the Disco supermarket. He spotted Sam's car parked on the right-hand side. As he drove past, he saw that she was making a phone call, but she nodded to show that she had seen him. Some thirty metres farther on, he found a space into which he slotted, making sure to leave enough room to pull out easily. Keeping an eye on her in his wing mirror, he watched her move out into the road and drive past him. For about ten seconds, he waited before taking up a position some fifty metres behind her. No other cars appeared to have followed her.

At the end of the road moving north, Sam turned right along Avenida Saravia, heading east towards the beaches. The traffic was relatively light. He paused for a few seconds before entering the Avenida, allowing one or two cars to fit in between him and Sam. The initial pleasant surprise that she seemed to be driving in a more cautious fashion than he had witnessed yesterday was rapidly shattered when, at the first sign of a straight, she put her foot down to pass a couple of cars. This wasn't going to be very helpful, as it meant that he would have to keep up with her, thereby probably drawing attention to himself. Sam's manoeuvre had the effect of detaching her from four out of the five cars which had been behind her. Only a small blue Chevrolet seemed to keep up. The last thing Leandro wanted to do was to find himself third in the queue. Car surveillance wasn't a skill for which he claimed any particular aptitude, but he suspected that not being spotted was preferable to being unable to come to any firm conclusion as to whether Sam was being followed on this occasion. He kicked himself for not having warned Sam to drive more slowly.

As he followed her, he tried to make a mental note of the two or three cars which separated them. Apart from the Chevrolet, these were a silver Audi sports and a black Cherokee Jeep. On balance, he felt that the latter two would hardly serve the purpose of discreet surveillance. He concentrated his attentions on the Chevrolet. As they moved nearer the beaches, he was going to be more exposed. Continuing along this straight Avenida was not going to be very productive. Suddenly, he saw Sam take a right on Leonardo da Vinci heading towards the shore, but not the most direct route to the gull-wing bridge crossing the estuary leading to La Barra. The little Chevrolet seemed to be going the same way.

He immediately realised that this would allow him, by continuing straight ahead, to reach the bridge a couple of minutes ahead of Sam, perhaps giving him a better view of anyone following her. He accelerated and, on reaching the roundabout, went round it and parked in such a fashion as to be facing the road down which Sam should come. To his relief, only thirty seconds later, the little white Peugeot came charging towards him and dived into the roundabout. There was no sign of either the Audi or the Cherokee, but the little blue Chevrolet was still there. That in itself was not necessarily proof of anything, since lots of people could be expected to be moving up and down the main road which linked the various coastal resorts all the way to Jose Ignacio and beyond. He pulled out, allowing one or two more cars onto the roundabout and then watched as, to his surprise, the little Chevrolet, instead of following Sam directly, made a lap of the roundabout, before re-joining the route, this time behind Leandro. This was not exactly what he had planned, but on the other hand, it did provide more evidence of the likelihood that Sam was being followed. As they crawled northwards in the late afternoon traffic of La Barra, with people doing their pre-Christmas shopping on leaving the beach, he turned over in his mind how far this might indicate that their movements had been watched even since his arrival – and indeed, as far as Sam was concerned, even from before.

At this point, Sam suddenly decided to stop, presumably to pick up something. Such a tactic had not been planned, but Leandro immediately realized that it was the perfect way to force a tail into revealing itself. Leandro drove past Sam as she stopped to park, and saw the Chevrolet do the same in his rear mirror, only to stop about thirty metres farther on. The passenger door opened and a young man, in T-shirt and jeans, jumped out and rapidly joined the crowd of passers-by, walking back towards where Sam was still in the process of parking the Peugeot.

There seemed to be little room for doubt now. Leandro decided to continue out of La Barra towards Mantra and Laguna Blanca and wait for Sam and the tail to pass him. He pulled into the side of the road where it swung down and round to the left out of La Barra and waited. About ten minutes later, Sam came past, with the small Chevrolet tucked in three cars behind her. He pulled out as unobtrusively as possible, but did not need to hurry, as he knew that from now on, the road would be relatively empty as it followed the shoreline going north. A few kilometres farther on, as they passed Balneario Buenos Aires, Sam began to indicate a left turn and he saw the Chevrolet slowdown so as not to crowd her. As soon as the oncoming traffic permitted, she turned left, heading towards the pinewoods. The Chevrolet allowed a number of other cars to pass, before following her at a distance of several hundred metres.

As agreed, Leandro did not follow, but moved on to a point some three hundred metres farther on, where he turned and parked facing back towards Punta del Este. He reckoned that Sam's followers would probably content themselves with taking her as far as her house, but might then pack it in. He watched carefully to see if any other car might be positioning itself in the area, but the stretch of road at this point was empty and he was unable to spot any other follower.

Sure enough, within ten minutes, the blue Chevrolet reappeared and, turning left in the direction of Jose Ignacio, passed him on the other side. Making a note of the Argentine number plate, he waited until they had passed over the brow of the low hill behind him, before turning and following them again to try and discover where they were going. Within a couple of kilometres, he saw them indicating a left turn and then accelerating through a cluster of new villas in the direction of the wooded slopes behind. He guessed that this might be the area of Carla's house and, as he passed, took a quick snapshot with his cell phone, to show Sam when they next met.

Their rendezvous had been scheduled for later that evening at one of the more crowded nightclubs. Situated in the basement of a large new condominium complex, it also boasted a multi-storey car park in which they had agreed to meet at three am precisely. Leandro wanted to hand over one of the new cell phones, but most of all to warn Sam of the presence of the followers. Still relying on their normal cell phones, he texted her the number of the bay in which he was parked. A few minutes after three, there was a tap on the window of his car and he found himself looking up into the laughing face of Sam, decked out in a long, blond wig. She could hardly contain her laughter, as she slid into the rear of the hatchback where the seats were folded down, gesturing to him to join her.

"Gentlemen prefer blondes, isn't that the saying?" she giggled. "Since I couldn't tell whether I was being followed...."

"You definitely were," he grunted, as he eased his way into the back between the front seats.

"I slipped into the ladies, changed into this horrid orange T-shirt and put on this wig, which, if anyone was watching for me to come out, would probably throw them. Obviously we haven't got much time."

"To begin with, you are being followed, although it seems only by one car, a dark blue Chevrolet, with two guys on board. They tailed you all the way home from the supermarket. Good idea, stopping off in La Barra. It made them stand out. They turned off and followed you as you headed for your house. Did you see them at any point?"

"I did see a car pass, something small and blue, as I was waiting for the garage doors to swing open."

"I followed them when they came back to the main road. They went a couple of kilometres towards Jose Ignacio and turned off here."

He showed her the snapshot on his phone.

"That looks very much like where Carla has her house."

"I guessed as much. Anyway, we need to try and work out what all this means. We haven't got much time now, so let's try and set up another meeting after Christmas. By the way, when does your father arrive? Here, take this cell phone, I've already put in the number of mine. And here are a couple of reloads as well." He showed her his cell phone. "We should definitely try and avoid using our normal phones until we can get the measure of what's going on. You ought to be getting back."

"My father's arriving tomorrow, so I'll have to devote most of my time to him over the next few days. This is getting better by the minute," she murmured.

"Also much more dangerous, for God's sake, this isn't a game, Sam. Whether it's Carla or whoever is behind her, he - or she - seems to be able to mobilise a team of followers, which is hardly normal behaviour. Now, it may just be a jealous lover, who checks out his mistress' friends, with or without her knowledge. Yet somehow, I doubt it. You

244

must go. However ...." He leaned over and kissed her hard, his hand searching for the zip of her jeans. He suddenly realised that Sam's insistence that he rent a hatchback might have its advantages.

She broke free a moment to gasp between his kisses. "Oh Christ, ... since I'm with Carla ... in the nightclub upstairs, it doesn't seem likely that they're also going to be ... Jesus, hold on ... following me as well. But she may be wondering what I'm up to. Christ, Leo, not so fast!"

He grabbed her buttocks violently and pulled her down on top of him, wrenching her jeans off her butt.

"Oh God, fuck me, Leo, rape me!"

Surrendering, she swivelled over onto his lap, driving her now exposed arse into his crotch. She worked around his erection immediately, feeling it between her buttocks and then allowing it to slide into her moist vagina.

It was all over in a matter of minutes. She pulled away.

"Jesus, I never thought I'd be doing this again at my age. You really do have a bad influence on me. You'll be missed. Go on, get out! Whore!"

"What did you just call me? Never mind, I like it."

Pulling her jeans back into place, she gave him a last kiss and got out of the car.

"I like being your whore. But can you afford me?"

"Almost certainly not. One final thing. I'll text you the number plate of the blue Chevrolet. Try and confirm whether it sits in Carla's parking lot. I only saw one of the guys, aged about 35, fair crew-cut hair."

She closed the car door silently and threw him a kiss through the glass. Between the front seats, he watched her walk rather awkwardly towards the escalator, which led back in the direction of the nightclub, her movement triggering the neon lights of the central parking lanes as she went. Without getting out of the car, he attempted to see whether anyone else was around, but apart from some new arrivals at the far end, no-one caught his attention. He looked at his watch and calculated that she must have been out of the ladies' cloakroom not more than fifteen minutes. He could only pray that the absence would not attract attention and prompt Carla to go looking for her.

January 2008

2 January 2008

Christmas passed uneventfully. Leandro had brought a couple of books about the Middle East in his holdall, suspecting that, if he wanted to understand Sam better, he should understand the situation in that part of the world in more detail. He had also packed a biography of Oscar Wilde, a present from Sam a few months previously.

"Read this, when you have some peace and quiet. It may help," had been her rather cryptic accompanying note. Help what? No doubt a better understanding of Sam.

Her outburst on their first evening in Punta del Este had not been the only occasion on which he had sensed the level of her engagement with the problems of Israel and the Palestinians. Although she claimed to have no time for violence as a form of response, Leandro had still sensed a degree of passion in her feelings, which had seemingly been translated into a deep-rooted hostility towards all forms of persecution and intolerance. For some reason, this appeared to be feeding into her involvement in the Carla affair, as evidenced by her reaction to the Sosa and Suarez killings.

In the days running up to New Year, a feast which was traditionally much more celebrated than Christmas itself in Argentina and Uruguay, Leandro had taken it easy, sleeping late, a light fish lunch somewhere near the beaches, perhaps a takeaway at the flat in the evenings to avoid the crowds. Eating alone in a restaurant, however delicious, was one of his nightmares. He spent a day exploring farther north towards Cabo Polonia, a wild, treeless fishing village buried in sand dunes, rapidly becoming one of the elite's refuges of choice. Depressed by the complete lack of any kind of urban planning, and dreading the cumulative effect of all those 4x4's churning up the sand, Leandro felt the need to enjoy it before the developers sank their claws into it forever. Sam had gone quiet and he presumed that she must be looking after her father. One afternoon, he thought he caught a glimpse of her in the company of Lamai, but could not be sure.

New Year itself passed in an ear-splitting display of pyrotechnics all along the coast, which Leandro was content to watch from his balcony, a bottle of champagne and a plate of smoked salmon beside him. The condominium had come alive on every floor and balcony and the parking area under the building was now completely full.

At midnight, he had rung Elena, but received no reply. His call to Alejandra found her at a party somewhere out in the northern suburbs near Pilar with a group of friends.

"Papa, happy New Year to you too, hope you're not alone. Oh dear, never mind. I'm here with Nouria and a whole pile of friends. Great party. I'll send you some shots from my cell phone. Anyway, must go and fill up my glass. Send you a big kiss. Lots of love."

She paused. "Don't you have Samira with you in Punta?"

Leandro was grateful that, in spite of his separation from Elena, his relationship with Alejandra had remained virtually intact. At the beginning, like any child, she had resisted the change, but, seeing that her parents had managed the separation process apparently without bitterness or recrimination, she seemed to have concluded that it was possible to love both of them equally. Inevitably, Leandro had watched her grow up faster after the separation. A shock of this kind often seemed to accelerate the process, perhaps not such a bad thing in today's harsher world. Divorce and separation were commonplace in Argentina, however much it might be a Catholic country. The temptations for sexual *machismo* in a country in which the women, until at least the age of forty, were on average much better looking than in so many countries around the world, were unlimited. Whilst fifty years ago, a husband might have discreetly kept a mistress out of sight, as had historically been the practice in most Latin countries, nowadays infidelity and separation seemed all too easy. Only the children paid the full price, the blow sometimes being cushioned by the sheer size of the families involved. An only child, Alejandra had been unfortunate in not having such a cushion. Leandro wondered whether this might not be part of the explanation for her relationship with Nouria.

Back in the winter, Leandro had bumped into Alejandra as she emerged from her classes one afternoon. Only too often he felt guilty that he was not doing more to see her or to keep in touch. He'd wake up in the morning promising himself to ring her and to find something to do together, but all too often the events of the day swept his good intentions aside with no contact being made. So he was delighted when she had accepted his invitation to a coffee. She seemed happy enough and chattered away about her studies, the things she had done at the weekend, dropping the names of friends who, he quickly realised, no longer meant anything to him. After a while, the conversation turned to Leandro's affair with Sam. From the beginning, he had taken the position that there was little point in concealing very much. Alejandra had shown what he felt to be a sincere interest in what her father was up to, with little sign of recrimination. She had even said that, as long as he was happy, she would be too. He was amused to discover that, probably through her connections with the *turco* crowd, she actually knew something about Sam.

"I've heard she's very good-looking, very smart. And apparently very clever."

He detected a touch of admiration in the manner she said it.

"She may even do you some good," Alejandra had added, laughing.

Later, as they sat watching the passers-by, making fun of their looks or quirks, a game they used to play when she was much younger, he had turned the conversation to her emotional life. Initial hesitancy had finally given way to trust, Alejandra confiding in her father things which, for some reason, she admitted that she had still not shared with her mother. She led him to understand that her relationship with Nouria was important to her and pleaded with him not to judge her on principle.

"It's not easy to explain. There's a depth of understanding, of common ground between Nouria and me which I haven't found before. Too many of the young guys I've been around with over the years have simply fallen short. They're always very keen to get you into bed, but rather less good at understanding what makes you tick. All too often, it comes down to whether you support River or Boca. I support neither, football bores me. I don't know whether you know what I'm talking about?"

He knew exactly what she was talking about and said so. He also suspected that this state of affairs wasn't going to change any time soon.

"Alex, at the end of the day, I want you to be happy. Nothing could be more depressing than to see you get married too young to the wrong guy, have children, and then split up. Up to a point, you're right when you say that your mother and I did just that. But we did wait until you were nearly out of your teens and when we felt confident that we could preserve so much of what was important to all three of us. It may not be perfect, but it could certainly have been more destructive."

She had given him a hug before disappearing out of the cafe.

He made a mental note to ring her again in a couple of days to hear more about her holidays.

Having finally got through to Elena, he asked her to pass on a message to Eduardo to make contact, if possible from a public telephone. From her audible reluctance to prolong the phone conversation, he could not entirely dismiss a suspicion that Elena might have found male company somewhere out of Buenos Aires. So what? What was he doing, if not exactly the same? And she wasn't giving him a hard time. Why did women always appear to be so much more reasonable?

Eduardo rang on the morning of the thirtieth. Leandro rapidly filled him in on everything that was happening in Punta del Este and asked him discreetly to check out the number plate of the Chevrolet. He warned him that the plate might belong to someone close to Carla's 'protector' and therefore be linked with Eduardo's attackers. Eduardo had a friend in the local police in Maldonado, the provincial capital for Punta del Este, and he would see if he could be persuaded to handle the enquiry on Eduardo's behalf, making it look as though the car might have been involved in an incident. This should serve to prevent any blowback to the Buenos Aires investigation. There had been no further contact with Sarmiento so far, but he intended to get in touch after New Year. As soon as he had news on both fronts, he promised to come back to Leandro.

With no contact with Sam foreseen until after New Year, much of Leandro's mental effort had been directed at trying to analyse the jigsaw puzzle of their investigation. However hard he tried to view it dispassionately, he inevitably found himself drifting back to the question mark hanging over Sam's relationship with Carla. This area of Sam's emotional architecture was still mysterious. Given what he knew of Sam's personality, made somewhat easier to fathom the more he

251

discovered the psychology of her icon, Wilde, he had to assume that the two women had embarked on a relationship which Sam found stimulating, but which was potentially destructive. There were moments when he would have welcomed some guidance from any one of Buenos Aires's battalions of psychiatrists. For the time being, however, he would simply assume that there was something powerful between Sam and the older woman. All he could hope to do was to ensure that she didn't get hurt, either emotionally or, even worse, physically.

He spent one afternoon juggling Sam's emotional relationships around on a virtual chessboard, with Sam in one corner, he in another, Lamai and Carla filling the last two positions. There might well be other, invisible, pieces on the board. Sarmiento, as well as Eduardo, and most threateningly, Carla's 'protector'.

To what extent were Carla's 'protector' and the blackmailer one and the same? From what Sarmiento had told them, his mistress had been murdered on the instructions of the blackmailer. With Carla the assassin, her link to the this person must therefore be very close. More obscure was the implication from Sarmiento's long letter that the blackmailer was also part of a sinister force at the heart of the present Argentine government. What kind of force was he referring to? Leandro was experienced enough to know that Argentine politics, particularly in the Peronist fraternity, were often all about this kind of thing. Sarmiento seemed to be saying that, if Eduardo's murder investigation could lead to the identity of the blackmailer and apparent master of Carla's services, this would somehow strike a blow against this new force.

That members of the present government under the Kirchner presidential duo had links to the left-wing guerrilla movements active in the 1970s, against which the military dictatorship had waged its 'dirty war', was well-known. Serious doubts remained, however, about how active the presidential couple had genuinely been at the time. Journalists had traced the origins of the Kirchner personal wealth back to the very period in which they claimed to have been fighting the dictatorship. Numerous leading figures in the present government, now strutting centre stage in Buenos Aires, could legitimately trace their political pedigree back to terrorist groups such as the Montoneros. Although the statute of limitations did not usually apply to crimes against humanity, under the Kirchners it was being selectively applied to pursue the military and protect those who had killed in the name of revolution. By any reading, President Kirchner and his wife were using human rights and the persecution of ex-military leaders to fabricate an ideological pedigree for their movement.

Leandro had read enough about the confrontation between the military regime and the Montoneros to know that it had been both bloody and uncontrolled, with assassinations and torture on both sides. Firmenich's strategy in the latter years of the dictatorship had been to send new recruits, inexperienced and untrained, into Argentina in the final Montonero offensive against the army in 1979 and 1980. Even without further research, it was probably safe to assume that the film which he had seen at Sosa's related to the last phases of that campaign, confirmed by the date, 1980.

Sarmiento seemed to be saying that one or two of the people in that film were linked to the murder of his mistress. How could he know this? Plucking up his courage, Leandro replayed the film. On closer inspection, there appeared to be two possible connections with present events. Firstly the presence of a woman, either the victim of the torture session or the other woman standing behind her, holding her up. Secondly, the interrogator wearing a mask. Unlike the first interrogator, he must have a reason to conceal his identity. One possible explanation was that he might be recognised by the victim. In that case, could he be a double agent, a militant in the Montoneros, but actually reporting to the military? With so little to go on, and with more than twenty-five years elapsed, it would be very difficult to investigate these hypotheses. However, at the earliest opportunity, he would share them with Eduardo.

How much he shared them with Sam remained to be seen. Based on this conjecture alone, should he pull Sam back? This being the woman with whom he had now fallen deeply in love, he gave it a lot of thought. But on reflection, he came to the conclusion that Sam was largely aware of the risks, risks which, he suspected, were a part of the buzz for her. Add to that the fact that she had consistently demonstrated that she would not allow herself to be treated as some kind of subordinate, to be told what to do. She had made that very plain on the balcony that first morning after his arrival. Even if she might initially have been motivated by a desire to help Leandro to protect Eduardo, it looked increasingly as though her pursuit of Carla now corresponded to additional, more complex motivations.

Taking the Sam-Carla duo as the fulcrum, it looked as though this might go one of two ways. Either the relationship was a temporary affair, destined at some point to peter out, perhaps at the end of the summer, when Carla would return to Switzerland and Sam to Buenos Aires. Alternatively, it might grow into something longer-term and more complex. The more he thought about it, the less he could pinpoint who - Sam or Carla - would take the initiative. It was with a feeling of growing anxiety mixed with something bordering on fascination, that he realised that, however perverse the reason, Sam might very well chose to plunge deeper into the embrace of Carla. As to her motives, he could only guess. That she seemed capable of pushing her emotional relationships to limits which only she seemed prepared to set for herself, was abundantly clear. Based on what he had read in Sam's book, he wondered how much she was influenced by her fixation with Wilde. As far as he could tell, the man had constantly pushed the limits of his own sexuality, with little regard for social convention and the feelings of those close to him. Was Sam being driven only by her sexuality? Or additionally by some kind of inner mission to challenge anything which bore the hallmarks of extremist political violence and abuse? Such feelings played a part for sure, but he was far from certain that this was now the main driver.

Pending Eduardo's success in extracting more information from Sarmiento, Leandro needed to get a clearer picture of the personality of Carla, her lifestyle, the owner of the house in which she was staying. It remained to be seen whether Sam's dialogue with Carla could provide some of the missing pieces.

A text message to her local phone suggested a meeting at his flat for the following day. An hour or so later, she had accepted for seven in the evening, when a maximum number of people would be entering the building, back from the beaches.

From about a six forty-five onwards, Leandro posted himself against the railings of his balcony, armed with the small pair of binoculars which he usually carried in his travel bag. He scanned the road below and, after about ten minutes, caught sight of the little white Peugeot slowing down and entering the ramp leading to the underground car park of the condominium. Searching down the road behind Sam, he could see no sign of the blue Chevrolet. Five minutes later, the doorbell rang. The warmth of her embrace went some way to consoling him for the days apart. She dropped as if exhausted into one of the armchairs, gasping for a strong drink.

"*Mojito*? Not sure that I can mix them as well as the bar the other night."

"Fine, whatever, as long as it's strong."

Armed each with a long glass of the pale white liquid, floating mint and crushed ice, they toasted each other.

"Happy New Year!"

"So, what progress? I'm not going to lead the life of a monk like this, unless it's in a good cause."

"Progress? Certainly! Anyway, you wouldn't last a week in a monastery before they caught you on top of a choirboy!"

"Wait a minute! You're the one who's bi!"

"Shut up and listen."

With Christmas out of the way, Carla had got in touch, suggesting Sam come round late one afternoon on the evening before New Year's Eve. She had arrived at about six thirty.

"The little blue Chevrolet was parked near the servant's entrance! Same number plate. So that's one link closed. Though no sign of any men."

"I suppose that in some way comes as a relief. At least we now know that it's someone close to Carla who is following you. It would have been more worrying had we not been able to make the connection. I should hopefully soon be hearing from Eduardo where that car comes from."

Sam nodded.

She had found Carla again on her own, though the maid had been around to serve champagne. They had sat by the pool, watching the evening light creep along the coast from out across the Atlantic. Sam had been unsure as to what Carla was proposing for the evening, and had been happy to follow the conversation wherever Carla might lead it. After a predictable conversation about how Punta del Este was filling up with people, the queues of cars and the crowded beaches, Carla had begun to show more than a passing interest in Sam, in her background, quite unashamedly probing for details of her boyfriends and, no less blatantly, of her girlfriends. Half expecting this line of questioning, Sam had seen little reason to be too reticent, given also the probability that the followers might have spotted her with Lamai.

"Ah, Lamai *is* here. I thought I caught a glimpse of her the other day with you in the car."

Sam ignored Leandro's comment and continued.

"To be frank, any woman with even half a brain could have worked out where Carla was coming from long ago, but I let her make the running anyway."

Seeing the rather confused look spreading over Leandro's face, she put down her drink and leaned forward across the low table towards him.

"Although we haven't discussed these things in any detail so far, mainly because I believe that you're far too intelligent to make it necessary, let me once more try and make one or two things a bit clearer. In case you hadn't noticed, I keep my emotional scenarios very compartmentalised."

"That's what you said last time. Although I'm very curious to hear what you have to say, I don't want you to feel that I'm putting pressure on you to do so. I've pretty much worked it out for myself. It's not a situation I've known in the past, but then, it's never too late to learn. I know that, by rights, I should be feeling furiously jealous, but for some strange reason, I must be less *macho* than I thought, or at least more prepared to compromise. Call it old age."

He attempted a smile, before continuing.

"I've never heard of your concept of emotional compartments, but I think I know what you mean. In some strange way, Sam, I've become more and more fascinated to watch how you manage these compartments, largely because of the way you handle my compartment. Never seen anything quite like it but that's because I'm pretty sure that there aren't many girls like you. Where will it go? Where will it end? Who knows? But for the time being, I'm along for the ride. However, my greatest dread, my love, is that anything should happen to you. So you'll forgive me, if I take too close an interest."

She blew him a kiss over the top of her glass.

"And the fact that I fuck well might also have something to do with it," she added.

Leandro could not deny it.

"At the moment, I have three very distinct compartments... Call it maybe four, if I count my father. There's you, there's Lamai, though sweet as she is, she's not near the top of the emotional intensity scale. And now there's this business with Carla, for which I have opened a new compartment, but the shape and content of which I can only dimly perceive."

She paused before going on.

"You see, in a strange way, I always see myself as living in a kind of spiritual and emotional apartment with different rooms, each with a different occupant. It's something that I've been aware of since I was a child. Maybe in some way connected with the death of my mother. I don't know why. I move between the rooms as the mood takes me. By nature, I would hate the rooms to be bland or boring. At any moment, I feel a need to be in one or another, if possible the most stimulating, the most exciting, even at times the most risky. A bit like Oscar, I need the buzz. Although fidelity doesn't formally come into it, except of course in the case of my father, at the same time, as I switch rooms, I don't have the feeling that I'm betraying anyone. That makes me different from Wilde. He switched to relations with men because sex with his wife, once they had their children, no longer interested him. I don't switch because I've lost interest. It's because I enjoy the change. It's partly because I think I adapt to each room and its occupant."

Based on what he had now been reading, Leandro could more easily comprehend the context of Sam's intellectual and emotional affinity with Wilde.

"And no doubt, you get the buzz which comes with the risk?" he commented.

"Yes, risk is a driver. Like it was for Wilde."

"So how, as a matter of interest, do you see the occupant of my room?" Leandro asked slowly.

"Do I really have to spell that out? You're not listening, Leo. I just said that I'm not switching because I've lost interest. Quite the contrary. We've been together for more than six months now. Surely, every time you're with me, every time we discuss politics or jazz, every time you're fucking me, you must have a pretty good idea of how I see you, how I feel about you? Although I wouldn't want you to get conceited, and leaving that brain of yours out of the equation, you really do fuck very well – though at times a little *imsak* might help - and, when I'm visiting that room of the apartment, my favourite room – I repeat, my favourite room - I can't get enough of it. At your age and with your experience of women, you must be able to spot pretence from genuine emotion. I'm sure you've been with a hooker and known what it's like when it's feigned."

He nodded.

"I guess so. When we've finished this conversation, I may have to do a bit of checking again, just to remind myself. If you see what I mean."

"All in good time, get me another drink. You make them too small."

He brought back two refilled glasses.

"By the way, why did you leave my brain out of it?"

She ignored his question.

"If you're okay with what I've just said, let me get back to the story."

Leandro nodded.

"As I was saying, although Carla is probably not the kind of woman to hang around, she also clearly enjoys the foreplay, if that's the appropriate word. At one point, she got up to change out of her jeans and T-shirt, and came back wearing soft black leather *bombachas* and a silk blouse, very deep cleavage, similar to what she had worn at one of the polo parties. The message was intentionally strong. Anyway, I won't bore you with the details."

"Who said anything about being bored?"

"Oh, I don't know, perhaps the look on your face. Anyway, we had a few more drinks and at about nine thirty, the maid had laid out a small dinner for the two of us on a table by one of the large sitting room windows. Candles, more champagne, very intimate. Delicious food, real Russian caviar, smoked salmon, nothing too heavy to weigh down the body. The vodka perfectly chilled. Just what I like!"

"I'll have to remember that, I always knew you were going to be hard to please. But carry on, the tension's killing me."

"Over dinner, Carla laid it all out. She assumed that I had perfectly understood her line of business, and talked freely about Tawfiq and many similar clients. In fact, she was quite fascinating. She lives most of the time in a totally unreal world, in which her clients have only to snap their fingers for her to be flying first class to Nassau or Monte Carlo or Marbella. Chauffeur driven limos at the airport, nights at the Ritz, corporate jets to pick her up, massive yachts parked at St. Tropez or in the Seychelles. As the dinner went on, I began to think that studying Victorian literature might not be the only career path for me. But as you know, I'm more fascinated by the man than by his plays."

Sam laughed.

"I'm bound to say, I don't see you as a school mistress either," Leandro quipped.

"Mistress, yes. School, definitely not!"

Leandro could only agree.

"Add to that the fact that, in her niche of the business, although obviously sex plays a part, it's on another planet from hookers on the street. Quite another world. The sexual act is part of it, but it sits firmly alongside glamour, expensive clothes, expensive meals and the best of everything. And running through it all, the client is given a taste of danger, the sense of being with a powerful woman. With some of her clients, it's more about playacting - role-playing as she calls it - than anything so banal as getting between the sheets. Not that that doesn't happen, but for much of the time, most of these guys expect something very different. And that's where her role model comes in. She's what they call a dominatrix, but certainly not the kind to be whipping or beating up her clients. These men don't want traces of having been brutalised, except perhaps in their imagination. They're much too public for that. Given the right company, they're perfectly happy to have her on their arm, very provocatively dressed, maybe at some private party, where wives don't get a look in anyway. By having someone like Carla in attendance, they can transmit a number of things. Money, since in the company they keep, no-one is in any doubt that they represent megabucks and that Carla charges a hell of a lot for her time and skills. Sex, certainly, but not of the basic, cheap kind. Rather the reverse, sex with a strong flavour of the darker side, which has been creeping out of the cupboard, into books and onto the catwalk for the last ten or twenty years. You only have to look at fashion gurus like Jean Paul Gaultier to understand that. The kind of thing Helmut Newton shows in his photographs. I saw your reaction to the one on the wall in my flat."

Leandro nodded again.

"I thought so. The wilder the cat these guys have on a leash, the better for their image. And given the male imagination, the fact that the girl might perform as well with another woman as with her man, that's also part of the fantasy. That's what Carla delivers. And makes a lot of money into the bargain, whilst actually having far less direct physical contact with her clients than one would imagine. All she has to do is to keep up the right appearance, look dangerous, mobilize some stunning girls and send in the bills."

"That's all very fascinating, and makes me think that I may not have the right career path either, if I'm ever to afford that kind of thing," Leandro commented, "But then how does the murder of an Englishwoman in a hotel fit with that? It seems to be quite unnecessarily risky."

"I know. But as you'll see, Carla is a lady of many parts."

"Just before you go any farther, what was going through your head, knowing what you know - or rather what we suspect - sitting there alone with her and listening to all this? To be frank, I would have been terrified."

Sam hesitated.

"In theory, you would be right. Not that you strike me as the kind of person who is easily terrified, by the way. Possibly because men give more importance to physical violence than to emotional violence. Of course, nothing that I knew about Carla up to that point could provide the certainty that I might not end up like the Englishwoman. Carla exudes physical strength, power, even very occasionally violence and there is a dark side to her personality, with which murder could fit. Some of this was going through my mind as I listened, yet, for some reason, I simply didn't think that that was how the evening was going to end. As you once said, a trail of dead bodies is unlikely to be good for business. Not to mention the fact that, if you look back in history, about ninety-nine percent of murderers have been men. Which makes me think that we're still missing a man in the scenario. I'll come to that in a minute."

"Okay, I take note, though I'm not sure that I share your optimism. And you're right, there is a man lurking there somewhere, whom we have to find and identify."

Dinner over, and with a cooler breeze coming in off the sea, the two women had moved into what Carla had referred to as the library. Whilst Carla was pouring out a couple of brandies, Sam had glanced at the sparsely lined bookshelves. Many of the titles appeared not unrelated to the lifestyle Carla had been portraying, ranging from such obvious titles as the 'History of O', the book and in DVD, through to works of a far more specialist nature, inevitably mostly in English.

"They sell most of them on the net as far as I can see," she continued, laughing. "'The Art of Female Dominance', or 'The Compleat Slave', were just a couple that stuck in my mind. When I got home, I looked them up on Google and found most of them on Amazon. That, and any number of DVDs, many of them the usual blockbusters no doubt to while away a rainy afternoon, but also a few for which the audience would no doubt require more than an R rating. She came up behind me with my glass of brandy as I was taking a look and clearly wanted to know how I was reacting. Partly to tease her, I made some remark about not being sure that this kind of thing was my scene, to which she replied that one could never be sure. Then she took my hand and stroked it against the soft leather between her legs. I can't say that it didn't work for me. More of that some other time," she added, sensing Leandro's heightened curiosity.

Carla had installed herself next to Sam in the deep leather sofa, and Sam again felt the strong sexual pulsion which she had felt at their first meeting. At one moment, a flat screen TV on one of the walls began to project a powerful scene of lesbian intercourse.

Sam cut short her narrative at this point, but Leandro was in little doubt about what had happened next. It struck him that Sam might have gone a long way to designing the mental compartment now firmly occupied by Carla.

Sam sat in silence, turning the empty *mojito* glass between her fingers, leaving him at a loss as to how to continue the conversation.

She finally spoke.

"Obviously, these are things which it doesn't come easily for me to discuss with you. If you've read *Les Liaisons Dangereuses* by Laclos, or maybe you saw the film with Malkovich, though the original by Vadim was much better with Jeanne Moreau and Gerard Philippe – fantastic movie - you may remember that too much transparent infidelity finally destroys the relationship, which, my love, is the last thing I want to do with you."

"I saw the Malkovich," Leandro commented, his voice suddenly a little hoarse. He had half expected her to move closer to him, but she stayed at her end of the couch. By now, the sun had gone down completely and the lights of the condominiums all around them showed that Punta del Este was preparing itself to go out to dinner. His instinct was to change the conversation.

"All this makes me hungry."

He instantly regretted how flippant it sounded. He caught a flash of anger on Sam's face and realised that he still had a lot to learn. He got up and, standing beside her, put his hand on her shoulder. She didn't respond.

"Forgive me. As you said once before, it's all a matter of adjustment. I'm doing my best, although rather badly."

She looked up at him, a slight smile playing on her lips. Then she too got to her feet and, resting her hands on the balcony railings, looked out towards the sea. After a minute, she turned back towards him.

"You're not the only one, Leo, who has to adjust. In some ways, I may be just as confused as you are. It's been three or four days since I was with Carla and the furniture still hasn't settled into place in her room in my apartment. She's sending me a whole lot of new signals that I have to assimilate. Can't say any more. Please be patient, Leo. In the meantime, having something to eat strikes me as a great idea. Let's go!"

As he was picking up the empty glasses, she continued quietly.

"When I'm ready, I'll tell you more. But I do want you to know that I love you and that I haven't lost sight of what this is all about."

"Don't worry, take your time. It's your foot on the accelerator, even though I may occasionally try and grab the handbrake."

She smiled again.

"Don't you worry either, in so many ways, you Leo, you've got the ignition key."

Another week went past.

Sam again accepted an invitation to dinner with Carla. As she arrived around seven-thirty, she caught sight of a large black BMW with darkened windows emerging from the gate. She just had time to notice an Argentine number plate, but in the fading light, wasn't able to make a note of the number. One of the young men who had been in the Chevrolet was holding open the gate. To be seen noting the number was not a good idea. Unsmiling, he watched her drive through, before closing the gate behind her. She waved her thanks to him as she stepped out of the car, but elicited no response.

On entering the house, the maid pointed her in the direction of the steps leading to the lower floor. Sam had discovered that she was called Nayaraq, which according to Carla meant 'she who has many desires' in Quechua, the commonest language of the Andean Indian tribes. More than a little apt, Sam thought. The doors of the gym were open and light could be seen through them. With her fingertips, she pushed open the door and looked in.

In the centre of the large training mat, Carla stood, cat-like, a coiled human spring, perspiring only slightly, her muscular body sheathed in a black lycra leotard, her torso protected by light body armour. She was facing Carlos, one of the young men Sam had once glimpsed outside in the courtyard. He was wearing tight shorts and a T-shirt, over which he also wore light Kevlar protection. Fascinated, Sam watched as they circled each other in some kind of martial arts sequence, seeking a gap in the other's defences. Suddenly, Carlos launched a flying kick at Carla's head, which she sidestepped effortlessly, bringing a blow to the side of his neck with the edge of her hand as he flew past. As he regained balance, Carla was onto him with a flying jab to his chest from the side of her foot, which sent him spinning to the ground. Judging by Carlos' look of pain, this might not be full contact, but nor was it just posturing. Carla laughed, which only added to her opponent's visible discomfort.

"Okay, *basta*, Carlos. Let's leave it at that. Thanks for the workout."

Acknowledging his ritual bow, she bent low and then spun on her heel. Carlos pushed past Sam as he left the gym, avoiding her eyes. She watched him leave, but on turning back, saw no sign of Carla.

From a door in one of the wall mirrors came the sound of a shower.

"Come on through, Sam, but first drop that pretty little silk dress you're wearing!"

Carla's voice came from the same direction.

Sam stepped cautiously into the darkened dressing room, at the back of which she could see the semi-frosted glass of a large shower room, the walls finished in what seemed to be highly polished jet-black *tadelakt*. Tiny spotlights in the ceiling flashed on Carla's strong body, setting it off in glistening contrast with the black of the walls. As Sam approached the edge of the cubicle, dropping her dress on the floor and flicking off her shoes, Carla, the water pouring off her body, stepped forward and pulled her under the water jets bombarding them from all sides. With one hand, she slipped Sam's string down her legs and began to caress her buttocks, whilst pressing her large, perfectly shaped breasts against Sam's. From their smooth, tight erectness, Sam had some time ago surmised that Carla had not necessarily been born so well endowed. With the other hand, she began to work Sam's clitoris. Sam immediately sensed that, as in previous encounters with Carla, her's was to be the role of the submissive partner. Given the martial arts exhibition she had just witnessed, this might also be the safer option. Based on her experiences to date, she was content to let Carla show the way again tonight. As her eyes grew accustomed to the dark, steam-filled shower, pierced by the pencil-thin light beams from the ceiling, Sam realised that it was far larger than she had originally imagined. At one end, she could now see a wide couch covered in a glistening black material, towards which, after some minutes of gentle but increasingly intrusive caressing, Carla now directed her. She propelled Sam onto her back on the couch, over which a warm, lightly perfumed and oily liquid was streaming from a line of small nozzles along the wall. As she sank into its elastic surface Sam's body felt it slippery and sensuous against her skin.

"Latex! Enjoy!" Carla explained, seeing a flash of perplexity in Sam's eyes.

Kneeling on either side of Sam's thighs, Carla grasped her wrists and pinning her arms back above her head, lowered her out-thrust breasts over Sam's nose and mouth.

In a small side cubicle, invisible behind one of the shower mirrors, Nayaraq refocused the high-definition video camera on their two glistening bodies. Regaling her own clitoris, a low moan punctuating the acoustic silence of the film chamber, the maid masturbated in unison with her mistress.

About an hour later, Carla and Sam sat on the terrace by the pool, a bottle of champagne in an ice bucket between them. Carla turned and smiled at Sam.

"You're very good, Sam, you must have had some good teachers," she whispered.

"You make me feel a beginner."

"You're certainly not that, but - as always in life - we can all improve with practice."

Carla smiled and raised her glass in a toast.

They sat in silence, Sam reliving the deluge of sensations which Carla had unleashed upon her in the basement. Successive waves of extreme sensuality had been interspersed with explosions of violent dominance. Carla had remorselessly governed every shift in Sam's emotional and physical responses, the viscous surface of the couch on which their slippery bodies arched and twisted adding a new level of sensuality to the kaleidoscope of caresses, violations and incursions to which Sam had been subjected. Sam had been fascinated by the psychological power and raw physical strength of this woman. More than once, images of the Buenos Aires hotel bedroom had flashed into her mind, as Carla pinioned her and on occasion, clamping her hand over Sam's nose and mouth, brought her close to suffocation. At other times, Carla, queening, knelt over Sam's face, gripping her head between her legs, enveloping nose and mouth with her cunt, till Sam screamed for breath and came, not for the last time. No part of Sam's body escaped Carla's intrusive fingers and lips. Compared to the delicate, respectful ministrations of Lamai, Carla's onslaught was savage and relentless, opening up unfamiliar vistas of desire and sensuality, of new erotic appetites, which, Sam dimly suspected, might henceforth seek satisfaction.

As she sat sipping her champagne, Sam recalled what she had read about erotic asphyxiation, having looked it up on the web when Leandro and Eduardo had told her about the murder at L'Hôtel. But not until this evening had she tasted the heightened stimulation, a mild euphoria, brought on by oxygen shortage to the brain. Someone had said it was like cocaine, as addictive. That might be an understatement. Given the physical strength with which Carla had controlled her, a strength which Sam had rarely encountered even with men, she had no doubt that Carla could be the killer. Yet, for reasons which were far from rational, the possibility of Sam herself getting to that terminal stage seemed highly remote. A risk which, as they now shared the quiet of the evening on this terrace, she wanted to discount completely. If Carla was the killer, then deep down, Sam felt that something didn't quite fit.

She sensed that this evening, Carla had begun to furnish the room set aside for her in Sam's emotional residence. Although Sam had subconsciously already suspected it at their first meeting, she now detected that Carla moving in might dramatically change the floor plan. Deep down, she felt a mixture of fear and adrenalin, the start of an adventure into new, uncharted territory.

For the time being, she preferred not to think too deeply about any implications for her relationship with Leandro and for the investigation on which they had embarked together. He even bore some responsibility for her current position. How much she would tell him, or he could even stand, was best left for another day. She briefly remembered her remark to Leandro about the ignition key. A part of her hoped that it was still in his hands, but tonight, she was no longer quite so sure.

The maid appeared to announce dinner. Sam caught the girl's gaze lingering on her, as if she needed to accommodate this new partner in her mistress's life. She imagined that Naya, as Carla called her, would on occasion be used by her mistress as a prop in some of her more complex scenarios. Sam returned her gaze steadily, wondering whether she might have to watch her back. Turning, she caught a look pass between Carla and the maid. The latter dropped her gaze to the floor.

When Naya had left, Sam asked.

"Where does Naya come from, Carla? From her accent and her looks, she seems Bolivian or Peruvian. But she's very tall and slim. And with those breasts, she could be Miss Bolivia."

Carla laughed.

"To begin with, she's only half Bolivian, her mother may have been an Aymara Indian, but her father was German. As you know, Bolivia and Paraguay seem to have attracted some of the master race in the years immediately after the war. That's why we sometimes speak German to each other. As for the measurements, I paid for those. With certain clients, I've found that the mixture of her exotic looks, with those slightly Asian eyes and the darker skin, on top of that body, go down very well. And she's very good at playing the submissive maid role. I'll get her to give you a demonstration some evening. By the way, whilst on that subject, you must introduce us some day to that pretty little Asian you have in tow."

Sam was just able to control her sense of shock. Not only was Carla having Sam followed, but, what was more, she saw no need to conceal it.

"Ah, Lamai, she's quite exquisite. If you think it's a good idea, Carla, why not?"

"I have many good ideas and every intention of testing them with you, darling Sam. I feel we could make a very powerful team. When you know me better, let's discuss it. I'll tell you a little bit more in a minute."

The affectionate adjective was not lost on Sam.

As they sat eating dinner, Carla dominated the conversation, as if surfing on the intimacy of the bond now established between them. She had a humorous and at times sardonic way of describing some of the stranger episodes in her life. The description of her jet-setting adventures around the globe had them laughing through most of the meal. However, on this as on previous occasions, Sam detected that history appeared to begin around the end of the 1980s. Seemingly innocent questions about where Carla had grown up or what she had been doing prior to that date consistently ran into a brick wall.

"So, business is likely to be a bit quieter. That way, we can see more of each other for the next week or two. Or at least until Davos!" Carla changed the subject. "What are your plans in the coming few days?"

Sam decided to take the plunge.

"Well actually, I'm not sure. You see, my father's rented our house for a couple of weeks. He does that every summer. He doesn't use the house much. I was over here to prepare it for this let. In fact, he just does it to break even on the upkeep. He doesn't really need to. So I was thinking of moving into a hotel. I've reserved a room at the Posta."

Carla interrupted.

"No ways. You can move in here with me. As of tomorrow, *el patron* is off to Buenos Aires anyway. That way, we'll get to know each other even better."

Sam appeared to hesitate.

"Come on, Sam, you know you want to."

"Oh dear, I didn't know I was so transparent."

"Not transparent. But..." and Carla appeared to hesitate before continuing, "the body doesn't always send the same messages as the brain. If you see what I mean."

Sam nodded. Again, she didn't want to think through the full implications for Leandro. On the other hand, he could hardly blame her for pursuing their target.

"Then that's settled."

Changing the subject, Carla mentioned that Tawfiq and his Saudi companion had left Punta just after New Year, though dropping a hint that she might be meeting up with the Jordanian in St. Moritz for the winter polo tournament.

"That would be good." Sam paused before continuing. "But I suspect you may have another client who is keeping you here. Am I wrong? I was nearly hit by a very large BMW as I arrived."

"In a manner of speaking, we've been each other's client for many, many years. I'll introduce him to you someday. He's complex, special. Doesn't mix easily. In some ways, he could be described as a client, since he has very special tastes which he relies exclusively on me to serve. In other ways, he's the boss, my *patron*, who invested in my business. I'll tell you a lot more about that, if you're interested. From your performance this evening, I think you should be. I really think you have great talent and with me, you can have a hell of a good time. Also earn a lot of money. More of that perhaps some other time. Have a bit more of the dark chocolate ice cream, it's so delicious and so bad for our figures."

Although the switch of subject was light-hearted, her tone of voice made it clear that the main topic was, for the time being, closed.

The dinner over, they lingered past midnight on the terrace.

"Let's keep this evening quiet," Carla suggested. "Frankly, the idea of all that traffic and noise puts me off."

"Fine with me," Sam replied.

"It's getting cooler. Let's go inside. There are a couple of things I would like to show you. Bring the rest of the champagne, if there is any. Otherwise Naya can bring us another bottle."

Putting her arm firmly round Sam's waist, she led the way indoors to the couch opposite the large flat video screen.

For the next hour or so, Carla played a series of video sequences some of which, however artistically directed, would not have made it past any but the Japanese board of censors. Many of the scenes showed handsome men - and often their female partners - being attended to in surroundings of great luxury by a team of beautiful girls, always provocatively dressed. Although they were more the exception than the rule, other videos showed more sadomasochistic scenes, often set in aristocratic chateaux somewhere in the European countryside, in which statuesque women straight out of the latest she-hero movie, in leather or latex catsuits, enacted bondage scenarios involving beautiful, willing victims, gagged, trussed, chained. Such scenes often ended with lingering acts of lesbian lovemaking.

Sam detected that Carla was observing her reactions out of the corner of her eye and deliberately showed less interest in the more violent SM. Carla deduced that physical torture was not Sam's scene, but detected a slight quickening of the pulse on Sam's temple in response to the savagery, passion and opulence of the scenes between the women. After what had just happened in the shower, this came as no surprise.

"This might interest you."

Carla switched off the DVD player and plugged a laptop into the flat screen. With Internet Explorer, she typed in a URL. The screen opened onto a pure black background on which, in Gothic red lettering, scrolled the words 'Lady Blast' accompanied by a provocative image of Carla reclining on a golden brocade couch, the lower part of her body encased in gleaming black thigh boots over skin-tight leather trousers. These were matched to a corset of the same material which underpinned her magnificent breasts, visible through a half-open silk blouse. The mass of her blonde hair fell onto her shoulders, framing her face in profile, looking away, as if not in the least interested in the viewer.

To Sam's surprise, Carla chuckled loudly. "The clients love it! Also it's a word play between two languages. In Russian you see, the B is pronounced like a V. So at a quick glance, to a Russian, it reads like Vlast. And in Russian, 'vlast' means power. Have to keep up with the new clientele," she added by way of explanation.

Then, having first chosen a language - English, French, German, Russian, Arabic and Spanish were all on offer - she pressed a link which offered a small menu of services ranging from social escort through to more sophisticated, but light, S and M.

"As I think I've explained before, this is not about simple sex and prostitution. My clients can get whatever they like on that front anywhere, the supply is endless and cheap. No money to be made there. This is about offering something very expensive, tailor-made, personalised. We are a select tribe, perhaps a dozen real professionals in the whole of Europe. Our clients choose us with the same attention to detail as they might an expensive car. It's got to drive and feel just right, and it's got to take them to the destinations they – but also I - choose. To some extent, I have to play a role similar to the elegant salesman who might be showing you over a Rolls or Bentley. This website doesn't appear in Google. You only get to me by personal introduction, and you have to accept my terms and conditions, just as if I were a Swiss private bank. That includes providing me evidence of your ability to pay. And pay a lot. The terms and conditions also spell out what I'm not prepared to do, which may, depending on the client, exclude any form of direct intercourse."

"Can I ask a question?" Sam asked.

"Of course, dearest Sam, that's why you're here."

"When you left me the other night with Tawfiq and Aziz, what happened next?"

"I wondered how long you'd wait to ask about that. In fact, Tawfiq is only the intermediary for Aziz. Aziz, or more precisely his employer, is the real client. He's one of those who can really pay for anything - and a part of that, I can supply. That's not to say that Tawfiq hasn't been a client in his own right. As it was, when we left you, we came back here. Aziz wanted me to provide him with some kind of a fashion show, which he filmed and photographed to take back to his employer. There are all sorts of costumes in the garderobe downstairs, I'll show you them someday. It seems the employer has some fairly exotic tastes. From the little Aziz has let drop, he is a Saudi prince, although not one of the senior royals, but involved in high-level defence deals, or something like that. He's also the kind of client I prefer, fun loving, lots of imagination, very sure of himself, no expenses spared. Many of my colleagues seem to specialise in men who want to be treated as if they were guilty of some terrible crime or badly behaved, insulting them or beating them or locking them up. Frankly, I like my men to be men, I'm not interested in a man on his knees in front of me, trembling at my command. Without denigrating or humiliating them, I give my clients a taste of danger, of power, of some kind of darker underworld."

At that point, it being near three in the morning, the phone rang. Carla lifted the receiver, seemingly expecting the call.

"I'll meet you there. I'll need a little time to change and, at about this time of the night, up to an hour to get there, the traffic along the coast is usually terrible, all these young people. I ask for you by name? *A très bientôt.*" All this in what Sam could hear was impeccable French.

"I'm so sorry, Sam, I'd forgotten about him. A Lebanese gentleman, my guess is that he's probably an arms runner for the Iranians. I'll have to get myself prepared, he always insists on a very special look. He wants me to accompany him to the tables. He says I bring him luck. If he wins, I get double my usual rate. If he loses, I get the basic. Do you want to hang around? I can give you a lift to your place, one of the boys can bring your car. He'll probably keep me busy for a day or two, we could meet next Friday, when you move in."

"I've had so much to drink, the lift would be good. I can watch some TV - or maybe another one of your DVDs - while you dress."

"Fine. What kind? Oh, why don't you choose? The DVDs are all in this cabinet."

She made a quick internal call to tell one of the young men to prepare the Mercedes to leave in half an hour's time.

Sam had made a random selection of a couple of the discs, which she slipped into the machine. About half an hour later, a totally transformed Carla strode into the room. She found Sam staring in some perplexity at a sequence in which a semi-human form, apparently male, encased from head to toe in black latex, writhed and squirmed in the centre of a shining black platform. The whole room was black, the walls covered in long shining black curtains, one side an enormous mirror stretching the scene into infinity. The face entirely hidden behind a gas mask, parts of the body connected by hoses and tubes to a variety of pumps and air bags. A groaning sound, part pain, part orgasm, seemed to come from inside the mask. She could just make out a figure which she assumed was Carla in the background, also in glistening latex, administering the bizarre session, alternately switching off hoses and air pumps and caressing his genitals or blocking the airway of the mask.

"Not sure what all that's about...," Sam commented, with a nervous laugh, looking at Carla.

"Shit! How did you get hold of that? I told you the *patron* had rather special tastes, which only I'm allowed to satisfy. He'd be furious if he knew that someone else had seen it. Don't worry, but I must ask you to forget that you ever saw it!"

With the final sentence, Carla's voice had suddenly acquired a harshness behind which Sam sensed danger.

Sam nodded. "It's much more about you, than about him, if you see what I mean."

"I know exactly what you mean," Carla replied, hiding the DVD at the back of the bookcase.

Dispelling the disturbing images from her mind, Sam turned her attention to her hostess. Carla was wearing a floor-length caftan of dark red satin with a high collar, which only partially concealed her generous proportions. Her face had been transformed, now a smooth pale mask of large almond-shaped eyes, heavily made up, a vast mouth of deep red, botox-proportioned lips, her nose small. Her blonde hair had given way to a massive wig of jet-black curls which fell to the small of her back. As Sam moved closer, she could see that Carla was wearing some form of mask, through which she could detect her eyes, laughing back at her.

"My God, is that what this man wants? And that mask? It's incredible."

"Yes, maybe a little hot at times, although the latex is wafer thin! I have them made specially to order at a place in Zürich. You actually have to come pretty close to spot them, except of course for the fact that the proportions are bit exaggerated. I told you he likes things exotic, Asian, and as it's what he's paying for, it's what he gets.

"It's amazing."

"Let's go!"

Carla tipped a final mouthful of champagne between her massive lips and led the way outside, where the Mercedes was ticking over with one of the young men at the wheel. Sam's Peugeot was idling behind it.

"Thanks, Carlos, I'll drive it. Follow us, Manuel, we're going to the Conrad. I'll drop off the Señorita on the way. You follow with her car, and then you can hitch a lift back here. There's never any lack of traffic," she instructed the other driver in the Peugeot.

As she climbed into the Mercedes next to Carla, Sam thought that she could see the tail end of a large BMW parked between the trees. The gates opened electronically and the small convoy left.

Propped up on a pile of satin pillows in the master bedroom, the man put down the two-page note he had been reading. This new girl of Carla's was certainly more interesting than some of the others she had recruited to her team. Very good-looking too. But then, that was a *sine qua non*. All the girls had to be beautiful to charge the rates they did. More educated, this one also seemed to have travelled a lot. *Turco* family, wealthy. No particular political affiliations. On the second sheet, a brief record from the surveillance team of her movements since Christmas. Nothing special to report. Had been seen at a bar in the company of a man of about forty-five to fifty, but owing to a shortage of resources, it had not been possible to establish his identity.

'Wouldn't be surprising, given her looks, that someone should be taking an interest. Wonder what Carla has in mind for her? I'll ask her tomorrow. Then we'll decide whether Señorita Samira needs closer examination. In the meantime, let's take a look.'

He dimmed the bedroom lights and pressed 'Play' on the DVD control. On the large flat screen mounted on the wall, the glistening figures of Carla and Sam in the shower began to intertwine.

He watched them for about twenty minutes, but although he could, at the cerebral level, appreciate their erotic display, his penis remained steadfastly limp. Finally, he rose and inserted another DVD into the player. His headphones almost exploded with the screams as the hand-held camera finally pulled the scene into focus. The girl, naked but for the latex hood which entirely covered her face except for her mouth, strapped to the chair, twisted and turned, screaming, retching, gasping for breath. Her taught little breasts, her whole body glistening with sweat, caught by the white glow of the floodlight. The camera brought the black latex of his hand into focus as he pumped his fingers in and out of her vagina. As he watched, he wondered which one of the girls this had been. She was not as well shaped as the Bolivian girl from last September. Slowly, the images provoked the arousal he was seeking until, in unison with the moment at which Cacho – or was it Manuel, he couldn't remember - finally suffocated her, the orgasm came. He ejected the disc and lay back on the bed.

10 January 2008

"Why did you pick me up at that party?"

They were lying naked, at right angles to each other, on the enormous bed in the master bedroom, Carla's head resting on Sam's stomach, her eyes closed.

Carla laughed, the deep-throated laugh which came to her in moments of pleasure.

"I wondered when you were going to ask that. Look up at the ceiling mirror, my love. What do you see?"

Rather like a scene out of a late nineteenth century Orientalist painting, languidly, sensually outstretched, their sunburnt bodies formed a T against the white satin of the sheets.

"Us."

"You. Why wouldn't I pick up someone looking like that? Like you?"

"But I was hardly naked at that party," Sam protested.

"Your personality was though, your inner passion. You stood out from all those other Argentine women, with their boring long blonde hair, their botox, their predictable clothes, you know what I mean. You, Sam, were in a class of your own. The same class as mine. I had to have you. But let me ask you the same question. Why did you respond?"

Sam thought for a moment. One answer was of course the trap they had set to try and find Lady X. Hardly a reason she was going to give now, though. But there was another, as powerful.

"I suppose I felt something of the same."

She knew she had. She wasn't lying.

"You suppose? Only 'suppose'? Come on, Sam. You *know*!"

Carla turned her head and looked into Sam's eyes, through the valley between her breasts. She repeated her reply.

"You know you did. I saw it from the moment I sat down next to you on the sofa."

There was no way Sam could argue with that statement. The physical magnetism exerted by Carla was something she felt inside her, growing more powerful since that first encounter, flooding not only her loins, but also her thoughts. The relationships she had had in the past with other women simply did not fall into this class. As she lay there, feeling the softness of Carla pressed close to her, she sensed all of a sudden that the combination of her relationship with Leandro, with whom she knew she was in love, and now with Carla, could, like some emotional booster, lift her into a higher orbit, providing a platform to empower that part of her life, the secret which she had shared with neither of them. Until many more things had become clearer, there was no way she could share it with Carla. But with Leandro? The time was fast approaching when she would have to share it with him.

For a moment, she doubted her capacity to manage both. What she now knew about Carla, the world she inhabited, opened up vistas hitherto unsuspected, opportunities to pursue for that other mission. If there were not to be a collision between Carla and Leandro, her two new partners would somehow need to be adjusted to each other, juxtaposed to become more powerful than the simple sum of their parts. She had no intention of losing either. Bring them together in Punta del Este? Maybe. Or perhaps somewhere else, on neutral ground.

"You're right, of course. You so often are."

She paused before continuing. Risk was what gave life a meaning. A roll of the dice.

"So where do we go from here?"

"So you're coming?"

"I thought that was somehow understood."

"You move very fast, Sam, my love."

Nearly another week had gone by. It was mid-January and Punta del Este was well into its summer routine.

Eduardo had once been on the phone to say that, in the latest contact just before New Year, Sarmiento had been sent an internet link by the blackmailer which took him to a new website. There, a five-minute video showed his English mistress chained to the bed, finally asphyxiating with the huge dildo forced into her mouth through the sole breathing hole of the hood which encased her head.

"Presumably it was Lady X doing the filming. I am trying to find a way for Sarmiento to make a copy of the video so that we can have a look. I told him to try and download some form of screen-capture software. We'll see how he gets on. Oh, by the way, a friend of mine who has stayed at L'Hôtel told me that, like at the Alvear Palace, there are one or two apartments in a side building which connect with the hotel, which they rent out quite separately. We didn't know about that when we did our first check of the guests. It just could be a lead."

Sam had met up briefly with Leandro over a drink to confirm that the contact with Carla was still on track, all the more now that she was actually staying with her. She told him about their last evening together, though sparing him some of the more intimate details. She also mentioned that Carla appeared prepared to admit to having her followed.

"She knows about Lamai. So far, at least, she hasn't mentioned you."

"Probably more luck than anything else."

"Carla clearly has some kind of sponsor. Someone who drives a big BMW and goes in for a very complicated form of sex, with tubes and lots of rubber and latex. I only caught a glimpse of something on a video, but she was clearly very annoyed that I'd seen it. You said something about asphyxiation in the case of the Englishwoman. My guess is that that is something which turns him on - and perhaps Carla too."

Sam saw no need to admit to Leandro that her first taste of erotic asphyxiation at the hands of Carla had not been nearly as unpleasant as it might sound.

"And another thing. She uses the word *'patron'* when referring to him, which in the polo world means the millionaire who is paying for everything."

"This might be beginning to add up. As we believe that the murder of the Englishwoman is connected to this blackmail operation, it's probably reasonable to assume that the blackmailer and her *patron* are one and the same person. Somehow, we have to try and find out who it is. The number plate of the BMW got us nowhere, though Eduardo's still trying. Any chance of a name for this *patron*?"

"She hasn't used it so far. Before I forget, I have the answer to why Eduardo could never get anyone to recognise Lady X. The reason is quite simple. In the hotel, she was wearing a mask. At a distance, and in poor light, the night porter could be forgiven for not having spotted it. That explains the huge eyes in the lift. She was wearing one the other evening. To go and see some client. Amazing! Oh, and another thing. Carla told me the other day that she would have to be back in Switzerland before the end of the month, adding rather mysteriously 'You know, it's Davos party time again'. Sounds to me as though she's got an interest in some of those ten thousand so-called world leaders."

They had parted in the underground car park, after a more leisurely repeat of their earlier 'rape'. Sam promised to be in touch again two days later. But no call had come, neither on the third, nor on the fourth day.

19 January 2008

Having spent the last twenty-four hours trying to get through to Sam on her cell phone, he had been without news for too long. A recorded message informed him that her phone was either out of range or switched off. He did a quick round of the beaches and bars which he guessed Sam and Carla might frequent north of La Barra, but with no success. A trip farther up the coast to Jose Ignacio's most popular restaurant, La Huella, standing on stilts on the edge of the beach, brought a possible sighting of Sam, in the company of a blonde lady, two days earlier at lunchtime. The young lad looking after the cars in the restaurant's car park claimed to have seen a silver Mercedes SLK convertible, driven by a blonde in the company of a younger woman, who seemed to fit the description which Leandro provided. He remembered it, largely because of the size of the tip he had received, but also by the way they had triumphantly deterred the attention of a number of young, and not so young, men.

"One look from the blonde and the guys got the message. They left around five in the afternoon."

Unwilling to be picked up by Sam's followers, Leandro decided to try and get to her father's house through the woods, approaching from the back. He pulled off the main road at the last turning before hers heading uphill. After passing a couple of recently built houses, the road petered out, becoming a track leading into the woods. To his left, he caught a glimpse of Sam's house through the trees, which confirmed that he was close enough to make his way there on foot, having first parked the car over the brow of the hill. He approached the house with care, looking for any sign of someone watching. He reckoned that, if this were the case, he would be coming up behind them, from the opposite direction to the one in which they would be looking. He circled around the house at a range of some two hundred metres, but saw no sign of any vehicle nearby. He finally decided that no surveillance was in place.

He re-joined the road leading from the main coast road to the house on the beach side and walked uphill towards it. Lengthy ringing on the entrance bell at the gate to the property got no reaction. Making sure again that nobody was watching him, he followed the wall of the property to a point out of sight of the road and, hauling himself up with the help of a tree conveniently close to the wall, dropped into the garden. Not as fit as he thought! He knew that he need not worry about dogs, but that some form of alarm system would almost certainly be in place. The aim was to detect any sign that the house was still inhabited. No sound came from the house, and the garage and car bay were empty. He walked round the house without touching doors or windows and tossed pebbles up against the bedroom windows. No response. There was nobody there. The let must also have come to an end.

He made his way back to the car and set off for Punta del Este. In exchange for a discreet fifty-dollar bill, the girl behind the counter of the car rental firm used by Sam confirmed that the car had been returned on the previous afternoon. From there the options were that she had either caught the last flight out to Buenos Aires, or made her way to Montevideo, perhaps by bus but more probably by limmo. From Carrasco airport she could have returned to Buenos Aires or caught a flight somewhere else. He made his way back to his flat and called Sam's apartment in Buenos Aires. After about ten rings, Sam's voice came on the line in the form of an answerphone message. He was just about to hang up, when the receiver was lifted at the other end.

"*Hola*?"

"*Hola*? Is that you, Lamai?"

"Hello? Yes. Is that Leandro? Are you also back in Buenos Aires?"

"No, not yet. I'm still in Punta and I'm looking for Sam. Have you any idea where she is? When did you get back?"

Lamai hesitated.

"We flew back together yesterday. She's not here. She's flown to Europe, today at midday."

Leandro was stunned and for a minute said nothing, trying to work out the implications.

"I see. Do you have any idea where in Europe?"

"Switzerland, I think. She packed some of her ski clothes. It's the winter season, isn't it?"

Leandro was far from convinced that Sam was heading for the ski slopes, but thought better of sharing his doubts with Lamai, all the more in case anyone else might be tapping the line and trying to her track down.

"Do you know what airline she went with?"

"I believe she went Air France, through Paris. But I'm not sure."

"Okay, Lamai, thank you very much."

"Oh, she also asked me to give you a message. That she is sure you will know where and why she has gone, and that you're not to worry."

The last part of the sentence seemed to cause Lamai a little difficulty. Leandro experienced a mixture of emotions.

"Thank you very much. Are you all right?"

"Oh yes, Sam asked me to look after the flat and left me enough money for a couple of months."

A couple of months! What *was* going through the girl's head?

"Good, that's fine. If you need anything, give me a ring." Leandro gave her his cell phone number.

Pouring himself a whiskey, he sat on his balcony, trying to work out what the hell Sam was up to. She had obviously decided to follow Carla, presumably to Zürich. That Sam was unpredictable, he had learned from experience, but this latest initiative seemed in a class of its own. The fact that she had not answered her cell phone yesterday and today might partly be explained by her being en route, and he did not know whether she would use the same Argentine cell phone once she got there. He had a vague recollection of her once mentioning that she owned a cell phone registered in France, but she had never given him the number.

The following morning, he spent a couple hours on the beach in line of sight with Carla's house, watching it discreetly through his small binoculars. There was no sign of any movement and it looked as if all the shutters had been rolled down. Carla had also left.

22 January 2008

A couple of days later, having handed back the flat and rental car, he returned to Buenos Aires and, calling Eduardo ostensibly to tell him about his holiday, fixed for him to come round to the flat later that evening. Although the two of them had kept in touch, he was now able to fill in Eduardo with a lot of the detail of what Sam had reported to him. For his part, Eduardo said that his attempt to track down the owner of the BMW had made little progress, other than the discovery that a number of very expensive high-end cars were registered in the name of a tiny agency, the owners of which he had so far not been able to identify. He suspected that some of these cars had in fact been imported without paying the full importation tax.

"You'll probably remember the story of that Mercedes officially imported in the name of a handicapped gentleman so as to avoid the import tax. They finally tracked him down playing polo!"

Whoever owned or was driving the BMW, they clearly intended to remain discreet.

"Same story with the Mercedes driven by Carla."

The news that Sam had left for Switzerland left Eduardo perplexed.

"What the hell goes through that girl's head? Did she give you any hint that she might have this in mind?"

Leandro shook his head.

"I've had no message from her, except from a girl looking after her flat while she's away."

Leandro was not in the mood to let Eduardo into the intricacies of his relationship with Sam, and even less into Sam's relationship with Lamai or Carla. His son might be of a younger generation, but he suspected that Eduardo was ill-prepared for more unconventional emotional scenarios. Eduardo was likely to have a rather

283

unsympathetic reaction to the idea that Leandro, whom he loved as well as admired, should find himself on the receiving end of Sam's idiosyncratic emotional role play. He had to think of a way to dress up the idea that Sam had chosen to follow Carla. The emotional and physical attraction which Sam felt for Carla was certainly not for discussion at this stage. Better to disguise it as something else.

"She and I had a bit of an argument about a week ago. Probably nothing serious. But she's not the kind of girl to take the initiative, to show any form of weakness by trying to make up. She muttered something about there being good snow in Switzerland and my suspicion is that she's gone off there, leaving me to cool my heels - if that's the word, given the fact that it's about forty degrees in the shade outside."

"And you don't think she's going to do anything about Carla? Is that lady still in Punta del Este?"

"I don't know," Leandro lied.

"So what are you going to do?"

"Well..." Leandro began slowly. "I've had a visit planned to London to see one of my clients for some time. Maybe now's the time to go."

"And don't pretend that a little detour via the Alps might not be in order!" Eduardo chuckled. "You're getting soft in your old age, uncle. Unless there's something very special about Sam, I'm not sure you would have fallen for that one a few years ago."

"Fuck off, young man! What do you know about these things? And yes, there is something pretty special."

"I'm glad to see, uncle, that you're blushing."

They laughed.

After Eduardo had left, he gave Elena a ring to say that he was going to Europe on business in a couple of days. Alejandra happened to be round at her mother's and he was glad of the opportunity for a chat with her as well. Finally, he rang his mother's flat. Estela, his mother's personal maid of many years, answered the phone.

"Your mother is asleep, Don Leandro. Do you want me to wake her?"

"No, let her rest. How has she been lately?"

"Not too well, I'm afraid. A certain amount of pain. I think the doctor has prescribed something stronger. We'll see if it works."

"I'm sure it will help. I'll try and ring her again the day I leave, before I go to the airport. You have my cell phone, if need be, ring me wherever I am. I don't expect to be away for more than ten days. I'll be in London and then probably in Switzerland, on business. Take care of her, Estela. And thank you as always."

"*Buen viaje*, Don Leandro. I'll let you know if there's any reason to get worried."

"You can always ring Doña Elena as well. She also knows where to find me."

"I know."

Leandro put the phone down slowly. His mother was only just seventy years old, but she'd been diagnosed with cancer nearly two years before. She appeared to have come through the chemotherapy without too much difficulty in the months that had followed, but there had been a relapse and this time round, she had found it much harder to put up with the treatment. Since the death of his father, she had borne her solitude stoically, but, as an only son, it weighed on him. He resolved to send her postcards along the way. It seemed a bit old-fashioned, in these days of Internet, but he knew that she appreciated it. A question of generation. In many ways, he regretted the passing of these old habits almost as much.

He pulled out a suitcase. Not knowing exactly where Sam had gone made it more difficult to choose appropriate clothes. If she really had gone skiing, perhaps he'd be able to hire something on the spot. He took a quick look at the weather forecast for London and Zürich. It looked as if it was going to be cold. Thick coats however were not really part of his wardrobe. He'd just have to make the best of it.

Before leaving, he would have to attend to the usual administrative formalities, pay bills, pay his maid, have a session with his partner as he was leaving him to run the office. He had spoken of being back in ten days. But with Sam, who the hell knew what would happen?

After an uncomfortable flight in the back of a British Airways 747, Leandro found himself wishing that he had remembered to find a thicker overcoat, as he shuffled up the connecting bridge into Terminal 4 at Heathrow. The contrast with summer in Buenos Aires on this gloomy, windswept morning in London could not have been greater. One of the Buenos Aires-based flight attendants had finally taken pity on him and slipped him some extra miniatures of whiskey, as well as a couple of cushions. That, combined with a mild sleeping pill, had made the night pass quite rapidly. As he had discovered in the past, British Airways did not exactly provide a memorable gastronomic experience, but on balance, he preferred the service to that of Aerolineas Argentinas. The Argentine girls might be prettier, but only too often the passengers seemed to get in their way.

By about nine thirty he was checking into a small hotel in the Bayswater area recommended to him by his contact at Frobisher. At least the room was warm and the water in the shower boiling. He decided that although his meeting with Frobisher was not until three that afternoon, it was probably better not to catch up the lost sleep, but to adapt as fast as possible to the new time zone. As he was about to leave his room, the phone rang.

"Is that Leandro?" came a male voice at the other end, in English.

"Yes, who's that?"

"It's Charles, Charles Colson. I know you're coming into Frobisher this afternoon, but I was wondering whether we might have lunch beforehand."

"Fine, where shall we meet?"

Charles gave him the name of a pub in the Bond Street area and suggested they meet in the small dining room on the first floor at one o'clock. Braving the cold wind and drizzle, he walked down to the Bayswater Road and hailed a taxi.

The strong smell of old ale so characteristic of English pubs greeted him as he walked through the door. A pretty blonde girl behind the bar, whose English seemed to be far less competent than his own, indicated a side door leading upstairs.

"Where are you from?" he asked.

"From Latvia. And you? You don't look English."

"From Argentina."

"Oh, how wonderful. I'm sure the weather is better than here. Do you think I could get a job there?"

"I'm sure you could. I'll give you my e-mail when I leave."

He made his way upstairs. There was only one person in the small, wood-panelled dining room, sitting at a table drawn up near the open fire.

"Leandro?"

He nodded.

"Charles?"

"Sit down and get warm. What will you have to drink? You can have practically anything you like, assuming you like beer."

"A good Guinness will be just fine."

Charles disappeared downstairs for a couple minutes and returned with the drinks and two menus.

"The service up here is not ideal, but at least it's quiet. We won't be disturbed. The girl downstairs assured me that the fish and chips are very good. There's also steak and chips, but I don't suppose that will tempt you, coming from where you live."

"Fish and chips! I'd almost forgotten. I'll have that."

At that moment, the girl from Latvia appeared.

"Perfect timing. Very easy. We'll take your recommendation. Fish and chips for two."

Charles smiled at her.

Leandro studied him. Probably about fifty years old, with a full head of sandy coloured hair cut fairly short, a well-tailored tweed jacket and grey flannels concealing a good physique. Well-polished shoes. Military background? The hands were strong, the nails well-trimmed. The face was lightly tanned, belying the season outside. He liked the look in Charles' eyes, which, whilst at times appearing half closed, nevertheless radiated a perceptible friendliness. He could see that Charles was returning the compliment.

"So, how was your flight? British Airways? There are worse airlines. On the whole, the service is superior to the beauty of the stewardesses."

He laughed.

"It was fine. One of the Argentine flight attendants took pity on me. I managed to get some sleep."

"You don't look too bad. Anyway, welcome to London, though I know it's not the first time."

"No, it's the third or fourth. And I lived here for a couple of years at the end of the 80s."

"That's before we first approached you, as I recall."

"Yes, exactly, and I don't think we've ever met."

"No. But James has passed your file over to me, so I'm probably up to speed with the things you've been doing for us. Anyway, James thought it might be a good idea if we met. How are things down there?"

"Complicated. As you know, Kirchner's wife was elected president back in October. The first couple months have been fairly confused, what with her picking a fight with the Americans and various other nations. International diplomacy has never been the Kirchner strong suit. I think that quite a lot of people were expecting her to change the team, perhaps to bring a new look. But there is little sign of that. Did you see the copy of the economic bulletin we produce, which I sent just before Christmas?"

"Yes I saw that. The fact that she's Kirchner's wife would of course suggest that things aren't going to change a lot. Where do you see the main problems arising?"

"It's a mixture of things. On the one hand, on the political and particularly the international front, it's obvious that our government feels closer to people like Chavez in Venezuela or Correa in Ecuador. Internally, there are plenty of distortions on the economic front, be it the massive use of subsidies in transport and energy, or the decline of inward investment, which is likely to make the energy situation even more complicated. The exchange rate is another uncertain and there are clear signs that inflation is going to become a real problem. And that will have repercussions at the social level."

Charles listened in silence as Leandro expanded his views whilst they were waiting for the food. When this arrived, they ordered another couple of pints.

"It's battered with beer," Charles commented. *"Buen provecho!"*

Leandro looked up, surprised by the excellent Spanish accent.

"I was brought up in Spain," Charles offered by way of explanation."

My father was a teacher at a school in Barcelona. I went to school there. But I did my university here in the UK." He smiled before continuing. "And I was in Malvinas in 1982."

Leandro noted the use of 'Malvinas' in the place of 'Falklands'. A small peace offering?

"I know you were shot down. And that you lost your co-pilot. I'm sorry," he ended simply, the tone of his voice slightly lower.

"Thank you. Actually, I was the co-pilot. It seems a bit banal to say so, but we were all just doing our duty."

Charles nodded.

"I was attached to 3 Para."

That probably went some way to explaining Charles' discreet physical fitness, Leandro concluded.

289

"I thought it would be good if we met just the two of us first," Charles continued. "In our business, we can't afford to close our eyes to any possible misunderstandings. I know that in the past, you've made it clear that you're not prepared to do anything which you see as harmful to the interests of Argentina and we completely respect that. In fact, it should not be otherwise. As far as I can tell, we have always relied on you're telling us whether or not you're prepared to look at a piece of work which we may show you. We could probably perfectly well continue on that basis. However, it struck me that we might both benefit by discussing the issue in a little greater detail, in a way which might help us both to establish clearer demarcation lines. I don't know what you think?"

Leandro was nodding.

"I don't have any problem with that. A sort of commercial DMZ?"

"I wouldn't put it that way. A demilitarized zone is a concept used by warring nations. I hope you don't look at our relationship in that fashion."

"Sorry, but very tactful."

"Forget it. By the way, how's the fish?"

"Delicious."

"I'm assuming, that for the purposes of discussion, your English - or should I say Scottish - ancestry represents a cultural affinity with these islands. This means that, in general, you're more content to work with an organisation like Frobisher, as opposed - for instance - to working with the French or Germans."

Leandro nodded.

"At the same time, we also know that for different reasons, mainly economic, the British were something of a privileged partner of Argentina from the very beginning. Whether it's George Canning, or the first diplomatic representative, Woodbine Parish, or our contribution to your country's agricultural and infrastructure development - the railways, the role of the City of London in raising finance and in the process nearly busting Barings bank, all these things, when combined with the size of the Anglo Argentine community, means that there is a real affinity. In fact, probably only the Malvinas stand in our way."

"That, and the fact that for a not insignificant proportion of our left-wing or nationalist intelligentsia, the UK can always be dressed up in the clothes of imperialist pirates, meaning that in the order of hatred, you come in just behind the United States and its Monroe Doctrine of interference in the affairs of any country south of the Rio Grande."

"And some of Kirchner's actions on the islands have come with a heavy dose of anti-imperialist jargon, as I recall."

"You're right, and that goes down very well with a certain slice of the Argentine population."

"To be frank, even though I fought there and lost friends there, I'm probably not so very clear in my own mind as to the rights and wrongs of the Argentine versus the UK arguments over ownership."

"I also belong to a group of people in Argentina who are at heart equally a bit confused. But politics being politics, for better or for worse, you're locked into your position and we're locked into ours. And in the vast majority of the population, the Argentine claim to the islands is hard-wired. Anyway, enough blood has been spilled and more than enough speeches have been made, for us not to wreck a good lunch."

"You are absolutely right and I apologise."

"Let me add a few thoughts, Charles. In simple terms, I'm an Argentine, I was born and grew up there, and put my life at risk for the country. It's a land endowed with all the riches which any country could dream of, inhabited by a population of mixed origins, but which come together in what has up to now been a tortured and often tormented history. You only have to go back to the days of Peron, or the various regimes of the military which ended in the disasters and horrors conducted by Videla and his successors. In spite of all this, the Argentines are a warm, loving and compassionate race, whose goodwill and perhaps irrational optimism in the vast majority of the social classes has enabled them to survive all manner of abuse and misgovernment. My Argentine side makes me want to do anything which will improve our chances of prospering, and progressively eliminating the inequalities which continue to exist in our society. Most of all, I'm interested in finding ways to work towards a situation in which Argentines accept responsibility for the development of their country, on a politically and socially mature basis. Rather than allowing a small minority of largely corrupt politicians to monopolise the stage and abuse our civic and human rights."

Charles raised his hand to signal that he wanted to say something.

"That's fine and laudable. But in practice, how would you define what you call working towards that situation? I mean, does it include going into politics? Are you in fact active in politics? From the little that you've said today and from reading the monthly reports put out by your consultancy, it looks as though you're far from convinced that the present government will actually move the country in the direction you're talking about."

Leandro thought for a minute. Charles was right and had put his finger on the most vulnerable spot.

"Politics in Argentina is a minefield. Large parts of it are massively corrupt and, if you want to get involved, you rapidly have to demonstrate that corruption is not going to be a problem. Though to be honest, there are really very few countries in which corruption is not a problem to a greater or lesser extent. Even countries such as the United States clearly demonstrate that the power of lobbies can deflect even the best intentions. Perhaps you in the United Kingdom are particularly lucky, though I suspect that there must be corners of the system which could do with a bit of cleaning up."

Charles did not dissent.

"At the moment, I do what I can with the research which we publish, and which is not particularly lenient as far as this government is concerned. It has all the makings of being as corrupt or more than the government of Menem, but it comes with an additional, extremely negative, component. Namely the justification of too many actions and policies behind a charade of trying to compensate for the injustices committed under the military regime. Menem tried, but failed, to push through an agenda of reconciliation, similar to what was being done in South Africa. He didn't entirely succeed and a number of key figures surrounding the Kirchners come from the left-wing terrorist movements which suffered most at the hands of the military. What they failed to do by armed means in the 1970s, they are now trying to push through on the grounds that they have been democratically elected. The agenda is pretty hidden still, but I fear we're going to see some major changes, not all of them for the good of the country by any means. That's very worrying."

"So, if I understand you correctly, there might be areas of work which you would see as serving in some way to prevent the kind of decline which you describe. In other words, the good of Argentina is not in your mind synonymous with simply supporting any government in power?"

Again Leandro paused to think.

"Can we order some coffee? I'm beginning to feel the jetlag catching up with me."

"Of course."

Charles again went downstairs to place the order. He was back in a matter of minutes.

"It's going on for two thirty anyway. Let's have a coffee and then we can continue our discussion at the office."

"While we wait, I can start to reply to your question. There are obviously areas, of which responsible – I emphasize the word 'responsible' - Government intentions towards the Malvinas is one, which I would regard as probably excluded from our work together. That might not include something as extreme as whether or not some form of military action were being planned. Repeating that mistake would be disastrous for the country. Not that with this lot, there is the slightest risk, given the way they've emasculated the military. I don't share the approach which Kirchner has been adopting since he came to power, burning the bridges which Menem's Foreign Minister, di Tella, was carefully trying to build towards the islanders - by that I mean cancelling the agreements reached during the 1990s over charter flights and fishing and oil exploration. But I would not go so far as to try and provide secret information on future non-military Argentine policies with regard to the islands. I also believe that Argentina's natural resources belong to us, to the nation, and therefore I'm not interested in working to support oil companies or mining companies to negotiate a better deal at Argentina's expense. That sort of tactical intelligence you will have to get hold of some other way. On the other hand, that almost certainly leaves a wide range of subjects on which we can work together. That probably applies particularly to areas in which the long-term interests of the country are being undermined, either through corruption, through drug trafficking, through terrorism and so on. I say all that, of course, without actually having a very clear idea of the kind of areas in which you might be interested at Frobisher. If I've got it wrong, forgive me. To that you have to add of course the fact that I'm a researcher by training, particularly in economics and finance, and therefore things like drug trafficking or terrorism are not really my area of speciality."

"Do you take sugar?"

"No thanks."

"Let's continue this conversation at the office. It may be that we have got something which fits with what you've been saying."

Charles and Leandro went downstairs and while Charles was paying, Leandro passed his e-mail to the Latvian girl.

"What's your name? Mine's Leandro."

"Velna," she replied.

"Well, Velna, if ever you feel like some sun and some good steak and wine, drop me an e-mail."

The drizzle had stopped and, with typical London weather, the grey clouds were scudding fast overhead, revealing the occasional pale blue patch of sky. It was even colder.

"We can walk from here. We've changed offices since you were last in London."

Charles set off at a brisk pace in the direction of Grosvenor Square.

A small, late nineteenth-century townhouse down a discreet Mayfair mews housed Frobisher's new offices. Nothing outside betrayed the identity of the company behind the gleaming black gloss painted door with its formidable and highly polished brass knocker. The thick red-carpeted hall led towards an imposing staircase, at the top of which hung a large portrait of what Leandro presumed was the Elizabethan navigator. As they entered, a good-looking redhead in her early forties, dressed in a dark grey pinstripe suit, emerged from a side door.

"There are a couple of urgent e-mails on your desk upstairs, Charles, and a call came in from southern Africa, the case you've been working on. Mr Flemming, welcome. I'm Alexandra. I hope that you had a good flight and that the hotel is satisfactory?"

"It's fine, thank you very much for arranging it. I also have a daughter called Alexandra."

"In her early twenties, if I'm not mistaken. I'm sure she's a very pretty girl. Argentine women have a reputation for being very good-looking."

"Judging from what I'm looking at, English women have nothing to worry about either."

Alexandra smiled.

"Perhaps it's not just Argentine women."

"That's enough, you two. We've got business to attend to," Charles interrupted. "We'll go to one of the meeting rooms. Which one is free, Alex?"

"Armada."

"Perhaps not the best choice for a Hispanic visitor. But it did take place over five hundred years ago, so some of the wounds must have healed."

Charles led the way upstairs. The pale grey and white panelled room, its fireplace lit, was furnished in simple dark mahogany Chippendale, with Victorian seascape oil paintings on the walls.

"Take a seat, I've just got to go and deal with those e-mails, but I'll be back in a couple of minutes." Charles pointed to the long dining table in the centre of the room.

While he was gone, Leandro sent a text message to Sam's Argentine cell phone, though far from convinced that she was either using it or that, even if she were, she would reply. On a side buffet, he leafed through a simple, though hermetic, marketing brochure for Frobisher, which did little to conceal the intelligence community and security service origins of its founding partners. A simple map of the world indicated the countries in which Frobisher could claim a presence. He noted that Argentina figured among them. He sat down in one of the armchairs by the fire to await the return of Charles. It was nearly twenty minutes before he reappeared.

"Sorry about that, it was a bit more complex than I had expected."

"Glad to see that Argentina figures on your map." Leandro held up the brochure.

"And so it should. Are you okay for coffee? Would you like another one, to keep you awake?"

"Good idea. Yes please."

Charles pressed a buzzer under the dining table.

"So where were we? I would like to put something to you. I think it's a very interesting question and, subject to your views, I think it might fall outside the areas of potential conflict which we discussed over lunch."

Once a tray with two bone china cups of coffee had been delivered, Charles began to outline a recent requirement which had been brought to them by one of their longest-standing clients, the identity of which he did not however reveal.

Charles first gave Leandro a very potted history of the Arab-Israeli conflict, about which Leandro confessed that, given his relationship with an Argentine girl of Middle Eastern origins, he now knew far more than might have been the case a year or so earlier.

"Well, if she's of Arab origin, you may be getting one version. If she's Jewish, you'll no doubt get another. Either way, it doesn't really matter, since we Brits, in our altruistic enthusiasm, and in particular the enthusiasm of a certain Prime Minister back in 1917, Arthur Balfour, of whom - whatever your girlfriend's origins - she must have told you something, created an insoluble situation which the world has been paying for ever since. Or at least, more precisely, ever since 1948 when Israel was given – or, perhaps more accurately, took - its independence. Balfour may have been acting for personal moral reasons, but the way we and the French carved up the Middle East during the First World War was certainly more a case of realpolitik. From then until the fall of the Berlin Wall, the problems we helped to create were largely kept under control by the superpowers, with the exception of a few minor, though highly visible, wars between Israel and its neighbours. In which the former generally came off better than the latter. At least that might be one interpretation, until Israel got sucked into Lebanon and the Palestinian cause acquired - in my view, far too belatedly - the support of parts of the Arab world, which had until that time mistakenly seen benefit in allowing the problem of the Palestinians to fester. However, the rise of movements such as Fatah or Hezbollah, although they advanced the Palestinian agenda very dramatically, had the additional and now much more dangerous side-effect of intensifying the Shia – Sunni divide. In particular, Iran was drawn into the foreground, not only through its support for Hezbollah, but more generally into the confrontation with Israel. Whether or not Saddam Hussein may have had nuclear ambitions - although he probably never had the means to match those ambitions, as we found to our cost - there seems to be little doubt that Iran has such ambitions and seems to have every intention, whatever the rest of the world may say, of acquiring a militarized nuclear capacity."

"Yes, I've been following that, although obviously at long range."

"Well, as a result, you will no doubt have detected the concerns of bodies such as the IAEA and the Western powers to try and prevent Iran building up a stockpile of weapons-grade fissile material. The Russians, through the sale of their reactor to Iran, are as close as anyone to knowing just how far the Iranians have got to date. But the whole question of Iran's secret installations, growing centrifuge capacities necessary to the enrichment of uranium to weapons grade, and secret attempts to lay their hands on the latest technology and even - if possible - more enriched uranium, keeps a number of people awake at night, and not just in Tel Aviv or Washington."

Charles finished his coffee.

"Forgive me, Leandro, if a lot of what I am about to say is already well-known to you."

Leandro made a gesture to indicate that he should go ahead.

"The attempts of the Iranians to get around the embargoes laid down by the Security Council or unilaterally by the European Union, have served to draw in a number of players who would, normally, have little interest in the Middle Eastern problem. If that weren't enough, the water is also getting muddied by the global links of terrorist organisations, of which Al Qaeda is only one, and which, it is thought, may well have ambitions of its own to acquire radioactive material in order to put together some kind of 'dirty bomb'. Where government policy ends and where terrorist ambitions begin has become a grey area which is making life extremely difficult for security agencies all around the world. Amongst the more marginal players, whose agendas may - at the end of the day - be nothing very much more than a desire to tweak the tail of Uncle Sam, one can now count people like Mr Chavez in Venezuela. With all its oil, it's shown little or no interest in things nuclear. However, Chavez has friends, who happen to include the presidents of your country, Mr and Mrs Kirchner. And Argentina does have a nuclear capability, albeit for civilian use only, in which the Germans such as Siemens have been one of their main technology suppliers. There were stories going around a number of years ago about whether or not Argentina - or at least certain members of the Argentine military - might be tempted to forget about the nuclear free zone of the San Jose treaty. Generally, the experts are of the opinion that nothing much has happened, and one would expect Siemens to keep its eyes well open. However, our experience in Iraq and more recently in Iran have shown us that appearances can be one thing and reality another."

Leandro had been listening carefully.

"I've a feeling I know where you're going on this one, but I should point out that it's hardly an area in which I can move very easily or unobtrusively."

"We appreciate that, but the answer is that, even if it is only to provide evidence that nothing is happening, our client places huge importance on this question, for obvious reasons. We don't have many people like you in Argentina. Of course, we also have to assume that organisations such as Mossad or the CIA are looking at this very closely. If anyone can find out what's going on, it's no doubt the boys at Mossad, but even here, history has shown us that Israel and the rest of the Western powers are far from sharing the same agenda all the time - and even less, their information. Our reading of the Kirchner administrations is that they do not exactly shine by their efficiency, discretion or clarity of strategy. The Kirchners appear to have little respect for traditional institutional, legal, or economic arrangements, players or policies. Opportunism only too often appears to be the name of the game, offending Uncle Sam or screwing the military, a favourite pastime, with little concern for the consequences or for collateral impacts. In that kind of situation, doing something dangerous for the wrong reasons and without thinking through the full consequences, can become a very dangerous way of doing things. Impunity seems to be ingrained in the way your government currently operates. Ninety-five percent of the time, only Argentina suffers. But in the remaining five percent, the collateral damage can be real and, in the particular situation we're talking about, potentially catastrophic."

Charles paused, before adding a final comment.

"Obviously, you have to be the best judge of whether or not you can be of any assistance to us. We will naturally respect your decision."

Leandro nodded.

"Your assessment of the way in which policy is being made in Buenos Aires today sadly rings only too true. I wish it were otherwise. On balance, of course I would like to help. Whether I can actually deliver anything of interest, I have to be in some doubt. But I am prepared to give it a try. You reminded me earlier that we had some kind of unwritten arrangement regarding the lengths to which I would go in situations in which the interests of Argentina might be at stake. I can tell you straight away that only a lunatic would believe that the interests of Argentina might benefit from becoming involved in this kind of situation. At the far end of the world, we easily lose touch with the reality in which countries such as yours have to live. Occasionally we get a taste of it, as when they blew up the Israeli Embassy or the Israeli centre, but one could argue that Argentina's splendid isolation over the years has bred a dangerous sense of impunity, or at the very least, carelessness with the results of our actions. Nine times out of ten, as you say, it's the Argentines themselves who pay for it. Which explains why we've changed governments so often. Arguably, today, some would say that we have the worst expression of this phenomenon. Probably only time will tell."

"Well, if you feel that you can help us on this, I'll put together a more detailed brief. I trust you're in no doubt about the delicacy of the subject. I should mention that our client only wants us to begin work on this around April, so we still have plenty of time, and that will give you an opportunity, once you're back in Buenos Aires, to see how you may be able to meet the brief. Is that all right with you?"

"Fine."

"I think in your e-mail before you came, you mentioned that you might have something to ask us. Is it something you want to discuss now?"

"If you can spare the time."

For the next quarter of an hour, Leandro selectively outlined to Charles the main elements of the case surrounding the murder of Janet Williams. Certain pieces of the story he did not reveal, including the real nature of his relationship with Eduardo, other than to mention that he was his godfather, nor the role of Sam. He did however lay emphasis on the apparent connection between the murder and certain extremist elements inside government, for whom the return of democracy in 1983 had not represented the end of hostilities between sectors of Argentine society. Without explicitly referring to Sarmiento and to the exchanges between him and Eduardo, Leandro described a connection between the assassinations of at least two people connected with the 'dirty war' and a more complex web of financial blackmail and manipulation, apparently originating somewhere inside the current government machine.

"For various reasons, we think that there's a link between the two key figures connected with the murders, not only this woman, Carla, but also someone close to her, who appears to be pulling the strings in the background. And both of them seem to have some kind of connection with Zürich. That's where I'm going on Saturday. Obviously, I don't know what kind of contacts you have in Switzerland, but from the little map in your brochure, I see you claim a presence there. I've never been to Switzerland and apart from their chocolate and banking secrecy, don't know very much about the place. If there was any possibility of having a contact with someone from your organisation, ideally in Zürich, to help me to unravel even a part of the story, I would be extremely grateful. From what we know, there is a financial dimension, probably involving Swiss private banks and some of their Argentine clients. Somehow, the identity of some of these clients has become known. Our suspicion is that an Argentine, man or woman, has been able to piece together enough information to blackmail some of them. On the basis of what I've told you, do you think there is any way you can help?"

Charles sat thinking for a minute. Then he got up, saying that he would be back in about five minutes. It was nearer ten when he reappeared.

"I've been having a word with my colleague who looks after Switzerland. We do have someone in Zürich, who has helped us in the past both on financial questions and on background information relating to residents and nationals. He seems to be very well plugged in both in the banking sector and with the police. The Swiss are extremely vigilant when it comes to foreigners, with the possible exception of where their money comes from. Telling tales on your neighbour is something of a national sport and so the police is usually very well-informed about what foreigners may be up to, given a strong xenophobic streak in the national character. My colleague will first have to check with this person whether they are prepared to help you, and we should have a reply by tomorrow afternoon. What time is your flight?"

"It leaves around six pm from Heathrow as I recall. The day after tomorrow. Perhaps I could give you a ring sometime tomorrow. I would really appreciate any help you can give me."

"That's fine. If we can do it, we would be happy to. But we do have to wait for this person's agreement. Without going into very much detail, can we make reference to someone having possibly penetrated Swiss banking secrecy? That usually puts the Swiss on your side. As to this formidable lady - did you say her name was Carla - I think it's best if you bring that up directly with our contact, it might only put him off, particularly if we didn't get the story quite right. In spite of their conservative appearance, I believe the people of Zürich are actually quite avant garde on the sex front, though it probably doesn't do to remind them of it." Charles chuckled. "I have some pretty wild memories of a case we had in Zürich, involving one of Russia's new rich, a few years back. So take care."

"I'll do my best. I see it's getting dark already. Getting to bed early is probably a good idea."

Charles accompanied him to the door and they shook hands warmly.

"It's been a pleasure meeting you, Leandro, take care. It sounds pretty messy, this business you're involved in. *Un abrazo.*"

Three days later, Leandro woke to the sun streaming into his bedroom. The sound of the Sunday bells of a nearby church gently penetrated the double-glazing of the window. Through the thin gauze of the net curtain, he could glimpse the outline of the hill rising behind the rooftops of the Neumarkt quarter of the town.

He had spent a couple of days wandering round old haunts in London and had managed to have a drink with a colleague from his Citibank days. It felt good being back in London. After Buenos Aires, it was his favourite city. Its bookshops were a particular passion and he had spent most of one morning in Waterstones on Piccadilly, buying far too many books for his luggage allowance. He never learned!

His flight from London had landed at Kloten airport at around eight thirty the previous evening and he had caught a cab into town to the *pensione* into which the tourist service desk at the airport had booked him on arrival. The impeccably clean white Mercedes – something of a contrast with the Buenos Aires taxis he knew - had made its way through a maze of cobbled back streets and deposited him on the doorstep of a small, eighteenth-century town house, carefully preserved. The snow had been neatly piled up on either side of the porch and the ice scraper was clearly visible.

In contrast to the unfriendly formality of the taxi driver – another contrast, although this time in Buenos Aires' favour - the lady who answered the door had been polite and welcoming. On seeing his passport, in surprisingly good English, she had launched into a long and convoluted story about her great uncle who had emigrated from the Canton of Graubünden to Buenos Aires in the 1920s and had apparently made good, something to do with farming.

Leandro smiled back at her.

"You're quite right, there are a lot of Swiss round that part of Santa Fe Province, whole towns of them, and all involved in the cattle and grain business. Have you ever gone to see your relatives?"

"Oh, it's far too far and expensive for me, though they seem to be able to afford to come over here once in a while." She paused. "The last time was in the mid-1990s, their currency was strong, something to do with the dollar, my cousin came with his very pretty wife and two children. Such lovely little ones they were too. The little girl was so pretty, with long black hair falling down her back, beautifully dressed, not like the kids around here who shave their heads and dress like criminals. All these street punks, with their sticky hair and black finger nails." She shuddered at the thought.

Leandro smiled again sympathetically. "We don't seem to have many of them in Buenos Aires, rather the opposite, young men with long hair, as if the Beatles had never gone out of fashion. And the girls are certainly very pretty. We are not much into punk rock as far as I can see."

"And you should see it when we have the Gay Parade in June! Down the Bahnhofstrasse, all these ugly people, perverts most of them, I would say, dancing all day and through the night. It's all the fault of our politicians, they'll do anything for a vote – anybody's! But that's enough chatting, Señor Leandro, you must be tired, here are your keys, it's on the third floor at the top of the stairs. Breakfast's between eight and ten tomorrow morning, it's Sunday, so you can sleep in a bit longer."

He took the key and thanked her, and made his way up the stairs to his little room on the third floor. Half an hour later, he was asleep.

As he lay under the heavy duvet, half dozing, he felt in no hurry to get up for the breakfast downstairs. Instead, he began to plan his day, all the more since it was a Sunday and he guessed that the Swiss would take their weekends seriously. First, find a café for some good strong black coffee and some croissants and hopefully a newspaper in some language he could understand, followed by a little sightseeing to get the feel of the city, then a phone call to Francisco Mateo to see if they could have dinner that evening. After that, he could wander round the old parts of the town and find a nice bistro for some lunch. He fell asleep and woke up again after ten.

After a backbreaking shower and shave - the slanting roof of the old house put the basin mirror at the level of his chest - he took a small rucksack out of his suitcase, into which he dropped a map of the city that he had picked up at the airport information desk, as well as his laptop and cell phone. He had not even bothered to check last night whether his roaming also worked in Switzerland. It didn't. What chance of finding a 'pay as you go' on a Sunday?

He went down the stairs quietly and dropped the keys into the small wooden chalet marked 'Schlüssel'. Turning, he found himself face to face with Frau Schmied.

"You did not come down to breakfast," she said with a mild tone of reproach.

"Don't worry, Frau Schmied, I slept through, I was very tired ... and your bed is so comfortable," he added, to pacify her.

The stern look on her face faded immediately and she smiled.

"That was my grandmother's bed, you know, it has her initials on the foot of the bed."

She was clearly family proud.

"Are you going out?" which seemed an unnecessary enquiry given his appearance. "If so, take a house key, that way you can come and go as you wish," and she took one out of the counter drawer. "The small one is the only one you need during the day, the other one also at night. You don't look as though you're properly dressed for the cold, though. Here, take this scarf, it was my late husband's and I always leave it here for this kind of situation."

She handed him a plaid cashmere, which he dutifully - but also gratefully - wound round his lower face.

He thanked her and let himself out into the street. It was virtually empty on this freezing Sunday morning. The narrow streets of this part of the old town twisted and curved, but he guessed that by going downhill – as long as he kept upright - he would eventually come to the quay by the river Limmat which divided the town. He made his way down the slope, stepping carefully to avoid the rare patches of black ice which had survived, and stopping to look into the different shop windows. A strange mixture of graffiti-daubed high fashion boutiques alternating with dark kiosks selling manga magazines, sex toys and heavy pornography. He finally came on what looked to be a popular café, judging by the number of people of all ages and backgrounds propping up the counter inside and spilling out onto small tables on the pavement, even in this chill. One of these was empty, so – deciding to brave the cold in exchange for the sun - he quickly settled himself into the light aluminium chair, placing his rucksack carefully between his feet. He remembered hearing that the law-abiding Swiss were not above a little petty crime, especially in this city.

The waitress was slim, her black hair cut in an aggressive crew-cut, heavy makeup contrasting with her pale skin. She was wearing tight PVC jeans tucked into massively soled army boots, a skull-adorned black tee-shirt, her bare arms showing one or two exotic examples of the tattooist's skills. Leandro smiled at her, but got nothing in return.

"Could I have a black coffee and some croissants? Sorry, I don't speak German," he asked, his English deliberately slow.

"It's alright, I'm from London," came the sharp reply. "Sugar and milk?"

"Oh, great, I just came in from London last night. Sugar will be fine … And do you have any English language paper?" he asked.

"You're not English," she almost spat it out, with a faint tone of disgust.

"No actually, I'm Argentine."

"I thought you were too sexy to be British," she retorted, a slight hint of interest now creeping into her voice.

"Thanks, it's always good for morale, at my age."

Still she did not smile.

She was back in five minutes, weaving her way between the tables, exchanging a word or two with some of their occupants. She laid out the espresso, a plate with two croissants ('Not up to the *medialunas* at London City,' Leandro thought to himself) and a copy of yesterday's International Herald Tribune.

"Best I could find," she almost apologized.

"Have you any idea where I could find a cell phone or some 'pay as you go' card, on a Sunday," he asked her as she was turning away.

She appeared not have heard, so he decided to wait until she brought the bill. He settled down to look at the IHT, not that he expected to learn much that he did not already know from the day before.

The news items were stale and the financial markets as depressing as ever, with relentlessly pessimistic commentary on the slow demise of the world's banking industry, a subject about which he was beginning to feel that no-one could tell him anything new. No news about Argentina, but that came as no surprise, it was a long way away. On the Saturday supplement pages devoted to the arts and culture, his attention was caught by a half page article by an Armenian art expert, Souren Melikian, writing up an auction of rare stamps due to be held in Zürich at the end of the coming week. One of the major pieces would be a set of nineteenth century stamps from Mauritius. Leandro's philatelic expertise had not got much beyond his own small collection, started at the age of seven. An uncle had given him an album and several transparent envelopes, each containing one hundred stamps from all around the world, which he had carefully split up into their different countries of origin, each country getting a page in the album. Even now, Leandro remembered that Mauritius was one of the holy grails of stamp collectors, and could just about recall a blurred image of the head of Queen Victoria on a black or red background as he had poured over it in a dog-eared catalogue from London. The expert was quoting the auctioneer's estimate at over a couple of million dollars. Maybe he'd been collecting the wrong countries!

His reading was interrupted by a tap on the shoulder and he found himself looking up into the heavily bearded face of a young man, dressed in a black polo sweater and jeans. Black seemed to be the only colour round here, they must have met Henry Ford, Leandro thought to himself.

"You looking for a phone?"

"I might be...," Leandro replied cautiously.

"Well, you just asked Tanya where you could find one, didn't you?"

Leandro remembered that he had glimpsed the waitress stopping at one of the other tables after bringing him the coffee.

"Okay, you're right, any ideas where I can get one on a Sunday?"

The young man sat down on the chair opposite Leandro and placed a small leather shoulder bag by his side.

"What do you want? Nokia? Motorola?"

"I'm not really very fussy, as long as it works and has credit."

Twenty minutes later, Leandro was again on his way down towards the river, fifty francs of credit on a Motorola in his pocket and Tanya's phone number as the first entry on the SIM. She had come back with the bill and, in response to his thanks for having sorted out the phone problem, had slipped him a napkin with her cell phone number under the change.

"I get off after five," was all she had added curtly.

When he reached the river, a dark grey flood coming in from the lake, he paused and, finding shelter in a doorway, tapped out a message to Sam's Argentine cell phone, telling her that he was now in Zürich and giving her his new-found cell phone number. Reluctant to rely solely on this means a communication, he would have to find an Internet cafe to send a mail as well.

Occasionally scanning the town map, Leandro was soon crossing the Muenster Bruecke into the city centre. A couple of blocks took him to the Bahnhofstrasse, lined with impressive jeweller's shops, furriers, and banks. Lots of banks. Paradeplatz found him staring up at the stern façade of Credit Suisse, the epitomy of Switzerland's banking secrecy and respectability. Millionaires were obviously well catered for along this street. He sat down on a tram-stop bench in the middle of the square and took out the cell phone.

He dialled Francisco Mateo's home number and after a series of rings, a woman's voice answered "*Hallo? Wer ist da?* Who is there?"

"Do you speak Spanish ... or English ?" he asked.

"Both," came the reply in both languages.

"I'm so sorry to disturb you on a Sunday, but I was wondering whether Francisco was there."

"Just a minute," and he heard the voice turn away from the phone. "It's for you."

Francisco came to the phone.

"Hello, who's that?"

Leandro repeated his apology.

"Hey, Leandro, what brings you here? So long, *che*! How are you? How are things?"

"I was just passing through, and...."

"Nobody just passes through Zürich, Leandro! Rome, yes, London, yes, Paris, yes, but Zürich – not really."

They both laughed.

"Okay, you're right, I've got a little business to attend to and I was wondering whether we could have a drink or something to eat, and maybe you could guide me?"

"Of course, although we're just going out for a day along the lake with the kids, there's a warm little restaurant with a good view of the mountains, not sure whether that would be the best scenario. How about lunch tomorrow? Monday?"

"If that's okay with you, that would be fine," Leandro replied. "How's the family? How many of you are there now, anyway?"

"Just the four of us, our daughter is six and our latest – a boy – is four. Quite a handful, you must come round, I'm sure that Carolina would love to see you too."

"It's Leandro," he spoke in an aside to Carolina presumably standing near him.

"Yes, she's nodding her head vigorously. Let's have lunch tomorrow or the day after, and then fix up something, if you're staying on a few days:"

"I'll be here until about Thursday, I would say."

"Okay, let's plan dinner on Tuesday then. Is that okay with you, Caro?" Francisco had his hand half over the mouthpiece. "We'll either give him something here or get Fräulein Anika to come and babysit.... Yes, Leandro, that's fine. I'll give you the number of my cell phone, so give me a call tomorrow morning when I'm at the office and we'll fix where we meet the day after. Okay?"

"That's wonderful, *che*, I'll call you sometime after ten tomorrow morning, then. Have a good time with the kids. And thanks. Oh, do you have any idea where I can find an Internet cafe? I'm about halfway along Bahnhofstrasse, as far as I can tell."

Francisco gave him the approximate location of a cafe, back on the other side of the Limmat.

He looked up the telephone number of the Frobisher contact that Charles had given him when he had called the office. The ringtone finally gave way to an answering machine which, after an initial incomprehensible message in what he presumed was Swiss German, gave way to an English version, asking the caller to leave a message and phone number.

"This is Señor Perez," Leandro began, using the name provided to him by Charles, in preference to his real identity. "I believe you've heard from London and have agreed that we could meet."

He gave his newfound Swiss cell phone number, but not the address or telephone of his *pensione*, given that Frau Schmied knew him by his real name. "I will be here for at least a week. Thank you."

By this time, it was getting on for one thirty in the afternoon and the effect of the croissants had long ago worn off. Passing what looked like a warm little bistro in the Augustiner Gasse, not far from the cathedral, he rapidly discovered that lunch was served a lot earlier in Switzerland. The owner finally relented and steered him towards a table in the corner, thankfully close to an open fire.

About an hour later, having worked his way through what the waiter assured him was a Zürich speciality of veal in a cream sauce and *roesti* potatoes, followed by a delicious baked apple with thick cream, washed down with a light red wine from the Canton of Valais, his cell phone began to vibrate in his pocket.

"Hello, is that Señor Perez? This is Herr Johann. You called me and I've had a message from London. In what way can I be of assistance?"

The English, though grammatically correct, nevertheless bore the heavy overlay of a German accent. Leandro thanked him for calling and asked him whether it would be possible to meet sometime in the next couple of days, at his convenience. He wanted to have the meeting with Francisco after seeing Herr Johann, in case that provided any leads that he might share with Francisco.

"How about a drink at the Hotel Baur au Lac tomorrow evening? Say around six o'clock?"

"That'll be perfect. How will I recognise you?"

"Don't worry. I have your photograph. See you tomorrow, Señor Perez."

Efficient, the people at Frobisher, Leandro thought. He looked out of the window and saw that the blue sky had given away to dark grey, with heavy white clouds moving fast over the rooftops.

"There will be snow," the waiter announced as he brought Leandro the bill. "You'll probably need a thicker coat," he commented dryly.

"Not sure where I'm going to find that. Not to mention that all the prices I've seen on the Bahnhofstrasse seemed to be way beyond my means."

The waiter, perhaps unused to admissions of poverty in this mega-rich metropolis, seemed to take pity on him.

"There are a number of shops selling second hand clothes, often quite good quality, on the other side of the river. You might try there, off the Muenster Gasse, that area."

Thanking him for his advice, Leandro made his way down the hill back towards the Limmat River, crossing on the Raeths Bruecke, and plunging back into the maze of little streets which led off the Muenster Gasse. Tucked in amongst the bewildering array of little boutiques, he finally found something which appeared to match the waiter's description. A 'goth' girl greeted him in a friendly fashion. Her ears displayed a mass of silver rings and studs, with multi-coloured ribbons woven in with her black and violet dreadlocks, a studded dog collar round her neck, and various layers of plastic black and red skirts. Even through all this smokescreen, he could imagine that she was quite pretty. He explained what he was looking for and she led him over to a long rail from which hung all sizes and shapes of coats and jackets. She finally pulled out a three-quarter length, dark blue overcoat of heavy wool, reminiscent of something a naval captain might wear with its broad collar and matt black buttons, one of the few items wide enough to accommodate his shoulders. She helped him into the coat, smoothing it into place, a process which Leandro thought was taking rather longer than such a simple gesture warranted. He turned to find her upturned face smiling at him, and, as she began to fasten the buttons on the front, he felt her hand slip inside. Laughing, he pushed her gently away. There must be something about his Punta del Este suntan!

She made some remark, which he could not understand, but which from the look on her face suggested a certain disappointment at his lack of libido. He smiled apologetically and made to pay for the coat. She raised her two hands, fingers out-stretched, five times, to indicate fifty Swiss francs. Good value, he thought.

The girl opened the door for him, offering a small business card and her cheek for him to kiss. Since Argentines systematically kiss all members of the opposite sex anyway whenever they meet, Leandro kissed her. She waved to him from the door of the shop as he headed off in the direction of the Internet cafe indicated to him by Francisco. It was full and he had to wait about ten minutes before being given a booth. He sent off a simple message to Sam, giving her the address of his *pensione*, its telephone number and his Swiss cell phone number. He also sent a message to Elena to say that he had arrived safely, suggesting she pass on the message. She would know that this applied to Eduardo.

By this time, evening had come. He asked the man behind the Internet console if he could recommend a good pub or bar.

312

After a day spent wandering around the city, with a sense of growing frustration and foreboding at the absence of any response from Sam, the next evening found Leandro entering the elegant doors of the Hotel Baur au Lac, along with the Dolder Grand up on the eastern shore overlooking the lake, a flagship of world-class service for the world's very rich. In its honour, Leandro had managed a blazer and a tie, which went surprisingly well with his recently acquired coat. On entering the bar, a man sitting on one of the high stools at the far end gestured to him with a rolled up newspaper.

"What would you like to drink, Señor Perez?"

"A glass of cold white wine will be perfect," Leandro replied.

Herr Johann placed the order with the barman and, picking up his own drink, led the way to a table over in the far corner.

"Your first time in Zürich?"

"Yes it is, very beautiful city, I don't think I've ever seen quite so much wealth on display."

"Oh, that's for the visitors, we in Zürich do not believe in too much ostentation. Thank you, Franz." This to the waiter, who had brought over Leandro's wine. "It has also got worse in recent years. We now have to cater for the super-rich from Moscow and Peking, who want to see a lot of diamonds and gold in the shop windows, so as to minimise the time spent choosing inside the shop. They seem to like to walk in and give the impression that they know what they want, even if they've only just made up their minds ten seconds earlier outside."

Herr Johann permitted himself a modest smile. He looked to be about fifty-five years old, dark - possibly dyed - hair receding, a little too heavy around the waist, with all the airs of a minor bank executive.

"Luckily, that's not really my problem. First of all, Herr Johann, to your good health. I don't want to take up too much of your time. The people in London kindly offered to introduce you to me to provide a little help over a rather complex matter in which I've been involved in Argentina. From what I was told in London, you might be able to help me through your excellent access to the Zürich police and authorities dealing with nationality questions."

Herr Johann nodded his head to indicate that this was possible.

Leandro went on to explain that he was trying to identify a man of Argentine origin, who had apparently settled in Zürich sometime between 1981 and 1982, at a time when he might have been some twenty-five years old. This person might have worked in the financial sector in Zürich into the 1990s, before returning to Argentina around the year 2000. His original case for Swiss residence could have been based on the claim that he could no longer remain safely in Argentina under the military dictatorship. Recalling the names scribbled on the interrogation centre film, Leandro added that it was possible that he might have had some relationship with a woman, also possibly of Argentine origin, with the name of Burkart, although Leandro couldn't be sure of the spelling. Her first name might be Carla. He ended by emphasising the delicacy of the matter and the need to ensure that this enquiry should in no way get back to the persons under investigation. He saw no particular reason to explain his own status nor his profession. A man like the one sitting opposite him would be used to anonymity and forego any questions not directly relating to the matter in hand. Frobisher no doubt employed and collaborated with people from every conceivable background and, in the same way, it would not occur to Leandro to ask about Herr Johann's profession. The introduction from Frobisher would be sufficient to ensure the necessary level of trust between them on this occasion.

Herr Johann listened to him in silence, occasionally noting a word or two on a little pad.

Seeing that Leandro had nothing further to add, he asked. "I presume that you have no further information. You will no doubt realise that it is not a lot to work with, but I suppose it is also probable that the number of Argentine immigrants coming to Zürich at that time will not be a very large one. You are no doubt in a hurry."

"The trouble is that my resources are not unlimited. So the sooner I can obtain the information I need and be on my way back to Argentina the better. Oh, and by the way, might you be able to check whether a certain person flew into Zürich in the last ten days on an Argentine passport?"

It had suddenly occurred to him that Herr Johann might also be able to confirm whether Sam had arrived in Zürich, as he suspected.

"I can try," Herr Johann responded a little noncommittally. Leandro gave him Sam's name. He closed his notebook and finished his drink. Not a man for the small talk, Leandro noted.

"You have been most kind. Can I offer you another drink?" but Herr Johann had already signalled the waiter to bring the tab. "Please allow me to pay, Herr Johann."

"Certainly not, Señor Perez, you are a guest in our city. I will contact you on your cell phone at about noon tomorrow to let you know how I'm getting on. It's been a pleasure meeting you," he ended, though it sounded more like a case of Swiss formality.

They both rose and Herr Johann discreetly shook Leandro's hand, before walking away in a manner which indicated that he did not propose to allow them to be seen together too much. Leandro sat down again and indicated to the barman that he would have another glass of white wine.

He pulled out his phone. Still no message from Sam. Having finished his wine, he went out into the lobby and asked the concierge if there was a Business Centre where he might check his e-mails. Parting with twenty Swiss francs gave him half an hour of Internet. No sign of a mail from Sam there either. Nor was there any message from Eduardo. He had to hope that a combination of Herr Johann and Francisco might bring some progress.

He rang Francisco and suggested postponing their lunch until the Wednesday, to gain time to hear from Herr Johann.

Leaving the hotel, he made his way across the windswept bridge to the Kronenhalle brasserie, which he had found during the day's wanderings, located on the same side of the river as his *pensione*. The night was cold and he happily settled himself into a small table as a waiter deposited the crisp napkin over his knees. With its high ceiling

315

illuminated by elegant chandeliers, panelled walls covered in prints and paintings, the waiters dressed in smart black and white, the place reminded him of some of Buenos Aires' turn of the century cafes and restaurants. Taking the waiter's advice, he again ordered the classic veal and *roesti*, with an ice-cold German lager, and settled down to enjoy the warmth and the elegance of the place. He was in no hurry to get back out into the cold.

With Swiss punctuality, his cell phone rang next day at noon precisely.

"Señor Perez? Herr Johann. I believe I have most of what you need. I suggest we meet, if that is convenient for you, in half an hour's time at Café Weggen, in the Weggengasse. Number 4."

Impressive, Leandro thought to himself. They duly met in the small cafe indicated by Herr Johann, where he handed Leandro a manila envelope containing a thin folder.

"Please review it. If there are any additional questions, I will take them now. I can also confirm that the lady whose name you gave me flew into Zürich on Air France at half past eight in the evening ten days ago, coming from Paris. The hotel address which she provided is also in there. I believe that the person in whom you're interested is the one identified in these notes. He appears to be the only Argentine who matches all the parameters you gave me, namely age, approximate year of arrival, grounds for requesting asylum and subsequent professional career, before departure for Argentina in 2001. As to the woman Burkart, although the spelling is not quite the same, being more correctly 'Burkhardt', again there appears to be a match, principally based on her date of arrival from Argentina, although she subsequently changed her name to Bodmer. She also appears to have had a connection with the Argentine gentleman. Her professional career however appears more unusual, as you will see."

Herr Johann put on a slightly pursed smile as he finished the sentence.

Leandro skimmed through the two sheets of paper contained in the folder.

The man's name was Alberto Dávila. A name at last! He had arrived in Switzerland in late 1981 and by the late 1980s had acquired a Swiss passport, keeping the same name. There was no indication that he had renounced Argentine citizenship. Given the usual rules of minimum residence, normally at least twelve years in Switzerland, this suggested that Dávila must have some Swiss antecedents or else perhaps some good connections. From 1982 to 1985, Dávila had gone through a minor Zürich business school and emerged with a diploma in economics and finance. At that point, he had been employed by a small finance company specialising in the trading of devalued bonds issued by countries suffering from the third world financial collapse of the mid-1980s, in which such countries as Argentina and Mexico provided a large part of the instruments they bought and sold. In early 1991, he had taken a job on the private money management side of UBS, where he remained for the next two years. From UBS he had moved to American Express credit card services based in the same city, although on what, from the summary of his tax returns, initially appeared to be a lower salary. He had remained at American Express until 2001, when he had left Switzerland, ostensibly returning to Argentina. At this point, the information on Dávila came to an end.

"There is a list of his home addresses. Can one deduce anything from these?"

"The areas in which he is living improve steadily, so we can assume that he is also increasing his disposable income to meet the higher rents. His last address is an expensive block of flats on the outskirts of the city heading along the lake."

"You have also included details of his cars, the last one being a large BMW, which would also confirm that his financial position is improving."

Herr Johann nodded.

"I should also mention that, although there is nothing written in these documents, he is suspected of having possibly had contacts with Marxist and underground Castroist organizations. He is believed to have travelled at least on one occasion to Cuba, in 1995, and the impression is that this was not for tourism. My contact gave me this verbally."

Leandro turned to the double-sided sheet of paper on Burkhardt/Bodmer. He noted that her first name appeared on the file as Carolina - not a big jump to Carla. She had arrived about a year after Dávila, but her direct Swiss lineage, tracing back to a small village in the Canton of Zürich from which her grandfather had emigrated in the 1920s, meant that she had rapidly acquired Swiss nationality. She had not made any claim for asylum. Her first job had been in the cantonal hospital, working as an assistant anaesthetist, having apparently been able to show some medical training back in Argentina. She had continued at the hospital until 1990, when her professional activities seemed formally to cease. Her social security number had remained unchanged. Leandro noted that her home address in 1989 and 1990 seemed to coincide with that of Dávila, although their flat numbers were different.

"I see that Dávila and Burkhardt seem to have had the same address."

"Yes, or at least the same building. That was an additional reason to confirm that these two people in whom you are interested are probably connected. You will find one more connection later."

By the mid-1990s, Bodmer, the name she had now adopted, appeared to be moving in very different circles and the quotation from her file which Herr Johann had included made little secret of the fact that she had now transferred her talents and ambitions to the escort trade. A brief entry for 1994 said that the police had been called to a 'studio' where she served her clients, predictably in response to complaints from neighbours about the irregular hours she kept. This had led to a further change of address. On this occasion, the name of Dávila appeared as a guarantor for Bodmer on the rental agreement. As an annex to the notes on Burkhardt / Bodmer, a single sheet of paper provided details of her **present** website, including a summary breakdown of the services which she provided to clients.

"Miss Bodmer pays her taxes and her parking fines and so, for the time being, nobody is interfering with her life. It has however come to the notice of the Cantonal authorities that she travels extensively, if only judging by the fact that her passports seem to need frequent replacement. No doubt, this is connected with her business. We also understand that her bank account is quite substantial."

Herr Johann kept a straight face.

"I see there are two addresses now."

"The first one is, I believe, her private residence. The second, her place of work. Both of them are in an upmarket part of town. There is also an indication that she may have an address in Geneva, though the property is in the name of a company."

Leandro, perhaps for the first time since this chase had begun, now had the strong feeling that some of the larger pieces of the jigsaw puzzle were finally falling into place. At last they appeared to have a connection between Carla and someone who might begin to fit the profile of the blackmailer.

"I am most grateful to you, Herr Johann. I could never have imagined such speed and precision of information. Perhaps someday I can return the favour. I've no idea whether your business may take you to Argentina."

"Only too pleased to have been of service, Señor Perez. And who knows, maybe I will take you up on your offer someday."

He got up, acknowledging Leandro's gesture that this time he would pay.

"Within limits, if there is any additional information you require, please let me know. Goodbye, Señor Perez."

He again disappeared as discreetly as the night before, leaving Leandro with the sense that Herr Johann would somehow always pass unnoticed. Armed with all this information, he felt ready to meet Francisco the following day for lunch. But first, a quick stop at the hotel which Sam had noted on her immigration form. At least Sam did not seem to have moved straight in with Carla. He picked up a taxi outside and fifteen minutes later was standing in front of the chic receptionist of an elegant little boutique hotel in the Enge district of the city. Trust Sam to maintain standards.

He explained that he had just flown in from Argentina and was looking for a friend who had told him that she was staying at this hotel. Somewhat diffidently, the girl consulted her computer screen.

"She checked out yesterday, Sir."

"She didn't tell me anything about leaving," Leandro genuinely expressed disappointment. "Did she leave any forwarding address, or perhaps a note?"

"No, Sir, I'm sorry. I have no information of that kind."

"Well, would you be able to tell me whether she booked a taxi for the airport?"

"I don't believe so, Sir, since I booked the taxi for her, but she made no mention of the airport or the railway station."

"Thank you."

He kicked himself for having missed Sam by so little. If she hadn't gone to the airport or the Bahnhof, it suggested that she had stayed in Zürich, presumably at Carla's. He did, thanks to Herr Johann, have leads in the form of Carla's two addresses, not to mention the website. But how to make use of them? He could hardly turn himself into a one-man surveillance team. Nor could he judge whether his text messages and e-mails were getting through to Sam. He rather suspected that she would have been checking her mailbox while staying at the hotel. If she wasn't replying, there had to be some reason. But whether this was by way of a precaution, or because she really did not want Leandro to make contact, was far from clear.

He sat down on a bench in front of the hotel, trying to work out the motives for Sam's silence. Suddenly he was gripped by an overwhelming sense of frustration, even futility. If Sam didn't want to see him, what the hell was he doing chasing around Zürich? Here he was, ten thousand kilometres from home, having flown here at his expense because he felt that Sam required his help and protection. And now she was doing nothing to respond to his attempts to make contact. Should he assume that it might all be over? And yet, being the injured party in the kind of emotional sparring match, which sometimes seemed to define Sam's relationships, was one thing. To reach the definitive conclusion that it was all over was another. And more than he could countenance at that moment.

Yet as he thought about it, he felt a sudden need to switch off, break the pattern somehow, even if only for a short while. Churning the problem wasn't going to solve it. Closing his mind - and even his body - to it, however briefly, might allow things to fall into place, give him a different perspective on his relationship with Sam. His mind and his emotions needed a change.

On the spur of the moment, he took a taxi back to the shop where he had bought his coat. To his disappointment, the pretty girl who had served him had been replaced by someone he took to be the middle-aged owner, so, after a cursory search through the clothes-racks, he headed off up the hill towards the cafe at which he had been served by the English girl, Tanya, on the first morning of his arrival. Although she saw him arrive through the door, she initially gave no sign of recognition. However, on coming over to him at the table he had selected near the back of the cafe, she gave a brief smile.

"So, how's the gaucho surviving the northern cold?"

"Not too bad. How are you, Tanya?"

"I'll be a lot better in a couple of hours when my shift ends around ten. Can you stick around that long?"

Leandro was disappointed that she should have interpreted his intentions quite so easily. On the other hand, he had heard that English girls were not ones for wasting time.

"Sure. You keep serving the beers, I'll wait."

Ten o'clock found them standing on the pavement outside the cafe. The street was dark and the air bitterly cold.

"So, what's on offer?"

"I don't know," he replied rather lamely. "You know this place much better than I do."

"I tend to prefer a good meal after, rather than before, sex. But let's start off with a few drinks. There is a good *bierkeller* just round the corner, the owner's a friend of mine."

Judging by the way the owner greeted her, Leandro calculated that Tanya had a pretty elastic interpretation of friendship. They settled into a booth in the cellar bar, where, to Leandro's relief, the noise was a trifle less deafening and the haze of smoke more efficiently dissipated by a noisy extractor at pavement level.

"So what brings you to Zürich? Going skiing?"

Leandro saw no reason to tell this girl anything close to the truth. He explained that he had come to do research into the Swiss financial system, given his work as an economic consultant back in Argentina. Zürich was the heart of the Swiss banking system, so that's why he was here, to get a view on how the financial crisis was affecting the business of managing people's money. If at the same time, he could have some fun and see some of Zürich's more exotic people and places, so much the better.

"When you say exotic, what've you got in mind?" she asked, with a slight smile playing over her lips.

"Oh, I don't know. What's the menu? What do people like you get up to on a Saturday night?"

She paused to down half her beer.

"Well, there's just about everything in a city like this. Drugs, sex, got a vice, you name it, there's certainly some place you'll find it. What are you into?" As if in little doubt as to what part of his answer might be, her hand was already travelling rapidly in the direction of his crotch.

"You know, you're fucking sexy!" she added, almost superfluously.

In a strange way, Leandro felt that this kind of unsubtle, purely physical approach, with a girl at the opposite end of the spectrum from Sam, was exactly what he needed tonight.

"Okay, I'm certainly getting the message, and happy to do so. But how about you showing me one or two of your favourite haunts first, perhaps after we've had something to eat, and then we'll see where we end the night. I'm not sure, by the way, that my *gasthaus* - or rather my landlady - is going to be the best solution."

"Don't worry, that's easy. Pass me a hundred francs, and I'll first pick up something to accelerate the brainwaves. From my friend, Johnny, over there."

Leandro watched her go over to the bar armed with his cash, where there was a swift exchange and she was back by his side.

"I don't know why, but somehow I don't get the feeling that you're a regular. So this stuff's pretty light."

She lit up a couple of cigarettes.

Somehow, Leandro felt vaguely disappointed that his image seemed to be so blatantly innocent. After another couple of beers and the cigarettes behind them, they emerged once again into the freezing night.

"To start the evening, the place I'm thinking of going to won't get rolling for an hour or so at least, so why don't we get something to eat? We can get some great pizzas just round the corner."

She led the way down the ill-lit street.

At around two in the morning, they found themselves standing at the entrance to a short alleyway, which looked to be the back end of a garage or warehouse. Inside, to the mind-numbing throb of the latest form of 'electro-house' and blinding strobe lights, she pulled him into a heaving mass of exotic figures, dressed in 'goth', punk, fetish, and all manner of disguises drawn from video games or similar sources. Part of the warehouse seemed to be broken down into smaller cubicles in which the groups congregated according to their dress code or their sexual inclinations. Given Tanya's taste in clothes, Leandro was not too surprised to find himself being led towards a 'goth' group in which shaven heads, PVC, straps and leather seemed to predominate. On reflection, with his leather jacket and jeans, he did not feel too incongruous, and he was surprised to see that he was by no means out of place in terms of his age. The aroma of hash and many other stimulants, not to mention beer, was overpowering.

What Leandro took to be a friend of Tanya's pushed her way through the crowd, and after an extended mouth-to-mouth embrace with Tanya, turned her appreciative attention to Leandro, a process in which Tanya seemed only too happy to share. The second girl also appeared to be English, judging from the few words they had exchanged between them. If anything, her 'goth' look was even more outlandish, with a mass of chains festooning her black rig, and studs vying for space with contrasting black and red makeup on what, Leandro detected, was actually a quite pretty face. Her long hair had been dyed in alternating vertical bands of crimson and grey, her dress a combination of diminutive skirt, torn stockings and huge boots with platform soles.

After about an hour, the noise and the claustrophobia of the place were beginning to take a physical toll on Leandro.

"Perhaps we can find something a little less noisy?"

"I thought you'd never ask," Tanya threw back at him and, leading him firmly by the hand and grabbing the second girl round the waist, she steered the trio in the direction of the door. On top of all the beers and whatever he had smoked, the cold hit him like a sledgehammer and he had to lean against the building to avoid falling over. The two girls slipped under each arm and marched him carefully down the street. A couple of blocks later, when he was wondering whether he could keep going at all, they steered him through the door of a small semi-detached house in an alleyway.

"Can you make it up two floors?"

He nodded, but still required their help to get there. Tanya turned the key in the lock and he eased through the narrow entrance door. Much to his surprise, the place was tidy and the air, thanks to an open skylight, was fresh, although overlaid with a strong incense-like perfume. The two girls pushed him gently down onto the bed which seemed to cover half the floor of the small sitting room. Whatever they had drunk or smoked, being generally unused to such a mixture, Leandro felt as if his strength had drained out of him.

"Don't worry, Leo, we'll look after you," Tanya whispered in his ear. It was the last thing he could remember until near lunchtime on the following day. He retained a faint impression of the two girls moving all over him in the darkness before all went black.

"Coffee?"

It was the other girl. He had never even found out her name.

"Tanya had to go to work. She sends her regards and asked me to tell you that she'll always retain a fond memory of an Argentine gaucho."

The girl laughed as she set a mug of steaming coffee on the floor beside him.

"Frankly, I'd be amazed if anything happened on my side at all," Leandro commented, an apologetic tone in his voice.

"Don't worry, with a bit of our help, it certainly did!"

"Shame I was too far gone to appreciate it, in that case."

"Tell you what, we'll do it again - and this time, we'll make sure that you do. By the way, Tanya thought that you might need some help, not sure for what, but if you need manpower if things get rough or need any supplies of things exotic, she said to call her. Here's her cell phone number, though she thinks you already have it."

Having made his way back to his *pensione*, he just had enough time to shower, the water first boiling, then freezing, to bring him back to a semblance of normality. Shaved and changed, he set off to meet Francisco for lunch at the little restaurant he had suggested.

Francisco was already waiting for him and, after greeting Leandro warmly to make up for all the years since they had last met, he gestured to the opposite side of the small wooden table which he had taken at the back of the bistro.

Leandro first apologized for having changed the day of their lunch.

"No problem. *Che,* it's good to see you after all these years, when was it we last met? In Buenos Aires, wasn't it, in the middle 1990s? In spite of everything, time hasn't treated you too badly. And how's Elena? You had a daughter?"

"They're both fine. But Elena and I have split up, a couple of years ago, though we still see a lot of each other. It was all very friendly and civilised."

"I'm sorry to hear that, these things happen. Anyway, what brings you here? I presume something to do with your financial research, what with this great banking crisis we're all sweating through."

"Up to a point. But what about you? How's your family?"

"Oh, as I told you, we're fine, the kids growing. This is a safe place for kids, though obviously we miss the sunshine and the friendliness of us Argentines. It's a pretty cold bunch around here, you never really get to know the Zürichois."

"How long have you been here now?"

"I came in 1988, before I was married. Then Caro joined me about five years later. We got married here."

"And you're also still in banking, if I'm not mistaken."

"Yes, I work as a portfolio manager at Julius Baer. It pays well, and I run a sizeable amount of South American money. Not that I can tell you much about that."

"Don't worry, I'm not here on behalf of the Argentine taxman. In fact I spend most of my time trying to avoid him, if you see what I mean."

"I certainly do. Along with about sixty percent of the rest of the Argentine population. The other forty percent are sadly too poor to have a problem. Anyway, why don't we order? The lake fish is particularly good."

During the lunch, they chatted generally about the financial crisis, the emergency steps being taken by Obama since his arrival, the responsibility of the Federal Reserve in the initial crisis, and its impact on the markets. They were forced to agree that the world's super-rich would probably emerge unscathed from the crisis, which was no doubt good for Francisco's business

As they sat over coffee, Leandro steered the conversation carefully towards the Argentine community in Switzerland. He showed interest in others like Francisco, who might be working in the banking community. He wouldn't mind meeting any of them who might be around, to see if they could provide material for a piece of research he was doing about offshore Latin American assets.

Francisco thought for a minute.

"There aren't that many left, there used to be far more about ten or fifteen years ago, but, with the good years of Menem, a lot of them moved back to Argentina, as quite a lot of money management was actually being done in Buenos Aires. In spite of the 2001 financial crisis, not all that many of them came back."

"Presumably, some of them must have moved closer to their clients."

"And set themselves up in places like Panama or Miami."

Leandro, having some difficulty in seeing how he was going to bring the conversation round to Dávila, finally decided to plunge straight in. He felt more confident in the knowledge that the target was back in

Buenos Aires and had been for five or six years, according to the information provided to him by Herr Johann.

"Did you ever come across a guy called Dávila, maybe from the Salteño family?"

Francisco answered without hesitation.

"Yes, I knew someone called Dávila, who was here in Zürich long before I arrived, and, as I recall, went back to Argentina - I think - about five or six years ago. Can't say I knew him very well, strange kind of fellow. I remember Caro meeting him at some party and coming away as if she had met the devil himself. Why do you ask?"

"Oh, nothing special, I was given his name the other day by somebody who thought he might be able to answer some of my questions."

"He's not been here since 2000 or 2001. Very much the playboy. I've a faint recollection of his having left UBS under a bit of a cloud, but he seems to have picked himself up and gone to work for Amex. Definitely on the wild side, don't think he ever married, had a reputation for giving parties at which all the usual - and some of the less usual - stimulants were available. And his women had a reputation for being pretty strange as well. Frankly, I'm surprised he survived as long as he did at Amex. He must have done quite a good job. From what I heard, he was never short of cash."

"Doesn't sound as if he'd have been a terribly reliable source anyway. You haven't kept in touch with him, by the sounds of things."

"Frankly, no! I really didn't like the man, nor the company he kept."

Leandro felt that he had at least established that, if he spoke more openly to Francisco about Dávila, it was unlikely to get back to him. However, to go straight to the point now could have the effect of unsettling Francisco, as he might sense that the conversation had been manipulated. On the strength of what he had been able to piece together in the last twenty-four hours, finding out more about Dávila no longer appeared to be the main priority. Until further notice, Leandro was content to work on the assumption that Dávila was the blackmailer. Instead, he would concentrate on tracking down Sam - and the sooner the better.

"I'm probably going to be staying on over the weekend, why don't we try and get together again sometime before I leave?"

"Can't say I've been very helpful for your research. But I know where I can get some more classified figures about Latin American offshore wealth than you're likely to read about in the newspapers. We've done some research in that area, as you can imagine, and I'll see what I can share with you. You may be able to use some of it in an unattributable fashion."

"That would be fantastic, *che*. I'll give you a ring in a couple of days."

Some 11,000 kilometres away across the South Atlantic, as Leandro was leaving the restaurant, Alberto Dávila opened his emails as he sat in his office at number 11, Avenida 25 de Mayo, the offices of SIDE, the Argentine intelligence service. A tall, slightly sinister building looming over the north-western corner of the Plaza de Mayo, as if physically guarding the Presidential Casa Rosada across the street. He had decided to come back to Buenos Aires from his farm in the Province of Buenos Aires, where he had spent most of the time since leaving Punta del Este. It was the last week of January and the weekend would see the crowds coming back from the beaches in droves. Better to clear his desk of any accumulated papers.

There were a couple of messages from Carlos in Zürich. The man who had been seen with Carla's new companion, Samira, had turned up in Zürich. Carlos had apparently seen a message on the girl's cell phone, saying that he had arrived and would she get in touch with him.

Dávila was intrigued. Here was a man whose girlfriend was quite clearly running a parallel relationship with a woman. And it was almost certain that he knew about it. That much the boys had been able to establish in Punta del Este, having one evening followed the woman Samira to meet this man. He still hadn't put a name to him, but that wouldn't take long. Carlos had only been able to establish the man's first name as Leandro. Now this Leandro had gone to the trouble to follow Samira all the way to Switzerland. Either he didn't know about the relationship with Carla, which Dávila very much doubted, or else, for some reason, it didn't seem to worry him. Argentine males must be getting more broadminded! Or might there be a more sinister reason for his trip to Zürich?

Could there be any connection with the murder of Janet Williams? Or indeed with any of the others? As far as he knew, the police investigation into the murder of Williams had got nowhere. Either because Subinspector Falcioni had been sufficiently frightened to take no further action, or else - even if he had pursued the investigation - he hadn't got anywhere. Dávila was fairly confident that, if Falcioni had continued digging on the case, it would have been brought to his attention.

So, on the face of it, it looked pretty much as though this man Leandro, whoever he might be, was after his girl.

Still, better to try and find out who he was, just in case.

He emailed back to Carlos to try and track down this Leandro and get a family name. If he was after Carla's new girlfriend, she should be allowed to see him. They could use that to find out more about him, including where he was staying and thus clinch his identity.

The more he thought about the highly blurred events of the night with Tanya and her unknown friend, the more Leandro hoped he would not live to regret them. In spite of what he regarded as something bordering on a justified cause, he nevertheless felt a deep sense of guilt. However, combined with the near identification of the blackmailer, the last night had served to snap him out of the confusion which had temporarily assailed him at Sam's hotel. The night with the two girls, the little he could remember of it, had definitively brought home to him why he was in love with Sam. Any uncertainty in that quarter had at least been laid to rest.

If only he could now find a way to pin down Dávila, this might set events in motion which could lead to the collapse of whatever processes might be at work back in Buenos Aires. A number of the pieces were still missing from the jigsaw puzzle, but, if in pulling them together, he could lift the threat hanging over Eduardo and recover Sam, the trip would have been worth it. The start of the trail now clearly seemed to be in Zürich. But without finding Sam, it could still go cold.

He had a couple of items of information to work with, namely Carla's addresses and the probability that Sam was still in town. Given what he knew about the time Carla and Sam had spent together in Punta del Este, the first would probably lead to the second.

He needed some mobility. A visit to the Avis offices in Gartenhofstrasse produced a Ford Focus, in an unobtrusive shade of blue, on a three-day rental. He checked the two addresses Herr Johann had given him for Carla on his street guide and set off.

Navigating the mid-afternoon traffic, he found himself in what appeared to be a prosperous residential district beyond the Enge station on the southwest side of the city, where Sam's hotel had also been located. Amid larger residential blocks, elegant two or three storey houses stood in their own gardens behind dense hedges. With a Swiss sense of privacy, it was usually impossible to see anything below the first floor windows. However, at this time of the year, many of the trees were bare, making the task a little easier. He decided to concentrate his attention on the first address, which Herr Johann had suggested was Carla's private home. There was nothing particularly to attract attention about the house, which stood in its own grounds near the end of the Richard-Wagner-Strasse, close to the corner of Conrad-Ferdinand-Meyer-Strasse. A simple wrought iron gate gave access to a courtyard up to the front door, shielded from the rain with a traditional turn-of-the-century glass canopy. Since it seemed to occupy the whole of one corner of its block, he drove back up to Seestrasse and round the block to approach it from the Conrad-Ferdinand-Meyer-Strasse side. A pair of large, metal-sheeted gates blocked any sight of the garden or cars which might be parked there, but from his recollection of what Carla had been driving in Punta del Este, he imagined something in the upper price range. Just as he drove past, he detected a movement in the gates, as they began slowly to swing inwards. It being a one way street, he drove on without slowing down and tucked the Ford into the first space he could find in the next block. Watching in his wing mirror, he saw a dark metallic grey soft-top Porsche 911 emerge slowly from the gates, pause to see if anything was coming, and then, having pulled out fast, accelerate down the slope towards him. As the Porsche flashed past him, he caught a glimpse of a blonde at the wheel, large dark glasses all but obliterating her features. Luckily, mirrored windows were probably illegal on cars in Switzerland, so that he was at least able to see inside. If it was Carla, she was alone. He just had time to scribble down its Zürich number plate before the Porsche disappeared behind the line of parked cars in front of him.

He pulled out of the parking space and decided to do another circuit, this time parking uphill from the corner on which the house stood. Again, he was fortunate to find a space, from which he could diagonally get a reasonably clear view of the whole building. The winter daylight was beginning to fade, since the street ran down the east side of the hill below the Seestrasse and was already in shadow. As he watched, lights were lit on the first floor, indicating that two windows on the front façade and one round the corner belonged to the same room. Judging by what appeared to be pictures and a bookcase on one wall, he suspected it might be the drawing room. A shadow fell across one of the windows as someone pulled the curtains, effectively blocking out any further view of what was going on. This wasn't going to be easy!

Just at that moment, a small gate opened in the garden next to which he was parked. An elderly gentlemen, well protected against the cold by an olive green Loden overcoat and a thick scarf over his nose, emerged, pulling a reluctant Yorkshire Terrier behind him from what seemed to be a public park. He wasn't so old as not to notice Leandro sitting at the wheel of the car and to give him more than a cursory glance. Clearly a residential area not used to strangers sitting around in parked cars. Any thoughts of passing a few hours a day with binoculars discreetly trained on Carla's house were clearly out of the question.

He needed some ploy to establish whether Sam was staying with Carla. He toyed with the idea of asking Herr Johann if he had any means of checking, but the more he thought about it, the more he was reluctant to rely too heavily on Frobisher's assets or at least, not until something more vital or risky was contemplated. It wouldn't have surprised him if Herr Johann had found a way to check on who was staying in the house, possibly using his contacts in the cantonal police. But anything too frontal might simply alert Carla and send her out of range. Whatever he tried, it had to produce results fast. He couldn't afford to sit around in Zürich for ever. How to get Sam to confirm her presence at the house?

As he sat there, he idly watched a small delivery van from Spruengli, the chocolate specialists in the Bahnhofstrasse, pull up and the driver, having extracted a large carton from the back, deliver it to the door of a neighbouring house. Why not? It might work, though whatever was delivered would need to be sufficiently valuable not to be entrusted to anyone other than the beneficiary. Anyone could take delivery of chocolates. But maybe a piece of jewellery? Or an expensive dress? On the other hand, whatever was delivered might not reach Sam, so the budget needed to be reasonable or he would be throwing a lot of money away for nothing. Maybe lingerie, knowing the weakness she had for only the best. Was there a La Perla shop in town? He would have to search.

Night was falling fast and there seemed little point in staying on the street. A visit to the concierge at the Baur au Lac should provide guidance on the question of lingerie. Herr Max proved as knowledgeable on that subject as on so many others relating to the discreet enquiries of the hotel's clients. Somewhat to Leandro's disappointment, he simply recommended a visit to the biggest department store, Jelmoli.

"You'll   find   they   have   everything,   Sir."

February 2008

By midday the following day, Leandro, with the guidance of one of the store's personal shopping advisers, had put together a beautifully wrapped package of some of the best pieces from Agent Provocateur, in the absence of La Perla, which Jelmoli didn't stock. It was to be hand-delivered only to Miss Haidar herself. He paid cash and when they asked for a name as sender, he also gave Haidar, as if he was a relative. He was assured that the delivery would be made before three pm that afternoon. Failure to deliver in person would be reported to him by phone.

He could choose between trying to observe the delivery or just waiting for the phone call. It being a beautiful sunny day, though very cold, he decided on the former. Warmly dressed and armed with a newspaper, having parked the Ford, he took a stroll in the park opposite Carla's house.

At around two thirty, he caught sight of a small Jelmoli van slowing down near the end of the Richard-Wagner-Strasse. He deliberately lingered in the park so as to coincide if possible with a sequence in which, someone, probably a maid, would answer the door first, and then have to go to find Sam.

The front door was opened on the first ring and, to his shocked surprise, by the young man he had last seen following Sam at La Barra! Carla never seemed to move without her shock troops! Or were they minders acting under instructions from Dávila? If Sam was staying with Carla, with this escort, she was hardly going to be a free agent. As he watched, the deliveryman held onto the parcel, while the bodyguard stepped back inside. He was pleased to see his instructions being followed. Swiss reliability as usual.

A full two minutes passed, which felt like an eternity, before the front door was again opened to reveal Sam. Even at this range, he could see the puzzled look on her face, as she signed the receipt and took the parcel. He saw her turn, apparently laughing and close the door behind her. A momentary perplexity would no doubt instantly be hidden by a

338

story for the benefit of the bodyguard. He was sure her brain would be as lightning fast as ever. Although he realised that his ploy had probably been more dangerous to Sam than foreseen, he didn't doubt that she could rise to the occasion. Having confirmed Sam's whereabouts, he now had to find a way to make direct contact.

On the following day, a Saturday, Francisco rang Leandro to say that he had pulled together some information on Latin American overseas wealth for his research. Although Leandro was broadly satisfied about Dávila's identity, he nevertheless saw an opportunity to test his ideas on someone who knew the market.

They met in a café on the Ruden Platz. Having accepted the papers Francisco had prepared for him, Leandro began to talk more directly about Dávila. He indicated that he was interested in the Argentine in the context of what he described as a possible scam in the Buenos Aires financial markets. Not the truth, but neither was it so lurid as to provoke unnecessary curiosity from Francisco which might get back to Buenos Aires. He apologized for not having made this clear first time, but Francisco seemed untroubled.

Reminding Francisco about what he knew of Dávila's banking career, Leandro asked whether there might be material to serve a criminal purpose nearly ten years later? Francisco thought about it for a couple of minutes, then suggested the following explanation.

"The common thread running through his jobs in Zürich has to be his access to rich Latin American clients. Whether in the finance company, at UBS, or later at AMEX, we can assume that the reason for his being hired lies in the fact that he's Latin American, therefore speaks the same language. Judging by his social life or at least what I saw of it, he appears to have been a sociable kind of guy – though rather sinister late at night. In normal circumstances, it would not have been at all surprising if he had then set up on his own as a portfolio manager, taking his address book of clients with him, whilst all the time domiciling their accounts either with UBS or with AMEX, so that they should feel secure. This kind of arrangement was very common practice in the 1980s and 90s and, depending upon the size of the funds he might have managed in this fashion, would certainly have proved pretty lucrative. An independent portfolio manager like that would normally share the management fee with the bank in which the account was domiciled, being of the order of one percent. This suggests that if he had one or two hundred million under global management, he would have been pulling in a comfortable million dollars per annum in fees. But at no point after joining UBS or AMEX does he seem to have gone independent. Instead, he seems to have stayed and continued to draw a salary. So that does not appear to have been his main ambition. Of course it's possible that he simply felt that he was not up to the business of successfully managing client accounts. It's not given to everyone. It requires solid analytic skills, as well as the ability to sit down with the client and explain to him why the markets have lost him ten or twenty percent of his portfolio. There are many times when I think that my job is a hiding to nothing. When the markets go up and the client makes money, it's thanks to the markets, and when they go down and he loses money, it's your fault!"

Francisco managed a wry smile.

"On the other hand, working on the credit card side of AMEX, our friend Dávila would almost certainly have walked away with the identity of a large number of extremely wealthy Latinos, including many Argentines, with illegal bank accounts offshore, obviously not declared to the taxman. So if there is a sinister purpose to be deduced from his career, it's that the identity of the clients might prove more lucrative to him than just managing their money. This might also go some way to explaining what he was doing on the credit card client helpdesk at Amex. In the process, without ever meeting any of these people, he would have been able to build up an address book of names, their spending power as well as the identity of the client's bank. A security question often used to identify the client over the phone would be to ask which financial institution was paying the monthly account. So, with that information, he would have an idea where their money was kept. Obviously there's no clear evidence of this, but it might be part of the answer to your question."

"So what you're suggesting is that, armed with an address book containing names and depositary banks, our friend Dávila could have acquired the components of a manipulation operation?"

Leandro was careful to avoid the word blackmail.

"Yes, that's feasible, and in fact, the time spent at AMEX would have ensured that his address book grew far more rapidly than if he had just been sitting in UBS waiting for the clients to walk through the door."

Francisco paused for a minute, and then continued.

"There's another thing. Given his Latin American background and probable involvement with the UBS and AMEX client base, he would also, in the normal course of business, have got to know other bankers managing Latin American funds. It was quite common, even in the 1980s when the region was in trouble, and certainly in the 1990s, when not only Argentina but a number of other regional countries began to recover in a spectacular fashion, for ministers of finance from the region, or other economists interested in the region, to come to Switzerland and make presentations about the state of those economies. These were often lunchtime affairs, arranged in some of the big hotels in Geneva or Zürich. They would have been attended not only by the specialists looking for investment opportunities in these emerging economies, but almost certainly by a number of the client managers, interested to know what was going on back home for their clients. As the economies grew, so the amount of free capital would also grow and some of that would almost certainly find its way to accounts in Switzerland. So, sitting in one of these lunches, our friend Dávila would have been able to make friends and, who knows, maybe even pick up a few tips as to potential clients for anything he was planning. It's an idea, but if you're smart - which I believe he was - he could certainly have been trying to get alongside some of these people."

After a brief pause, he went on.

"And who knows, he might even have been able to exert some influence over some of them, particularly through the kind of parties which he was throwing in those days here in Zürich. Who knows what banker might not have fallen into a trap?"

Another piece of the jigsaw had been placed on the table, namely the possible genesis of the blackmail operation. What Leandro still needed was an irrefutable connection between Dávila and Carla, even if the question of the flat rental guarantee seemed evidence that they knew each other. But was this enough to establish that Dávila was Carla's *patron*? He was hoping that Sam would be able to do this? But could Francisco?

"Fascinating. That's been very helpful, Pancho, I owe you one."

"I can do some more digging if you like, just let me know."

"No, for the time being, I don't want anything to filter back and who knows, he may not be the only person involved in this fraud, so that by asking around, we might end up by alerting him."

Then, as Francisco was leaving, Leandro threw in a parting shot.

"Just one more thing, Pancho, although it's not directly connected. Did you say something about the kind of women Dávila went around with?"

Francisco paused. "It was only hearsay, you know, on the local grapevine. Someone mentioned him being involved in some pretty rough stuff, you know, whips, chains, that kind of thing. I think I mentioned that Carolina met him once and came away with a pretty nasty feeling."

Leandro decided on a final roll of the dice.

"Were any other Argentine women involved?"

Francisco paused again and took a deep breath.

"Now you mention it, there was one. In the late 1990s, there was talk that she was running a brothel or something of that kind. Zürich has all kinds of exotic places. They said that hers was very exotic, if you know what I mean! Never been there, of course." He put his arm round Leandro's shoulders as they walked towards the door. "But don't ask me how to find them. I'm a boring married man with two kids. Take care anyway."

"You've been very helpful. I'll just stay and have another coffee. *Che*, I'll give you a ring before I leave next week."

He went back to the table and ordered another espresso from the waiter. From what he had just heard, Dávila had apparently acquired all that he needed to set himself up to become the blackmailer of Sarmiento and also Carla's *patron*. The more he thought about it, the more he could discern a clear connection between Dávila, Carla and the chilling events of the 1980 film. It was by no means far-fetched to assume that Dávila was the man in the mask and Carla the nurse. Dávila would only have had to hide his identity from the prisoner, not from the torturers and their assistants. A bizarre relationship had been born in the dank, urine-smelling cells and passages of El Pozo, only to blossom, like some black orchid, on the banks of the Limmat. He sat staring out of the window onto the grey alleyway outside.

A freezing wind was chasing through the narrow streets of the city when he finally emerged through the revolving doors of the bistro. Wrapping his scarf more tightly over his nose and mouth and hunching his shoulders into the wind, he made his way to the wi-fi café, which he had been frequenting in recent days. He found an email from Eduardo containing some amazing news. Transmitted in very roundabout terms, the gist of the message was that Sarmiento, having failed to master any kind of 'screen capture' software to copy the films he had received at Christmas from the blackmailer, had finally resorted to making a reasonably good video movie of what was on his screen. This he had been able to pass to Eduardo via his parked car. On playing back the movie, which lasted for some twenty minutes and showed the final moments of the Englishwoman in the hotel bedroom, Eduardo was fairly sure that he had been able to establish at least two facts which appeared radically to alter their interpretation of what had happened that night. He suggested a time when Leandro should get him on Skype, next day, Sunday.

At the agreed hour next day, they made contact.

"The original film appears to have been handheld, judging by its shake and some panning shots. Right from the opening scene, Williams is already spread-eagled and chained to the four corners of the bed, her cunt in full view and her head encased in the tight black latex hood. Even on this copy, her breathing is very audible as she forces air in and out through the small hole over her mouth. Almost immediately, there's a close-up shot of what is clearly the delicate hand of a woman, in a latex glove of the kind you could buy in any pharmacy, thrusting the huge black dildo in and out of her pussy. The microphone picks up the English woman's low cries mixed with the sound of her breathing, as the dildo's pumped deep inside her."

But then, to Eduardo's amazement, the camera had pulled back to reveal Lady X, still in her fur coat, her blonde hair falling over her shoulders, sitting on the side of the bed, working the dildo and fondling Williams' breasts.

"That means that she wasn't alone in the room. Someone else, filming, was with her. When did that person appear? Hard to tell, but judging from the fact that when the film starts, Williams is already tied to the bed and, in her black hood, effectively blind, it's possible that Lady X let that person into the room once Williams had been immobilised."

"*Mi Dios*. That's certainly changes everything. Have you been able to do anything to find out who the person might be and how they got in?"

"Not yet and of course I've got to be very careful about going back to L'Hôtel after all these months. But that's not the end of what the film tells us. Just wait for it! The video camera used to film in the bedroom had a date and time-counter. Most people usually switch it off, but in this case, perhaps because whoever was filming was under a lot of stress, it was left on. The film sent to Sarmiento has a break in it. After about ten minutes of Lady X doing her bit, there is a gap and the next sequence, again a close-up, shows the dildo being applied, but this time the hand is much bigger, that of a man, although also in a latex glove. And the final shots show the same hand withdrawing the dildo and forcing it through the breathing hole deep into the woman's throat. I'll spare you the details of her last moments! What is most interesting however is that, if we're to believe the time-counter, and relate it to the hotel CCTV, Lady X was walking away from the hotel at the same moment! So to some extent, we are back at the beginning!"

"Jesus, this never ends. What you're saying, Eduardo, is Carla may not be the murderess we have taken her for all these months."

"Exactly!"

Leandro needed to think through the implications of what Eduardo had just told him.

"My immediate reaction, of course, is a huge feeling of relief, knowing that Sam - and I haven't had time to tell you this yet - is currently staying in Carla's house here in Zürich. That doesn't mean that Sam is out of danger, but at least it appears to be at one step farther removed."

He detected that Eduardo had suddenly gone silent on the other end of the line.

"You hadn't told me that that was what Sam had done when she left Punta. Though I'm bound to admit, watching the panicky fashion you caught that flight to London, something of the kind had occurred to me."

Leandro could just catch the slightly sardonic little laugh which followed.

"Okay, okay, you're right, I wasn't totally frank with you. I certainly suspected that Sam had done something of the kind, but I had no proof and I had to get here to find out."

"Anyway, uncle, it's not your sex life we're talking about now, that'll be for another day."

"Well, thanks for that at least!"

"My pleasure."

Leandro thought for a minute.

"At my end, I've also been pretty busy, with some very interesting results."

He summarised what he had learned from Francisco and Herr Johann, and the preliminary conclusions he had drawn from all this.

"So, in a nutshell, it would appear that there is a direct link between Lady X and the blackmailer, going as far back as the early 1980s, and we now have a name for the most likely candidate. I'll spell it out. Note down the following numbers, being letters of the alphabet. 1. 12. 2. 5. 18. 20. 15. Then 4. 1. 22. 9. 12. 1. Dead simple."

He gave Eduardo the date of birth, "But subtract two from each of the numbers. With that, you should be able to find out where he is and what he's up to today."

Eduardo repeated the numbers and confirmed that he had been able to work out the name and date of birth. Leandro felt slightly embarrassed by the total simplicity of the little code he had used. Frobisher would no doubt expect higher standards of sophistication!

"I need hardly tell you that, even from the little we know about this guy, just putting in a simple police trace is likely to get all the alarm bells sounding immediately. If he's the kind of person who can send in the heavies to beat me up, putting some kind of protective 'firewall' round his identity is likely to be a minimal precaution. But I'll see what I can do and keep you posted."

"With all that we've been able to pull together at your end and mine, you've got your work cut out, especially given all the constraints the closer we get. Be very, very careful and let's try and have another chat in two days' time."

He sensed a pause at the other end of the line.

"I'm not sure we will get any closer. You must realize of course that none of this has a hope in hell of being used as evidence. We know that it adds up, but trying to use it would not only be ruled inadmissible, but – last but not least – destroy Sarmiento."

Leandro had come to the same conclusion as the pieces began to fall into place, but had not wanted to be the first to say it.

"I know," he answered. "Anyway, just be careful."

"You too, uncle, and good luck with Sam"

Eduardo hung up.

Leandro sat back. The scenario had radically changed with Eduardo's latest news.

The key pieces on the board now each carried a name. It was rather like a chessboard at an advanced stage of the game. In black, like an all-powerful queen, the figure of Dávila. Rather like a knight, apparently capable of moving in unexpected directions, the figure of Carla, also black. Perilously close to these two on the board, Sam. He was not quite sure what kind of piece she was. Possibly another knight, though a white one.

On his side of the board, his castle, finding it difficult to align itself in a position from which to strike the black pieces. Not to mention the fact that, if he was to take Sam's relationship with Carla fully into account, the black knight had to be left standing on the board, after the queen had been taken.

As to Eduardo, given all the constraints on his actions, perhaps he wasn't much better than a pawn. Obviously, if all the other pieces were well manoeuvred, he had the ability to strike. But it was very limited.

This appeared to be a game of chess without kings. Bizarre.

Any way he looked at it, the threat from Dávila was clear. And now Sam had somehow succeeded in inserting herself into their game, whatever that might be. The pieces on the board might now have a name, but their future moves had not become clearer. Only by finding Sam had he any hope of unravelling the situation. Somehow, he needed to find himself alone with her – and as soon as possible.

He spent the rest of the afternoon at the nearest internet cafe searching the web for Lady Blast. The URL provided by Herr Johann immediately produced an elegant black portal, emblazoned with a complex coat of arms quartered into an assortment of symbols of sexual restraint or domination, including whips, chains and masks. Entry to the site led to a series of pages and images presenting the wide range of services provided by Lady Blast and her beautiful crew of escorts. As Leandro scrolled over a screen-wide photograph showing Carla seated in the centre of a trio on either side, to his amazement he found himself looking into the eyes of Sam, introduced as the latest recruit to the team.

In the centre of the screen, Carla sat cross legged on a high perspex throne, nonchalantly brandishing a black riding whip, her body tightly cinched in a black leather catsuit, her breasts forcing their way through its long zip open to the waist, legs encased in thigh-high red patent boots with fifteen centimetre stiletto heels. An expression of total disdain, with which she seemed to size up her virtual admirer, marked her undoubtedly handsome features. On either side, the six girls, all heavily and provocatively made up, with flowing jet black, red or golden hair, were posing in an assortment of uniforms and evening gowns, from which their perfectly shaped curves seemed on the point of exploding.

Like the others, Sam was provocatively attired in what appeared to be a long, strapless gown of some jet black, glistening material which encased her tightly, from the low-cut strapless bodice down to her ankles, in such a manner as to set off her all too visible attractions to best advantage. Her face had been heavily made up to emphasize her Semitic features, with black kohl eye shadow fading into a deep purple below her finely arched brows, her lips a pouting vermilion. She was fortunately almost unrecognizable to anyone but her closest admirers.

This was the first time that he had actually seen a likeness of Carla. Though not beautiful in a classic way, she was definitely very, very handsome and exuded sex appeal. Long, flaming blonde hair framed a broad face, with high cheekbones and a wide forehead. Large dark eyes, lightly made up under curving eyebrows, a wide, sensitive mouth, her features combined to give an air of total assurance, a strong personality and extreme sensuality. She would be remarkable in any gathering and probably lethal if cornered. Leandro for the first time began to get a sense of the hold which Carla seemed to exercise over Sam. Explicable perhaps, but hardly reassuring.

With growing unease, Leandro scrolled over each girl in turn, producing a drop-down menu headed by the girl's name, age, alleged nationality and vital statistics. This was backed by a short biography extolling the social and other talents, including languages, cultural interests, and particular skills, which each girl would, if her services were retained, provide to carefully selected clients on a worldwide basis, distance of travel and duration of mission unlimited. Some even added a list of their regular destinations, ranging round the European capitals, but also farther afield to the Gulf States, the Caribbean or South Africa. Additional photos showed each girl in a variety of costumes, ranging from the most elegant evening gown, through the straight black skirt and white blouse of a top-class secretary or personal assistant, and finally a selection of more provocative fetishist costumes.

As he came to the end of the row, with only Sam's profile unopened, Leandro froze the cursor. Although he had been correct in assuming that Sam had followed Carla to Switzerland, it had simply never entered his head that she would take it to the point of what, he was now forced to recognise, seemed to imply some form of commercial as well as emotional engagement. He was scrambling to comprehend and rationalise the reasons which might have underlain Sam's decision. The fact that she had left Punta del Este with no warning was now explained. Whatever the reasons might be, it was obvious to Leandro that no explanation would have been adequate to secure his agreement to such a decision. The unanswered e-mails and phone calls sadly made sense.

Plucking up his courage, he slowly scrolled over Sam's silhouette, to learn that her professional name was Dalal, her origins Middle Eastern and South American, her languages Spanish, English, French, Brazilian and Arabic, her age thirty. Her cultural skills included music, classical and jazz and modern dance, her taste in art contemporary, as also an interest in literature and drama. With growing trepidation, Leandro scrolled towards areas of particular expertise, and was only half reassured to find that she was described as a 'novice', albeit bisexual and with a taste for role-play, preferably of the super-heroine kind. Her favourite films were said include The Matrix, Underworld, Kill Bill, and Avengers amongst others. But she also claimed to be able to convey the 'female mysteries of the Orient' in her dress, her rituals and 'submission to the desires of the all-conquering lords of the deserts of Arabia'!

"What is all this shit? What the fuck has got into her? Is she out of her mind?"

Leandro switched off the screen and sat back. His first instinct was to pack it all in and fly back to Buenos Aires on the first available carrier. Whilst he had progressively, not without significant anguish, attained a certain level of tolerance as regards Sam's leading-edge sexual tastes, each revelation had hitherto been rendered palatable by the manner in which Sam had explained things. This and her ability to transmit to him the conviction that, for the time being at least, he was at the centre of her emotional, if not always her sexual, focus. What he was now seeing had hit him totally unprepared.

On its most generous interpretation, it appeared that Sam had decided that only by penetrating Carla's world so completely would she be able to discover the truth surrounding the latter's role in the murder of the Englishwoman. But it didn't take Leandro more than a second to conclude that joining Carla's escort agency, which he increasingly suspected might be no more than a polite euphemism, must be based on more than a simple desire to solve the murder. If merely piling up evidence was Sam's principal motive, some kind of message to him explaining her intentions might have seemed an obvious step. Whilst Sam's unusually adventurous attitudes to sex had come to hold fewer secrets for him in the eight or nine months they had known each other, joining an escort agency – and above all expecting him to condone it - was, by any stretch of the imagination, pushing his tolerance to extreme limits. Most of all, to lengths where even the most broadminded of lovers could be expected not only to raise serious objections, but most likely simply to walk away. Perhaps that was what she was looking for. Yet perhaps not. Unpredictability was certainly no stranger to her personality. Yet somehow he felt that he should have picked up some indication that she was of a mind to terminate their relationship. He might not be Casanova, but, perhaps flattering himself, he still felt that, in his thirty-odd years of sexual activity, he had seen enough girlfriends come and go to read the signs. From the description of their first meeting at the polo party, he had detected that Carla seemed to exercise an unusually powerful lesbian fascination over Sam. But he had not sensed a compensating shift away from him on her part. However difficult at times, he had come close to accepting that Sam's bisexuality allowed her to switch instantly from one side to the other. But now? Did the evidence before him suggest that he had been misled, or more probably, that he had misled himself? Visions of older men making fools of themselves with younger women flashed before his eyes. He smiled cynically. He had seen it happen enough times among some of his friends and now bitterly recalled his confident predictions that he wouldn't fall into the same trap.

Where to go from here? Tomorrow's flight back to London and from there to Buenos Aires seemed an obvious choice. Yet somehow, this option smelled of cowardice, of futility, making a nonsense of everything he had been through to date, not only as regards the murder case and protecting Eduardo, but even more his relationship with Sam. Walking away from it, given what he knew about her, would be to fall into the classic Argentine macho trap of hurt pride, pinning the blame conveniently onto the woman – however much in this case it might appear justifiable.

The more he thought about it, the more it became obvious to him that only through some form of direct confrontation with Sam would he be able to take a decision to go or stay. His e-mails, SMS and phone calls having remained unanswered, only a direct approach via the website now seemed possible. He knew where she was, but he could hardly walk up to the front door.

He scrolled back to the homepage and found a Contact Menu, which enabled a visitor to make direct contact with the girl of his choice. Under Dalal he found an e-mail. How to make contact in such a way that if the mails were being vetted, the nature of his prior relationship with Sam would not become apparent? Not only could Carla read them, but he had to assume that the bodyguards were also there to do rather more than just carry out the garbage. He would have to pose as a rich South American, passing through Zürich on business, looking for some exotic company for the night and prepared to pay over the odds for something special. He must find a way nevertheless to get Sam to detect his true identity. Given the flamboyant style of the website, something totally excessive seemed in order. He began to draft a mail in a style so lurid that it made him cringe.

"Hello Dalal, how beautiful you are. I would like to get to know you better and penetrate your Oriental charms. I am passing through Zürich to see my bankers, but they are so boring. I feel sure that an evening together could be mutually rewarding. I have just come from Punta del Este where I have spent the last two weeks of December and most of January. I see that you are South American, so perhaps you know Punta del Este and such beautiful bars and nightspots as Posta del Cangrejo with a setting sun and its wonderful mojitos. Please let me know if you are free in the next two evenings by responding to this mail. Yours Leo."

All in Spanish, he had to presume that Carla and the bodyguards would be able to read and understand the text, but that the reference to the Posta at sunset might alert only Sam to his true identity. He quickly created a Yahoo e-mail in the name of Leo, and sent it off. All he could now do was wait.

Bored with the internet café, he took his laptop and wandered over to a warm bar which he knew had Wi-Fi. By the time he was into his second beer, a ping from his laptop told him that a message had arrived.

"Dear Leo. Of course I am at your service. I too have tasted the mojitos at La Barra. They are the best. You must tell me in what circumstances you would wish me to accompany you, the extent of your desires, even down to the way you would wish me to be made up, dressed, perfumed. Share with me your passions, so that I may prepare myself to satisfy your every whim and pleasure. Tell me where and when we can meet and how long you would seek my company. The following link will provide you with ideas, and also indicate the tariff you should pay to secure my company. Please fill out the attached form and return it and I will indicate the cash equivalent, payable when we meet. Dear Leo, although you will see that I am a novice, I feel sure that I can bring you full satisfaction. Yours, Dalal."

Leandro had some difficulty in believing that Sam had written this grotesque response. The link took him to a drop down form, on which he could enter the details of where they should meet, with date, time and place. boxes to tick indicating whether they would form part of a group, for drinks, for dinner, for the theatre or opera, for a nightclub

353

and whether her company would be expected for the rest of the night, with cut-off times at six and nine in the morning or beyond. As to her appearance, options included anything ranging from a little black silk cocktail dress, through an evening gown, to more exotic styles such as Oriental, as well as fetishist options. Materials and styles could even be mixed and matched. The list of possible perfumes ran to more than a dozen and the small JPEGs of possible make up styles ran to a similar number, each one with its own heading, such as Arabian, Chinese, geisha, punk and many more. In terms of attitude, the options ranged from mild dominance to full submission. As to her own tastes, the form expressed a preference for champagne and vintage burgundy.

Leandro stared at the form, at a loss to know how to respond. This was crazy!

Given that Sam was hardly an unknown quantity, he felt that, although the transmission of an excessively exotic wish list would largely be a waste of time for both of them, any self-respecting client would provide some form of personalised response. What he most wanted was direct contact with her in surroundings which, even if they were observed, would provide him with the opportunity to assess exactly where she stood and where she wanted to go. Only on this basis would he be able to establish what this meant not only for the murder case, but also - far more critically - for his relationship with her.

His instinct favoured meeting in surroundings sufficiently private to ensure that they could neither be too easily observed, nor - even more dangerously – filmed or taped. A meeting at the Hotel Baur au Lac, of which he at least now knew the basic layout, should provide him with a setting in line with his ostensible financial situation. It would also be a context in which hotel security might be regarded as too intrusive to allow someone to get sufficiently close to film or record their meeting. He would need to move into the hotel from Frau Schmied's *pensione* in advance, although for one night he would not necessarily need to check out completely.

"Dear Dalal. What wonderful news! And what options! I do not know where to begin. In your photo alongside Lady Blast you are already beautiful enough. Come as you are, the black dress moulds your body so exquisitely. You will be the most beautiful woman in the room. My plan, as you will see from the attached form, is that we meet in the bar of the Baur au Lac tomorrow evening at seven pm. From there, we should dine together and for the rest - let us plan it together. I cannot think of releasing you before the morning. Send me your terms and reactions by return. Your impatient Leo."

After a pause, he clicked the 'send' button.

Not least, it posed him with the need to ensure that he would also be appropriately dressed for the occasion. Something which he had frankly not foreseen when hurriedly packing back in Buenos Aires. His usual blazer and grey flannel trousers would have to do!

The reply came within fifteen minutes. Dalal promised to respect his personal wishes and to meet him in the bar as arranged. As regards fees, her presence and attentions until midday on the following day came in at a straightforward US$ 2,500! Leandro, although shocked, wondered whether some arrangement might not be reached, but decided not to pursue the matter.

He had the morning of the following day to get hold of the cash. Frobisher owed him some fees, which Herr Johann might be able to deliver to him at a meeting next day.

By phone, Leandro was able to make a reservation for the following night at the Baur au Lac in the name of Señor y Señora Leo Flemming, using his American Express card. He made it clear that Madame would be flying in on a later plane to join him for dinner.

The following morning he spent sprucing up his wardrobe, to present an image in keeping with the profile of someone able to spend a reasonable slice of a month's salary on twelve hours in the company of a beautiful girl. The meeting with Herr Johann to collect the cash went off smoothly and unobtrusively at the coffee shop of Spruengli on the Bahnhofstrasse. By two thirty pm he was driving up to the Baur au Lac in one of Zürich's white Mercedes taxis, having made sure to pick it up outside the back entrance of Julius Baer, the private bankers. He could not tell whether Carla and her team would be showing any interest in him so far in advance of their rendezvous, but there seemed to be no harm in taking a few precautions. If anybody questioned the taxi driver, the response should be satisfactory.

The rest of the afternoon in his hotel bedroom, he trawled the web, searching for further background on Carla and her girls. She appeared to occupy a star position in the guides and listings of elite escort agencies and more specifically of dominas around Europe and the US. Not entirely to his surprise, he even found a few addresses in Buenos Aires, and significantly more in places such as Rio or São Paulo.

Unlike many of these websites however, and certainly compared with the majority of dominas in Europe, the emphasis in Carla's website was not directed towards humiliation of the opposite sex. Instead, it pointed towards elaborately orchestrated escort services of the five-star variety, in which the potential for role-play and fantasy played a significant part. She appeared to be targeting a very high net worth market, not averse to spending a lot of money to be seen in the company of strikingly good-looking women. The detailed menus to the services provided by Carla and her team of girls confirmed that they had gone for what, in the business of sex and its various permutations, appeared to be a niche targeted specifically at men - but also women – with a taste for strong sexuality, fantasy, exhibitionism, luxury and the transmission of a 'power image'. The scenarios no doubt coincided with the client's personal fantasy, sending powerful messages as to his manhood and taste for risk to any other male in the vicinity. These girls could clearly deliver services which their wives or other mistresses were either not prepared to contemplate or for which they lacked the necessary skills and looks. Not to mention the wardrobes and scenarios! The photographic settings showed yachts, private jets, airport lounges and the entrances to such hotels as the Ritz in Paris or the Pierre in New York. There was even a section indicating that the girls were prepared to accompany their clients on safaris or similar expeditions to out of the way places. They might be up the Mekong, but the girls remained impeccably attired and made up, as in the adverts, their Louis Vuitton travel bags much in evidence.

As far as he could tell, they were offering a mixture of fantasy role-play, escort services, facilitation, as well as – in the final stages and seemingly at the discretion of Lady Blast and her girls – of more elaborate sex, in which lesbian scenes played a significant part. Not of the 'by the hour' variety, but rather a fusion of fantasy and fetish.

Under the heading of 'Guided Tour & Personal Shopper', the services of two of the girls could be obtained to act as driver and personal shopper. This would include the provision of a Bentley, Porsche Cayenne, Rolls or Mercedes, usually black with darkened windows. The video stream showed one of the girls, dressed in full black leather chauffeur's uniform, tight pants tucked into high-heeled boots, a short bolero-style jacket with long sleeves, black gloves and a peaked cap, from which cascaded her long blonde hair, opening the rear door of a Bentley to allow an elegant couple, possibly Russian, to emerge and walk up the steps of Crédit Suisse. The second girl, in the guise of personal shopper, elegantly attired in a form-hugging black suit of some shiny material over a white silk blouse, stiletto-heeled, was seen to lead the chicly dressed Russian woman, also beautiful in her own right, away towards one of the largest jewellery stores on the Bahnhofstrasse. The scene switched to early evening, with the Bentley drawing up outside the Dolder Grand, the leather-clad chauffeur stepping out to open the door for the couple, now weighed down with carrier bags from the most expensive boutiques in Zürich. Later that evening, the couple was shown emerging from a restaurant, to be joined by their two companions and driven to a glossy apartment. There, after a generous consumption of champagne, the final shots showed the man drawing the chauffeur into a silk-hung bedroom, whilst the woman and her guide initiated a lesbian scene on the deep pile carpet of the drawing room. What was that lot going to cost, based on Sam's hourly rates?

Turning to a webpage entitled 'Tropical Cruise', the scene shifted to a Caribbean island with a yacht lying at anchor in a palm-fringed bay. Here a couple, more Middle Eastern in appearance, was shown being waited on by a topless but superbly endowed trio of Carla's girls, all beautifully bronzed, wearing only a minimalist Brazilian thong, as the couple sat on the after deck, the table groaning under a display of lobster, caviar, and champagne. The video panned to an underwater shot worthy of an early James Bond movie, with the husband being guided through the coral reefs, his two female companions clothed only in a stream of bubbles.

Roaming through the rest of the website, Leandro found that clients of either sex could be offered a five-star dinner reception for a small party of four or six in a classically decorated apartment, in Zürich, Geneva, as well as the major European capitals - London, Paris, Rome, Berlin or Madrid - even Hong Kong, Singapore, Beirut and – somewhat to his surprise – Buenos Aires. Here again there appeared to be an option as to whether the party ended after the liqueurs, being driven to their respective hotels in the Bentley, or in the adjoining bedrooms.

Sam had certainly joined a very special world!

At around six thirty pm, he decided to take up a position in the bar from which he might observe any unusual movement, whilst at the same time establishing a relationship with the barman and waiters before Sam's arrival. Seated near the entrance, he could also observe movement outside in the lobby. He ordered some champagne to reinforce his confidence.

Just after seven fifteen, he felt a light touch on the shoulder and, turning, found himself confronted with a version of Sam which he had never seen, in spite of the strong taste for theatricality which he knew was part of her personality. Her face was brilliantly made up *à la Orientale*, with black lines extending to endpoints from the outer corners of her eyes, emphasising their delicate almond shape, set off with massive lashes. Her lips were a gleaming, dark ruby red, her prominent cheekbones emphasised with strong highlights. She was wearing a flowing red leather coat which fell to the floor, half unbuttoned to reveal the skin-tight long black dress which he had seen in the website photograph. As she opened the coat wider, he saw that it was lined with a dark fur, which might have been mink. Her views on animal rights seemed to have taken a back seat!

He stretched out his arms as if to greet a long lost friend, her name on the tip of his tongue. Before he could utter a word, she had slipped between his arms and pulled him hard up against her.

"I'm Dalal," she whispered in his ear, as if foreseeing the blunder he was about to make. Out loud, she continued, "My dear Leonardo, at last I've caught up with you. God, I need some of that champagne!"

Planting a light kiss on his cheek, she released him and dropped lithely into the armchair on the opposite side of his table, though not releasing his hand while she did so. She settled back in the chair without removing her coat, spreading its long folds to either side over the arms to reveal the shiny second skin of her long dress, it's low, strapless bust topped by a small gold and enamel pendant. The Druze star! All this had come close to bringing the bar to a standstill. Madame Flemming was in a class of her own!

"My dear Dalal, you look fantastic! Beyond my wildest dreams!"

Signalling to the now very attentive barman to bring over a bottle of champagne, he sat back and surveyed her. She looked unbelievably sexy. A wave of pure physical desire swept through him, stronger than he could ever remember. First their two week separation and now this embodiment of exotic sexual provocation before him.

"My dear, business first."

He pointed to a stiff white envelope bearing the logo of the hotel, lying in the middle of the table.

"I believe it is the agreed amount."

She acknowledged the courtesy with a smile and a slight inclination of the head, stretching out a black silk opera-gloved hand to sweep it off the table and into a concealed pocket inside her coat.

"Lady Blast deeply appreciates the fact that you have chosen a relative beginner in her arts. As you know, I am but a novice in this new profession. I have received strict instructions as to how to play my part to your satisfaction, so that I may learn to serve all the different desires of our worldwide clientele."

Leandro began to wonder how long they were going to have to keep up this ridiculous interchange, and something about the way he looked at her rather quizzically passed the message.

"But, dear Leonardo, I'm sure you have many things to tell me, as well as, perhaps, to ask me."

As she spoke, she placed a visiting card on the table, face down. As he reached across, he corrected her.

"It's Leandro, not Leonardo, by the way."

Sliding his glass next to the card, he saw that a few words had been scrawled on the back. *"Be careful, I have a microphone!"*

He tried not to betray his shock. That was going to make things a lot more complicated, although giving him a surreptitious wink, she appeared to send him a message that she would find a solution. In the meantime, the act must obviously be kept up. He could only guess at the reasons for her being fitted out with a wire. A form of quality control for a beginner, which would later serve for training purposes?

Or were the reasons more sinister? The latter seemed by far the more likely.

"How do you find the champagne, Dalal? I suggest that we have dinner here in this hotel's elegant restaurant. I'm a stranger to Zürich and, on a cold night like this, I feel reluctant to climb in and out of taxis and take risks with the cooking in some untested restaurant. Would you object to that?"

As she nodded agreement, he continued.

"Tell me, since we're so comfortably sitting here, and we have the whole of that bottle to get through before moving to the dining room, tell me about yourself. What brought you to Zürich? I understand that you're either South American or from the Middle East? For so beautiful a girl, you are clearly perfectly prepared for the profession you have chosen, though it might not always be every girl's first choice. The more we know about each other, the better we may enjoy our hours together."

He poured another glass for both of them.

"To the success of your new profession - or should I perhaps call it a vocation?"

He leaned across the table and their glasses touched.

"And to the success of your business in Zürich," she responded, with just a hint of emphasis, which he suspected was more than just a polite formality.

As they enjoyed the rest of the champagne, he gave her what he considered - for the benefit of any listeners - to be a predictable version of why he had come to Zürich. He was here to check on his accounts with one of the private banks, the identity of which he carefully concealed, since no such account existed, at least not in Zürich. He deliberately kept any biographical details and his Argentine origins as close as possible to a reality that could be verified.

"But all this must be very boring for you. You must have heard so much of this before from other clients here in Switzerland. Tell me, Dalal, tell me more about yourself. You're also from South America, like me, I believe?"

He was interested to hear what version she would play to him, presuming that it would be in line with what Carla would already know of her.

"I come from Argentina, Buenos Aires, but my origins are Syrian," she began. "I spent some time in the Middle East a few years ago. I studied literature in Buenos Aires. And I have done modelling for some of the main fashion magazines in Argentina."

"I am not surprised!" Leandro interjected. "I am sure you could have made that a profession had you wished to."

"Oh, I earned a lot of money in fashion photography, some of the best designers in Buenos Aires used me for their collections."

"And now...?" Leandro left the question hanging in the air.

She paused briefly.

"That's more complicated. It's very personal. I am sure none of my friends in Argentina would understand."

She took another sip of her glass before continuing, with a slight smile, narrowing her eyes and arching her back in such a manner as to emphasize her breasts through her open coat.

"I have always been interested in sex, all kinds of sex. Even at school, I can remember it got me into difficulties, especially with the nuns!" and she laughed, Leandro joining in.

"When I was young in Buenos Aires and also on my travels, I met many men, in France, in Italy, in the Arab world, they taught me many things. But I also met women and they taught me even more. They taught me much more about what men really want and how we women can give it to them. How we can control you through your desires. It's not just through our bodies, but also through our minds. And then a few months ago I met Lady Blast, in Punta del Este – in Uruguay – I am sure you know it."

Leandro nodded. "I was there at the New Year."

"Oh, so you said. Where were you staying? Which beaches did you go to? What a shame that we did not meet then!"

"No matter, we've met now. Go on...."

"Well, Lady Blast showed me things I only dimly suspected, things about myself, about my deepest desires. She showed me that there were two sides to my personality. One side quite normal, which allows me to love men – or women – with simplicity, with tenderness, with loyalty. And then another, more secret side."

She paused again and looked at him from below half-closed eyelids. Leandro began to get the feeling that some of what he was hearing might not just be for the benefit of the listeners, although the references to Lady Blast were clearly intended to demonstrate her allegiances. But was she also passing him a message at the level of their relationship? He looked at her quizzically.

"This is most interesting."

It seemed a banal response.

"I am pleased that you find it interesting. I've not told many people about this. But I feel that I can tell you, somehow you bring out a desire in me to share my thoughts and innermost beliefs."

"And perhaps not just your thoughts," he promptly responded, again an exchange which would seem superficially consistent with their client relationship for the evening.

"Not too fast," she chided, "I've not finished my story."

"Please continue, Dalal, forgive me. You were going to tell me about the other side."

"Yes. But first, some more champagne please."

"Of course," and he refilled her flute. "And then later we can go into dinner. Please tell me more, I find it fascinating … and truly exciting."

He felt that an enthusiastic reaction was called for, given potential listeners. Yet as he listened, he became more and more convinced that her speech held more than a grain of truth. Remembering her description of her emotional 'apartments', it suggested that Carla was increasingly a well-established tenant.

"What Lady Blast showed me was that not only could a woman exercise total power over a man, through her body and also through her mind, but she also showed me - most important – that this need not be the traditional control relationship between a dominant woman and a submissive man. Instead, such a relationship could become more than the sum of its parts, to the benefit of both. Such a relationship, even though its basis might outwardly appear commercial, could be built on trust, a trust also strengthened by an intimate knowledge of the sexual and emotional desires of the two parties. For many men, such a relationship might not be possible with their wives. The contractual nature of the relationship, which can be terminated at any time, rather than being a weakness, in fact underpins and strengthens the bond. You look perplexed…. Do you follow me?"

"I think so…," Leandro replied, a trace of doubt in his voice.

Not for the first time, Sam was setting out a stall of emotional options, which required both the high level of the trust she was talking about, but also lots of imagination. Not to mention a willingness to throw away traditional codes and try something very different. How much of this was marketing and how much the real Sam?

At this moment, the barman came over to where they were sitting to announce that their table was ready in the dining room. He got up, somewhat relieved that the theorizing was at an end. It was reality he was looking for, not theories.

Sam's entry into the dining room of the hotel did not pass entirely unnoticed and Leandro had some difficulty in remembering when he had ever seen such solicitous service at his dinner table.

The meal, though delicious and impeccably served, was, in other respects, uneventful. Whatever she had in mind to deal with the microphone must wait until they were alone together. At one point, he left the table and walked through the main lobby to another men's cloakroom, to see if there were any familiar faces. He was not surprised to spot one of the two Punta del Este bodyguards, better dressed than usual, apparently engrossed in a newspaper, which his dark glasses must have made it hard to read. The discreet earphones suggested that he had not only been recording, but also listening in to their conversation. Leandro gave no sign of having seen him. The close interest they were taking in Sam's movements, for whatever reason, was beginning seriously to irritate him.

To engineer a situation in which they could be unobserved, as they left the table Leandro suggested some more champagne, this time in his suite. Another bottle of Pommery and some caviar were ordered to be delivered to his room. He preferred not to think too hard about the cumulative damage to his American Express card!

Up in the suite, the champagne and caviar having arrived and some suitably romantic music chosen by Sam, Leandro indicated in sign language that they must find a solution to the question of the microphone. On a piece of paper he scribbled that one of the bodyguards was somewhere in the hotel. He had no idea of the range of the microphone. However, it would be risky to assume that they were safe, simply because they were now two floors higher up. Even so, the bodyguard might find it difficult to locate himself unobtrusively somewhere along the passage.

Slightly to his surprise, Sam first dimmed the lights.

"Dear Leo, the moment we've been waiting for!"

From the broad grin on her face, this was clearly for the benefit of the microphone.

"Dalal, let me embrace you!"

"First, Leo, I must freshen up. Give me a minute, please."

After a mere five minutes, she reappeared, naked except for the Druze star round her neck, high heels and the long black opera gloves. In one hand, she dangled a small microphone and antenna, dripping water, which with a flourish she proceeded to drop into the champagne bucket.

Then with a snarl of triumph and pent-up lust, she threw herself on Leandro, propelling him onto the huge bed. It was but the work of seconds for her to strip off his clothes, a ritual on which she had insisted from the earliest days of their lovemaking.

"Those shots of the man desperately struggling out of his shirt and jumping up and down to get out of his trousers are so inelegant -

frankly a turn-off!" she had explained one evening in his flat. "Anyway, it allows me to check that you're still all there!"

Pressing him down under her on the bed, she swiftly ran her hands over his whole body, as if checking that nothing had indeed changed. He lay on his back, rediscovering the smoothness of her flesh as his hands sought out familiar curves and recesses. Grasping Leandro's fingers and guiding them deeply inside her pussy, she began sliding her hips back and forth, short gasping breaths and a deep moan of pleasure the only sound as she intensified her pleasure. After a time, she changed position. Kneeling over him, Sam began a slow, lazy movement of her broad hips, up and down and side to side, a silky, sensuous motion, her breasts tingling with desire, caressing his face. As she swayed over him, her nipples swelled as he pulled at them with his lips, her eyes closing with the growing intensity of the stimulation. She could feel her cunt glowing and throbbing in response to his searching fingers. To take his cock in her mouth, to feel him inside her, to be pinned down with the weight of his body, to allow him to penetrate her in every orifice she could offer him – her throat, her cunt, her ass! He slid down her body, stroking her with his tongue and lips as he passed and reversed himself between her legs. Slowly working his tongue over her labia, pressing deeper and deeper with each pass, he felt her legs tensing as his tongue plunged inside her.

"Oh my love, it's been too long. Yes, there. Again. Yes."

Sam's head was swirling. The feel of his body, the scent of his skin. The weeks apart and now this reunion rammed home to her why she loved him, the feel of him, the touch of his hands, the sound of his voice.

Their lovemaking ended just before dawn in the large sauna shower of the luxurious bathroom.

Mid-morning, as they lay next to each on the bed in soft white bathrobes, the remains of a delicious breakfast at the foot of the bed, Leandro finally challenged Sam.

"Now Sam. Are you going to tell me why you came here? No explanation. No message. What was I supposed to think?"

Sam said nothing for a minute, an enigmatic look on her face.

"I'm sorry," she began. "I know what you mean."

She paused again.

"I'm even more sorry that I can't give you all the reasons now. You're going to have to trust me. Somewhere, deep down, the fact that you followed me so far, I interpret as being a sign of that trust."

This evasive reply was not at all what he had expected, not what he had come over ten thousand kilometres to hear. Leandro felt anger and frustration well up inside him.

"Trust doesn't come cheap these days," he retorted, ill concealing a note of sarcasm.

She threw him a glance tinged with what he took to be a measure of contempt.

"I'm sorry, if I don't have the bank balance of your new lovers," he continued, although instantly regretting the remark.

She slapped him hard across the mouth, taking him completely by surprise with the violence of her reaction.

"You don't usually hit below the belt," she shot.

As he watched, the flash of fury in her eyes slowly faded to one of sadness.

"Sorry, I didn't mean that," he murmured.

"But somewhere, Leandro, you thought it."

Again she said nothing for a moment, looking at him, her sadness now clearly visible, before finally whispering.

"I'm sorry, Leo, we can't take this any farther!"

Leandro was at a complete loss for words. What a fool!

She got up from the bed and made her way into the bathroom, dropping the bathrobe as she left. Leandro lay back in the bed, cursing his stupidity. It wasn't even as if he really believed what he had said. His temper had momentarily got the better of him.

Some fifteen minutes later, Sam re-emerged. She had piled up her hair, her slim neck wrapped in the fur collar of her red coat, now fastened by a long row of buttons down to the floor, hiding her black dress. Her exotic makeup of the previous evening had given way to the usual understated highlights. He even wondered whether she might have been crying. She raised her gloved index finger to her lips.

"Leo, I have to hope that wasn't you. I know that I haven't been very fair to you since I last saw you in Punta. I'm sorry, I truly am. Please believe me, there are reasons, and I'll find the right time to explain them to you. When I do, I hope you'll understand why it couldn't be here, today. In the meantime, go back to Buenos Aires. There's nothing you can do to help me here. I'll be back there when I can. Take care of yourself, Leo. Please don't say any more."

She crossed the carpet and took his face in both hands. The kiss was as long and as passionate as any she had given him.

He made as if to rise from the bed, but she had already turned on her heels. Reaching the door, she paused briefly to smile at him. He raised his hand and called after her.

"Before you go! There's one thing you should know. Eduardo is now convinced that the killer is a man called Dávila, her *patron*, not Carla."

"I know."

Then she was gone.

Leandro sat on the edge of the bed, a feeling of nausea sweeping through him. One day, his Anglo-Saxon sarcasm was going to be the death of him. He prayed that this wasn't the day.

After a few minutes, he asked the switchboard to put him through to British Airways. Snow was beginning to fall outside.

A few hours later, with the snow falling more heavily, the sky over Zürich was a dark leaden grey as evening approached. The streets almost silent and deserted, with only the occasional car carefully making its way, headlights on, tyres squeaking on the freshly fallen white of the Richard-Wagner-Strasse below. Sam stood by the window, looking out.

She had returned to Carla's house deeply shaken. She knew that Leandro's remark had come off the top of his head, but she had also understood that her newfound persona had profoundly disturbed him. Not to mention her refusal to provide any explanation. Whereas she had been able to lead him slowly towards newer sexual and emotional horizons over the preceding months, she suspected that the role of Dalal might just be a bridge too far. And why not? In the mind of a man, her role-play could easily be seen as just a more sophisticated form of prostitution. Perhaps she shouldn't blame him. Whereas their lovemaking had shown that their passion remained as unbridled as before, who knew what had been going through his head at the time? She had established that her relationship with Lamai could be accommodated, but her relationship with Carla had clearly always worried him. She knew that part of this related to the dangers which they suspected were associated with Carla, and with Dávila, but there was more to it than that. It had been her intention, as soon as the lovemaking was over, to begin to explain just why she had done what she had. And then, at the last minute, she had avoided his legitimate query, in so doing, sending quite the wrong signal. Always one to follow her instinct, for some reason, she had sidestepped. And he had interpreted it perhaps in the only way he could.

Instead of trying to recover the situation, she had raised the stakes - and the risk that she would lose him. She had taken a big bet. She had to hope that it would pay off. She had meant it, when she had told him that there was nothing more he could do for her now in Zürich. How would he interpret that? How confident could she feel that Leandro was still a willing inmate of her emotional apartment?

"Señorita, Madame Carla was wondering whether you would join her in the Sanctuary," Carlos interrupted her thoughts.

Reluctantly. Sam picked up the phone on the coffee table and dialled an internal number.

"You were looking for me?"

"I'm just back from Geneva. I'm in need of you, my love. And maybe, just maybe, you'll tell me about your friend Leo."

Carla's voice was low and voluptuous, a tone Sam knew only too well, reserved for a special séance together, a message straight to her loins.

"Give me a few minutes, I'll be there."

The line clicked at the other end.

Sam went back to her bedroom. She needed time to think through the situation with Leandro, but it would have to wait. A warm shower to remove all traces of their lovemaking. For the intimacy with Carla to come, there could be no hint of his presence. Carla might not be jealous by nature, but, from Sam's experience, she knew that Carla insisted on total exclusivity, in time and space, for these sessions together. That was the purpose of the Sanctuary. Carla had once explained that, with promiscuous sex the focus of so much of her life, her relationship with Sam needed a time warp, a physical capsule of its own.

Sam stood looking at herself in the mirror. What scenario might Carla have in mind? She knew that Carla loved her sex with Sam to be smooth, unctuous, with maximum contact and minimum abrasion. The explosions of force, when they came, impacted all the more. At the end of their first session together, in the shower under the house in Punta del Este, Carla had insisted on personally shaving Sam's pubic hair, to reveal her beautifully shaped mons and outer labia. Putting down the razor, Carla's tongue had driven Sam to a final orgasm there and then. Sam rubbed in a soft perfumed cream, smiling as she recalled Leandro's reaction - admittedly of pure pleasure - on discovering the change. After their parting this morning, she had to hope there would be more moments like that.

She opened the closet in her dressing room, trying to decide what to wear, turning over the assortment of expensive lingerie which she had thrown into her suitcase on leaving Argentina two weeks earlier. Her weak point - as Leandro's untimely doorstep delivery had so dangerously demonstrated. Unable to resist temptation, she had yielded. The collection had nearly doubled since her arrival in Zürich. Finally, she selected a bodystocking of the finest white lace. An image of the discreet little shop behind the Faubourg St. Antoine in Paris where she had found it – and a few others of equally outrageous style – flashed into her mind. Recommended to her by a beautiful Brazilian transsexual plying her trade on the Faubourg, those 'girls' always had the best. She almost laughed out loud, remembering the contrast between the delicate figure of the girl and the deep husky voice, which had emerged from her carmine lips! The mesh of the white lace, stretched taut over Sam's breasts, was offset by what remained of the deep tan she had acquired beside Carla's swimming pool. The feeling of her whole body lightly squeezed in its embrace always turned her on. In front of the mirror, she checked her silhouette, the perfectly shaped breasts, their nipples already aroused as the tight lace rubbed against them, a narrow waist falling away to sweeping hips and the globes of her buttocks. And then her legs. She sometimes felt that her legs were the best part of her. Leandro, like so many men, preferred her tits and arse. Men were so stereotyped!

"Yes, Carla, you're a lucky woman! And, come to think of it, you too, Leo!" she murmured to herself as she looked once more in the mirror. She hesitated. Perhaps her tits and arse were spectacular after all.

She took a floor-length black silk peignoir off its hanger and dropped it over her shoulders, leaving it unfastened to allow ample exposure of her body beneath. Then, slipping on a pair of dark red stiletto-heeled pumps, and picking up the envelope containing the dollars Leandro had paid her last night, she gave a final pirouette in front of the mirror, before taking the inner lift to the Sanctuary, which Carla had sunk in the basement of the house two floors below.

The small foyer to the Sanctuary gave onto a short flight of translucent white stairs leading to a black door with massive silver hinges and fittings. The sound of her heels on the steps resonated in the total silence. She pushed open the door, silent on its hinges.

The walls of the room were a gleaming black lacquer, the floor highly polished tiles of the same colour, the ceiling one continuous mirror. On one wall, another mirror. On the other, access to Carla's private bathroom through translucent curtains. In the centre, a vast, pulpous couch, wholly sheathed in shining black PVC. Against two of the walls, large white sofas, contrasting sharply with the darkness around, illumination discreetly provided by a string a concealed lights around the ceiling. The temperature was a warm twenty-five degrees, a heavy scent of musk wafted in the air by the small fans.

"You broke the rules!"

The tone was far from welcoming. Carla was standing in a corner of the room, her diminutive waist constricted by a black leather corset, over which loomed her commanding breasts. Matching leather thigh boots and long black latex opera gloves to above the elbow made up the rest of her costume. Almost no jewellery. Her shimmering blonde mane fell loosely over her shoulders, waving softly in the airstream of the fans. Her body gleamed, covered in some perfumed essence. In spite of the aggressive tone, Sam thought she detected just a hint of sadness in the large eyes.

In one hand, Carla dangled the microphone and antenna which Sam had last seen disappearing into the ice bucket at the hotel.

"You broke the rules!" she repeated, her voice taking on a sharper edge.

"Yes, Carla. There are some rules and some situations I can't accept. No apologies!" Sam replied smartly, wondering how the hell they had recovered it. "But I did get paid."

She placed the white envelope on the table beside Carla.

Carla appeared momentarily disconcerted by Sam's response.

"There will still be a price to pay for your actions," she murmured, tossing the microphone into a corner.

Sam did not protest, in little doubt that this must presage some kind of complex ritual in which Carla would seek Sam's atonement.

Carla took Sam by the hand and led her without a word towards a corner of the room. Sam silently acquiesced. To each wrist, Carla buckled a tight red leather cuff, from which hung a short silver chain, which she joined with a small padlock. She raised Sam's arms above her head and fastened the extended chains to a hook hanging from a silver pulley fixed to the ceiling near one of the corners. Pulling down the other end of the chain, she secured it to a wall cleat. Fitting similar

372

cuffs to each ankle, and spreading Sam's legs wide, she fastened their chains to a ring set in the floor. Finally, Carla tied the silk peignoir across Sam's back to reveal her body. With her feet spread apart and positioned behind her point of balance, her arms stretched upwards to the ceiling, Sam was now fully extended, her body sharply arched, off balance, breasts thrust forward in the direction of the dais.

Tossing her hair out of her face, Carla settled back on one of the sofas and observed Sam's silhouette, idly stroking the nipple of one breast, legs crossed provocatively.

"You knew that that microphone was meant to function all night. What possessed you to break communication that way? Needless to say, Carlos had no choice but to leave, and go back this morning. For a few hundred francs, he was able to retrieve it when the room service was cleared away after you checked out. Can't say your conversation was all that interesting until you drowned it. Explain such insubordination, Sam!" The tone was imperious.

Sam saw no reason to back down.

"I'm not sure we can go on like this, Carla. We have to reach a workable agreement. Though I don't usually negotiate hanging from the ceiling, you leave me no choice. I'm not just one of your other girls, at your beck and call, compliant with your every wish, to be controlled with a vocabulary of domination and a flow of cash. Although I've no way of comparing how you behave with them when you're alone, I do know, Carla, how you behave with me. I may be wrong, but something tells me it's different between us. If it's not, undo these chains and call me a taxi. I'll be out of here in an hour! Though you do possess some of me, you don't own all of me. You also know about Leandro and, for the present, that territory is off-limits to you. If that's a problem, as I said, call the cab."

She paused to gauge the impact of what she had said so far. Carla remained silent, holding Sam's gaze. She continued.

"As to the question of the microphone, I hesitated whether to reject it there and then, when Carlos brought it to me. Finally, I thought it better not to force a confrontation with Dávila's watchdogs. As you know, I'm not a fan of theirs. I won't accept it next time."

She noted the slight nod of Carla's head.

"But, Carla, let's forget all that. I think we make a powerful team, particularly with some of your most important clients. I don't want to share in the profits, but I do want an arrangement with you which has different operating procedures. I'll spell them out, though perhaps not from this position. Please be clear. I'm not talking about what we feel for each other."

Somehow, she was able to force a smile.

Carla sat there quietly, her eyes never leaving Sam's face, weighing her words. After a minute, she got up from the sofa and came over to stand in front of Sam. Sam detected her most exotic perfume, Fleur de Narcisse, a special order from l'Artisan Parfumeur in Paris.

"You're probably right, my love. Perhaps I'm getting too old for the life I lead, I need more stable, deeper relationships. In you, I believe – I know - I've found one. The other girls are just beautiful, high-class whores, with whom everyone has a good time. Without me, they'd be back on the streets. But you, Sam, you're so different. We are very similar in many ways. You don't do it for the money, that's obvious. Thanks to your father, there's no lack of that. You don't need the flashy lifestyle, which you could get by many other means."

She turned and lay down on the dais.

"So what is it, Sam? When I was attracted to you the first night we met at that party, somehow I detected it was mutual. With that little Thai girl, you can no doubt make love all night. But a Carla, that's very different, isn't it? Is it the danger? The risk? The adrenaline is powerful, isn't it? The eroticism. So why did you engage with me? Why, Sam? There are other reasons I've no doubt, although at the moment, I don't know what they are. This Leandro? Where does he fit in? After all, he followed you all the way to Zürich. I don't know many Argentine men who would follow a girlfriend, whom they knew to be two-timing them in a lesbian relationship, halfway across the world and then indulge in a bit of fantasy role-play like last night. And pay out a few thousand dollars into the bargain. So what's it all about?"

"Do I have to be this uncomfortable to carry on this conversation?"

"You still haven't paid the penalty, even if it's the last one before we change our contract," Carla retorted. "When we make a contract, we stick to its conditions, until we change them. Once the price is paid, we'll return to this conversation."

Sam shrugged as best she could, given her posture. She had no recollection of any contract. But then, if that was the way Carla was going to play....

Carla leaned over and pressed a buzzer on a side table. Through the curtains emerged the figure of Naya, totally sheathed in black latex, except for her mouth and tiny lenses over her eyes. She stood next to her mistress, motionless, a gleaming statue, awaiting instructions. Carla's hand lightly caressed her buttocks with the tips of her fingers.

"I once told you that Naya was a superlative submissive. Enjoy the demonstration. In silence. We'll talk later."

Carla gestured to Naya, who moved across to face Sam. Carefully she inserted a rubber ball gag into her mouth, strapping it tightly behind Sam's head. Behind the lenses of her mask, she appeared oblivious to the look of fury on Sam's face.

"Help me off with this," Carla instructed her. It was but the work of a few seconds. Keeping on the opera gloves, Carla's tanned body stretched languorously on her back in the middle of the dais. She parted her legs, giving Sam a clear view of her clitoris.

"Your penalty for last night's insubordination, Samira, will be to watch, but not to enjoy."

Naya's glistening body straddled her mistress, pinioning her arms above her head. An image of Michelle Pfeiffer flashed before Sam's eyes. Except that Naya was a much more sensual Catwoman, and Carla definitely a lot sexier than Michael Keaton!

Swinging from the chains, Sam watched, fascinated, her erotic tension spiralling, as the maid's gloved fingers regaled Carla's body, caressing, teasing, thrusting, penetrating. Although Sam had made love to another woman on many occasions, she had never before watched it as now. With her tongue, Naya invaded and rippled into every passage, Carla's hand directing her lips, the only visible part of Naya's face. In a final phase, a snakelike double dildo linking the two women, they rotated and pumped, till even Carla could no longer control her cries. Sam's body strained and writhed uncontrollably in concert. Perfectly attuned to her mistress' every response, Naya brought Carla to orgasm again, and again. Finally, on a signal from her mistress, she slipped away as silently as she had come. Carla lay back. Her eyes had held Sam's gaze throughout.

After a while, she rose, released Sam from the chains and straps and helped her out of the peignoir. Carefully she stripped the lace stocking from Sam's exhausted body. Every muscle aching from the posture forced upon her by Carla, but most of all from the muscular tensions which the display had transmitted to her loins, Sam collapsed onto the platform. She sank into its soft surface, its slippery coolness a balm against her skin. Carla lay beside her, head resting on her arm, studying her.

Slowly she leaned across and inserted her gloved fingers into Sam's vagina. As she did so, her mass of blonde hair fell across Sam's breasts. Given her level of arousal, Sam orgasmed instantly, the tension flowing from her body like a receding tsunami.

"I couldn't let you stay like that, my darling."

Taking Sam's head in both hands, her kiss lingered long on Sam's lips.

"Now to our new contract. We should both be in the right mood."

"I thought you said you weren't into pain", Sam whispered.

"No, only pleasure."

Sam could just manage a low moan by way of response.

"Let's go shopping, Sam! Let's celebrate!"

They were sitting in Carla's Porsche on the following afternoon, the snowflakes dissolving on the windscreen as the car's powerful heating system kicked in.

"I'll show you some shops which I'm sure you'll find very tempting, knowing your tastes." Carla turned, smiling, gently stroking Sam's inner thigh.

Pressing the control button, she opened the gates and emerged carefully into the street. The snow had been falling all night. Carla usually drove very fast, but intelligently. Sam sat back and enjoyed the sensation of two good-looking women in a very fast car, male drivers on the road easily distracted, even the Swiss!

The Porsche now parked, Carla led Sam down a side street in the older part of town across the Limmat. She pressed the buzzer next to a black enamel-painted door, the appearance of which in no way suggested the presence of a shop.

"You'll see, he does wonderful things in leather, mainly very upmarket streetwear, but also some specials on the basis of designs I give him. The leather all comes from Italy, the only place. His clients come from all over. I know he has a lot from Russia, but just as many from the US. I want to make you a little present."

The door clicked open and Carla led the way upstairs to the first floor. Another buzzer.

"Carla! What a wonderful surprise!"

In trainers, jeans and a polo neck sweater, all black, Amadeo, a man of about fifty, slim, shaven head, greeted Carla warmly, in French with an overtone of Italian. Then, putting his arm around her waist and Sam's, he marched them into his workshop, the pungent aroma of leather filling Sam's nostrils. Releasing them, he turned to admire the two women.

"Ah, you must be Sam. I've heard about you. You are as beautiful as Carla told me. In fact, more beautiful. And with that figure, I will do wonders."

"That's enough, Amadeo, or I'll start to get jealous." Carla laughed. "But you're right, I didn't do her justice."

Turning to Sam, Carla continued.

"You will see, Amadeo is an artist. Much more creative than Jitrois in Paris. I presume you know who I mean?"

Sam knew well enough. Jean Claude Jitrois had given up psychology to become a fashion designer, the first fashion couturier to take fetishism out of the closet and put it on the catwalk and on the street, dressing stars of the pop world, but also high society and many others in exotic and beautiful leather.

"Of course I know. I can't wait."

"You see, Amadeo, Sam needs to impress a number of very important men, if you see what I mean."

Amadeo winked at Carla.

"Of course, I see exactly what you mean."

It was obvious that Amadeo knew all about Carla's line of business and was a major contributor to her wardrobe.

A couple of hours later, he had also made a contribution to Sam's. A gift from Carla, in the form of a pair of amply pleated leather *bombachas*, similar to the ones which Sam had so admired at the polo party. A tight-sleeved short jacket with Chinese collar and a Victorian style corset with back lacing to enhance her waist. All pale pewter of the softest leather. She would wear it to the dinner in London that Aziz was setting up for her with the Saudi royal!

For a moment, as she admired herself in the mirror, Sam wondered what Leandro's reaction would be. She more than half suspected that he would have few objections, although she didn't see herself going to their usual pizzeria in it. Something needed to be done about his lifestyle, the social circles in which he moved! Would she get the chance?

"Come back in a couple of days for another fitting," Amadeo instructed her.

The two women emerged onto the pavement. The snow had returned in strength, cloaking the narrow streets in its white silence, the only sound the crunch of fresh snow under their boots.

"Coffee and chocolate at Spruengli's? Then we'll need to find you some beautiful boots to go with Amadeo's stuff."

Having reparked the Porsche in a side street, the two women strolled down the Bahnhofstrasse. It was past five and the offices were disgorging staff. The sight of these two handsome women, shrouded in their fur coats, turned more than one head, even in a city accustomed to seeing good-looking examples of their sex. Sam had noticed that the women of Zürich were far better looking than their counterparts in Geneva, not afraid to dress more provocatively.

Their entry through the doors of Spruengli produced a similar effect on the clientele. A number of more bourgeois Zürichoises frowned at the sight of so much blatant extravagance! No doubt concerned about their husbands being led astray by such predatory females loose on the streets of the city.

They headed into the little side salon and ordered coffee and a dish of the shop's world-famous *truffes du jour*.

Sam suddenly saw Carla stiffen. She had seen something over Sam's shoulder.

A look of fury.

"Shit! There he is again!"

"Who?"

"Carlos. I spotted him when we were parking to go and see Amadeo. And there he is again. I've had enough of this spying. *El patron* calls it protection, but that's not the point at all."

Sam turned, but couldn't see Carlos anywhere.

"No, he's gone. He saw that I spotted him."

"Someday, Carla, you must tell me a little bit more about your relationship with your *patron*. What's it all about, why are these two men always hanging around?"

"It's a long story, it goes way back. Even to before I came to Switzerland. This isn't the place for that. It's far too complicated. Anyway, it may change very soon. But it's important that you know about it. I'll tell you one evening, by the fire, over a drink. There are many things I need to tell you. And perhaps you Sam, you'll tell me a few as well. We still have so much to learn about each other."

Sam caught the change of expression in Carla's eyes. The anger had given way to tenderness.

"These *truffes* are really something. So delicious with coffee. And so bad for my figure."

"Stop saying that, will you? You needn't worry about your figure," Carla interjected. "It's at my age that it really gets perilous. Anyway, pass me the dish, you're not going to have all of them."

They abandoned the warmth of the cafe. Sam saw Carla checking up and down the street, presumably looking for Carlos.

"Can't see him. Anyway, let's forget about that and get you some sexy Louboutin boots to go with your new outfit. Some nice twelve-centimetre heels. Only the best for our Saudi friends. Dear Sam, you're going to look so pretty. I must give a dinner party for you. Then tomorrow I'm going to show you something different in the way of fashion accessories. Perhaps a little less public. More intimate."

She put her arm under Sam's and led her up the Bahnhofstrasse. It had started to snow again. Sam was wondering what kind of people might come to such a dinner party. And what Carla had in mind for tomorrow.

Knowing Carla, she suspected that it would lead her into new paths.

8 February 2008

Paying off the taxi, Leandro unlocked the wrought iron gate at the entrance to the Pasaje La Piedad, leading to the elegant building which housed his apartment. One of the two occupants of a car parked on the opposite side of the street noted his time of arrival. They had been told merely to keep a record of his comings and goings. The watchlist at the airport had alerted Dávila's team to Leandro's arrival that morning on the flight from London. He saw nothing of this.

One of the reasons why Leandro failed to spot the surveillance could have stemmed from the fact that he was still laughing at the wild gossip with which his taxi driver had been regaling him in an incessant stream since the moment he had climbed on board with his suitcases at the airport. Taxi drivers in Buenos Aires, of which over thirty thousand were licensed, might vary in their taste in music, between Argentine folklore, the tango, pop or even occasionally classical music, but in their politics, they formed an almost uniform group hostile to whichever government was in power at the time. His driver, delighted to find someone who had been out of the country for most of the summer and who therefore needed to be kept informed of the latest news and scandal, rapidly brought him up-to-date on such varied subjects as the health of the President, rumours as to the marital situation of the Presidential couple, the latest scandal engulfing one or other football player, not to mention the rising cost of living or growing insecurity. All this at a speed along the motorway into town comfortably above the limit, followed by a process of changing lanes every hundred metres in order to gain a fraction of a second on the time, weaving in and out of the dense Buenos Aires traffic. After one of these rides, Leandro often felt the need to offer up a prayer to those overworked guardian angels in the sky, who somehow saved so many Argentine drivers from themselves on an hourly basis.

"Here, keep the difference. I always pay for good information."

"*Muchas gracias*, Señor. Any time. It's my pleasure."

The bundle of unopened mail awaiting him was depressing. He had been away for less than a month, the pile of electricity, water and gas bills, however derisory the amount invoiced, given the current government's lunatic policy of subsidising public services, meant that he would have to move fast to ensure that the service wasn't cut off. It was the kind of administrative hassle he hated. Without unpacking, he picked up the phone. Tired, he failed to spot a slight alteration in the way his calls were going through. He rang Elena and they agreed to have dinner on the following day. She reported that Alejandra was in good spirits. He could detect that she was too. He would have to try and discover diplomatically what she had been up to. Not that she wasn't going to do the same to him.

He rang his business partner, who sounded relieved that there would now be two pairs of hands back on the job. He gave Leandro a quick rundown of what had been happening on the economic front in the country during the summer holidays, since Leandro told him that he had deliberately kept out of touch with current economic events. Leandro listened patiently. Nothing had changed. But then why should it in the holiday season? Either through tiredness, or, given the radical shift of focus of his life over the last couple of months, he caught himself wondering how much all this really mattered. He needed to get back into the groove, it was often like this after long summer holidays. Yet deep down, he sensed that this whole affair, Sam, the events in Zürich, had got his adrenaline running much faster. Sad that it didn't pay the bills. In fact, quite the contrary. He closed his mind to what he would find on the next monthly statement of his American Express card. He needed a good shower. But first, he must ring his mother. Her maid, Estela, answered the phone.

"It's Leandro, I'm back. How is my mother?"

"Don Leandro! It's good to hear your voice. Your mother appreciated the postcard you sent from Switzerland very much."

"Good, I'm glad it got through. How is she?"

"Better recently, I'm glad to say. Perhaps the new treatment is helping. She seems to be sleeping a lot, but in general, she's much more her old self. You know, chasing me around, checking out what I'm doing, sending me out to get things."

Estela's kindly voice betrayed the fact that she would hold none of this against the old lady whose companion she had been since Leandro's mother had offered her a job at the age of seventeen. Leandro's mother had found her sitting on a park bench, crying, lost, just arrived on the bus from the wild and backward Province of Tucuman, down to her last few pesos. They had never been separated since that day. Now it was Estela's turn to repay the kindness. Even though she had been able to set aside some of her earnings and buy a plot of land in her home village, it had never occurred to her to abandon the old lady.

"That's very good news. I'm in a bit of a hurry just now, but I'll drop round tomorrow or the day after. Tell her I called and if she wants to ring me, I'll be at home most of the time."

The long flight, again packed into British Airways economy class, had left him weary, even though the time difference was usually manageable. He knew that the traveller's rulebook suggested that he should struggle on until evening, only going to bed at the normal time, but on this occasion he collapsed onto the sofa with only a towel around his waist, given the oppressive heat in the city, and was soon fast asleep.

He woke at around six in the evening, sweating, his backache worse than when he had climbed off the plane.

Back in Buenos Aires, his separation from Sam felt even more painful. When she had walked out of the door in the hotel, it was as if the floor had collapsed, even if he knew that she was far too intelligent to have taken his remark at face value. At the same time, the Sam he had found in Zürich felt like a Sam that he had not yet encountered, even though their lovemaking had been as powerful and passionate as any they had shared. But the artificiality of the setting, the unseen presence of listeners, of people so close to his relationship with her as to become a threat, even a physical danger, had skewed the context. Not to mention the new Carla scenario, which seemed to lead in directions as unfamiliar as they were dangerous. Having ineptly brought their intimacy to a premature close, he had not been able to pose all the questions uppermost in his mind since following her to Zürich. Would she give him the chance again? These and many other questions had churned around in his mind as he made his way back to London to catch the Buenos Aires flight. On the southbound plane, only a liberal dose of Valium had allowed him to shut them out for a few hours. Now, back in familiar surroundings, he needed some peace and calm to think things through properly. Would Sam send him some kind of signal? Should he send one? He decided to postpone these questions until he had had a good night's rest.

On a whim, he rang Elena to see whether she would receive him that evening rather than next day.

"Nothing in the fridge, Leo? Of course, come along. Then you can tell me all about the sinful things you've been up to in old Europe. If you deny any of it, I won't feed you."

At about nine, he was knocking on her door. The two men in the dark blue Renault noted down the address. The boys in the office would check it out.

Elena had set the table and was preparing a huge dish of his favourite pasta with basil and olive oil. A good bottle of merlot stood open on the table. There were even candles!

"Jesus, you must been unfaithful to me this summer!" Leandro quipped, waving his hand in the direction of the elegant dinner table.

"Typical! And just when I thought you might appreciate me welcoming you home. You always were a bastard."

He pulled her towards him, his arms appreciating the familiarity of her contours. They kissed.

"I missed you."

"Liar! Or did *la turca* give you a bad time? That's it, isn't it? You're not as cocky as you were last time I saw you. Never mind. She'll probably repent. Intelligent women often do... and sometimes also the not so intelligent."

"Now who's being a bastard? By the way, you're looking pretty pleased with yourself. Had a good summer?"

"Very good, thank you," she replied enigmatically.

"I need a drink!"

Elena served the pasta perfectly *al dente* as always. They concentrated on the food.

"You always did make a great pasta."

Leandro, having swept up the remains of the olive oil and Parmesan cheese with a piece of bread, swivelled his chair so as to be able to cross his legs more comfortably and take the weight of his spine, resting his arm on the table, his glass full of merlot.

"So, are you going to tell me?"

"What?" Elena replied coyly.

"Oh, I don't know, how was the summer? Where did you go? Something. Anything."

"Only if I first get something in return."

Leandro gave her a rapid summary of what had happened over the last couple of months, minimising the role of Sam and certainly concealing her relationship with Carla. Someone as clear-headed as Elena would think he was deranged to contemplate the kind of relationship which he now had with Sam. He admitted to having gone to Zürich to find Sam and, without going into any details, to having parted on very uncertain terms.

Elena listened in silence, sipping her wine.

"You've got it bad, Leo, haven't you?"

"You think so?"

"I know so. You haven't told me half the story and I suspect that it's the half which is causing you the most unhappiness. But is it unhappiness? I wonder. Somewhere, I suspect that you're actually enjoying this. You've never had a relationship with anyone quite like Sam before."

Seeing Leandro about to interrupt, she continued.

"Don't get me wrong, this isn't jealousy - at least, I don't think so. It's more compassion. While you've been away, I've done a tiny bit of digging. By the sounds of it, this Samira's quite a girl. Sure you can handle her?"

Leandro drew a deep breath and made a gesture of helplessness.

"Frankly, I don't know. But you're right. She's got to me. Big-time."

"Poor Leo. At your age. Deep down, you men never grow up. It always feels like the first time for you. Somewhere, we women know how to learn from experience. So, tell me, what are you going to do?"

Leandro shook his head.

"I don't know," he repeated. "I don't know whether to get in touch with her, or wait for her to be in touch with me."

"Jesus, that's the kind of question you'd be asking yourself aged fifteen! Take my advice, let her rot! If she loves you, she'll turn up. If she doesn't, she won't and you may be well out of it. Oh, I know, you'll be crying in your little bed at night for a month or so. But you'll recover. It's not some little Arab girl is going to drive you to suicide."

Leandro grinned.

"You're right. Anyway, I'm not the suicide kind. Not one for the grand gestures."

Elena led the way to the sofa and patted the seat next to her.

"Come over here, let Elena look after you."

Leandro sat down next to her and rested his head on her shoulder. Not for the first time, he wondered why they had split up.

"Were we mad to split up?"

"Don't let's start that one again."

He detected that Elena meant what she said. Whatever he might be thinking, he couldn't ignore the possibility that their arrangement now suited her. After all, it had suited him when things were going fine with Sam.

"So, now it's your turn."

"Well..." She drew out the word. "Yes, I've met someone. There, before you ask. I've got a good relationship going with him. Probably simpler than yours. It's only at a very early stage, but we spent a good summer together. And yes, I'm very fond of him. But then I'm very fond of you."

Leandro felt almost a physical pain shoot through him. They had always agreed that the other had total freedom on that front. But somehow, however much they might have accepted it in intellectual terms, in physical and emotional terms, it wasn't that easy. He wondered what Elena had felt when she had first heard about Sam.

Elena had detected the impact of her words.

"Listen, Leo, this is a two-way street. If you can have Sam, presumably I can have my man. At the end of the day, whoever we have, we'll never be able to wipe out our time together. That'll cause pain. Don't think that Sam doesn't cause me some pain. And I can see that what I've just told you hurts. Sorry. But for the time being, that's the way it is. We had our reasons to split up. Jealousy is not a good reason to come together again. Somewhere, deep down, I never completely rule out the possibility that we may come together again. But not this way."

"You're right... as usual."

"And we can still help each other. You can always come and cry on my shoulder."

"Perhaps not this time. At least, not crying."

"Brave man!" A slight note of irony was not entirely absent.

It was Saturday morning. With nothing better to do, and given that SIDE worked all hours, he had come into the office, calling in his assistants as well. Just to spoil their weekend.

An email from Carlos informed Dávila that Leandro had left Zürich, something which he already knew anyway, and that the girl Samira appeared to be preparing to travel also.

He called in Cacho, who occupied the small office next to his and acted as his gatekeeper.

"What's the news on this man Flemming?"

"Give me a moment, *patron*, I'll bring in the reports."

He was back in a minute and handed over a sheaf of half-page typed notes. Dávila skimmed through them.

"Nothing much here. Except that I see that there was a phone contact with a Subinspector Falcioni. What could that have been about? Who's he?"

None of his close team knew about Dávila's involvement with Williams. He had made sure of that. So he wasn't going to show too much interest in Falcioni to Cacho.

"As you know, Flemming came back yesterday from London. We picked him up at his flat and since then he seems to have been doing all the usual things, seeing his ex-wife, ringing his mother. As to Falcioni, we don't know what that was about. There's some family connection, as far as we can tell. You want me to find out some more?"

"It's not really important. But, if you dig something up, let me know. That'll be all. And bring me a coffee."

Dávila was not nearly as untroubled as he had indicated to Cacho. There was something which made him nervous about this link between

Falcioni, the woman Samira and Flemming. Although he had put a tail on him and tapped his phone, he needed to check Flemming out some more. He hoped he had not been negligent. The relationship with Samira had been spotted as far back as January, but it had slipped his mind to take it farther at the time. The external phone tap had been put in place only a day or so earlier. Careless? He hoped not.

He picked up the phone and dialled an internal number to the archives. He didn't want to go through Cacho.

"This is Dr Dávila," he announced to the girl who picked up at the other end. "Could you see if we have any information on a man called Leandro Flemming, age mid-40s? Bring it up to me personally. No, that'll be all. Thank you. As quick as you can."

About half an hour later, a pretty brunette in T-shirt and jeans tapped on his door.

"*Adelante!*"

"Leandro Flemming, Dr Dávila? We don't have very much. It's all here."

"Good, put it down there, thank you."

The girl had heard gossip about Dávila in the canteen and was pleased to get out of his office fast. Anyway, being Saturday, she was only working the morning shift and was due to meet her *novio* for lunch.

Dávila picked up the slim file. It didn't take long to skim through the few pages it contained. Date of birth, parents (mixed Scottish and Italian origins), education, something of a war hero in the Malvinas, then finance and now running his own economic and financial consultancy. There was an example of one of the consultancy's monthly bulletins. Not particularly flattering on the subject of the Government's economic policies. But then, none but the most die-hard Kirchnerista economists would have anything good to say on that subject anyway, given the fact that there wasn't a policy to speak of. It wasn't a subject in which Dávila was going to get involved. This Government had uses for him other than to defend the indefensible. No mention of any connection with Falcioni. That would still need looking into. It wasn't worth photocopying any of the file. He sealed it into an envelope and sent it back to archives. A quick look at Google only told him that Flemming had spoken at some economic conference.

He decided to wait and see if the surveillance produced anything more interesting.

Now that he was back in Buenos Aires, Leandro urgently needed to sit down with Eduardo to compare notes. Being late summer, and given his almost continuous absence since before Christmas, he had persuaded Elena to suggest a family *asado* on that weekend. Eduardo rapidly got the message and had rung his godfather to suggest a barbecue to be organised by Florencia at her parents' weekend *quinta* about fifty kilometres southeast of Buenos Aires.

That Sunday therefore, Leandro took advantage of the fine weather to take the Alfa Giulia out of its lock-up garage and head off for the *asado*. Traffic was light and the car, well on the way to its fiftieth birthday, performed the way a well-treated Alfa Romeo of that vintage should. The gearbox smooth, the clutch heavy, the roar from the exhaust the way God had intended. In his mind's eye, he was chasing Vittorio Gassman along the twisting roads north of Rome. Argentine males, like their Italian counterparts, appreciated *la bella mecanica* and waved as he thundered past. Sam had enjoyed the only time he had taken her out in the Alfa. Would there be another occasion? Italian cars needed pretty girls to come into their own. And not only Italian cars....

He parked the Alfa in the stand of willows near the house and, collecting the box of red wine from the boot, made his way towards the *quincho*. It was the usual thatched roof structure typical of such weekend properties, equipped with the all-important barbecue installation, large enough to grill half a cow. A simple piece of engineering developed in Argentina to handle the massive quantities of meat and every other part of the bovine anatomy which made up a minimal Argentine *asado*. He found Eduardo, sweating, stripped to the waist, already hard at work, having probably set up the fire more than two hours earlier. A good *asador* needed the essential mass of glowing wood and embers to generate a constant stream of freshly grilled sausages, steak, kidneys, sweetbreads, offal, virtually every part of the animal other than the liver, the order of the cuts a time-honoured ritual. The expectant family and friends, glass of red wine in hand, would deliver an equally steady stream of advice and criticism in return. Tradition however ensured that the *asador* usually got the best cuts and was never allowed to go short of the rough red wine which fuelled his efforts.

Two of the family dogs hovered in close proximity, the scent of grilling meat irresistible. Florencia was laying a couple of tables under the trees nearby. On spotting Leandro, she ran over and greeted him warmly.

"Uncle Leandro, nice to see you're back. How was Switzerland? Did you get any skiing?"

He kissed her.

"Only saw the mountains from the plane! You're looking well, Flor. You went to Pinamar? Not too many people, I hope. I see Eduardo's been at it for a couple of hours. Looks good. Where do you want me to put the wine?"

She pointed towards a side table near the barbecue. A pile of plates and cutlery were already in position. At least a couple of dozen wine glasses as well.

"Why don't you leave the box over there and we can open the bottles as we work our way through them."

Over the next half hour, Florencia's parents arrived, as well as Elena and Alejandra. Leandro was delighted to see his daughter again and she greeted him as warmly as he could ever remember.

"Papa, I heard you were back. And you didn't ring me!" Her tone reproachful. "Not even a postcard."

Leandro felt bad, but the warmth of her embrace instantly dispelled any fears that she had meant it seriously. For reasons he couldn't exactly explain, somewhere inside him was a feeling that his affair with Sam had somehow altered his relationship with his own daughter. Was it a question of generation? Did having a girlfriend like Sam mean that he could understand his daughter's psychology better? Probably. A warm glow inside him as he held Alejandra in his arms, seeking her forgiveness, was tangible. Somehow, she also seemed to sense it.

Two hours or so later, Eduardo's skills as an *asador* had been loudly applauded, toasts had been drunk to reward his efforts, a recognition of the *asador's* skills being traditionally honoured in this manner at every barbecue. Florencia's parents had drifted away towards some deckchairs under the shade of the trees. Alejandra had found a Paraguayan hammock strung up between two posts near the swimming pool and Elena was asleep in a deckchair nearby. Florencia had dutifully retired to the kitchen to do the washing up. Even the dogs had finally collapsed under the weight of scraps and bones tossed in their direction throughout the meal.

Leandro and Eduardo were sitting with their backs to the wall of the *quincho*, out of the merciless sun of the hot late summer's day. They were finishing off a coffee, fighting off the desire to lie in the shade and sleep.

"I was expecting you to look a bit better, after your time in Europe," Eduardo began.

Leandro waved his hand as if to clear the air.

"Well, it was a bit complicated, more than I expected."

Eduardo looked at him, quizzically.

"The Señorita? Not quite what you expected? Of course, uncle, it's none of my business...."

"A part of it, you're right, is not your business. However, quite a lot of it is. So let's just talk about that."

"As you wish."

Eduardo shrugged his shoulders. Leandro suspected that he was in fact quite interested in his relationship with Sam.

"What news on your front?"

"Well, not a lot to report after what I told you over Skype the other day. I've rechecked the film. As I said, it's virtually impossible that Carla murdered Williams. We have to assume that it's Dávila. So that slightly takes the heat off Sam. Now, as to Dávila, that's a very interesting story."

"I was wondering how long it would take us to find out who he is."

"Very complicated. I had to be very careful of course, but one way or another, just by using information publicly available, I was able to pin down our friend. He allowed his name to get into some report about the inner workings of this government, you know, people surrounding the President and others going back to the left-wing movements of the 1970s, the Montos and others. Alberto Dávila turns out to be sitting somewhere inside SIDE. Do I need to say more?"

"No, not much. Not very reassuring."

Leandro was perfectly aware of the darker side of the Argentine government machine. SIDE, or Servicio de Inteligencia del Estado, was Argentina's equivalent of a mix between the CIA and the FBI. Not above conducting operations outside Argentina, but mainly a machine used by incumbent governments to protect their interests, watch their enemies, and generally do things which they would prefer not to see splashed across the headlines of La Nación or Clarín. It occupied offices opposite the Casa Rosada, on 25 de Mayo, its staff tending to change in the upper echelons in line with the change of President. It had been one of the arms used extensively by the military dictatorship during the 'dirty war', but had also been involved in such things as attempting – in vain as it transpired - to get hold of Exocet missiles during the Malvinas campaign. He knew that they had people posted in embassies around the world, though it was far from clear why that should be the case. In general, the unsavoury side of Argentine politics. But then perhaps SIDE was not so different from sister organisations in so many countries around the world. No-one was in any position to occupy the moral high ground when it came to intelligence gathering. And now it turned out that Dávila belonged to that world! Certainly not good news, since it clearly explained much of what had been happening, the initial attack on Eduardo in his flat, the ability to mount surveillance around Carla, and probably many things of which he, Sam and Eduardo were not even aware.

One thing however appeared out of place. The blackmail operation. Could that be official? Or was Dávila running it on the side? If so, it was a potential weak spot. Perhaps it was a bit of both, with Dávila concealing the financial side, but using his power over well-placed individuals to foster the business of government.

"So that explains where those guys came from who beat you up in your flat?"

"Presumably. Perhaps a few things more. It also suggests that we have seriously underestimated who we're dealing with." There was a note of bitterness in Eduardo's voice.

"At the very least, it suggests that, whether she knows it or not, Carla - and by extension, Sam - are operating on the margins of the Argentine intelligence community. The fact that you were attacked almost certainly confirms that. Since that time, we've tried to be more careful, but, given the fact that Dávila's men actually sit in Carla's house, we might be naive to think that they haven't reached certain conclusions as to your role, my role and, God forbid, Sam's."

"Do you think they are able to deduce anything as regards you and me?" Eduardo's tone conveyed that he was worried.

"Possibly. Perhaps we should assume that they can - and have. Have you been looking out for surveillance?"

"Yes, perhaps not rigorously, not every day."

"And?"

"Can't say I've seen anything, but obviously we must be more careful."

"As regards Dávila. Have you tried to cross check with Sarmiento? After all, if he's the one blackmailing him, I suppose it's not impossible that he may have actually come across Dávila somewhere."

"That's a good idea. But I suspect I can't make it too direct."

"No. But you might put it differently, perhaps asking him if he had come across an Argentine in any of the banks with which he had had dealings in Switzerland. Let's see what he says. When is your next contact with him?"

"I can get in touch with him pretty much when I want. I'll try that. It's a good idea."

"So what we have is that Carla appears to be off the hook for the actual murder, and that her partner and sponsor, Dávila, is the likely killer. And given the advantages he enjoys in terms of surveillance, eavesdropping, telephone tapping, in other words, all the usual spying techniques, that means that he's in a strong position not only to identify us, but - more worryingly - take action against us."

Eduardo nodded.

Leandro continued.

"The question is, are we in any position to make use of what we know and, through that, solve the murder, get Dávila arrested and find a way to get back to our normal lives?"

He looked at Eduardo.

"To be frank," Eduardo replied, "I don't think so. We have information given to us by Sarmiento, hardly likely to stand up in court. That includes the vital video recording which seems to indicate that it's a man who actually murders Williams. How do we pin that on Dávila? Given the state of our knowledge today, I don't think we can. It's a load of circumstantial evidence, partly provided by Sam, partly by simple deduction on our part. None of it would stand up in a court of law. Which, unfortunately, leads me to the conclusion that we either back out - which might be the wisest, although very frustrating - or try and get Dávila to show his hand. Quite what that means, I don't know."

Leandro looked enquiringly at his godson.

"Show his hand? How do we do that? In what way? It's only of any interest if whatever he does can be used against him. My guess is, he's unlikely to do that. And I can't think of any trap which we could set him. He's probably much too smart for that. I don't know what you think?"

"Sadly, I think you're right. It's more likely to be a case of us allowing the whole thing to drop and disappear, than finding a solution which would lead to Dávila's arrest. Do you think that there's anything that Sam could contribute?"

"We'd have to talk to her. Which, at this particular moment, is not that easy."

"Well, uncle, you'll have to be the best judge of that."

"Not very helpful, all this. Do you want another coffee?"

"No, I need to help Florencia. She'll have done it all, she usually does, but I feel bad about it. Not that she reproaches me anything."

He got up and placed a friendly hand on his godfather's shoulder.

"Maybe we'll be lucky."

Next morning, Leandro was having a breakfast coffee at London City. He needed to catch up with the papers after his time away. He turned the pages of La Nación. Little had changed. Cristina Fernandez's government was still treating the uncritical Argentine public to a stream of fabrications, half-truths, as part of a well-orchestrated strategy of disinformation. And non-one seemed ready to challenge them. It made him feel impatient, frustrated.

Half an hour later, he emerged from the cafe onto the pavement and stopped to buy a magazine at the corner kiosk. As he looked up, his eye was caught by the way in which a man in a leather jacket, standing some twenty metres away, jerked sideways, as if to look into a shop window – except that there was no shop window.

"Ah, *muchacho*, let's see what you're about."

Leandro joined a line waiting for the *colectivo*, which would take him in the direction of a large bookshop which he often frequented in Barrio Norte. The man in the leather jacket showed no interest, but, as soon as he saw Leandro about to board the bus as it drew up opposite the stop, he swiftly joined the end of the queue, boarding last.

Standing halfway down the bus, Leandro paid no attention to the man, who steadfastly looked ahead through the windscreen. Leandro noted that he appeared to have at least one earpiece, as if listening to some form of MP3. As they approached Las Heras and Callao, Leandro pushed his way through to the exit door and stepped off onto the pavement at the first stop. Slightly to his surprise, the man in the leather jacket made no attempt to get off. The bus moved off. Out of the corner of his eye, Leandro checked to see whether there might be some last-minute exit, particularly since the bus was now held up at the traffic lights. Getting off at points other than official stops was the norm anyway. Still the man did not appear.

Perhaps he had been mistaken. Another explanation was that the man was not alone and that he was part of a team which included colleagues in a car. As discreetly as possible, he looked around at the traffic on Las Heras, but spotted no obvious candidates.

He walked up Calle Junin in the direction of the Recoleta cemetery, going against the traffic. That would probably cause any following car some difficulty, given the city's system of alternating one-way streets. They would have to drive on to the next street, Urriburu, to catch up with him. He walked faster up to the first corner with Vicente Lopez, then turned left heading in the direction of the Village cinema complex. As he rounded the corner, he caught sight of a man of similar build and appearance running rapidly round the far corner of Urriburu in his direction. As soon as the man caught sight of Leandro, he broke his stride, apparently hesitating between immediately slowing to a walk, or continuing to run, even if it meant coming closer. As he did so, Leandro looked to his left as if studying the menu on the corner cafe. The other man also stopped, looking into the windows of the shops at the far end of the block. Leandro was now in no doubt that he was being followed. The question was, did they have enough people to replace both the one in the bus and the one who had now so unprofessionally given himself away? He rather doubted it, all the more since somebody would have to be driving the car.

He walked on towards the entrance to the cinema complex, which housed the bookshop, Cuspide, he wanted to visit. He passed the cash desk and moved into the back of the large hall, with its ranks of bookcases and display cabinets, positioning himself in such a way as to be able to look back in the direction from which he had come. For approximately five minutes, nothing happened. Then, to his surprise, the man on the bus appeared, this time with his leather jacket slung over his shoulder. There was no doubt. It was the same man. They were clearly limited for manpower and yet prepared to be recognized. So invisibility might not be their main objective.

Leandro decided to spin it out to see what happened. He selected a couple of books and then settled himself at one of the small tables which the bookshop provided to its clients. He ordered a coffee and began to read. His follower had little choice but to dawdle, seemingly uncertain what to buy, but equally reluctant to get too close to Leandro by joining him in the cafe.

The other man had no doubt been posted outside, or might even have been swapped over with the driver of the car.

As he sat there, Leandro tried to analyse what was going on. He was pretty sure that between September and now, he had not been followed on a regular basis. If that was the case - and of course he could not be certain of it - why the sudden interest? What had changed? It might not be too difficult to explain. He and Sam had got alongside Carla in Punta del Este, Sam had followed Carla to Zürich and then he had followed Sam there as well. That someone was interested in his relationship with Sam was obvious from the microphone with which Sam had been equipped for their meeting in Zürich. Perhaps he shouldn't be surprised that the interest in him had now shifted back to Buenos Aires, a setting in which Dávila could mobilise far more resources than in Zürich. Would it go any farther than that? It probably depended upon what he did, where he went, whom he saw and the interpretation that would be placed on all of these. That he might now have been seen with Eduardo wouldn't help his case, given Eduardo's involvement in the early days of the investigation into the Williams' murder. His only plausible line of defence was their relationship, but, with hindsight, that might begin to wear rather thin, if viewed from Dávila's end of the telescope. What interpretation might Dávila arrive at? From an initial concern to stop Eduardo pursuing his investigation, which might have had the desired effect once the thugs had beaten Eduardo up in his flat, there would probably have been a period in which Dávila might have gained the impression that he was safe. Then, towards the end of November, Carla had picked up Sam. That in itself might not set any alarm bells ringing and Dávila might well have been content to let their relationship flourish. But behind Sam stood Leandro, who had then gone to the lengths of pursuing her to Zürich. Might some intelligent research by an assistant throw up the fact that there was a link between Leandro and the detective originally investigating the murder? It was possible, especially for someone as paranoid as Dávila.

This line of thinking was not particularly reassuring. Whether it was on target, Leandro would only be able to tell if Dávila's interest became more aggressive. From what Leandro knew about the methods to which Dávila might resort, an unattractive prospect.

The situation seemed to reinforce the argument which Eduardo had been putting forward, namely that there was very little that he or Leandro could do to incriminate Dávila. So why go on?

He didn't have the answer to that question today. Was Eduardo also being followed? He'd have to find a way to check with his godson. If they did nothing, how long might they expect the surveillance to continue? Who could tell?

He felt powerless, not a feeling he enjoyed. There was, however, one conclusion he could draw. The more Dávila suspected him, the more Dávila would also suspect Sam, now sharing a house with Dávila's bodyguards. He consoled himself with the thought that his thugs probably needed to be more law-abiding in Switzerland than on their home territory in Argentina. Switzerland was not the place for simple assassination. Not like Buenos Aires!

Having paid for his coffee, he made his way to the till to pay for his book, watching the other man lining himself up to follow. As Leandro emerged back onto the esplanade in front of the cinema complex, he detected the second man getting up from one of the cafes farther down the pavement. With taxis usually patrolling the cinema entrance, he quickly found one and climbed in. Out of the corner of his eye, he watched his two followers walk rapidly back towards Urriburu, where they had no doubt parked their car. As his taxi followed the perimeter wall of the cemetery, he saw a black Renault pull out and the two men climb in. They were hardly being very discreet. In fact, he wondered again whether they might not actually be under instructions to make themselves visible, as opposed to the reverse. Perhaps Dávila was trying to send him a signal. Given the ease with which Dávila had disposed of other unwelcome actors, he wondered whether Dávila would actually bother with anything so subtle as a mere signal?

Back at his flat, he flicked up his emails. There was one from Charles Colson's pseudonym.

Leandro and Frobisher having agreed that a more discreet form of communication should be used, the email announced that Charles would be arriving on 13 February. A subsequent exchange of mails, which Leandro sent from a *locutorio*, established though a simple code that Charles would be staying at the Sheraton near Retiro main railway station, opposite Plaza San Martin. Also opposite the Malvinas War Memorial. Leandro suspected that Charles would find time to go and pay his respects. Rather than drawing attention to Leandro by going to his apartment, Charles suggested that Leandro come to him. They agreed to meet after breakfast, on the day following Charles' arrival.

Leandro had spent at least an hour checking for surveillance, but by dint of using the rear exit to one of his usual cafes, he reckoned that he had probably lost anyone who might be following him. They might not appreciate the fact that he had slipped away, but at least they wouldn't know where he had gone and whom he had met.

From the downstairs courtesy phone, Leandro rang the room. Charles told him to come up straight away. He found Charles, in typically British fashion, wearing an elegant paisley dressing gown and barefoot. From the first year he had spent in London whilst waiting for Elena, briefly sharing a flat with a colleague from Citibank, Leandro had got used to the fact that so many Englishmen seemed to prefer, on getting home, to take off their shoes and wander around in socks or even bare feet. The Argentine male would rather be seen dead!

Charles greeted him warmly.

"So, was Zürich a success? Did our man get what you needed?"

"He did a fantastic job and gave me exactly what I needed. If you're in touch with him, please send him my best regards - or at least, those of Señor Perez," remembering the pseudonym he had used.

"Of course. Anyway, Buenos Aires looks and feels much the same as usual," Charles continued, gesturing in the direction of the window to the traffic piling up around Retiro. "This may not be the greatest hotel in town, but it's fairly anonymous."

He waved Leandro over to a table near the window.

"Coffee?"

"No thanks, had some an hour ago."

Charles got up and pulled a notebook out of the briefcase lying on a side table.

"First of all, thank you for your last economic report."

Leandro interrupted.

"It was largely produced by my partner, given that I was away."

"No matter, our client appreciates a more objective view, given his significant investments in the region. However, it's not the same client I want to talk to you about. Or rather, not about the client, but about what he's interested in. You remember our conversation in London?"

"Yes, of course."

"I told you then that things might start to move round about now. They have. I suggest you don't take notes, if you can avoid it."

"No problem."

"The topic being extremely delicate, we have to take every precaution in our communications. I detect that, for whatever reason, you suspect the possibility that someone is tapping your phone calls or your mails? Am I right?"

"I've no definite proof, but the business I've been working on over the last few months has involved someone high up in SIDE. I'm not sure how much they may have identified me, but obviously it would be wiser to assume the worst."

"That's obviously the only option. SIDE is not a nice organisation, as I recall. You have the impression that they are actually taking a close interest in you, do you?"

"At the moment, the most I seem to be getting is some surveillance. As far as I can tell. As you know, espionage has not been my *metier* up until now."

Leandro laughed nervously.

"Don't worry, we can try and compensate for that. I have some ideas on that front. What are you doing about communications? Telephone tapping? That kind of thing."

"At the moment, there's only really one or two people with whom I have to communicate and we do that with cheap, pay-as-you-go cell phones, which we throw away after a certain amount of time."

"Probably good enough for the time being. What about where you live? Or your offices? Do you think your phones are tapped? Or maybe some kind of listening device?"

"As far as the phone is concerned, as I said, anything sensitive tends to go over cell phones. As to a microphone in my flat, well... I don't know. I haven't yet detected any sign of someone having been there, but they may just be good at their job."

Charles got up and walked over to his briefcase, from which he extracted something looking rather like a mobile phone.

"Before I go, I'll leave this in your name at the reception. I'll pack it up of course. You can use it to sweep your flat, it's pretty sensitive and should pick up anything transmitting. Take it as a token of our esteem." Charles smiled.

"Much appreciated, Charles. Many thanks."

"If there is any sign that the situation is becoming more complicated for you personally, we would need to see how far we go from here as regards the assignment."

"I understand. For the time being, there's actually nothing specific that I've done which could lead to consequences. Or at least that's the way I see it. Someone else might see it differently."

"That's reassuring, but obviously we must keep a close watch on it. At this stage, my instinct is to give you a broad picture, not very different from what I told you in London. Then I suggest that you concentrate on seeing what kind of access you may have – or can generate - to answer specific questions. Once we have a clearer picture of your capability, then we would move to specifics. What do you think?"

Leandro nodded.

"The interest of our client relates to the Argentine nuclear industry. As you know, Argentina has a nuclear power generation capacity, centred on two power stations already running, Atucha I and Embalse, with

404

Atucha II expected to be revived soon. You've had nuclear power since the mid-1970s, apparently always for peaceful purposes. On the first reactor, Atucha I, the supplier of the pressurised heavy water reactor was Siemens, and on Embalse, a CANDU reactor was installed. Discussions have been going on with Siemens to push forward with the commissioning of Atucha II and I believe a target has been set for about 2013. There's also talk of Russian interest. The Embalse nuclear power plant also produces the cobalt-60 isotope, which has medical and industrial uses. Most of the technical work and research is handled by an entity called INVAP – I think it stands for Investigación Aplicada - formed in 1976. Stop me if all this is familiar territory to you."

"Some of it is, but carry on, please."

"Perhaps some indication of the position of Argentina on the subject can be deduced from the fact that, along with Cuba, your country didn't at the time sign the 1967 Treaty for the Prohibition of Nuclear Weapons in Latin America and the Caribbean, the Treaty of Tlatelolco. However, you did ratify it some twenty-five years later, soon followed by Cuba. It's possible that this was nothing more than administrative or political inefficiency. And one can imagine why, during the time of the military, they might not have been so keen to join up. Indeed, they resisted pressure from Washington to do so. However, when the military were kicked out in 1983, the new president, Alfonsin, started to move the industry out of the control of the military. As I recall, the Comision Naciónal de Energia Atomica – CNEA - had actually been run by the Navy. Alfonsin also initiated some form of technical cooperation with Brazil."

Leandro had been taking a look at the question since returning to Buenos Aires and took the opportunity to show that he had done some of his homework. He picked up the story.

"As far as I can tell, the operation of our nuclear plants is run by a company called Nucleoelectrica Argentina, which is state-owned. Since the year before last, this government has announced that it's going to pursue nuclear energy as part of its overall energy strategy. By the way, not a bad thing, considering the fact that so little is being invested in power generation at the moment. The previous president, Kirchner, announced that the third reactor, Atucha II, would be commissioned and there are plans for a fourth. Alongside that, they were going to increase the production of heavy water at the Arroyito plant and revive uranium enrichment at Pilcaniyeu."

"Which is what interests us as well," Charles interrupted. "In fact, all this new activity not only means that you're going to be upgrading and strengthening the country's nuclear capability, but it is also generating a lot of contacts internationally, some of them no doubt perfectly legitimate in terms of looking around for new technology. Some of them, perhaps less so."

Leandro noted the pause.

"Brazil? Venezuela?"

"And possibly, through Venezuela, Iran," Charles added quietly.

Leandro let out a low whistle.

"President Kirchner's great buddy, Mr Chavez, is close to them, as we know."

"Exactly. There's no hard evidence, but a certain number of circumstantial indications that there may be something to that possibility. You've no doubt been following the saga of Iran's nuclear ambitions. So you'll know that the Iranian president, Mahmud Ahmadinejad, has been seriously courted by Chavez. And even the Brazilians, normally a bit more sensitive to the opinions of Washington, have not been above sending out feelers."

"So, if I understand it, what you'd like to know is whether there's any truth behind the suspicions. Is that it?"

Charles nodded.

"It's not going to be easy. Obviously, there are safer assignments. But, as I was listening to you in London, correct me if I'm wrong, but I got the impression that this would not fall outside the scope of our collaboration."

Leandro said nothing for a moment.

"I've had some time to think about it since we met. I still believe that this is an area in which I could help, at least in principle. To be frank, I don't believe that it's in the interests of our country to get into bed with the likes of Chavez or Ahmadinejad. They're both what the Americans would call 'rogue states' in varying degrees and, whilst I don't believe that Chavez could do very much more than cosy up to the Cubans and generally embarrass the Americans around Latin America, the Iranians are a different story. Ahmadinejad's denial of the Holocaust, which to be frank he must be too intelligent to believe himself, is nevertheless symptomatic of someone determined to push Israel to the brink. Perhaps even over the edge. The amazing thing is that, I'm not sure how much you're aware of it, Argentina has about the third largest Jewish community in the world after the US and Israel itself. We've already got ourselves swept up in the Arab-Israel confrontation, with those two terrorist attacks about fifteen years ago at the time of Menem."

"Yes, they blew up the Israeli embassy and some kind of Argentine-Israeli Institute, as I recall."

"Yes, the AMIA as it's known. Nearly a hundred people died one way and another. There were all kinds of nasty rumours going round about whether Menem himself might not have soft-pedalled the investigation, with stories of him being paid large sums of money to stop the investigation getting anywhere. After about ten years of the investigation deliberately getting nowhere, since 2004 it's started moving ahead slowly, in the right direction this time, and the results indicate that Hezbollah planted the bomb. In fact both bombs. Everyone knows that they are funded by Iran. So, for the present government to be getting closer to Teheran seems pretty strange, given the fact that they've made a point of saying that they will try and solve the crimes."

"I suppose if you were very Machiavellian, you might see some connection. Nuclear technology against a conviction. Iran is desperate to build up its nuclear capability, in spite of the fact that they are working with the Russians on a nuclear power plant. Give us a hand on the nuclear front, and we'll help you to solve the bombings."

"Yes, that or any number of other variations, being Argentina. There are signs that our close relations with Venezuela may be a bit more elaborate than just receiving suitcases full of money to support the presidential campaign or inviting them to collaborate in the oil industry. The Venezuelan oil company, Pedevesa. even owns a couple of petrol stations in Buenos Aires as a visible sign of this collaboration. And we have a number of parallel official lines feeding into Caracas, not just our Embassy."

"Anyway, Leandro, what do you think? Is this something you might be able to do some work on? Obviously, we'll be pursuing it on behalf of our client through every channel we have, he's going to pay us very well. And if for any reason you decided to turn it down, there would be no hard feelings. Do you want more time to think about it?"

Leandro had been expecting this question.

"No, if I can help you, I'm prepared to do so. But I only got back a few days ago and what I think I should do is first of all come up with an honest assessment of whether or not I actually can do something worthwhile. That means doing some research, seeing who I know or can get to know, that kind of thing. Can you give me a couple of weeks?"

"Certainly, but, to be totally frank, not a lot more. I want to be able to tell my client how we propose to deal with the assignment in about three weeks' time."

"Okay, that's clear. Do we communicate as usual?"

"Here's a little list of suggested pseudonyms for some of the main institutions and topics. If read, it would look pretty innocent but at least coherent. It's primitive, but probably effective enough at this stage. Obviously, if we get into real detail, we'll supply you with a high level encryption system, but I don't think we need it at this stage."

Leandro wondered what he was getting himself into. The feeling that his life was changing, moving in directions which showed every sign of being more stimulating, although also more dangerous, was growing inside him. For the last six months or so, he had been edging steadily towards the more turbulent waters of the government's undercover operations. Up to now, in the context of murder and blackmail, of themselves already sufficiently unattractive. Now it was moving into the zone of espionage. Not something that he had prepared himself for. However, you only live once. And somewhere, tucked away at the back of his mind, was the irrational idea that he and Sam might even pursue the assignment together.

"That's fine, Charles. I'll leave you now. If you want to see me before you leave, send me the usual mail. Is there anything I can do for you while you're here?"

"No, thanks, Leandro. I've got a few errands to run and I'll probably wander across and look at the Memorial. About time I did that. Take care. We'll be in touch."

Charles accompanied Leandro to the door and placed a friendly arm on his shoulder.

"Good to see you. As I said, take care."

"You too."

Frau Peitsche, her trademark whip in hand, accompanied her client to the door of her dungeon. For the last two hours, at his request and in exchange for a significant sum of his money, she had been using him as her ashtray, her floor mat, the polisher of her elegant boots, whatever came into her mind. In a word, her slave, on all fours on the carpet at her feet, naked except for a facemask and the collar and chain with which she controlled his every movement. The look of serenity on his face showed that it had been a good session. Now showered and back in his habitual dark grey suit, white shirt and dark blue tie, he would return to the bosom of his family and tell his wife, as she prepared the *spaetzli* and *bratwurst*, that he had had a good session in the public baths. It had been a hard day at the office, all this cantonal bureaucracy.

This Friday evening ritual went back a number of years, ever since her colleague Carla Bodmer had sent the gentleman to her, knowing that she would provide this high level official from the Zürich public administration with the kind of humiliation which he so badly, so secretly desired. Bodmer had sensed, from her first meeting with him, that he was not really her type of client, if nothing else given his more modest financial situation. But Frau Peitsche was less demanding. Her client list was long and varied, and she had more than enough work. But one never knew when a man in his position might not prove very useful.

"So, Herr Schmidt, I wish you a good weekend. And see you next Friday." Schmidt was not his real name, she knew perfectly well who he was, but convention forbad such transparency.

"*Herrlich*, Frau Peitsche, a wonderful evening. Your devoted slave thanks you from the bottom of his heart."

He lent forward and kissed her hand. *Kuessdiehand!* The old style. The new generation of her clients seemed to have lost these charming old habits. The world was moving on. Better enjoy the last vestiges of the old wherever possible.

He turned to open the front door of her studio.

"Oh, Herr Schmidt, just a minute. I have something for you. A service you can perhaps render."

He acknowledged her request with a polite bow.

"Always at your service, Madame. It would be an honour."

She handed him an envelope.

"It's from Frau Bodmer."

"A wonderful lady. I will be eternally grateful to her for introducing me to you. May I look at it?"

"Of course. I believe it is a very simple request."

He opened the envelope and studied the contents of the single sheet of paper. As a senior official of the Migrationsamt, the Cantonal department which controlled residence and work permits in the Canton of Zürich, she was asking him to investigate the possible illegal employment of two gentlemen at a private house in the upmarket part of the city. He raised an eyebrow on noticing that the address seemed familiar. Anonymous - and not so anonymous – tale-telling was an old Swiss sport, almost as popular as football. His office relied heavily on the Swiss habit of spying on your neighbours and reporting their behaviour, if considered inappropriate, to the authorities. More than half the illegals sent home could trace their fate back to this national trait. Why Carla Bodmer should be playing the game was beyond him. But a favour deserved another in return.

"I will see that her request is answered positively."

He bowed again to his mistress and left.

On the following Monday afternoon, two officials from the Migrationsamt parked their car near the corner of Richard-Wagner-Strasse and Conrad-Ferdinand-Meyer-Strasse. Somewhat to their surprise, they realised that the residence to which they had come was one and the same as that of the person who had sent the original letter. Being a corner house, it bore one number on one street and another round the corner, having an entrance on both.

They rang the bell. The door was opened by an exotic, dark skinned maid, somewhat underdressed to their taste.

"Could we please speak to the owner?" the lady official asked, courteously.

The maid showed them into an elegant drawing room.

"Just a minute, please wait here. I will call Madame Bodmer."

The two officials glanced at each other in ill-concealed amazement. Had she really denounced herself?

After a couple of minutes, a strikingly good-looking woman, elegantly dressed in a close fitting woollen suit, silk blouse and perilously high heeled pumps joined them.

"I am Frau Bodmer. What can I do for you?"

The woman official, uncertain how to proceed, decided to play it safe. She introduced herself and her companion, handing Carla a card showing that they were from the Migrationsamt.

"We have been informed by someone living on this street that there may be two men working illegally in this house. Could you please tell us if that is the case?"

Carla feigned shock.

"I don't know what to say. I have two houseguests, from Argentina."

"We were informed that the two men in question have been coming and going over a period of eighteen months or even more, that they have been seen driving cars from this property, working in the garden and apparently acting as some kind of protection."

Carla's face fell.

"This is most serious."

"You are right, Frau Bodmer. Are either of these persons present at this time?"

"They both are. Shall I call them?"

"Please do. And please ask them to bring their passports."

Carla pressed a buzzer and Naya reappeared silently.

"Please ask the two Señores to come down."

Naya turned.

"Oh, and tell them to bring their passports."

While they waited, the woman official turned to Carla.

"And this … other person?" nodding her head in the direction of the door through which Naya had just left.

"Oh, she has a residence permit and a work permit."

Carla walked across to an elegant ormolu desk and, opening one of the lower drawers, produced a file, which she brought back.

"Here, this is the correspondence with your office and here is her *carte de séjour*."

The woman official glanced at it quickly.

"That is all perfectly in order, Frau Bodmer. Thank you."

They waited a few more minutes in silence.

The door opened and Carlos and Manuel walked in, casually dressed. Their surprise was ill-concealed. They looked at Carla for a steer.

"Carlos, Manuel, please show your passports to this lady," she said in Spanish.

Bewildered, the two passed over their dark blue and gold Argentine travel documents.

The woman official, with her companion looking over her shoulder, studied each document carefully.

After a few minutes silence, she looked up and addressed herself to Carla.

"Both of them have clearly been coming and going very frequently over the last eighteen months. At a quick guess, without actually calculating the dates, it would appear that, perhaps apart from a month around Christmas and January, they have been here most of the time over that period. It is possible that with their entries and exits they have technically complied with the maximum ninety days given to them on each entry. However, the pattern is much more in line with someone working here. Unless of course, you can demonstrate to us that they are truly houseguests?"

Carla's response was a mixture of confusion and embarrassment. She stuttered.

"Well... I don't know ... You see... I'm sure there is an explanation."

"Frau Bodmer, you are a Swiss citizen, you know that this is a serious accusation, not one that we can take lightly, let alone ignore."

Carlos and Manuel were watching, their nervousness growing by the minute.

"What's all this about?" Carlos asked Carla in Spanish.

"Someone, apparently a neighbour, has denounced you as possibly working illegally here, without a work permit. In this country, that is extremely serious. At the very least, I will have to pay a fine."

Carlos and Manuel glanced at each other. Then Carlos replied laughing.

"Come on, Carla, all you do is go around and see this lady's boss and slip an envelope across the table. It's so easy. Relax."

At that point, the woman official's companion spoke for the first time. In perfect Castilian Spanish, he addressed Carlos.

"Señor, that is a most improper suggestion. Suborning a public official in Switzerland can carry a prison sentence. Such a remark will certainly not help your case. I suggest you keep quiet." He murmured something to the woman official, presumably explaining what had just been said.

Carlos looked as if he was about to hit the man, but then thought better of it. His reaction, however, was not lost on either of the officials.

"Frau Bodmer, this is most improper. Obviously, you cannot be responsible for the remarks just made by this gentleman. However, the matter cannot rest here. You will receive a letter tomorrow informing you that both these gentlemen must leave Switzerland by the end of this week, that is to say in five days' time. Until the matter is cleared up, they will not be allowed entry back into Switzerland. As it is obvious that you have allowed this situation to continue, you will be called to a meeting at our offices, at which we will determine the fine that you should pay. As a Swiss citizen, it is your duty to ensure that our laws are observed. In every other respect, we know that your situation is perfectly in order. I will take these two passports now and they will be returned in time for the departure of these two gentlemen."

She turned to her colleague and nodded her head in the direction of the door.

"We thank you for receiving us. This is very embarrassing, but, as long as the two Señores leave as agreed, the consequences should be limited. We bid you good day, Frau Bodmer."

Carla shook their hands and then pressed the buzzer once more. Naya accompanied the two officials to the door.

It had hardly closed, before Carlos and Manuel exploded with fury. Carla raised her hand to silence them and, turning on her heel, walked to the door.

"This is Switzerland. It's not Argentina. Your remark, Carlos, certainly sank you. In my business, I can't afford to have the cantonal authorities on my back. You'll have to leave by the weekend. I'll see what I can do to sort it out. With a bit of luck, you can be back in a month or two."

Carlos continued to protest, but Carla had left the room.

Dávila checked his Blackberry. There was a mail from Carlos in Zürich announcing that he and Manuel were returning to Buenos Aires in a couple of days, having been expelled by the Cantonal authorities.

What the hell was Carla up to, allowing this to happen? It was too late to ring her now. First thing tomorrow morning.

Was this part of some new game she seemed to be playing? According to Carlos, she had disappeared for a couple of days the previous week. It might have been a client, but for reasons Carlos could not quite pin down, there seemed to be more to it. Was Carla trying to slip from his grasp? She knew too much, far too much. Pressure would have to be brought to bear, a very clear message to remind her of where her loyalties lay. He leaned back in his chair. This was the kind of scenario game he enjoyed playing. Especially with Carla. Though perhaps this time the outcome might have to be different.

It was the last week of February when Sam finally returned to Buenos Aires. Still unsure how to interpret her parting remark at the hotel, Leandro had decided to wait for her to take the initiative. To his immense relief, a brief text message had come a week after his return hoping that he had arrived safely and saying that she was okay. Suspecting that she wanted communications to be kept to a minimum, he saw no alternative but to restrain his desire to open up the lines more fully. Around the second week of February, the lines went completely dead. Although he had the telephone number of Carla's house, he resisted calling Zürich.

Then one morning, the doorbell rang and she was standing there, immaculate in a white cotton jogging suit, apparently straight from a session at her gymnasium, judging by the slight dampness he detected as they kissed.

"I flew in yesterday morning. Horrible flight, full of returning *porteños* back from Europe. Luckily I was in Business."

She breezed into the flat and spent a few moments wandering around, turning over the papers on his table, as if checking out if anything had changed. She went into his bedroom and sniffed the air.

"No new perfumes. So you've behaved yourself. Missed me?"

"What the fuck do you think?" he muttered.

Without a word, she went over to his laptop and, with a few deft keystrokes, checked out the recent history of his web surfing.

"Interesting! Glad to see you've visited Lady Blast a few times. Noticed any changes? And a few other specialist sites too? Fetishism. Bondage. You're really changing, Señor Flemming."

Leandro couldn't make up his mind which he wanted to do first. Hit her or fuck her! He decided against both.

"Want some coffee?" he said, deliberately turning away from her.

"Maybe afterwards."

"After what?"

"Don't give me that! And get rid of that stupid look on your face."

She watched him. He seemed more interested in tidying his papers. That Celtic self-control needed disrupting. She turned her back to him and pulled down the lower part of her jogging suit to reveal her perfectly shaped, naked butt. Which, placing one foot on the arm of the sofa, she now extended provocatively in his direction.

Leandro hesitated. In spite of everything he had come to expect from Sam, this was certainly not the way he had imagined their first reunion.

"So? What are you waiting for?"

She looked over her shoulder in his direction.

He did not respond.

Without a word, Sam placed the fingers of one hand in her mouth, liberally covering them with her saliva, before beginning to sweep them between her cunt and her anus.

By sheer willpower, Leandro turned away.

"Why don't you stop that?" he muttered, sitting down at his worktable.

Sam observed him for a moment. Then she stood up straight, pulling her tight jogging suit back over her hips. She sat down on the sofa and watched him. She hated herself for what she had just done. He continued to look at his papers.

"Well done," she finally said.

"What's that supposed to mean?"

"You're the man I thought you were."

"Because I didn't rush over and fuck you?"

419

"Exactly. If you'd only been with me for the sex, that's probably what you'd have done."

"Come on, Sam. I thought you knew me better than that."

"Just checking."

"All I can say is that you've learned some pretty rough tricks since your time with Carla."

"You're right. Forgive me."

Seeing that he had been deeply disturbed by her gesture, she came over to him and gave him what he felt was the most platonic kiss he had ever received from her. From his side, he toned down his usual passion. But what it might have lacked in arousal, it made up for in duration.

"I'll have that coffee now."

As they sat there, with the late summer sun streaming in through the windows, she briefly brought him up-to-date with her movements since their morning in Zürich. He noted that she provided rather little detail other than dates and places. Sam had remained in Zürich until the second week in February, when she had flown to Beirut. There she had spent about a week, before flying back via Zürich to Paris. All in good time, no doubt.

"Spent a wonderful couple of days in one of my favourite cities, doing a spot of shopping. I'll give you a fashion show one evening."

"Don't tell me. Your usual haunts."

She smiled.

"Anyway, I need to get back and have a shower. Then I've got to get my life organized again. Can we have a drink with Eduardo as well, perhaps in a couple of days' time?"

Leandro promised to fix it.

As she left, she held him close, without saying a word. Seeking forgiveness.

The phone rang on Dávila's reproduction Empire writing desk in his flat. It was past seven in the evening. He put down his glass of whiskey. It was Cacho. He didn't usually ring at this time.

Dávila had had a busy day. One of the SIDE directors had called him into his office and sought his views on how they might find a way to put pressure on a leading businessman, who was beginning to step out of line and criticize the Government's economic policies. Dávila was known for his ability to get to people like that. They weren't too interested in the how and why, but if he could deliver results, that was all that counted. After a few hours of research in his own archives, he had been able to suggest a pressure point. The man clearly had a couple of mistresses, one of whom he had installed in a lavish flat in one of the new high-rise blocks in Puerto Madero. It also appeared that he had been able to set up quite significant bank accounts in the Cayman Islands. Perhaps a visit from the AFIP, the revenue service, might serve to bring him back to a less critical position? The director had been delighted and promised to keep him posted. Dávila had faintly regretted not having got round to trying a blackmail on him.

"Good evening, *patron*, very sorry to disturb you, but there's something I think I should mention. They've rung in from the car which is watching Flemming. Apparently the girl Haidar and the policeman Falcioni have turned up at Flemming's flat. I'm only ringing you because you seemed to be interested in Falcioni the other day."

Dávila was silent for a while. How sinister might this be? First, he had to play it down with Cacho.

"Many thanks, Cacho, thanks for calling. Don't worry, bring me a report in the morning. It's Flemming's girlfriend after all. Did you ever find out anything about the policeman's relationship with Flemming?"

"Not a lot, *patron*. Or rather, nothing very interesting. We spoke to the *portero* at the entrance to Flemming's *pasaje*, showing him a photograph of Falcioni, as if we were looking for him. He immediately recognized him, he's a relative of Flemming apparently, been going there for years. But I still thought I should let you know. You looked a bit worried the other day."

Dávila forced a laugh. He hadn't realised that he was quite so transparent. He'd have to be more careful next time. Still, Cacho had been with him for years and, in so many respects, he had no secrets from him. As long as he kept the envelopes with the dollars flowing, he could probably count on his loyalty. At least he hoped so. In fact, he had no choice. Maybe, someday, Cacho might also have to have an accident....

In the meantime, he really needed to work out whether this trio was just a group of friends getting together, or something more sinister. Each of them in one way or another was coming across his sensitive radar screen from a slightly different direction. It might be coincidence, but he could ill afford complacency. Additional resources would need to be mobilized. A closer look at Flemming seemed a good way to go. He also needed to speak to Carla, to see what she had to say about this. Remind her that her neck was also on the line in the Williams case.

"What can I give you to drink?"

Eduardo was sitting at the table, fiddling with his car keys. Sam, in skin-tight jeans and short-sleeved T-shirt, with only a tiny logo to show that it had come from an expensive boutique on the Faubourg St. Honoré, was lying stretched out on his sofa. Leandro detected mild tension in the air.

It was after eight in the evening. If they were going to practice the precautions which he and Eduardo had discussed previously, they should perhaps find somewhere else to talk. Leandro had swept the flat with the device left to him by Charles Colson and had found nothing, but preferred to err on the side of caution. Not to mention the fact that he did not want to get Eduardo asking him where he had laid his hands on such a sophisticated device.

He moved across to the table and, with a felt pen, scribbled on a writing block.

LET'S HAVE A DRINK AND JUST TALK ABOUT OUR HOLIDAYS, AND THEN GO OUT AND FIND SOMEWHERE ELSE TO EAT AND TALK.

He showed it to them and they nodded their agreement.

"So what's it to be?"

"Whiskey for me," Eduardo replied.

"A Campari on the rocks with a slice of lime for me," Sam added.

For about half an hour, as they sipped their drinks, they exchanged innocuous news about how they had spent the last month or so, Punta del Este, Switzerland, and Pinamar, where Eduardo had taken Florencia.

"I'm hungry," Sam announced finally. "I don't suppose you've got anything we can eat here?"

Leandro shook his head.

"That settles it then, let's go!" Sam headed for the front door.

They waved down a passing taxi. Sam produced a small mirror from her tiny handbag and proceeded to examine her eyebrows.

"Blue Renault, just pulled out behind us," she commented in English. She was clearly enjoying this.

They drove across town to the corner of Quintana and Recoleta. Their destination, the Munich restaurant opposite the church. One of Buenos Aires's oldest restaurants, it mainly catered to families and a slightly older generation. Its menu was endless. Usually full in the evenings, it was unlikely that their followers would also get a table. Eduardo noted the blue Renault parking half a block back towards Ayacucho.

The three of them slid onto the benches facing each other in the wooden side cubicles which lined the walls.

In gastronomic terms, the Munich specialised in classic Argentine dishes, steaks, more steaks and such old favourites dishes as *vitel thoné* or *revuelto gramajo*.

"The *revuelto gramajo* here is the best in Buenos Aires. Shall we get a portion for three?" Leandro asked.

"You're right. I love it. All those soft pommes frites, juicy eggs and crisp ham! Go for it!" Sam responded enthusiastically, though having little doubt that her gym would be the ultimate beneficiary.

The cubicles, being relatively narrow, meant that they could lean forward and speak softly, even though the restaurant's overall acoustics were in any event terrible. If any follower had made it inside, even the most sophisticated directional microphone stood little chance of breaking through the din.

Leandro and Eduardo brought Sam up to date with the news of Dávila's profile. Leandro noted that it didn't seem to come as any surprise to her, nor necessarily to get her worried.

424

"Oh well, we'll just have to be more careful," was her only comment.

"Don't be too relaxed, Sam. SIDE's not a nice organisation."

She brushed it aside.

"So you've also decided that Carla didn't commit the murder?" she changed the subject.

"As far as we can tell, that's the case," Eduardo confirmed.

"So what now?" Sam looked from one to the other. "Are we just going to sit here, helplessly, and wait for something to happen?"

"Unless you've got any other ideas?" Leandro rejoined.

"To be frank, not at the moment. But what makes the two of you think there's nothing we can do?"

Leandro took over.

"The problem is, although we may know that Dávila murdered Williams, and almost certainly Sosa and Suarez as well, and that he seems to be running a nasty blackmail operation, none of this would stand up in a court of law. Almost all our information in one way or another derives from an anonymous informer, and the rest, things I found out in Zürich, however genuine, could never be used. So how do we proceed? Frankly, at this point, I don't know. What do you think, Eduardo?"

Eduardo nodded in agreement.

"So, if we can't use the law - which often doesn't work in Argentina anyway - what can we use?" Sam asked bluntly. "It's pretty frustrating to have got this far, and then not to be able to go any farther."

"I know how you feel," Leandro sympathised.

Sam scanned the dining room, her frustration palpable.

"Oh well, let's enjoy the *revuelto* as a first step," Sam said, with a shrug of the shoulders, digging her fork deep into the mountain of *papas fritas*, ham and eggs on her plate. "Typical Argentina! Too often, we're powerless to deal with the big problems and have to seek solace in a plate of food. No wonder we never get anywhere. Just like Italy! Except that we never produced a Michelangelo or a Botticelli."

She paused. Then she smiled.

"But we did produce Maradona! He'll have to do for the time being. Not ideal, but anyway...."

She raised her glass.

"To Diego!"

"To Diego!"

Leandro, detecting that Sam had certainly not said her last word, dreaded to think what she might be plotting. It was unlikely to be simple. Unless of course someone else made the first move. He also sensed that there might be many other things which she had not been prepared to discuss in front of Eduardo. As they left the restaurant, he took her aside.

"Come round to my place tomorrow for dinner. I suspect you've much more up your sleeve than you're prepared to share with Eduardo. Am I right?"

Her eyes flashed.

"How observant of you," she threw at him with a slight tone of irony. "See you tomorrow then. No, actually, not tomorrow, I'm dining with my father. The day after. Okay?"

She set off down Quintana towards Callao, where there would be more taxis. He watched her. Passing one of the city's best ice cream parlours on the next corner, she failed to resist the temptation of a small pot of their darkest chocolate.

Eduardo was still standing on the pavement next to him. Leandro turned towards him.

"She's some girl," Eduardo commented.

Leandro did not feel in the mood to discuss Sam with his godson.

"What news on the Sarmiento front?" he replied.

"I had a brief chat the other day. Obviously, I didn't think it wise to tell him that we had identified Dávila. The last thing we need just now is for one of Dávila's blackmail victims to do something to scare him."

"I suppose you're right. It would be committing suicide. I don't know how, but we have to find a way to put an end to all this. Unless something happens, everything will continue until he loses patience. With Sarmiento, or worse still, with us."

"I know what you mean. Anyway, got to go. Florencia's waiting for me. Good night, uncle."

"Good night, Eduardo. Take care."

March 2008

A plate of simple pasta, with some olive oil, fresh basil from his window box and *reggiano* cheese, Argentina's closest approximation to parmesan, along with a good merlot, would be easier than the effort of going out to find a restaurant. Two days had passed since their meeting with Eduardo at the Munich. Sam was back in Sam's flat.

"Properly *al dente*, the way you like them," Sam announced as she placed the large dishes on the table. Leandro had lit a couple of candles.

"Very *intime!*" she added.

"Well, you need to be relaxed, if you're going to tell me more."

"Might have guessed as much! Okay, let's get it over with! But only when I've finished my pasta, I'm not going to let them get cold just because you're dying to find out more."

For the next quarter of an hour, they concentrated on the pasta in silence.

"As always, one eats too much!" she said, finally pushing her plate to one side. "You can finish what's left in the bowl. My figure can't take any more."

"You might just have to slip into that sexy corset you bought the other day in Paris."

"You'd really like that, wouldn't you?"

"Probably. But I detect you're trying to change the subject."

"And I detect a certain change in your sexuality. No longer the plain vanilla guy you used to be when I met you. Those websites I saw on your laptop?"

"That's enough of that for now. Maybe some other time. To the business in hand, Señorita Sam, let's have it. What's the background that we're missing?"

"I need some more wine before I go any farther."

Sam got up from the table and settled herself into one of the armchairs.

"Typical, payment upfront. Your time with Carla certainly gave you some bad habits, you've lost your faith in human nature."

"Oh piss off, pour me a glass and fire away."

He uncorked a second bottle and filled her glass. He was relatively relaxed about the coming conversation, having wandered round his flat that afternoon with Charles' anti-eavesdropping instrument. It had registered nothing.

"In spite of everything you told me that night at the hotel in Zürich, not made easier by your friends listening in to my every word, I'm convinced that your decision to go to Zürich with Carla was only partly driven by the whole Dávila affair. I don't think you've told me everything. And to be frank, it's getting to me. That there's something between you and Carla is only part of the story - or at least I hope so. Maybe, if Carla knew about me, she might feel the same way. On the other hand, in her line of business, there can be little room for exclusive relationships and jealousy."

Sam nodded.

"Don't worry, Leo," she replied quietly, "she knows all about you and has done since around Christmas in Punta. Are you surprised? But you're right, she has little room for jealousy. In fact, quite the contrary. She understands what you mean to me and has gone some way to protecting you against the unwanted attentions of the bodyguards provided by Dávila. Don't put on that cynical look!"

Leandro was staring at her in frank disbelief, and made a gesture with his hand as if discarding what she had just said.

"On one of our evenings together in Punta, she asked me who the certain gentleman might be, with whom I had been seen together. We may have picked up the followers, but apparently they also picked you

430

up. I told her a little about you. I would have been wasting my time, given what we knew - or more precisely, didn't know - at that point, trying to explain to you the more complex nature of Carla. You would probably have thought that I was a full-blown lesbian and that my passion for Carla was getting in the way of my rationality."

Seeing the look on Leandro's face, she added.

"Don't deny it, that's almost certainly how you would have reacted. And, with that, your trust in me - let alone anything else - would have been destroyed. Admit it."

Leandro didn't reply immediately. He remembered the feeling of incomprehension which had seized him when he had discovered that Sam had left without saying anything. Also the frustration which had driven him into the arms of Tanya and her friend when he couldn't make contact in Zürich. He had come very close to giving Sam up completely. He had to concede that to be told that Carla favoured his relationship with Sam might have left him convinced that Sam and the rest of the world had gone mad.

"You see, I'm right."

Leandro nodded, but could not conceal a look which showed that he was finding it difficult, nonetheless.

Sam continued.

"However, there is more. The fact that Carla was prepared to contemplate my relationship with you would hardly have been sufficient reason for me to follow her to Zürich. In fact, there would have been no cause and effect in that."

She paused, gesturing to Leandro to pass her the bottle and filling up her glass. Then, somewhat to his surprise, she walked over to the hifi and turned up the volume to a level which was almost uncomfortable. She came back and, sitting opposite him on the sofa, gestured that he should sit opposite her.

She leaned forward and began to whisper.

"What I'm about to tell you must never leave this room. In fact, before I tell you, you need to confirm that you still feel the same way for me as before the time I met Carla."

Seeing Leandro making as if to move next to her, to hear her more clearly, she stopped him short.

"No, I don't mean that. I trust your word and your eyes long before I trust your hands. Long before. I thought we had established that the other day? When I first arrived."

Leandro tried to disguise the move by reaching for the bottle and filling his glass. But Sam had not been fooled.

"Perhaps you drink too much," she taunted him. "Your word, your eyes, I said."

There was a moment's silence, before Leandro replied.

"I can't say that it's always been easy. You have many ways to make a man like me suffer, sometimes even without realising it."

"I know, but you're still sitting there," she murmured.

"Don't I know it."

He gave a short sardonic laugh. He thought before continuing, speaking low, choosing his words with care.

"Somehow, almost since the very beginning, I knew this wasn't going to be easy, that there would be pain, though I didn't know in what proportion to pleasure. Even now, Sam, I'm scared to try and reach a balance. Though it may seem odd, for some reason I've never doubted your word, even when those words seemed to be destroying what we have together. Can't explain it. But that's the truth. I've grown addicted not only to your body, but to the workings of your mind, to your words, in short to you, and even at times to the pain."

He thought for a moment before continuing, trying to find a better way to express what he was thinking.

"Perhaps because - please don't think I'm being trite - being with you is like flying an aeroplane. Never forget, a plane nearly killed me. That

432

doesn't prevent me wanting to fly, and - as far as you're concerned - being prepared for the risks, maybe even paying the full price. Maybe that's not a classic romantic way to put it, but that's what it's about. That, I think , is what's in it for me. Is that your answer?"

After a pause, Sam simply said.

"Exactly what I wanted to hear. And what I've thought all along, somewhere inside me."

She drew a deep breath as if on the point of starting to say something, but then suddenly got up.

"Let's go to the cafe on the corner."

"Wait a minute, I thought...," but Sam was already slipping into her coat. "Okay, if you say so."

Some ten minutes later, with a couple of brandies on the table between them, Sam explained the sudden move.

"A minimum precaution. It suddenly hit me that we could probably not rule out the possibility that someone from Dávila's office might have planted a microphone in your flat, once they knew about you. Hence the loud volume. But at least this way we can talk naturally."

Leandro still said nothing about the detector. Last time he had checked, all had been okay. He would give it another check tomorrow.

She downed half her brandy, before continuing.

"You'll remember what I told you about that day on the West Bank, when the Israelis picked me up. I think I mentioned the confusion I had felt at the time, on discovering that parts of my tribe, the Druzes, also lived on the Israeli side of the border. As you know, the Israelis held me for about two days. What I didn't tell you was that, after they released me, that wasn't the end of it. Back in Jordan, they contacted me. And I was prepared to meet them, to listen. You've no doubt heard of Mossad, the Israeli intelligence service."

"Of course, who hasn't? And particularly here in Argentina, where they pulled off one of their biggest coups, extracting Adolf Eichmann and taking him back to stand trial in Israel." Leandro was staring at Sam. "Jesus, I dread what you're about to tell me."

"Well, as so often with me, your worst fears may be about to be fulfilled. I do work for them, though on what you might describe as a freelance and intermittent basis. I'm no doubt just a tiny cog in their wheels. But if there's a particular job I can do for them, they offer it to me. For my part, I tell them what I'm up to - within reason."

Leandro was at a loss for words. Would the shocks served up by this girl never end? Mossad! With everything that Sam had thrown at him over the last couple of months, now this! With her Syrian roots, what had made her switch sides?

He gestured to her continue. He needed time to adjust.

"For various reasons, they were interested in the Dávila situation and the link with Carla. She's clearly known to them. Not surprising really. But most of all they were interested in Aziz, the Saudi. They were the ones who put me up to accompanying Carla back to Switzerland. It all happened so fast and, as I said earlier, I didn't feel like explaining all this to you on the eve of my departure. I just gambled you'd follow me."

"Am I that predictable?" Leandro asked, with a certain edge of bitterness creeping into his voice.

"Don't confuse predictability with trust and reliability."

"Oh, so that's alright then?"

"Don't get bitter, you've no reason to be. Let me carry on."

Tipping back his glass of brandy, Leandro nodded that she should continue.

"As you probably know, there's no trick in the book that Mossad doesn't play. Using good-looking women is certainly one of them."

Leandro looked even more depressed.

"Just after the night you and I met in Zürich, I accompanied Carla to Geneva and then I went on to London. When she referred to Davos, we had guessed that some of those ten thousand highflying politicians and businessmen, keen to share their concern for the future of our society and the health of the planet, particularly if it can be done alongside celebrities such as Bill Gates or Bono, also have their more private side. I suspect Carla is personally on call to at least five of the presidents of the Fortune 500. Two of them had reserved one of her evening specials, at which a couple of the other girls were also present, and one had reserved the penthouse suite in one of Geneva's five-star hotels. Judging by the new Cartier watch on Samantha's wrist next day - the English girl who was there - the tips were more than generous. Carla had apparently received an instruction via Tawfiq, the Jordanian, that Aziz would also like me along to his meeting with her. I can't say that, apart from a good dinner and a visit to the Velvet which lasted well into the night, it was all that eventful."

Detecting Leandro's scepticism, she explained that since it was Muharram, the first month of the Islamic calendar, admittedly a month taken more seriously by Shias than by Sunnis - and Aziz, a Saudi, being a Wahhabi would give it less importance – the two Arabs had nevertheless felt the need to show some restraint.

"Not that they were exactly fasting! But more important, Aziz took a lot of interest in me and, when we parted, hinted that his boss might have need of my attentions."

"And his boss is a Prince involved in the defence of the Kingdom. You mentioned that. No doubt your handler in Mossad's very interested in that! And I'm just supposed to sit by and watch this happen! I need my head examining!"

Leandro's tone was caustic.

"Pretty much."

"And Carla in all of this?"

"Her Middle Eastern clients are some of the most important she has. So obviously, she's not going to get in the way. Carla's not sentimental. She's hard-headed and she leads a tough life. That's not to say that she is incapable of genuine emotion. As one day I'll explain to you, far, far from it. But her years with Dávila have left her pretty bullet-proof on some fronts."

Leandro turned his chair sideways to the table, crossed one leg over the other to relieve the pressure on his spine – that old rugby souvenir - and looked towards the bar across the tables, which had now filled up completely. With his left hand, he stroked the stubble on his cheek. The silence went on for a minute or two. Sam sat there fiddling with the brandy glass, watching him.

"And London? You mentioned London."

"After Geneva, Aziz asked me to fly to London. I was put up in one of the best hotels, the Lansdowne. For your information, they say it has one of the best bars in the world. On my second evening, I was invited to join a small dinner party in one of the private rooms of an exclusive club in the middle of Mayfair. Aziz had given me an incredible budget to get some clothes! I had a ball that afternoon, even though I had done the main shopping with Carla at Amadeo's in Zürich."

Seeing Leandro's blank look, she explained.

"Amadeo's Carla's leather couturier. The most beautiful, sexiest things. You'll see one day. Anyway, the Prince was there, but although we chatted a lot, it was clearly only intended that he should take a look at me. I must say, he's very charming. He placed me on his left at the dinner table, we talked. He's got lots of interests. And he was clearly interested in me. We tend to think that they only think about spending money and having a good time. But in his case, there's a lot more to him. Anyway, at the end of the dinner, Aziz told me that I should expect a call. I would be sent for, to join the prince virtually anywhere on the planet. So far, the call hasn't come."

Finishing his brandy, he looked up at Sam, his mind having digested her news. A response was in order, however incomplete.

"To be honest, Sam, tonight I don't know what to think. This latest piece of news. I have to get my brain round it. Up until we met in Zürich, I had a feeling that it might all be just a game, you and Carla. I don't know why, but I did. Probably fooling myself that, like from a bad dream, I would wake up and find us the way we were last year. Like in a dream, there was a feeling of invulnerability, the thrill of the chase. There was danger, yes, after all, we were dealing with people, some of whom were as vicious as they come. But we were bystanders, the real action, as we now know, being between Carla and Dávila. Were we in danger? At times, we thought so. That was part of the adrenaline. But we were amateurs, and like all amateurs, we only half understood the rules and the risks."

He refilled his glass.

"Then came Zürich. And so much changed. Frankly, you – Dalal – I was completely unprepared. First the fact that you wouldn't reply to my messages. Then Dalal! The whole relationship with Carla had gone overboard. I reacted stupidly that morning, I know, but somewhere, it came from deep inside, although the moment I said it, I feared that it was all over."

He paused and she took the opportunity to reply.

"I sensed that. But I knew it wasn't over, even if that wasn't the moment to sort it out. I had to walk away."

She placed her hand on his, immediately detecting his silent response to her touch.

"I knew we would come together again, Leo. We needed a bit of time to sort ourselves out. That's what I'm here to do, what I want to do above all. You know what you just said about the danger? Was there real danger? I don't know. But, with you, Leo, thanks to you, I do know that I've lived the last six months more intensively than for many years. In fact, not since the time in Jordan. I also know that I'd be reluctant just to go back to my Oscar Wilde studies. But what about you? How content are you to just going back to writing your economic bulletin?"

Leandro said nothing. Now there was also the business of Frobisher. How much could he tell her? She was bound to be interested, simply because Mossad must be looking for the same answers. He didn't reply at once.

"Is your little office out in San Isidro going to be enough?"

"Don't knock it, it pays the bills."

"Luckily, as you don't want to die of starvation as well as boredom."

"Don't be so cruel! The trouble with you, your tastes are too expensive."

"Have I ever asked you for a peso? I can't understand why you think that anybody would be after your money."

"You never did tell me what it was that you were after."

Leandro felt a surge of relief that they had somehow come back to teasing. It might not resolve the core problems, but it should smooth the way. He needed more time to think. There were still too many things unsaid.

"We've had a lot to think about this evening. Let's take a rain check, Sam. I need to sleep on all this. I don't know about you?"

She leaned across the table and took his hand in both of hers. Then, without a word, she got up and left the cafe.

Not for the first time, she had left him with the bill and the hard decisions. Why didn't these decisions appear to be so hard for her? He needed another drink. And some rest.

"*Che*, Manuel, have you any of that really good Guatemalan rum?" he asked the waiter.

"I think the boss hides a bottle somewhere."

Manuel came back with a fresh brandy glass and poured him a couple of centimetres of the Zacapa 23-year vintage.

Leandro sat there, thinking, prolonging the pleasure of the soft velvet liquid. Then, leaving money on the table, he waved to the waiter and walked back along the pavement towards his flat.

The watcher in the car made a note of the time. He would have preferred to follow the girl, but the instructions were to concentrate on the man. On top of that, a new instruction had been received. Establish any pattern of movement which would allow the technicians to get into the target's flat for an hour or two. The watcher knew this should serve to plant an eavesdropping device.

The combined effects of the previous evening's discussions, the two bottles of merlot and the incomparable Zacapa ensured that Leandro only woke at midday. It being a Saturday morning, it wasn't a problem. As he walked precariously towards the bathroom, massaging his temples, he caught a glimpse of something white on the floor by the front door. He might have guessed! A note from Sam, proposing dinner at Oviedo, one of her favourite restaurants. She had already reserved a table for nine thirty that evening. Always one for the effect. Would a text message not have been more efficient? Less personal for sure.

"Somehow, that lady has to take me a little less for granted," he muttered. Not that he was in the slightest doubt about being there. However, just for the sake of his masculine pride, he would leave her sitting there for a good half an hour.

At just after ten, he still seemed to have arrived first, until he saw her emerge from the wood-panelled stairway leading down from the cloakroom. She was dressed to kill, all the men in the restaurant her willing victims, their female companions her instant enemies. Oscar Wilde exhibitionism in top gear! Her dark hair, longer than when they had first met, redder than he could remember – was it just the lighting? - was offset by a pale grey knitted sweater dress which fell in ample folds to just above the knee, fur trimmings on the sleeves. Over this, a wide knitted cape of a darker grey wool, its large hood framing her face. Grey leather thigh boots with unbelievable heels. The day's cold front just about justified her attire. Some of the spoils of her visit to Paris. Or perhaps Zürich?

"How do you like this? From Les Copains. They make such wonderful knitted clothes – a real Italian speciality. It's the finest alpaca wool, the softest there is. Vicuna would be even softer, but would cost twice as much. And anyway it would be against my ecological principles. Got it just before I left Zürich."

"Really good for my ego," Leandro muttered.

He helped her out of the loose cape, which an eager waiter was standing by to collect, and pocketed the cloakroom docket.

"How can you expect me to concentrate on our very complex relationship, let alone take any kind of rational decisions, when you bring out all this heavy artillery? Your way of dressing ought to be banned by the Geneva Convention, there's no longer any place in our society for weapons of such massive seduction. In fact, your only redeeming virtue is what you do for my ego."

"Since when the sudden interest in my virtues? Thought it was only my vices you were interested in. Anyway, be quiet and get me a drink. I knew you'd come late on purpose and I've just had to kill fifteen minutes up in the ladies' toilet. Not to mention, whilst I was there, avoiding the attentions of that German bitch sitting over there in the corner."

She sat down on the bench, smoothing the folds of the dress around her. The hem she kept just above the tops of the boots. Leandro took the chair opposite.

He looked at the other table where a handsome blonde, in her mid-forties, had been watching Sam with undisguised interest. He smiled.

"Don't you dare smile, fuck you. For that you can order a bottle of the Baron B rosé champagne." She beckoned the wine waiter to the table. "El Señor is ready to order."

"We'll have a bottle of Baron B rosé," Leandro complied, ill suppressing a grin.

Leandro looked around the restaurant. Although it had only been under its current management for less than twenty-five years, Oviedo had the look of an old French brasserie, with its long red leather-covered benches along the walls, dark polished wooden partitions and large white globe ceiling lights. Argentine decorators and carpenters produced very high quality reproductions.

"My father loves this place, but he hasn't brought me here for a long time."

"Just as long as nobody thinks I'm your father," Leandro replied with a hint of sadness in his voice. "Those clothes just make you look younger - and more beautiful - and me probably older, as a result."

"Somehow, I don't think anybody could have confused the look on your face with paternal love when you greeted me."

"Conceited bitch! Anyway, let's drink to your filial good health."

The champagne had arrived, now resting in an ice bucket next to their table.

"Yes, *padre*. And to your longevity."

"I'll drink to that. Just when I was looking forward to a quiet life and an early retirement. Let's order and then you can tell me why you're looking so sure of yourself. Wish I could say the same, after everything we left unsaid last night."

Sam didn't even pick up the menu.

"First of all, if you're thinking of an early retirement, you can count me out. Somehow, I don't see myself wrapping a rug around your knees in front of the fire."

"Not unless you can get your lips under the rug as well?" he suggested.

"You've really got a filthy mind! I came here to eat, not to listen to your erotic fantasies. Put your menu away and let me order for you. Let's see. Yes. To start with, *chipirones a la plancha* for you, they grill the baby squid just right, juicy but crunchy. I'll have the oysters. An ice cold chardonnay with that. Then you should have the wild boar with mushrooms. It comes with a scramble of eggs, cassava and bacon. I'll have the *ravioles de cordero*, the lamb is delicious in pasta. And we can have a good red with that. Finally a mousse of passion fruit for me and you can have the apple pancakes – very thin and brittle. Don't argue, obey!"

"Christ, shades of Carla! Okay, sounds delicious. The sommelier – if they have one - can suggest the wines, spare me all the effort. And they say oysters are good for the libido."

As the waiters bustled around them, unfolding their napkins, placing a large basket of small, warm loaves in the centre of the table, Leandro stole a long look at the girl sitting opposite him on the red banquette. How much easier everything would be if she weren't so bloody good looking. Her make-up! And now that dress! He felt an uncontrollable urge to get his hands inside it. He did his best to dispel it for now.

In spite of a slight hangover on awakening at noon, he had nevertheless felt the need to devote some of the afternoon to preparing his thoughts for the evening. He had sat at his worktable, jotting down ideas on a pad.

Setting aside all the purely emotional parts – a virtually impossible task - and merely concentrating on what appeared to be a new set of rules for the game he and Sam were playing, he remained confused. The news of her relationship with Mossad was obviously a game changer. Yet, given what he was doing for Frobisher, and even more, what he was about to start for them, he could hardly present a strong case against Sam's relationship with the Israeli intelligence service. Frobisher was certainly no Mossad and the potential risks by no means in the same league, but there were clear parallels.

On waking at some point during the night to get an aspirin, he had been hit by the potential synergy between what Frobisher wanted and what Mossad would certainly want. Anything which contributed to a better understanding of where certain players, particularly Saudi Arabia and Iran, stood vis-a-vis Israel, particularly on defence issues, must be the main item on Mossad's agenda. Item number one on that agenda must be Iran's nuclear capability. So far, Israel seemed – with an occasional display of direct action, such as their alleged hacking of the Iranian control systems - to have been content to allow the running to be made by the Western powers or the International Atomic Energy Agency inspectors. But their patience would ultimately run out and they might take things into their own hands. As they had done in the case of Iraq's Osirak nuclear plant many years ago, or much more recently in their attack on a suspected Syrian nuclear laboratory.

Israel had good reason to be concerned with the centuries-old battle between the Shias, now spearheaded by Iran, and the more extreme variant of the Sunni allegiance exemplified by Saudi Wahhabism. Given the decline of superpower influence in the region since the fall of the Berlin Wall, the danger to Israel lay above all in the radicalisation of this ancient confrontation, particularly since Osama bin Laden had stoked the fire nearly seven years previously. The combination of the Iranian Islamic state slugging it out in the madrassas from Marrakesh to Malaysia with the seemingly limitless resources of the keepers of Islam's Holiest Places, represented by far the broadest threat to the continued existence of the state of Israel.

Yes, Mossad should certainly be interested in anything that Leandro might turn up on the subject for Frobisher. Was that manageable, not only in terms of his allegiance to Frobisher, but, more immediately, his relationship with Sam? Perhaps the dinner would provide some answers. In the process, he needed to understand how this girl of Arab descent had seen fit to switch allegiances.

"That's enough staring! Anybody would think you'd never seen me before."

Leandro shook his head, as if to clear away a temporary lapse of concentration.

"Sorry. Lost in my thoughts. You're not very good for my concentration tonight. Anyway, here's to your new wardrobe."

"*Salud!*"

Sam studied Leandro over the top of her glass. She knew that last night she had left him very confused. He had reacted less virulently than she had expected to her news about Mossad. What conclusions had he reached, if any? Whatever they were, he wasn't giving much away. With his mild hangover, unshaven, that faint look of boyish perplexity in his eyes, he was very sexy. Succumbing to the feeling, the tips of her fingers slipped down to the folds of her dress between her thighs. A low current passed. She must be patient.

"So, Leo, are we here to celebrate the end of what your old friend Dave Brubeck would have called 'a fine romance' - or is it to launch ourselves on a new adventure?"

"Good question. You mean to say there's a reason for this dinner? You're the one who reserved the restaurant."

"Either way, I felt it deserved a good setting and a good meal."

Leandro laughed.

"Always one for doing things in style."

"If you can't do it in style, it's probably not worth doing."

"That sounds like your favourite Mr Wilde."

"No, this time it's my favourite Miss Me."

Leandro laughed again.

The waiter brought over a little *amuse gueule* of homemade *foie gras*.

"Delicious."

"How is your father by the way?"

"Happy to see his itinerant daughter back. I think he works too hard. I counted a few extra grey hairs after my time away."

"You surprise me! Am I ever going to meet him? I've heard so much about him."

"And he about you."

"That may not be very reassuring for him. I'm sure he'd want you to be on the arm of some extremely successful businessman."

"You'd be surprised. Somewhere along the road, I think he's realised I'm not made just to prop up a rich man's ego. Add to that, he knows I won't need the money, he's made sure of that. No, I think he's resigned to the possibility I may yet serve him up a few surprises. As long as I don't bring the honour of the family into disrepute... And obviously, I'm taking a risk being a seen in the company of a serial sex maniac like you."

Leandro looked at her sharply, avoiding her last remark. She had suddenly provided an opening.

"And you don't think your relationship with Carla or working for Mossad might put that at risk? Be serious for a moment, Sam. I can hardly imagine two things more likely to do so."

His reaction caught Sam off guard. She was silent. She slowly looked around the restaurant. Then she breathed deeply, before turning back to Leandro. He could detect a sadness in her eyes which had not been there a minute before.

"You're right, of course. I know that. But...."

He waited a moment.

"But what?"

Sam shook her head, her dark red hair falling over her face as she looked down at the table. He wondered whether he had ever seen her so vulnerable. He stretched out and touched the hand with which she was lightly holding the stem of her glass. She didn't look up. For a moment, it felt as though the whole restaurant had gone silent. She half raised her head, looking directly at him. She spoke softly.

"Maybe that's why I need you. I need you to help me to decide what's right. Up to now, I've been able to handle this kind of decision on my own. But now, I'm not so sure."

Unprepared for so disarming an approach, Leandro lent back in his chair, inadvertently withdrawing his hand from the table as he did so.

"Please, I need to touch you, to feel you," she whispered.

He leaned forward again, and this time took both her hands in his. Yet somehow the effect was not the same and they both sensed it.

"I'm not sure...," he muttered.

"Leo, listen to me...," she began. At that moment, the first course arrived.

"*Ostras* for Madame, I believe. And *chipirones* for Señor? Can I pour the chardonnay?"

"That's fine, perfect temperature."

Leandro felt an urgent need to escape back, even for just a few seconds, into the simpler world of food.

Sam also appeared to regain some of her composure, as the business of eating oysters absorbed her full concentration for the next ten minutes.

"There! A dozen oysters should give you a run for your money later tonight."

"You were right about the *chipirones*. These people do them better than that Spanish place on Quintana."

Yet no amount of gastronomic small talk was going to let them escape the conundrum which Sam had placed on the table earlier. Somehow, the right mood had to be reset.

Thinking about it that afternoon, he knew that he always had the option of just walking away and rebuilding his life without her. That it would be very painful, he had not the slightest doubt. She could do the same. But it was clear that, in her case, the background battle between her convictions and the call of her family could not be so easily reconciled. Possibly never. He suspected that her father's allegiance must lie firmly in the anti-Israeli camp, seeing himself first and foremost a Druze from Arab Syria. It seemed highly unlikely that he would make the transition of loyalties which, for reasons which Leandro still did not understand, had prompted Sam to change sides that day in the Israeli interrogation centre. Her account of the episode had been nothing if not opaque. But he had no doubt that the decision, once arrived at, was wholly sincere. The part played in that decision by the Israeli female interrogator who had so impressed her might be a factor. Yet another powerful woman with whom Sam had felt an affinity. The image of Oriana Fallaci, the photograph in Sam's bookcase, had also come to mind. Sam had briefly alluded to the handsome Italian journalist's vehement attacks on the destructive forces of Islam, describing her as an inspiration. Was this part of the explanation? He needed to find out more about the Italian. Another key to the personality of Sam? And now here she was, dining with him, far less in control of her life than she would like, apparently asking him to supply the convictions, the arguments, which she could not find in herself.

The main course lived up to expectations, its path enhanced by the excellent red wine recommended by the waiter. The conversation focused harmlessly on the food, easing the tension. It was only with the desserts in front of them, that Leandro picked up where they had left off.

"This dinner has been too good just to be a farewell. Or maybe not good enough. Either way..." He stopped. "Jesus, what a trite opening line. I'm sure Oscar Wilde would have had a better one."

Sam thought for a moment.

"'Men can be analysed, women... merely adored'. It's something like that. Remember, from the play? Is that what you're trying to say?"

"What a memory. Just when I thought that I might have you at my mercy! Christ, who would ever want to negotiate with you?"

Sam had regained her composure. Her hand sought his across the table.

"But you do have me at your mercy, Leo. You just don't realise it. So take advantage of it." She spoke softly.

"You're not making this any easier, with that kind of remark."

"Who said it had to be easy?"

It was Leandro's turn to be thrown off balance. He paused to fill their glasses.

"You shouldn't let that wonderful pancake get cold."

"Fuck the pancake," he said, pushing his plate aside.

She dipped her spoon into the passion fruit and stole some of his pancake.

"Too good to waste!"

She smiled, a thin trail of the pale ice cream contrasting with the dark red of her lips.

Suppressing a violent urge to taste it directly on her mouth, Leandro launched himself into the debate once more.

"I guess, at the end of the day, it's what you want to live for. We both know that a home and children, supplied by some wealthy businessman, may not be your ambition in life. To date, monogamy hasn't exactly been your watchword. Don't worry, I'm not trying to convert you. I'd certainly be the last to want to do that," he added quickly, seeing the shadow of a frown pass over her face. "Anyway, if I had, I probably wouldn't be sitting opposite you. At heart, you love to live dangerously. I'm sure your pal Oscar, as you refer to him, had something to say on the subject, having not exactly chosen the conventional life."

"He did, in the same play. You're right. It's a drug, I would love to patent it, sell it and become even richer."

"Yes, but by prescription only. But do I detect that the dangerous life is becoming a little too complicated?"

"Not so much complicated, nor even necessarily a matter of danger. But, with your irritating common sense, you've made me see that some things come with a price. Whereas I'm pretty sure that my father has broadly accepted the fact that my emotional life will always be unconventional, hardly a tribute to the education provided by those horrible nuns, I've little doubt that the Carla situation, if he were to learn of it, would be a bridge too far. You probably haven't looked, but I'm no longer on the website. I agreed that with Carla before I left. She knows me and her clients well enough to judge when to send my profile to anyone, which she only does after checking with me first. You look reassured?"

That was the least she could say, though still very far from ideal.

"I suppose I have to take that as some kind of improvement. But you know what, Sam? If I'm honest, in moments of weakness, probably when I was pissed, it gave me something of a thrill to see you in that company."

Leandro instantly wondered about the wisdom of that remark.

"That almost sounds like good news, especially as I'm going to ask you to accept that Carla is not off the scene. Please, Leo, don't look so worried! Give me time to explain."

Sam sat back on the bench, apparently rearranging her dress. Leandro had noticed this gesture in the past, usually when Sam was about to launch into some kind of self-confession. In fact, Sam sensed that the conversation was moving into complex emotional terrain, where she wanted her physical sensations to be in tune with her mind. The soft, clinging feel of the dress on her body heightened her inner tension, a physical and nervous stimulant to her thoughts. If only Leandro could feel inside her. Her passions, what drove her, might become clearer to him.

"There are two aspects to my relationship with Carla. One of them you'll probably understand quite easily. The other may prove more difficult. Easy one first. As I mentioned the other night when we left your flat and went down to the cafe on the corner, Carla provides me with a very effective springboard to pursue certain high-level individuals, like Aziz and hopefully his boss, the Prince. My handler at Mossad is definitely keen that I build a relationship with the Prince. Like the Prince, they feel there will be others potentially of interest to them. So, in that respect, you can call me Mata Hari!"

"God, how I fell in love with Greta Garbo in that film!" Leandro interjected, closing his eyes, reliving the scenes. "I was so young. And she was so beautiful."

Sam reacted swiftly, not wanting him drifting off into some nostalgic daydream.

"Well, this Mata Hari's a dark redhead and, lucky man that you are, she's physically yours! Not just some cellulose dame, that you can only dream and masturbate over. This one you can actually fuck! Here and now!"

"For Christ's sake, you'll have us thrown out!"

"Anyway, do I need to explain this any further? I'm sure you understand what I'm driving at. I need Carla for professional reasons."

Leandro nodded.

"I know what's coming. Not just professional."

"You're right. Now for the more difficult part. There probably isn't any easy way to say this. You remember what I once told you about my emotional relationships being rather like an apartment?"

"How could I forget," Leandro murmured. "It's the size of the rent and some of the other guests that depress me."

"Well, the good news is, you still occupy the master bedroom. And who said anything about rent? You get to live there for free. Or hadn't you noticed?"

"There are times when the price feels quite high. And I've a nasty feeling that what you're about to tell me isn't going to lower it in any way."

"Listen, you've known from the start that I wouldn't come cheap."

"Go on," he murmured.

"I love it, when you put on that look of the injured party. Let's get it over with. Carla does have the keys to a guestroom, actually the principal guestroom. But – and I emphasize but - not the master bedroom. Like any guest, she will come and go at times. But the day may come when I ask her to hand back the keys."

Sam studied his reaction.

"You don't look very convinced?" she quizzed him.

"Oh, I don't know, it had occurred to me that the life of a concierge in a hotel might be quite interesting. Think of 'The Night Porter'."

"With me in the role of Charlotte Rampling?" She had loved the film.

"Exactly. But don't let me stop you, keep going."

"Is there any of that champagne left?"

He filled both their glasses. She took a mouthful, before continuing.

"Please try and understand. You've known ever since you found me with Lamai that I was bi. And, correct me if I'm wrong, I suspect it adds spice to our relationship. I remember our first night together after you'd been to my flat that day. You were incredible. You're just like all the rest of your gender, lesbian sex turns you on."

"I wish you wouldn't make me sound quite so banal. At the rate we're going, this is becoming some kind of Kinsey report, with me in the role of just another statistic. Maybe Elena was right. I should give up economics. Research a whole new dimension to the word inflation."

"Now you're just being vulgar, and it doesn't suit you."

"Sorry."

"You've never met Carla. One day you should. There are definitely two sides to her. The one you, most other people, see is the one she projects on her website. Make of it what you will, though I'm not sure you're in such a strong position to occupy the moral high ground. Then there's another Carla. That's the Carla who sought me out that night at the polo party. In some ways, that person operates at both extremes. That's to say, at one extreme she is much softer, more loving and more compassionate than her web personality would have one believe. Also in need of love. And also capable of great kindness. At the other extreme, she can be much more dangerous, capable of much greater violence, than that personality. To a certain extent, Lady Blast represents a controlled fusion of those two extremes."

"Fascinating." Leandro looked unconvinced.

There was a silence.

"I hear you and I've no reason to contradict you. One day perhaps I will meet her. In the meantime, you're asking me to reconcile myself to your continued relationship with her. That's it, Sam, isn't it?"

"Yes," she answered simply.

"Well, what are the options? I either cohabit with Carla or I don't. Like some kind of concierge. That's the bottom line, isn't it?"

He smiled at her and detected that she found this slightly disconcerting.

"I don't know," she answered, rather lamely.

"You do, so don't let's play games. Nor can we just overlook the question of Mossad."

"What about Frobisher?" she rejoined quickly.

"You're still playing games, you know they're not comparable. Just for a minute, put yourself in my place. If a man you loved told you that he intended to pursue a high risk profession, for which he might be called away at any hour, that the exercise of the profession might bring him into close sexual encounters with a variety of women…. Oh, and by the way, that he's also running a homosexual relationship on the side. Does that sound like a very attractive proposition?"

"In your case, it's the bit about the homosexual relationship I don't believe." She grinned.

"Thanks for nothing. What about the close sexual encounters?"

"Wasn't there something about two 'goth' girls in Zürich?"

"What the shit? Where did you get that from?"

He looked shaken.

"Oh, I don't know, word gets around. I note you have the decency not to deny it."

"But I do."

"And if so, as far as I know, you'd be lying, something, Leo, you've never done before! Never! Tanya… wasn't that one of them?"

"Jesus, you're the devil incarnate. How the fuck did you find out?"

"So we're no longer denying it?"

"Okay, I give in. No doubt those fucking bodyguards."

She leant across the table and took his hand.

"So you see, we're to a certain extent the mirror image of each other. In which case, there appears to be the making of a compromise. What do you say? "

Leandro looked out of the restaurant window. A fine rain had started to fall. A taxi had just drawn up next to the restaurant. The doorman stepped across the pavement, holding an umbrella, as a smartly dressed, elderly couple slid awkwardly from the back seat of the car. Argentine taxis were not well adapted to arthritis. For a split-second, Leandro wondered whether, twenty years hence, he would be doing this with Sam. Probably not. But then, so what? He had rarely planned one year ahead, let alone twenty.

"As I think I once said to you, an optimist is just a poorly informed pessimist. On balance, I would prefer not to have more information. So that way I can remain an optimist. And, being an optimist, that means I should probably give it a chance. Which, dear Sam, I propose to do. Will I regret it? Who knows? My instinct, however badly informed, tells me that the pleasure and the thrills you will bring, in the final analysis, could outweigh the pain. Not very scientific. But it's the best I can do."

"Everything is dangerous. If it wasn't so, life wouldn't be worth living. As my friend Oscar put it."

"But coming back to Carla. What am I supposed to think about that?"

"Only when you understand one thing, will you be able to appreciate the personality of Carla. You and Eduardo, I can see, have always assumed that Carla was, so to speak, on the same side as Dávila. From your attitude to her, and from things which you've said, you believe that Carla was on the side of the military, of the torturers. In fact, because you saw that video of the torture scene, you probably think that Carla is the nurse standing behind the victim?"

"Well, yes, that would appear to be the only reason why, when they both get to Zürich, they come together. And why she's involved in the hotel murder. Are you saying that's wrong?"

"Completely!"

"Then I don't understand."

"Carla is not the nurse standing behind the prisoner. She was a prisoner. Not necessarily the one in the film, though."

"You're crazy! Why in heaven's name would she have anything to do with Dávila, if he was torturing her? It doesn't make sense."

"Have you never heard of the Stockholm Syndrome?"

"Of course. Hostages ending up by falling in love with their captors. I'm not quite sure how much it applied in the case of torture, although it certainly seems to have been the case when people were held for a long time. Some recent examples in Colombia, with women held hostage and finally having an affair with their captors, and even having children by them."

"Exactly. And we have a variant here. I don't know how much you've followed the subject."

"Nothing more than what I've read in the papers, but fill me in," Leandro replied.

"Well, give me a moment, as it really is important in terms of your perception of Carla."

Leandro made a gesture indicating that she had his full attention.

"The enquiries into what happened in the detention centres, all the work which has been done by the Madres de Plaza de Mayo, by judges and by human rights organisations, all have thrown up an amazing reality as regards certain relationships between torturers and victims. Carla gave me much more detail. The military, rather like what happened in the Nazi concentration camps, had what you might call 'slaves' amongst their prisoners. People producing false documents, which the military then used to expropriate or simply steal assets belonging to their prisoners or to the 'disappeared'. There are hundreds of cases in which members of the military got their victims to sign off papers, transferring property, businesses, anything they wanted to lay their hands on. For that, they sometimes needed false documents, which lawyers and notaries, locked away in the cells, would produce for them, as a way of staying alive."

"I had heard that," Leandro interjected.

"But what is much more grotesque – even unbelievable - is the fact that the interrogators working in these places were quite capable of taking a woman prisoner, whom they might have been torturing that morning, getting her to put on a pretty dress, make herself look beautiful, and then take her out, quite publicly, to a restaurant somewhere in town, here in Buenos Aires. Who knows, perhaps even to this place. That's what happened with Carla. She was very handsome and sexy, you can see that today, and there were at least two men among the torturers who would take her out. She told me about the amazing feeling of sitting surrounded by normal people, all having dinner, chatting away, looking into the eyes of a man who only a few hours earlier had been causing her excruciating pain. And who might start again next morning. She said it was surreal. And yet overpowering."

"And was Dávila one of these two men?"

"During the time she was held, she wasn't able to work out whether the officer, with whom she would go out in the evening, might be the man who had been wearing a mask over his face at one of the interrogations. It's only when they met in Zürich, and then only after a number of years, that he finally told her that he had been a member of the Montoneros, before betraying them and working for the military. And that he had tortured her!"

Leandro was silent for a moment, digesting what he had just heard.

"Then why did she need to leave Argentina when the military were kicked out? As a victim of the military, surely she had no reason to leave, nothing to fear?"

"She left, because she was above all sickened to the core with a country which had allowed something so terrible to happen and which, no sooner were the military on the run after the Malvinas defeat, than they all emerged from their little holes and began to take their revenge on those whom they had been content to allow to do the dirty work. That's not to say that the dirty work was in any way legitimate, but too few had had the courage to stand up and denounce it. Now they were all dancing around the funeral pyre. It made her sick. So she left."

Leandro couldn't avoid giving a momentary thought to his parents.

"I see. And how do you explain her later career."

"One of the reasons you thought that Carla was the woman behind the chair is that you assumed that she was fulfilling some kind of medical role. The woman behind the chair was a member of the military and was a nurse. But it wasn't Carla. Carla had been studying medicine, by the time she was picked up by the military. But the military had a very perverted idea about many things, including medicine. For instance, they condemned Freud as some kind of sex maniac and burned his books. She was studying psychology at the University. This was regarded by the military as a serious cause for suspicion. So in 1980, also because she was not afraid to say what she thought, they picked her up. That's how she ended up being tortured. Then when she got to Zürich, she decided to go on with her studies, but also to take up nursing. At that time, she felt a need to be involved with preserving life, not destroying it."

"Yes, but then, what happened later to explain what she's doing now."

"It's not an easy question, and maybe she doesn't even have the answer, or at the least not the full one. Naturally, I haven't been able to pry too much about that. Inevitably, after what she's been through, the sexual act is not quite the same for her as it might be for you or me."

"Yes I can see that."

"As you know, although she might technically describe herself as a dominatrix, she's not at all into torture and pain, unlike many of her colleagues. In fact, very much the contrary. Even the title dominatrix doesn't really apply. But to make things simpler, it serves her purpose. She's into sexual pleasure of different persuasions, giving free rein to heightened sensuality. To intensify this, she recognises that power, a measure of risk and taking things to the edge have a part to play. But not physical pain. She's had enough of that in her own life not to want to inflict it on others. You might say that she focuses on the pain of pleasure, not the pleasure of pain. It's about the limits of pleasure, not at all about sadism."

"What about the relationship with Dávila? From the little you've told me, that's pretty much on the edge."

"Certainly on the edge, but from what she's told me, it doesn't involve pain. Dávila has a problem getting it up. He's also a heavy rubber fetishist. Something he apparently got into in Zürich. Giving free rein to his fetish, combined with autoerotic asphyxiation, brings him to orgasm. That's what Carla delivers. They have sessions together. She's also by no means averse to a bit of latex fetishism. But as far as I can tell, he's a special case."

"You can say that again. But I still don't understand why she even puts up with him."

"Remember what I said earlier. Somewhere in all of that, the foundations were laid in those surreal evenings in the restaurants of Buenos Aires, when, perhaps having tortured her in the morning, he would take her out for dinner and maybe to a nightclub afterwards. When he appeared in Zürich, this relationship somehow grew. As far as I can tell, he arrived a few months after her. I don't know how they met again, but they did. And he seems to have been a presence in her life from that time onwards. He funded her business, provided her with protection. Particularly after he returned to Argentina five or six years ago. Up until that time, he could provide her support and cash. As he became richer, so the set up in Punta del Este emerged. Since it was on his doorstep and, because of his connections with SIDE in Buenos Aires, he was able to provide her with protection. Those two guys and their car. I presume that there must be some kind of setup in Argentina, though my suspicion is that, being on his doorstep, it's very low-key. Dávila has presumably concealed his Swiss passport. But since she's changed her name and is now Swiss, that provides her with a level of protection."

"But you said that you thought that you had seen them together at the polo parties. So he's not exactly concealing his existence."

"No, that's right. He probably feels secure enough."

Leandro thought about what Sam had told him.

"I presume I can share some of this with Eduardo?"

"Yes, of course. At least the bits about Carla. Not the bits about you and me. As you can see, I'm very keen that we shift Carla from the side of the 'vilains', dressed in black, to the side of the 'heroes' – or more precisely, the 'heroines'."

"Though, as far as I can see, she's usually dressed in black."

"As I said before, she only transmits an image of evil, she's certainly not evil. She's a victim of evil. I only wish she would find a way to get out from under the spell of that terrible Dávila. Only then can she properly set everything she suffered behind her."

"Do you think she'll ever come back to Argentina?"

"Not a chance. Not with these people in power. Having been a victim of the oppression, she has a real problem with watching the way in which human rights, the 'disappeared', left-wing terrorism, the events of the 70s are all being exploited to create some kind of legitimacy for something which she sees as nothing better than raping the country."

Leandro thought for a while. There was no easy way to phrase his next question.

"Sam, what about you and her? How's that going to play out?"

Sam said nothing for a moment.

She had been expecting this question ever since their parting in Zürich. Lying in bed, having perhaps woken in the middle of the night, she had tried to analyse it. On the one hand, Leandro with whom she knew she was deeply in love. On the other, the figure of Carla, complex, alluring, in so many ways overpowering. One night, she had detected a certain parallel with her favourite literary figure, Wilde. *De profundis*, from the depths. The words had flashed through her mind that evening in the Sanctuary. Although she saw Carla in her professional role as amoral rather than immoral, deep down she knew that danger lurked in the directions in which Carla was taking her... or to which, perhaps, Sam was at times herself leading the way. Wilde's relationship with his lover, Alfred Douglas, had been self-destructive. Part of her fascination with the Irish genius stemmed from a certain affinity she had felt at times with Wilde's suicidal trajectory. But the Carla she had come to know was so much more than the selfish, egocentric young Bosie. One evening by the fireside in her Zürich flat, Carla had finally begun to speak of her days in the interrogation centre, and before. She had spoken of her revulsion at what the military had been doing to her country, but more important, to her friends. In spite of the dangers, she had finally gone to work for the Montoneros, even though by that stage the battle was lost. It had not been long before she had been picked up.

"I was passionate about it. I was young. I was prepared to take risks. Anything rather than just sit idly by. You, dearest Sam, remind me of myself, perhaps in better, more honourable ways."

She had kissed Sam's hand.

Was Leandro to be Sam's Constance, Wilde's long-suffering wife, destined to pay the price of her passions? For the time being, like Constance, Leandro seemed prepared to accommodate Sam's conflicting emotions. But for how long? Would he, like Constance, finally terminate their relationship? Sam needed more time.

"I won't deny that we share a special relationship." Sam spoke slowly, choosing her words with care, to minimize damage. "She once said that she could see a lot of herself in me. I prefer to interpret that in its most positive sense. She certainly exerts a very powerful physical attraction over me. Has from the first moment we met. Leaving aside the physical, which is very potent, I'm also fascinated by the force of her personality. She's lived through terrible experiences and although hardly everyone's first choice, she's risen to the top of her profession. In spite of everything, deep inside her, she has preserved values. Real kindness is one of them. In little things. She may not be Mother Teresa - though I'm told she wasn't a very nice person either - but is there something so immoral about satisfying people's inner passions? Particularly if no serious harm comes to anyone in the process? Amoral perhaps, immoral, I'm not so sure. Women have given pleasure to men since the beginning of time. It's people like St. Augustine, a womaniser if ever there was one until he got religion, who placed women in a position of inferiority. Or Thomas Aquinas? If you can't control your libido, control the women. Just look at the Islamic world. In the same breath, the mullahs insist on every centimetre of a woman's body being concealed, whilst simultaneously promising privileged access to seventy-five – or however many – dark-eyed virgins in heaven for those foolish enough to blow themselves up. With a mass of innocent bystanders into the bargain. Is religion really only about controlling your sex urge? Anyway, don't get me onto that subject."

"I'm not sure that we can completely forget her part in the hotel murder. She may not have killed Williams, but she must have suspected that Dávila would do something. Don't you think?"

Sam paused, before continuing.

"I know. She's tried to explain that one to me. To a very large extent, Dávila still exercised his sinister control over her at that time. However, after the hotel affair, she made clear to me that it was over. She felt totally betrayed, used. How and when she handles that remains to be seen."

The look on his face indicated that Leandro would need some more convincing.

"So, to sum up, as regards Carla and me, not everything is totally clear, and it may be some time before it does become clearer. In the meantime, I'm going to have to ask you to be patient. I can't say any more. Am I asking too much?"

Leandro nodded quietly and then looked out of the window again. The rain had stopped.

"Leandro, I love you. Get that into your head. You're smart enough to distinguish between love and sex. And between love and attraction. Carla attracts me powerfully, I have great sex with her, very different, she plays to something very complex inside me, unlocks special desires. It's probable she's in love with me. You also give me great sex. But above all we love each other, a deep love, there's so much more. I love your intellect, your outlook on life, your body. I for one know that I love you. And in other ways, I love her. But it's not the same. I can only hope that, after all that's happened, you love me."

He looked at her.

"I'm afraid I have to ask you one question."

"Go ahead."

"Through the website, did you make love to any other client?"

He said it slowly.

She smiled.

"Only one, an arsehole of an Argentine who gave me a bad time at the Baur au Lac."

"I love you," he whispered.

"Be careful," she murmured, "Oscar once said that if one tells the truth, one is sure sooner or later to be found out!"

"Fine with me."

460

The waiter brought the bill.

As he waited for the credit card to be returned, he watched Sam as unobtrusively as possible. She was sitting totally still, her face flushed, otherwise expressionless.

Bridges had been rebuilt. They might not withstand all the weight put on them, but there would be ways to cross. The question of Mossad still needed addressing, but it would have to wait. A number of important things had been made clear.

If only she weren't so fucking beautiful!

And so beautiful fucking!

Kneeling on the satin sheets, taking Sam from the rear, his hands on either side of her slim waist, the roundness of her butt filled his immediate horizon. He watched her in the wall mirror as, naked except for her boots, kneeling, her face buried in the sheets, she arched her back, gyrating her hips, side to side, luxuriating in his fullness inside her. Alternately lifting her on his penis, thrusting in and out, cupping her breasts in his hands as they swayed below her body, he dragged out their pleasure.

A mirror. Perhaps he should also install one in his bedroom to heighten the tension. That way, he could watch her from all sides at once!

On climbing into the taxi outside Oviedo, Sam had given the driver an address he didn't recognise. In the district of Cañitas, opposite the Hippodromo, the splendid 1920s municipal racecourse, symbol of a more elegant age, now almost entirely taken over by one-armed bandits.

"Where the hell are we going?"

She put a finger on his lips.

"Sssh, you'll see."

He paid off the taxi and found Sam speaking quietly into an interphone. A large, circular door, combining highly polished brass with darkened glass, swung open. She took him by the hand and led the way.

"You've got to be joking. I haven't used one of these places in years," Leandro laughed.

"Can you remember the house rules?"

An extremely pretty girl, under a mountain of blonde hair and not very much else, looked at Leandro, expectantly.

462

"What kind of room can I give you?"

Before he could answer, Sam had stepped in.

"I believe you have one on the second floor, red and black, with lots of mirrors."

"How long for?"

"Till midday," Sam replied unhesitatingly.

"Credit card please."

Leandro watched, fascinated. He stood back, smiling, letting her make the arrangements. Perhaps it couldn't always be the Alvear Palace. She had clearly been here before! Who with? That would have to be for another time.

He'd never been to this one before. The tradition of *hoteles de alojamiento* had never died in Buenos Aires. Since so many young people continued to live with their parents well into their late twenties, even up until the day of their marriage, the youth of the city needed places to go. And by no means only the youth! Most of Argentina's medium-sized provincial towns could boast one or two such places, usually discreetly located a couple of kilometres out of town, a neon sign covered in hearts announcing "Hotel Feeling" or some similarly unsubtle name.

Behind ornate doors, dotted around the city, discreetly located even in its smartest downtown areas, these places flourished on the back of a steady clientele. He remembered, when he worked in the financial district, there had been one almost opposite the window of his office. Young lads from the trading floor of the bank could occasionally be observed slipping through its doors, followed at a discreet distance by one of the prettier secretaries. The lunchtime break over, Leandro would grin to see them returning, separately, flushed with pleasure, exchanging a discreet 'thumbs up' with colleagues. For some reason, he had seen the need to use them only rarely. Elena's parents living in Cordoba had meant that she had a flat to herself.

Sam unlocked the door. With a majestic sweep of her hand, she introduced him to their bed of sin. The room was red - all over. Carpet, walls, ceiling. In the middle, a huge bed, sheets of black satin. Wall mirrors on three sides. The very best of taste!

"I like the feel of this place," Leandro murmured.

"It's the feel of you I'm more interested in," Sam retorted smartly.

"Not so fast, Madam. I need to look at you. You're particularly beautiful tonight."

Having helped her slip out of the hooded cape, he removed his jacket and sat down in the only armchair.

"Just stand there!" he ordered, unbuttoning his shirt.

With a feigned look of submission, Sam placed herself in front of him, booted legs apart, hands on her hips, tossing her hair, rearranging the ample folds of the dress to pull it closer to her body.

"Too beautiful! That dress really suits you. Where did you say it came from?"

"Who cares a shit? You're not interested in my clothes. It's my body you want."

"That's where you're very wrong. However beautiful a woman's body, it's so often made more beautiful by being partly hidden. Maybe all those Vogue magazines taught me that. Not that my imagination can add anything to your existing assets, but...."

"Assets? What am I? Some kind of exotic financial instrument? Reduced to a bottom line? When it's really the line of my bottom that you're interested in."

"Don't spoil it! Don't be vulgar! I repeat, Sam. Those clothes make you very, very sexy. You may think that I'm some kind of insensitive male hedonist, but you're wrong. Sex isn't just about getting it up. Otherwise, we'd still be running around naked. Just think how mysterious a woman can be when covered, think of the days when women used to wear a veil. Even those burqa things. Arab men don't seem to realise that they've made matters far worse for themselves. I'm sure they imagine some beautiful virgin underneath all those folds. But why am I even telling you this? You're the one who went on and on about late

464

Victorian fashions. Women's fashions, as you know, are usually designed by men."

"Most of them gay, by the way!" Sam snorted.

"Perhaps, and what's the matter with that? Gay men are probably best placed to bridge the aesthetic divide between the sexes, the sensual divide. I don't know. Anyway, that's enough verbal foreplay. Come over here, let me touch you, show you what I mean."

He leaned forward and pulled her closer, burying his face in the soft grey folds at the level of her pubis, running one hand down the side of her boot, the other over her hips and up to her breasts. Apart from a tiny triangular *cache sexe*, she was naked beneath the dress. The sensuality of the soft alpaca wool, through which he could detect the firm contours of her body, reverberated through his nervous system. He felt his penis swell.

Sam's skin responded instantly to the combined quest of his hands and the caress of the alpaca. Throughout the dinner, she had struggled to conceal an almost constant state of low arousal, yet finding ways unobtrusively to stimulate the soft caress of the wool over her skin. Funny that Leandro hadn't noticed... or perhaps he had! The waiting was over.

With one hand, she pressed his face harder against her, down towards her sex. Then with both hands, she lifted the loose hem and stretched the dress over his head. His lips skimmed her labia, as the little triangle of silk slipped down her thighs. His tongue sought and found the entrance. Placing his hands on her buttocks, he drew her closer.

"Yes, oh yes. That's it, go on! Please, please, strip me, I want you inside me. Don't make me wait any longer. All evening...," her voice merged into a low moan.

In a single, smooth movement, he pulled the dress up over her head and wrapped its folds round her up-stretched arms. He picked her up and carried her to the huge, round bed, with its black satin sheets and drapes. A part of him made a mental note not to be seen dead in them.

In Pasaje La Piedad, two figures quietly closed the front door of Leandro's building and made their way back to the wrought iron gates giving onto the street. They had had all evening to get the job done.

Leandro turned over the latest offerings in the political section of the Cuspide bookshop at the entrance to the Village cinema complex, across the road from Recoleta cemetery. He remembered his last visit, with Dávila's followers in tow. This time he appeared to be on his own. Even though Cristina Kirchner had only been running the country for little more than the proverbial hundred days, a couple of books had already emerged, attempting to draw a line under the period of her husband's presidency and to assess what the future might hold, now that a woman was in charge. Speculation had been rife even before the election about the balance of her mind and emotions, references being made to bipolarity and violent emotional swings. It was too early to tell and he saw little point in throwing away money to get some half-baked theories. He looked around for any book by Oriana Fallaci, but was told they were out of stock.

Sam was late, the film due to begin in ten minutes. Punctuality was not necessarily Sam's strong suit. He could always leave the ticket for her at the counter, it wouldn't be the first time. With numbered seats, she'd find him. After a few minutes, he walked back to the ticket desk and handed one of the girls a ticket, with her name printed clearly on the back. Then, switching off his cell phone, he went into the auditorium. The film hadn't started, just the usual adverts and trailers. Ten minutes later, the main film began. Still no sign of Sam.

Two hours later, he emerged onto the pavement. It had started to rain. He switched on his cell phone. No text messages. Hoping the rain would stop, he took a table inside one of the pizzerias located next to the cinema and sent Sam a text message to tell her where he was. He ordered a *quattro stagioni* and a glass of red wine. Maybe so much cheese wasn't ideal for his cholesterol, but what the hell. He placed his cell phone on the table in front of him. The restaurant was full, thanks to a number of the film theatres emptying around the same time. The rain had ensured that nobody had gone very far for a meal. Eating alone was one of the things he hated most and he regretted not having picked up a book when he had had the chance. By about midnight, with still no sign of Sam, he paid the bill and since it was still lightly raining, called up his usual taxi company to send a car. Their number was engaged, the same with two of the other companies he tried. He would have to walk home. At a brisk pace, avoiding the puddles and loose paving stones which the Municipality's poor maintenance had turned into an obstacle course, he got there in under half an hour. His jacket was soaked, but since the evening had been warm, there was little cause for concern.

As he stepped into his drawing room, he could see the light flashing on his answering machine. He listened to the tape. Three calls from Lamai, the panic in her voice more evident with each call. Something had happened to Sam, could he call back as soon as possible? The last call had been made only five minutes before he arrived, so he had no hesitation in calling back.

She picked up at once, but her words were so garbled by panic that he finally gave up and promised to get round to Sam's flat straight away. This time the cab company answered immediately and within five minutes, having slipped the Bersa into the pocket of his coat, he was on his way to Puerto Madero. He failed to spot the black Renault which settled down behind the taxi, at a distance of about half a block, given the empty streets at this time of night.

The promise of a large tip, combined with the efficiency of the tidal flow traffic light system, ensured he was pulling up outside Sam's ultra-modern apartment block in less than ten minutes. The Renault had broken off on reaching the last corner.

Lamai must have been watching for his arrival, as the main door slid open before he had even touched the buzzer. The night watchman, disconcerted at first by Leandro's dishevelled appearance, finally let him through. Within minutes, he was holding a sobbing, hysterical Lamai in his arms to calm her down. Settling her into an armchair, he went to the kitchen and found some brandy, which he poured into a small glass, knowing that she never drank alcohol. The shock of the drink, after an initial coughing fit, finally did its work. Lamai sat there, now only the occasional sob passing her lips.

"Start at the beginning. What happened? Slowly, don't rush it, Lamai."

He had also poured himself a brandy, sensing that he was going to need it.

Lamai finally controlled her sobbing. She went to the bathroom and came back after a few minutes, looking as though she had put her face under the tap. Her long hair was wet and there were damp patches on her dress.

"I apologise, Leandro, please forgive me. I will tell you all I know."

Leandro made a gesture to indicate that he quite understood. It would probably be better to allow her to tell her story in her own time, rather than bombarding her with questions.

"Go ahead, take your time. Just one question. Have you told the police?"

"No, not yet. Sam always told me I should ring you first."

"Good, well done."

In her at times hesitant Spanish, Lamai began to tell what had happened.

They had been out shopping late that afternoon, in the Galería Pacifico, the shopping mall on Florida. It had been crowded. Suddenly, Sam had caught sight of someone, or something. She had told Lamai to step away from her and to watch what happened from another one of the counters. After a couple of minutes, two men had appeared and started talking to Sam.

"They looked very nasty, not *simpatico*. It looked as if arguing. Then they got on each side and began to walk her towards the door. Sam didn't protest, but some of the people near her, they begin to react. One of the two men produced *credencial*, as if a policeman. The people calm down. One of the men looked towards me, but I hid behind a counter."

From there, Lamai had watched as they took her downstairs to the street.

"I followed after a minute. Doorman told me that a black car pick them up and they drive along Cordoba towards 9 de Julio. I came back here. Maybe somebody was here, some things perhaps have been moved. I can't tell if anything missing."

"So what time did this happen exactly?"

469

"About eight thirty this evening. I get back here at nine, tried to ring you. But your cell phone not answering. I'm so sorry. And I'm so afraid."

She began to sob again. He moved over and, sitting beside her on the couch, put his arm around her shoulders.

"Don't worry, we'll get Sam back."

It appeared to calm her a little.

He got up and walked over to the window. The two men in the car watched him. One spoke into his cell phone.

The blindfold was removed from her face. The glare of the two neon strips on the ceiling was excruciatingly painful. With her hands cuffed behind her back, Sam could do nothing except close her eyes and hope that the ache would slowly pass. One of the two men standing beside her grabbed her above the elbow, pressing cruelly.

"Lie down, over there, on the mattress!"

Keeping her eyelids screwed almost shut, she tried to see what he meant.

"Over there, *puta!*"

He pushed her brutally so that she fell forward onto the thin mattress laid out on the concrete floor in a corner of the room. She felt a searing pain in her shoulder as it hit the ground, taking the full weight of her body. She rolled into a ball, just in case he might follow up with a kick. Although she could hear him breathing heavily, she guessed he must have stayed in the middle of the room. Slowly she opened her eyes. The glare had lessened. She could make out the silhouette of two men, standing in front of her, their hands in their pockets, black against the overhead light.

As best she could, she tried to sit up and look around. The room was not very large, with two doors and no windows. From the smell, she suspected that one door gave onto some kind of bathroom or toilet. The other door had remained open and she could see into another room and beyond that, a door apparently giving out into the darkness. The fresh scent of the *campo*, of grass and eucalyptus trees, filtered through.

She had no idea of the time, but suspected that nearly four hours had elapsed since her abduction in Galería Pacifico. An initial attempt to try and keep track of what direction they were going had rapidly been abandoned. Quite early on, she thought that she had heard the noise of an aircraft, which might suggest that they had gone past Aeroparque. An image of her first afternoon with Leandro at a nearby restaurant

471

had flashed into her mind. It seemed very long ago. Then progressively, she lost track. The noise of heavy traffic and the slow crawling pace of the car might suggest that they had been following the General Paz ring-road round Buenos Aires. After that, she had resigned herself to not having any idea where they were taking her. Only the length of the journey indicated that they must have left the suburbs of the capital and moved out into open country. Long straight stretches, with only the rush and slipstream of oncoming traffic, mainly lorries, for at least a couple of hours, indicated that they might perhaps be within a radius of two hundred kilometres of the city. The final, bumpy section had probably not been longer than twenty minutes, so the *campo* in which she now found herself might not be much farther than ten kilometres from paved asphalt. Beyond that, she had no idea. In a country the size of Argentina, she could be anywhere.

Only Lamai at this moment in time would know of her disappearance. She would certainly have the sense to ring Leandro. Where would they take it from there? In the first moments when they had grabbed her, she had been able to get a look at their faces, but had recognised no-one. Who were her kidnappers? Who were they working for? Dávila was an obvious possibility. But conventional kidnap was also good business in Argentina. These and a host of other possibilities had been flashing through her mind all the way along. She was tired, confused. Sleep was what she most wanted.

One of the two men bent down and unlocked the handcuff on one wrist, which he then pulled, with little regard for the pain he was causing, to place it on the bottom pipe of a radiator set on the wall. Sam had little choice but to allow herself to be dragged across the mattress.

With that, the two men turned and, switching off the light, left her in total darkness. She heard the sound of a padlock being fixed to the other side of the door. She began to sob. Her body ached all over, not made any more bearable by the fact that she was now ravenously hungry, not having eaten anything since lunchtime. It must be well past midnight. From exhaustion and nervous tension, she finally fell into a fitful sleep.

At six next morning, Leandro was dialling the number of Carla's house in Zürich. Given the circumstances, he had decided soon after arrival from Zürich to buy a couple of payphones, on one of which he was now making the call. It would be late morning there. A soft feminine voice, clearly an answerphone, indicated that the caller should leave a message. The message was in English, German and French. He cursed inwardly, before leaving a brief message to the effect that Frau Bodmer should ring Leandro Flemming in Buenos Aires as soon as possible. He knew that the name would immediately register with Carla. As it did within half an hour.

"Hello, is that Leandro?" The voice was rich, alluring, low-pitched. The *porteño* accent was impeccable, although embellished with just a hint of something else, maybe German? In some strange way, it sent a tingling feeling through him, this first occasion of direct contact with the woman who had come to figure so dramatically in his, and in Sam's, life.

"Yes, is that Carla?"

"Yes, at last we meet, even if only courtesy of a phone company."

There was a soft laugh at the other end.

"Carla, Sam has disappeared. Last night. She was taken away by some men in the Galería Pacifico, when she was out shopping. I only heard about it at around midnight."

He detected a sharp sucking in of breath at the other end. Then silence.

"Are you still there?"

"Yes, I was thinking. This is bad, very bad. Have you any idea who it might be? Could it be a simple ransom, given the fact that Sam's father is very rich?"

"It could be, but somehow, I rather doubt it."

"So do I. I think it's more complicated than that. Much more complicated. Have you gone to the police?"

"Not yet, only too often they're the ones doing the kidnapping down here. And usually, as soon as the kidnappers find out, the victim disappears completely. Unless of course you have any reason to believe that we should?"

"No, that's absolutely right. Do nothing for the moment, the longer we have to try and discover what has happened, the better."

Leandro was struck by the use of the word 'we'. A level of complicity which he had not expected. And yet, they had something very much in common. Sam was important to both of them, each in their own way loved the girl. Until that moment, it had simply not struck him quite that way.

Again there was a silence at the other end of the line. Then Carla came back on.

"Give me a few hours. I'll ring you later today. Don't worry, we'll get her back."

There was a click at the other end and the line went silent. Again the 'we'.

With no idea of the time, she was awakened by the sound of the padlock being removed. The door opened and through it, she caught a glimpse of sunlight on the other side of the far entrance door. Only one tree was visible in the garden and, from the length of the shadow, she suspected that it might be near noon.

The man who came in was neither of the two from the previous night. So now at least three different men were involved. Sam attempted to sit up as best she could, leveraging herself against the hard bars of the radiator.

"So, how was the night?"

She was surprised by the solicitous question. They actually cared?

"What do you think?" she replied sharply.

"We ask the questions, not you!"

The man turned towards the door, through which Sam could make out the figure of a woman.

"Señora, bring in her food!"

So at least they were going to feed her.

"Put the tray down next to her!"

The woman, in her late forties, portly, clearly of the *campo* judging by the rough patina of her skin, walked awkwardly towards her, carrying a tray. From the look on her face, Sam detected that she was unhappy with what she saw. She put down the tray and stepped back quickly, almost as if she was afraid that Sam would bite her.

"You can go now!"

Sam surveyed what had been brought to her. A small bottle of mineral water, something which looked like vegetable soup and a plate containing a steak, which had been cut up into small cubes, and mashed potatoes. Perhaps she wasn't going to die of hunger after all. She held up the hand which was bolted to the radiator. Only a spoon had been provided. They were clearly not taking any chances!

"Please. I can't eat with only one hand."

The man hesitated.

"You can manage with the spoon!"

She shrugged her shoulders. She was too hungry to fight over this. With her free hand, she managed to manoeuvre the tray onto her lap and set about the food. Not exactly cordon bleu, but she reflected, the way she felt, she couldn't care a damn.

The man had left, padlocking the door again as he went out. About an hour later, he was back.

"Toilet?"

She was dying for it. She nodded her head vigorously.

He bent down, undid the handcuff and led her through the other door in the room. The bathroom was larger than she had expected, almost formal. An old ball and claw cast iron and white enamel bath, long and deep, the way they used to make baths at the turn of the century, stood along one side. A basin, chipped enamel with stained brass taps, hanging off the wall and a toilet with no seat. Manufactured in England in the late nineteenth century. Probably hauled to the *campo* from the nearest railhead by cart when the house was built.

The place wouldn't make a star in the Michelin. She was surprised at her own capacity for sick humour, given her circumstances. She remembered Leandro once saying that it was their sense of humour which had enabled the English to survive in so many desperate situations. As far as she knew, she hadn't a drop of English blood. So maybe it wasn't just the English.

She put her hand on the door handle, but sensed that the guard intended to stop her closing it. She turned round and stared him down, no trace of pleading in her eyes. It seemed to impress him, as he let go of the door and allowed her to close it. They weren't all complete shits, determined to humiliate her at every turn. She suspected that it would vary from one guard to the next. Time would tell.

Having come off the phone with Carla, Leandro had taken a shower and then gone off to London City to get some breakfast. Not for the first time, he failed to spot two men following him at a discreet distance, one of whom settled down at the bar. It was still relatively early in the morning and the cafe was only beginning to fill up, mainly with people on their way to work, stopping in for a quick coffee and some *medialunas*. Not the regular sedentary, newspaper-reading crowd that would fill it up from about ten thirty onwards. He found a table in the corner. He didn't usually smoke, but this morning he felt an overwhelming need. After a second coffee, he pulled out a notebook and tried to jot down some ideas. He was interrupted by a call from his partner, asking if he had been able to draft part of the report which they wanted to send out later that week. Conscious of the fact that everything must appear as normal as possible, he replied noncommittally that the text would get to him in plenty of time.

His pen hovered over the paper. That Sam had been taken by Dávila seemed to be the only conclusion, the same to which Carla also appeared to have arrived independently. Why? Most likely only Carla could provide the answer. The persistent escalation of Sam's presence in the Carla scenario would presumably not have gone unnoticed by Dávila. The followers in Punta del Este, the microphone in Zürich, and perhaps many other activities, which he could only suspect. Perhaps tapping his phone or his emails, certainly following him here in Buenos Aires. These were all sensors feeding into the Dávila network. Right at the start, Leandro had been keen to protect Eduardo. Between September and his trip to Zürich, the plot had become infinitely more complex, more dangerous, not only for Eduardo but progressively also for him and for Sam. Sarmiento's message had been clear. A dangerous, uncontrolled force, though perhaps small, was at work in the current system. It was no secret that the present government was using Argentina's intelligence services, SIDE in particular, to spy on and destabilise the opposition, their actions taking many forms. Although the blackmail and murder which made up Dávila's *modus operandi* might be just a sideshow in the broader scenario, two things could not be ruled out. One, Dávila's access to information and to methods which few would suspect or even question. Secondly, the possibility that, perhaps for reasons of desperation which they could not yet decipher, Dávila had moved into a more proactive, more dangerous mode. The killing of Williams, of Sosa, and now the probable kidnapping of Sam, these might all be signs that something, or somebody, perhaps even Sam and Leandro through their interest in Carla, were forcing Dávila to take direct action. Having to confront a person as complex and vicious as Dávila was not a reassuring prospect.

Leaving aside the highly unpleasant ramifications of this analysis, he realised that there were other factors to be taken into consideration, human, less dramatic, but which nevertheless required attention. Sam's father, for instance. He knew that they were close, with Sam usually finding a way to ring him every couple of days. Given her unpredictable sense of adventure, there would no doubt be occasions when more than a couple of days would go by, but even so, he could hardly be left in the dark a minute longer than necessary. But how long was necessary? And if it all turned out to be a classic ransom situation, it was even possible that the kidnappers were already in touch with him. Indeed, given Dávila's devious mind, they might even do both.

Any way he looked at it, the level of danger had suddenly moved from amber to red. Which meant, amongst other things, that he could expect to be under heightened surveillance, and probably Eduardo also. He looked around the cafe, his gaze passing harmlessly over the man at the bar, engrossed in a copy of that morning's Clarín. Solitary men made up the bulk of the clientele at this hour. He kicked himself for not having been more consistent since his return in checking whether in fact he was being watched. He wouldn't make a very good spy. He was in the wrong game.

He needed to speak to Eduardo, but to be careful how this was done. He rang Florencia, hoping that they would not have got round to tapping her phone. Given the difficulty of concealing his identity, he rang on his own phone, using the pretext of trying to fix up an *asado* for the weekend and asking her to get Eduardo to ring him as soon as possible to finalise the details. Although this was one of numerous ways they had agreed to communicate before Christmas, he hoped that the signal would still work.

What to do about Sam's father? Whichever way he looked at it, he had to make contact sooner rather than later, which meant in the next couple of hours. It wasn't going to be easy, given the fact that, in spite of going out with Sam for nearly a year, they had still not met. He did however have the address and telephone number of her father's offices. He could not rule out the possibility that Dávila might even have taken things to the extreme of putting her father under surveillance. Leandro needed somehow to look at the situation from the point of view of someone who had no reason to suspect that Sam's kidnap was anything other than a possible ransom situation. Assuming that Dávila was well aware of his relationship with Sam, wouldn't it be normal for Leandro to get in touch with her father? What interpretation could be placed on such a move, other than an innocent one? If he was being followed, or his phone tapped, making contact with the father would not appear out of place. If he wasn't being followed, or having his calls listened to, then what the hell? It made no difference.

He picked up his cell phone and dialled her father's office number, a number Sam had once given him, asking him to look after her father in just such circumstances as these.

Half an hour later, he was sitting across a low table from her father, a couple of glasses of mint tea steaming between them. The office was sparse, though the quality of the furniture definitely upmarket. Some beautifully framed examples of Arabic calligraphy, no doubt phrases from the Koran or the *suras*, adorned the walls. Her father looked rather older than he had expected. Sam was no doubt the cause of some of those grey hairs.

"Señor Flemming, I am pleased finally to meet you."

It seemed to be a day for closing links.

"So am I, Señor Haidar, I feel bad that we've never met before."

"Given how important you are to my daughter, I would agree."

The response was in no way aggressive, rather kindly, the gaze steady, the older man exuding a certain Oriental tranquillity. He was going to need all of it!

Leandro momentarily regretted that he had not shaved that morning. It was clear that her father was a man who paid attention to appearances, the old school. He remembered Sam's remark about well-polished shoes being the hallmark of a certain generation of Argentines. Her father's positively glistened.

In the taxi, Leandro had tried to work out just how much he would tell her father. To take him all the way through the story, starting with the hotel murder, was clearly out of the question. He had to assume that Sam kept most of her activities to herself, whether on the emotional or sexual front, and very probably, indeed certainly, on the professional. At the same time, he would have to find a reason to ensure that Señor Haidar didn't just pick up the phone and call the police. He and Carla needed time. Time to try and establish whether their suspicions over the involvement of Dávila were well founded. He was confident that Carla would come back with an answer to that question. If Dávila was not involved, then presumably the situation became less complex, even if no less dangerous and potentially tragic.

"Señor Haidar, have you heard from your daughter in the last twenty-four hours?" A low-key opening question, albeit loaded.

"No, I heard from her a couple of days ago. But presumably you will have seen her since then? Why?"

A look of concern was slowly spreading over the older man's face.

"No, I also saw her a couple of days ago, but since yesterday afternoon, her phone hasn't answered."

"That would not be the first time, I'm sure, knowing my daughter. So, why are you here? Should I be worried? The fact that you have chosen to come and see me by yourself is hardly reassuring."

The old man was right, of course.

"It's just that..." Leandro hesitated, before going on. "It's just that, she was supposed to meet me at the cinema yesterday evening. She never arrived. I've tried ringing her flat, without success and her cell phone is not replying, or even taking a message. It's not like her to disappear quite so completely."

He wasn't sure that all this sounded very convincing, but it was the best he could produce on the spur of the moment, and, fortunately, close to the truth. Bringing in Lamai might only confuse the issue, he had no idea how much her father knew about that side of Sam's personality. Señor Haidar produced an answer to that question almost immediately.

"We can ring her flat, she has an Asian girl with whom she shares. I wasn't very much in favour at the beginning, but it seems to ensure that the place is looked after. Particularly when Samira disappears off to Europe, as she did in January. But I'm sure you knew that anyway."

Leandro could see that he was concerned, but also that he was seeking more reassuring solutions to the problem. Best to reinforce that for the time being.

"I'm sure you're right. I must have rung when the Asian girl was out. I will try again."

"We can try now."

Leandro dreaded what Lamai's reaction might be. He had stupidly forgotten to warn her.

"Why don't you try, Dr Flemming, I sometimes find it difficult to understand what the girl says. I suspect my hearing isn't what it used to be. It comes to us all."

A stroke of luck.

"May I use your phone?"

Her father passed the cordless receiver to him. He dialled the number.

Lamai picked up and Leandro immediately began talking, in an attempt to ensure that she didn't throw another fit of hysterics, which the father might hear. He quickly explained that he was with Sam's father and that they would continue to try and track her down. He detected that Lamai was confused by the lack of drama in what he was saying and could hear her beginning to protest.

"But, what about last night? They took her away. Have you told her father?"

"No, not yet, we must wait. Anyway, Lamai, I'll ring you back later. *Hasta luego.*"

He hoped that the side of the conversation to which Señor Haidar had been listening could be interpreted in a number of ways. He handed back the phone.

"She has not heard anything. She wanted to know if I had."

The father nodded.

"I'm a bit old to be chasing my daughter around the globe. Perhaps, now that we have met, I may ask you the favour to keep me informed. I should probably worry more, but Sam has taught me over the years that worrying only makes me grow older. And I can afford that less and less."

He smiled and Leandro smiled back.

"Of course, I will ring you later today. Here is my cell phone number, please ring me any time you feel like it. I'm sure there's nothing serious."

He hoped the look on his face conveyed more conviction than he felt inside. He stood up and walked over to a bookshelf on which stood a row of small silver trophies.

"Your golf must be very good, Señor Haidar. Very impressive!"

Her father rose carefully and joined him.

"Those were better days. Now I just about get round," the older man adding as an afterthought, "I sometimes wish I had been able to get Samira to play. It teaches humility."

Leandro smiled. Sam. Humility?

They shook hands.

"Again, Leandro... may I call you Leandro? I'm very pleased to have met you finally."

"It's an honour, Señor. We will speak later."

Down on the pavement, he breathed deeply. It could have been worse, but it would never be much more than a holding operation. He found a text message from Eduardo to call him back.

The man behind the wheel of the decoy black and yellow taxi, parked on the other side of the street with its red '*Libre*' light extinguished, made a note of the time. He picked up his cell phone.

"He's just been to see the father."

Someone was tapping on the passenger window. To the driver's horror, he realised that it was Leandro, who had crossed the street, trying to see if the taxi was free.

"*No, no!*" he shouted through the closed window. Leandro walked away. Taxi drivers were losing their manners. Not so surprising, given the widespread posture of gratuitous rudeness regularly transmitted by members of this Government!

Leandro's cell phone began to ring. An international call. After two thirty in the afternoon, presumably Carla.

"Leandro? It's Carla. I've been doing some checking, made some phone calls. I'm pretty sure now that it's Dávila who's taken Sam. For one thing, he's not picking up on my calls, when he usually answers immediately. Secondly, I've received a mysterious email, almost certainly from him, looking like a collage from newspapers, cuttings about kidnaps. He has that kind of a sense of humour. I also spoke to one of his bodyguards who used to be here in Zürich, and he was most evasive when I started to talk about Sam. So I think we can assume that that's what happened. Think I also know why he may have done it just at this point. He knows that by harming Sam, he's hitting at me. I know this isn't easy for you to listen to, and one day no doubt Sam will make things clearer."

"It's alright, she already has, partly," Leandro interrupted. "Anyway, that's the least of my concerns. Probably of yours too. More important, what do we do now? By the way, I've been to see her father. For the time being, he just believes that she may have gone off to do her own thing, it wouldn't be the first time. But clearly that story won't hold up forever."

He could hear Carla breathing softly, presumably thinking.

"I've been able to make certain moves already, which, if they work out, should provide a solution. However, I have to confirm a number of things, one of which is where he may be holding Sam. There are three possible places he's most likely to use. Some place in Buenos Aires, although I think that's the least likely, since it's far too visible. Then there's his house in the Delta. That's a possibility. Finally his farm out beyond Chacabuco. I've only been there once, I might be able to get through to the manager or his wife. She's a poor thing, they have a daughter who's not well, and I think they're terrified of Dávila. Who knows, she might give something away. But whatever happens, I will need at least another twenty-four hours to try and establish exactly

485

where he may be holding her. Only when we know that, can we work out the next steps."

"What can I do at this end?"

"For the time being, Leandro, probably not very much. If we're wrong and it's just a criminal kidnap, no doubt her father will be hearing soon. But, as I say, I don't think that's the case. This is my old friend Dávila trying to settle a score with me. And I know what that score is. So you'll just have to be patient, Leandro. And courageous. *Abrazo.*"

With which, she rang off.

Leandro stared impatiently at his phone. He didn't much like the reference to courage. He felt powerless, never a pleasant feeling. Should he call Eduardo back? His first instinct had been to find someone to plan the next moves. But, on reflection, it might merely bring his godson back into the spotlight, get Dávila to focus on him again, when all along, one of the main objectives had been to avoid just that. He decided against it. If Eduardo now rang him again, he'd stick to the story of the *asado*. The day Eduardo found out, he'd justifiably be furious, but he'd just have to deal with that when it happened.

Some 11,000 kilometres away, Carla dialled a St. Petersburg number.

"*Dobry dien.* Good day. Is that Svetlana Mikhailova? How are you? It's Carla Bodmer from Zürich. Fine, thank you. Please put me through to Victor Alexievich."

Time passed with no sense of time. In fact, three days had passed since her kidnap. Nothing had been said or done to indicate who her kidnappers might be, for whom they might be working. No attempt had been made to get any name out of her to be contacted, which suggested that they either already had that information, or that ransom was not the main purpose. A lot pointed in the direction of Dávila.

Thanks to the glimpse of the outside world which was afforded every time someone came to see her, and, following the sequence of the meals brought to her by the woman, she calculated that a couple of days had gone by when the routine imperceptibly changed. She had finished her lunch, the tray had been taken away, but this time the woman came back armed with a broom with which she proceeded to sweep around the room in which Sam lay. The guard also appeared a bit more nervous, occasionally casting a glance through the open doors.

"You'll have a visitor," the woman whispered when the guard's back was momentarily turned. "*El patron* is coming."

Sometime later, the most brutal of her guards appeared. By now, she had worked out that his name was Ramon. He first went into the bathroom and she could hear the bath begin to be filled. Was she finally to be given a chance to wash? All this in honour of the *patron*?

He came back into her room and released Sam from the handcuff to the radiator pipe, making her stand up in a corner. It was almost the first time, apart from her daily trips to the toilet, that she had been allowed to stand. He kicked the mattress away and placed a metal rotating stool in front of the radiator. He pulled her over and made her sit down and, stretching her arms behind her, handcuffed a wrist to each end of the radiator. The position was extremely unpleasant, since it pulled her shoulders as far back as they could go. Without warning, he produced what appeared to be a small black sack from his pocket, which she rapidly recognised as being some kind of thin rubber hood. With both hands, he stretched the opening as far as it would go and pulled it over her head. She immediately began to scream, but he paid little attention.

Pulling it roughly down on all sides of her head and face, he finally had it in position. She realised that the hood was fitted with a single hole aligned with her mouth, through which she gulped in air. All vision blotted out. Her screaming was rewarded with a backhand across the mouth.

"Shut up, bitch!"

The panic would not subside, although she knew that to give way to it would serve no purpose. Images of what had been done to the Englishwoman in the hotel flooded into her mind. Was this the way they killed every woman? Her brain in overdrive, she calmed down slightly, seeking evidence of a connection between the hotel murder and what was happening to her now. Were these the same people? Given the fact that she and Leandro and Eduardo had been on their trail for more than six months, and had finally identified them all, it obviously couldn't be ruled out. In fact, it would be better to assume it. The methods used were becoming familiar. Dávila's signature!

She sat still, in complete blackness, her arms and back beginning to ache excruciatingly. She sensed Ramon leaving. How long was she going to be left like this?

Time passed. She had no way of telling how long. Then she heard the door being opened. From the low murmur of voices, at least two people had come into the room. She sensed someone standing over her. Not a word was said. Then the sound of a chair being pulled up in front of her. A hand caught the top of her blouse and tore it open. Suddenly, a sharp point pricked the skin between her breasts, then moved up and pulled sharply away. She stifled a scream. The clasp of her bra had been cut, releasing her breasts.

A hand touched her, advanced to caress the underside of one breast, then moved up towards her throat. Fingertips touched the other breast. She began to shake uncontrollably. This soft intrusion was almost worse than any brutality.

As the hands, strangely soft, almost feminine, continued their caress, her head was brutally pulled backwards and a hand placed over her mouth, closing off her air. She rolled her head in every direction, but to no avail. The hand remained firmly clamped over her lower face. She tried to bite at it. Finally she screamed. She heard the scream dying away before the hand was finally removed. She sucked in a lungful of air, panting, retching.

The hands continued to caress her. Again, her mouth was covered. There had been no warning and she had had no time to take a breath. Her chest heaved, desperate for oxygen. This time, the release came faster.

Suddenly, the handcuffs were released and she was pulled to her feet. Hands unceremoniously stripped her. Her blouse torn off completely, her jeans pulled down to her ankles and over her bare feet. She stood there, arms by her sides, unseeing, trembling not only from fear, but now also from the cold. Still, not a word had been spoken.

Dávila surveyed her. Even in her present state, he could see that she was far more beautiful than the videos suggested. No wonder Carla had fallen for her. Large perfectly-formed breasts overhanging a narrow waist which then swept out to her hips. Athletic. Carla had what he knew was referred to as an 'hour glass' figure. Here was another one! An image of the two interlocked in the sauna flashed before his eyes.

He sat down on the stool in front of her and leaned forward.

Sam suddenly felt fingers entering her vagina. Desperately she tried to clamp her legs together, but too late. The fingers slid in and out, slowly, then gradually picking up speed. Then a soft voice broke into the sound of her breathing.

"So, Samira, we finally meet."

Dávila!

"Tell me, Sam – isn't that what Carla calls you? Tell me. Why are you here? Why are you with Carla? My Carla."

The fingers drove on remorselessly.

"You love her? Probably. Many women do. But there's more to it than that. Isn't there? Tell me."

The sensory isolation of the hood over her face and the rhythmic intrusions into her genitals dominated her consciousness, confused her thinking. Had Dávila discovered the reasons for her initial contact with

Carla? What did he already know? In her confused state, the simplest solution lay in silence.

Her vagina was beginning to swell and an ever-sharper pain to dominate her thoughts.

"You want to be brave? Why bother? We can do so much worse to you."

The fingers were withdrawn, with just a lingering twist. Her wrists were brutally pulled behind her back and strip tied. Strapped at ankles and knees, her legs were locked together. Blind, dizzy, she began to topple over. Two pairs of hands caught her, one around the waist, the other below the knees, lifting her bodily off the ground. She felt herself being carried into the next-door room.

For a moment, she was suspended. Then, on a murmured instruction from Dávila, she was plunged into the ice-cold water of the bath. She heard the water cascade over the sides, full to the brim. Unable to stabilise herself, pinioned, she struggled to keep her head above the water, dragging in lungfuls of air, her weight pulling her repeatedly below the surface. God, was she now to be drowned? Was this to be the famous 'submarino', a common form of water torture used by the dictatorship? Was there no limit to the horror they could dream up?

As they held her mouth just on the surface, the relentless questions began once more. In the brief moments above the level of the bathwater, Dávila's soft voice would fill her consciousness.

"Come on, Sam, tell me. It's not just the love of Carla. It's more. What is it? What do you and Flemming want? And this Subinspector Falcioni? He's part of it, isn't he? Tell me and all this will be over."

Dávila orchestrated Sam's macabre ballet of alternately being pushed and held below the water until her lungs, bursting, expelled what air she had been able to grasp, her face then being brought up to just above the surface in the wake of the bubbles. There it would be momentarily held between invisible hands, while through the hole in her hood, she dragged in air, before being once again forced to the bottom of the bath. And every time, his questions reverberating in her ears, the sound dampened by the hood and the swirl of the water.

She lost any sense of time. It seemed an eternity, a switchback of suffocation alternating with survival. Childhood images of returning, chest bursting, to the surface after a dive too deep in the swimming pool at some friend's house streamed across her mind. Her lungs felt ready to explode. This was breath control with a vengeance.

Suddenly, it all stopped. Again, she was picked up bodily, water pouring off her as she was carried back into the other room. Still naked, the zip-ties were cut off and a wrist shackled once more to the radiator. There was silence. Then the hood was stripped off her head.

The neon lights blinded her. She raised her head.

Almost with a sense of relief, she recognized the man sitting on the stool in front of her. It was Dávila! Although they had never met, she had seen one or two photographs of him in the company of Carla, both in Punta del Este and in Zürich. Now that she saw him in the flesh, she realised that he was the man she had seen in the company of Carla at the party at which they had first met before the polo finals.

He smiled gently.

"So, Samira, now you see me. I've waited a long time. I've observed you often before. In the flesh, you're more beautiful than I thought. But very obstinate. So obstinate. What a shame."

For once, Sam simply could not find the words. She could only shake her head in disbelief. Her relationship with Carla flashed through her mind, like a film in fast forward. But this final sequence seemed to belong elsewhere, following a logic which she had never properly foreseen. Had her fascination with Carla blinded her to this risk?

He was talking to her again.

"I'm sorry, if you feel that you've become a pawn in in my relationship with Carla. Which is true. You have, perhaps through no fault of your own. The ironies of life. For reasons beyond your comprehension, I need you. I need you like this!"

He stretched out a hand to her breast. She pulled away in disgust, but, with her back against the radiator, there was no escape. His hand, soft, delicate, cupped her breast, stroked her nipple. All the while, he held her gaze steady. She thought she was going to throw up. Looking over

Dávila's shoulder, she caught sight of Cacho fiddling with a video camera. And all this had been filmed! Always the same routine.

He studied her reactions, his face betraying no emotion, the same little smile playing over his lips. She remembered what Carla had said about the way he got his kicks. She remained frozen. Show no fear.

Suddenly, Dávila seemed to lose interest.

"For once, I'll go no farther. I need you like this. Alive. Anyway, I don't really need your answers. I already have them."

Perhaps her lack of response had been a disappointment to him. Yet he seemed not to have been looking for a fight, a pretext for violence. She looked down at the floor, her breath slowing. Whatever he might have been expecting, she wasn't going to give him the satisfaction. He seemed to sense it and got up.

Turning to Cacho, he took the diskette. Without a word, or even a sideways glance at Sam, he left the room, followed by the two bodyguards. The lights were switched off and the door closed once more.

Sam slumped forward as far as her handcuff would allow, every ounce of energy and strength drained from her. She began to shake uncontrollably. She was freezing, as the water evaporated on her body in the cold air of the room.

What had he meant when he said he already had the answers?

Nearly a week had gone by following Sam's disappearance.

Two days after Leandro's last conversation with her, having heard nothing, he had rung Carla again. She had been in touch with the farm and had spoken to the manager's wife. The woman had apparently sounded terrified, replying evasively to Carla's enquiries. Carla had come away now more convinced than ever that Sam was being held there. Leandro had suggested that he speak with the police, determined nevertheless to keep his relationship with Eduardo out of the picture. She had immediately reacted against the idea.

"Be clear, Leandro, if she is in the hands of Dávila - and I am convinced that she is - any move in the direction of the police will immediately be detected by him. He occupies a central position from which he can control and observe everything going on around him. He will already have every antenna out, to try and see what anyone is planning. The police are not the answer. We have to find other ways." She had gone silent for a moment. "Forgive me, I must hang up, I can see he's ringing me on my cell phone. If there's anything interesting, I'll ring you back. Be patient."

His phone had rung half an hour later. Carla, her voice clearly much more strained, had news.

"That was Dávila. To tell me to look on an Internet account which only he and I use in exceptional circumstances. I looked at it. The man's a monster. No, that's not the word. I can't find the right word. He has sent me absolute proof that he has her, and that she is at the farm. He sent me a short video. She is alive, but I won't tell you anymore. It wouldn't help, either you, or me, or Sam. We must just focus on the fact that she is alive."

"Good God, who is this man that you are associated with? Tell me, what has he done to her? It's far worse, if you don't tell me."

"It's worse if I do. Please believe me, at this moment, the best you can do is to be patient and make no move. I know that that's an almost impossible instruction for someone like you, but for my sake, for the sake of Sam, please, please, do as I ask. Sadly, you are no-one against Dávila and his machine. I know it - or at least a lot about it – but because I'm so far away, he cannot control what I'm doing. I will get Sam back - for you...," she paused. "... and for me," she added softly. "The wait will not be long. I will be flying down there towards the end of next week. Dávila and I have much to talk about. He's sent me an ultimatum. For that conversation, he needs Sam to be alive. He knows that. He's promised me that. For what it's worth, that's the best guarantee of her safety we have. Please believe me."

Leandro was silent. He had never met this woman and had no particular reason to trust her. Except for the fact that Sam did trust her. He knew that. The more he thought about it, the more he realised that he really had no choice. But somehow, the thought of doing nothing terrified him.

"How do I deal with her father? The poor man, I have to find a way."

"I'm sure you will. Though I doubt that the truth, or even anything like it, is what he needs to hear. I leave that to you. I must go now. Let us speak next week. We'll find her, I know we will. *Abrazo.*"

Again the 'we'. However, in their partnership, he had no doubt that he was very much the junior partner. The way she had spoken had made that clear. Carla was in control, which she liked to be. Where she knew how to be. She wasn't a dominatrix for nothing. He had little doubt that she would play by different rules, rules which he might only begin to imagine, certainly never used.

He needed time to think it through, although he had to confess that he had very little if anything to go on. Her refusal to tell him about Sam terrified him. He had seen Dávila at work, that night in the hotel. He also knew that Dávila, in some ways, had a lot to lose. Not only everything that he had done over the years, as explained by Sarmiento, the killings of Suarez and Sosa, but now also the move against Sam. Carla up until that point appeared to have been an ally. If he had moved against her by taking Sam, that would suggest that he now also saw the danger coming from Carla's direction. And behind Sam, stood Leandro and behind Leandro, Eduardo. Had he made the connections? The surveillance seemed to confirm it. The one piece of information to which he must cling was Carla's statement that Dávila needed Sam alive, not dead. At least, until a meeting with Carla in a week's time.

That week promised to be one of the hardest in his life. Perhaps, it should not also be the hardest for Sam's father. If everything went wrong, there would be plenty of time to try and put the pieces together. But if whatever Carla was planning paid off, the old man need be none the wiser. He picked up his cell phone and told Señor Haidar that he had news. He would be round in a couple of hours. First, he must prepare the ground with Lamai.

It didn't take long to persuade Lamai to stick to the story he was going to tell Sam's father, should he ring her.

Seated once again across the low table, the mint teas steaming, mustering as much conviction as possible, he explained that he had received a satellite phone call from the *altiplano* of northwestern Argentina. Sam had decided to take a break from civilisation and had gone up to Jujuy, where she had hired a 4x4 and set off on her own to see the salt flats and volcanoes of the high altitude deserts, amongst some of the most spectacular anywhere in the world. She would be out of touch for a week or so and no-one was to worry. To Leandro it sounded weak as a story, but the old man appeared satisfied.

"She always did have a fascination for the *altiplano*," was his only comment. "Perhaps reminds her of the deserts of the Middle East."

Leandro had been there once and could well appreciate the fascination. He said so.

"I trust she didn't take her new motorcycle," the old man added.

"Her what?" Leandro gasped.

"Oh, didn't you know? She bought some huge machine a week or so ago, soon after her return from Switzerland. I was totally against it, but that – with Sam – is a guarantee of failure."

That girl really took living on the edge to new heights! Traffic in Buenos Aires, indeed in all of Argentina, was lethal enough without deliberately courting death! Half the courier riders never wore a helmet, as they slalomed through the traffic, or if they did, it was usually perched on the back of the head like a baseball cap. He didn't even want to think of the statistics. Per capita, Argentina had one of the worst casualty records for road accidents in the world. He didn't believe much in the power of prayer, but if Sam came back alive from the present drama, he'd have a word with her about her new steed.

"No, I hadn't heard!" he muttered.

When the old man looked at him quizzically, he repeated his comment, realizing that Señor Haidar might be going a little deaf.

Then he left, promising to ring if he had any further news. He hoped that the next time it would be better.

The Saturday afternoon traffic had slowed them down. Ruta 7 was renowned for its potholes and poor maintenance and overtaking was the nearest thing to Russian roulette.

"Worse than the bloody road to Tula," the driver muttered under his breath. "How are we doing for time?"

"It's six thirty. We should be there in under an hour according to the GPS. You want me to take over?"

"No, it's all right. Just give me a bit more of the coffee, will you?"

Tolya handed him a small plastic mug.

"That's the end of the first thermos, but we've got another couple."

"The sun will begin to go down in about half an hour. We can reconnoitre the place before midnight, then get a few hours' sleep, and hit them before sunrise at seven. We need to be back in Buenos Aires by early evening. It's the time in between that's going to be complicated."

Sergei concentrated on the driving, to keep up the average speed and, most important of all, to ensure that nothing happened which might bring them in contact with the *Gendarmería*. Their almost total absence of Spanish, not to mention of entry stamps into Argentina, would make things very, very difficult to explain.

They had only been in the country about nine hours, having landed discreetly from a powerful motor launch in the early hours of that morning on a beach in Martinez, in the northern suburbs of Buenos Aires. The launch had disappeared back out into the River Plate, and would meet them at a prearranged point near the dockside fruit market in San Fernando at seven pm tomorrow.

As usual, the boss had fixed everything. They were well used to these last-minute assignments. He was so powerful. Sergei had kept a framed copy of the small advertisement, which had appeared two years earlier in a magazine specialising in military and security questions, on the wall of his small flat in the Donskoy district of Moscow. He'd taken the flat because it provided a pleasant view of the old Donskoy Monastery. He was not a believer, but for some reason, the image of the old church had made him feel safer. Somewhere he'd had an irrational sense that this might open a path to redemption for the violence and brutality which had made up so much of his life. He'd answered the advert, not too optimistic about his chances, given the large pool of ex-Spetsnaz operatives already on the market. A series of interviews in the basement of one of Moscow's largest and most modern office blocks had finally led to the offer to join the boss's protection team. Apparently, his rudimentary knowledge of English had been a deciding factor. Like all the other candidates, he knew how to kill and maim, so there wasn't much between any of them. Their training had ensured that. There he had met Tolya.

Thanks to the boss's excellent business connections, it had only taken forty-eight hours to get their Uruguayan entry and Brazilian transit visas. The boss had sent his managing director with a personal letter to the Uruguayan and Brazilian ambassadors in Moscow, requesting special treatment for his two economic analysts to finalise a market study of agribusiness in Uruguay. The Uruguayan ambassador knew full well that agribusiness exports were his country's main, albeit modest, contribution to the balance of trade between their two countries. A balance heavily in favour of Russia, given the importance of petroleum exports to the small, energy-hungry country. The ambassador had personally rung the boss to confirm that the visas would be ready next day. The Brazilian visa had been more of a formality. Svetlana, the boss's very sexy personal assistant, had called Sergei up to her elegant office to collect the two passports, exacting a lightning fuck in the guest toilet from the wiry bodyguard. She fancied most of them, but had something of a soft spot for Sergei.

They had flown out of Sheremetievo airport two days earlier on Aeroflot, discreet paperwork ensuring that the lethal contents of their heavy suitcases, consigned onto the aircraft, would attract minimal attention.

At São Paulo, a senior member of the Russian consulate staff had facilitated their temporary entry into the country, allowing them to board a small chartered aircraft parked in the private section of

Campinas. From there, yesterday morning, they had flown first into a small landing strip in the countryside north of Montevideo to drop off the cases, which had been placed in the boot of a large BMW parked under the massive eucalyptus trees. The driver, a striking looking girl with close-cropped hair, had not said a word. They were not on the ground longer than ten minutes, continuing the flight into Carrasco. The stopover en route would not have shown up in their flight plan, and the delay had been too brief to be noticed. At Carrasco, they had been met by the same large BMW. All they had been able to discover was the girl's name, Naya.

"Sounds Russian," Tolya had commented, hoping to elicit some response, but she had shown little interest in them.

She had taken them to a shabby bar for something to eat in a down-at-heel suburb of the Uruguayan capital, before setting off for a small marina some thirty kilometres east of Colonia. Here the launch had been waiting for them.

The driver of the boat had handed them the keys of the Ford Ranger, explaining through sign language where they would find it once they got off the beach.

They were now approaching Chacabuco, some two hundred kilometres east of Buenos Aires. The flatness of the landscape reminded him of parts of the Ukraine. The main road would swing north-west along the edge of the town, before taking a right angle to the left, to continue Ruta 7's general south-westerly direction. As always, when approaching a major intersection, Tolya scanned the road ahead through his powerful binoculars.

"All clear."

Sergei brought the Ford Ranger XLT double cab down closer to the speed limit usually set at the entrance to every town. Neither too fast, nor too slow. The latter was just as likely to attract attention. They passed the *Gendarmería's* control box by the side of the road. The only policeman visible had his feet up on the table and was clearly taking a post-*asado* siesta.

"Just like our militzia," Sergei growled. "They're the same the world over."

Tolya was switching between the map on his knees and the GPS as they drove along. On his instructions, about ten kilometres beyond Chacabuco, before crossing the river, Sergei took a right turn off the main road in the direction of O'Higgins, a small village of some 1,300 inhabitants. They would have to drive through to get to the farm which lay a further five kilometres north. Skirting the northern side of the town, they drove past the old railway station and a row of large grain silos, before turning north again into the countryside. By now, it was rapidly growing dark. Hopefully the car would not attract too much attention on a weekend evening.

"Take it easy, we're about a kilometre away. In this flat countryside, anyone can see headlights from far away. According to this Google photograph, there should be a small track leading off to the right in about one hundred metres, and, according to the Swiss woman, an empty barn in among the trees."

Sergei turned off the headlamps, running only on sidelights. With the thick cloud of dust coming up off the dirt road, he feared that even this would create a patch of light moving in the distance to anyone who might be on the lookout at the farm.

"I'll drop you at the beginning of the track and you can go and reconnoitre the place. In the meantime, I'll turn round - as if I'd lost my way - and run in the direction of the village on headlights until I get back to the main road. Now that I've been here, I'll be able to come back without any lights."

Tolya got out of the car, taking a carryall off the backseat.

Sergei turned the Ranger on the narrow track and, switching on the headlights again, set off back the way they had come. About fifteen minutes later, he was back, creeping slowly forwards so as not to set up any dust cloud, all lights off. He turned right onto the track and a couple of hundred metres farther on, caught sight of the small beam of Tolya's torch guiding him into a stand of trees which loomed black out of the darkness.

Sergei parked the car between the eucalyptus trees, making sure to switch off the courtesy light before opening the door.

"The farm's over there, they seem to have quite a lot of lights on. Bad for their night vision."

The two men sat with their backs against the car, on the opposite side from the farm, and studied the Google Earth stills and the rough maps which Carla had emailed through to the Moscow office.

"How many people did she reckon might be there?"

Tolya pulled out a small notebook.

"The usual staff is a cook and one house maid for the main house. Then there's the farm manager, his wife and possibly a daughter. They have a separate house, you can see it here on the map, about one hundred metres from the main house. Leaving aside however many guards may now be present, that's it for the area around the main house. Except for the outbuilding where they may be holding the girl. Then there's what the Swiss woman called the *peones*, farm workers. They have living quarters about half a kilometre on the other side of the house. Presume there will be dogs. And need to be careful about horses. They make quite a lot of noise if there's something they don't like at night."

"We could have done with another two or three men. There are bound to be at least two bodyguards, maybe four. I'm not worried about the staff, we can find a way to frighten them enough to stay in their beds. Presumably, at least one, if not two, of the bodyguards will be awake all the time. We've got another couple of hours to try and work out what their routine is. Let's get on with it."

Pulling dark grey matt overalls over their underclothes and slipping on gloves and a light hood over their heads, each man checked through his equipment and began to stow it around his body.

Although the next couple of hours were to be dedicated to reconnaissance, they could not rule out the possibility that something might go wrong and that they would have to launch the attack there and then. In shoulder holsters under one arm, each man slipped a 7.62mm PSS silent pistol, loaded with its special low noise SP-4 ammunition. This Soviet-era handgun was designed so that none of the exploding gases actually left the cartridge when fired. On their thigh, an 8-round 9x18mm Makarov, the AK-47 of handguns, in its self-loading side holster. Firearms were only to be used as a last resort on this first outing.

Special miniaturized two-way communication mikes and earpieces, a couple of low-level stun grenades to keep people inside, and the essential night vision glasses made up the list.

Finally, Tolya slung a twelve-gauge RMB tactical shotgun, with its folding metal stock and forward sliding pump action, over his shoulder.

"Can't you ever leave that thing behind?" Sergei teased.

"I just like something I can hold with both hands," Tolya retorted defiantly.

Sergei checked that the car was well hidden, in the event of someone taking this track. They then checked the direction of the light breeze which had sprung up as they were preparing.

"We'll have to circle round to the east and come in from that side," Tolya whispered.

With no moon and only some slowly-moving high cloud to shut out the stars, they set off in complete silence, keeping as close as possible to the edge of the fields, where the occasional line of trees afforded cover. Their examination of the Google photographs had served to identify several stands of trees on the east side, so that they moved as rapidly as possible between them, trusting that little had changed since the satellite had passed above.

Dávila had chosen to concentrate on soya. Thanks to soaring commodity prices, with exponential demand from China, the bean had become the money-spinner of Argentine agriculture in the first decade of the new century. At least no livestock to contend with. The harvest would be brought in any time now, and the crop, standing some twenty-five centimetres high, served to dampen any sound. Unaccustomed to so much birdlife, they froze close to the ground every time the inevitable plovers rose clamouring into the air along their path. There seemed to be more than one couple in each field. They cursed silently. Sergei spotted a water tank and its galvanised windmill, now redundant since the departure of the cattle. Standing a couple of metres higher than the surrounding pastures on its earth mound, they could use it as an observation post. The main house and its garden now lay a mere three hundred metres in front of them.

With their backs to the water tank and concealed by the shrubbery which had overgrown the mound since the departure of the cattle, they studied the scene through their night vision binoculars. The manager appeared to have organised an *asado* by the side of his house. They could see a middle-aged couple, no doubt the manager and his wife, moving around among the rest of the staff, offering wine and serving the steaks. The farmhands, five of them, could be easily recognised by their *bombachas*, open shirts and berets. Hovering on the fringe, slightly on the edge of the group, two thickset men, dressed in jeans and T-shirts, each with a shoulder holster slung under his arm. Clearly the bodyguards. From the house, a younger girl emerged, presumably the housemaid, warmly greeted by the gauchos. The two bodyguards showed little inclination to fraternise.

Lights were on all over the main building and the manager's house. Focusing beyond the party, a small outbuilding could be detected between the trees. Even though the blinds appeared to have been drawn, it was just possible to catch some light around the window frame and under the main door.

Sergei nudged his companion and pointed towards the outbuilding. They studied it closely and finally caught a shadow moving across in front, cutting out the light from below the door. Presumably another bodyguard. At that moment, the door opened and a fourth man emerged. The two of them walked over to the party and tapped their colleagues on the shoulder. They nodded and, handing over their plates, took their turn by the outbuilding. The manager brought over a couple of plates and glasses to the two new arrivals, but didn't linger. It looked as though he didn't have much time for them.

Counting, Tolya calculated a total of ten men and two women on the property, as far as they could see. The absence of much contact between the gauchos and the bodyguards suggested that the latter would not be counting on the farmhands in an emergency. By early next morning, the manager would no doubt be fast asleep in his house, and the five *peones* be back in their living quarters, half a kilometre away. The information still missing was the sleeping arrangements of the bodyguards. It looked as though the two off duty would be sleeping in the main house, which appeared large enough to contain some extra bedrooms.

The *asado* had inevitably attracted all the mongrels from the neighbourhood. Impossible to tell which were resident and which were visitors since, as so often in the countryside, dogs were merely there for functional purposes, to guard and to survive off scraps. Hopefully, some of them would slink away at the end of the evening. But some would certainly remain.

Sergei tapped Tolya on the shoulder. They should now move round the property, in order to get a clearer picture of how the buildings related one to another and to identify possible lines of approach, given the wind and light conditions. Keeping as low as possible so as not to stand out above the skyline, they began to move downwind. From a new position in a clump of eucalyptus trees, they studied the side of the house, where they could see a number of parked vehicles. The main house now lay between them and the *asado*. A four-wheel-drive Toyota pick-up no doubt belonging to the farm manager, and a couple of black saloons, presumably driven by the bodyguards. A decrepit pickup over twenty years old was parked farther back, which could have brought some of the farmhands from their living quarters. Probably not all, as a number of horses were also hitched, still saddled, to a long rail.

"Get closer, electronic protection?" Tolya whispered.

Sergei nodded, indicating that he would stay farther behind to provide cover. Tolya loped over to a low hedge through which the fencing of the property passed. Soundlessly, he buried himself in the shrubbery, making sure not to touch any wires. On balance, they had discussed and discounted this possibility, since the amount of wildlife to be found around a farm of this sort would have had the alarms being tripped a hundred times a night. Their guess was confirmed when he failed to find anything more lethal than some rusty barbed wire, left over from the days when cattle had occupied the fields surrounding the house.

As Sergei watched, Tolya moved along the fencing until he was opposite a large juniper bush rising a couple of metres off the lawn. Its low-hanging fringes enabled him to crawl closer. Sergei moved up to the fencing, to continue providing cover.

In less than ten minutes, Tolya was back. Pulling out Carla's plan of the property, he indicated that they would have to move round farther in order to get closer to the outhouse, where they suspected the girl was being held. The building stood in the lee of a large clump of trees, which might give them cover to get closer. Before starting anything, they must confirm that the girl was on the property. With at least one guard near the building, this wasn't going to be easy.

Taking full account of the direction of the wind, they moved along the side of the hedge until they had lined themselves up with the clump of trees and the small outhouse beyond. From this side, they could detect that the back of the building consisted of a low veranda, under which a door could just be seen. From their first observations, it appeared that, when only a single guard was involved, he would be standing at the main door on the other side of the building.

Sergei tapped Tolya on the shoulder and indicated he should make the move. Tolya pointed in the direction of shrubbery on the same axis of the outbuilding. If Sergei could get there, he would be able to see movement at the front of the house as well. Sergei nodded. He crawled the thirty metres and ducked under the shrubbery. The wind had suddenly dropped. Dogs would become more of a problem.

As soon as he saw that Sergei was in place, Tolya began to crawl towards the outhouse, before standing up and moving quickly under the shadow of the veranda. In his earpiece, Sergei's low voice confirmed that nobody was moving in his direction. Carefully, he tried the handle of the back door. It was locked and time would certainly not permit an attempt to pick the lock. Judging from its age, the bolt was likely to be straight sided and therefore largely impervious to an inserted knife blade.

"Someone's coming from the party. Front of the house. Don't move!"

There was a pause.

"Maid. Bringing food. Stay where you are!"

Again a pause.

"Handed to the guard. Taking it inside. Wait a minute. He's coming out again. No plate. Must be someone inside."

From his position, Sergei watched the guard sit down on a chair standing near the door. He lit a cigarette.

"Be careful, dog followed the maid. Round the other side of the house."

Tolya moved swiftly to the corner of the house farthest away from Sergei. If the dog was coming from anywhere, he would come round that corner. Which it duly did, head low, sniffing the floor. A low growl greeted the sight of Tolya.

Grabbing the animal by the head to smother any further sound, he drove his Kizlyar blade deep into its throat, lying on top of the animal to quell its final thrashing. Within seconds, it was still.

"Get out fast!"

Tolya crawled rapidly away, dragging the dead dog. He could only hope that it would not be missed too soon. But, given the number of dogs....

Sergei also withdrew, joining Tolya in the clump of eucalyptus trees. From there, they moved beyond the hedge.

By the time they got back to the Ford it was past ten. From a distance, they could see lights continuing to burn at the farm. Unfamiliar with Argentine social habits, they had no idea how long this might go on. Perhaps, like most people who lived off the land, the manager and the *peones* would rise with the sun at around seven o'clock next morning. That suggested they would be going to bed around midnight. Keeping their voices down, they planned the operation.

They need only expect serious opposition from the four bodyguards. At the moment of the attack, two of them would almost certainly be asleep, as would the manager and his wife. The main concern must be to pull it all off as silently as possible. The five gauchos would no doubt sleep longer on Sunday morning, it being a day of rest and the effects of the manager's wine probably extending their slumbers.

"What worries me most is the fact that we have to find a way to prevent the bodyguards' boss getting suspicious during the day. Somehow, we have to ensure that there is no communication between the farm and the island. That's going to be tough one," Sergei muttered.

"I know. What's more, we're going to have to make sure that everyone on the main property is locked down without access to a phone, even after we've left. Not easy. On top of that, what about the gauchos? Are we going to have to immobilise all of them or run the risk that they will turn up at the farm during the day?"

They went on tossing around ideas for about another hour, until they had come up with the best plan they could in the circumstances. They decided to hit the gauchos' sleeping quarters first and immobilise them as effectively and silently as possible, before then moving onto the main house. On balance, unlike the bodyguards, the gauchos might easily collapse under the surprise of their attack.

"From what I've heard, Argentine gauchos are good with their knives."

"We'll just have to stop them getting to them. We may have to shoot one first, to calm down the rest."

"Probably."

"Maybe they'll have visitors during the day. They probably get together a lot, these Argentines."

Both men were conscious of the fact that they knew little about the Latin mentality. One way and another, Afghans were more familiar.

"We're going to have to decide whether we stay at the farm for as long as possible to prevent any contact with the island, or whether we just run that risk and head off for Buenos Aires as soon as we're done. It's possible that only the bodyguards have regular contact with the island. We'll just have to see." Sergei yawned. "I'm whacked. It's been a very long day. Let's get some sleep."

While Tolya stretched out on the back seat of the car, Sergei lay down beside it, out of the wind. Within minutes, they were both asleep.

At four thirty in the morning, Sergei woke Tolya.

"Time to be moving. Any more of that coffee left?"

"I kept some back on purpose. Won't be very warm, but better than nothing."

Ten minutes later, they set off, equipped as before, but this time with the addition of a couple of powerful thermite grenades – very small, but - burning at more than two thousand degrees centigrade - capable of setting fire even to concrete. This time they would have to go beyond the main house, so they followed a wide arc away to the east, the wind having stayed in the same quarter overnight. As they moved, the dogs of the neighbourhood seemed to communicate their presence by the occasional yelp or short burst of barking. It took them nearly half an hour to line themselves up to the east of the long, low building occupied by the gauchos. Some horses stood quietly in the neighbouring paddock, and they could see the old truck parked to one side of the building. They moved up to the fence separating the paddock, the horses moving away silently, apparently used to early morning company.

It was five am and the sun would not rise for another couple of hours. There was virtually no moon, as a thin layer of clouds moved slowly in from the eastern horizon. From across the intervening pasture, they studied the building through their night-vision binoculars. A couple of dogs could be seen lying in front of the dormitory door, there would no doubt be others hidden away in more sheltered places. The plan on which they had finally agreed consisted of generating maximum distraction in the gaucho quarters, in order to draw away as many people as possible from the main house. With an incendiary grenade, they would set fire to the dormitory, which should have the effect of tying down all its inmates to fight the blaze. Hopefully reinforcements would then come up from the main house, ideally in the form of the manager, and probably one or two of the bodyguards. This would significantly reduce the number of people they had to deal with in the main farm buildings.

With Tolya covering him, Sergei moved up to within some fifty metres of the living quarters, carefully remaining downwind and under cover of the wild shrubbery which had been allowed to spread around the building, partly to cut down the prevailing winds. The dogs still showed no signs of moving. Releasing the safety catch on the incendiary, he lobbed it carefully so that it rolled the last ten metres, coming to rest against the back wall of the dormitory building. He immediately backed away and re-joined Tolya. After about a minute, they could see a dull glow from the point at which the device had made contact with the building. Even as they watched, the glow turned incandescent white and they could see the first flames beginning to rise up the side of the building. The chemical compound was such that, like napalm, it would soon project an unquenchable liquid over the ground and the surrounding wall. However much water or conventional fire extinguisher foam might be thrown at it, the fire would grow in intensity. As yet, the dogs on the other side of the building had shown no sign of being alerted.

"It's caught," Sergei whispered, gesturing that they move towards the main house.

Quietly, they trekked back towards the main house, again aligning themselves downwind. From their position, they could now observe both the dormitory, from which smoke was beginning to rise, in one direction and the main buildings on the farm in the other.

As they watched, the door of the dormitory burst open and the gauchos streamed outside, frantically pulling on their jeans and *alpargatas*. One seemed to take charge, sending a couple in the direction of the water tank which conveniently stood only some thirty metres from the building, whilst another couple disappeared in the direction of another outbuilding. The last one broke away from the group and came running in the direction of the main house. They counted all five. Looking at the main house, it was clear that the commotion had already been detected by one of the bodyguards, who could be seen running to the main house, shouting. A window in the manager's house, presumably the bedroom, was thrown open and the bodyguard could be seen pointing in the direction of the gaucho quarters. Within a couple of minutes, two of the bodyguards emerged from the main house, pulling on their trousers and T-shirts. The manager had also come outside and they could see him talking to someone through his bedroom window, presumably his wife. Finally, the manager and the two bodyguards who had been on duty set off in the direction of the fire to which the gaucho had already returned. Of the two remaining bodyguards, one moved over to the side building to replace the one who had left. The other one stayed by the main house, leaning against the veranda watching the blaze. He was soon joined by the manager's wife and the other maid. Manpower around the main building had now been reduced to two bodyguards.

Sergei and Tolya moved back towards the blaze, keeping the lowest profile possible, and stationed themselves about a hundred metres from the burning dormitory, some fifty metres to the side of a straight line running back to the main house, at a point at which the track led through a small coppice of eucalyptus. Each one flattened himself behind a tree on either side of the track, in such a way that they could both see what was happening at the main house and at the fire. As they watched, it appeared that the gauchos were starting to contain the blaze at one end of the building, having brought up a couple of small hoses connected to the windmill. Whilst two of them trained the hoses on the roof of the building to prevent the fire spreading, the remaining men had formed a chain and were passing buckets from the water tank.

After about twenty minutes, the manager appeared to signal that the worst was over, although smoke was still rising and a dull glow could still be seen in certain corners. The two bodyguards dropped their buckets, clearly no longer interested in something which they didn't see as their problem anyway, and lit up. They watched the gauchos and the manager checking to put out the last smouldering parts of the building and then, without a word, set off back in the direction of the main house.

They never made it.

A single silenced shot from Sergei and Tolya to the temple, one from the left, the other from the right, and their professional and private lives were at an end. Keeping an eye on those still moving around the dormitory, the two Russians ran forward, crouching as low as possible, and quickly dragged the bodies into the soya, out of sight of anyone walking back to the main house.

The men working with the buckets were still moving around the area in which the blaze had been strongest, dousing any remaining pockets of heat. The point at which the fire had been started by the grenade would probably still require quite a lot of attention.

Sergei and Tolya, crouching low, moved downwind and out of the line of sight between the main house and the fire. Whatever else they might be doing, the two bodyguards that had stayed behind would be watching what was happening at the blaze. Within five minutes, they were again in the shrubbery on the edge of the main garden. The two bodyguards hadn't moved, one standing at the entrance to the outbuilding, the other one having pulled up a chair on the veranda of the main house, both of them intently watching what was happening across the fields.

Sergei motioned to Tolya that he should take the one by the outbuilding, while he looked after the one on the veranda. They would hit simultaneously. Confident that both guards were looking only in one direction, they moved quickly and silently into position. Running the risk that the dogs might give the alarm, speed was vital. Within a minute, Tolya had come up to the sidewall nearest to the door of the outbuilding, whilst Sergei, coming from the back of the house, reached the corner of the veranda closest to where the other man was sitting.

"Go!"

Each man rushed his target, taking him completely by surprise. Before either guard had time to realise what was happening, the garrotting wire round the neck sent an all too clear message. Tolya's target attempted to swing round with a body blow and was rewarded with a vicious tightening of the wire and sideways movement which had him on the ground, fighting for air, fists flailing about his head. It was clear that hand-to-hand combat didn't figure sufficiently in the training of people more used to simply pointing a gun at the back of someone's head and pulling the trigger. Tolya spun him over onto his face and tightened the wire. He knew that within less than a minute, the man would pass out.

Sergei, the wire firmly round his victim's neck and twisting it with one hand only, simultaneously kicked the chair out from under him and forced his knee into the small of the man's back. His target was the bigger of the two who, using his weight, had managed to turn onto his back, raining blows on Sergei's head and body. A carefully aimed, crushing chop to the groin, however, doubled him up instantly, the wire still around his neck. Again, Sergei pulled the wire tight and threw all his weight on the man's chest. Deprived of air, the man's resistance began to fade until he finally slumped motionless on the ground.

They rolled their targets over onto their faces and bound their hands and ankles with zip-ties, then gagged them. Looping a thin cord round their throats, passing it through the wrist ties and anchoring the other end at the ankles, they hogtied the two guards. They would come round soon enough. A quick body search removed a cell phone and 9mm automatic from each man.

Sergei stood up and turned to be faced with the two petrified women, standing in the doorway, so shocked that it had not even occurred to them to retreat inside and bolt the door. Drawing his Makarov, he forced them back into the front room. Making each sit down on a chair by the kitchen table, they offered no resistance to his tying their wrists behind the chair back and each ankle to the chair leg. He quickly checked that there were no cell phones anywhere within reach, and then, locking the door from the outside, joined Tolya. Given the separation between the two buildings, neither bodyguard was in any position to help the other.

"Now for the rest."

Looking at his watch, less than fifteen minutes had passed since the shooting in the coppice. Through his night vision binoculars, Tolya studied the scene back at the dormitory. The six men could still be seen moving around.

Although their main mission was to release the girl, the first priority was to bring the whole situation under control. From the briefing they had received, they understood that, during this Sunday, they must not only free the hostage, but also manage it in such a fashion that Dávila could not be alerted in time to do anything about it. A raid to free the prisoner later in the day had been ruled out on the grounds that they could not control the comings and goings from the farm. It being Sunday, additional innocent participants might become involved. Hence the decision to attack before dawn. The elimination of two of the bodyguards meant that they must not only neutralise the five *peones*, but also control the manager and the two remaining bodyguards.

Should Dávila choose to make contact, they must ensure that he would not be alerted to what had happened.

In the next ten minutes, the six remaining men must be taken out of the game.

Sergei and Tolya moved fast across the intervening fields, pausing only on the tree line closest to where the fire now appeared to be totally under control, to ensure that everybody was still present and roughly in the same place. A straggler might upset the whole process.

For a couple of minutes, they watched the gauchos moving around what was left of their dormitory, with the manager apparently giving final instructions.

Breaking out of the tree line from two different angles, Sergei with his Makarov and Tolya his twelve gauge RMB, they boxed the group in. To maximize the effect of shock and surprise, Tolya let off one round of his RMB into the ground at their feet, causing a blast of dry earth into their faces. The sight of these two massive Russians, easily standing ten to fifteen centimetres taller than any of them, visibly in no mood to tolerate any response, instantly dispelled any incipient thoughts of resistance. They might not have much experience of firearms, but they all knew what a shotgun would do at close range. Obeying Tolya's sweeping gesture with his RMB, the men lined up against the wall of the small outbuilding, where Sergei zip-tied their hands behind their backs. They then marched all six men into the small outbuilding, which turned out to be the *monturera* where they kept their saddles and riding tackle. Sergei gestured that the five should lie down on the floor, leaving the manager standing in one corner. He then zip-tied each man's ankles and repeated the hog-tie they had used on the guards at the farm. Any excessive movement would have the effect of tightening the neck noose. A quick frisk of the semi-dressed men quickly ensured that no-one had a cell phone tucked in his pocket nor a *facón*, the gaucho's inseparable dagger, tucked into his belt. A box of tools containing pliers and anything else which might have served to cut them free was tossed outside. Using gestures and pointing at his wristwatch, Sergei indicated to each man that he should lie still until midnight. Some nodded, the others too shocked to do anything other than shut their eyes.

They then marched the manager back across the fields to the main house. Both the guards had now regained consciousness and were clearly trying to work out how to get out of the hogtie. A swift kick in the crotch instantly put an end to any further ideas in that direction. To reinforce the message, Sergei held his Makarov to each man's temple and, just in case the message had not been sufficiently clear, let off a round into the soil next to their heads. The pressure wave and the crater of earth did the rest. They lay still.

Tolya checked that the two women were still tied to their chairs in the kitchen. Marching the manager in front of them, they finally approached the outbuilding. The door was ajar.

Taking no chances, Sergei kicked it open and moved swiftly through it and to one side, his Makarov in both hands, just in case they had failed to spot any guard inside.

The building consisted of two rooms and a bathroom, sparsely furnished, paint peeling off the walls, the one with a single table and chair, in the other, a thin mattress laid out on the floor. Chained by handcuffs around one wrist to a water pipe, a girl, half sitting on the mattress, screamed in terror.

"Okay, come in," Sergei passed the all clear to Tolya. "Bring in the manager."

Sam suddenly realised that they were not speaking Spanish. Although weakened and exhausted from the tension and treatment she had received over the last week, it suddenly dawned on her. They were Russian. This must be the work of Carla's new *patron*, Victor Alexievich!

She struggled to dredge up the few words of Russian she could remember, but they didn't come.

"Who are you?" she finally asked in English.

"All okay, *vcio harasho*, we friends," came the reply, and Sergei pulled up the lower half of his mask to show a broad smile. Even in her terrified and filthy state, he could see that this girl was very pretty.

This was the first time that the manager had heard either of the men speak and Sam detected from the surprised look on his face, that, like

514

so many working in the *campo*, he might have English or Irish ancestors and therefore have some knowledge of the language. The English had financed the railroads, Irish labour had built them. Tolya had gone outside and now re-entered the room holding the keys to the handcuffs, which he had found on a hook on one of the pillars of the veranda. He freed Sam, who could finally sit up normally. Her wrists were bruised. From her appearance, it looked as though she had spent most of the time chained to the pipe, lying on the mattress. She was still wearing the same jeans and blouse, now torn and filthy, which she had been wearing the evening of her kidnap. Her shoes, handbag and light coat lay bundled in a corner. Her matted hair stuck to the side of her face.

Sergei gestured to her that she should try and stand up, but quickly saw that she was both too weak and dizzy as she tried to rise. Holstering his Makarov, he bent down and picked her up, as if she weighed nothing.

In Russian, he indicated that Tolya should escort the manager and release the ankles of the guard lying outside. He carried Sam quickly to the main house, Tolya bringing up the rear with the two men. Showing a totally futile burst of resentment, the bodyguard, his legs once freed, kicked out at Tolya, who had no trouble in sidestepping the attack. In return, he was rewarded with a leg sweep which cut his feet out from under and sent him spinning to the ground, doubled up and fighting for breath.

Once at the main house, Tolya reapplied the hog-tie not only to the guard but also now to the manager, laying all three men out about two metres apart on the veranda. Sergei carried Sam into the main house and laid her down on a small sofa standing against a window. He detected a look of sympathy from the wife of the manager. The little maid remained as petrified as ever.

The sun had crept up over the horizon, flooding the land with a pale yellow light. He looked at his watch. It was a seven fifteen. It'd been easier than he had expected.

"You understand English?" he whispered to Sam. "*Ya* Sergei, *on* Tolya." Pointing at his companion.

"*Da*, yes. Thank you. Thank you. *Spasibo*."

She burst into tears. Her body shook as the tension began to flow out of it. He picked up a blanket from the bedroom next door and putting it around her shoulders, with a pillow behind her head, made her as comfortable as possible on the sofa. He found a glass on the kitchen sideboard and filled it with water from the tap. His eye was caught by a bottle of something looking alcoholic. Uncorking it, he detected some kind of cognac. He poured a very small amount into another glass and brought both over to Sam.

"Please, drink!"

Sam took a sip of the brandy, but was immediately overtaken by a fit of coughing. Nevertheless, she felt that it might do her good.

"Please, I explain. You understand?"

She nodded.

Pointing at his watch, he continued slowly.

"We here *do* five this evening. Until five. Then go. Problem, Dávila ring here, perhaps, today." Indicating the men lying outside, "They must answer. Say all okay. If not..." Sergei made a gesture with his finger across his throat. "*Kaput!* They must understand. You explain?"

She nodded again.

"Dávila, I think he usually telephones two, maybe three, times per day," she replied. "I understand. I will explain. Where are their cell phones?"

Sergei stepped through the front door and instructed Tolya to find all the cell phones that he could in the bedrooms and around the house.

"You must eat." Pointing in the direction of the manager's wife, Sergei said, "She cook."

The stress was evaporating and the cognac was having its effect, warmth creeping back into her body. Wrapping the blanket around her shoulders, Sam got unsteadily to her feet. Tolya came back into the room holding six different cell phones.

"These maybe belong to the guards," he said to Sergei, laying four of them down on the kitchen table. "These two I found in the bedroom next door. Presumably the manager."

"Please, explain to them now!" Sergei turned to Sam.

Addressing herself first to the two women in the kitchen, Sam explained what would happen that day.

"Nobody wants to harm you. But make no mistake, these people are trained to kill. They have killed so often, two or three more deaths make no difference. If your husband does anything foolish, they will shoot him. So please, do not provoke them."

The little maid began to sob.

"Tonight, we will leave and you will be safe. But you must do as I tell you."

The manager's wife managed a timid smile through her tears. Suddenly a flood of words poured from her.

"I'm sorry, you are not the first girl to have been here. I do not know what the *patron* does with them. He is a terrible man. I've told Carlos so often that we should not stay here. He and those other men, they are brutes. Please, don't let them shoot my husband. We have a daughter, eighteen years old, she's in hospital. I could never look after her by myself."

"Then please pass that message to your husband. Today, he must do exactly as he is told. He makes a mistake, this will be immediate, no-one will be able to save him."

The woman nodded.

"Are you expecting anyone today?"

The manager's wife hesitated. Sam detected it immediately.

"You must call them up and say that you are ill, that they should come next weekend. We must have no visitors today. Do you understand? Nobody must come here today. And if you try to warn them, don't forget I will be listening and they will shoot you too, have no doubt.

Nobody can get to you in time to save you, so nobody must come. Now, if they untie you, can you prepare some food for us?"

The woman nodded. "I understand, don't worry. But we are not expecting anyone. When girls are here, *el patron* says we must never have visitors."

Turning to Sergei, Sam explained.

"She understands. I've made it clear no-one can come here today. They must not try to warn anyone if they make a phone call. Or else you will shoot them immediately. I will listen to what is said. She has been kind to me during these days. You can untie her and she will prepare food. The little maid, she's not dangerous. Perhaps you make it easier for her? Perhaps just tie her by one wrist. She also tried to be kind. She is very frightened."

Sergei looked doubtful, but finally nodded.

He went over to the two women and cut through the tie strips. He took the maid and led her over to a chair by a radiator, to which he handcuffed one wrist. At least she could move a little.

As Sam watched him, she suddenly caught sight of something gleaming round the girl's throat. Sam's hand searched for the necklace which always hung between her breasts. It had gone. She stepped over to the girl, who was trying to turn away, and flicking open her nightdress top, saw the Druze star glinting in the girl's long hair.

"So one of these bastards gave you a present, did he? Well, I'll have it back!"

She felt no anger at the girl, given the situation in which she and the manager's family had been living since her arrival.

"Come with me now," Sam said to the manager's wife.

They went outside. The sight of her husband, tied up but alive, provoked an immediate reaction of relief on the face of his wife. She bent over him and stroked his hair. He groaned.

Sam, propping herself up on the arm of Sergei, repeated the general scenario.

518

"Do not have any illusions. If you make one false move, these people will kill you. It will be quick, but it will be final. They are trained to do this and they've done it many, many times. Your lives depend on what you do today. I know that Señor Dávila or one of his other guards telephones one of you two or three times during the day. You will remain tied up as you are now, and you will each have your cell phone next to your head. If one of them rings, one of these men will press the answer button, but you will speak and I will listen. After the way you've treated me, make no mistake, if you say the wrong thing, I will be happy to tell them and they will shoot you. No-one can get here in time to save you. And remember, if one of you warns Señor Dávila or his team, the other two will also die. At that stage, they will have nothing to lose by killing you all."

Turning to Sergei, she asked, "Where are the other two guards?"

Sergei repeated the slitting motion across his throat, pointing in the direction of the fire. To be more explicit, he made the gesture of firing a pistol with his fingers.

Sam was pleased to note a shudder going through the bodies of the three men lying on the ground in front of her.

"So you see. Two of your companions are already dead. Two or three more will make no difference." Turning to the manager, she added, "Just remember your daughter."

He nodded as best he could.

Tolya held up the six cell phones.

Sergei had pulled up a chair for her. Sam looked down at the three men. "Which are yours?" she asked. "Don't choose the wrong one, it could also be your last mistake."

To her own satisfaction, but also with a faint trace of dismay, she detected that she was beginning to enjoy the situation. Not surprising, perhaps, given the way these bastards had treated her for the last few weeks. She could feel energy and hope creeping back as the course of events became clearer.

519

The guard she knew as Cacho nodded when one of the Motorolas was shown to him. The other, Ramon, on being shown a Nokia, merely said "That's mine."

"When do you usually receive the first call?" Sam asked.

The two guards hesitated, as if wondering whether this might be used to set a trap.

"Be careful," Sam warned. "Today, you have no room for mistakes or any *viveza*."

She could see Cacho exchange a quick glance with Ramon.

"Usually at nine," Cacho finally replied.

"For your sake, I hope they don't wake up earlier," she muttered.

It only remained to confirm which of the two cell phones found in the bedroom belonged to the manager.

"They understand?" Sergei asked.

"Yes. I will listen to phone calls." She made a gesture of listening to a cell phone. "But perhaps you do something to make all very clear?"

Sergei smiled. This girl had more balls than at first appeared. He turned to Tolya, made some remark and pointed in the direction of a one of the larger dogs, which had just appeared at the end of the veranda. Drawing his Makarov from its holster in a single movement, Tolya loosed off a round without apparently even taking aim. The unfortunate animal was catapulted a metre into the air, dead before it hit the ground. The effect was not lost on the men lying on the ground.

"She's preparing food."

Leaning on Sergei's arm, Sam stepped inside. The manager's wife came towards her, nervously.

"Please, use our bathroom. There is some hot water."

Turning to Sergei, Sam asked, "What time is it?"

He looked at his watch and lifted eight fingers.

"First call, perhaps nine o'clock. I must have bath." She made the motions of washing herself.

Sergei nodded his agreement.

The manager's wife leading the way, Sam walked slowly through their bedroom to the simple little bathroom on the other side. At least a shower.

"I will bring you some of my daughter's clothes, she is not as tall as you, and you are much slimmer. Perhaps they will fit."

She returned after a couple of minutes carrying a couple of blouses and T-shirts, a skirt and a pair of jeans.

"Please try them."

Taking them from her and thanking her, Sam closed the door and slowly pulled off her filthy clothes. She was terribly stiff, every muscle ached, after so long lying on the mattress, chained to the radiator. She threw them in a pile in the corner. The lavatory had no seat. But then, neither had the one in the outbuilding where they had held her for the last couple of weeks. She had got used to the squatting position. She turned on the water in the shower, the gas fired water heater on the wall rapidly turning the flow from the diminutive showerhead into a steady stream of boiling water. Memories of showers in bathrooms of the Ritz in the Place Vendome or the Connaught in London, her platinum Amex card on full throttle, flashed before her eyes. She almost burst out laughing. Somehow, this one felt better than any of those. She stood under the water for ten minutes, trying to wash away the horrors of the last two weeks. She found a bottle of cheap shampoo on the window ledge. At last, her hair, matted and greasy, began to regain its usual softness. Even the soap, giving off a scent of cheap rose perfume, felt better than anything produced by Guerlain. What soap had Wilde ordered before leaving Reading gaol? She knew it had some exotic name.

Some twenty minutes later, Sam emerged, revitalised. The jeans and one of the blouses might not be her usual style, but, once the manager's wife had given her a belt, she had been able to pull in the waist so that at least the jeans no longer threatened to drop around her ankles. Sergei's appreciative look, even under his facemask, did not escape her.

"No telephone calls?"

"*Niet! Nichevo!*"

The manager's wife had, in the meantime, prepared a potato tortilla of generous proportions, along with a pot of strong coffee. Sitting down at the kitchen table, Sam attacked enthusiastically.

Sergei pointed at his wristwatch to show that it was near nine o'clock.

At that moment there came the sound of a car engine. Sam, startled, looked out of the window. A Ford pick-up was parking behind the manager's truck. With relief, she saw Tolya adjusting his facemask as he stepped out of the driving seat. Sergei had sent him to bring the car from its hiding place, just in case anyone else found it during the day. By way of precaution, he had covered the number plates with duct tape.

It was just after nine thirty when one of the cell phones began an insistent ringing. Everyone stopped what they were doing. The phone lay closest to Ramon's head. As if it were a poisonous snake, he rolled away from it as best he could. Then it stopped.

Sergei picked it up to check the call log. The number had not been registered. He handed it to Sam, without saying a word.

"Maybe Dávila. I don't know number."

Sergei placed it beside Ramon's head once more, kicking him into his original position.

They waited, but the call was not repeated.

Everyone relaxed visibly.

About an hour later, the cell phone lying next to Cacho's face began to buzz furiously. Cacho's face was a mask of terror. Sergei moved forward immediately and placed the barrel of the Makarov against his temple. Cacho froze.

Sam stepped forward quickly from the chair on which she had been resting and, lifting the cell phone a few centimetres off the ground, pressed the 'answer' button, as well as the loudspeaker and placed it near Cacho's mouth.

"*Hola, hola,* Cacho? You there?" The voice could be heard faintly at the other end.

Cacho seemed paralysed. His throat had gone completely dry, not a sound passed his lips.

"*Hola, hola? Puta madre,* shit connection! *Hola, hola?*"

Cacho still said nothing. Again the line went dead.

Sam switched off the phone and looked across at Sergei.

"He must answer!" Sergei emphasised the point by pressing the barrel of the automatic under Cacho's jaw.

Sam turned to the manager's wife.

"Is reception always like this here?" she asked.

"No, not always, but many times the calls do not get through. It depends where you are standing. Here near the house it varies. Don't worry, they will try again. It's happened before."

Sergei nodded.

"You eat now," Sam said to Sergei. "Then he," nodding in the direction of Tolya.

Sergei exchanged a few words with Tolya and then went into the kitchen, where the manager's wife had prepared another tortilla and more coffee.

"Give your husband some water," Sam suggested.

The woman looked at her gratefully and went out with a small bottle of mineral water, which she carefully placed between his lips. He drank avidly.

During the time of her imprisonment, Sam had seen the manager only occasionally, but she had detected that, like his wife, he was not a little uncomfortable with the situation. But, being a man, he had not been able to find a way to express it. His wife, on the other hand, on the rare occasions when she had been allowed into the room where Sam was being held to bring food, had usually tried to find a way, on occasion producing a piece of cloth dipped in fresh water with which to clean Sam's face and hands, or a comb to straighten her hair. The look in her eyes had been enough to convey to Sam that she was profoundly unhappy. The presence of one of the bodyguards had always prevented them exchanging any words. When the woman had once tried to say something, Cacho had slapped her across the mouth, telling her to shut up. Sam had shaken her head, as if to advise her not to try again.

By midday, the sun was burning up the landscape. Tolya, after his session in the kitchen, had made at least two excursions to the *monturera* to check that the gauchos were still tied up and unlikely to cause any trouble. On returning, he signalled that everything was under control.

All of a sudden, Tolya called out something to Sergei, pointing across the fields, to where the plume of dust of an approaching car could be seen moving across the near horizon. Sergei turned to Sam, who called the manager's wife out under the veranda from the kitchen. The three men lying on the ground found the strength to lift their heads in the direction from which the sound was coming.

"I thought you said nobody was coming today," Sam's tone was sharp.

The woman looked panic-stricken.

"We weren't expecting anyone, I promise," her strangled voice conveying terror.

"How do you stop them?"

Before his wife could reply, the manager interrupted.

"I put the padlock on the gate last night. I think that's Jose Ramon in his truck. He won't be able to get under the crossbar of the *tranquera*. He always comes through the main gate. Someone will have to open it."

As if to confirm what the manager had just said, the croaking of a decrepit klaxon came from the far end of the avenue of trees leading to the entrance to the property.

Sergei and Tolya had moved out of sight to the opposite ends of the veranda, Makarovs trained on the three men lying on the ground. Sergei looked across at Sam, expectantly.

The croaking of the horn grew more insistent.

Turning to the manager's wife, Sam thought fast.

"You will have to tell them that they cannot come in. I will go with you. If you do not persuade them to go, you know what will happen here."

The woman looked desperate. Sam took her by the arm and began to march her in the direction of the gate. No time could be wasted, in case Jose Ramon chose to come in on foot, leaving his truck at the gate. Sergei stepped forward quickly, offering Sam his small PSS silent pistol. She hesitated, then shook her head. She was not in the killing business. Instead, she gestured that he should follow her, keeping out of sight.

As they began to walk down the avenue, Sam wracked her brains for a story to deter the visitor. Then it hit her.

"Who is this Jose Ramon?"

"He's the manager on the next door farm. He's a good man, he doesn't deserve to die."

"Does he have a family?"

"Yes, two children."

"Listen to me carefully."

She could see that a man of about sixty had got out of the truck and was now leaning on the gate. He had caught sight of them and it was almost certain that he would now come towards them. Sure enough, he stepped across the horizontal bars of the old cattle grid and, smiling broadly, walked in their direction. About a hundred metres separated them. In the background, Sam thought she could hear the rustling of leaves as Sergei moved forward behind the line of trees.

"First of all, I'm your cousin from Buenos Aires, on a short visit. My name is Paula. Secondly, you tell him that one of the gauchos is very ill, that the doctor came last night and that he's afraid it might even be polio. He has a very high temperature and his joints are very stiff. You have brought him into the main house."

The woman looked at Sam, clearly mystified.

"Yes. You must use that story." Sam was emphatic.

She had been desperately trying to think of anything that might stop the visitor from coming closer to the house. Illness was usually a deterrent, but nowadays, few illnesses seemed sufficiently infectious to prevent someone coming in range. Aids? Cholera? Dengue? Then, it had hit her. She suddenly remembered that Argentina had been hit by a terrible polio epidemic in the mid-1950s, which had ploughed through the rural population as well as the towns. Middle-class families had taken refuge on their country estates as if escaping from the Black Death. She remembered her mother talking about spending the long, hot summer in their *quinta* in Marcos Paz, food being left at the gate, only one trip per week into the local town to stock up on basic provisions. The arrival of vaccines had, like everywhere else in the world, largely made polio a thing of the past. But, among the generation of the manager's wife and the man walking towards her, who would have been children at the time, the spectre might still have an effect. Anyway, it was worth a try.

"I'll back you up. But we must stop him. And we must also stop him from spreading the news in the village, at least for a few hours."

Sam was regaining confidence. She might not be in her best physical form, but her brain still seemed to be functioning. Leandro would be proud of her. She smiled inwardly.

"*Hola, Catalina, como estas*? How are you?" The man called as he moved closer.

Catalina, so that was her name. Sam had never heard it and had forgotten to ask. The fact that the woman was visibly a bundle of nerves might add effect to the story.

"*Hola*, Jose Ramon. *Mal*! Bad. Please don't come any closer," Catalina's voice was trembling, convincingly, most probably from the presence of Sergei behind them in the trees.

"*Che*, what's the problem? You don't look so good."

"It's young Francisco. He's very ill. It's bad. Don't come any closer!"

Jose Ramon hesitated, about ten metres away.

"What's he got? Has the doctor been? I thought I saw another car near the house."

"No, that's mine. I'm Catalina's cousin, Paula, from Capital. Just here for a couple of days. Bad timing," Sam interjected.

"But what's he got?"

The manager's wife looked at Sam, hesitating visibly. Sam realised that she must take over. She laid a hand on Catalina's arm, as if to stop her replying.

"We are not sure. But the doctor talked of it possibly being polio."

Jose Ramon took a step back. She had been right. The old childhood terror could be read on his face.

"*Por Dios*, but that disease was finished years ago," the expression on his face not matching the conviction of his words.

"Yes, that's what we all thought. Anyway, the doctor's not sure. He only mentioned it as a possibility. He's going to do some tests and they will hear in a couple of days."

"*Mi Dios*, well, if you don't mind, I don't think I'll come any closer. What with my two girls."

Catalina finally spoke, a measure of relief detectable in the steadiness of her voice.

"Don't worry, Jose Ramon, we perfectly understand. Of course, you mustn't come any closer. Anyway, it's only one possibility. We are all praying that the tests will show something else. But just in case, we

527

think it's better that no-one comes to the house. Perhaps, it would be better not to say too much in the village, either. No need for panic. Please don't say anything. I'll let you know."

Jose Ramon hesitated, then made as though to blow her a kiss.

"Well, you take care of yourselves. Give me a ring when you've some news. I'm sure it'll be nothing."

He waved to them and turned on his heel.

Sam saw Catalina's shoulders droop as the tension faded.

Jose Ramon suddenly turned round.

"What happened last night? Did you have a fire? Someone said they had possibly seen something burning, not here but up at the *muchachos'* dormitory. Quite a big fire apparently."

Catalina was caught off guard. She was briefly lost for words, but then reacted.

"Oh, that, the others were having an *asado* and, what with Francisco's illness, they didn't put out the fire properly. A shed caught fire early this morning. But they were able to put it out."

"Well done," Sam murmured to her.

"You've been having a busy time. I would have come over to help, but I only heard about it this morning. Take care. *Abrazo* to your husband."

Jose Ramon turned on his heel and continued walking back to his truck.

They watched him go. With a final wave, he climbed back into the cab, finally getting the engine started and, having turned round, set off back the way he had come.

"I'm worried that the village will know all about it before the sun goes down," Catalina muttered.

"You did well. And for the time being, your husband is still alive."

Sam put her arm around the woman's shoulders as they walked slowly back towards the house. Her joints were loosening up. The shower had done wonders. Sergei emerged silently from behind one of the trees, holstering his Makarov.

"Is good!"

Tolya came towards them and said something to Sergei.

"Another call. Not answered."

It was clear that failure to communicate was becoming a serious problem. By now, it was past two in the afternoon, and they were not due to leave for another three hours. Unless some message got through to Dávila, he might try and find another way to check what was happening.

About twenty minutes later, the cell phone next to Cacho vibrated furiously. Sam again picked it off the ground and pressed 'answer' and the loudspeaker.

"That you, Cacho? Where the hell have you guys been? No-one has answered all morning!"

"Sorry Carlos." Cacho paused. The cold steel of the Makarov pressed against his left temple was confusing him.

"*Che,* Cacho. What's the matter, is the connection bad?"

"No, no. It's okay."

Carlos must be able to hear Cacho breathing heavily on the mouthpiece.

"What the fuck's the matter with you? You okay? You sound different? Did you have a party last night? Too much to drink?"

"Yes, yes, that's it. I've just woken up," Cacho spoke quickly.

"And the others?"

Another pause.

"They're still asleep."

"And the girl?"

"No, she's awake."

Cacho was tempted to add that Sam also had the power of life and death over him, with a round from the Makarov only a second away from terminating everything. Was this the way it was supposed to end? He hesitated, then saw Sam exchange a glance with Sergei. He thought better of it.

"She's okay. We kept watch."

"Okay then. But wake the others up. *El patron* is pretty twitchy today, and pissed off that he could not get through to the manager. He's already tried twice. And you guys haven't picked up either. There's a big *asado* here, lots of *capos*. So ring me back in a couple of hours. He wants a regular report. And go wake up the manager. *Capisce?*"

Again a short pause, before Cacho replied.

"*Esta bien*, Carlos, got the message. Tell *el patron* that everything's fine."

The line went dead at the other end. He heard the click as the Russian put the safety catch on again. Sweat poured off Cacho's face onto the dusty ground. It wasn't just the heat of the sun.

Sam put the phone down on the ground next to his face and looked across at Sergei. They might have earned themselves a couple of hours respite.

She needed to have a clearer idea of where they were going from there. She gestured to Sergei that she wanted to talk to him away from the rest. They moved onto the front lawn.

"What's the plan?" she asked.

Sergei pointed to nine pm on his watch.

"We must be in river - delta? - by this time. Meet Carla. Then go Uruguay."

The ambitiousness of the whole operation was impressive.

"And here, we leave when?"

Again he pointed at his watch.

"Half past five. Latest."

That left another couple of hours.

"And these people?"

Sergei looked a bit evasive.

"We take two men only."

"Cacho and Ramon?"

He nodded.

"And the rest?"

"Stay tied up. They will not die. Tomorrow someone comes. They okay, I am sure."

That made sense. They could not afford anyone trying to get through to Dávila while they were driving back to Buenos Aires.

It was now after three in the afternoon. Tolya was sent back to the dormitory to check that all was still under control. He came back, relaxed, a thumbs up. There was nothing to do but wait and hope that there would be no more unexpected visitors.

Sam sat in the cool of the kitchen with Catalina.

"How long have you been working here?" she asked, trying to fit the horror to which she had been subjected into some broader framework.

Catalina hesitated, looking nervously in the direction of the door through which she could see her husband lying on the ground.

"About two years..." her voice trailing off as though she would prefer not have to say any more. But Sam wasn't going to relent that easily.

"And you mentioned there had been other girls. Like me?"

Catalina shook her head.

"Not like you. *Negritas*, younger." She used the word which so many Argentines applied contemptuously to anyone seen as less than pure European in bloodline. It irritated Sam every time, but not now.

"And what happened?"

Catalina's face betrayed terror and horror all in one.

"Terrible things."

Sam got up and motioned her into the bedroom, closing the door behind them. She lowered her onto the side of the bed and sat down next to her, again putting her arm round her shoulders.

"Tell me," she whispered.

Silently, Catalina began to cry. She picked up the corner of the sheet to wipe the tears running slowly down her face, plucking at it with both hands.

"Terrible!" she repeated.

Patiently, compassionately, Sam tried to coax more detail out of the woman.

"*El patron*. He came. Not often, but always terrible things. The girls."

Slowly, painfully, Catalina began to talk about some of the visits which Dávila had made to the farm since their arrival to work for him. There had not been many. Perhaps, one every six months. The scenario was usually the same. Two bodyguards would arrive around midday with a young girl in the back of the car, blindfolded. She would rapidly be locked in the outhouse in which Sam had spent the last two weeks. The bodyguards would check that everything was secure and ensure that, by the time the patron arrived, the staff had been reduced to a minimum. The *gauchos* and the maid were given money to go into town and told not to come back until next day. Sometime in the early evening, the *patron* would arrive in a second car, driving himself. She would be asked to serve him a light meal, at which he usually drank a lot. This he would share with the two bodyguards. In the silence of early evening in the Argentine *campo*, she could hear the desperate cries and sobbing of the unknown girl, locked in the outhouse. The men appeared to pay no attention to this.

At various points, Catalina had to stop, as if choking on the words. Sam waited, giving her time.

Then at about ten in the evening, she and her husband would also be told to leave and only to come back next day, not earlier than noon. She knew very little about what would happen after their departure. Then one evening, about six months ago, Cacho had got very drunk. The *patron* was not there at the time. Her husband, sitting out on the veranda and sharing a couple of bottles of wine, allowed him to talk. And talk he did. It had been like someone telling a nightmare. Although Cacho provided very little detail of what went on in the outbuilding, he appeared traumatised by what *el patron* was asking him to do.

"He talked about the sex, the violence, the pain. Those poor girls! And all the time, *el patron* was asking him to film it!"

The glimpse of Cacho and the video camera flashed before Sam's eyes. She had clearly not been the first. At least she had survived. Her scenario had been different.

"And when you came back, next day?"

"They had always gone. The girls had disappeared. My husband once found tracks of a car going to a part of the *campo* where there's a big *monte*, a lot of trees. It looked as though they had been digging there. But, honestly, he was too scared ... we were too scared... to do anything."

Catalina leaned forward into Sam's lap, sobbing, her whole body shaking. After a minute, she pulled herself together.

"*El patron* paid us well, those months he came he usually added a few thousand pesos. After the first one, we felt that it was too late to speak to anyone. The night when Cacho got drunk, he said something to my husband. *El patron* will kill anyone who talks about this, he said. He was terrified. Our daughter was beginning to fall ill, we simply weren't going to risk it."

Sam felt that she had heard enough. One of the first thoughts to come into her mind was how much Carla had known about this. That she had known about the Williams girl in the hotel, she was in no doubt, but all this? And now what had happened to her? Dávila's visit to her had not been about working off some terrible sexual perversion. Or at least only superficially. If suffocating and drowning her could be described as superficial. This was about Carla, and Sam being used against her. Dávila had said as much. She felt sick. She stood up. She needed fresh air.

"Don't worry, Catalina, it will all end soon."

The woman tugged at her sleeve, but Sam pulled away and went out onto the veranda. The sight of those two bastards lying on the ground!

By now, it was getting on for five o'clock. She walked up to Sergei.

"Soon time?"

He nodded.

"We go."

He sent Tolya back to check out the gauchos one more time.

"She, we must tie up," pointing indoors to Catalina.

"I will explain to her. Bring in the husband too."

Sam brought Catalina into the kitchen and sat her down at the table. The husband had been put onto his feet and, very stiff, joined them. She closed the door so that Cacho and Ramon could not hear. She explained to them that they would soon be leaving, that the three of them would be tied up in the kitchen so that they could not escape. But she promised that by the morning, someone would come and release them all.

"And those two?" the husband asked, nodding towards the door.

"They come with us. Don't worry. I don't think you'll see them again."

She didn't know where the confidence came from to make so formal promise. Somewhere, inside her, a tiny premonition.

She looked through the door and signalled that they were ready.

Tolya came in and rapidly retied Catalina. He distributed them around the kitchen, tying them to water or gas pipes in such a fashion that they could not free themselves easily. Then with a damp cloth dipped in detergent, he went round with Sam wiping anything she might have touched, in the shower, the kitchen, cutlery, door handles, the chair. He locked the main door on the outside. He even took her back to the outhouse. She hesitated a minute before going inside. The bathroom and the radiator were wiped down.

Sam knelt down beside Cacho.

"One call. You're going to tell them everything is okay."

The Makarov was pressed against his temple. Cacho nodded.

She redialled the last incoming call and again switched on the loudspeaker.

It rang five times before going to an answering machine. She tried again. The same result. She killed the call.

"This time, you leave him a message that it's five thirty, that everything's okay, but that you're running out of battery. Got that? Tell him there's been a power cut."

Cacho nodded again.

She redialled and looked at Sergei to indicate maximum pressure. The barrel of the Makarov was twisted nearer to Cacho's left eye, so that he could almost see the tip of the round at the other end of the barrel.

Again the voicemail.

"*Hola* Carlos, it's Cacho. It's about five. Everything's okay. Tell the *patron* not to worry. My battery's low. There's been a power cut. Speak later." His voice broke towards the end, choking.

Sam cut the call and nodded to Sergei, who flicked back the safety catch.

"We go?"

"*Da*, we go now."

They pulled Cacho and Ramon to their feet. They could hardly walk. Now gagged and blindfolded, still zip tied at wrists, knees and ankles, with a thick hood pulled over their heads, the two men were unceremoniously dumped next to each other in the rear load area of the Ford Ranger, a double tarpaulin stretched over them. She detected that neither of her two Russian friends were particularly worried about whether there would be enough air, particularly on a hot day. Their muffled groans went unheard. Tolya bent down and removed the tape from the number plates. Then he picked up all the cell phones.

Sergei waved her into the front passenger seat, whilst Tolya settled into the back, with their backpacks of equipment. As they drove past, she could see that they had punctured the tyres on the pickup and the two saloons parked alongside as a precaution.

Driving carefully down the avenue of trees, they looked to right and left to see whether there was any traffic on the dirt road. All clear. Sergei accelerated away in the direction of O'Higgins. As they drove along, Tolya began to throw the cell phones out of the car window into the adjoining ditches.

It was dark by the time they were parking the pick-up in a narrow side street close to the riverside fruit market in the port area of San Fernando, a pretty suburb of Buenos Aires running alongside the River Lujan. Sam had acted as guide, combining the carefully pre-set route of the GPS with the map and what she could remember of the area. They had briefly got lost on the connecting road between San Fernando and the Panamericana highway, but a man on a bicycle, apparently oblivious to some muffled knocking coming from the rear of the car, pointed her in the right direction.

Sergei produced a map which he handed to Sam.

"Boat here."

He pointed at the map. It had been left for them in a small side dock, some hundred metres from where they were now parked.

She nodded.

"Okay."

"*Minoutochku!*"

Again they wiped down the car, steering wheel, door handles, tarpaulin and fasteners. Sergei released the catches on the tarpaulin. The two bodies lay quiet. Possibly unconscious.

From his waistband, Sergei pulled out his PSS silent pistol. In less than ten seconds, Cacho and Ramon had each received a 7.62mm round in the back of the skull. There had been practically no sound. They could not have felt anything. Sam sensed that neither had she.

Placing a thermite device under the pickup, Tolya set the timer to go off ten minutes later.

"*Khorosho*, now we go." The two men picked up their holdalls.

She led them off in the direction indicated on the map.

24 March 2008

The moon had risen, a huge yellow disc over the far bend in the river, throwing a pale sheen over the water. Now past eight on this Sunday evening, the crowds of weekend sailors had made their chaotic and ear-splitting way down the rivers and canals back to the marinas in San Fernando, Tigre or San Isidro. Whether behind the wheel of a car or of a high-powered motor boat, the Argentine male demonstrated the same disregard for life and limb, whether his own or that of his neighbour. The Sunday evening exodus was restoring the Delta to its true owners. Chased from the waterways by the invading hoards of motor cruisers and jet skis since the previous Friday evening, the *isleños* began to re-emerge in their little boats, shuttling between the islands to visit friends or pick up supplies at the nearest *almacén*. The languid flow of the pale brown waters produced only a faint rippling sound as it lapped against the reed banks and now abandoned jetties of the *porteños* weekend retreats.

The faint red glow of a cigarette revealed the presence of one of Dávila's bodyguards on the end of the jetty. The boss had had a busy day, with a large *asado* for some of the high-ups in the office, who had been joined by a couple of faces more often to be seen heading political rallies on TV. Each of these had come with at least one bodyguard, so that the bodyguards' *asado* around the huge grilling area had been as populated, though slightly less articulate, than that of the bosses. Some of these had regularly made their way between the long table under the palm frond roof of the main *quincho* and the laden *parrillas* from which a steady flow of *bifes* and every other part of the animal was provided by the two *asadores* Dávila had brought in from his *campo* west of Buenos Aires. A good rough red wine from Mendoza had ensured that, until about six in the evening, even the bodyguards had stretched out under the trees in the late summer sunshine.

The boss had become progressively more nervous and short tempered around lunchtime. He called Carlos over to his table.

"For some reason, I can't get through to the farm. No-one seems to be picking up. Get through to them as soon as possible. I know it's Sunday, and they've probably had an *asado* last night. But it's not good enough. I don't pay them for that. As soon as you get some news, Carlos, let me know."

Carlos had tried all the cell phones he had, Cacho, Mario, Ramon and the manager. Finally, at around two thirty, Cacho had picked up.

After hanging up, Carlos had walked over to report to Dávila. He was not best pleased.

"I don't pay those bastards to get drunk. Ring them again in an hour and try to speak to Ramon as well."

He turned back to his guests. They would soon be leaving and then he would be alone with Carla. She had arrived early that morning. Given his recent signals to her, they had some serious talking to do. And then a session.

At around six thirty in the evening, all the guests had piled back into the cruisers and launches in which they had arrived earlier in the day, and with a lot of shouting, waving and roaring of large horsepower engines, had streamed off down river.

Carla had sat next to Dávila on the veranda of the main house, smoking and talking quietly as the sun went down and stillness returned. She had been invisible all day, resting in their bedroom, her presence unsuspected by his guests. It was a sign of something.

Carlos could now see that the *patron* and his woman were involved in an intense discussion. She was unlike any woman he had ever seen. At least not in real life. In the cinema, maybe, but in real life . . . Her eyes seemed to drill through him whenever he came close. And God was she sexy. Even though he tended to prefer them younger. How did *el patron* do it, he so small, even ugly? He had read somewhere that women might be attracted to ugly men. He sighed. Probably the money. At least *el patron* had that.

He could see that this evening it wasn't all going the boss' way. They were arguing, their voices occasionally rising, although he couldn't catch the words. Then after a while, things seemed to settle down. He watched the woman rise and put her hand on the *patron*'s shoulder. Perhaps a gesture of reconciliation.

Later, Dávila passed him word that the staff, the cook and maid, should take the evening off and stay scarce. From experience, this signified that the women would be locked in their quarters until next morning. And that he and Marcelo must remain at least two hundred metres from the main house, guarding the perimeter. *El patron* occasionally had such evenings with his woman, when to disturb him was to court certain dismissal or worse. The lights around the main house dimmed and the electric blinds came down to seal off the interior from curious eyes. Only the hum of the powerful air conditioning system at the back of the house broke the silence. Carlos knew the form. *El patron* had some strange, vicious tastes, but to show any interest in them was fatal. At least this time there was no other girl. A fleeting memory of the scene six months ago, the Bolivian kid suffocating in front of him...

He chased it from his mind, consoling himself with the image of the fat envelope of hundred dollar bills which had been thrust into his hand a couple of days later.

A few kilometres closer to San Fernando, Leandro, his launch moored to an abandoned jetty on the banks of the Urión, watched the navigation lights of a large motor launch approaching from the direction of the Vinculación canal. He flashed his lights on and off three times and waited. The noise of its powerful engines came closer and then, suddenly, a small handheld searchlight picked him out. He didn't know exactly what to expect and so, just in case the launch were someone else, he waved, holding up an empty petrol can, to suggest that he had run out of fuel. In his other hand, out of sight, he gripped the Bersa 9mm purchased after Sosa's death, which he had slipped it into the back of his trousers on leaving his flat.

The larger launch cut its engines and coasted towards him. He could see the silhouette of three people on board.

"Leandro, is that really you?"

The voice of Sam carried across the intervening water.

"My God, Sam. Are you all right? Of course it's me, who else would be crazy enough to be standing out here in the dark and the cold waiting for you?"

"There are times I really hate that Anglo-Saxon humour!" she could be heard muttering.

The boats touched and one of the men standing next to Sam jumped over with a line. Slipping the Bersa back in his waistband, Leandro held the two boats close together. Sam stepped across, collapsing onto the wide upholstered seat of the cockpit. He caught her as she fell and wrapped his arms around her.

"Thank God. These men? They got you out?"

"Yes, sent by Carla. They're Russian, I'll explain it all to you, as much as I can work it out for myself."

540

She kissed him long and hard.

Sergei and Tolya grinned at the sight of these two embracing.

"*Poidyomcya*! Let's go." Sergei whispered to his colleague. He stretched out a hand to Leandro, who shook it as hard as he could to convey his gratitude.

"She, she brave woman." Sergei waved to Sam. "Good luck."

Sam found the strength to climb back across onto the other launch and embrace Sergei. He gave her a small envelope.

"For you. From lady."

"Thank you, thank you. *Spasiba*."

She kissed Tolya as he made ready to step back into their launch.

"*Spasiba*."

The two men waved and Sergei restarted the engine, slowly pushing down the throttle. Their launch backed away. Within minutes, its rear navigation light had disappeared up the Urión.

Sam lay down on the bench, her head on his knees. Leandro started the engine. She looked up at him.

He kissed her.

"What did he give you?"

"I don't know. Let's see."

In the light of his torch, she handed him a small white card.

"DE RUSIA CON AMOR, C. FROM RUSSIA WITH LOVE, C."

That woman was never very far away, but for once, Leandro felt nothing but affection and gratitude for her. Perhaps one day he would be able to express it.

Russians! Whatever next? He could only begin to imagine what the release of Sam might have involved. If they had pulled this off in the heart of the Argentine pampa, they must know what they were doing. Things had changed!

Fifteen minutes later, he docked quietly at the end of the jetty in front of his house. Sam had fallen asleep. Having looped the painter round one of the poles, he picked her up carefully and carried her inside.

As he laid her down on the bed, she stirred and looked up at him, her eyes half closed. Her lips parted in a slow smile.

"My love, be careful, the last four men to have seen me naked all died today," she whispered. "Horrible deaths!" She shivered dramatically.

He would have to take his chances.

An hour after they had gone indoors, Dávila and Carla stood in the main bedroom, sheathed from head to toe in black latex. A black hood with gold-framed eyeholes enhanced the beauty of Carla's eyes, her full lips a violent red. Latex thigh boots, needle heels. Dávila's hood completely sealed off his features, a short breathing tube emerging from the area of his mouth his only connection with the outside world.

In Punta del Este, in Zürich, and here in this sanctum at the core of his house in the Delta, with its jet black walls and mirrors reflecting every move, the ritual would be played out in accordance with a set of rules whose surreal inspiration lay in the scenes which had thrown them together more than twenty-five years earlier in the underground cells of El Pozo. Waterboarding had given way to autoerotic suffocation, screams of pain to groans of pleasure and arousal. Where Dávila had once been the master of ceremonies, alternating extremes of agony with brief intervals of respite, it was Carla who now orchestrated the proceedings.

Taking his gloved hand in hers, she led Dávila through the closet door into the inner cell, closing it behind her, and steered him round a large rectangular platform, towards a seat at the other end of the room. Taking him by the hips, she lowered him into place, so that his sightless head was on a level with the glistening surface of her tight abdomen. Like a blind man, his hands began to caress her body, circling her breasts, down either side of her hips, finally between her thighs seeking the mound of her latex-covered labia. Thrusting her breasts against his face, she guided his hands over their curves, as if helping him to print their profile and unctuous texture on the retina of his mind. His breathing grew louder. His hand finding the small rubber air pump suspended between her legs, he began to squeeze it slowly. As the dildo swelled inside her, Carla threw back her shoulders, arching her back. A low moan of pleasure escaped her lips.

On a touch from her, the pumping stopped. Stepping back, she pulled aside the curtains along one wall and unfolded a long, sack-like body bag which she laid out on the central platform. Taking Dávila once more by the hand, she helped him to sit on the edge of the platform. Having sprayed lubricant into the top of the rubber bag, which she had unzipped from crotch to neck, she eased his feet and legs into the lower half. Helping him to roll onto the platform, she finished the process of totally encasing his body in the bag. It only remained to pull its hood over his head, adjust his short breathing tube through a small hole, extricate his limp latex-sheathed penis through an opening in the area of his crotch and slide the airtight zip up to his chin.

"*Gehts? Bequem?*" It was part of the ritual that she always speak German to him.

He nodded his head, a faint grunt coming from the tube. Picking up a gas mask from which dangled a short hose, she slid it over his head, making sure to insert his breathing tube into the airway, and tightening the straps. The sound of his breathing now rasped in the tube. From each side of the platform, she stretched thick rubber straps across his body, pinning him to the table at ankles, waist and neck. She then plugged an air hose into a valve on the shoulder of the body-bag which, to the low whirring of a compressor, proceeded to suck out all the air, a powerful vacuum constricting Dávila's progressively objectified body.

Bending over him, Carla began the hazardous ritual elaborated in their early years together in Zürich. Stroking his limp member with her right hand, with her left she alternately opened and closed the supply of air to his mask by placing her hand over the end of the tube. Each shutdown was to be longer than the last. Dávila fought for breath as his body arched and twisted in response. Slowly, she detected the beginnings of arousal. His breath came faster, a low moaning audible from behind the mask. The work of her two hands finally led to the erection he sought. For the next ten minutes or so, Carla orchestrated his pleasure, stroking his latex penis with her gloved hands, swallowing it between her lips, alternating fellatio with asphyxia. Dávila's breath came harsher and faster, his constricted movements at times more violent, at others more voluptuous. A powerful orgasm finally shook him from head to toe.

Carla glanced up at the small electric clock on the wall. It showed nine thirty. She bent closer to him, pressing her lips against his ear.

"*Es ist Zeit, mein Liebchen,*" she whispered. The time had come.

She circled round him, caressing him softly. Then, with a final extended kiss onto the mouthpiece of his mask, she inserted a plug into the end of the hose, shutting off the air completely, and stood back. Turning away from him, she watched his final contortions in the wall mirror. At first he lay still, but only for some thirty seconds, before the realisation that all was wrong produced a frenzied jerking of the glistening black chrysalis that Dávila had become, his head crashing from side to side, powerless. The rasping shriek of his breath, overlaid with screams, continued for more than a minute, then died slowly away, the convulsions growing smaller, less violent, as he lost consciousness. Within two or three more minutes, she knew he would be dead. Carla sat and silently surveyed the motionless, dehumanised relic of more than twenty-five years of shared psychosis. In the ultimate game of trust, Carla had deliberately broken the one and only rule. She knew it, but had no regrets.

"I needed my freedom, and you were never going to give it to me, Alberto. Our torture games had to end. What you did to Sam was a step too far. Hopefully I've released you from your cancer. And brought my own cure."

As she walked slowly towards the door, she allowed her hand once again to glide along his inert shape. A final glance at the blackness behind the lenses of the mask. She passed out of the closet into the bathroom and stepped into the shower.

Having first extricated the dildo, she voluptuously peeled off the black latex, like a snake casting its skin, as if shedding her past at the same time. Naked, she washed away her juices, her sweat, the perfumed shower gel soaking into every pore of her body. Her skin felt new. Kicking the suit and boots into a corner of the shower, she emerged and dried herself carefully.

It felt as if she had suddenly woken from the grip of a dreadful nightmare, which had preyed upon her for more than twenty-five years. It was physical, as if some major diseased organ had been surgically removed. With it had gone the dull, pulsating pain she had felt inside her all these years. It was as if her life had suddenly come into clear and coherent focus. The sinister relationship with Dávila, with which she had been too long compliant, too long a partner, had been dispelled. An act for which she had been preparing for some time. Insofar as it involved taking human life, something she had never thought she would do, it had terrified her. But, in the final analysis, if, in exchange for his life, she could recover her own?

Her experiences in the time of the military dictatorship had provided Carla with ample material after reaching Zürich for reflection on the nature of evil. Where did her act, taking the life of someone like Dávila, sit on a scale of evil? Any belief in God had been fully tested by her experiences. On balance, she would regard herself as an agnostic at best. She had once consulted a Jesuit priest working in a poor neighbourhood of the Swiss city. He had shown her a more philosophical distinction of evil, between intention and action. For that matter, if evil was the yardstick, how did her act compare with Dávila and the horrors in which he had indulged? In his crimes, action and intention had been inseparable. But in hers? She might be condemned for the action, but what of the intention? Her act might be evil, but given the context, was her intention equally so? Had she not at times wondered whether, through her relationship with Dávila, she might not have become an accomplice, simply by surviving? Tonight, had she somehow taken a revenge, for herself, even for others?

As she stood there, the dominant feeling was of one release, of evil washed out of her life. Tomorrow, in the light of day, the dilemma would no doubt return. She would face that when it came.

From a cupboard in the main bedroom, she pulled on an old pair of jeans, one of his Ralph Lauren shirts and a thick sweater. A pair of strong boots completed her get up. Moving to the sitting room, she picked up a small rucksack containing her passports, cash and credit cards, as well as her laptop and three mobile phones which she had placed behind the sofa.

On the Blackberry reserved for calls to Dávila, she dialled his number, the one he used exclusively for calls to her. He had once proudly told her that it wasn't in his name. A muffled buzzing sound came from inside the jacket which Dávila had hung over a chair earlier in the evening. She pulled it out, checked that it was her number ringing and then, turning it off, dropped it into her bag. One less piece of evidence.

From inside the hall, she flashed the veranda lights on and off three times. Then she sat down in one of the rocking chairs on the porch and waited. Within a minute, from the darkness of the trees by the river, Sergei and Tolya emerged silently.

"Was she all right?" She spoke to them in Russian.

"A bit bruised and very tired. But she should be okay with a week's rest and some loving attention."

"Are you ready? It's this way."

She led them back into the small cell.

"Unstrap him and then let's go."

As they were about to lift Dávila off the table, she stopped them.

"Just a minute."

She stepped outside and made her way to the drawing room. She knew the combination of his safe, concealed behind an ugly landscape of the pampa of which Dávila had been inordinately proud, and, spinning the wheel, pulled out his small confidential laptop. He had never suspected that she knew the combination.

Collecting his SIDE pass card from the inside pocket of his jacket hanging over the back of a chair, she took both into the inner room, where the two young men were waiting, trying not to show too much curiosity at the bizarre scenario of the room. She pulled down the long zip on the bodysack. Dávila's fists were clenched against his chest by the final suffocation. His face remained invisible under its latex mask. Rigor mortis would set in only later. It was easy for Carla to slide the laptop, the ID tucked inside the lid, under his arms against his chest.

"That should make it more interesting when they find him."

Having closed the zip hermetically once more, she unstrapped the gasmask from his head and inserted a large plug in the top of the breathing tube. Then screwing the air hose back onto the valve, she pumped up the inert shape until it looked like a huge black cigar.

Carla followed Sergei and Tolya as they manoeuvred Dávila out of the house and down to the jetty. She nearly tripped over the unconscious body of the guard, who had been smoking there earlier.

"How long will the guards be out?" Carla whispered.

Sergei shrugged his shoulders. "Forever... the cook and the maid are watching TV over there in their bungalow and they haven't moved."

Tolya began to walk upstream along the riverbank and five minutes later, the silhouette of the motor launch loomed out of the light mist hanging over the canal, coming silently down on the current.

"Have you set the fuel and incendiaries?"

"We laid all that out while we were waiting. It'll burn long and very fiercely."

"Okay, let's get this on the boat and then you set off the fire."

The shape of Dávila was unceremoniously bundled onto the rear seat of the launch and, while Sergei and Tolya, having picked up the unconscious body of Carlos, ran back to the house to set off the thermite grenades, Carla stood in the bow holding the rope, loosely tied to the jetty.

In less than ten minutes, the two men were back.

"Did you remove the padlock on the servants' house, so that they can get out?"

Tolya nodded.

"We dumped the bodyguards next to the incendiaries. There won't be much left of them!"

She released the rope and allowed the launch to drift some fifty metres down the canal. Then, at a very low speed, they set off towards the wider river. As Carla looked back at the main house, a dull glow was visible between its supporting stilts, as an acrid smoke began to swirl across the garden. She turned and looked ahead.

As they passed the darkened outline of one of the small riverbank settlements at the entrance to Arroyo Los Sabalos, they dumped Dávila overboard. Carla watched as the black rubber tube bobbed away in the wake of the launch, the moonlight playing on its glistening surface. He might have dreamed of this way to go.

"Okay, Sergei, let's head for Puerto Sauces."

So as not to attract attention and also to spot any floating obstacles on the surface, the GPS clearly indicating the route, they cruised at half speed along the final stretch of the Rio Parana de la Palmas to emerge through the Bajos del Temor to the broad expanse of the River Plate. Here, they paused briefly to ditch all their armoury except the Makarovs.

Watching Sergei and Tolya throwing their guns overboard, Carla took the two dedicated Blackberrys out of her bag. Holding one in each hand, as if weighing them, she was on the point of dropping them into the waters of the River Plate. She hesitated, then put them back in her bag. Maybe some day she would come to regret that decision.

They went to full power and less than two hours after they had cast off from the house, the twin 400 horsepower engines had them slipping into moorings in the discreet little Uruguayan marina.

Naya was sitting at the wheel of the BMW, parked under the trees beyond the dockside. At that hour, no-one was around to check their identities, not that that would have been a problem, since theoretically they had never left Uruguay. Sergei got into the rear seat with Tolya, Carla sitting in the front beside Naya. She reclined her seat. In low gear, the BMW crept out of the small village and rapidly re-joined the main road in the direction of Montevideo and Punta del Este. They would be there in about four hours, driving carefully so as not to attract attention. Carla was asleep before they reached the road.

GC 157, the Guarda Costa's Alucat launch, gave a powerful reverse thrust of its 220 horsepower twin Volvo Penta, Hamilton Waterjet engines and coasted the final meter up to the jetty. The sailor in the bow jumped onto the wooden planking and hitched the line onto the handrail.

It had been a busy night, what with the fire up river, the burnt out Ford in San Fernando and now this. What a way to start the week! They had arrived far too late to prevent the house being totally burnt down, but when they had given its GPS coordinates over the radio, all hell seemed to break loose, with senior officers calling in every five minutes and strict instructions not to allow the story to get into the press. It had nevertheless made the morning news, one of the islanders – whom they were still trying to track down – having rung into a local radio station with the story. Luckily nobody had been hurt, as far as they could tell, although the forensics were still searching through the rubble. Two terrified maids had been picked up along the river bank, who seemed to suggest that the owner and two bodyguards might be missing.

The owner of the *almacén* was waiting to meet them.

"It's over here," he said, leading them about fifty metres along the riverbank.

The deflated tube containing Dávila's body lay stretched out on the mud.

"We opened the zip, but then didn't touch it again. Everything was dry inside. When we found it, it was blown up like a balloon, floating in the reeds over there. We could feel that it was a body, that's why we opened it." He stepped back to allow the Prefectura officer to bend over the rubber bag.

"What the shit is this? Some kind of floating coffin? Is this the way some people want to get buried nowadays?"

He opened the zip farther to reveal the laptop frozen in Dávila's rigid embrace. As he lifted it up, the SIDE ID card fell out. He'd seen one of those before to know that this was no ordinary corpse.

"Jesus, this guy's somebody high up. Don't touch anything. I'm going to call base. *Cabo*, stay here and don't let anyone get close."

He ran to the launch and called up the San Isidro Prefectura office.

Sam, exhausted, slept until mid-afternoon. Leandro had been up since early morning, spending most of the time sitting by her bedside, looking at her, allowing the full realisation of her return to swirl through him. In the dim light which filtered through the curtains of the bedroom, he studied the curves of her body, the splash of her hair against the pillow, the softness of her breathing. Her sleep was as deep as any he could remember. Even the smell of the coffee he had brewed for himself, a scent which usually roused her, had had no effect.

With time to think, he had skimmed through the events of the last month. A year ago, he would never have imagined the scenario in which he now found himself. His affair with Sam had led him in directions he could never have suspected. From a life centred on the observation of political and economic events in Argentina, he had progressively been drawn into a zone of darkness, of intrigue, of violence. That these existed below the surface, he had never doubted. But from being in his own estimation a fairly law-abiding citizen, he now found himself operating, whether he liked it or not, on the margins. A target for sinister forces inside the government, they had followed him, attacked his son, murdered people with whom he had been in contact, kidnapped the woman he loved, and now, in this final episode, provoked what almost amounted to an act of war. He had to assume that such was the mission of the two men he had glimpsed out on the river last night. Had sex and violence completely replaced monetary reserves and interest rates as the focus of his existence! Was this really what his life was to be about from now on? As he observed Sam's sleeping form, he asked himself whether she had not somehow pulled him down a rabbit hole, like some Alice, into a world in which nothing was quite what it seemed? Not to mention the assignment for Frobisher, to which he must return as soon as the present drama was over. As long as it was over. He might have Sam back again, but what of Dávila? It was logical to assume that the rescue of Sam was part of a wider operation to deal with Dávila. But he could not be sure.

At about ten, he had walked to the edge of the river and had rung Carla's home number in Zürich, but an answering machine had informed him that she was travelling and that the caller should leave a message. He tried a cell phone which she had given him the day after Sam's disappearance, but again no reply.

Standing on the end of the jetty, he rang Señor Haidar to tell him that he had heard from Sam, that she was on her way back from the north. The old man thanked him, but seemed to take his daughter's two-week absence as normal.

Later that morning, Carlitos rowed past in his low dinghy and shouted to him as he stood on the veranda.

"Lot of excitement in the river last night, Don Leandro. Big fire in Arroyo Los Sabalos. Never seen so much Prefectura. They're everywhere this morning."

Leandro had some ideas about that, not to be shared with Carlitos.

Finally, around midday, his cell phone vibrated as he sat watching Sam. He answered, whispering into the phone as he walked back out onto the veranda and down towards the sluggish canal.

"It's Carla. How is she?"

"She's sleeping. Exhausted, but apparently in good shape."

He had personally verified the perfection of her shape last night, but a combination of the physical stress and tensions of the two weeks on the farm had rapidly swamped her passion and she had fallen asleep in his arms.

"She loved your message."

Carla laughed, a deep laugh which he had never heard before.

"I thought it was appropriate for your Mata Hari."

Could Carla somehow know about Sam's relationship with Mossad? He would have to ask Sam.

"She loved it. I can't find the words to thank you for everything you pulled off. It was incredible. And thank those two if you see them."

"I'm looking at them at this moment. I'll pass on your thanks. But how are you, Leandro, now that you're woman is back?"

"I'll leave that to your imagination. Though I do hold a grudge against you for not having told me anything, for not having given me an opportunity to do something, however small, to help get her back."

"Don't hold it against me, Leandro. I only did it in your interest. You see, Dávila was having you followed from the moment you got back to Buenos Aires. For my plan to work, I needed to ensure that nothing happened to you. For a start, there was no telling what Dávila might do if he got hold of you. And he would have lifted you off the street, had he been given the slightest reason to suspect that you could get between him and me. He's had enough people killed in the past, one more would have made no difference. Knowing you, you might have tried to intervene directly to rescue Sam. That would have made it impossible for my plan to work, if anything had gone wrong and Sam had been moved away from the farm. She had to be in one of the only places to which I could guide my two Russians. If Dávila had moved her, I wouldn't have known where to send them. For that reason, and for that reason alone, the less you were able to do, the better for Sam. Don't worry, I've a feeling that Sam is going to give both of us plenty of headaches in the future, plenty of opportunities to come to her rescue. And I'll enjoy it. And so will you." She laughed again.

Leandro shook his head. This woman was really something. Even down the phone, he was getting to sense some of the fascination she must exert over Sam. One hell of a rival! But for now, she had saved Sam and that was all there was to it.

"I'm sure you're right, Carla. Maybe one day, I can return the favour to you."

"If I see an opportunity, I'll cash in my credit. Don't worry!"

"You can't be far away. Where are you?"

"In Punta del Este. We arrived early this morning. When she wakes up, tell Sam that I'll be here for another week or so, if she feels like a rest."

Leandro tensed. The competition for Sam's time was back on the agenda! But he sensed that jealousy was not going to be a good ally against someone like Carla.

"Of course I'll tell her. Some sea air will do her a lot of good. Maybe I'll even come over with her."

Carla didn't miss a beat.

"Of course, Leandro, great idea. We'll fix it. Now, I must get back to my two heroes. Take good care of her and tell her I love her."

"After what you've just done for her, I'd be surprised if that was necessary, but of course I'll pass it on."

"And you take good care of yourself too, I know what you mean to Sam. At least the threat of Dávila is no longer hanging over you. *Un beso.*" She cut off.

Leandro walked silently back into the bedroom. Sam was still fast asleep. He resumed his vigil. The focal field of his emotions had widened. Up to then, Sam had occupied the foreground, the background somewhat blurred. Now, he realised quite clearly that the background must be brought into focus, to include Carla, this strange woman who had just sent him a kiss over the phone. Sam had told him as much that evening at Oviedo. His phone conversation with Carla had finally brought it home.

He would have to meet her. Soon.

But now, he had a date with the girl lying opposite him in the half light of the room. They made soft, slow love that afternoon. And later, as they sat on the veranda and watched the sun slip behind the trees, she rang Carla.

It was a perfect late summer afternoon. Punta del Este had long ago been abandoned by the holiday crowds and the coast had returned to the quiet lifestyle reminiscent of earlier times. The sky to the east was a dark, luminous blue over the Atlantic, the sea unusually calm, the white specks of seagulls drifting and dipping along the waterline.

Sam and Carla were sitting over the remains of lunch beside the pool. More than a week had gone by since Sam's rescue. Leandro had finally reconciled himself to the idea that she might recover more rapidly in the company of another woman, and had accompanied her on the Wednesday following her release to catch the flight to Punta del Este. Sam had first rung her father, reassuring him that she was now on her way back from the North East and would come and see him as soon as she got back. Leandro agreed that her physical condition after more than two weeks in the hands of Dávila's thugs was still far too visible for her to confront her father.

Carla had collected her at the small airport.

"So what happened to Sergei and Tolya? I was hoping to find them here, to thank them again."

"I drove them into Montevideo on the afternoon of Monday, the day we got back from the Delta. They had to go through with the cover story for which they got their visas. Typical Victor Alexievich to think up something so complicated. Sergei and Tolya were ostensibly doing research into agricultural businesses in Uruguay on behalf one of his companies. The Uruguayan-Russian Chamber of Commerce had set up some meetings for them with the Ministry of Agriculture, people like that. Not that either of them could probably tell the difference between a cow and a sheep. The Embassy were to provide an interpreter and Victor Alexievich had sent them with a long list of questions. Frankly, they didn't even understand the questions. Anyway, I made sure that they were cleaned up and smartly dressed in suits and ties and they booked themselves into the Radisson Hotel. I kept well out of sight.

They left a couple of days later on an evening flight back to Moscow. Quite what the Uruguayans made of it, I don't know. But who cares?"

Carla was clearly delighted with the whole charade.

"Most important of all, they got you out. I put them in touch with a couple of Russian girls back in Moscow who I know for sure will give them one hell of a night." And Carla laughed, that deep laugh that Sam knew came from the heart.

"You were brilliant! And perhaps soon I'll meet Victor Alexievich to thank him personally."

"Don't worry, I'm sure you will. Very early on, I explained to him who you were, but most of all, what you are for me. He got the message and certainly pulled a brilliant operation together. You'll like him, he's one of the new generation of Russians, very rich, very confident, but not flashy. That's what makes him different."

"And Dávila in all of this?" Sam asked, almost in a whisper.

"History! In every sense of the word. With luck, no-one will ever see or hear of him again. But especially not you, my love, after what he did to you."

"Someday, I'll tell you a bit more. But it's all still too fresh."

"Don't bother, I know it all."

"How? Did he send you some kind of video?"

"Yes. Typical of his twisted mind. I told you in Zürich how we came together back in the 1980s. But it's only in the last eighteen months or so that he became homicidal. As if something was eating away inside him. I can't explain it. Then came the incident in the hotel. I told you about that one as well. He wanted to drag me fully into his tormented mind, like some kind of accomplice, trading on what we had been through together. It's at that point that I realised I had to end it. Unwittingly you became part of that process, something I wouldn't have wished on my worst enemy. Anyway, I don't want to talk about him anymore."

Although it was slowly fading, Carla was still struggling to come to terms with what she had done that night in the Delta.

She stood up and walked round the table to stand behind Sam. She leaned forward, putting her face next to Sam's, wrapping her arms around her.

"I'm so sorry, Sam," she whispered. "Can you forgive me?"

Sam said nothing, but, placing her arms over Carla's embrace, she pulled her closer. Words were superfluous.

They stayed in this embrace for a minute or so.

Carla straightened up.

"Now you must rest. You're already looking much better, a few more days and you'll be the old Sam again."

Turning, she called out.

"Naya, la Señorita is going to rest. Pull the curtains in her bedroom please."

Naya appeared in the doorway.

"*Wo sind die zwei Handys, Naya? Ich hatte sie hier hingelegt...*"

Naya shook her head.

"*Weiss nicht, Madame. Hab' sie heute nicht gesehen.*"

Sam looked up.

"Anything the matter? "

"The two Blackberrys. The ones I told you about the other day. I'd left them lying here. And now they've gone."

"I threw them into the sea on my walk this morning," Sam replied, her tone deliberately matter of fact.

"You what?"

A look of anger had flashed into Carla's eyes.

"Yes. You shouldn't have kept them. They were bad for you, Carla. You have to make a clean break."

Sam held Carla's gaze.

Almost as fast as it had come, the fury faded and softness returned. Also a touch of sadness.

She turned away and stared out towards the sea. After a few moments, she walked back to Sam and taking both her hands in hers, kissed them.

"Thank you, my love. You're right, of course. Only you would have had the courage."

Later that evening, Sam's Blackberry was buzzing on the night table beside her bed. She looked at her watch. She'd been asleep for more than three hours, the sun was setting fast, judging by the thin ray of light at the edge of the curtains. She showered and pulled on a soft jogging suit.

Carla had remained sitting near the pool. The last rays of the sunset lit up the tops of the pine trees around the house.

"Leandro asks if he can come at the weekend."

"At last, I was wondering how long he would hold out. Of course. As soon as he gives us his flight details, you can confirm that I'll get Naya to pick him up."

April 2008

Leandro had brought Sam back to Buenos Aires. She had been the one wanting to return, to rebuild the relationship they had established that night at Oviedo's. He sensed that, after all the drama since their dinner and the night spent at the *hotel de alojamiento*, she needed to put the furniture of her emotional apartment, so violently disturbed by the kidnapping, back in place. Their days together at Carla's had persuaded him that, in some strange way, he and Carla filled a complementary need in the complex psychology that was Sam's. Carla had immediately made him feel at ease. She was a mistress of ceremonies even in the most complex situations, sensitively orchestrating their triangle of emotions, by no means concealing her relationship with Sam and yet at the same time clearly sending Leandro a signal that he could – indeed should - occupy as much room as Sam would give him. Subtly, in the language she had used, she had shown him how to respect a boundary between what he felt for Sam, and what she felt. He was increasingly convinced that Sam might be right when she said that Carla was in love with her. It was as if he and Carla had become partners, prepared to share an emotional space with someone they both loved, seeking all the time to avoid a confrontation which would only upset the object of their affections.

Lying awake, with Sam beside him, he had tried to analyse it, to rationalise it. Finally, he had given up. Until further notice, the need to allow Sam to recover far outweighed any satisfaction he might derive from arriving at an intellectually satisfactory conclusion. He turned over and fell asleep, his hand resting on her thigh.

The traces of her ordeal on the farm were slowly receding as the days passed. Leandro began to relax. Even so, she was more restless even than usual and at times appeared to have difficulty concentrating, whether on the book she was reading or on the thread of one of their discussions. She would suddenly stop in mid-sentence and look past Leandro. At those moments, he would stretch out his hand to touch her and, with a slight quiver of the shoulders, she would recapture the point at which she had broken off.

"Don't worry, my love, it will pass," he murmured and she smiled back, a look of gratitude.

"Yes, it will, don't you worry either."

"I suspect you need something to focus on."

"You're probably right, as so often."

Soon after their return, Sam had told Leandro of her conversation with Carla about Dávila. Dávila was dead. Without knowing all the details, it was apparent that the two Russians had gone on to Dávila's Delta house and that Dávila had died there. How, Carla had not said.

This explained something else. Leandro had, within days of returning from the Delta after Sam's release, detected that the surveillance had disappeared. Over coffee one morning with Eduardo, his godson confirmed the same impression. Just by way of precaution, he had used Charles' equipment after his return. He was shocked to discover a small microphone placed high on top of his bookshelves! The fact that his prior sweep had not found any trace led him to the conclusion that it must be a more recent intrusion. Close inspection of his doors and windows produced no trace of any entry. He would change the locks as soon as possible. Not that he had any real illusions that it would deter a professional! But with Dávila dead, he probably had less to fear.

He had ultimately decided to keep Eduardo in the dark about the true circumstances of Sam's disappearance, playing back to him the same story that he had given to her father. Although he felt uncomfortable about withholding so much, in discussion with Sam they had come to the conclusion that the less said the better at this stage. Eduardo appeared to have accepted the story of her trip to the northeast and a subsequent week at her father's house in Punta del Este, where Leandro had ostensibly joined her. On top of that, Eduardo had finally decided to marry Florencia, which was now taking up a lot of his time. Leandro was delighted.

A couple of days off the deadline set him by Charles, he sent an email, the gist of which was that, on the basis of his analysis, he should be in a position to respond to the assignment. It had not been an easy decision, but at no stage had he doubted that a collaboration in nuclear matters with Iran was a policy which could do nothing but bring harm to Argentina.

It was now late April. Sam was reading. Leandro was watching the evening news on TN, a channel not known for any particular sympathy with the present government. The sun had gone down above the roofs on the other side of Pasaje La Piedad, the noise of the traffic a dull rumble at the far end of the narrow little street.

The doorbell rang. Eduardo strolled through the door, an enigmatic grin on his face.

"You'll never believe what happened today!"

"Is it worth a good drink?" Leandro asked. "Excellent timing as always!"

"I would say a bottle of your best champagne, uncle."

"Come and sit next to your aunt Samira," she said, moving to one end of the settee, "and tell us all about it."

Sam and Eduardo had clearly established a good level of banter.

"Judging from the way you're dressed and that sinister helmet in the hall, I presume that that monster downstairs is yours?" Eduardo challenged Sam, as he sat down beside her.

Sam, in tight black leather jeans tucked into ankle boots of the same colour, and a black Harley Davidson tee-shirt, was in no condition to deny it!

The champagne served, Eduardo began.

"At about ten this morning, Fonseca calls me into his office. First he asks me a number of routine questions about current cases that I'm handling. Then, as I'm about to leave, he calls me back. Did I remember the case of the Englishwoman in the hotel? I expressed regret that we hadn't made more progress. We could close the files, he said, the case had been solved. Naturally, I showed some surprise. Yes, some very recent events had thrown a completely new light on the case.

Apparently, he'd been called a few days ago to a high-level meeting at the Ministry of Justice and Human Rights, where he found himself at a large conference table with a group of very senior officials and officers, from the Army, from SIDE, from the Presidency and from the Prefectura. To begin with, everyone in the room was made to sign a confidentiality agreement. Once everyone had signed, the representative from SIDE presented the story. It appeared that at the end of last month, Prefectura had picked up the body of a certain Alberto Dávila in Arroyo Los Sabalos up in the Delta. They were told in the strictest confidence that Dávila had been a high-level advisor to SIDE and enjoyed very privileged access to a number of senior members of the present Government. Without going into details, the group was informed that the condition of his body indicated that he had been involved in some form of perverse sexual activity. The autopsy revealed that he had died of asphyxiation, not of drowning. During the night, when he had apparently been dropped in the river, a fire had completely destroyed his house farther out in the Delta. A laptop computer found on the body had, on examination, enabled the investigation to put together a complex picture of extreme sexual perversions practised by Dávila, including the kidnapping, rape and assassination of young women. Other files suggested that he might have been a member of a paedophile ring. It had also been possible to start putting together what appeared to be a series of illicit financial transactions linking Dávila to a number of prominent and extremely wealthy members of the Argentine business community. Since these transactions usually passed through a number of shell companies, it would take some time to track down the whereabouts of the funds. Preliminary investigation suggested that some of the funds might have been invested in property in Argentina and Uruguay. There were suspicions that he might also have had an accomplice in Switzerland, but they had still not been able to identify that person."

"I wonder where that leaves Carla. Hope she doesn't get caught up in this," Sam cut in.

Leandro looked at her, surprised.

"It strikes me that she might very well."

Sam said nothing and looked away.

Eduardo continued.

"I don't know frankly. Anyway, the investigation is currently also looking at some of Dávila's travel movements over the last year. On top of that, on the weekend of Dávila's murder, his farm near Chacabuco had been raided by some sort of paramilitary team, apparently foreign mercenaries. They had rounded up all the gauchos and locked them in their quarters. There was a suggestion that a woman had been involved. The bodies of two bodyguards, members of some kind of clandestine hit team set up by Dávila, had been found shot on the farm. Ballistics were able to identify the bullets and shell cases as coming from a Russian automatic, a Makarov. Two different weapons, one for each, so probably two separate killers. And not content with that, they found another two corpses in the remains of a burnt out Ford Ranger in San Fernando. Two heavies also associated with Dávila. Shot in the back of the head. The pick-up had been left there the same evening. It looked as though they had used a thermal grenade. In their case, the bullets, or what was left of them, seemed to have come from a very rare weapon, a silent pistol of Soviet design, used most often by Russian Special Forces. A real assassin's choice. So all in all, quite a killing spree!"

Sam and Leandro avoided looking at each other.

Eduardo looked a bit put out at their apparent lack of enthusiasm at what he was telling them.

"You don't seem impressed!" he muttered.

"No, you're wrong, it's an amazing story, seems to confirm everything we suspected," Leandro replied quickly.

"Exactly. Anyway, when I didn't seem to be showing the necessary degree of enthusiasm, which seemed to irritate him, he dropped his bombshell. The laptop had also contained a film portraying the murder of Janet Williams at the hotel! Further investigation had established that Dávila had spent the night in one of the two flats adjoining the hotel at the time of the murder. So that seemed to be that! For reasons of professional pride, I of course expressed disappointment that it had not been our team that had cracked the crime, but Fonseca brought me up short. He said that if we'd got there, it could have been disastrous for all our careers. Not only would we have been moving against one of the most sensitive areas of the Government, nothing less than SIDE – but – and here he practically made me sign the secrecy form as well –

he had been reliably informed that the investigation was now looking at Dávila's activities during the *dictadura*. Over a coffee after the meeting, one of the SIDE team, an old friend of Fonseca's – he has them everywhere as we know – told him that there were good grounds to believe that Dávila, far from being an active member of the Montos, and therefore ideologically attuned to many people at the heart of the present Government, might actually have been an informer working for the Army. As such, he might have been responsible for the arrest, torture and disappearance of a number of those who had waged the final offensive against the military in 1979 and 1980. Fonseca made a reference to ESMA, to another interrogation centre known as El Pozo and to certain films. We can guess that, after killing Sosa, Dávila's thugs brought him the library and the investigators must have found them on his laptop. Dávila being very close to one or two key figures in today's Government, if it emerged that he was a traitor, they might also find themselves under scrutiny. If that came out, it would blow a massive hole below the waterline of the current government's precious human rights image. So all in all, Fonseca was very happy that we'd been able to combine a semblance of professional commitment without actually getting too close to the fire. He even congratulated me on having had the good sense to play it long!"

There was silence in the room.

"Well," Leandro began, "that now seems to explain why the surveillance stopped at the end of last month. More important, this would indicate that you, Eduardo, are no longer in danger, which was after all the main objective of this exercise all along. And best of all, it's been achieved without any of us apparently being implicated. I'd say we've been very lucky. On the other hand, I've a nasty feeling that this may blow up in the face of certain people, including your informer. The first thing should be to warn him, very carefully so as to leave no trail. He was after all instrumental in our making progress, and you owe him that much."

They had still not let Sam fully into the secret of Sarmiento.

"It seems hard to imagine, given that they have the video of the hotel murder, that they won't go looking for Carla, just as we did," Sam added quietly.

"Eduardo, did anybody give any idea of who could killed Dávila and burned down his houses, not to mention killing his thugs?"

"No, but it must all have been pretty violent. There was a suggestion that two more of his security guards had also been burned to death in the house fire up river. The others had simply been executed. From the way Fonseca spoke, it sounded to me as though they might not be too eager to track down the killers. Largely because, if you look at it one way, by killing Dávila, these people may actually have been doing the government a favour. Not to mention clearing up a little freelance operation at the heart of SIDE."

"You're right, I hadn't thought of it that way."

"Apparently, the government is content to let the whole incident appear as confused as possible. The events on the farm have also not made it from the local Chacabuco papers. Attacks on farms are pretty common anyway, these days. Although the fire in the Delta got into the papers, I can't recall having seen anything about a body being found up river. They must have put a total clampdown on that part of the story, to stop embarrassing questions being asked. I'll try and get some more out of Fonseca, but he may not be very forthcoming."

"I may have a piece of the puzzle," Sam spoke slowly. "Using one of her roundabout circuits, Carla asked me a few weeks ago how difficult it might be to get a copy of Dávila's death certificate."

Eduardo thought for a minute before replying.

"My guess is that it won't be easy. I suppose, a death certificate might be a way of closing our file, but somehow I don't think anybody is going to want to give us a copy and make so obvious a link between the killing of Williams and Dávila."

"Could there be any other way?"

"I don't know, I'll try and find out."

"What other loose ends are there?" Leandro asked.

"A lot of depends on how much they decide to follow up on Carla. Through Carla, they could get to Sam, and through Sam to you. They may get to her through the Uruguay connection, if they can trace it.

After all, Carla wasn't exactly invisible around Punta del Este this summer."

"My feeling is that she's locked all that down," Sam muttered, somewhat enigmatically.

Eduardo turned his chair towards her.

"Forgive me if I appear to insist, Sam, but how much more do you know? I have the distinct impression that you're ahead of us on this one. And not for the first time!"

Sam showed no sign of being in the least disconcerted. Instead, she adopted that look of seriousness, which, Leandro had to confess, could at times irritate him. Leandro decided to let her fight her corner, even though he now knew as much as she did.

"As you know, Carla and I have been in touch fairly regularly over the last few months. She never actually said anything directly, but I could tell when I was in Zürich that she was preparing something. Something which she implied was going to change a lot of things. I'm pretty sure that she's found herself a new *patron*. From hints that she dropped when I was with her in Zürich, I had a feeling that her relationship with Dávila was coming to an end. One night, she told me about what had happened at L'Hôtel."

She focused on Eduardo.

"It was as you suspected, Eduardo. Dávila had told her to pick up the English woman at the Rural and to bring her back to her hotel. He'd told her that Janet Williams was into BDSM and breath-play and told her how to set it up. Carla was amazed how the whole sequence played out almost exactly as Dávila had said it would, right down to Williams telling her how she wanted to be tied down and providing the hood and the dildo. Dávila had instructed Carla to ring him on her cell phone when Williams was all tied up and within a few minutes, he appeared in the hotel bedroom. Williams was so busy moaning and breathing through her hood, that she never heard him come in. Carla continued to work on Williams with the dildo while he filmed her until, at one point, he signalled to her to leave, which, suspecting the mood he was in, she was very happy to do. The last thing she saw as she left the room was Dávila working the dildo with one hand and filming it all with the other. When she left, Williams was very much alive, though obviously in a highly vulnerable position with a man like Dávila in the room."

Leandro filled her outstretched glass.

"It was only a day later that she put the newspaper coverage and what had happened together. Dávila had given her strict instructions to fly to Uruguay, which she did, under an assumed name. Naturally, she was terrified that somehow this would come back to her. It was only towards the end of October that Dávila convinced her that the trail had gone cold and that it would be safe for her to return to Buenos Aires. That's when we met."

Seeing that neither Eduardo nor Leandro were about to make a comment, Sam continued the story.

"The rest we know. However, the hotel episode seemed, as she put it, to shatter the spell, the hold which Dávila had exercised over her for the previous twenty years or more. On a number of occasions, in Zürich, I suspected that she was casting around for a new *patron*. In February I detected a lot of coming and going. A very smooth Russian from St. Petersburg took her out to dinner a couple of times and I'm fairly sure that she joined him in St. Moritz for a long weekend. Then a couple of weeks ago, when I rang Zürich, Naya, Carla's Bolivian maid, told me that the two Argentine bodyguards had left. She added that steaks had now been replaced by caviar, *blinis* and sour cream on the daily menu. Naya often joked about the amount of meat that was being consumed by Carlos and the other guy. I interpret her remark as meaning that Russian heavies are now in residence. So all in all, it wouldn't surprise me if Carla had been able to persuade her new partner to dispose of the past. That could explain the choice of weapons."

Eduardo sat in silence, absorbing what Sam had told them. Leandro adopted the same puzzled look.

"No way, I suppose, that any of this could be checked out?" Eduardo wondered out loud.

"Frankly, without my sitting down face-to-face with Carla, almost impossible."

"Any plans in that direction?"

Sam flashed a look at Eduardo.

"None at the moment!" she replied, curtly.

Leandro felt the need to change the subject, before Eduardo's questioning became too intrusive. He also wanted to put a slightly different spin on Carla's involvement, if nothing else to protect her, and through her, Sam. Now was not the time for Eduardo to learn of Sam's kidnap. Nor to get into the intimacy of Sam's relationship with Carla.

"So, just to summarise, the plot of what has been happening over the last nine months is as follows. Stop me if you disagree. Dávila, back around 1980 -1981 is a double agent, a member of the Montoneros, but actually working for the military. He is the man wearing the mask in the June 1981 movie given to us by the unfortunate Sosa. Carla is the army nurse holding up the victim. With the Malvinas fiasco, either together or separately, they leave the country and seek asylum in Switzerland. Does their relationship date back to the days of El Pozo, all this business with pain and asphyxiation? Or did they start that in Zürich? Either way, it doesn't matter very much. Whether it's the fact of having shared the horrors of the torture sessions, or because they share a taste for more exotic sex, they are very close to each other and ultimately become partners. How much did Carla know about the blackmail operation? Very probably something, if only to judge by the fact that Dávila had enough money to bankroll her. And she may well have suspected that Dávila had murderous tendencies into the bargain. While she was running her call girl business in Zürich, Dávila concentrated on preparing the ground for a profitable return to Argentina."

"I don't think that's the right word for Carla's business," Sam commented softly in the background.

Leandro ignored the remark.

"He returns to Argentina to find that his ex-Montonero comrades are now running the place. With no difficulty he slips into the system, this time in SIDE, whose principal purpose is to defend the interests of the new ruling elite. He returns with his blackmail operation possibly already up and running on the side, if we are to believe your informer.

Do his new bosses even know about it? Or does he just indicate to them that he can exert influence over certain high profile people in the business and financial world? The present government regularly uses a combination of sticks and carrots, on the one hand storing up information to use against anyone who gets in their way, on the other giving everyone's corrupt instincts free rein. Dávila appears to fit the profile. What does he do with the money?"

Again Sam interrupted.

"I'm pretty sure he just banked it."

"Back in Argentina, he no doubt serves his old comrades well. He does however have one worry, namely the need to remove any traces of the double game he was playing in 1980 and 1981. One way or another, he appears to have tracked down both Suarez and Sosa, though it seems to have taken him some time, as he only acts against them last year. I presume we agree that Dávila was behind both murders? So far, this government doesn't yet seem to have resorted to such extreme measures, probably because they've no reason to feel threatened. But Dávila did. Presumably the Suarez named in the 1980s film is the same man who was shot on his farm. Dávila didn't need to see the film to identify Suarez, since it's most probable that he already knew his identity."

Eduardo interjected. "I think we can be pretty sure they're one and the same. And I think your analysis is correct so far."

"Then, last year, he breaks the mould, by personally killing Williams. Up to then, he had remained firmly in the shadows, letting others do his dirty work. How do you explain that?"

Sam raised her hand, as if seeking permission to speak.

"I suspect that, first of all, he became overconfident. He'd got away with everything so far and, by nature, something inside of him needed to get the extra buzz. Blackmailing people over the Internet, like everything on the web, is virtual danger, not the real thing. I also know from what Carla told me, that he had made her participation a test of their relationship, a way to repay what she owed him. And, as I think I said before, Carla not being nearly as murderous as we all thought at the beginning, she never really forgave him for that. Which is why I believe she finally turned against him at the end of last year.

"I think you're right," Leandro replied. "The chance to combine so many of those tortured personality traits in a single event, dominating Carla, creating and stage-managing his own 'snuff' movie, one in which he could personally take his victim over the edge of the cliff on which he so often stood personally, I mean asphyxiation, it must have been a trip out of his wildest dreams."

"Exactly," Sam responded.

"And that was too much for Carla, not to mention that he had placed her centre stage in a murder?"

"Precisely."

Leandro turned to Eduardo, who was nodding his head in agreement.

"Is anyone planning to extradite Carla? Always assuming that they know who she is."

"Emphatically not! Of course I asked Fonseca whether we shouldn't be going after the woman in the film, trying to identify her, pulling her in as an accessory to the crime. But he very forcefully told me that nobody wanted to rock that boat. They're afraid that there are too many loose ends and unknowns over which they have little control, things they don't want to see on the evening news. We know that Carla has Swiss nationality. Perhaps they do as well. But the Swiss are notoriously fussy about every little detail being right and every box ticked before they do anything, all the more if there is any risk that this might start to knock a hole in their beloved banking secrecy. And extradition to a place like Argentina, with our legal system – she would almost certainly escape that one. All that could become very public. SIDE with its fingers in Swiss accounts? Just think how the press might use that. They know it and are highly unlikely to risk it. I think she can consider herself fairly safe. Perhaps she might take fewer holidays in Latin America, that's all."

Leandro detected a smile of relief flash across Sam's face.

"Well, Eduardo, where do we go from here? Apart from finishing this champagne."

"That'll be fine for the present. Obviously, if I hear any more, I'll let you know."

"Fantastic news. Let's raise our glasses to the fact that we survived."

With a certain mock formality, the three of them stood up, clinked their glasses and embraced.

"We wouldn't have got anywhere without you, Sam," Eduardo said, holding her in a manner which Leandro felt was pushing the limits of his long-term relationship with Florencia. Not to mention with him!

The bottle finished, Eduardo finally left. Leandro accompanied him downstairs.

"Have you warned Sarmiento?" he asked, as they stood in the cobbled *pasaje*.

"I was in touch with him about ten days ago. He seemed nervous. Made some remark about the blackmailer, which I didn't fully understand. Given what we've learned, I suppose it's possible the investigation was beginning to get to him. I tried him again last night, but he wasn't on line."

"Keep trying! We owe him."

"She's crazy, you know, your girlfriend," Eduardo commented, nodding towards the pearl grey and chrome Harley Softail Night Train parked a few metres away. "She'll get herself killed on that thing! In this town."

"Don't tell me. Tell her!" Leandro replied, ruefully shaking his head in despair.

He gave Eduardo a hug and went back upstairs.

As they sat with a second bottle of the champagne, Sam, lying stretched out on the sofa, rested her head on his shoulder. She seemed deep in thought. Presumably thinking through the implications of the news brought by Eduardo.

Leandro reflected on the year that had passed.

A year ago he had met Sam, that morning on the Avenida de Mayo. A year which had taken his life in totally different directions. On those desolate islands, he had been given a second chance, surviving the crash of the Pucará. Twenty-five years later, almost to the day, Sam had walked into his life. There were moments when he had trouble remembering how he had felt before meeting her. There were times when he sensed that he was losing control over parts of his life. Sometimes to Sam, sometimes to others. To Carla? As to Sam, he had bought in. As to the second.... His face-to-face encounter with Carla in Punta del Este had blown away many of his prejudices. Nor had her personality, her sensuality been lost on him. Although the older woman had, out of respect for Sam, been careful not to trespass on his affections, even at her most neutral Carla's sexual magnetism was overpowering - for both sexes, he had to remind himself. Sam had been right, she did have very beautiful eyes, able to switch instantly between control and deep compassion. Like so many of history's successful courtesans, Carla had a way of conveying an impression of total commitment to whoever she was with. Little wonder that Sam was fascinated by her. Those days with Carla had provided a measure of reassurance that, when Sam spoke of separate rooms in her emotional apartment, it was coherent with the way in which the three of them had shared their time. Carla had convincingly succeeded in sending him the message that she fully understood that this was a *ménage à trois* which, she at least, wanted to preserve.

Yet, at the back of his mind there lingered a feeling of uncertainty. Uncertainty as to the way in which the triangle would play out in the future, much greater uncertainty as to the directions in which Sam's partnership with Carla would lead her, made infinitely more dangerous by the Mossad dimension.

All because of this girl, whose dark red hair now pressed against the side of his face. Like a tectonic shift, she had realigned the way in which he visualised his professional life. And his emotional life above all.

In some strange way, Sam had also brought him closer to Alejandra. There were clearly new affinities, which allowed him to understand his daughter better, to be more compassionate, more flexible. Forced to adapt to the new emotional rules laid down by Sam, he now saw his daughter through more understanding eyes. He was less sure whether the same could be said of his relationship with Elena. Time would tell.

575

And Eduardo. Their collaboration over the Williams case had brought them closer together in new ways. He had good reason to be grateful that Eduardo had sought his advice in the investigation. The way in which the affair had ended had, thank God, seemingly left his son unscathed. Without the intervention of Carla's hit men, and, he suspected, of Carla herself, it was far from clear how it might otherwise have played out. The time spent by the three of them in piecing together the jigsaw had not brought them closer to a solution. Instead, it had left them more exposed. As Sam's kidnap had so graphically demonstrated. Another debt to Carla. How would she redeem it? Surely a small price to pay for having helped to place his son out of harm's way and to recover Sam.

Given the new assignment now entrusted to him by Frobisher, and what he knew about Sam's dual life, he sensed that recent events might only be the prelude. His old way of life showed all the signs of being a thing of the past.

He looked down at her and stroked her hair. She looked up at him, her pale green eyes tender. Not just the effect of the champagne!

"I was just thinking about the year we've been together. Because it's about a year, since that day you first sat down at the café next to me. We've been very lucky. After what happened to you, it might not seem that way. But on balance, we've come through far better that we might have deserved. You've changed my life, for that, I have to be thankful to you . . . maybe even to Oscar Wilde. Danger, fashion, sex in an Alvear Palace suite or in rooms rented by the hour - a new outlook on all these things - you've brought all that. You've stimulated me in a way that no woman ever has before. Like the day I survived the crash, nearly twenty six years ago, you've given me a new lease of life. Did I tell you? I haven't had that nightmare of the crash in over six months. As for the future, who knows?"

Sam gave him a long searching look. A slow smile. Leandro was no fool. He had never lied to her or pretended.

"It's funny, Leo, me too. My life has changed as well. My world is now dominated by two people, who, in some strange way, combine to play to two sides of my personality. A duality always lurking there, I suspect. Both of you are positive for me, even if Carla plays to the darker side of me. Not dark in an evil sense, but certainly feeding passions, impulses, unsuspected appetites buried deep inside me. A side of me which you – even I - still only dimly perceive. Though I think you've seen enough of it to fascinate even you. But above all, you, Leo. You play to the side of me which is bright, positive, good. I don't want to embarrass you, but deep down, you are a good man. Don't shake your head like that. You're certainly better than me. I love you for that, I need you for that. You protect me, help me to understand things about life, things about myself. I've never had that from anyone before, not even my father. What do I give you in return? Love, for sure. Yet I can't promise that I won't cause you pain, although it will never be for pain's sake. I'll no doubt do things, which will shock you. I already have, I know. But you're still here. Can you live with that? Carla plays to my body and parts of my heart. You play to my brain, to all of my heart *and* to my body. I need both, but if ever I have to choose, you'll always be my first choice. The other side carries thrills, passions, risks. I need them, but I could not survive on them alone."

She watched him, trying to detect the impact of her words.

"Does any of that make sense?"

Leandro nodded. Nothing with Sam was ever easy.

"Yes, in some strange way it does. But one major question mark still remains. I'll let you guess."

That was an easy one.

"Mossad? You don't understand why, I know. I'll explain it to you another time. Now let's go and find a good restaurant. Not just another one of your sordid little pizzerias."

"By taxi, if you don't mind!"

Eduardo pushed a copy of the previous day's La Nación across the table towards Leandro, pointing to an article on one of the inside pages. It was a Saturday morning and they were having coffee, as usual, at London City.

"Our friend?"

"I saw it, but didn't make the connection. I suppose it could be. What makes you think it is?"

"Soon after hearing what Fonseca told me they had discovered about Dávila, and as you suggested that evening, I sent Sarmiento a brief message. To alert him to the fact that the authorities had possibly identified his blackmailer and obtained some information about his activities. As you can imagine, he was extremely worried. He asked me whether there was anything I could do, but I had to confess that the investigation was being handled at the highest level and that I was in no way involved. He went off the air after that. Hasn't replied to any of my emails. That was

LA NACION

Buenos Aires, viernes 26 de abril de 2008

Death of a leading business man

The body of Carlos Manuel Contreras, founder and only shareholder of Contreras y Cia., was found by the portero of his apartment building in Calle Juncal, on the pavement below his fifth floor balcony at 6.30 yesterday morning. He appeared to have fallen and died instantly. Foul play is not suspected, according to a spokesman for the Comisaría 1a.

Ing. Contreras, the only son of Teniente General Rafael Contreras, who retired from the Army in 1977, was able to build up a significant energy/related business during the 1980s and particularly after the arrival to power of President Carlos Menem, becoming involved in a number of successful oil exploration operations in Chubut. He leaves a wife and two sons. None of these were available for comment.

Readers may recall that Contreras y Cia., was the subject of a brief investigation in 1998 linked to the origins of the funds which had enabled its founder to set up his businesses. These investigations, which included allegations that the source of the family wealth might be linked to events which had taken place under the dictadura, proved inconclusive and were ultimately abandoned.

Ing. Contreras was a leading member of the Jockey Club and on the boards of a number of charitable organisations, including two hospitals and an orphanage.

three days ago. Obviously, since we never knew who he was, there was little we could do to protect him. From the little research I was able to do, it seems to fit. Age, married with children, living in one of the gated communities in the northern suburbs as well as this flat in town."

Leandro sat thinking for a minute.

"I'm afraid you're right. Without knowing who he was, there was little we could do. If he committed suicide, it's probably because whoever followed up in the investigation took the profile of Sarmiento as a member of Dávila's paedophile ring at face value. Which is of course exactly what Dávila would have wanted. Presumably, Sarmiento just couldn't face it. Another one of Dávila's tragic victims."

Another newspaper item a few days later, reporting the death of an Argentine diplomat in Brussels, who had fallen to his death in the Grand' Place, did not however attract their attention.

almacén	grocery store
alpargata	espadrille-style slipper commonly worn by gauchos
altiplano	Andean high plains
asado	barbecue
asador	person in charge of barbecue
bandoneón	small accordeon used in tango
barrio	urban precinct
bife de chorizo	tenderloin steak
bombacha	long pleated gaucho trousers, possibly Turkish origin, buttoned at the ankle
cabo	corporal
campo	generic word for Argentine countryside
cana	Argentine slang for policeman / gaol
Casa Rosada	Presidential Palace in Buenos Aires
che	familiar name for other person
chinchulines	tripe
chipirones a la plancha	small grilled cuttlefish
colectivo	bus
Comisaría	police station
cordero	lamb
cortado	coffee with hot milk
credencial	official pass or identity document
Dictadura	dictatorship, usually applied to the period in which the Argentine military governed the country (1976 - 1983)
dogo	Argentine mastiff
estanciero	landowner
El Pozo	the well
ESMA	Escuela de Mecánica de la Armada - Navy School of Mechanics / most infamous interrogation centre at time of military dictatorship
Fabricacciones Militares	Argentine state-owned military industrial complex
facón	short one-sided dagger carried by gauchos
faja	broad rawhide belt worn by gauchos
Fuerza Aérea Argentina	Argentine Air Force
Guarda Costa	Coast Guard

hotel de alojamiento	short stay hotel, rooms by the hour
isleños	islanders (of Delta)
locutorio	internet and telephone booth
maricón	homosexual (male) (pejorative)
mate	yerba *mate* leaves, herb tea, popular in Argentina, Paraguay and Uruguay
medialuna	croissant
medialuna de grasa	salty croissant
Migraciones	Argentine Immigration Service
monte	stand of trees in the pampa
monturera	tackle room
mozo	waiter
muchacho	"my man", "my friend"
novia	formally recognized girlfriend
novio	formally recognized boyfriend
papas fritas	fried potatoes, chips
papas paille	very thinly sliced fried chip potatoes
parrilla	grill for barbecue, restaurant specializing in grilled meat
pasaje	narrow side street, often dead-end
policlínica	hospital
porteño	inhabitant of Buenos Aires
portero	concierge, porter
Prefectura	Argentine Coast Guard
pueblo	town, village
quebracho	iron wood
quincho	outhouse, usually housing the barbecue and dining area
quinta	weekend residence
revuelto gramajo	dish of fried potatoes, ham and egg
Salteño	resident of the Province of Salta
tranquera	gate to a country property
turco	slang term for immigrants from the ex-Ottoman empire
vitel thoné	veal in tuna, anchovy and cream sauce, with capers
vivo / viveza	smart, wily, innate Argentine intelligence, often overrated

Contents

Extracts from **Dark Wars**

appearing in 2014

30 April 2008 - GRAND PLACE, BRUSSELS

A flower seller setting up his stall early in the morning found the body, spread-eagled on the cobblestones, the head brutally crushed by the fall. It had rained since the moment of impact and the blood had been partially washed away. The *Lokale Politie* were rapidly on the scene. Once the investigating officer had satisfied himself that there was no further evidence to be obtained on the square, the body was taken away by an ambulance to one of the laboratories belonging to the Institut National de Criminalistique et de Criminologie.

Inspecteur Principal Jean Michel Leroy, leading the investigation, got through to the duty officer of the Argentine diplomatic mission in Brussels as he was having breakfast in a cafe round the corner from the Embassy. The diplomat, Juan Carlos Moreno, caught a taxi and met Leroy at the entrance to number four on the Grand' Place. Leroy handed him the wallet which they had found in the back pocket of the dead man's jeans, containing his diplomatic ID, identifying him as Luis Maria Sanchez.

"He's a First Secretary in your Embassy, I believe."

8 May 2008 – QUERANDI LUNCH

On 18th July 1994, a massive carbomb had destroyed the building housing the Asociación Mutual Israelita Argentina, more commonly known as the AMIA, in the Calle Pasteur in downtown Buenos Aires, taking eighty-five lives and wounding some three hundred. The explosion followed an earlier terrorist attack on the 17th of March 1992, when a bomb placed in Calle Arroyo had blown up the Israeli

Embassy, killing twenty-nine and wounding almost ten times as many. On that occasion, a jihadi organisation in Lebanon with links to Hezbollah and Iran had claimed responsibility.

Leandro well remembered the terrifying images of a mountain of collapsed masonry in Calle Pasteur, people digging desperately in the ruins in search of survivors. Israeli rescue specialists, as well intelligence experts, had been flown in during the days following the blast, which they soon discovered had come from 300 kilos of ammonium nitrate concealed in a Renault Trafic pickup van. Within days, a number of arrests had been made linked to the sale and repair of the vehicle. By mid-August, the investigating judge's suspicion had fallen on four Iranian diplomats, but during the following months, this line of investigation was neglected in favour of the interrogation and arrest of a number of military and police personnel suspected of links to the bombing. Among those detained was one Carlos Telleldín, the person possibly responsible for the transfer of the van to the bombers, and soon to become a central player in the farce, which was to follow.

"You were talking about the way in which the investigation had been handled. Seems to have shown all the signs of deliberate political manipulation. Key documents and tapes relating to the investigation mysteriously disappearing. Bribery by the judge leading the investigation. How much lower can we sink?"

Carlos nodded.

"When they began to take the lid off it, it emerged that Telleldín had been bribed 400,000 US dollars by the investigating judge, Juan Jose Galeano, out of funds provided by the Argentine intelligence service, SIDE. He was bribed to produce a story, which would deflect attention from the Iranian connection."

"As I recall, the change of tack was attributed to heated internal discussions in the immediate aftermath of the attack between Carlitos Menem and his top ministers. They seem to have persuaded him that there was little to be gained by pursuing the Iranian connection, except the added risk that Teheran might launch a third attack in retaliation."

"And the fact that Iran had become a major trading partner for our beef and cereals was not entirely irrelevant. And if that weren't enough,

Menem's soft-pedalling was later attributed to his having received a ten million US dollar bribe from Teheran."

"Which he denied of course!"

"Yes, except that subsequent investigations by the Swiss authorities indicated that he might very well have received such a payment."

About Nicolas Brentano

Nicolas Brentano is the penname of a long-term observer – and lover – of Argentina, whose travels and professional activities in politics and finance have provided him with first-hand knowledge and insight into many of the settings and actions of this book – though perhaps not the more extreme !

Riding the switchback of Argentina's fortunes throughout the decades portrayed in this book, he shares the love of his main characters for the kindness and compassion of los Argentinos, who - in spite of all the hardships which successive governments have inflicted upon them – retain the confidence that one day their country will return to the world status it once enjoyed.

For a free Ebook version of
DIRTY WARS
Please email
dirtywars@sifipublishing.co.uk
quoting the following code:
DW4466
And stating the preferred format

For information and sales enquiries:
info@sifipublishing.co.uk

SIFIPUBLISHING

WWW.SIFIPUBLISHING.CO.UK

CPSIA information can be obtained at www.ICGtesting.com
Printed in the USA
BVOW11s1258291213

340317BV00007BA/53/P

9 780957 264069